I0819859

Parables of Light

PARABLES OF LIGHT

A Novel

Clearview Press
Franklin, Tennessee

Library of Congress Control Number (LCCN): 2020901765

ISBN: 978-0-578-43452-0

For Elinor

Chapter 1

I was almost fourteen when I went away to camp in the summer of 1961. I'd already been there for three or four weeks, and one night I was eating dinner in the dining hall. I was pretty much over being homesick by then. The head counselor stood up and tapped his spoon against his glass. Everybody got quiet and he called out the name of a camper who was told to report to Mr. Dale, the owner of the camp. The kid got up and walked over to Mr. Dale's cottage.

An hour later I saw the guy crying in his cabin. One of the counselors was helping him pack up his things. His father had dropped dead from a stroke. A couple of weeks later we were at lunch and the head counselor stood up and clinked his spoon against his glass again. Then he called out my name. Everybody in the dining hall stopped eating. While they were watching me walk out the door, I was trying to decide which one of my parents I wanted to still be alive.

Mr. Dale was sitting out on his patio reading a newspaper. He glanced up at me and went back to his paper. Mrs. Dale came up and hugged me. She told me that I'd gotten a telephone call, and that there would be another call in a few minutes. I sat in the shade and waited. I kept going back and forth between imagining the rest of my life without Mother, and thinking about growing up without my father.

The minutes went by and the call didn't come. Mrs. Dale kept looking at me. She could tell I was suffering and she finally said something to Mr. Dale. "Julius, maybe we should go ahead and let the boy call home."

He didn't even look up. "I'm sorry, dear. I'm not paying for any more campers who make long-distance calls."

It was another twenty minutes before the phone rang. Mrs. Dale handed me the receiver and I heard my father's voice. He was choking up and I closed my eyes. Then he told me that my grandmother was dead. I tried to look solemn while he was telling me about her heart attack. After I hung up, I thanked Mrs. Dale. I left Mr. Dale on the patio reading his newspaper.

I would've done a cartwheel or turned a flip as soon as I was out of sight, but I couldn't come close to doing either one. On the way to my cabin, I kept wondering if Mr. Dale already knew that my parents were okay.

The next morning I was supposed to make a lanyard during crafts period, but the last thing I wanted was another lanyard. I just slipped off into the woods. There was a trail that ran along the top of a bluff, and after a few minutes, I came to a clearing that looked out over the Caney Fork River. I liked being alone. I liked the way I felt when nobody knew where I was. I sat down on a big flat rock and stared out at the water.

It wasn't long before I was wondering what it would be like to get in a canoe and just keep paddling up the Caney Fork. I imagined going farther and farther upstream until the river narrowed into a creek. But the more I thought about it, the more complicated it got.

The creek would keep getting narrower until it was just a trickle of water coming from a spring, and then the spring would spread back into a network of underground channels. I thought about it for a while, and I finally decided that the origin of the river wasn't always the same.

Most of the time the river would start with the tributaries of the spring, but when it was raining hard enough – when the water was flowing across the ground and soaking through the soil and running down through cracks in the bedrock – the origin of the river extended up into the clouds.

It was a long time before I understood that trying to find the beginning of a river was like trying to find the beginning of a journey.

I got back from camp a couple of weeks later. My father had cleaned out my grandmother's apartment by then. He brought home a large cardboard box, and inside the box was everything he wanted to keep. I looked through it, and along with some old letters and photographs, I found the journal his father started back in 1905, when he was supervising a leper colony in the Philippine Islands.

The passages he wrote were in the present tense, which made the people and the places he was describing seem especially real. My grandfather kept writing in his journal after he moved on from the leper colony. He was living in Manila when he wrote his last entry. He died the next week.

June 22, 1918 – I am sitting on the verandah. It is late in the afternoon. Pop is asleep in his chair and Alicia is on her blanket, chewing on her teething ring. Georgie is going back and forth on his rocking horse, and the sunlight is shining through his curls. I wonder how old he will be when his final memory of me fades away. Trini is beside me and she is staring out toward the street. She is brooding, but she doesn't say anything. The smell of paella is coming from the kitchen. I have no appetite, but I will eat what I can.

Alicia crawls over and grasps my ankle with her wet little hands. She pulls herself up and gives me one of her big drooling smiles. Georgie glances over and he begins to rock harder. I look back at him and I start leaning up and back in my chair, pretending to ride a horse of my own. He grins at me. Trini is watching him closely. She is worried that he will fall off his horse again. She wants me to tell him to slow down. I am cold and perspiration is soaking through the back of my shirt. I will sit with them for as long as I can.

Mother noticed how much time I spent reading my grandfather's journal, and on my fourteenth birthday, she gave me a journal of my own. I wasn't surprised when I opened my present. She thought I spent way too much time watching television. She was always trying to find something productive for me to do.

By the next summer, I still hadn't written anything. She probably thought the journal would end up on a shelf at the back of my closet, along with the barely-touched microscope she gave me when I was twelve and the still-unused chemistry set I'd gotten when I turned thirteen.

There wasn't anything worth writing about until the middle of July. I watched a little television that night after dinner, and then I went back to my room. I tried to write the way my grandfather had written – as though what happened earlier that day was happening right then.

July 19, 1962 – It's Thursday afternoon. I'm sitting on a towel on the grass at Willow Plunge. A big white cloud is sliding along the edge of the sun. My shadow fades away and then it fades back in. Kids are laughing and splashing around in the swimming pool. The smell of suntan lotion is in the air. The Wah-Watusi is playing on the jukebox. I hold up the bottle of Sprite I'm drinking, and I look at the sun shining through the glass. The carbonation is rising toward the surface. I pretend that the bubbles are shimmering worlds moving through a vast green universe.

The Locomotion comes on. I turn around and a girl with dark hair is walking right toward me. She has on a blue bikini and she's wearing sunglasses. She looks like she could be a senior, and she's good-looking enough to be in Playboy. Thank God I'm wearing a T-shirt over my puny white body. I stare at her for a few seconds before she notices me. Just as I'm turning away, she smiles. It's too late for me to smile back.

You'll Lose a Good Thing starts playing and Hall Guthrie walks by holding a football. I smile when he glances over. He smiles back, but he doesn't know who I am. I'm not surprised. He was four years ahead of me at Battle Ground Academy. He graduated last year. He was president of the student body and an honor student and an all-state football player. Now he plays for Vanderbilt. On top of everything else, he looks like a movie star.

He throws the ball to Charlie Ballou. Charlie was a football star at Battle Ground and he also plays for Vanderbilt. Hall's shirt is off and some girls are off to the side staring at him. A couple of grown women are sitting over in the shade. They're watching him, too. They watch him all the way through Twist and Shout. They're still staring at him when I get up and walk over to the pool.

It wasn't that big a deal, but I wanted to write down what happened. Maybe I wanted to write it down because I hadn't been around a girl in a bikini since my hormones finally kicked in – which was right around the time President Kennedy was sworn into office. I didn't get to see all that many girls. Battle Ground Academy was an all-boys school. It was founded in 1889 in Franklin, Tennessee, less than a mile from where Willow Plunge was eventually built.

To get everything straight about what else happened that day, I read through the rest of what I wrote down in my journal. I rode the sixteen or so miles back to my house in Nashville, and after dinner, I watched *The Donna Reed Show* with my parents. It was a rerun, but I didn't care. I liked to look at Shelley Fabares even though she was way too old for me. But it wouldn't have mattered if I was twenty-five – she would've been way out of my league.

Before I went to my room, Mother brought up my portrait again. It had been a couple of months since one of her friends offered to do a painting of me. Ever since then, Mother had been trying to get me to go over to the lady's house and pose for her. That night I went ahead and said I'd do it. Mother had been sad for a few days. It seemed like she needed something to go her way.

She never said why having a painting of me was so important to her, but I was pretty sure I knew. I still didn't look all that different from the way I looked when I was little. When she was an old woman, the portrait would help her remember the way I was when I was a kid – back before I started falling apart.

It helped that I liked the lady who wanted to paint my portrait. Her name was Ann Woodmore, and she'd always been really nice to me. Just about every time I saw her, she'd ask me some question, and then she'd listen to whatever answer I gave her. The lenses of her glasses were thick. They made her eyes look big and blurry. I wondered if she'd been as big a loser as I was, back when she was about to start tenth grade.

I assumed that Ann wanted to paint me because she liked to paint, but that wasn't the reason. Later on, I found out that she'd been a psychologist for a few years. Mother wanted Ann to figure out what was wrong with me without letting me know what she was up to. I needed all the help I could get. For the past year, I'd been drowning.

Chapter 2

The day after I went to Willow Plunge, I was back in summer school. My freshman year at Battle Ground had been a nightmare. I failed two subjects. My summer classes were in the morning, and I started spending a couple of afternoons a week posing for Ann at her house, which wasn't too far away from where I lived.

After she sketched the outline of my head and my nose and my mouth, she painted my eyes. I hated the way I looked in photographs. My eyes never looked right. But the eyes Ann painted didn't look like the eyes of somebody who knew how ugly he was.

We sat in her living room and talked while she was painting. She would ask me a question, and I'd say something I thought she wanted to hear. She was always nice about it, but I could tell that she was waiting for me to say more than I was saying. She just sat there and painted, and pretty soon she asked me the same question she'd asked before. But she'd ask it in a way that made it harder for me to get by with some phony answer. When I wasn't being honest she knew it.

When I was open with her she looked at me and nodded like I'd said something that made a lot of sense and might even be important. I wouldn't admit it to Mother, but before long I looked forward to going over to Ann's house. The more I went, the more talking I did, and after a while, I was telling her things I never thought I'd tell anybody.

I could tell that she wanted me to talk about my parents, and I finally went ahead and told her about the times when they drank too much, and that it made me feel sick inside when they argued. I told her how much I loved Mother and that I loved my father too, but that it seemed like a different kind of love and I didn't think I knew him very well, and how worried I was that he and Mother might end up getting a divorce, and how that would change everything and that I didn't think I'd see my father very much if their marriage ever broke up.

I also told Ann how much I loved it when they were getting along, and that sometimes they would laugh at things together, and how great it was when they did.

One day she started asking me a lot more about school. I told her about leaving Woodmont after sixth grade, and that my first two years at Battle Ground Academy went pretty well. Then I told her how everything changed.

I looked out the window and I made myself explain things I didn't want to talk about. "Nothing was the same when I got to be a freshman. Being with the other kids wasn't like it was in eighth grade. I didn't fit in anymore. I wasn't sure how to act and I didn't know what to say."

Ann stopped painting but I kept talking. "I tried to avoid the guys who teased me about my goofy-looking teeth and being a skinny weakling. They always told me how ugly and stupid I was. One time I wrote a poem, but I never showed it to anybody. I called it *The Medusa.*"

I told Ann I mostly hated school, but that I'd read some good books and there was something about history that I liked. My English teacher said I was a pretty good writer when I was interested in what I was writing about, but he said I daydreamed and looked out the window way too much. After that, instead of looking out the window as much as I had, I wrote funny captions to go with the pictures in my textbooks, and I made up stories in my head.

I started getting sick around the middle of ninth grade, and I told Ann how tired I felt and about having a cough that wouldn't go away and that I couldn't seem to pay attention in class, and how hard it was to get my homework finished, and that my grades kept going down, and I told her about getting further and further behind and about the nightmares I had. I got the feeling she already knew that I'd failed Algebra and Latin.

Life had gotten bad and it was getting worse, and I couldn't see how things would ever be okay again. My parents were worried – I could tell – but they didn't know what to do. It might've helped if they cut down on their drinking, but I wasn't sure it would make any difference.

Most of their friends drank just as much as they did, and I guess my parents didn't think alcohol could have anything to do with whatever was wrong with me. The way I looked at it, plenty of guys at Battle Ground had parents who drank and argued too much, but they weren't falling apart.

Ann knew I liked basketball, and one day she asked me if I thought I'd end up playing on the varsity at Battle Ground. She must've known she was in for a long answer as soon as I started talking.

"I was really slow and uncoordinated when I was a little kid. It took me forever to learn to ride a bike. A lot of times I hated going to recess. I couldn't stand it when the captains chose up sides. No matter what game we played, I was always one of the last guys picked."

When I was in second grade I started playing basketball on Saturday mornings at Tom Hendrickson's house. He had a concrete court in his backyard. His father had been a star athlete at Vanderbilt, and over the next few years, he coached everybody who showed up.

I wasn't any good, but I got to where I could shoot okay. We played in the YMCA league when we were in sixth grade. We won the city championship, but I didn't get in many of the games, and I didn't make the team at Battle Ground when I was in seventh grade or eighth grade.

I'd grown a little by the time I was a freshman, and when Mr. Roche announced who was on the team, my name was the last one he read. It was the first time he'd ever coached and it showed. We did way too many drills, and the offense he came up with took most of the fun out of the game. He didn't believe in fast breaks, and the plays he made us run didn't work. I tried to do what I was supposed to do, but I kept messing up. He probably thought I was trying to undermine him.

I was pretty sure I wouldn't get to play very much, and I asked my parents not to come to the games. Having them drive all the way to Franklin to watch me sit on the bench would've made not playing a whole lot worse. It probably bothered them when I said I didn't want them to come, but I was glad I did it. I was the only one on the team who didn't get to play in any of our first three games. By then I got the feeling that Mr. Roche wanted me to quit.

And then I was *sure* he wanted me to quit.

I went ahead and told Ann the rest of it. "For three or four games in a row, Mr. Roche would wait till there were only fifteen or twenty seconds left in the game, and then put me in. I'd get to the scorer's table as fast as I could, but there were usually just three or four seconds left when I got to play. I acted like it didn't bother me. The last game we had, he waited until there were two seconds left, and then he called timeout and put me in."

By then my cough was worse and Mother took me to the doctor. I had a pretty bad case of strep throat and I didn't go to school for three weeks. There were only a couple of games left in the season when I got back, and there wasn't any point in going to practice again.

I didn't want Ann to think that Mr. Roche was a bad guy. "What he did wasn't right, he was just a new coach and I was probably driving him crazy. I guess he didn't know what else to do. He laughed when I was running over to the scorer's table, but he's always been nice to me when I see him during school."

It wasn't too long after that when Ann asked me if I thought I had a spirit, and if I believed in God. She already knew that I went to Sunday School and church every Sunday.

I grew up hearing the same Bible stories that most kids heard when they were growing up. For a long time, I believed in the Sunday School Jesus, but I never understood the Holy Ghost. And the relationship between God the Father and Jesus didn't seem like the relationship between a father and son. I kept wishing that there was a mother.

Ann had a grandfather clock that chimed every fifteen minutes. Time seemed to slow down when I was trying to talk about God. "There's a big painting hanging on the wall across from our Sunday School class. It's a painting of God. He's a muscular old man dressed in some kind of white garment, and he has white hair and a white beard. His face looks different in just about every picture I've seen, but overall he looks Scandinavian."

His mouth was closed in the painting, but I didn't mention it. I didn't want to get into whether he had teeth. Humans were supposed to be made in God's image, and since people had teeth, it seemed reasonable to assume that God had teeth, too. But if there was anything in the Bible about God eating, I didn't know about it. And if he didn't eat, I wondered why he'd have teeth.

I beat around the burning bush for a little longer before I told Ann that I was pretty sure I had a spirit. I told her I believed in God, but that believing didn't feel the way it did back when I was younger. The way I thought about God and religion changed a lot during ninth grade, right along with everything else.

One morning in Sunday school, the teacher was talking about Noah and the flood. I was sitting in the back row listening to how two animals of every species on the planet showed up from wherever they'd been, and then they just got in line and walked up a ramp and into the ark. I'd always believed that was how it happened and I wanted to keep on believing it, but miracle or no miracle, it just didn't sound true anymore.

Other things didn't sound true either, and before long I didn't know what I believed. I kept trying to ignore all the doubts I was starting to have. School was falling apart for me, and I didn't want church to fall apart, too. But ignoring my doubts made everything worse.

I finally told Ann about a particular night when my parents had been arguing. "It had been raining all night. It was really late. The radio stations had all gone off the air. It kept raining and raining, and I started thinking about how I was betraying God. I felt like a traitor because of all the doubts I was having."

After a while, I started reciting Bible verses so I wouldn't think about things like Noah floating around in an ark full of animals, or Jonah living for three days inside the belly of a whale, or Methuselah fathering a child when he was 187 years old, and then living on to the ripe old age of 969.

The 23rd Psalm was my favorite prayer and after I said it a few times, I thought I might as well keep saying it until I fell asleep. I kept praying, but every lap I took through the Valley of the Shadow of Death made me feel more alone, and it seemed like the rain would keep falling forever.

While I was praying, part of a Bible verse I'd heard once or twice in church came into my head. I was a little off, but what I remembered was, "Whatsoever things are true, whatsoever things are honest, whatsoever things are just, whatsoever things are pure – think on these things." It came from a letter of the Apostle Paul. I'd heard about people who'd been given signs, and I wondered if God could've put that passage in my head.

I kept thinking about things that were true and honest and just and pure that came from Jesus – things like loving my neighbor as myself and turning the other cheek and loving my enemies.

I prayed in the dark and tried to lose myself in the goodness of Jesus, and I kept praying about what was true and honest and just and pure and I started breathing faster and I could feel my brain and my body getting hot and I was still praying and it felt like a fire was building up inside me and I started sweating and writhing around on my bed. And then a flash of current shot through me like lightning.

I felt different after that, and I kept wondering what had happened. I didn't know what I'd experienced, but since I was thinking about Jesus when it happened, I thought it could've come from Jesus.

My doubts had led me to whatever I'd gone through, and I ended up thinking that it must be okay to have doubts. And if it was okay to have doubts, it was okay to have questions, too. I ended up making Jesus a promise. I promised that I wouldn't pretend to believe something that I didn't believe.

But having the current run through me didn't do anything for my health. I was already getting sick by then, and I didn't get any better. It didn't help my grades, either. Subjects like Latin and Algebra still seemed irrelevant, and I had a hard time getting my homework done. I was okay at writing and history, but that was about it. And along with everything else, I felt as cut off from the guys I went to school with as I was before.

Chapter 3

After I told Ann about the passage from Paul, she stared off into the distance and repeated it word for word. And when I told her about having the current go through me, she stopped painting. She didn't say anything for a while.

She finally looked at me and smiled. "I'm wondering how you feel – how you *really* feel – about what happened that night. And I wonder how you feel about some of the other things you've told me. You mostly talk about what's above the water. I want to know what's under the surface."

Part of me didn't want to tell her anything else, but another part did. School was about to start back up, and if there was a chance that being open could keep everything from getting messed up again, I wanted to give it a try. I ended up telling her a lot, but it only came out a little at a time. She must've felt like she was putting together a jigsaw puzzle with a whole lot of missing pieces.

I did the best I could to explain what it was like to lie in my bed in the dark and hear my parents argue when they thought I was asleep. I usually couldn't tell what they were saying, but I could hear the anger and the alcohol in their voices. They would gradually quiet down, and after a while, my father's snoring filled up the darkness.

He was in the Pacific during World War Two, but he hardly ever talked about it. Mother said he'd probably done things and seen things that he didn't want to remember. All those years later, if an unusual sound woke him up in the middle of the night, he would reach for a pistol that hadn't been beside him when he slept since 1945.

When my father's snoring got softer, other sounds would drift into my room. Harding Road was less than a mile away, and sometimes, late at night, the siren of an ambulance would haunt the darkness.

When I was eight years old, a guy in his twenties was killed in a wreck on Harding Road, just a few hundred feet from the house where he grew up. He'd gone to Woodmont School and he was a football star in high school, and we went to the same church. I heard the sirens that night, and from then on, when I was alone in the dark listening to the wail of an ambulance, I heard death.

And there was death in the sound of the trains that moved through the darkness along the western edge of our neighborhood. The tracks ran just beyond Harding Road, and a catastrophic train wreck had taken place there back at the close of World War One. When I was little I heard older kids say there were nights when the spirits of dead passengers could be heard moaning in the dark.

Death was somewhere out in the night. I'd lie in bed and think about how it was slowly closing in on Mother and on my father, and that it would eventually come for me. I thought about the times I went to Mount Olivet Cemetery with Mother. I remembered watching her stand beside the grave of *her* mother – crying the way she must have cried back when she was eleven, on the day when her mother was buried. Seeing her cry would make me think about being alone in a coffin forever – the way God might've been alone, back before he created the world.

On nights when my parents argued, after the last car came down Clearview Drive and sent clusters of shadows and light sliding across the ceiling of my bedroom, I would stare at the top of the cedar tree that was right outside my window. I pretended that the tree was standing guard – restless on windy nights and motionless when the air was still.

In the summer there was a fullness to the sound of the wind

when it filled the trees, but in winter it sounded thin and hollow when it passed through the bare limbs and branches. And there was another sound. Year after year the nights were punctuated by the relentless barking of the same solitary dog, somewhere off in the distance.

There were bad nights, but bad nights didn't happen all that often. On most nights Mother went back to the bedroom to read, and my father dozed off in his chair. He'd wake up after an hour or two and reach for the glass on the table beside his chair, and after he took the last few swallows of whatever he was drinking, he followed her to bed. Those nights were peaceful. There weren't any angry words coming from their bedroom, but sometimes I'd lie awake anyway.

Several streets over, on the northern edge of the neighborhood, was a boys' school called Montgomery Bell Academy. On Friday nights in the fall, if there was a football game and if the wind was right, the cheering crowd sounded pretty close.

By the time I was in third or fourth grade, I would pretend that I was a high school player I'd seen in a photograph in the sports section of the newspaper. The player was number 98, and he was reaching out to catch a football.

I'd lie on my left side in bed and position myself just like the guy in the photograph – my left toe pointed down, my right knee up, my arms extended, my hands ready, and my eyes on the imaginary ball I was about to catch for a touchdown. Then I waited to hear the next wave of cheering drift into my room. As soon as I heard the roar of the crowd I'd whisper, "Number 98 – All-Star," and pretend they were cheering for me.

And from the time I was around ten years old, there was something else about lying in bed at night. A couple of days after Marilyn Monroe was found dead, Ann brought up the subject of girls. I didn't see how I could get out of talking about it, and I told her a few things that could help her understand me.

We lived on an end lot. There were neighbors behind us, but

nobody lived on either side of our house. A teenage girl my father called the Blonde Bombshell lived across from us on Crescent Road, which ran on the east side of our house. My room was on the west side of the house – about twenty feet from Clearview Drive.

On Friday and Saturday nights, an hour or two before she had to be home, the Blonde Bombshell and her boyfriend would pull up and park on the Clearview side – where her mother couldn't see the car from her house. They parked beside a cedar tree, which wasn't far from where I was lying in the dark. When my window was open and the car windows were down, and if it wasn't too windy, I could hear the songs they were listening to.

When I was ten I imagined they were out in the car kissing each other – the way I'd seen teenagers kiss on television and in the movies. I knew my teenage years were on their way and that a lot would be coming with them, but they were too far away to worry about.

Songs like *Chances Are* and *Maybe* and *It's All in the Game* and *All I Have to Do Is Dream* and *Lonesome Town* and *Mr. Blue* would drift in through my bedroom window, and they sounded as innocent as I was. The Blonde Bombshell moved away around the time I was twelve, and sometimes I wondered if she and her boyfriend were still dating.

It wasn't too long after that when I started paying more attention to song lyrics. If the Blonde Bombshell and her boyfriend were parking together on some other dark street on Friday and Saturday nights, *Devil or Angel* and *Step By Step* and *Let It Be Me* and *Will You Still Love Me Tomorrow* gave me a better idea of what they might be doing.

My favorite song from back then was *Dream Lover*. It would drift in through my window, and before long I was wondering if I'd ever have a dream girl. There were times when I wondered if my dream girl could be lying in the dark somewhere, listening to the same song I was listening to. Sometimes I fell asleep thinking about her.

By the time I turned fourteen, there was a *Playboy* hidden under my mattress. Getting it there wasn't easy. One day, after weeks of procrastination, I rode my bicycle a couple of miles to a drugstore where nobody would know who I was. But when the hard-eyed woman behind the cash register looked at me like she knew why I was there, I lost my nerve and went back home. The next day I went to a different drugstore.

I picked up copies of *Look* and *Life* and *The Saturday Evening Post*, and I took them up to the counter and paid the cashier. Then I acted like there was something else I needed to get. I went to the magazine section again, and after I put *Look* and *The Saturday Evening Post* back on the shelf, I grabbed a *Playboy* and slipped it inside the copy of *Life*.

Nobody noticed when I left, and I peddled back by a hard-to-follow route. I looked over my shoulder all the way home. As soon as I got to my room and shut the door, I started to get acquainted with Miss September. All I could do was hope that my grandmother and Jesus and God and the Holy Ghost weren't watching.

I remember wishing that the Blonde Bombshell still lived across the street. I pictured her standing out in her front yard, wearing the shorts and the cut-off T-shirt I saw her wear a couple of times when she was mowing the grass. I tried to imagine how she'd look in a magazine like *Playboy*, but I never got too far with my fantasy.

Miss September was joined by Miss October, and there was a succession of other centerfolds, but I didn't stop thinking about my dream girl. It wasn't long before I bought a transistor radio. It would be under my pillow when I was supposed to be asleep. I listened to *Johnny Angel* and *What's Your Name* and *Baby It's You*, and I still wondered if she was listening, too.

But there were times when hearing songs like *Look in My Eyes* and *I Love How You Love Me* made me feel empty. Those songs were written for teenagers in parked cars, but I couldn't see myself kissing a girl in the back seat of a car, much less doing anything else. I kept singing *Dream Lover* when I was by myself, but there were times when I wondered if my anthem would end up being a song like *Stranger on the Shore.*

By the time I made my confession to Ann about the Blonde Bombshell and buying the *Playboys*, I'd started my sophomore year at Battle Ground. My life was better than it was the year before, but it wasn't that much better. There were other things I was getting ready to tell Ann, but one afternoon in late October I showed up and something had changed. For most of the time I was there, she looked like she was about to cry. I kept wondering if it was because of what I'd told her about the Blonde Bombshell.

Chapter 4

October 26, 1962 – It's Friday afternoon. Ann called me right after I got home from school, and I'm on my way over to her house. The trees are full of color and the wind is blowing. I'm walking through her yard and some leaves spin up into a column and whirl across the grass. When Ann opens the front door, she's holding a book I've heard about. It's called Silent Spring.

She looks tired and sad. I don't know what to say. I don't go through the door until she asks me to come inside. She says she was up all night finishing my portrait. It's propped up against a table, and I get a pretty good look at it. My mouth is closed, so my teeth and my stupid-looking braces don't show. There's a look in my eyes like I know something. I wish I knew what it was.

And I wish I knew why Ann is so sad. We both sit down. She looks at me and she tries to smile. She takes a deep breath and tells me how much she likes it when I come by. Then she says she might be going out of town for a while. I get the feeling there's something else she wants to say, but she looks away like she isn't sure she should. I'm used to that. Mother does it all the time. She finally asks me if I know what's happening in Cuba.

Of course I knew. I'd watched President Kennedy's speech four days earlier. Almost everything in the news was about the Russian missiles. We'd talked about it in history class all week. Our teacher, Mr. Godshaw, said that if we didn't attack Cuba, the next thing the Russians did would be even worse. And then there was an assembly at Battle Ground. Our principal, Mr. Rennin, told us what to do if there was a nuclear attack while we were at school.

That was bad enough, but when my father came home on Tuesday, the trunk of his car was loaded with cases of canned food, and there was an Army surplus tent and three sleeping bags in the back seat. Before dinner, he told me to get a couple of blankets and some winter clothing out of my closet, and he brought his guns and some ammunition out into the living room.

And every night he drove to Jim Caldwell's Shell station on Harding Road and filled up the car with gas. He told me if something happened while I was at school, he'd drive to Franklin and meet me at an abandoned building not far from Willow Plunge.

I'd seen my father look worried before. The previous year there was a big showdown with the Russians in Berlin, but he didn't put a bunch of food in his car, and he didn't say he'd come to get me if something happened. Mother was pretty good at hiding the way she felt, but I could tell that she was worried, too.

Ann shifted in her chair and leaned forward. She looked at me through the thick lenses of her glasses. "I'm sorry for not being better company, but I... I'm afraid."

I just said, "So am I."

Neither one of us wanted to talk about what could be about to happen. When she saw me glance over at the portrait, she asked me what I thought.

I told her how good it was, and then I said something else. "I just wish I was like the kid in the portrait. He looks really... confident."

She took off her glasses. "You don't know it yet, but the boy in the painting is *exactly* who you are."

Then she said something I thought I understood, but I wasn't sure. "Maybe the boy in the portrait just isn't ready to come out yet."

I'd read *To Kill a Mockingbird* over the summer, and what she said made me think about Boo Radley. I imagined myself lurking in the shadows and prowling around at night. She almost said something else, but she stopped herself.

Ann was holding something back. And a couple of weeks before that, there was something that Mother hadn't told me. She was writing on a notepad, but when I came into the bedroom, she cut the conversation short and hung up. I was pretty sure she was talking to Ann.

While she was fixing dinner I went back and checked the notepad. She'd peeled off the top page, but the pressure of her pen made an imprint on the next page. Some of it was hard to make out, but I could see where she'd written down "anxiety." The next word wasn't as clear, but it looked like it could've been "disorder." Mother probably thought that if whatever was wrong with me was bad enough to have a name, it would make me worry even more if I knew about it.

It wasn't long after that when Ann stood up and gave me the portrait. I just thanked her and told her goodbye.

I wasn't ready to go home, but I didn't want to run into somebody I knew and have to explain why I was walking around with a portrait of myself. I also didn't want to think about whether Ann was back at her house crying, or if the world was about to blow up. The weather was good and people were all over the place. It seemed like a normal Friday afternoon.

I wanted to go somewhere and be by myself. I ended up walking to Woodmont, my old grammar school. There was a Men's Club meeting that evening, and a few of the fathers had gotten there early. They were in the cafeteria, but nobody was in the rest of the building. A side door was open and I went upstairs. I hadn't thought about the way Woodmont smelled since the last time I was inside – back when I was eleven. I went down the empty hall, and after I passed the trophy case, I walked by classroom doors decorated for Halloween with black cats and witches and orange pumpkins and crescent moons – all made out of construction paper.

I ended up in my sixth-grade classroom. I propped the portrait up next to the door and found my old desk. I recognized it from the dent at the bottom of its front right leg. It was still on the back row. Except for the two extra stars on the American flag in the corner of the room, not much had changed. I sat down and closed my eyes, and I tried to pretend that I'd never left.

Instead of October 26, 1962, I imagined it was October 26, 1958. There wasn't a missile crisis and I wasn't in high school. It could've been an episode of *The Twilight Zone*. A screwed-up fifteen-year-old boy is afraid that the Earth is about to get blown up, and he takes refuge in his grammar school. He goes back to his old classroom and sits down at his old desk, and he wills himself four years back in time.

It would've been a pretty depressing episode. If I went back to 1958, what would I have said to Sally? Would I come up to her out by the water fountain, and say that she had to stop going into the girls' bathroom after lunch and sticking her finger down her throat to make herself vomit? Would I tell her that if she kept doing it, when she was in ninth grade she'd lose so much weight that she'd be in and out of the hospital, and almost die a couple of times?

And if I sat down next to Johnny at lunch, how could I tell him to spend as much time as he could with his father? How could I explain that in two years his Dad would collapse and die on their kitchen floor?

And what would I say to Jeff, who was an eighth grader? Would there be a way to convince him to stop riding his bicycle on Hillsboro Road? Could I just walk up to him after school and say I'd had a premonition that he'd get hit by a car the next summer?

Or would it be better to go ahead and tell him the truth? What would he say if I told him that he would spend the rest of his life in a wheelchair after a woman in a station wagon hit him on her way home from the grocery?

I went over to one of the windows. It was just after sunset and there was still plenty of light. A couple of girls were out on the playground going back and forth on the swings. They had no idea how much danger they were in.

I hadn't noticed it before, but there was a chart by the door of the classroom. It showed the phases of the moon. On October 26th the lunar cycle was in the depths of its waning phase. There would only be a sliver of illumination.

An almost moonless night seemed like a good time to take a walk through the Valley of the Shadow of Death. I could hear a couple of men talking at the bottom of the stairs. I got my portrait and left as soon as they moved on.

When I got home, my parents made a big deal out of the portrait. They went on and on about how much it looked like me. They were probably glad to have something to take their minds off of missiles and mushroom clouds. I didn't want to just sit around. I took my basketball outside and started shooting on the goal in our driveway. There was a floodlight on that corner of the house, and sometimes I shot at night.

I usually pretended I was playing for Battle Ground in some big varsity game, but that night I pretended that if I could make eight out of ten free throws, there wouldn't be a nuclear war. I'd hit three or four in a row, and then I'd choke and have to start all over again. I never could make eight out of ten, and I ended up kicking my ball across Crescent – into what had been the Blonde Bombshell's front yard.

Chapter 5

October 26, 1962 – It's Friday night before dinner and I'm standing out behind our house. The wind is picking up a little and it's getting cooler. I wonder if the world will end tonight. I can see Mother through the kitchen window. She was beautiful back when she and my father got married. She's still pretty – but she isn't still twenty-four and she's gained a little weight since then. She's in front of the stove and there's a cloud of steam when she takes the lid off the pot of rice. If Mother is thinking about me, she's probably wondering how scared I am.

She worries about me a lot. Sometimes she wants me to talk when she thinks I'm anxious, but I usually don't say much. She already had a couple of miscarriages by the time I came along, and she was afraid she wouldn't get to be a mother. I'm pretty sure she didn't picture motherhood being the way it is. She's very loving and sentimental and good, but sometimes, even when things are going okay, she seems sad. I've always wondered if it's because she was still a girl when her mother died.

My father is walking around in the next room with a drink in his hand. He's probably wondering how he'll take care of us if there's an attack. He looks like a typical middle-aged businessman, but he isn't typical.

His father grew up in Nashville and became a physician, but he went to the Philippines not long after the Spanish-American War. There was a shortage of doctors there, and he ended up marrying a Spanish lady from Manila. My grandfather died when my father was two and my aunt was one. There are times when I wonder if part of the reason my father and my mother ended up together is because they both lost a parent when they were little.

When my father was nineteen, he left his mother and his sister in Manila and came to America to go to college at Vanderbilt, where his father graduated in the 1890s. My father went into business after he got his degree, and he and Mother married in 1940. Pearl Harbor was attacked the next year and Manila was quickly occupied by the Japanese. He was determined to get back to the Philippines to find his mother and his sister.

My father found a way to get into the intelligence branch of the Army Air Corps. He was trained to go behind enemy lines, and do things like examine downed enemy aircraft to see if they had been modified. He made it to Manila at the beginning of the battle to drive out the Japanese. The fighting was still going on when he found his sick mother and his wounded sister, and he got them food and medical treatment.

So much for the apple not falling far from the tree. The tree found a way to get to the other side of the world while a war was going on and operate behind Japanese lines, and then rescue his mother and sister. The apple just had to pass a few courses in high school, and he couldn't even make some free throws in an imaginary game to save the world.

The day after my father came home on leave from the war, he collapsed from the malaria he'd been carrying since he was in the jungle. He spent the next two months in a military hospital. His mother and sister stayed in the Philippines, but after his sister, Alicia, was killed in a plane crash in 1950, his mother finally came to America. I grew up knowing not to ask about his sister.

The day after President Kennedy made his speech on television announcing that Russian missiles were in Cuba, my father had called a friend who worked in military intelligence. They'd been in the same unit in the Philippines, and the guy was working in the Pentagon. I was pretty sure my father found out more than was being reported on television. While I was standing out in the backyard, I watched him pacing back and forth in the den. I wondered what he wasn't telling us.

A surge of wind came through the trees and I could see the dark shapes of leaves falling in front of the windows of our house. I kept watching Mother and my father. If civilization was destroyed, everything they went through during their lives would've been for nothing.

After dinner, I told them I was going for a walk. My father asked me to stay close to home. I went back to Woodmont, but a few men were still inside the school and I walked up to the playground.

Every time a car went by, the headlights would illuminate the swings and the seesaws and the jungle gym. They looked like sculptures. After a few minutes, I heard the barking of the dog I'd listened to so many times late at night. I took it as a bad sign that it was barking so much earlier than usual. It didn't sound very far away, and I decided to find out where it was and finally see what it looked like.

I'd been all over the neighborhood when I was a kid, but except for a couple of times when I went trick-or-treating with classmates on Halloween, I hadn't walked around at night. And I'd never walked around in the dark alone.

I went pretty far up one street, and when I heard the dog again, I cut through a couple of yards to the next street. I seemed to be getting pretty close, but then the barking stopped. I wanted to keep looking for the dog, but I was already pretty far from home and there was no telling when the barking would start again.

I took a different way back. I could see illuminated television screens in most of the houses. A lot of people were probably watching Jack Paar. It looked like any other Friday night. I didn't hear the dog again until I was walking up Lynnbrook Road, close to where Tom Hendrickson lived.

I walked over and stood on the basketball court. It had only been eight years since we started showing up on Saturday mornings to learn how to dribble and shoot and play defense, but it seemed like forever. The court was right across Westmont Avenue from Herbert's field, where kids from the neighborhood played baseball in the spring and summer, and football in the fall, and where kites were flown whenever the weather was good and the wind was right.

I went across Westmont and walked out to the spot in left field where I almost made the best catch of my life, back when I was ten years old. I wasn't good enough to be an infielder, so I always ended up in the outfield. Phil Andrews was at bat and I was in left field, and he hit a high line drive to deep left-center. Everybody assumed it was a home run, including Phil, but I got a really good jump on the ball.

By then I'd figured out that when a pitch came in on the left field side of the plate, the ball was almost always hit toward left, and that low balls were usually hit on the ground and high balls were hit in the air. Phil was a big right-handed batter, but he didn't pull the ball very much, and I'd already taken a few steps over toward center field. As soon as I saw where the catcher was moving his mitt, I took off toward the left-center field gap. The pitch he hit was waist-high and right down the middle, and he crushed it.

The year before I tried to make the catch, back when I was in fourth grade, I slid in under Phil's tag and committed the great sin of claiming to be safe. Phil was popular and I was barely tolerated, so when he kicked me in the side as hard as he could for claiming to be safe, nobody said anything. It hurt pretty much, but I cried because I couldn't do anything about it and because nobody took up for me. It was finally decided that if Phil apologized – which he eventually did without meaning it – I would be out.

The only reason I got the jump I got and ran as fast as I had, and lunged as far as I did, was that catching the ball was the first chance I'd gotten for revenge. I'd been waiting a year. I felt the ball bounce off the top of my glove, and I tore up my left elbow when I hit the ground.

Nobody said "Good try," and I don't think Phil even saw me dive for the ball. He would've gotten mad if I'd caught it. He would've probably glared at me for the rest of the game. I kept thinking about how, if I'd caught it, I could've run up to him and said, "Hey Phil, what are you gonna do – kick me in the side again?" When the inning was over I went in and sat down by myself near the backstop. I pushed my elbow against my jeans until it stopped bleeding.

Some wind came up and the dog started barking again. It was starting to get cold. I knew my parents were wondering where I was, but I looked up at the sky for a few minutes before I went back across the field to Westmont.

There were stars everywhere. The visible part of the moon reminded me of an eyelash. Sometimes on clear nights, I climbed up on the roof of our house, and a lot of times when I stared up at the stars, I thought about God. By then I was pretty sure that he had never been alone in the universe. I didn't see any way that an all-powerful being would choose to exist alone in a void.

That night, standing in the field and looking up at the sky, I was pretty sure that since God was eternal and since he'd created the universe and everything in it, then the universe must be eternal, too. The Earth might not last, but at least the universe would.

When I was on my way back home, I noticed how quiet the neighborhood was. There were hardly any cars on the road, and leaves were scraping and tumbling as they blew across the pavement.

It wasn't long before I walked by a ditch where the skeletons of several prehistoric Indians had been dug up a couple of years earlier by a construction crew putting in a gas line. A local archaeologist said that a thousand years in the past there was probably a small settlement around the place where the graves were found. Ever since then, I'd wondered about the people who lived there, all those centuries earlier.

There were times when I tried to imagine what they looked like and what they wore and what their houses were like and what language they spoke. And I wondered what they thought God was like and what they dreamed about at night.

Guys my age had lived there, and they probably loved the place where they lived as much as I loved the place where I lived. I started thinking about all the Indian bones that still hadn't been found, and how none of them would be disturbed if there was a nuclear blast.

I had a pretty good idea of what the neighborhood would be like if a nuclear warhead exploded anywhere close to Nashville. I didn't want to survive. I didn't want to see the neighborhood in ruins. Or wander off and try to live somewhere else. I wanted to die right there.

If there was an attack, I thought I knew what would happen to the house I loved, and to Woodmont School and to Herbert's field and to Tom Hendrickson's basketball court and to the place where I always fished on Richland Creek and to Belle Meade Theater and to Moon's Drugstore, where kids from Woodmont School went for cheeseburgers and milkshakes and to buy comic books and baseball cards, and to the rest of the houses and the yards and the trees, and to the quiet streets where we rode our bikes.

After a few decades, the roofs of the houses would rot away and start falling in, and in a century or so only the walls and chimneys of the houses would be left. The yards would be overgrown and there would be trees where the streets had been. After a few more centuries, the remains of the last house would collapse. My house and Woodmont School and all the places I cared about would end up buried under the dirt.

But people would probably survive in other places and start over, and in a thousand years, a descendant of one of the survivors might eventually walk around in the dark and wonder about the people who had lived in what was once called Nashville, back before the nuclear war. Maybe the descendant of a survivor would eventually find my skeleton.

I was wiped out by the time I got home. I watched the news with my father, and after I told Mother good night, I went to my room and wrote in my journal. I was listening to one of the rock and roll stations, and the last song the disc jockey played before the station went off the air that night was *Smokey Places.*

I lay in the dark and watched the cedar tree outside my window moving in the wind. I thought about the Blonde Bombshell, and I wondered if, somewhere out in the dark, some guy was in the back seat of a car telling a girl that if they were going to die, they might as well go out with a bang.

I kept watching the tree swaying back and forth, and I started saying the 23rd Psalm. It sounded empty when I said it. Even though I felt a little better when I was saying the passage from Paul, I didn't get too far with whatsoever was true and whatsoever was honest and whatsoever was just and whatsoever was pure.

I finally stopped praying. If the two most powerful nations on Earth were stupid enough and crazy enough to blow up the planet over missiles in Cuba, then humanity probably didn't deserve to survive. God might be letting the chips fall where they were going to fall, and what was going to happen was going to happen.

It was late when I heard my father snoring, and I got up and went into the den. He was asleep in his chair and the television was still on. The only thing on the screen was the test pattern for Channel 5. I didn't wake him up. I left the TV on in case something happened, and I took his glass into the kitchen and poured what was left of his bourbon into the sink. After I got back in bed, I kept looking at the tree outside my window.

The last thing I remembered from that night was thinking about a nightmare I had when I was seven. In my nightmare, something had taken me away from my family, and I ended up in Mexico. I'd been trying to get home, and I finally made it all the way back to Nashville. I got to Woodmont School, and after I walked the rest of the way to my house, I knocked on our front door. The people who came to the door were strangers. They said they were the only family that had ever lived there. It was the worst nightmare I ever had.

Chapter 6

When I woke up on Saturday morning the world was still in one piece. My parents looked tense, but I was tired of worrying. It was getting warmer, and I ended up taking my journal to the Woodmont playground and writing some more. By the time I got to school on Monday, President Kennedy had announced that things were going to be okay.

Mr. Godshaw, who taught Modern History, was the only teacher who talked about it in class. None of the guys at school even mentioned it. Since the world didn't blow up, they probably thought it hadn't been that big a deal in the first place. It was like the whole thing hadn't even happened. Everybody just kept going on with their lives, and after a while, so did I.

Tenth grade wasn't great, but at least I didn't get sick as much as I did the year before. My doctor finally figured out that I was anemic, and that there were problems with my thyroid gland. The reason I kept getting strep throat was because my immune system was all messed up. I started taking some pills, but it was a while before I felt any better.

I finally got my braces off, and after the dentist put in a couple of fake teeth, I didn't keep my mouth closed as much as I had. I was still stuck with Algebra and Latin, but English wasn't too bad and I liked history even more because Mr. Godshaw was the teacher. Kids laughed about how conservative he was, but he was entertaining and he seemed to like me.

Mr. Godshaw said it wouldn't be long before America fell to

the communists, and that we'd all probably end up being slaves of the Soviet Union. He talked a lot about Martin Luther King being a communist, and how the civil rights movement was part of a plot to weaken America. And he kept telling us that America was being weakened by President Kennedy.

After the missile crisis, Mr. Godshaw said that when Kennedy didn't attack Cuba, he showed the communists that America wasn't willing to fight. He said because Kennedy didn't meet aggression with aggression in Cuba, he was an appeaser. He told us it wouldn't be long before the communists took over South America and Central America, and after that, they would spread north like a plague.

General Curtis Lemay, who was a noted Air Corps commander in World War Two, was a military adviser to the President, and he was one of Mr. Godshaw's heroes. Mr. Godshaw was sure that the general did everything he could to get the president to bomb the missile installations and invade Cuba. He said while it was possible that President Kennedy was a communist, he could've just been an unconscious agent of the Communist Party.

I wasn't nearly as far underwater as I'd been when I was a freshman. Algebra was still irrelevant and uninteresting, but Latin wasn't too bad and I was getting better at basketball. I also found out that I had a talent I hadn't known about. I was pretty good at making up dirty lyrics to rock and roll songs.

I turned *It's My Party* ("and I'll cry if I want to") into *It's My Hymen* ("and I'll wince if I want to") and *Then He Kissed Me* became *And Then He Porked Me*. I changed *Hello Muddah, Hello Faddah* from being a song about a boy's struggles at camp, to descriptions of the wide range of sexual deviancy that went on in his cabin.

And *Walk Right In* became an invitation by a physiologically unique girl to her boyfriend. Sometimes guys at school would want me to make up lyrics to a particular song, and I could usually come up with something that made everybody laugh.

By then I'd noticed that a couple of the teachers at Battle Ground were pretty messed up. They weren't like Mr. Roche. He was just inexperienced. There was one guy in particular who was entirely different. His name was Mr. Peters and he looked like a cross between a drill sergeant and a bulldog.

He liked to ridicule anybody who was little or weak or fat, or who wasn't an athlete. But if a kid came from a rich family, Peters would leave him alone even if he was bad at sports, and no matter what he looked like. I tried to stay out of his way.

There was a quiet freshman who was sort of a sissy, and I'd already seen Peters pick on him a couple of times. One day when I was sitting at the same table with the kid at lunch, Peters came over and sat down. Then he started working the word *queer* into just about everything he said.

He looked at the kid and said, "Something *queer* happened last weekend." After that, he told some other guy at the table to get him some dessert. Then he said, "Just don't *queer* the deal," and he stared at the kid and raised his eyebrows. The kid looked like he was about to cry. He got up and tried to leave, but Peters yelled at him and made him come back and take his tray to the kitchen.

I must've been frowning. Peters looked at me and got mad. "Something the matter?"

I was too much of a coward to say what I wanted to say. There was another guy at the table – a senior named Elliot Grizzard – and he saw the look on my face, too. He was really smart, but he didn't have many friends. I'd seen him playing chess against himself in the library. He was supposedly an atheist, and I heard that he'd gone to a couple of Civil Rights demonstrations in Nashville.

The day after Peters picked on the kid at lunch, Grizzard saw me in the hall. "Do you know how to play chess?"

"Yeah, but I'm not any good."

"We should play after school today."

"It won't be much of a game."

He just nodded. "That's okay. There's something I want to talk to you about."

I met him in the library, and while he was slaughtering me in chess, he told me about a few other things Mr. Peters had done. Grizzard said he thought he knew a way to stop him, but he needed a little help to pull it off. He didn't say anything else for a few seconds. "But there's something you need to know. You could get kicked out of school for having anything to do with this."

I didn't want to get in trouble, but I was really curious about what Grizzard wanted to do. Along with not wanting to look bad in front of a senior – and along with how much I couldn't stand Mr. Peters – I was flattered that somebody might need my help. It was easier to stay than it was to leave, and I kept playing chess while I listened to his idea.

Grizzard said that Mr. Peters came downstairs at just about the same time every day on his way to lunch. He'd watched the way Peters walked down the steps, and he thought he knew how to make him trip. His plan was to wait until nobody was around, and after he screwed in an eye hook on the left side of the stairs, he'd screw another eye hook into one of the posts on the right.

Then he'd tie one end of some fishing line to the hook on the left and run it through the hook on the right, and he'd stand down beside the stairs where nobody would notice him. When Peters got to the fishing line, Grizzard would pull it and hope that Peters tripped.

Grizzard wanted me to come along right behind Peters. If he tripped, I'd reach down and cut the fishing line off the hook. While everybody was distracted by Peters, Grizzard would pull the line down to where he was. Without any line on the steps, it would be hard for anybody to figure out why Peters fell. The next day, Peters would get an anonymous letter telling him that he had been punished by a secret committee of students.

The thought of Peters bouncing down the stairs made me start laughing, and I came up with an idea that Grizzard liked. I said that instead of using an eye hook to the left of the stairs, maybe he could just use an old nail – one that looked like it had been there a while. A nail would be harder to see than a shiny new eye hook, and if it was bent up at a sharp angle, he could just make a loop in the line and slip it over the nail. And when I came along afterward, it would only take me a second to reach down and take it off the nail.

The next week, one afternoon when nobody was around, I was the lookout while Grizzard screwed in the eye hook. He put it on the outside of a post, and positioned it so it would be a little above and about six inches out from the front edge of the second step down from the top of the landing. Then he hammered a rusted nail into the board that ran down along the left side of the stairway, and he bent it up the way I'd suggested.

The next day Grizzard slipped out of study hall and went up to the top of the stairs. He looped the line over the nail, and after he ran it through the eye hook, he went down beside the bottom of the stairs and waited. Class let out a few minutes later. I was a few feet behind Mr. Peters when he stepped off the landing. Just before his foot came off the second step, Grizzard pulled the line as tight as he could.

I couldn't tell whether Peters hit the line with the front of his shoe, or if the line caught on his heel. He had an armload of papers and books, and when he lost his balance he lunged for the railing and dropped everything he was carrying. He got one hand on the rail, but he couldn't hold on and he lurched sideways down the stairs.

He knocked down two or three students on his way to the bottom. While everybody was looking at Peters rolling around at the foot of the stairs and cursing, I slipped the line off the nail and Grizzard pulled it down and stuffed it into his pocket.

When Peters finally sat up, he started yelling at the students standing around him. He said he'd give 50 demerits to anybody who didn't leave. Another teacher ended up helping him to the school clinic, and from there they took him to get checked out at the hospital. I couldn't believe Grizzard had pulled it off.

We went back when everybody was at lunch, and while Grizzard unscrewed the hook, I pulled the nail out of the wall with a hammer. He put the line in the trash can in the restroom, and around the time I was dropping the nail and the hook in the trash outside the lunchroom, Grizzard was putting the hammer back in his car.

Peters only had a banged-up shoulder, but when he came back to school the next day, he found a typed letter on the desk of his classroom. "What happened on the stairs was a warning. Stop picking on kids who can't defend themselves. We're watching you." I glanced at him a few times during the next assembly, and he seemed uneasy.

I played chess with Elliott Grizzard a couple of more times, but that was about it. I was too young for us to be friends. And it turned out that by the time Peters fell down the steps, he'd already decided to leave Battle Ground Academy. The next year he was working at a bank somewhere.

That was just about the only victory I had the whole time I was in high school, and there were plenty of defeats. The worst one happened because I'd gotten pretty good when it came to insults. Guys insulted each other all the time at Battle Ground.

The insults usually involved things like implying that a guy was a homosexual, or that he was ugly or stupid, or that his genitalia was especially small, or speculating about the sexual appetites of his mother, or of a sister or a girlfriend if he had either one. Even though I wasn't all that popular, I had a minor reputation for being able to cut people down.

One day I insulted a guy who took what I said personally, or at least he pretended to. He was chunky, and I said something about his being fat. Guys said stuff like that to each other all the time and everybody knew it didn't mean anything.

But he was furious, or he acted like he was, and he wanted to fight. He was a lot heavier and stronger than I was, and he was angry. I tried to turn away his wrath with a soft answer, but it didn't work. He saw an opportunity to show everybody how tough he was and he took it.

It would've been a lot better for me if I'd gone ahead and tried to fight him, but I wasn't mad and his anger seemed to drain away the little bit of strength I had. I felt like I was paralyzed. He pushed me a few times and when I didn't fight back, he threw me down. Guys gathered around the way they always did, but they didn't get to see a fight. What they saw was a humiliated coward. I figured that any time they thought about me for the rest of their lives, all they would remember was how I chickened out.

There were plenty of other defeats, but they were all more subtle than that. I'd gotten better in basketball, but I still didn't think I was good enough to make the school team. I didn't want to go through the embarrassment of getting cut, and when November came around, I didn't try out. And by the time winter turned to spring, it was pretty obvious that I would fail sophomore Algebra. I would be going back to summer school again.

Chapter 7

May 18, 1963 –My father went to play golf, and I've come with Mother to see President Kennedy. He's in Nashville today and he'll be riding right down West End Avenue on his way to speak at the football stadium at Vanderbilt, which is only about three miles from our house. The weather is good and we're waiting on the sidewalk in front of West End Methodist Church.

It's probably crowded downtown, but there aren't many people out where we are. I've seen Kennedy a million times on television. I wonder if he'll look any different in person. My parents didn't vote for him and Mr. Godshaw says he might be a communist, but Mr. Godshaw really goes overboard about all the communist stuff. I'm pretty sure Kennedy is better than Nixon would've been.

A couple of police motorcycles come up over the rise to our left and then the motorcade moves into view. I see the big black presidential limousine, and then I see President Kennedy. He's sitting on the right side of the car. He'll only be about 30 feet away from me when he goes by.

Just as he gets up to where I am, he turns his head a little and looks at me. Then he stares right into my eyes for a couple of seconds. I'm staring back at him and I smile. He looks like he's about to grin and his right hand twitches like he might wave, but the limousine moves on by and he looks at the road ahead.

Mother has a big smile on her face. A man standing a few feet away saw what happened. "It seems like he knew you." I'm pretty sure President Kennedy noticed me because of the green shirt I'm wearing, and maybe the reason he kept looking at me is because I'm tall and skinny, and because I have a goofy-looking flat top instead of a normal haircut.

We'd planned to just go back home, but after the president looked at me, I wanted to hear his speech. Vanderbilt stadium was a few hundred yards down West End, and Mother and I walked as fast as we could to get there before Kennedy started talking. The place was crowded. We ended up sitting pretty far away, but he wasn't hard to hear.

I wanted to put something from his speech in my journal, and Mother handed me a little pad and a pencil from her purse. The president talked some about politics, but a lot of his speech was about education. What I ended up writing down sounded pretty important. "You have responsibilities to use your talents for the benefit of the society which helped develop those talents. You must decide whether you will give to the world in which you were educated, the benefits of that education."

I got through with my exams a few days later, and I went to the library and got a book called *PT 109*. It was about what President Kennedy did back in World War II. I knew that he was a war hero, but I hadn't understood how brave he was, or what he went through. I also knew a little about his family, but I didn't understand how easy it would've been for him to just sit around and be rich.

He did more than talk about having a responsibility to do things for the world. By the time he gave his speech, he'd been doing things for the world for twenty years. After that, it bothered me when I heard people say how much they hated him.

I was turning sixteen in September, and along with going to summer school, I took a driving class. Learning to drive and learning just enough algebra to get by was pretty much all I did that summer. I understood that I was supposed to have a social life, but instead of having dates and going to parties, most of the time I stayed at home.

The guys I knew and the teenagers I saw on television all acted pretty much the same way. I was fairly sure that doing what everybody else did – and thinking the way everybody else thought – was the way to be popular and have a girlfriend.

I wanted to fit in and be popular, but even as messed up as I was, I wasn't willing to turn myself into a made-up version of who other people thought I was supposed to be. The way I saw it, I could either go to the teenage costume ball wearing a mask, or I could stay home. I didn't like staying home, but that's what I did.

High school kids in Nashville had been getting together and starting rock and roll bands ever since rock and roll came along, and local rock and roll bands took off in the early 1960s. Almost every school had at least one group that played on weekends. There were two really good bands at Battle Ground Academy in 1963. There were parties in people's driveways and yards that whole summer, and there were plenty of nights when I could hear the music from my room. It would drive me crazy.

Sometimes I wanted to run out into the darkness and follow the music until I found the party, but even if I could've made myself do it, I knew what would happen. I'd just end up watching all the confident guys dancing with girls who would've ignored me.

So I stayed in my room and listened to the music, and imagined how good the girls looked in their sundresses. Curfew would finally close in, and by the time the music ended, a lot of couples would've already slipped away to secluded places. The neighborhood would get quiet and I'd lie in bed waiting for a train to roll by, or waiting to hear the dog I'd never seen start barking at nothing.

August 31, 1963 – It's Saturday night and I'm in my room. It's been another wasted summer. Cars are going by on the way to a party that's just down the street. I can hear kids talking and laughing between songs. I wonder if my dream girl is there. I imagine climbing out of my bedroom window and walking through the darkness until I get to the music.

Everybody will be dancing except for one girl. She is standing by herself in the shadows, and I can tell that she's been waiting for me.

But I can't make myself go. I keep telling myself that she wouldn't notice me if I showed up, and I start screaming into my pillow. When I can't scream anymore, I get down on the floor. I want to beat my head against the rug, but I don't. I tell myself that even if she's there, she has a date and I couldn't stand to see her shaking everything she has during the fast songs and clinging to the guy she's with during the slow songs.

I know every word to every song the band is playing, and a guy who sounds almost as good as Major Lance starts singing Hey Little Girl. I start singing, too, and I sound pretty good and I take the light off my desk and put it on the floor, and when I turn off the rest of the lights in my room, my shadow is on the wall and then it's Hey Baby and Do You Love Me? and Twist and Shout and Heat Wave, and I sing and I dance with my shadow till the party shuts down.

After that, I didn't want to get in bed and wait for the dog to start barking. My parents were asleep by then and I went out to the living room. My portrait was on the wall next to the fireplace. I made myself look at it even though it mostly reminded me of who I wasn't.

I was tired of wasting my life. I wanted to see myself the way Ann saw me. She didn't see some pathetic character who would back down from a fight and who wouldn't go to a party by himself and who wouldn't talk to girls.

The kid Ann saw looked like he would stand up to a teacher who was a bully, instead of just playing a part in making him fall down a flight of stairs. In the portrait, I looked like a guy who wouldn't let anything keep him from making a basketball team. I looked like a kid who could figure things out. Like a kid who wasn't playing it safe. I looked like a kid who refused to ignore the fact that some of what he'd been taught in church couldn't be true.

Chapter 8

Three weeks after I started back to Battle Ground Academy, I turned sixteen. It was my junior year. All I had to do to get my driver's license was pass a written test that was a joke, and then take a driving test that was basically cruising around for a few minutes with a state trooper in the car. The written test wasn't a problem, but having the trooper sitting next to me made me nervous. When I ran a stop sign I never saw, the trooper instinctively slammed his foot into the floor, trying to stomp on a brake pedal that wasn't there.

I figured that after he got back, he told the other troopers that he'd found his candidate for choker of the year. At least Mother was the only one there who knew me. And the only person she was going to tell was my father. He probably wouldn't be all that surprised. I had to wait another month before I tried it again, and that time I managed to see the stop sign.

I was required to take another year of Latin, but I was finally through with Algebra. I took Geometry instead. It turned out to be almost as big a waste of time as Algebra was. I also took English, but it was mostly diagramming sentences and memorizing the rules of punctuation. The only class I looked forward to was American Government. It was taught by Mr. Godshaw, and he continued his ongoing account of how communism was taking over America.

I wanted to make decent grades that year, but I wanted to make the basketball team even more. Every day after school, I went to the gym and played in pickup games. I was at least as good as three-fourths of the guys who were trying out for the varsity.

If they tried to play me tight I could get by them. Sometimes I'd go off the wrong foot on my layups, but I usually scored. And if they played me loose, I had a pretty good shot from outside. After a couple of days, nobody acted surprised when I put it in the basket. And one day we were playing and I couldn't miss. Just about every shot I took went in, and Coach West was off to the side watching the whole time.

I was pretty confident when tryouts started, but we didn't do much scrimmaging. Coach West was big on fundamentals and being in shape, and just about all we did was go through drills and run. Even though I didn't think anything we were doing would make us better players or make our team any better, I tried as hard as I could. But sometimes I went the wrong way on the drills, or I made a mistake on offense.

Of the thirty-five guys who went out for the team, only four or five were any good. I felt like I had an outside chance of being a starter. Twelve of us would make the varsity, and another twelve would be on the junior varsity.

After two weeks Coach West posted the names of everybody who made the varsity and the junior varsity. The rosters were taped to the door of the locker room. I wasn't on either list. I felt numb. After I walked around for a while, I ended up in the library. Nobody else was there, and I sat at a table and cried.

I didn't hate Coach West. He was a nice guy. There wasn't anybody to talk to, and I finally got tired of thinking about it. Before long there were other things to think about.

November 22, 1963 – It's a little before one o'clock on Friday afternoon and I'm sitting in American Government class. It's almost time for the bell to ring and Mr. Godshaw is talking about the Second Amendment of the Constitution. Bear Robinson comes to the door. "Mr. Godshaw... well President Kennedy... he's been shot." Mr. Godshaw thinks Bear is joking, and he laughs and says how unfortunate it would be if something happened to the president. Then he goes back to talking about the Constitution.

The bell rings and I go by the student center on my way to lunch. The TV room is crowded. Walter Cronkite says the president was wounded, but most of the guys are pretty sure he'll be okay. I think about how easy it would've been for somebody to take a shot at him six months ago when he was riding past me on West End Avenue. Everybody feels the excitement of seeing history being made, but some of the guys are convinced that the president is a communist sympathizer. I hear two different classmates say they hope Kennedy dies. It seems like I'm watching everything from inside a cloud.

I ate as fast as I could, but by the time I got back to the TV room, Walter Cronkite had announced that President Kennedy was dead. Nothing seemed real from then until I got home. Except for the same news about the assassination being repeated over and over and over, there wasn't anything on television. I kept thinking about how we'd looked into each other's eyes.

A few other guys and I went over to Tom Hendrickson's house after dinner, and we played basketball and slow-motion football out in the rain until after midnight. Things were still pretty depressing the next day. It stopped raining and I took my basketball outside and started shooting. I pretended that I'd changed schools, and that I was playing against Coach West and the Battle Ground varsity. I made just about every shot I took.

Mother and I went to church the next day, and after Sunday school I signed up to play on the church team. We went into the sanctuary right after that, and halfway through the sermon, somebody handed a note to Dr. Rowe, our preacher. He announced that Lee Harvey Oswald had been shot and killed.

I couldn't understand how a man who just killed the President of the United States – an assassin who had the answers to so many questions – could've been killed. I didn't cry about Kennedy until the next day when I saw his little son salute the casket when it went by in the funeral procession.

The Battle Ground Academy Christmas Dance was going to be just before we got out of school for the holidays. Everybody in the junior class was supposed to take a date. I could've gotten out of it by pretending to be sick, but some guys who were going were even bigger losers than I was. If I was the only one in the class who didn't show up, I would've heard a whole lot about how I didn't go because I was queer. I didn't have much of a choice.

I had no idea who to ask, but then I ran into one of my cousins, Alex Hadley, who was a year ahead of me in school. I told him I needed to take somebody to the dance, and he said he'd check around. When he called me up a couple of days later, he said one of his friends had a cousin who was supposed to be really good looking, and nobody had asked her to the Christmas Dance.

Then he told me the girl's name was Yancey Walsh. I'd never seen her, but I'd been hearing about Yancey Walsh ever since I started high school. She was supposed to be one of the best-looking girls in that part of Nashville. I was pretty sure I knew why she hadn't been invited to the dance. Anybody who would've been brave enough to ask her out, probably assumed she was already going.

If she was anywhere close to being as beautiful as I'd heard she was, having Yancey Walsh as my date would make me look good. I knew how stupid and shallow that was, but I didn't care.

Even though I knew she'd probably go, it took me a couple of days to work up the courage to call her. When we finally talked, I didn't make enough of a fool of myself for her to turn me down. For the next few days, I pictured us showing up together at the dance, and I imagined how a lot of the guys I knew, and maybe even some girls, would think that I must have more going for me than they thought.

And there was always a chance that she'd actually like me. If that happened my stock would go through the roof. I didn't know what it would take for her to end up liking me, but I convinced myself that it wasn't totally impossible.

I knew I'd have to dance, and that was a problem. Dancing with an actual girl, and especially with a girl like Yancey Walsh, was going to be a lot different than dancing with my shadow.

I couldn't get home in time to see American Bandstand during the week, but it also came on the next Saturday afternoon. By then I had a TV in my room, and I practiced in front of the television by pretending to dance with whichever girl was on camera.

And on the following Wednesday night there was the Patty Duke Show. At the start of the show, as part of the introduction, there were a few seconds when Patty did some kind of rock-and-roll dance. As soon as she started dancing, I started dancing, too. And at least once a day I turned on my radio and danced in front of the mirror.

On the night of the dance at Battle Ground, before I left the house, I looked at myself in the mirror. My suit seemed okay, but I wanted to come up with something that might make me just a little more appealing. There was a can of peppermint-scented room freshener in the kitchen, and I sprayed myself right before I left. The spray turned out to be a lot more pungent than I thought. A friend of mine drove, and even though it was a cold night, we kept the car windows rolled down all the way to Yancey's house.

When I went inside to meet her parents, a puzzled look came over her father's face. I was waiting for him to mention the overpowering smell of peppermint that accompanied me into the room, but he didn't say anything. It wasn't long before Yancey made her grand entrance. She was as beautiful as everybody said she was. She briefly tilted her head to one side when she came in contact with the peppermint, but she didn't mention it either.

We drove the whole way to Franklin with the windows halfway down and the heater going full-blast. The peppermint had lost some of its strength by the time we got to the Battle Ground gymnasium, but couples started looking around as soon as I went by.

I'd survived the peppermint, but I still had to dance. Yancey ran into a couple of her friends, and while they were talking, I kept telling myself that when we started dancing, to just dance with the music.

But I didn't have to dance that night. The band was a really good local R&B group called *The Spidels*, and after they did three or four songs – when they were good and loose – they started singing *Twist and Shout*. They were dancing and Mr. Rennin, our headmaster, took that as a provocation. He told them to pack up and get out.

Later on, he said that he wouldn't tolerate any suggestive dancing at a school function. I was pretty sure that if white guys had danced the same way, he wouldn't have done anything about it. But there was a positive side to Mr. Rennin. He had a really good sense of humor and he was a great storyteller, and he'd always been nice to me. Sometimes I got the feeling that he didn't like being a headmaster.

People stood around talking, and it wasn't long before things got pretty boring. I wanted Yancey to have a good time, and I thought she might enjoy hearing me do a parody of a song. I started off with *Deep Purple*, by Nino Tempo and April Stevens, but I changed the lyrics to –

When my grandmother falls,
Down the steps and hits the wall,
And the stars begin to twinkle in her head,
Through the fog of her memory,
Everything is so hard to see,
And she just lies on the floor.

I got the feeling that Yancey really thought that my grandmother had gone to the hospital. When I tried to explain that it was just something I'd made up, she looked a little confused. By then it was pretty obvious that we wouldn't end up slipping away to some quiet place to make out. I'd known it was a long shot, but it would've been great to go back to school and happen to mention that I'd kissed Yancey Walsh.

And there was something I didn't understand. Looking at her was mostly like looking at *a picture* of a girl. It didn't seem like I was with an *actual* girl, and I wondered if kissing her would've been like kissing a picture – which I'd already done a few times by then.

We hung around a little longer and then we rode back to Nashville. When we were pulling up to drop Yancey off at her house, *Popsicles and Icicles* came on the radio. I was aware of the irony. Then I walked her to her door, and we exchanged our mutually awkward parting pleasantries. As for making myself look good by having a date with Yancey Walsh – nobody at school ever said anything about it.

Chapter 9

The holidays came and went without any other major embarrassments. I played church-league basketball with all the other rejects, but the retired preacher who was supposed to coach us quit showing up. I ended up sort of coaching the team. We only lost twice, and we never did any drills. I kept wondering how many games we would've won if Coach West was in charge.

While everything else was going on, the Beatles were exploding all over the radio. Their songs were everywhere. I said I couldn't stand them, but that was mostly because they were so popular. Sometimes I'd go against things just so I'd have an identity. I also said I couldn't stand Elvis, but I liked him okay – even though I liked Ricky Nelson and Roy Orbison a lot more.

It wasn't long before I had to admit that the Beatles were pretty good. I'd lie in bed at night and listen to their songs on the radio, but as good as they were, their songs didn't get inside me the way rhythm and blues songs did. I liked the Beatles, but their version of *Twist and Shout* couldn't touch the version by the Isley Brothers.

After I finally got my license, I started driving to school. Most of my classmates drove the same way I did. Driving fast was like being on a thrill ride at the state fair. The closest I came to having a bad wreck was one morning when I was going about 80 miles an hour up Hillsboro Road on my way to school in my family's second car – a 1956 Chevy Bel Air.

I was passing a line of cars when a truck came around a curve in the oncoming lane. There wasn't anywhere I could go, and I slammed on the brakes. My car hardly slowed down at all, but when the driver I was passing jammed on his brakes, a space opened up. I had to do something, and I downshifted. The tires screeched and the car skidded, and I swerved into the open gap. And that was that. But instead of figuring out that I might need to stop driving like an idiot, all I figured out was that I was a pretty damn good driver when I needed to be. I didn't stop driving like a sixteen-year-old until a few months later.

April 23, 1964 – It's just about 3:30 on Thursday afternoon. It's been raining off and on. Three of us are on our way home from school, and I'm in the back seat doing some homework. Our car suddenly swerves off to the side of the road, and the other two guys jump out and start sprinting back down Hillsboro Road. I get out and follow them. They run across a little concrete bridge, and then they go down to the bank of the creek that runs under the bridge.

Just before I get to the bridge I hear a scream. A station wagon is upside-down in the water. Four guys from Battle Ground are beside the creek, and one of my classmates is in the water holding his arm. Another classmate, Jack Johnson, is lying on the bank and he screams again. Nobody at Battle Ground Academy drives faster than Jack.

Jack had started to pass a car, but when he tried to whip back into his lane, his station wagon slid sideways on the wet pavement, clipped the back of the other car, and crashed through the guardrail. Jack was thrown out when his car rolled into the creek. Dark blood was coming from his ears and he let out another scream, but it wasn't as loud as the one before.

I found a way to avoid going down to my schoolmates. A line of cars was blocking the road and I started directing traffic. At one point, after a grinning moron stopped his truck on the bridge and got out to gawk, I yelled at him and beat on the hood of the truck until he drove off. The cars had to keep moving so the ambulance could get through.

It wasn't long before Jack stopped screaming, and then he

started turning blue. I could hear the ambulance in the distance. It would've been there sooner if there wasn't so much traffic in the way, but I was pretty sure it didn't matter. The ambulance sped away, and in less than a minute it passed the place where I'd almost had my wreck a few months earlier.

Jack died on the way to the hospital. At his funeral, I sat in the balcony at the back of St. George's Episcopal Church with Tom Hendrickson and a couple of other guys. The worst part was seeing his younger brother sobbing while the family followed the casket down the center aisle of the sanctuary on the way to the hearse. I tried not to think about what had happened, but I slowed down after that.

Not long after Jack died there were several racial incidents in downtown Nashville. Black students were trying to integrate some local restaurants and they started staging sit-ins and marching. There was some violence and a few injuries, and one of the people who got arrested was Elliott Grizzard, who graduated the year before.

It was hard to tell who was more outraged about the demonstrations – our headmaster, Mr. Rennin, or Mr. Godshaw. Mr. Rennin, who never mentioned Elliott, spent an entire assembly giving an angry speech against integration. He ended up making a promise to the student body. "A Negro student will *never* be admitted to Battle Ground Academy."

Mr. Godshaw kept insisting that a restaurant owner had a constitutional right to turn away anybody he wanted, and that all the racial problems taking place in the South were caused by outside agitators. He said the agitators were being directed by communists to weaken America, so the country would be easier for them to take over.

And when Martin Luther King came to town, that really set him off. One of the things Mr. Godshaw always said was that the government couldn't make somebody equal – equality had to be earned.

I thought about that a lot. Felix Kingman, who'd been doing

yard work for our family since I was little, was a soldier in Europe during World War I. He was wounded in his back and legs when a German artillery shell exploded behind him, but after a couple of months, he returned to his unit. He had a limp for the rest of his life. When my father was explaining what Felix went through, I could tell how much he respected him.

The man who cut our grass and trimmed our hedges was not only a decorated war veteran, he was a good husband and father and grandfather, and he was an elder in his church. I wanted to tell Mr. Godshaw about Felix Kingman, and ask him what else Felix needed to do to earn his equality. If Mr. Godshaw ever served in the military, he never said anything about it.

There was something else I wanted to know. Mr. Godshaw was very religious, and I wanted to ask him if he thought Negroes could go to heaven. I'd never seen anything in the Bible about heaven only being for white people, or that there was a separate heaven for black people.

If Mr. Godshaw thought that Negroes went to heaven, I wanted to ask him if he thought God loved the Negroes who were in heaven less than he loved the white people who were in hell. And if he thought black people and white people were together in heaven, I wanted to know how he justified the way things were in Nashville and in the South, and in all the other places where the races were separated.

That's what I wanted to ask him, but Mr. Godshaw liked me. I made pretty good grades in his class, and I didn't want to mess that up. He stayed on Martin Luther King and the outside agitators for a while, but then he went back to the communists and how, if they ever took over Southeast Asia, it wouldn't be long before they would head across the Pacific to America.

Chapter 10

May 10, 1964 – I'm holding my grandfather's hand. He's gazing up at me from his hospital bed. He doesn't look the same without his glasses. I'm the youngest of his 13 grandchildren, but I don't think he knows who I am. Even though he's been an invalid since I was four years old, I've held onto one memory from before he was hit by a car while he was crossing a city street. I remember sitting in his lap at our dining room table when he gave me a red fire truck on my second birthday.

Mother talks about how kind and funny he used to be, and how loving he always was. He'll be 90 if he lives till next fall, but he won't come close to making it that long. Before he was a feeble old man in a hospital bed, he owned a clothing factory. Back in 1890, when he was the age I am now, he swept the floors of that same factory, helping to support his family.

He was only eight years old when he left Dundee with his scarcely literate mother and his brothers and sisters, and traveled to Glasgow. I look into the same eyes that watched from the deck of a ship as the Scottish coastline disappeared in the distance, and saw New York City eleven days later as his ship approached Ellis Island. I look into the eyes that saw America through the windows of the train that brought his family to Nashville, where his father, who worked as a stone mason, had rented a small house in a slum called Hell's Half-Acre. The same pale blue eyes – kind eyes – stared at the corpse of his father after he died of consumption in 1885, and now they look at me when I lean down and kiss him on his unshaven cheek.

Mother was there when he died three days later. She said his breathing got shallower and shallower until there were no more breaths. I helped carry his coffin to the hearse and then to the graveside. I was surprised by how light it was. After the burial, Mother sat in the car with her door open and cried for a long time. Watching her break down was a different kind of bad than watching Jack Johnson's little brother cry at the end of Jack's funeral.

Exams came and went and school finally let out for the summer. I did pretty well in everything except Geometry, but I passed. That meant I finally didn't have to go to summer school. Mother said she didn't think it was a good idea for me to have a part-time job I didn't care about and just stay around the house all summer. She didn't get any argument from me.

She got in touch with an old friend of hers who had moved from Nashville to Newport Beach, California. I was invited to go out for a visit that ended up lasting all the way into August. Her friend had a son named Ronny who was a couple of years older than I was. We'd spent some time together before he moved away, and we got along pretty well.

I liked being in California. Ronny worked during the day and I was on my own. I got to drive an old Ford Falcon they had, and it only took about fifteen minutes to get from their house to the beach. I loved the Pacific Ocean. Sometimes the waves were huge, and it wasn't long before I started body surfing. The first place I tried it was next to a rock jetty that caused the waves to well up bigger than they were anywhere else nearby. It was called the Wedge.

I couldn't believe how strong a wave could be. I felt like I was about to drown two or three different times before I finally started doing what everybody else did when a big wave was about to break. From then on, just before it got to where I was, I took a big breath and dove as deep as I could. The force of the water would throw me around underwater like a bomb had gone off, but I learned to relax until the ocean let me make it back to the surface.

I was usually at the beach by noon, and I stayed in the water most of the day. After I went back and we had dinner, Ronny and I went out and rode around. He had a black 1964 Ford Galaxie that he got when he graduated from high school. We drove all over Newport Beach and Costa Mesa, and a lot of times we went down to the Balboa peninsula. Night after night it was *Love Me Do* and *A Hard Day's Night*, but I was in California, so I heard *I Get Around* and *Don't Worry Baby* all the time, too.

I stayed up and watched TV after Ronny and his parents went to bed. Every time there was a commercial, I did as many pushups as I could before whatever I was watching came back on. I needed to do something about my body. When I got out to California I was six foot one and I weighed about 140 pounds. I didn't want to go back home looking the way I did when I left. Between the pushups and being in the ocean so much, it wasn't long before I could feel myself getting stronger.

June 25, 1964 – It's about 9 PM on Thursday and Ronny pulls up to a light. I'm hoping that whoever pulls up beside us is old. If it's a teenager, Ronny will do what he always does. He'll look over and let the guy know that his car is a piece of crap compared to Ronny's Galaxie.

Two nights ago we were at an intersection and the guy next to us revved his engine. Both cars peeled out when the light changed, and the Galaxie blew the other car away. I didn't like being in the middle of a drag race, but it doesn't take much to make Ronny mad, so I stayed quiet. I don't know anything about cars, but I pretend to listen when he starts talking about slicks and traction rods and anything else that will make his Galaxie go even faster than it already does.

Where Did Our Love Go comes on the radio. I like the Supremes. Diana Ross is pretty, but I always end up looking at Florence Ballard. Ronny changes the station and he keeps changing stations until he hears My Boy Lollipop, which is by a girl named Little Millie Small.

He starts talking about how cute Little Millie sounds, and then he starts talking about what he'd like to do with her if she was with him in the back seat of his car. I think about letting him know that she's Jamaican, but telling him Little Millie is black would just set him off. There are times when Ronny can sound a little like Mr. Rennin or Mr. Godshaw. Before he heard My Boy Lollipop he said something about going home, but we don't turn when the light changes. It looks like he wants to make one more run down Balboa Boulevard.

Pretty soon Ronny was staring into his rearview mirror. A car was tailgating us and he couldn't stand being tailgated. When he turned off onto a side street, the car behind us turned, too. When Ronny stopped, the other car passed us. It was two girls, but we couldn't see what they looked like.

Dusty Springfield was singing *Wishin' and Hopin'* and when Ronny screeched up behind them and flashed his headlights, they pulled over. I expected him to get out and investigate while I waited in the car, but when he opened his door he said, "Come on."

He went over to the passenger side, and I walked up and tried to think of what I was going to say to the girl who was driving. She was pretty good looking, especially from the neck down. I was just about to say something when Ronny came around the car and nudged me out of the way.

When I went over to the other side of the car, I saw why he'd left. The girl riding shotgun turned out to be nice, but she looked a little like Jerry Lewis would've looked if he was a skinny teenage girl with long hair.

The girls followed us to get some ice cream, and then we drove over to Little Corona Beach and took a walk beside the ocean. There was a lot of phosphorous in the water that night, and every time a wave broke there was illumination in the surf.

It wasn't long before Ronny and the girl – whose name was Susan – had their tongues halfway down each other's throats. I hadn't ever kissed a girl, and I wasn't about to start with a girl who looked like Jerry Lewis. So she stood next to me on the beach and waited for nothing to happen while I waited for Ronny's and Susan's tongues to get tired.

One day when there wasn't much surf I drove to Disneyland, which was only about 25 minutes from Ronny's house. I walked around all day, and I went on some rides and saw a couple of shows. But what stood out more than anything else was being in Tomorrow Land and seeing a black sailor and a white girl holding hands and smiling at each other.

I hadn't ever seen a mixed couple before, and being from the South I was supposed to be horrified. I followed them around for a while. Mr. Godshaw always said that racial mixing would lead to the collapse of America, but the girl and the sailor just seemed like they were having a good time. I didn't see anything wrong with them being together. And even if I *had* thought something was wrong with it, I didn't see how it would be any of my business.

Chapter 11

Not long after I visited Disneyland, I went to Los Angeles to stay for a few days with Mother's nephew, Wes. He was twenty-eight and he was the black sheep of the family. He was always nice enough to me, but Mother said he was wild and that he'd been wild all his life. I hadn't been in his apartment for 30 minutes before he asked me if I was dating anybody.

It bothered him when I said I'd never had a girlfriend, and he didn't say anything for a few minutes. He seemed to be thinking, and he finally asked me if I wanted to go to Tijuana. All I knew about Tijuana was that it was in Mexico. He said we could go to the bullfights, and after that, we could go to one of the houses. I was pretty sure he was talking about whorehouses.

I couldn't *wait* to go to Tijuana. I'd hoped that having a date with Yancey Walsh would help my reputation, but losing my innocence in a Mexican whorehouse would be a whole lot better than having a date with a beautiful girl. I'd have plenty to tell the guys at Battle Ground when I got back to school, and if I could get my virginity out of the way, I might finally be able to relax around girls.

Three people that Wes knew came by early on Sunday morning in a red convertible and we left for Tijuana. The guy driving the car was supposed to be an actor, and along with another guy, there was a receptionist named Samantha who looked like she could be in college.

She said she was tagging along because she'd never seen a

bullfight. She was pretty and she had long platinum-blonde hair, and I sat next to her in the back seat. Wes brought a metal flask that was full of some kind of whiskey. He drank the whole way down, and the more he drank, the more he had to say about politics.

He kept talking louder and louder, and he finally got around to saying that "the niggers rioting in Harlem needed to be machine-gunned and so should the Freedom Riders," and that "the Civil Rights workers whose bodies just got found in Mississippi got what they deserved, just like Medgar Evers got what he deserved," and that "the outside agitators were why the little girls got killed in Birmingham when the colored church got blown up," and that "Lyndon Johnson should be impeached for signing the Civil Rights Act" and "Kennedy should've ended the missile crisis by dropping a hydrogen bomb on Havana."

I read newspapers and magazines pretty often, and I watched the news almost every night. I understood that he didn't know what he was talking about. If I hadn't had Mr. Godshaw as a teacher, I would've probably just thought that Wes was crazy.

But Mr. Godshaw wasn't the same as Wes. If Mr. Godshaw was driving down the road and saw a black person having car trouble, he would've stopped and tried to help. He thought what he thought, but he wasn't a bad human being. But if Wes saw a black man off by himself on a quiet road, and if he was drinking with somebody he was trying to impress, there's no telling what he would've done. I kept thinking about the mixed couple I'd seen at Disneyland. If he'd been there, he would've probably insulted them and tried to start a fight.

When Wes was born the doctor used forceps to deliver him, and his skull was partially crushed. He was pretty smart, but his right arm and his right leg were messed up and he never could do things like play sports. He walked with a limp, but he covered it up pretty well. And along with everything else, his father was an alcoholic who died young, and his mother drank a lot, too.

When we got to San Diego, Wes was driving and he was drunk.

The whole way down I expected to hear *The House of the Rising Sun*. It finally came on and I knew that the God of the Radio hadn't forgotten me. After we crossed over into Tijuana, Wes started acting crazy. First, he drove on the wrong side of the road and made the oncoming cars veer out of the way. He did that a couple of more times, and then he saw a big Mexican guy walking along the street.

Wes stopped the car and stared at him, and then he yelled something in Spanish. The guy clinched his fists and started walking toward our car. He looked angry, and when he was three or four steps away, Wes took off. But after we went a few yards, he stopped the car and said something else. When the Mexican guy started screaming and ran at the car, Wes took off again.

August 2, 1964 – We're all sitting on the sixth row of the Toreo de Tijuana. It's sunny and the arena is dusty and hot. The crowd is mostly men with hard faces. Wes has a goatskin full of wine. He holds it up and squeezes a stream of red wine into his mouth. The only thing I know about bullfights is what I've seen in cartoons on television. I expect a matador to come out with a cape, and then a bull will charge a few times and miss, and after that, a few more matadors will come out and get charged by a few more bulls. Then we'll head off to whichever brothel Wes is taking me to. I try to picture what's about to happen.

Wes told me that for twenty-five dollars I could be with a really good looking girl. Ever since I knew we were going to Tijuana, I'd been imagining going up the steps of some old two or three-story house and walking along a half-lit upstairs corridor, and stopping at a door.

I pictured myself opening the door, and I kept trying to visualize the girl I saw at Willow Plunge back when I was fourteen. But whoever was waiting for me, when I opened the door I hoped the first thing she did was smile at me.

Our seats were fairly close to a small band of musicians sitting at the edge of the bullring. They were wearing red and gold uniforms that were stained with sweat and covered with a veil of dust. They started playing, and the matador and his entourage marched into the arena. After the bull came out and ran around the ring, he made several charges at the matador.

Every time the bull got close enough to gore him, the matador, who was holding out his cape, stepped to one side – just like the matadors in Saturday morning cartoons. There were a few more charges like that, and then the band started playing again and the matador left. I thought there was about to be another bullfight, but a couple of men rode out on horses that had heavy padding draped over their sides.

The men were carrying lances, and when the bull charged, the rider stuck his lance into the bull's hump and the crowd cheered like something great had just happened. Blood started coming out of the wound, and I wondered if every bullfight would have men on horses sticking the bull in the hump with their lances. The band started playing again and after the men rode off on their horses, three guys marched out carrying what looked like short harpoons. They ended up sticking them into the bull's hump, too.

I wanted the whole thing to stop, but the band got going again and the matador came back out with a sword. The bull charged and it wouldn't have bothered me if he hurt the matador at least as badly as he had been hurt. The crowd cheered like it was a big deal every time the matador got out of the way.

Then the matador lifted his sword and angled the blade downward. The bull charged and the matador drove the sword between the shoulder blades of the bull, and the crowd cheered when the bull collapsed and died. I looked over at Wes, who was yelling his drunken approval. The two guys with us were cheering, too. Samantha just looked at me and shook her head. All she said was, "One down, five to go."

Wes and most of the men around us kept getting drunker, and as the afternoon wore on, I was thinking less and less about what was supposed to happen after the bullfight. I kept hoping that one of the bulls would stick a horn into a matador, or into one of the other guys.

Every time a bull was about to be lanced or harpooned or killed, I closed my eyes and tried to think about things like going to the carnival at Woodmont School, or flying kites at Herbert's Field.

I was as thirsty as I'd ever been, but I wasn't about to drink any water while I was in Tijuana. The bottles of cola the vendors were selling were submerged in half-filled tubs of ice and contaminated water.

It was hot and dusty, and the thirstier I got, the more I wondered how the wine in Wes's goatskin would taste. I started whispering the 23rd Psalm to myself, and I imagined sitting in the shade beside still waters and my having my cup running over.

It was finally time for the last bull to come out, but instead of running into the arena, all he could do was limp out. He tried to charge the matador, but it looked like one of his ankles was broken. His charge was more like a lurch, and after a few steps, he stopped.

When the men rode into the ring on their horses, the bull didn't even move. They drove their lances into his hump, and all he did was bellow. And he bellowed again a few minutes later when he was stuck with the harpoons. The bull half-stumbled toward the matador when he came back out, and then the matador brought his sword into position for the kill.

The crowd had been whistling and booing since the bull limped out into the ring, and they kept sailing seat cushions out from the grandstand. When the matador drove his sword between the shoulders of the bull, the front legs of the animal collapsed, but he didn't die. More cushions sailed out and landed in the dirt, and there were more boos and whistles and catcalls while the matador made another attempt to complete the kill. The bull was choking and blood was pouring out of his mouth, but he still managed to make a couple of bellowing sounds.

By the time he finally fell over and died, most of the cushions were out in the ring. While we were leaving the arena, a man wrapped a chain around the hooves of the dead bull. Then he got on his horse and dragged away the carcass, while another guy started shoveling the blood-soaked dirt into a wheelbarrow.

I was too thirsty to spit. I tried to imagine myself being led beside still waters again, but I kept thinking about how the bullring and the rest of Tijuana belonged smack dab in the middle of the Valley of the Shadow of Death.

After we got to the restaurant at Hotel Caesar's, Wes left our table and went over to talk to a tall dark-haired woman who was dressed in a blue gown. She had big false eyelashes and she was wearing a lot of makeup. Both she and Wes looked like they were dead inside. They finally turned around and Wes pointed me out. I saw her nodding as she sized me up, but I started shaking my head. I kept shaking it until I was sure Wes saw me.

He stopped talking and came back to the table. He was frowning. "Are you sure?"

I said I was very damn sure. Everything that happened since we left Los Angeles – from all the things he said on the way down, to the crazy stuff he did when we got there, to what I saw at the bullfight – it all made me feel dirty and I wasn't about to feel any dirtier than I already felt.

I ended up sitting with Samantha in the lobby of the Hotel Caesar's while Wes and the other two guys went where I thought I'd be going, to do what I thought I'd be doing. Samantha was nice and we talked the whole time. She eventually told me what Wes yelled at the big Mexican.

The first time Wes stopped the car, he said that he was looking for a prostitute and he asked the guy where his mother lived. The second time, Wes told the guy that he had a question. He said he'd heard that the guy's mother would have sex with a pig for 100 centavos, and he wanted to know if it was true that she gave change.

I talked to Samantha for about three hours, which was a lot longer than I'd talked to Yancey Walsh. She was twenty-three, but she seemed more like a girl than a woman. We finally went outside and walked down Avenue Revolucion to a gift shop. I got some postcards and I bought a three-foot-tall piñata that looked like a cross between a llama and a giraffe. After Wes and the other guys finally made it back to the hotel, I got in the back seat next to Samantha and stood the piñata up in front of me.

It was a long drive and Wes eventually went back to ranting about the riots in Harlem and the dead civil rights workers in Mississippi, and about how great it was that Oswald had killed President Kennedy.

When we were coming into LA, there was a news report on the radio that the North Vietnamese had attacked two American destroyers in the Gulf of Tonkin. That sent Wes into a tirade. He said if LBJ didn't drop a nuclear weapon on Hanoi, he should be shot, and he ended up talking about how the communists were taking over the world.

I closed my eyes and kept whispering the same verse over and over – "whatsoever things are true, whatsoever things are honest, whatsoever things are just, whatsoever things are pure – think on these things."

August 5, 1964 – I am in the ocean. I got back to Newport Beach from LA the day before yesterday. I don't know if it was from being with Wes or from being in Tijuana, but I felt gritty until I got in the water. The waves have been pretty big – somewhere between five and seven feet – but there's a lull. I exhale and I let my body sink until I'm lying on the bottom. I stay down for thirty or forty seconds and then I come back up and breathe.

A half-hour ago I sort of rescued a girl. She was a few feet away from me when we both got caught in a riptide. We were pretty far from shore when we got out of the current, and she told me she wasn't sure she could make it back in. I could tell she was scared, but she didn't panic. I waited for a big set to come through, and then I pulled her in past the break line and up to the beach. She was pretty good looking and friendly, but I am an idiot. I just talked to her for a couple of minutes and then I got back in the water.

There were fifteen or twenty other body surfers around me. I kept treading water until somebody yelled, "Outside!" There was a big wave in the distance. I waited until it was close enough, and then I started swimming as hard as I could, but I didn't get far enough out in front of the swell to catch it.

The next wave welled up into a steep slant, and I dove to the bottom and dug my fingers into the sand. It broke right above me and lifted me up and turned me around and swept me back in toward the beach. I came up and got some air, and just before another wave broke on top of me, I dove again. I got to the bottom and I kept swimming into the rushing current until the water calmed down.

Everybody else either caught one of the waves, or they were blown in past the break line. Another set was moving in and I was in the right place. It was a fairly big swell. I started swimming, and after the water briefly pulled me back in toward the wave, it started pushing me out in front.

I swam hard and cut to the left, and when I shot out from the break and onto a shoulder, I felt the water crashing just behind me. I reached out with my left arm and slid across the surface, and then I dropped it to my side and angled toward the shore. I didn't kick out of the wave until it was playing out.

When I stood up, I was standing chest-deep in the water. I was going back home the next day. I thought about Wes and the bullring and the woman in the blue gown staring at me in the restaurant, and before I got out I immersed myself in the ocean one more time.

Chapter 12

My parents hadn't seen me in two months. When I got off the plane in Nashville, they weren't sure it was me. The flat top I'd had since I was nine years old was gone. I hadn't gotten a haircut since I left, and I didn't look like I lived in a prison camp anymore. I had a tan, I was an inch taller, and I'd gained 35 pounds – mostly in my shoulders and my chest.

Right after school started back, Coach Gantry, one of the football coaches, saw me with my shirt off in the gym. He said it wasn't too late to come out for the team, but I didn't do it. And I also didn't start going to parties and dating. I looked different, but I didn't feel different. I still didn't think anybody I'd want to go out with, would want to go out with me.

It was my senior year and I was pretty sure my grades would be okay. I didn't have to take Latin or a math course. I was taking United States History and I was looking forward to the centennial of the Battle of Franklin, which was four days after Thanksgiving. Battle Ground Academy was built right beside where the worst of the fighting took place, and minie balls and pieces of shrapnel still turned up in the dirt from time to time.

There were a couple of old cannons on the lawn in front of the academic building, and inside there were two large display cases full of rifles and pistols and swords and bullets and cannon balls and uniforms and canteens from soldiers who fought in the battle. I made a pretty good grade on a history paper I wrote about a

Confederate general. He was killed in the battle just after he rode across what eventually became the school campus.

Toward the end of 1864, after the fall of Atlanta, John Bell Hood, the Confederate general, brought the Army of Tennessee north. He thought if he could take Nashville, he could get resupplied and pick up recruits, and then he might be able to march up through Kentucky and take the war into the northern states.

Hood moved north until he was less than 40 miles from Nashville, and he was able to out-maneuver a large Union force under General Schofield. The Union soldiers were facing almost certain defeat, but there was a failure of communication between Confederate commanders, and the main road leading north was left open. Schofield's force escaped during the night and reached Franklin, where they quickly fortified their position.

Hood was rumored to have flown into a rage when he found out that Schofield's force had escaped. Hood ordered his troops north to Franklin, and late on the afternoon of November 30, 1864, the Army of Tennessee launched a massive frontal assault on the Federal defenses just south of the town. It was the deadliest advance over open ground during the entire course of the Civil War, and it came right across what became the campus of Battle Ground Academy.

November 30, 1964 – It's Monday afternoon. Today was our first day back after Thanksgiving break. I stayed after school and did some homework, and now I'm walking down to Columbia Pike. It's a lot colder today than it was a century ago when the fighting took place. I try to imagine what it was like on the afternoon of the Battle of Franklin, and I look a couple of hundred yards to the north, at the place where the Union breastworks stood.

Exactly one century earlier, Northern officers would've been yelling at their men, as soldiers using picks and axes and shovels and hoes worked as fast as they could to strengthen their defenses. Then there would've been an eruption of gunfire from beyond the rise of ground to the south.

The soldiers of two Union brigades had been posted a mile in front of the main line of defense, and they rushed back over the rise – swept along by an oncoming wave of Confederates.

There was a torrent of retreating men in blue uniforms, but their escape had slowed to a crawl when they converged on a narrow opening in the Federal lines – at the point where their breastworks and the turnpike intersected. Those in the rear were overtaken by the surging mass of attackers, most of them wearing shirts and jackets and trousers of brown or gray.

The battle flags of Confederate regiments intermingled with the flags of regiments from the Union, and the fighting was at close quarters. The chaos of warfare widened across the fields lining both sides of the turnpike, and the dead and the dying and the wounded lay in the dirt as the fight continued.

The Union soldiers behind the defenses didn't open fire until most of their comrades made it through the gap in the breastworks. But by then the flood of troops pouring into the gap was turning from blue to brown and gray. Hand-to-hand fighting spread inside the Union line, and battle-hardened soldiers kept killing each other during what was left of the afternoon. The break in the Federal defenses gradually closed, but wave after wave of Confederate soldiers kept advancing as the warmth bled out of the fading day.

The attacks continued well into the night, but by then it would've been too dark to see the determination and the fear and the resignation on the faces of the Confederates as they moved into the storm of bullets and artillery fire that would leave so many of them dead or maimed. Most of their faces were bearded or covered with stubble, but some faces were smooth – still too young to shave. I stood on the battlefield and imagined it was a century earlier, and that I was preparing to advance on the Union defenses.

If I had been seventeen years old in 1864, I would've probably been a Confederate soldier. But if I was a Confederate, I told myself that I wouldn't have been fighting to preserve slavery. I was pretty sure that I would've seen slavery for what it was. I would've been there because I didn't have the courage not to enlist. I would've been there because I couldn't face the shame of my family, or face being ridiculed or reviled or dismissed by my neighbors and by my friends.

And if I'd been a soldier, I was pretty sure I wouldn't have stayed with my unit all the way to the breastworks. I would've tried to find a way to escape without anybody knowing about it. I might've started taking the wounded back to the rear, or maybe I would've been lucky enough to get wounded in the arm or the leg. That would be better than pretending to be shot and sprawling in the dirt.

The Union army held its position and it was after midnight when they finally fell back toward Nashville. I walked back up from the highway over ground that had been littered with bodies on the morning after the battle. In about five hours nearly 4000 soldiers in the Army of Tennessee had been wounded, and 1700 men and a few boys, along with six generals, were dead or dying.

What was left of the decimated Confederate force trailed after the withdrawing Yankees, and Hood established his lines just to the south of Nashville. It was the final Confederate advance of the Civil War.

Of the regiments that moved forward across the Battle Ground Academy campus and advanced to Nashville, a few reached the fields and pastures that would become the yards and streets of my neighborhood. The Confederate lines ran near where my house and Woodmont School and Ensworth School and Moon's Drugstore and Belle Meade Theater would all someday stand.

And the lines were a little to the north of a solemn old structure that was still standing on Woodmont Boulevard, a couple of streets over from my house. It looked like it must have been an elegant residence in the years before the Civil War.

I assumed that slaves once worked on the land where subdivisions were eventually built, and that they occasionally stopped to drink from the little stream that ran in front of my house. A century later, neighborhood kids would explore the same creek in the summer, turning over rocks and looking for crawfish.

Two weeks after the Battle of Franklin, on the first day of the Battle of Nashville, advancing Union troops drove units of outnumbered Confederates back across the place where, when I was ten years old, I found a Union army button near a decaying old farm shed just two hundred feet from my house.

When I went back home that day, I wondered how many of the soldiers who were killed on the Battle Ground campus in 1864 had been my age. Just about the only thing I had to worry about in 1964 was getting killed in a wreck. After Jack Johnson died, I came up with a plan that might keep me alive if I was ever in an accident. Part of my strategy was to always be in the backseat when I wasn't driving.

February 25, 1965 – It's almost 7:45 in the morning and Mack Marlin is driving down Hillsboro Road in his Ford Fairlane. Tony Ballou is riding shotgun, and I'm in the back. It's been snowing, but the road looks clear. We've turned off the rock-and-roll station and we're listening to Paul Harvey, like we do every morning on the way to school. He's talking about Vietnam. He's saying a lot of the same things Mr. Godshaw says – that if America doesn't confront the communists in Vietnam, all of Southeast Asia will fall like dominoes.

As soon as we get to the long two-lane bridge that crosses the Little Harpeth River, our car starts to slide. Instead of trying to ease back into his lane, Mack slams on the brakes and we're going sideways on the ice at 60 miles an hour. Another car is coming toward us on the bridge. Right before the collision, I dive onto the floor of the backseat, just the way I'd planned. The impact knocks me up against the roof of the car, and I hit the seat in front of me on my way back down to the floor. It feels like the car is spinning, and then everything slows down and stops.

When I pulled myself up, I looked at what was left of the car.

The front part of the vehicle was torn off to one side, and Mack and Tony weren't there. I had to climb over the seat to get out. Tony was lying on the side of the road and he was groaning. He wasn't bleeding, but he couldn't get up. Mack was limping back toward us. He was hurt, but at least he could walk.

The girl who was driving the other car was unconscious. There was a gash on her head and there was a lot of blood. I was a little disoriented, but I was okay. The ambulance was the fastest way to get to Nashville, and I rode in the back with Tony and Mack and the girl. While we were on the way to Vanderbilt Hospital, I thought it would take everybody's mind off what just happened if I made up some lyrics. I did my version of a song we'd heard earlier that morning. It was *I Go to Pieces*, by Peter and Gordon.

"When I saw her coming up the road
I got so shaky and my blood ran cold
I told Mack to slide some other way,
But he didn't hear a word I said
And the car's in pieces and we'll need a ride
The car's in pieces and we almost died
Just because Mack Marlin cannot drive"

The girl was coming to, and after she yelled at me to shut up, she rolled over and vomited. It turned out that Tony had a couple of cracked vertebrae in his back and Mack had a hairline fracture of his left leg. Along with the cut on her head, the girl had a pretty bad concussion. It should've been a lot worse. The wreck was as close as I'd ever come to being dead.

May 25, 1965 – It's a warm spring morning outside, and I'm sitting in the Battle Ground Academy gymnasium. My 67 classmates and I are wearing gray gowns, and blue and gold tassels are hanging from our caps. We're supposed to look like scholars, but we look somewhere between strange and absurd. I'm pretty sure the members of the first class at Battle Ground weren't wearing caps and gowns when they graduated 75 years ago.

Back then, Battle Ground was like rural academies all across the South, and the school hasn't really changed all that much since the end of the 1800s. For the last six years, I've heard a lot about the importance of courage and perseverance and having good character. Most of the teachers care about the kind of people we'll grow up to be.

Professor Daley is sitting with the rest of the faculty. I'm staring at the deep lines on his face. He's in his mid-seventies, but he still teaches Latin. He graduated from Battle Ground in 1910, and after coming back to teach for a few years, he went off to fight in World War One. He's old and he doesn't move very fast, but from time to time I've seen him slap a disrespectful student across the face. They all seemed to know they had it coming. Professor Daley reflects the old fashioned values of the school.

Things were bad when I was a freshman and sophomore, but by the time graduation rolled around, I didn't want to leave. I was making good grades and everybody in my class got along pretty well. I tried not to think about how that morning was the last time we'd ever be together. There would be reunions every ten years, but everything would change after that day. I didn't like it when good things changed.

It took about 20 minutes for Mr. Rennin to hand out all the awards for academics, athletics, and citizenship. I knew they wouldn't say anything about it, but my parents were probably disappointed when my name wasn't called out.

The commencement speaker was an executive at Alcoa – the Aluminum Corporation of America – and he talked about the path we should follow for the rest of our lives. He said we should work hard when we got to college, and after we graduated we should think about serving in the military. He said that would make us look better to prospective employers when it was time to start looking for jobs.

He said that unless we planned to go into medicine or law, we should consider careers in business or finance or engineering.

But he told us that whatever path we chose, we should make ourselves valuable to our employers. He said if we did that, we'd be able to make more than enough money for our families to be comfortable.

I knew that was what I was expected to do, but the older I got, the more the future sounded like a prison sentence. Even though I'd probably end up having to wear a coat and tie every day and work in an office and do something boring, I was pretty sure I wasn't cut out to be a businessman or a banker or a salesman, or go into any of the other careers the commencement speaker had in mind.

I kept thinking about the adults I'd been around my whole life. They'd all gone through high school, and I wondered how many of them, back when they were younger, wouldn't have wanted to turn into the people they eventually became. I wondered if any of them had seen things the way I saw them – that being an adult meant I wouldn't smile much anymore, and that I'd spend most of my life worrying about money.

I wasn't sure, but it seemed like a lot of my classmates couldn't wait to have the sort of life I was dreading. Plenty of them drank and smoked, and some were pretty experienced with girls. I got the feeling that they wanted to end up like the sort of hip character Frank Sinatra played in movies. It was easy to imagine them putting on a suit and going to work in an office, and spending every night in a bar with a drink in one hand and a cigarette in the other hand and acting cool and trying to impress women who never seemed to have been girls.

Our names were called and we got our diplomas, and after we formed into lines and marched two by two down Everbright Avenue, we cut across the lawn to the school flagpole, which stood close to Columbia Pike. We circled the flag and more words were spoken and somebody said a prayer, and then we started singing our alma mater. I fought back some tears as I looked across at Jim Hamilton and Kenny Leonard and Jack Rogers and Tom Hendrickson, and at a few of my other friends, but once we got to "forward ever be our watchword, conquer and prevail," I knew I could get through graduation without embarrassing myself.

After we finished singing, a couple of guys yelled and there was some applause. Then the circle we'd formed disintegrated, and we started hugging our mothers and shaking hands with our fathers. I didn't think about it until a little later, but we were on the verge of getting into a new formation.

We were about to line up and march purposefully off toward college – and toward everything that would come after college. After a while, I went to my car, and while I was driving away I imagined Jack Johnson as a soldier lying dead on the field of battle. I passed through the place where Union defenses spanned Columbia Pike, and I kept thinking about Jack as I drove on toward my future.

Chapter 13

September 15, 1965 – I'm sitting in Alumni Hall with several hundred other members of the incoming freshmen class of Vanderbilt University. We're waiting to be welcomed into the student body by Chancellor Alexander Heard. At some point during the summer, I started thinking that going to college might be like being on a military campaign. I wonder if it ever seemed that way to my father, who got his degree in engineering in 1938, or to his father, who graduated 70 years ago as valedictorian of his medical school class. I'm about to march across an academic battlefield that's a lot like the one they marched across when they were my age. I look around at my new classmates. I pretend that we're all about to be briefed in advance of an epic battle.

I watched Dr. Heard rise from his chair and walk up to the lectern. I was struck by how confident he was. It was easy to see why he was the head of a prestigious university. He looked like a chancellor, he walked like a chancellor, and with his cultured Southern accent, he definitely sounded like a chancellor. Looking up from his text at regular intervals, he read a speech about what it was to be "A Vanderbilt Man." But when he said Vanderbilt, it sounded more like "Vondebult."

After listening to his carefully crafted presentation for a few minutes, I was pretty sure that the next four years would be an engaging intellectual experience. I wanted to know why things happened the way they did. I wanted to understand what was going on in the world. I couldn't wait to be part of classroom discussions and have the world start coming into focus. Dr. Heard's speech made being a Vondebult man – well-informed, intellectually confident, sophisticated, and refined – sound especially good.

Later that day the freshman class convened for another part of orientation – to learn about what was called the Greek system. The guy who was the president of the Interfraternity Council explained the process of going through rush at Vanderbilt. His main point was that when we visited the fraternity houses, we should just be ourselves.

That would've been fine if the members of the fraternities did the same thing, but being advised to just be ourselves was like telling somebody who was new to playing poker to show his cards to the other players, while their cards stayed face-down on the table.

Going through rush involved visiting each of the twelve or so fraternity houses, including the two Jewish houses, even though the Jewish fraternities were socially segregated from the other fraternities. We were all divided into groups and we spent the whole day repeating the same ritual. At each house we visited, various members told us why we should want to become members of their fraternity, and they did what they could to find out which rushees were cool, which ones were nubs, and which ones were somewhere in between.

I went ahead and did what the guy from the Interfraternity Council said to do. I tried to be myself. I already knew which fraternities were the most prestigious, at least to people in Nashville. But the guys I knew in those fraternities were mostly boring rich guys. They didn't smile much and I was pretty sure they thought even less than they smiled. I wouldn't have wanted to be around them any more than they would've wanted to be around me.

But one fraternity I visited seemed different. Instead of interrogating us, several of the members were playing in a band. I got a bid to join and I became a pledge, but it turned out that the only time they got together and played music was during Rush Week. And I eventually found out that the only reason I'd gotten a bid was because they thought it would help them get Kenny Leonard, one of my friends from Battle Ground.

I'd expected to meet a good number of Vondebult Men during rush, but all I saw were guys who wanted to screw girls and drink while they were in college, and eventually get rich. I didn't see anybody who looked like they were interested in what was going on in the world.

When the subject of politics came up in the fraternity house, there was a lot of spouting off about how Lyndon Johnson should be thrown out of office for pushing through the Civil Rights Act and the Voting Rights Act, and how Martin Luther King should be sent on a one-way trip to Africa, and how America should use nuclear weapons and bomb North Vietnam back into the Stone Age.

Wes would've fit right in. I was pretty sure there wasn't anybody around who wanted to talk about whether the universe had ever been a void, or if life could just be an illusion.

Along with pledging the fraternity, I signed up for NROTC – the Naval Reserve Officers Training program. I could tell that my father was proud of me for doing it. After I graduated I would get my two years of military service out of the way, and then I could go on and do whatever I was going to do.

Midshipmen were not only required to take a class called Sea Power – on Thursday afternoons we put on the uniforms we'd been issued, and we marched up and down a big field on the west side of the campus. Sometimes when we were marching, I pretended we were advancing on some academic objective.

I did what I was told to do, but a lot of it was really stupid. There was even a script for what an officer was supposed to say when he was standing watch on the deck of a ship. It was blah blah blah this, and the officer was supposed to answer, "very well' – and then it was blah blah blah that, and he was supposed to answer, "very well" again. Things were getting serious in Vietnam, but it was hard to be serious about marching around every Thursday and trying to figure out when to say "very well."

It was the first time I'd gone to school with girls since I was in the sixth grade at Woodmont. Songs from the summer and fall of 1965 were full of the promise of college romance – like *Do You Believe in Magic* and *Yes I'm Ready* and *Baby I'm Yours* and *Make Me Your Baby.*

I half-expected that it wouldn't be long before a girl would smile at me and we'd start talking, and then I'd have a girlfriend. There was even an outside chance that she'd turn out to be my dream girl. Some of the coeds at Vanderbilt were good to look at, but most of the time they didn't seem real. It was the same way it had been with Yancey Walsh, back when I was fifteen. The Vanderbilt girls were a little like pictures in a magazine.

A lot of them had beauty parlor hair and they dressed like they were thirty. The older guys in the fraternity said that most Vanderbilt coeds came to college looking for a husband, but that plenty of them didn't mind screwing around until they found one. I had a hard time believing that girls who acted as stiff as sprayed hair during the day, could end up spending all night in some guy's dorm room.

But things like that didn't seem to bother anybody else. Most of the guys I knew had dates every weekend. It seemed like everybody else was dancing, and I couldn't hear the music. Maybe things would've been different if I had a girlfriend, but that seemed less and less likely.

In addition to Sea Power, I took Freshman English, Finite Math, Psychology, and the History of Western Civilization. I was looking forward to English, but I was pretty sure that Western Civilization would be my ace in the hole.

Two history professors gave a lecture once a week in front of the whole freshman class, and on the other days, we broke off into small discussion groups taught by graduate students. The two professors clearly enjoyed being up on the stage in front of such a big audience. They joked around with each other and took turns trying to say something witty.

I didn't know why, but it got harder and harder for me to follow what they were talking about when they gave their lectures. And the graduate assistant who taught my history section was a pale, depressed-looking little guy who wore the same rumpled brown suit every day. It wasn't long before I figured out that the History of Western Civilization wasn't going to be my ace in the hole. It looked more like the six of clubs.

English class wasn't any better. I got the feeling that the professor didn't like being a professor. He'd probably been teaching the same novels and the same poems for years, and I wondered if that was why he didn't have any passion. Some of what I read didn't make much sense to me, but there were a few poems I connected with. My favorite one was *Christmas Eve in Whitneyville, 1955* by Donald Hall.

One day I wrote a poem while I was in Psychology class. The teacher had just showed us the brain of a college girl who was killed in a wreck. I was trying to describe how she might've reacted to having a bunch of students looking at her brain. It probably wasn't a very good poem, but I liked writing it.

Most of what I was supposed to learn seemed like a waste of time, and it got harder for me to keep up. I kept hoping that things would get better, but they didn't. It took me longer and longer to read what I needed to read, and it took me forever to write what I needed to write.

The teachers didn't take roll, and they didn't check on whether we were showing up. I started cutting classes and putting off reading my assignments and writing my papers. I told myself that I'd just catch up on everything later on.

November 11, 1965 – I'm on the Vanderbilt campus standing at attention on the field that becomes the NROTC parade ground every Thursday afternoon. All I can do is hope that nobody notices my tie. I was running late this morning, and instead of getting the regulation black tie I was issued, I reached into my closet and accidentally grabbed a tie that was dark green. I didn't notice that it was the wrong one until I got to school. It's Veterans Day and an admiral has shown up to review the corps of midshipmen. Of course, I've ended up on the front row.

It's supposed to be eyes front, but I cut my eyes to the right without moving my head. The admiral is walking in my direction. He's talking to the captain who's in command of the whole unit. The admiral doesn't seem to notice the lines of uniformed young men standing in formation. He is just moving past me when he stops. He turns toward me, looks down at my tie, and then he starts walking again. We march around for a while, but before we get dismissed I am told to report to what's called Captain's Mast.

I wasn't sure what to expect, but I knew it wouldn't be good. I showed up and I was told what I was supposed to do. I walked up the steps to a closed door and knocked loudly three times. Somebody inside ordered me to enter, and I went into the room and did a right-face, and then I walked up to a table where three student midshipmen were waiting for me. A couple of enlisted men wearing Navy uniforms were standing right behind them, and so was an angry-looking Marine sergeant who had already served in Vietnam.

I saluted and announced myself. "Reporting as ordered, sir." I tried to explain that I hadn't meant to be disrespectful, and how sorry I was for making the unit look bad in front of the admiral. Then they took turns yelling about how stupid I had to be to show up at an inspection wearing a green silk tie.

The sergeant who kept scowling at me had gotten a medal for rescuing two wounded fellow Marines from an ambush in a rice paddy. He seemed to think that I'd intentionally dishonored all the soldiers who'd ever been wounded or killed in Vietnam. The only thing that would've made it worse was if my father had been there to see everything.

I felt like there was a hole inside my stomach. It was really bad at first, but after a while, it was like watching somebody else getting torn to pieces. When they finally got tired of yelling at me, they said I was being dismissed from the program. I thought that I might as well salute before I left, and then I said, "Very well." It was the only thing I could think to say.

December 5, 1965 – It's Sunday afternoon and I've been sitting in the Vanderbilt Library since this morning. I'm trying to write a paper that's due tomorrow for English class. The paper is on a poem called Bereft, by Robert Frost. I've only written a couple of paragraphs so far, and I don't know if I'll be able to get it done on time. Frost was around my age when he wrote Bereft back in the 1890s. He must've felt pretty much the way I feel. My favorite lines are,

> "Summer was past and day was past,
> Somber clouds in the west were massed.
> Out on the porch's sagging floor,
> Leaves got up in a coil and hissed,
> Blindly struck at my knee and missed."

It wouldn't have been as hard to get the paper done if I'd known what was bothering Frost. I couldn't just make something up about a poem that meant a lot to him when he wrote it. I looked around at the other students in the library. They were turning the pages and writing like they were in a race. I stared out the window and started singing *California Dreaming*, but I made sure nobody could hear me. It reminded me of *Bereft*.

It ended up taking me fourteen hours to write three-and-a-half pages, but I finished by the time the library closed. I got a D minus on the paper because the teacher said I was too vague about the theme of the poem, and because I didn't do things like analyze the metrics and the rhyme scheme.

The teacher drew a red line through a section he didn't like. I'd written that it would've been an even better poem if Frost had the coil of leaves strike at a *leg* instead of at a knee. I'd never seen a swirling column of leaves move like it could strike at something as specific as a knee. Swirling leaves didn't move that way.

When it was time to write a term paper for history, I didn't get started until 10 PM on the night before it was due. It was about Aldous Huxley. I stayed up all night, but I got an F because I turned it in four hours late. I'd overslept and missed class. It wasn't very good, and I would've probably gotten an F anyway.

December 14, 1965 – I'm out in the country, driving down a gravel road in my 1963 Corvair. I was in class a couple of hours ago, but I started feeling like I couldn't breathe and I got up and left. I'm going down roads I've never been down before. I'm trying to get lost, and I'm not sure if I care whether I make it back home.

Some of the songs on the radio sound like they were written just for me. We Gotta Get Out of This Place comes on, and after that, it's Rescue Me. I'm just about to go across a little creek in the middle of nowhere when Help starts playing. I've been waiting to hear it for at least a week, and I start singing with John Lennon.

"When I was younger,
Four years younger than today,
I knew I needed help
And finally found my way.
But now the trouble's back
And there's one thing that's for sure,
Pretty soon the school will call
And throw me out the door.
Help me 'cause my head is hanging down,
It's about to be down on the ground,
I feel like I'm about to drown,
So please don't neglect me."

I didn't understand why I was lost again, and I wondered if anybody at Vanderbilt noticed what was happening to me. The sad-looking history instructor who wore the rumpled brown suit and who never recognized me when I saw him on campus didn't notice, and neither did the other teachers who didn't know my name.

But the guys at the fraternity must've known something was wrong. I'd stopped showing up, and when I ran into any of them, they didn't have much to say. It was like I had a disease they didn't want to catch.

I did what I could to study for exams, but my brain was pretty much frozen. I got two Ds and three Fs for the semester. There was deep disappointment in my father's face when I showed him my grades. And although Mother tried to cover up how hurt she was, I thought she was probably crying sometimes during the day and lying awake a lot at night. They thought I'd gotten over whatever was wrong with me when I was at Battle Ground, but my problems had come back with a vengeance. The way they saw it, my entire future was at stake.

I went through the formality of meeting with the Dean of Men. He was around thirty, and he looked like he was portraying a college chancellor in a play. I wondered if he was going to yell at me, but it was hard to imagine a guy who was that well-dressed yelling at somebody he didn't even know.

Underneath the tweed jacket with the leather elbow patches, he was wearing a corduroy vest, and underneath that, he was wearing a starched white shirt and a black and gold Vanderbilt tie. I would've bet five dollars that he was also wearing an undershirt. And to top it all off, he was holding an unlit pipe. I glanced back toward the door, and a tweed hat and a wool scarf were hanging on a hat rack.

I wondered if he always dressed like a sixty-year-old stereotype. He was polite, but it wasn't long before he got down to business. "Vondebult would consider you for readmission if, after enrolling at some other accredited institution, you are able to demonstrate substantial improvement in your scholastic performance." Or in other words, "Adios." So while my classmates at Battle Ground Academy continued to advance on their various academic objectives, I had been discharged from my unit and sent to the rear.

Chapter 14

Mother got me an appointment to see a psychologist named Virginia Burke. Her office was near Vanderbilt. When I went for my first session a few days later, I parked on a side street. Before I walked into the building, I looked around and made sure nobody was around who would recognize me. I took the stairs up to the sixth floor. After I checked the corridor, I slipped into Dr. Burke's empty waiting room.

I'd been thinking about how long it took me to open up, back when Ann was painting my portrait. I brought along my current journal so Dr. Burke could read through it. I hoped it would speed up the process. I wanted to spend as little time going to see her as possible.

After a few minutes, her office door opened and a guy a couple of years younger than I was came out into the waiting room. I didn't look at him and he didn't look at me. I thought it would be funny if I started acting crazy, but I didn't do anything. It wasn't long before Dr. Burke walked out of her office. She was a short, white-haired lady with understanding and patient eyes. She seemed to be sincere when she smiled at me.

She had a couch, but I went over and sat down in a big chair beside her desk. I explained about my journal, but she didn't look at it. She wanted me to talk about my time at Vanderbilt, and by the end of the hour, I'd talked about my classes and NROTC and the fraternity I'd joined, and what I thought about the girls I'd seen.

I explained everything as well as I could, but before I left, she said the next time she saw me she wanted to hear how I felt about flunking out of college. She wouldn't have found much about that in my journal. I hadn't written about how worthless I thought I was.

I wanted to do something constructive. I needed a way to start making up for what I'd done. Martha Graves was a neighbor of ours who lived a few houses up from us on Clearview Drive. She was a social worker, and she told me there was always a need for volunteers at the Metro Children's Home, which was an orphanage for the most underprivileged kids in the city.

When I went to see the director of the Home, he told me that most of the kids who lived there had parents who were sick or dead. Or in prison. He said kids were sent to the Home when there wasn't anywhere else for them to go.

He said I could come by every Saturday and spend the day playing with the younger boys. I was a little surprised when he told me that I shouldn't hold back if a kid needed to be spanked. He said they'd run all over me if I didn't punish them. I didn't mention it, but I was pretty sure I wouldn't be spanking anybody.

The most messed up kid I saw was named Alfred. He was six. He'd watched his mother put five bullets into his father to keep him from beating up one of her other children. Alfred had dead-looking eyes, and he was pale and emaciated. Sometimes he'd get some other kid by the arm or by the hair. He was too weak to do any damage, but he'd have a twisted little smile on his face while he was trying to inflict pain.

The boys liked me. We'd go outside and play games, or hike along Richland Creek, which ran near the back edge of the property. Their favorite thing to do was have play fights. They kept trying to get me on the ground, but they couldn't do it unless I was trying to keep from stepping on somebody.

On my second week, a kid named Stevie found a box turtle near the creek. He held it up like he was about to throw it. I told him not to do it, but he laughed and ran away. Before I could catch him he smashed the turtle against a rock and shattered its shell.

I grabbed Stevie and gave him a couple of hard swats on his butt. He just looked at me and laughed. Then I started spanking him as hard as I could. He kept laughing until I made him look at the turtle. It was dying and I told him how much it was suffering. Then I said that he was too good a kid to do what he'd just done. He started crying, and when I put my arm around him, he started sobbing.

He kept crying and I held onto him until he stopped. I talked to him for a few minutes, and by the time we went back inside he'd calmed down. When I told the director what happened, he just nodded. When he looked down at my right hand, he saw that the tips of my three middle fingers were bleeding.

He told me that the next time I was going to spank somebody, not to have my hand down at my side right before I did it. He said if there was too much blood in my fingers, they'd split open. I went back a couple of days later and Stevie started smiling as soon as he saw me. I wanted to give him a hug, but there were other kids around and they would've teased him if I had.

When I went back to see Dr. Burke, I told her about making Stevie cry. She wanted me to talk about it. I told her that I'd never seen anybody cry that way, and it made me feel sick inside. I kept thinking about all the pain he must've gone through to cry the way he had. At some point, I told Dr. Burke that Stevie and most of the other kids at the Home were a little like turtles that had been thrown against rocks.

Then she asked me if I ever felt like a turtle. I said I hadn't hit a rock yet, but I knew how it felt to be flying through the air. If I could've explained it without taking up the whole session, I would've told her that I felt a lot more like the last bull that was killed when I was in Tijuana.

I had the rest of the winter to think about how screwed up I was. To wonder if my spirit was about to shatter like a turtle against a rock, or end up like a bleeding bull in the middle of a dusty arena. I felt like I was looking up at the world from the bottom of a hole. All I saw was one cold, cloudy day after another. Things were better when I was playing with the kids at the Home, but I just went there on Saturdays. I didn't have a lot to do. At first I mostly just drove around.

But I finally started going to the Vanderbilt Library to read old newspapers. Back when I was supposed to study or write papers, I usually ended up going into the stacks and looking around. I eventually found a collection of old bound volumes of the New York Times up on the eighth floor. Before long I was going to Vanderbilt just about every day. I'd write in my journal, and spend hours reading about the way the world used to be.

I usually didn't see my parents until dinner. They never said anything about how I'd flunked out of college, but they were worried. When I went to bed at night, things were a lot like they were back when I was in ninth grade. I'd lie in the dark with the radio on and try to fall asleep.

Even when the songs were depressing, I made myself keep listening. It was punishment. I couldn't stand *Five O'Clock World*. I would picture myself wearing a coat and tie and carrying a briefcase, and being imprisoned five days a week in a job I hated. And *A Well Respected Man* pretty much described the boss I thought I'd probably have someday.

There was also *Everyone's Gone to the Moon* and *As Tears Go By*, but it was *The Sound of Silence* that bothered me the most. When I heard *The Sound of Silence*, I felt like I was walking around in a graveyard. It reminded me of the way I felt when I watched Mother crying after my grandfather's funeral. And it seemed to describe a depressing world that I probably wouldn't be able to escape. *Nowhere Man* was just about as bad. I thought it would make a pretty good inscription for my tombstone.

But even if I thought my prayer would be answered, I wouldn't have asked God to just wave his hand and make whatever was wrong with me disappear. There were starving children and people with incurable diseases who really needed a miracle. I didn't want God to have to fix something that was my fault.

I finally stopped saying the 23rd Psalm when I was trying to make myself fall asleep. I was walking through the Valley of the Shadow Death enough as it was, and saying it made everything worse. Sometimes I'd lie in bed and think about Vietnam. The war was heating up, and I deserved to be trudging through some jungle on the other side of the world.

On some nights, after the radio stations all went off the air, I'd listen to my father snoring. I wondered if he ever dreamed he was back in the Philippines, rescuing his mother and his sister during the war. I wondered if he ever dreamed about me. And some nights when the house was quiet, I still heard the dog I'd been hearing since I was a boy – barking in the distance.

I kept going to see Dr. Burke and we covered a lot of ground. One day she asked me what kind of life I wanted to have. It took me a while to come up with an answer. I finally said I wanted to be happy and make the world a better place. Then she got me to talk about what I needed to do for those things to happen.

The first thing I said was that I had to go back to college and find a way to graduate. My parents were both college graduates, and almost all of my high school classmates would end up being college graduates. My parents made sacrifices so I could go to college. I didn't see how I could be happy if I let them down. And I told her I could contribute to the world a whole lot more if I had a degree.

I eventually had to graduate, but I didn't think going back to college too soon made any sense. As long as I was the way I was – as long as I felt like I was living in a hole that I couldn't get out of – what happened at Vanderbilt would just happen all over again.

I'd gone from resolutely marching toward the breastworks of Vanderbilt, to wandering away from the battle. The more I wandered around, the worse things seemed to be. And winter kept going on and on and on.

Dr. Burke stopped writing when I said I was thinking about enlisting in the military. I told her that Mother would worry, but my father would probably think it was a good idea. I said that going through basic training and being in Vietnam might straighten me out. I could serve for a couple of years, and if I survived, I could come back and make a fresh start. I didn't tell her that I mostly saw enlisting as a way to punish myself.

February 4, 1966 – It's late on Friday afternoon and I'm at Vanderbilt. I'm standing in the parking lot behind the fraternity house. Five months ago I got fooled when a few of the members picked up musical instruments and played some rock and roll songs at their rush party. I feel pretty uncomfortable being this close, and I hope none of the guys in the fraternity will see me. I walked over from Neely Auditorium after I heard Richard Nixon give a speech supporting the war in Vietnam. He almost sounded like he was running for president again.

I don't know why he'd do it, but I overheard three people talking about how Nixon was going to visit the fraternity house after his speech. As long as I'm here on campus, I might as well find out if it's true. Some people are coming across the alley behind Cole Hall, and I spot Nixon. He's walking right toward me. He's still a few feet away when I smile. He doesn't smile back, and when I stick out my hand he just glances at me. He keeps walking until he disappears down the back steps of the fraternity house. I'm only two or three hundred yards from where I saw President Kennedy three years ago.

Nixon's speech was about how America had a duty to fight communism. He said that fighting in Vietnam could ultimately bring about a lasting peace. He sounded confident when he was up on the stage, but the way he looked at me before he went into the fraternity house seemed strange. It was like he was two different people.

The next day when I went to the Children's Home, Stevie wasn't there. His mother had her drinking under control and he'd gone back to live with her. Although he left in a hurry, he wrote me a letter. It was probably the first one he'd ever written. He wrote that he wouldn't forget me, and he added a PS. He promised that he, "wodn evir hort a tortle agin."

I might've made a little difference in Stevie's life, but with all the other things going against him, I couldn't see how it would end up mattering. There was a part of me that wanted to keep on playing with the kids at the Home on Saturdays, but I didn't know how much longer I'd do it. They were always glad when I showed up, but as soon as I left I was pretty sure they went right back to the way they were before.

Not long after that, the director asked if I would consider working there. He said I could move into the dormitory and get paid, and that I'd have my days free while the kids were at school. But I told him I might be going back to college in the fall, and that I should probably just keep things the way they were. I didn't say anything about the rest of it.

Dr. Burke usually did a lot of writing in her notebook when I went to see her. If she'd offered to let me read her notes, I might not have done it. I was curious about what was wrong with me, but I was afraid it was something really bad. It was getting harder to fall asleep at night, and a lot of times I didn't want to get out of bed in the morning.

I worried a lot during the day and I didn't feel like eating. I kept losing weight and I started taking some pills that Dr. Burke prescribed. She didn't say what they were for, but I looked them up in a medical book at the library. They were to treat anxiety. They might've been working, but I quit taking them after a couple of weeks. They made me feel like I was somebody else.

I'm pretty sure Dr. Burke told my parents that it might be a good idea if I got away from Nashville for a while. They talked about it with me, and I thought I might as well go back to California. I went by the Home and thanked the director for letting me help out. He still wanted me to work there, and he said to come by and see him when I got back. After that, I packed up.

March 6, 1966 – It's the middle of Sunday morning and a little snow is falling. I'm telling my parents goodbye in the driveway. I know there's a lot my father wants to say, but he just gives me a long hug and tells me how much he loves me. Then he gives me his usual strong handshake. There are tears in Mother's eyes, but she's trying to smile. She says she knows I'll be fine, but there's a tremble in her voice. I'm fighting back tears when I kiss her goodbye. I look at them in the rearview mirror as I'm driving away. I watch my father put his arm around Mother, and I see her break down.

The sky is low and heavy and it covers the leafless trees and the lifeless yards like a shroud. It seems like the neighborhood is being smothered by winter. I end up taking a detour by Herbert's Field and Tom Hendrickson's court, and I slow down when I pass the anonymous ditch where the Indian bones were dug up a few years ago. I drive past Woodmont School, and one boy is out on the playground dribbling a basketball.

Chapter 15

It took me three days to drive out to Newport Beach. God still had a sense of humor when it came to what was on the radio. I usually changed the station when a depressing song came on, but when I heard Simon and Garfunkel singing *I Am a Rock*, I joined in with my own lyrics.

> I have no books
> Or poetry to perfect me,
> But I am shielded in my armor,
> Longing for a womb,
> Imagining my tomb,
> I ran from home
> Now no one judges me.
> I am in shock,
> Where is my island?

Ronny had married Susan, the girl who'd been driving around with the girl who looked like Jerry Lewis when I was there a couple of years earlier. That meant there was a spare room at his mother's house. She said she liked having me around. She didn't care how late it was when I went to bed, or when I got up in the morning. Ronny and Susan didn't seem to be getting along all that well, and before long I was only going by to see them on the weekends.

The water wouldn't be warm enough for swimming until June,

but the sun was usually shining and I spent a lot of time walking on the beach. I went from the jetty at 40th Street all the way down to the Wedge and back, or up to the Huntington Beach Pier and back. I walked along the edge of the water, and there were times when I felt like I was in a trance.

I remembered the hug I got from my father and the tears in Mother's eyes, and sometimes I pretended I was somebody else. I imagined I was invisible or that I was a basketball player scoring 40 points in a big game, or I told myself that I was about to meet my dream girl on the beach.

Other times I imagined I was back at school at Woodmont or Battle Ground Academy, and that I had a chance to change the way my life would unfold. I also tried to talk to Jesus or the Holy Spirit, or to whoever or whatever had gotten inside me back when I was fourteen. And every day I apologized for messing up at Vanderbilt. The world seemed like it would stay dark forever, and I kept asking for some sort of sign that would lead me out of the darkness.

After dinner, if it wasn't too cold or too windy, I went to the Newport Beach pier and watched the sunset. A few lights came on after dark, and I usually just stayed on the pier and wrote in my journal.

April 28, 1966 – It's a couple of hours after dark on Friday night, and I'm at the far end of the pier. About 20 feet away there's a big man with gray hair and a dark complexion. He looks like he might be from Mexico or from somewhere in Central America. He just caught a fish and I walk over to see it. He glances at me and I smile and nod. He smiles and nods back. The fish is thrashing beside the man's tackle box. He holds it down with his foot, and bends over and takes out the hook. Then he puts the fish in a bucket, baits his hook with a squid, and casts his line back out into the water.

There are people scattered along the edge of the pier. Most of them look like they plan to fish all night. There isn't much conversation, but everybody seems pretty friendly. I go back and read over the first part of the poem I've been trying to write. Sometimes when I walk on the beach, I think about poems I read when I was at Vanderbilt. I want to see if I can write a poem that is true and honest and just and pure.

The Machine

A light comes on,
The factory doors open,
And we start moving.
The others are all
Wearing black ties,
And when they line up
In the middle
Of the conveyor belt,
I move off to one side
And lean away.
I can feel the heat
Of the roaring machine,
But I move closer
And closer to the edge –
Close enough
To the meshing gears
That they graze my neck
And snag me.
And as I am pulled
Toward the mouth
Of the hungry machine,
I dangle in the smoke
At the end
Of my green silk tie.

I didn't know what to write next. It was a clear night and there were lots of stars above the pier. I stared out across the water at the lights of boats and ships in the distance, and then I walked over to the rail and looked down at the waves.

An Asian woman sitting a few feet away pulled up a crab, and then the big man with gray hair hooked something that bent his pole and turned the clicking of his reel into a whir. He sat down and used his legs to brace himself against the railing. It wasn't long before there were several onlookers.

One of them walked up and stood behind him. "What do think, Palani?"

The big man was already breathing hard. "I think I'm not as young as I used to be." There was a little laughter. "I also think my bladder will give up before this fish does."

After a few minutes, he turned and looked at me. "You mind taking over while I hit the head?" I nodded, but I wondered why he picked me out. He got up and I took the pole, and I sat where he'd been sitting and put my legs up against the rail. There was a constant force pulling the line. Before he left, whatever was on the other end started pulling harder. The man gave me a long look and then he walked off toward the restroom.

By the time he got back, most of the others were fishing again. I was more than ready to relinquish the pole, but instead of sitting down, he smiled at me. "You look nervous. You ever fish before?"

I told him I had, but not off a pier. He slipped off his unbuttoned pale green shirt and tied it around his waist. He was wearing a gray undershirt and he had powerful arms. I tried to reel in a little line, but it was a battle. He stared out at the ocean and stretched. "You want a beer?"

"No thanks."

"Can you hold on for a couple of more minutes?"

I nodded and he reached down into his cooler and pulled out a bottle of Mexican beer. He used his belt buckle to pop off the cap. "It feels like a shark – maybe a Thresher. Or it could be a Mako. We'll know soon enough. And the name I go by is Palani. You sure you don't want a beer?"

He didn't say anything when I told him I wasn't a drinker. By the time I handed him back his pole, my hands were cramping and my wrists were tired. He kept talking to me, and I wondered if he was trying to keep me around in case he needed another break. He told me about a few other times when he'd caught sharks, and how he cooked them and how good they tasted, and how long he thought it might take him to reel in whatever it was he'd hooked.

He finally said he'd seen me on the pier before, and he was curious about why I was there. I ended up holding the pole a couple of more times while he took breaks from battling the fish, and we talked off and on until he finally landed a six-foot-long Thresher shark.

He was in the same place when I went back to the pier a few nights later. He smiled when I was walking up, and he gestured for me to sit with him. From then on I'd sit with Palani whenever I went to the pier. He fished and I read or wrote in my journal, and from time to time he told me something or asked me a question. As the weeks went by I learned a lot about him and he learned pretty much about me.

Palani was 56 years old. He'd come from Hawaii to California when he was 17 to find work. He was Mr. Godshaw's nightmare. He was a communist for a while, but he quit and became a socialist after he found out what Stalin was doing to the Russian people.

He said that he finally decided that being a communist was pretty much the same as being a capitalist. He thought that both sides wanted to turn the government into an enormous corporation. He said the reason he hated big corporations was because the bigger they got, the more they operated at the expense of the people who were doing most of the work. He'd been a machinist. He got married and had a couple of children, and then he became a union official in the plant where he worked.

After his favorite cousin was killed in the attack on Pearl Harbor, he joined the Marines. A few months after basic training he was on Guadalcanal. He went through most of the fighting, but then he got a bad case of dysentery and ended up in a military hospital in Australia.

After he was discharged he went back home, but he reenlisted later on in the war and fought on Iwo Jima. I told him about my father being in the Philippines. He said that my father's chances of finding his mother and his sister while the Battle of Manila was still going on couldn't have been much more than zero.

He went back to work at the plant after the war, but he told me that when criminals started running the union, he quit and opened up a car wash. His wife died of cancer after their kids were grown, but he ran the car wash for a few more years before he finally sold it. He had some grandchildren, but they lived pretty far away and he didn't see them as much as he wanted. He read a lot and he was trying to teach himself to paint. He said he came to the pier so he wouldn't turn into a hermit.

May 19, 1966 – It's a Thursday night and I'm sitting on the pier next to Palani. He's wearing a peach-colored shirt with the sleeves cut off. He's caught a couple of fish, and he's been talking about how he never believed that President Kennedy was murdered by Lee Harvey Oswald. Palani had loved Kennedy and I can tell how much the assassination still bothers him. I haven't told him about Mr. Godshaw, or about the kids at Battle Ground who started celebrating as soon as they heard that the president was dead.

Palani reels in his line and shakes his head. "It's taken longer than it should have, but people are finally figuring out that Oswald might not have killed John F. Kennedy." He takes the mostly-eaten bait off the hook and reaches into the bucket for another squid. "I don't know who pulled the trigger, but Kennedy's murder must've been set up by whoever recruited Jack Ruby to kill Oswald." He baits his hook and after he glances over at a man fishing nearby, he casts his line out into the darkness. "I just hope I'll live long enough to find out who really did it."

I was still working on my poem. A few days earlier I was in a bookstore not far from the beach, and I started looking through a poetry magazine. I tried to read a few of the poems, but I couldn't understand what most of them were about. I wasn't sure if what I was trying to write even qualified as a poem, but I finished it anyway.

I dangle
Over the machine
That waits
To drink my blood
And crush my bones.
Dangling
Above its meshing teeth,
I feel its heat and
Its relentless rhythm.
Suspended by
The green silk noose
Around my neck,
I swing my legs
First to one side
And then to the other,
And moving back and forth
Like a pendulum,
I try to make my escape.

June 4, 1966 – I'm just down from the jetty at 40th Street. The water is still cold, but I've been body surfing twice in the past week. Today the surf is heavier than it's been. There are red flags above the lifeguard stations along the beach. I'm not as strong a swimmer as I was the last time I was in waves this big, but I slip the fins onto my feet and walk backward into the ocean.

The big surf has churned up deeper water, and it's much colder than usual. I keep telling myself that I'll get used to it after a few minutes. The waves are breaking pretty far out, and some are crashing over the end of the jetty. Getting past the break line won't be easy. A big swell is coming in. It breaks and I dive to the bottom, but I still get thrown around under the water. When I finally make it back up to the surface, another good-sized wave is almost on top of me, and there's probably another one right behind it.

I swim toward it, and then I go under. An avalanche of water rips past the lower part of my body. I come up fast and swim hard toward the next wave, and I duck through just before it breaks. I'm finally past the break line, and I have a chance to catch my breath. I'm about a hundred and fifty feet from the jetty. Some board surfers are further down toward the jetty at 36th Street, but the only guys around me are a few body surfers and a kid on a bellyboard.

Another big set is rolling in, and I'm in the right place. The wave wells up and I start swimming, but I only take a few strokes before I stop. I thought I might've gotten brave enough to tackle the really big waves, but I'm not any more courageous than I was when I was sixteen. A guy in a wetsuit caught the same wave and he's gone. The next wave wells up underneath me, and I can see him finishing his ride about forty feet from the jetty.

The other body surfers took the next wave, and then it was just me and the kid on the bellyboard. He was probably fourteen or fifteen. We were both out a little past the end of the jetty, but he was closer to the rocks than I was. I saw him look over at me. There was something about his expression that didn't seem right. He made a few sluggish kicks away from me, and I realized that he was trying to get to the jetty.

Another wave broke over the end of the rocks. I looked toward the beach, but the lifeguard platform was empty. I started swimming as hard as I could, and by the time I got to the kid, he was only thirty feet from the rocks.

I started taking him away from the jetty, but he didn't understand what I was doing. He slipped off his board and started to go under the water, and the board floated away while I was pulling him up. It was out of reach by the time I got him turned onto his back. A big wave was coming in, and I was kicking as hard as I could to get him out past the break line. When the wave was welling up, I pulled him underwater with me.

He was choking when we got back to the surface. By then the wave was crashing down and sweeping over the end of the jetty. He was scared and confused, and I pulled him a little farther out before we stopped. I was breathing hard and my arms were getting weak. I told him that as soon as there was a lull, we had to get to shore as fast as we could. But I wasn't sure I was strong enough to make it. I looked toward the beach again, and a lifeguard was watching us from the edge of the water. I waved for help and he was on his way.

The lifeguard got to the kid pretty fast and we started for the beach. I tried to keep up, but I was too tired. Another set came in and a big wave broke on top of where I went underwater. The force of the wave threw me around like I was in a tornado. Instead of staying calm when I was running out of air, I panicked and swallowed some water. When I finally came up I was choking and gasping, but I didn't have that much further to go. I was almost to the beach when the next set came in.

I sat down in the sand for a few minutes before I went looking for the boy on the bellyboard. He was already gone. The lifeguard said the kid had been lifting weights, and that the water was so cold it did something to his muscles. The lifeguard was coming back from rescuing somebody else when he saw us.

Chapter 16

When I went to the pier the next night, Palani noticed that I was writing in my journal a lot more than usual. He finally asked me what I was working on and I told him about the kid on the belly board. The first thing he said was, "You're lucky you didn't get yourself drowned." He kept fishing, and after a few minutes I handed him what I'd written.

Rescue

He wanted to
Fly over and land
On the rocks,
But I thought
He was falling.
When I swooped in
And caught him,
We both began to fall.
Did I save a life,
Or did I almost end one?

Palani didn't say anything until he'd finished reeling in his line. "I don't know anything about poetry, but it sounds like you don't know if you did the right thing." He threaded his hook through a squid and made another cast off the pier.

"A medic in our unit got hit while we were on Guadalcanal. He could've taken a round to the head while I was dragging him in, or maybe he could've crawled back to our lines after it got dark. But I'm pretty sure I did the right thing. I'm pretty sure if I hadn't gotten him, he would've bled to death before the sun went down. Maybe the kid you rescued could've made it up onto the jetty and been okay, but you probably saved his life. Odds are, he would've gotten smashed against the rocks and drowned in the ocean."

It was several minutes before he said anything else. "I go back and forth on religion, but I like that verse from the Bible you told me about – the one about whatsoever is true and all the rest of it. So I want to ask you this. Isn't it true that you were trying to help the kid? And isn't it true that he would've probably gotten hurt or killed if you hadn't stopped him? It seems like you're ignoring whatsoever is true. It seems like you don't want to feel good about anything."

Palani stood up and handed me his rod. He stared out into the darkness. "You got knocked around some back in college and you're still pretty messed up about it. I think your Bible verse can help you get past some of that."

He turned around and leaned against the railing. "So here are a few other things that are true. I think it's true that you wanted to do well in school. And I think it's true that something you still don't understand kept you from doing it."

He bent down and fished another beer out of his bucket. He popped off the cap and looked out toward the water. "And I've got another whatsoever for you – whatsoever makes sense. Does it make sense to feel shame or guilt about something you couldn't help? All that does is keep you from figuring out why things happened in the first place."

I felt a tug on the line. I handed him the rod and he said it felt like a good-sized mackerel. It turned out to be a halibut. He glanced at me after he unhooked it and dropped it into his bucket. "You wanta hear my theory about why you don't like to fish?"

He smiled when I didn't say anything. "I think you feel sorry for the fish. When most people see a fish flopping around on a pier, they don't think about it. It's just a fish flopping around on a pier. But I can tell it bothers you. I've seen it in your eyes." He put another squid on his hook and cast his line out into the darkness.

"I think a lot of things bother you. Most people screw up and they feel bad for a little while and then they get over it. But you screwed up and you had all this guilt, so you started working with the kids in that home.

"And what about the missile crisis? Millions of high school kids lived through that. Some of them were worried, but how many were as worried as you were? And how many guys have some teacher who's a real bastard? They might hate the guy, but they don't end up getting involved in a plot to make him fall down the stairs.

"Kids go off to college every year. Some of 'em mess up because they discover booze or girls, or because they're homesick, or because of all sorts of things. But I don't think it was that way for you. I keep wondering if you messed up because you were on a road to somewhere you didn't want to be. Maybe the difference between you and the kids you were with in college is that you could see where you were going."

The halibut thrashed around in the bucket, and Palani arched his back and tried to stretch. "I don't think you see things the way most people do. Maybe for you, the lights are brighter and the shadows are darker. Maybe for you, everything is more – I don't know – more *intense*. I could be wrong, but it might be that things just hit you harder than they hit most people."

I didn't know what to say. Palani moved his head a little to one side and stared out beyond where his line disappeared into the darkness. "The way you're thinking and writing all the time – you're trying to figure things out.

"That could be a tough road for somebody like you. You might have trouble letting go of the questions you have until you get answers. But what happens if those answers end up being out of reach?"

He tilted his head forward like he might have felt something on the end of his line. "There's a Hawaiian name I should start calling you – it's *Kaimi*. It means "the seeker." And just so you'll know, Palani isn't my American name – it's my Hawaiian nickname. My American name is Wendell, but Palani fits me better. When my father started calling me Palani, you know what he told me? He said it meant whale turd. That's what he said – whale turd. But after a while, I found out it actually means *free man*."

He reeled in a few feet of line. "After I got back from the war I had a lot of questions. Every time I found an answer, or thought I'd found an answer, there was another question. I just kept going from one why to another. I never really gave up on it, but there were jobs and kids, and here I am sitting on a pier in the middle of the night. Maybe I should've figured out more than I have."

I didn't ask him how I could be a seeker if I didn't know what I was supposed to be seeking. After I left that night I kept thinking about what he said. I wondered about the world I saw. If it really was different from the world that other people saw.

The next day I got a call from my parents. I thought they were calling to get me to go up to Los Angeles and visit Wes. The last time we talked on the phone, they wanted to know when I was going to see him. I'd never told them about the trip to Tijuana.

It turned out they were calling to let me know that Wes was in jail. He told the police he was cleaning his pistol in his apartment and it accidentally went off. A girl who was with him was shot in the shoulder, and she bled to death before the ambulance got there.

I was pretty sure he wasn't cleaning his gun, but I didn't think he meant to kill her. He was probably drunk. He was probably trying to scare her. I was worried that the girl he killed was Samantha, the blonde receptionist I got to know when we went to Tijuana. The next day I went to the library and found the story in the LA Times. The dead girl's name was Joanna.

I wasn't going to say anything to Palani about Wes, but he could tell that something had happened and I went ahead and told him about the trip to Tijuana. He just shook his head when I told him about the bullfight and what Wes said to the big Mexican guy. But he was smiling while I explained why I stayed in the hotel lobby instead of going with Wes to whatever brothel he ended up visiting.

Then I went into how pathetic I was with girls. It took him a while to stop laughing after I told him about spraying myself with peppermint before my date with Yancey Walsh.

When the surf was up, I was in the ocean. When it was flat, I walked on the beach. My appetite was coming back, and I was putting on some of the weight I lost after being at Vanderbilt. With the body surfing I did during the day, and with all the pushups I did at night, I was getting stronger.

I still thought I should do penance in Vietnam, but I wasn't as far down in a hole as I'd been. I expected to get drafted, but I thought I might as well go to school somewhere and take a few courses in the meantime. I was pretty sure I wouldn't just end up staring at open books and putting off writing papers again.

I didn't say anything to Palani about going to Vietnam. He got mad every time the subject of Vietnam came up. One night he got a hard look in his eyes and started shaking his head. "What a bullshit war. 'The communists are coming, America! If we don't hold onto Vietnam, all the governments in Southeast Asia will be falling like dominoes. And after that, the commies will take over the whole world.'"

He stood up and spit off the side of the pier. "The older you get, the more you'll understand that there's a big difference between what seems to be going on in the world, and what's *really* going on."

July 16, 1966 – It's Saturday morning and I'm standing at the back of a big boat. Newport Beach is getting smaller and Catalina Island is off in the distance. The sun is reflecting from the water and the wind is blowing through my hair. The drone of the engine rises and falls as the boat moves from swell to swell.

I see some flying fish off to one side. I wasn't even sure they existed, but there they are. I love the way they come up out of the water and glide before they disappear back below the surface. There's a really pretty girl about thirty feet away from me. She's smiled at me a couple of times. I want to make sure she sees the flying fish, but it might make her uncomfortable if I go over and start talking to her. She's only about fifteen.

I hadn't ever been on an island before. I'd seen Catalina from the beach, and sometimes at night, I could see the lights of Avalon, the only town on Catalina, from the pier. While I was at Vanderbilt, sitting in class with my unfocused brain, I'd spent a lot of time drawing imaginary islands.

I outlined the way they would look from the air. There would be a main island where I'd pretend I was living, and the only way to reach it would be through narrow channels that led like a maze through the smaller islands that surrounded it. My maps of islands looked like something a fifth-grader would draw, but I liked drawing them.

It took about an hour and a half to get to Catalina. I walked around for a while and ate lunch, and then I took a bus tour that went to other parts of the island. The land outside of Avalon looked like it hadn't changed for ten thousand years.

When I got back from the tour, I went into a shop and bought a book that had a lot of old photographs of the island. After that, I sat down on an empty bench near an old casino, and I started looking through the pictures. Avalon hadn't changed too much since the 1930s. It felt good to be there.

It was pretty late in the afternoon when I started back, and I saw a few more flying fish before it got dark. The girl I saw that morning wasn't on the return trip to Newport Beach. I wondered if she ever noticed the flying fish. I wrote another poem in my journal that night after I got back.

The Seabird

After I swooped to his rescue,
We were both crushed
Against the rocks.
I remember
Breathing in water
Choking –
Choking and struggling
Until I finally surrendered.
Sinking slowly
To the bottom,
And then I was moving
Beneath the waves
With the others.
I could hear
Sounds and vibrations
Coming from the boat
As it skipped
Across the waves,
And when I took flight,
I looked down
At my reflection.
I wasn't a bird that drowned,
I was a fish that flew.

August 10, 1966 – It's one o'clock in the morning on Wednesday and I'm standing at the end of the Newport Beach pier. I'm looking for the lights of Avalon. I saw them an hour ago, but they've disappeared in the fog. I'm trying to picture the places I saw on the island, and I think about the girl I saw on the boat. She'll probably end up being some guy's dream girl.

This time tomorrow I'll be back home. Palani is fishing a few feet away. He hasn't had much to say since I told him this is my last night. He says he's gotten used to having me around. We both know we probably won't ever see each other again. I keep looking for the lights on Catalina.

How far away the pier will seem tomorrow night when I'm in my bed in Nashville.

The sounds of summer will be coming through my open window. The night will be full of the rhythms of katydids, and depending on which way the wind is blowing, I might be able to hear the dog if it starts barking. The sounds of late summer nights are probably the same as they were in 1925 when Mother moved into a big house on Woodlawn Drive with her family. When I get back I want to look at some old photographs, and see the way things looked back then. I want to write a poem about the neighborhood around Woodmont School. How it's like an island in the ocean.

Palani could tell I was almost ready to leave. He handed me his fishing pole and then he stood up and stretched his back. "Well if you come back this way, I hope I'm still around." He reached into his pocket. He'd written his unlisted telephone number on an index card.

"Here's how to get me. My house isn't much, but you're welcome any time." He put his elbows on the railing and leaned forward. "But before you leave I'm going to tell you something that's been on my mind."

He waited a few seconds before he said anything else. "In some ways you see the world the way it is, and in some ways, you don't. I keep thinking about how you don't say much about Vietnam. I've gotten to know you a little bit, and it wouldn't surprise me if you're planning to go over there so you can punish yourself.

"Here's what I want you to know. The time might come when you'll have to fight for your country – when you have to risk your life or take somebody else's life. But you need to have a damn good reason before you put on a uniform. The war in Vietnam is a piss poor reason. You've told me you want to be the kid you've told me about – the kid in the painting that lady did.

"Well that won't happen if you're dead, and it won't happen if you end up in some veterans hospital for the rest of your life, or if you turn into a drunk because you're trying to forget what you did on the battlefield.

"You need to understand this particular war before you even *think* about joining up. After that, if you still think it's worth killing for or dying for, then go ahead and enlist. But don't go over there just because you feel bad about screwing up in school."

He held out his hand and I shook it. He tried not to laugh. "I don't mind shaking your hand, but what I'd really like is to get my fishing pole back."

He looked up at the sky. "Here's this kid who won't throw a line off the pier because he feels sorry for the fish, but he thinks he might feel okay about gunning people down over in Vietnam." He looked at me again. "Okay, now go on back to Tennessee. Find some way to get through school, and then get your tail back out here. And don't wait till I'm too old to know who you are."

Chapter 17

September 5, 1966 – It's Labor Day and I'm standing in the middle of Herbert's Field. There's a little breeze, but I'm not sure there's enough. It's probably the last time I'll be able to fly a kite here. My mother waited until I was back from California to tell me that Herbert's Field had been sold. It's been divided into three big lots, and there are stakes in the ground marking the new property lines. There's a backhoe parked beside the road. Construction on the first house could start as soon as this week.

It's the last big open field in the neighborhood. The playground at Woodmont School isn't half the size of Herbert's Field. There are still a few good-sized backyards, but nobody wants a bunch of kids showing up and playing football or baseball right behind their house. The breeze fades, and I start running to keep the kite in the air.

Children had been playing football and baseball and flying kites at Herbert's Field since before the area started building up in the 1930s. It was woven into the lives of most of the kids who grew up in the neighborhood.

I didn't understand why a group hadn't gotten together and just bought it. It wouldn't have cost all that much to keep it the way it was. Plenty of people would've chipped in. But it wasn't just what was about to happen to Herbert's Field that bothered me.

While I was gone, a developer bought an old house less than a half-mile away on Woodlawn Drive. The house was already torn down, and condominiums, which were everywhere in Southern California, were being built all over what had been a big yard. The developer named it Regency Park, but calling a bunch of carports and asphalt and crowded-together structures a park – that didn't make it a park.

Things were also getting worse down along Harding Road. There was a time when the commercial area didn't include much more than Moon's Drugstore, Belle Meade Theater, a couple of gas stations, and a grocery store. But more and more buildings were going up all the time, and with so much more traffic, it was dangerous for kids on bicycles to get across the road.

And something else had happened a couple of years earlier. The school board directed that Woodmont, along with all the other elementary schools in Nashville, would only go up to sixth grade. A study was done and a panel decided that seventh and eighth graders would start going to junior high schools.

Woodmont School had been fine the way it was, and it was the same with the old house on Woodlawn Drive and with Herbert's Field. I wanted to let people know that we should hold on to what was good about the neighborhood, but nobody would've listened to an eighteen-year-old who just flunked out of college. The breeze died away and the kite fell like a leaf.

I walked over and stood where I almost made the catch and robbed Phil Andrews of his home run. I tried to remember as much as I could about Herbert's Field. I remembered all the Saturday mornings – from second grade on – when my schoolmates and I showed up, and Mr. Hendrickson taught us how to throw and catch and kick.

I remembered playing for the baseball team sponsored by Moon's Drugstore, and how scared I was of my coach. I made sure that I always knew how many outs there were and what base I needed to throw to, and to back-up throws and swing at close pitches when there were two strikes, and to run out every ground ball and hustle on and off the field.

And I remembered the first few weeks of football practice when I was in sixth grade and how hot it was and how big the eighth-graders looked and being a third-string bench warmer on the

Woodmont team, and how fathers would come by at the end of practice to watch us while they stood together and talked on the sidelines. I looked across Westmont Avenue at Tom Hendrickson's house. At least the basketball court would still be there.

I didn't want to see Herbert's Field all torn up, and I didn't drive by again until the houses had all been built. By then I'd written a poem about the loss of the field.

The Falling Kite

On cloudless
October afternoons,
Kites had danced
In the sky above the field
While boys practiced football.
And the kites kept dancing
When fathers
Stopped by after work
And stood off to the side
In their white shirts
And dark ties,
Watching as their sons
Learned to tackle
And block
And work as a team.
Some of the men
Watching their sons
Remembered autumn afternoons
When they played there –
Years before they went away
To defend their homes
And their school
And the neighborhood field
Where boys played football
On warm October afternoons.

One enemy was vanquished
But another emerged,
And a single kite falters
And falls in the fading breeze.

October 24, 1966 – I'm sitting in an empty classroom at Peabody College in Nashville. I have an hour before my next class. I should be working on a paper I have to write for English, but I keep looking out the window at a cluster of maple trees next to the building. Three of them are big red-leafed maples, and there's also a smaller maple with yellow leaves. I'm wondering which one will lose its leaves first. I start singing a song, but I make sure that nobody coming down the hall can hear me. It's called Mr. Dieingly Sad. It's a perfect song for the end of autumn.

Peabody was right across the street from Vanderbilt, but it wasn't trying to turn out students whose main goal in life was to make a lot of money. It was a teachers college. I wasn't doing much better as a student than I had the year before, but the classes weren't very hard and I wasn't too far behind.

I was going back to the Metro Children's Home on Saturdays, but I felt the same way I did before I left for California. The kids liked it when I was playing with them, but as soon as I left they probably weren't any better off than they were before I showed up.

I wanted to do more than just be a temporary source of entertainment for underprivileged boys. And I wanted to do more than go to an easy school where I probably wouldn't learn much that I'd need to know later on in my life. I felt like there was something I was supposed to be doing, but I had no idea what it was.

Almost all of the students at Peabody were girls. Two of them really killed me, but they were both a couple of years older than I was and they were dating guys from Vanderbilt. It didn't matter that they were older and had boyfriends. I couldn't see myself walking up to either one of them and starting a conversation. But I did manage to crawl out of my cave and have a few dates that fall.

I was coming out of class a few weeks after school started up, and a freshman girl with a desperate look on her face was in the hallway, kneeling in front of her locker. If she hadn't been fairly cute I wouldn't have stopped, so I probably ended up getting what I deserved. Her books were in her locker, and she'd lost the key to her lock. I went to the maintenance department and borrowed a bolt cutter, and I came back and cut off the lock. It was pretty obvious that she would say yes if I asked her to go out with me.

We had a date the next Saturday night. Her mother died two or three years earlier, and she was being raised by her father. When I went inside to meet him, he looked like he was in pain. It was like he'd spent the last few years dreading the night when his daughter would go to college and some guy would show up and take her out on a date. At first, I had the feeling that he saw me as a threat to her chastity, but after a while, I thought there was more to it than that.

I started wondering if he looked at me the way he did because he knew that somebody like me would eventually come along and marry his daughter, and then he'd be all alone. He was nice enough, but the wounded look didn't leave his face the whole time I was there. It was like as soon as the door closed behind her that night, he'd never see her again.

I took her downtown and we saw a movie called *Khartoum*. It reminded me of the Alamo, but instead of an old mission in Texas being surrounded, a city in Sudan was under siege. And instead of Americans trying to hold off an army of Mexicans, it was British soldiers trying to hold off an army of Muslims.

After the movie, I drove her out into the country to a secluded road where there wouldn't be any cars. I was nineteen years old and I still hadn't kissed a girl. I hoped that biology would take over, and things would unfold naturally. I hoped that things would go the way I was pretty sure they went for the Blonde Bombshell and her boyfriend when they had parked beside my house. But that wasn't the way things went.

She let me put my arm around her, but that was it. She was like the British general in the movie. She was the defender of Khartoum. Her father had probably been preparing her for that night for years, but I wasn't ready to retreat. She was a nice person and she seemed to like me, and we went out a few more times.

We finally progressed to where she let me kiss her, but when I tried to introduce the concept of French kissing, she pulled away. Then she said the magic words – "I'm very disappointed in you." I'd already heard more than enough artificial lines that sounded like they came straight out of *The Virgin's Handbook*, and unlike what happened in the movie, I decided it was time to withdraw my horde from the outskirts of Khartoum and melt away into the desert.

I didn't see the point of announcing that I didn't want to go out with her anymore. We'd only had a few dates, and trying to explain myself seemed worse than not saying anything at all. When I saw her at school I could tell that she was hurt. I was still nice to her, but that was about it.

A week or so later I was in the student center and she came in and sat down a couple of tables away. After a few minutes, she started shaking. She looked over at me and said she needed a candy bar. She looked upset, but I thought she was pretending something was wrong with her so I'd come to her rescue. Finally, a guy at another table ran off and got her some candy. By the time he got back, tears were running down her face.

She'd said something on one of our dates about being diabetic, but I didn't know anything about diabetes. I didn't know what happened when somebody's blood sugar got too low. When I saw her after that, she acted like I wasn't there.

Other than my one unfortunate attempt at dating, my first semester back in college went okay. I showed up for classes and took some notes, and I blossomed into a slightly below-average student. That wasn't saying much considering I went to Peabody. I still hated writing papers about topics I didn't care about, but I especially liked two of the poems I read for English. One was *The Second Coming* by William Butler Yeats. Part of it made me think of the bullfight in Tijuana.

> The blood-dimmed tide is loosed, and everywhere
> The ceremony of innocence is drowned;
> The best lack all conviction, while the worst
> Are full of passionate intensity.

The teacher said the poem was about the end of the Christian era and about the era that could come next. I read it about 50 times. I found a couple of things the teacher didn't point out, but I kept what I thought to myself.

My other favorite poem was *The Love Song of J. Alfred Prufrock*, by T. S. Eliot. There was a lot I didn't understand, but I liked the images it put in my head. It made me see the person I was afraid I might become. I kept imagining myself at the end of an empty, irrelevant life.

> I grow old ... I grow old ...
> I shall wear the bottoms of my trousers rolled.
> Shall I part my hair behind?
> Do I dare to eat a peach?
> I shall wear white flannel trousers,
> And walk upon the beach.
> I have heard the mermaids singing,
> Each to each.
> I do not think that they will sing to me.

The last three lines could've been written for me. I was pretty sure I wouldn't ever hear mermaids singing unless I could figure out what I was supposed to do with my life. I'd never stopped thinking about forming into imaginary ranks with my classmates and marching away from Battle Ground Academy. I finally wrote a poem about it.

The Coward

I took my place in the ranks
And our lines were straight,
And as we began moving forward
There was an explosion.
The others kept advancing
Into the smoke and chaos,
But I fell to the ground.
After I finally got to my feet,
I wandered until
I came to a river,
And washing the blood
From my body,
I was unable
To find a wound.

That was as far as I got with the poem. I was walking around in the wilderness while my classmates were fighting their way through breastworks, but I still thought I could end up seeing real combat. Palani had been right. I thought I should enlist. But it wasn't just to punish myself. There was always a chance that going to Vietnam would help me find out what I was supposed to do.

Chapter 18

December 11, 1966 – I'm sitting near the back of the sanctuary. The only reason I'm here is because I didn't want Mother to have to come to church by herself again. Before I went to California, a youth minister I really liked, Allen Charles, was asked to resign because he participated in some civil rights marches.

Our preacher, Dr. Rowe, christened me when I was six weeks old. I've always liked him and he's especially eloquent, but sometimes his sermons sound like political speeches. Maybe that's because a lot of the church leaders are rich Republicans who went to Vanderbilt. Every Sunday before the service, most of the congregation gathers downstairs for donuts and coffee. Today the conversations I overheard were mostly about basketball and business, but I heard a couple of comments about how the communists have to be stopped in Vietnam, and that anybody who is against the war in Vietnam is a traitor. And a couple of cars in the church parking lot had bumper stickers that said, "America – Love It or Leave It."

Dr. Rowe comes to the part of the service that's set aside for a minute of silent prayer. I give thanks for my time in California and for being allowed to know Palani, and then I ask God to help me find out what I should be doing.

A few days later I got a call from our neighbor, Arthur March. He lived three houses down from us on Clearview Drive. Mr. March told me that a college student had coached his oldest son, Hal, the year before, but he'd decided not to coach again. Mr.

March had seen me shooting on my goal, and he asked if I'd be willing to step in and take the team. He took me by surprise. I couldn't come up with a good excuse, and I went ahead and said I'd do it.

There was a coaches meeting at the YMCA, and the league supervisor spent an hour talking about sportsmanship and the importance of setting a good example. Our first practice was a few days later on the school playground. Almost all of the best players were on Woodmont's other sixth-grade team. The kids I got were pretty much the leftovers.

But one of my players, Davey Austin, was pretty good. It turned out that the only reason he was on my team was because the father who coached the other team didn't want him. Davey was supposed to be a discipline problem. Three of the other kids I had were average, and everybody else either hadn't played before, or didn't look like they had. My three worst players could barely dribble or shoot.

I'd been pretty good at working with the kids at the Children's Home, and I thought I'd be able to keep the Austin kid in line. We were halfway through practice when he started yelling at one of the other guys on the team for not trying hard enough. I walked him off to the side of the court. I told him I could see that he was the best player we had, and I asked him if he resented being with the other kids on his team. When he didn't answer me, I offered to call the coach of the other Woodmont team and see if he had room for another player.

Davey knew the other coach didn't want him, but I acted like I could work it out. Then I said it would be too bad if he changed teams. I told him that we needed a leader. He stammered a little and tried to tell me he didn't want to change teams, but I said he probably needed some time to think about what he wanted to do. I had him stand beside the court for the rest of the practice.

At first, we worked a lot on defense and rebounding, but it wasn't long before we started scrimmaging. We didn't do any drills and we didn't have any plays. I still thought they were a waste of time. We were a long way from even being mediocre, but I always liked coming to practice.

Even though we got clobbered in our first two games, the kids were having a good time. I was glad they liked playing, but I couldn't stand the way they acted when they lost. It didn't seem to bother anybody but Davey. Everybody else acted like they were supposed to lose. I'd felt the same way back when I was their age. They'd already gotten the message that they weren't any good. But if they were willing to work at it, two or three of the guys had a chance to make a high school team in a few years.

I wanted to make the season about more than just winning and losing, and it wasn't long before I came up with a way to explain what I wanted them to understand.

West End High School was only a couple of miles away from Woodmont, and for just about as long as I could remember, I'd heard about the West basketball team of 1954. But what I'd heard sounded too good to be true. I didn't want to tell my kids some fairy tale, and one afternoon when we didn't have practice, I went to the downtown library and started reading through the 1954 newspapers.

January 24, 1967 – I'm with my team on the basketball court at Woodmont. I've been telling them about what the West High team did in 1954, and I'm trying to keep from breaking down. Even though it might be too much for them to understand, it's something they should know about. Yesterday when I was reading about what happened, I ended up crying in front of the microfilm reader, but I've been able to get through most of what I want to tell them. I've told them about Dr. Scarborough's failing health, and how, before the start of that basketball season, he announced that he was retiring at the end of the year. But then I choked up and I had to stop talking.

Dr. W. H. Scarborough had been the principal of West End High School since the school opened in 1937. When students had personal problems, or when there was sickness or a death in one of their families, he always did what he could to help. It wasn't long before the students started calling him Doc, and he became a beloved figure.

Doc loved basketball, but during his final year as principal, his physician told him that his heart might not be strong enough to stand the excitement of watching the team play. Word got out that he was retiring at the end of the school year, and there was a school assembly. The team captains stood up and announced that the players were dedicating the rest of the season to Doc Scarborough.

West was known as a basketball school – there had been three state championships in the 1940s – but the 1954 team was small and nobody thought they compared to any of the championship teams. They were scrappy and there were a few good players, but the team lost several games during the regular season, and there was a serious question about whether they would even advance beyond the district tournament.

West managed to win the district tournament in a sudden death overtime, but in the first round of the regional tournament, they were losing to a highly-favored team. They were behind by four points with twenty seconds left, but a basket by one of West's undersized guards cut the lead to two points, and then there was a steal and a foul at the buzzer. When West made two free throws after time expired, the game went into overtime.

West won in another sudden death, and the school went on a quest. The student section kept chanting, "All the Way For Doc," and the players, despite being small and overmatched, kept winning close games. And when they won the regional tournament, the quest became a crusade. The state tournament was played at the Vanderbilt gymnasium, which was only a mile or so from the West campus.

They managed to win three more close games, but by the time they played for the state championship, the team was worn out. Doc, who hadn't attended any of the previous games, got a call at halftime. He was told that the players were leg-weary and flat, and they were lucky to only be six points behind. He was worried that the team would think they'd let him down when they lost.

The kids saw me tear up, but they didn't say a word and they didn't look at each other. I waited for what seemed like a minute before I tried to finish.

West was in a huddle next to their bench after the end of the third quarter, and then the entire gym went quiet. When the players turned around, they saw Doc Scarborough walking slowly down one of the aisles. He came to console them after they lost, but they thought he was risking his life to be there and cheer them on.

Most of the West players were in tears when they went out to start the fourth quarter. As loud as the students were cheering before, they got louder. There was a continuous chant of "All the Way For Doc," and when one of their little guards hit a long hook shot and gave them the lead with a minute left, the student body exploded. I struggled to tell the kids about the headline in the newspaper the next morning. I couldn't get it out at first, but I finally said it. "We Made It Doc, 42-40."

I told my players that not too many people remembered who won the state championship in 1953 or 1955, but people all across the state knew what the West End High School basketball team did in 1954. I said those players were remembered because they played for something bigger than themselves. West practiced harder and played harder than the other teams because of their dedication to Doc Scarborough. That was why they were remembered.

Then I told my players that even though they were just a bunch of sixth-graders from Woodmont School, if they practiced hard enough and played as well as they could, for the rest of their lives they would all remember that basketball season. And it didn't matter how many games our team lost. It was a lot to take in and I didn't explain it very well, but I could tell that a few of them understood that being on a team could mean a lot more than winning and losing games.

There was something else I wanted them to get out of the season, but I didn't say anything about it. They were already starting to tease and insult each other, and it would get a lot worse once they were teenagers. I wanted to keep them from getting crushed the way I'd gotten crushed when it happened to me.

I would've done some of it anyway, but it seemed to me that if I teased the kids on my team, they'd be used to teasing by the time they got to high school. I already knew that Davey was a smart aleck, but he wasn't the only one I had.

At our next practice, I did a play-by-play of our scrimmage. I acted like it was a real game. "Welcome to this live broadcast from the basketball courts at Woodmont School. We're here with our cameras and you're about to see some rising sixth-grade talent. We'll see if they can show the rest of the world how the game of basketball should be played."

After a couple of minutes, Davey dribbled the ball off of his foot and I kicked into high gear. "And that was young Davey Austin demonstrating the art of dribbling. He considers himself to be quite a player, so I hope you were paying close attention to his technique."

Everybody was laughing except for Davey. He gave me a dismissive look and I went over and pretended to conduct an on-air interview. When I reached toward him with an imaginary microphone, he started smiling. "So Davey, it must've taken a *lot* of practice to learn to dribble off your foot like that. Even though you were running down the court and being guarded, you were still able to hit your foot with the ball. That is *simply amazing*. Can you hit your other foot, too?"

I kept announcing our scrimmages when we practiced, and the more exaggerated my insults were, the more the kids liked it. They looked forward to hearing me say things like, "Just an *awful* shot," or "What an absolutely *horrendous* pass." Or "Perhaps the most *heinous* defense in the history of basketball."

It wasn't long before I was imitating the mistakes the guys made in games. If somebody lost the ball when he was dribbling, at the next practice I'd bounce the ball off my leg, and then stumble across the court and fall down. If somebody missed an easy layup, I'd look as awkward as I could and hit the bottom of the goal. But my version of missed free throws got the most laughs. Hal March, who was an average shooter at best, missed two free throws at the end of a game we could've won, and at our next practice, he knew I'd be giving my version of his performance.

"Alright, the game is tied and little Hal March will be shooting two shots. His parents are here in the stands, and Mrs. March has her fingers crossed. Think of *how proud she'll be* when her son wins the game for his team. Mr. March has been preparing Hal for this moment for a long, long time. And it's so easy. All Hal needs to do is hit *one* free throw. And Hal's parents aren't the only ones in the crowd with their fingers crossed."

I'd already found out the name of the prettiest girl in the class. "And isn't that Kay Porter sitting a few rows down from Mr. and Mrs. March? She sure is cute. I've heard that she's starting to notice Hal. If he hits a free throw and wins the game, there's no telling *what* might happen. Who knows, she might even take him off somewhere and give him a big kiss." The kids were laughing, and Hal was smiling and shaking his head.

"That's right, all he has to do is hit just *one* of his two free throws. Of course, there is another possible outcome, although it's *highly* unlikely. If Hal should *somehow* miss both shots, for the rest of her life, whenever she hears his name, Kay will remember what a loser he was. And who could blame her? A girl like that would *never* want to have anything to do with some *choker* who couldn't even make *one lousy free throw* and win a game for his team."

By then Davey was doing a pretty good job of impersonating a flirtatious sixth-grade girl. I finally stepped to the foul line to do my imitation of Hal. I took my time and appeared to concentrate, and then I shot the first free throw over the top of the goal. The second try went several feet off to the right side of the backboard, and Davey, still acting like he was Kay, gave Hal a look of disgust and pretended to vomit. Imitating kids screwing up became a regular feature of our practices, and sometimes a kid who had messed up would remind me if I forgot to make fun of him.

Teasing them worked out even better than I thought it would, but there were too many things I did wrong. Sometimes I'd yell at a kid if he was goofing around, and I'd get mad when somebody wasn't listening. We scrimmaged a lot, and there were times when one of my players would get tired and start loafing. I'd let him know when he wasn't trying, and if he said, "I don't care," that would set me off. I overreacted a few times, but whoever I unloaded on was usually back to having a good time by the end of practice.

February 19, 1967 – It's Saturday morning and our game is about to start. I didn't get much sleep last night. I checked my heart rate before I left home. It was 135 beats per minute. I get nervous every time we have a game. Today we're playing against what everybody – including my own players – refers to as "the good team" from Woodmont. We've gotten better since the start of the season, but we've only won two games.

Davey Austin is pumped up. The only way we'll have a chance is if he plays a great game. I can tell how much he wants to beat the kids on the other team. He says they've been bragging about how good they are, and that they keep talking about how they're going to slaughter his team. He hasn't said it, but more than anything else, he wants to beat the father who didn't want to coach him.

Davey played his heart out. He hit just about every shot he took in the second half, and the other kids played about as well as they could. With nine seconds to play, we had the ball and we were only down by one point. I called a timeout. The other team's best players would be all over Davey, but I came up with a play that might get him open for the last shot. It was our ball at midcourt, but when I saw how the other team lined up, I called another timeout. I needed to take a deep breath, but I couldn't.

I tried to sound more confident than I was when I was explaining what we were going to do. The kids were focused and Davey kept nodding. We ran back out onto the floor and the good team lined up the same way as before – just like I hoped they would. They were double-teaming Davey with their two best players. He lined up halfway between our foul line and half court, and the referee handed the ball to Hal March.

Davey got a screen from Will Evans. He started running to the near side, and Hal faked a pass to him. It was a great fake. Just as both of the kids guarding Davey cut in front of him to intercept the pass, he broke back toward the middle of the court. He got the pass from Hal, and Brooks McMillan, a really intelligent kid who usually made his lay-ups, took off toward our basket from the far side of the court. Davey took two quick dribbles toward the head of the circle, and then he hit Brooks with a perfect bounce pass. Brooks was wide open. His layup rolled around and went in, and that was that.

Davey was already walking over toward the father who coached the other team when he saw me coming in his direction. He knew I was too far away to stop him and he gave me a defiant smile. When I got to him he was shaking the coach's hand. All I heard him say was, "Good game."

But when we were walking away he started laughing and raised his hands in mock disbelief. "What kind of a dumbass doesn't keep at least one guy back on defense with a one-point lead and nine seconds left on the clock?" And he made sure that anybody who was nearby could hear him.

Chapter 19

I knew it might've been a coincidence, but I wondered if getting to coach was an answer to the prayer I said in church. I'd asked for help, and a few days later a door opened up and I ended up coaching a group of kids who seemed like they were my little brothers.

It might not have been up there with being a doctor or a lawyer, but I thought I was pretty good at working with kids. The reason coaching felt so natural could've been because I wasn't much more mature than the guys on my team. I was nineteen and my players were twelve, but most of the time I didn't think about how old they were. It wasn't twelve-year-old Davey and twelve-year-old Brooks and twelve-year-old Hal – it was just Davey, Brooks, and Hal.

It wasn't long before I went from being resigned to going into the military, to worrying about getting drafted. The only time I forgot about Vietnam was when I had basketball practice.

I wasn't sure why I loved being with kids as much as I did. Palani would've said it was because I had an extreme response to everything. He would've said that I couldn't like something without *really* liking something. But it might've been because kids were so absorbed in the present. If it was Saturday morning and they were playing basketball, they weren't thinking about anything else. When I was with them I was in the present, too, and that made me feel a lot more alive than I usually felt.

I was pretty sure I was having an impact on the kids at

Woodmont. They were definitely having an impact on me. Over the course of the season, I noticed that I'd stopped making up lyrics when songs came on the radio. If I was on my way to practice or coming back from a game, when I heard *Happy Together*, or *Kind of a Drag*, or *For What It's Worth*, I just listened.

I coached on Saturdays, and I'd started going to the Children's Home on Sundays. The kids at the Home would've been a lot like the guys on my team if things hadn't gone wrong with their families, but things *had* gone wrong. I still didn't think I was making their lives any better in the long run. Toward the end of basketball season, I told the director how much I appreciated the opportunity he'd given me to do volunteer work, but that I wouldn't be coming back. I felt guilty about leaving.

Sometimes the lead story in the news was about race, but it was usually about the war in Southeast Asia. The Viet Cong launched two major offensives within a few days of our first game, and they made another big push before the end of the season.

The assassination in Dallas still made the news, too. After we had a few games, there was a story about Jim Garrison, the District Attorney in New Orleans. He was conducting a formal investigation into the death of President Kennedy. I knew that would make Palani happy, and I decided to give him a call and see what he thought. I looked everywhere, but I couldn't find the index card with his phone number. I knew I hadn't thrown it away. I told myself it was bound to turn up at some point.

The closer it got, the more I dreaded the end of basketball season. I hated the thought of telling my players goodbye after our last game. I'd see them now and then at first, but after they graduated from high school, I might not see them at all. We'd just keep drifting away from each other. I was pretty sure that if we had more time together, some of the relationships would be more lasting. I didn't want the kids on my team to just fade out of my life.

Most of my players didn't want the season to end any more

than I did. One of the mothers told me that her son cried when he got home after our last game. Davey's mother said that he was sleeping in his jersey every night.

After the end of basketball season, right around the time when President Kennedy's remains were exhumed and reburied at Arlington Cemetery, I made myself get in touch with the guy who had coached Davey Austin and Brooks McMillan and Hal March and Will Evans and a couple of the other kids in baseball the year before. I tried not to sound too excited when he told me he wasn't going to coach again.

I went to the library and found a really good book on coaching baseball, and I tried to remember as much as I could from back when I played. Some of the kids who showed up on the field behind Woodmont for our first practice were better than I expected. We had a pitcher named Glenn Horn who had really good control, and it looked like our defense and our hitting wouldn't be too bad.

I didn't have afternoon classes at Peabody, and I usually got to Woodmont early. A few of the guys lived close enough to walk, but most of them rode their bikes. It was like basketball had been – they wanted to be at practice as much as I did.

There was a lot I didn't know about coaching baseball, and it took me a while to figure out what we needed to work on. A couple of the fathers thought their sons could be major leaguers and wanted us to win every game we played, but most of the parents just wanted their kids to have something to do when school was out. They didn't want them staying home and watching TV all summer.

There weren't any professional prospects on the team, but some of my players would want to keep playing when they were older. I thought my job was to help them get good enough to make the next team they tried out for.

April 4, 1967 – It's a warm, dry afternoon and I'm standing beside home plate on the field behind Woodmont School. I toss up the baseball and hit it hard between second and third base. Brooks McMillan is playing shortstop. He moves to his right and scoops up the ball, and then he pivots and makes a strong throw to the first baseman. He's a whole lot better at baseball than he was at basketball.

I'm going to hit the next ball to Davey Austin who's playing third. He's afraid of getting hurt. I remember feeling the same way. I hit a grounder right at him, and he steps to one side to field it and then he throws it to Will Evans, who's playing first. I start booing. He acts like he doesn't know that he's supposed to stay in front of the ball.

I was pretty sure that booing wouldn't be enough. "Since you like moving to one side so much, maybe you should go down to Mexico and learn how to be a matador." He rolled his eyes and I hit him another grounder. He did a little better, but he still moved out of the way.

I picked up a glove and after I swished and sashayed out to third base, I started using an effeminate Spanish accent. "Me llama es Davey Austin. I haf come to America to play the third base. I was a sissy bool-fighter in Mehico before I come to jour country."

I told one of the kids to hit me a ball, but before it got to me I moved gracefully to one side and pretended that the ball was a bull and that I was brandishing a cape. After a few more demonstrations of exaggerated cowardice, I motioned for Davey to get back to his position. He stayed in front of the next ball and he fielded it pretty well. He didn't seem to notice that I hadn't hit it as hard as I'd hit the first two.

At the end of practice, after I told the other kids what they'd done well and what they needed to do better, I finally got around to Davey. He was waiting for an insult.

"I just have one thing to tell you. Don't forget to pick up your dress from the dry cleaner on your way home."

He took on an air of quiet confidence and smiled at me. "Do you want me to pick up your *bra* while I'm there?"

I let him feel triumphant about his comeback for a few seconds, and then I smiled back at him. "Yeah, go ahead and pick it up. But the bra isn't mine – it belongs to your mother. And tell her I'm *really* looking forward to Saturday night."

He was laughing and the other kids started laughing, too. I thought I might get a call from some outraged parent about what I said, but the guys on the team must not have mentioned it when they got home. Or maybe I didn't hear anything because the parents knew what I knew – that their sons weren't innocent little boys anymore, and that junior high was right around the corner.

I didn't know it, but close to the time I was getting home that night, Martin Luther King was giving a speech in New York condemning the war in Vietnam. King was always being accused of stirring up trouble, and racial problems seemed to be getting worse in America. There had been riots all across the country the previous summer, and another summer was on the way.

For at least as far back as when I was in the seventh grade at Battle Ground Academy, Nashville had been a hotbed of the Civil Rights movement – from sit-ins at the lunch counters of downtown stores to the Freedom Riders. Stories about local race relations were in the news all the time. A lawsuit in the 1950s led to the desegregation of Nashville schools, but city leaders had done everything they could to slow down the process. It hadn't been long since I read a story in the newspaper. There was a chance that another lawsuit could be filed.

Chapter 20

The day after Dr. King's speech in New York, I walked into the Peabody student center and I saw a guy named Mike Higgins. A classmate of mine from Battle Ground had introduced us a few weeks earlier. He usually sat at the same table over in the corner of the cafeteria. Mike saw me walking in, and he waved me over to sit with him.

He looked like he was in his late thirties. He was working on a doctorate in history. He was in the military back in the 1950s and early 1960s, and he'd served in Korea and Vietnam. He was gruff and intimidating, and he had a wicked-looking scar that extended from his right eye back toward his ear. Listening to Mike talk about the war in Vietnam was a little like listening to Palani, but Mike was a whole lot angrier and more profane.

When he was talking about President Johnson or Secretary of Defense McNamara or General Westmoreland, it was always "that fucking Johnson and his fucking war" or "that fucking weasel, McNamara" or "that lying bastard, Westmoreland."

And when he really got wound up, he went into more detail. "If you love America, get down on your knees and thank God Almighty that you have the Corporation of Defense to protect you. Just send your sons into the military and send your taxes to Boeing or Monsanto or Lockheed, or to the corporate subsidiary of your choice. And while they're getting richer – while your kids are getting shot up and killed – they'll keep bribing the government to lie about how many Viet Cong are getting killed every week, and about how we're winning the war."

He'd been reading the morning newspaper, the *Tennessean*, but when I sat down he put it on the table. I got the feeling that Mike liked me, but I wasn't sure why. "Let me guess. You don't even know that Martin Luther King gave a speech in New York last night."

When I said I hadn't heard about it, he shook his head. "College students. You guys need to start paying attention to what's going on in the world. Last night King basically told all the powerful people who are betraying America to go fuck themselves.

"Fuck you, Lyndon Johnson, fuck you, Pentagon, fuck you, politicians, fuck you, corporations, and fuck you, civil rights leaders who're scared of pissing anybody off who might be their allies. *Man*, does King have balls."

He picked up his paper again. "Listen to this. 'A nation that continues year after year to spend more money on military defense than on social uplift is approaching spiritual death.' And what about this? 'We have been repeatedly faced with the cruel irony of watching Negro and white boys on TV screens as they kill and die together for a nation that has been unable to seat them together in the same schools.'

"He's coming right out and saying that the war is immoral. He's saying it's wrong and that people need to stand up and say so. You need to read the whole speech. King is magnificent, but all you hear from the right wingers – from assholes like George Wallace and Lester Maddox, and from the morons in the John Birch Society who keep calling him Martin Lucifer King – is that he's a communist.

"And then there's J. Edgar Hoover. That degenerate little turd has been using the FBI for years to try and destroy King."

A few days later he gave me a transcript of King's speech. He wanted me to read it, but it was pretty long and I ended up putting it in a drawer of the desk in my bedroom. I was drawn to Mike, but there were times when I just wanted to think about what we were going to do at our next practice.

May 3, 1967 – It's Friday afternoon and I'm with my baseball team at Woodmont. We have a scrimmage against a really good team in the morning. If we play like we did in our last scrimmage, we'll get embarrassed again. I'm afraid that a lot of the kids could give up on our team if we don't start getting better. We're working on situations. I hit the ball and a baserunner takes off for first base. Davey fields it okay at third base, but he makes a lousy throw to first. The ball bounces away from Will Evans and rolls off into foul territory.

The right fielder should've been backing up the throw, but he still hasn't moved. He finally wakes up when Will starts chasing the ball. I stop myself from throwing my bat into the backstop. I've told him to back up the base three times in the last twenty minutes. I hit the next ball as hard as I can down the right field line. It bounces up onto the pavement beside the school, and it keeps rolling. It takes him a while to run it down. The next time I hit the ball to third base, he comes in and backs up first base the way he's supposed to.

We had four good players. They were talented and they were wired for sports. They paid attention and worked hard when we were practicing. They deserved to be on a decent team. And we had five other guys with some ability, but they either didn't think they could get better, or they just didn't care.

I gave almost every kid on the team a nickname. I called the worst three players on the team Huey, Dewey, and Louie because they all ran like ducks. They just went through the motions of doing whatever they were supposed to be doing. They could've probably been average if they'd worked at it, but the only thing they were good at was making sure they didn't get hit by the ball. I liked them, but I couldn't stand their lack of effort. I kept myself from saying it, but when they didn't try, they were betraying the kids who *did* try.

I finally got the duck triplets to stay after practice so I could give them some extra attention. A couple of times I tried to sound like Donald Duck when I talked, and they seemed to appreciate the effort. The first thing I did was take them up to the basketball court – where we had recess when I went to Woodmont.

They looked surprised when I started telling them what I was like as a kid. "When you guys were two or three years old, I was a sixth-grader. I was one of the slowest kids in the class. We'd play kickball and dodgeball at recess, and the captains would choose up the teams. I was always one of the last ones chosen. It was embarrassing. I hated feeling like a loser all the time."

I asked them if they ever felt the way I used to feel. Huey didn't seem to be listening, but Dewey and Louie both had serious looks on their faces. A few minutes later, we were out in center field playing catch. At first, we stood close together and threw underhand, but we gradually moved farther away and after a half-hour, all three were throwing to each other overhand. Huey even caught a few balls.

June 6, 1967 – Baseball practice ended an hour ago and I've come up to the Woodmont playground. It's almost 8 PM, but there's still plenty of light. I sit down in a swing. There's no reason to go straight home. My parents have gone out to dinner, and I don't want to go into the den and turn on the television and hear anything else about the war between Israel and Egypt. Or about how there could be a nuclear standoff if the Soviets get involved.

It's been almost five years since the missile crisis in Cuba. I'm not as afraid as I was then, but I'm still worried. I'm sick of being worried. I'm sick of lying awake in my bed at night every time the world has a crisis. I didn't get much sleep last night, and I probably won't be getting much tonight.

I start swinging, and soon I'm going as high as I can. When I'm on my way down I think about the same thing I usually think about when I'm in a swing. The air rushes by my face as I pick up speed, and I imagine going all the way up and over the top of the bar and making a complete loop. I pretend that if I can make it over the top, I'll get to make a wish. Tonight I'd wish for the crisis in the Middle East to disappear.

My parents were back when I got home, and after a while I went up onto the roof of our house. The sun had been down for over an hour, but the shingles were still warm. I tried not to think about what the United States would do if the Soviet Union took military action against Israel. I kept telling myself that the situation in Cuba was a lot worse.

I eventually climbed down and walked over to the place in the backyard where I'd stood in 1962. I looked through the windows the way I did when I was fifteen. The lights in the den were off but the TV was on. Mother had already gone to bed by then, and my father was asleep in his chair.

I wasn't sure if my father was drinking more, but it seemed like he was falling asleep earlier than usual. A couple of months before that, he'd borrowed enough money to buy a half-interest in the family business from Mother's oldest brother.

I wasn't making his life any easier. I was doing better at Peabody than I'd done at Vanderbilt, but I still wasn't much of a student. Even though he tolerated all the coaching I did, he expected me to give it up and get a job once I graduated.

I wasn't thinking about a nuclear showdown over the Suez Canal later that night when I was trying to fall asleep. I was trying to figure out how to get through to the guys on my team who should've been better than they were. Along with Huey, Dewey, and Louie, I'd handed out a few other nicknames.

I had five kids who were average, and I called them "the Doe Brothers." I started referring to Steve as Steve Doe and Mark as Mark Doe and the other three the same way. A couple of practices later, they were all standing together. One of them started smiling. He thought he knew why I called them the Doe Brothers. He guessed that it was because they reminded me of female deer.

I started laughing when he said it. "Not a bad guess, but that isn't it. John Doe is a name for an average person." I almost mentioned that the police also used the name to refer to unidentified corpses, but I didn't want to make things too complicated. "The reason you're the Doe brothers is because even though you could all be pretty good, you insist on being average. I thought you might as well have last names that let the world know how average you're trying to be."

It wasn't long before I came up with a way to impersonate John Doe. I'd pull up my pants as high as they'd go and slouch over, and I'd keep my voice totally flat. If one of the Doe Brothers didn't run as hard as he could when he was on base, I went out to where he was and pulled up my pants. Then I started moving at half-speed and using my John Doe voice. "You know, it's not a good idea to run too fast. What if you fell down and got hurt?" And it was the same with batting and fielding.

I finally gave them a little speech. "If you dedicate yourselves to being average in junior high and high school, and if you keep being average all the way through whatever average college you end up going to, you can all marry completely average women and have spectacularly average children and especially average jobs. And who knows? Maybe one of you guys will manage to live such an incredibly average life that you'll get inducted into the Average Hall of Fame."

Some of the Doe Brothers gradually started showing more effort, and before long I conducted the first of three solemn ceremonies. I would hike up my pants and charge the offending player with the unpardonable sin of trying, and in an especially dull monotone, I would excommunicate him from the John Doe Society.

Chapter 21

July 3, 1967 – I'm in summer school at Peabody and I'm taking a class called The Citizen and His Schools. It's about as interesting as it sounds, but I'm glad I'm here. Yancey Walsh is sitting in the row in front of me. I don't think I've seen her since we went to the dance in the Battle Ground gym back when we were juniors in high school. She looked good before, but she looks even better now.

She's glanced back at me and smiled a couple of times. I've got longer hair and I'm taller, and I've gained about 40 pounds. I wonder if she recognizes me. Maybe a blast of peppermint would bring it all back to her. She's wearing a beige miniskirt, and I have a good view of her perfect legs, which are smooth and tanned and crossed. She's taking notes, and she keeps bouncing her left foot up and down. The muscles flex along her left thigh every time she does it.

I imagine running into her after class. We'll look at each other at the same time and she'll be really friendly. She'll notice my chest and shoulders and say something flirtatious like, "You've put on some weight since the last time I saw you." And when I say, "Neither have you," she'll laugh. I tell myself that I'm going to talk to her, and I start humming the melody of Dream Lover.

I chickened out and didn't say anything, but the next week she was behind me in line at the cafeteria in the student center. She remembered me and we started talking. She said she was just picking up a couple of courses at Peabody over the summer. Even though I didn't ask, it wasn't long before she let me know that she had a boyfriend.

The way things went with Yancey were pretty predictable, but the outside world was about as predictable as a stumbling drunk. Along with Vietnam getting worse, it seemed like there was a race riot every other week. And drugs were changing all sorts of things.

When I heard *Along Comes Mary* the year before, I thought it was about a girl named Mary. I didn't even know what marijuana was. Around the same time, I ran into Tony Ballou, my friend who went to Battle Ground and who got hurt in the wreck we were in. I had no idea what he was talking about when he said that a lot of his friends were smoking pot. I wasn't very aware of drugs in the early spring of 1967, but before long the drug culture seemed to be everywhere.

There were still songs like *Respect* and *Groovin'* and *I Was Made to Love Her* and *Make Me Yours,* but the radio was being invaded by psychedelic songs from all sorts of strange-sounding groups – like *Whiter Shade of Pale* by Procol Harum and *White Rabbit* by Jefferson Airplane – and there was also *Purple Haze* by Jimi Hendrix. They were all part of an avalanche of music involving drugs. I wasn't sure, but the *Sergeant Pepper's Lonely Hearts Club Band* album seemed to be part of the same avalanche.

Guys I'd known for most of my life were growing beards and letting their hair grow down past their shoulders, and they talked about the drugs they were using and what they were doing to stay out of the military. Getting drafted and going to Vietnam was in my head pretty much all the time. I spent a lot of time thinking about getting screamed at in basic training and slogging around in rice paddies.

My baseball team was the light in the deepening shadow of Vietnam. Davey Austin finally started getting in front of ground balls. One time during practice a grounder took a bad hop and hit him in the face, and he got up as fast as he could to keep anybody from seeing the tears in his eyes. When the next ball came his way, he didn't give an inch. Another time Brooks McMillan took a fastball in the ribs during a game, but he trotted down to first base like nothing had happened. A couple of innings later he came up against the same pitcher, and he hit the first pitch against the rightfield fence.

I didn't have that kind of physical courage when I was twelve, and I still didn't have it. And I wasn't any braver when it came to moral courage. Muhammad Ali had the guts to just stand up and say he wasn't going to serve in the military. I didn't.

Huey, Dewey, and Louie stayed after practice once or twice a week. By the end of the season, they'd made pretty good progress. In the last game, the very last time he came to bat, Huey managed to get his bat on a ball and it rolled a few feet out toward the third baseman. He waddled as fast as he could toward first base and he almost got there in time to beat the throw. When he heard his teammates cheering, he looked behind him to see what they were yelling about.

I did some things right, but I still got mad too many times – especially during the games. One of the reasons I got angry was because when my team looked bad, it made me look bad. Unless we were playing a weak team, I didn't like the games all that much. Before we played, my heart rate went up at least as much as it had during basketball season. Sometimes I'd picture Palani over by the fence shaking his head. He would've made fun of me for getting all worked up over a kid's ballgame.

The guys I was coaching only won two or three games the year before, but we ended up coming in second in our league and making it to the City Tournament. A few of the parents told me what a good coach I was, but the main reason we won so many games was because most of the other teams in our league were coached by fathers.

Baseball was pretty far down the list of the things they had on their minds, but it was the most important thing in my life. The fathers who coached had jobs and families. All I had to worry about was my team and taking a couple of courses in summer school. And most of the fathers I came up against called their players by their last names. The guys on my team were like my brothers.

August 5, 1967 – It's after dark and I'm standing on Lea's Summit in Warner Park. I can see downtown Nashville in the distance. Our team party is over and I should be on my way home by now, but I need to pull myself together. There are plenty of things going on in the world worth crying about, but I'm not upset about the race riots or about all the sailors who burned to death last week in the fire on the aircraft carrier off the coast of Vietnam, or because the country seems to be falling apart.

I'm crying because baseball is over. Davey and Brooks and Glenn and Hal and Will and the other sixth graders on my team are moving on to middle school, and they won't be on my team anymore. I've signed up to coach the football team from Woodmont in the YMCA league this fall, but it won't be the same.

I almost broke down at our party, but it wasn't just because of what I was losing. It was also because of what the kids were losing. I was sitting on a picnic table watching them running around and playing, and they didn't understand that it was the last time they'd ever be together. Their childhoods were flickering out and they didn't know it. And they didn't know that they were growing up in a world that seemed to be collapsing. I finally went down to my car and finished a poem I'd been trying to write.

The Signal

The boys hear
A bugle blowing
In the distance,
But when they look to me
For an explanation,
I stay silent.
I have already told them
As much as they
Would understand.

But it will not be enough –
It will not be nearly enough –
To get them through
What lies ahead.

There were already a half-million soldiers in Vietnam, and toward the end of baseball season, General Westmoreland asked for 200,000 more troops. A couple of guys I knew had already been drafted, and two or three others, including Tom Hendrickson, volunteered because they thought it would be better than going in as draftees. It was just a matter of time before I got called up.

Once baseball was over, the thought of having to give up coaching was on my mind more and more. My parents could see that I was worrying, and Mother finally asked me what was wrong. I ended up telling her how much I loved coaching kids, and that I was going to do whatever it took to keep coaching.

She probably told my father what I said. He thought it was a lot more important to put on a uniform and defend the country than it was to coach kids in sports, but he must've wondered if I could survive in the military.

I made it through my first year at Peabody, but going to class wasn't nearly as interesting as sitting with Mike Higgins at the table in the corner of the student center. I gradually found out how he knew so much about the war. When he was in Korea, he'd been in counter-intelligence, and he was in Vietnam when it was still under French control. "I was there as a military advisor before the fall of Dien Bien Phu – back when our government still claims we weren't in Indochina."

He knew a lot about Vietnam because of his military service, and he knew a lot about race relations because after he got out, he was a bouncer at a mostly-black nightclub in North Nashville. "Every once in a while some guy would come in and start running his mouth. I know a little bit about in-fighting and I never worried about customers like that. But it was different with the quiet ones. If they felt cornered they could be trouble."

Sometimes when he wasn't looking, I'd glance at the scar next to his eye. I wondered if it was from being in the military, or if somebody could've cut him with a bottle in a bar fight.

The other person who made me skip class sometimes was a guy named Sean Metzger. Sean was three years older than I was, and whenever he was in the student center, he sat at Mike's table. He seemed to like my sense of humor, and it wasn't long before we got to be friends.

He didn't look all that much like a radical, but he smoked marijuana and listened to Bob Dylan all the time. He hated racism and the war in Vietnam, which was probably why he hit it off with Mike. Sean lived in an apartment at the edge of the Peabody campus. He had a wife, but he said he was crazy to have gotten married so young, and he wasn't sure how much longer they'd be together.

He was smart and funny, and he was especially passionate about literature. He wanted to be a writer. There were times when I walked into the student center, and he'd be waiting at the table with a poem he wanted to show me.

He talked about Robert Frost and T. S. Eliot a lot, and he was in awe of *The Second Coming*. He said it was hard to believe that it wasn't written about Vietnam. He said he wanted to go out to San Francisco someday and meet Lawrence Ferlinghetti. Sean had memorized the poem, *I Am Waiting*. He'd close his eyes and hold up his hands and recite lines like he'd written them himself.

> '...I am waiting for the war to be fought
> which will make the world safe for anarchy...'

One of his favorite poets was Randall Jarrell, who was from Nashville and who went to Vanderbilt. Sean was especially drawn to *Death of the Ball Turret Gunner*, and his voice would get lower when he recited the last line.

> '... When I died they washed me out of the turret with a hose.'

Sometimes Sean strayed from war poems. He was really into Robinson Jeffers. His eyes would smolder when he recited the part of *Shine, Perishing Republic*, that addressed the demise of America.

> "I sadly smiling remember
> That the flower fades to make fruit,
> And the fruit rots to make earth..."

Sean loved to recite poetry, and he enjoyed getting Mike riled up. He would wink at me and then casually mention something about George Wallace, and before long Mike would be ranting about "that fucking racist, George Wallace," which would usually lead to "that fucking idiot, Lester Maddox."

And after he'd gone down a long list of other politicians he saw as self-serving frauds, Mike would get around to Strom Thurmond. One of Mike's friends from his nightclub days was a black guy from South Carolina – the state Thurmond represented in the U. S. Senate.

At some point, he told Mike about a black child that Thurmond fathered. "Thurmond isn't just a racist, he's a fucking hypocrite. He doesn't even have the guts to acknowledge his own daughter. Maybe his balls didn't make it out of the glider when he crash-landed in France on D-Day."

September 24, 1967 – It's getting late on Sunday afternoon. It's sunny and warm outside, but it's cool inside Peach Blossom. It's the oldest house in my neighborhood and one of the oldest houses in the county. No Trespassing signs are nailed to boards across several of the doors and windows. Nobody was around, and I went behind the house and came in through a back window.

There was an article about Peach Blossom in the newspaper a few days ago. It was supposedly built a little after 1800, and it was owned by a man named Joseph Erwin. A few years after the house was built, Erwin's son-in-law was killed in a duel with Andrew Jackson.

His son-in-law was named Charles Dickinson, and his grave is supposed to be a couple of streets over in a subdivision. The article said that preservationists wanted to turn the house into a museum, but the plan fell through and Peach Blossom is about to be demolished.

There are splintered boards and broken glass and chunks of plaster on the floor, and the air is stale and musty. The mantles over the fireplace are gone and the interior doors are missing, along with most of the molding. I walk around and the sounds of my footsteps echo off the bare walls.

While I was going through the rooms downstairs, I tried to imagine what had happened in the house over more than a century and a half. Births and deaths in the bedrooms. Thousands of family meals in the dining room. Stories by the fireside. Slaves going about their daily chores. Whispering to each other when nobody else was around. And parties and conversations and laughter as time flowed through the house.

There was a big curved staircase in the front room. The railing had been removed and I wasn't sure how strong the stairs were. I stayed close to the wall when I was on my way up to the second floor. I went into a bedroom, and I imagined whoever slept there lying awake in the dark on the night after Charles Dickinson was killed in the duel.

The furniture was all gone, but I kept looking for something that could've been left behind. I ended up in the smallest of the upstairs bedrooms. It looked like it might've been occupied by a child, or maybe by a servant.

It wasn't long before I noticed a narrow gap between the edge of the floor and the wall. It seemed like a good place to look for an old coin or a button, and after I found a nail, I bent down and ran it along the base of the wall.

After three or four feet I made contact with something that moved. I found a longer nail and it took a few tries, but I finally fished out what looked like a marble. I wiped away the dust, and it turned out to be an old lead bullet. It was dark gray and there were a few nicks on its surface.

I wondered how long it had been since anybody touched it. I imagined that it could've been lost by a boy, and that I was standing in what was once his bedroom. I kept thinking about how it might've ended up where I found it.

I was rolling it around in the palm of my hand when I started looking out the window. The glass was thick and wavy and it made the trees and the yard and the surrounding neighborhood look out of focus.

I went over and stood by the window, and I imagined the boy gazing out at the fields and meadows and watching the slaves at work.

The sun was getting lower and when it was obscured by the branch of a tree, I noticed some scratches in the lower left corner of the window glass. The letters *I E* were etched into the window pane, and underneath the letters was the date, *1809*.

The letters were rough and irregular and so were the numbers. They looked like they might've been carved in the glass by a child. I wondered if, nearly 160 years earlier, a mother had stood behind her little son or daughter, while her diamond ring was used to mark the glass. The *E* probably stood for Erwin, the last name of the man who originally owned the house. I kept rolling the bullet between my fingers. I felt like I was in another dimension.

I finally went back outside, but before I left, I walked around to the side of the house. I came to a low, half-open door behind some shrubbery, and I pulled it open. There were steps leading down into the cellar. I wanted to crawl in and look around, but I didn't have a flashlight and the air was dead and dank.

After I closed the door most of the way, I put the bullet in the right front pocket of my pants. I kept thinking that a boy could've lost it. I started a poem that night and I finished it a couple of days later.

The Bullet

Was he pulling off his britches
When the bullet
Fell out of his pocket?
Had it bounced
Across the floor and rolled away
And not been missed?
And after the bullet
Settled into the space
Along the edge of the wall,
How many years went by
Before he walked down the stairs
And got on his horse
And rode away from home
For the last time?
And through all the years
With the bullet lying
Just out of sight,
How many other children
Grew up in his old room?
How many other
Long-forgotten treasures
Are concealed under boards,
Or lost in hidden crevices?
How much will be lost
When the old house
Is razed and swept away?

Chapter 22

October 6, 1967 – It's Friday night and I'm sitting on the back row of the football stands at Montgomery Bell Academy. The campus is half a mile west of Peach Blossom and about a half-mile north of my house. The night is warm and windy. It seems alive. The homecoming game is going on, but most of the guys on my football team, along with a bunch of other kids, are playing on an expanse of grass just beyond the north end zone.

Hill Murray, a fifth-grader who plays quarterback on my football team, picks up the ball on one bounce and starts running. He stays on his feet as long as he can, but he finally gets tripped up, and just about everybody else piles on top of him.

We had practice this afternoon and I told the kids to watch at least some of the game. I said we'd be a whole lot better team if we did things the way Coach Owens gets his team to do them – from the way they come out of the huddle and line up, to how organized and aggressive they are on offense and defense. The kids saw pretty much of the first half, but now they're playing Smear the Queer with a bunch of other kids. A rush of wind blows across the stands. It feels like the night is cooling down.

Ten years earlier, when I was in fifth grade, my father brought me to the homecoming game at Montgomery Bell. I sat in just about the same place I was sitting, and I watched my classmates playing Smear the Queer right where the kids on my team were playing.

The game hadn't changed. Somebody would kick the football, and whoever picked it up took off running and everybody else tried to tackle him. I wanted to join in that night, but I just kept sitting in the stands with my father.

One of my players, a sixth grader named Peter Johnson, was playing the role that I played, but at least he wasn't sitting up in the stands. He was standing off from the other kids, down beside the fence at the back of the end zone. He was as close to the game as he could get without being noticed, and he was watching intently.

There was a big crowd and it took me a while to get down to where Peter was. The girls on the Homecoming Court were sitting in the front row of the stands in their formal gowns. A couple of the girls looked old enough to be out of college. I didn't remember high school girls looking that way. I moved along the fence past knots of self-conscious younger girls, and I wondered which ones would eventually wear white gowns and reign over homecoming.

The crowd wasn't nearly as dense down past the end zone, and I was closing in on Peter. I'd called him Pedro at the start of the season, but it wasn't long before he got a new nickname. He never went full speed, and I told him he was like a car that never went faster than 15 miles per hour. From then on I called him School Zone.

He turned around as soon as he heard his nickname. Peter Johnson was a really good kid, but he was at least as inhibited as I'd been back when I was his age. He tried to do what I told him to do, but I still hadn't gotten him out of first gear.

I rubbed my hands together. "Okay School Zone, why do you think I came down here to see you?"

He just shrugged.

"So you have absolutely *no idea* why I'm here?" Then I started talking like I was a TV announcer on a game show. "Well if you can guess the answer to that question, you can win a pony and $1000 in cash *and* a trip to Disneyland. So what do you say? Are you ready to take a stab at why I'm here?

He was smiling. "I don't know. Is it to get me to watch the game?"

"And why would I do that?"

"So I could see how nobody is going half-speed?"

I imitated the sound of a buzzer. "That's a pretty good answer – but I'm sorry, it's the *wrong* answer. So you can kiss the pony and all that money goodbye. And you won't be going to Disneyland either. No, I'm here to tell you something you need to know. It's something you and I have in common."

I told him about when I was there ten years earlier, and how much I wanted to play Smear the Queer instead of just staying in the stands watching everybody else play. He looked a little surprised, but he seemed to be taking everything in. And I explained how, as I got older, I kept myself from doing things like go to dances, and that I missed out on all sorts of other experiences.

At that point, Hill Murray and a couple of my other players saw me talking to Peter. They came over to where we were standing. Their clothes were stained with grass and dirt, and they were all breathing hard and sweating.

Peter didn't seem to mind when the other kids walked up, and I kept talking. I lifted my hands and looked up toward the sky, and then I looked at him again. He knew I was up to something, and he smiled and tilted his head a little to one side.

I tried to sound like a preacher who was making a prophecy. "*Behold*, I have received a vision. Ten years in the future – exactly ten years from tonight – you will return to the Montgomery Bell Academy homecoming.

"But by then you'll be a lot slower than you are now, and you'll be slower because you'll weigh over 600 pounds. And you'll weigh over 600 pounds because all you've been doing is sitting alone in your room and eating, and the reason you'll sit in your room all the time will be because you never made friends, and the reason you never made friends will be because you never learned to play with other kids, and you never learned to play with other kids because, even though your football coach told you that you'd end up being a 600-pound hermit if you didn't go over and start playing Smear the Queer, you didn't do it."

There was a big smile on Peter's face.

"When you show up ten years from tonight, you'll struggle to get your big fat butt up into the stands, and as soon as you sit down, there'll be the sound of creaking metal and splintering wood, and then the entire section where you're sitting will come crashing down on three little kids who are playing under the stands."

I looked up at the sky and brought my right hand up to my forehead. "If School Zone had *only* played Smear the Queer when he had the chance, the lives of those innocent children wouldn't have been snuffed out." I touched him on his shoulder. "There should be an unwritten rule of boyhood. A guy should play Smear the Queer any time he gets a chance."

The only kid who wasn't laughing was Hill Murray. He had a serious side, and he was trying to figure out why I'd come up with that particular story. When he looked at me, I winked and cut my eyes toward Peter. Then I tilted my head toward where the game of Smear was still on.

I wasn't sure he understood what I was trying to communicate, but a minute or two later when he started walking back toward the game, Hill put his hand on Peter's shoulder. "Come on. We need another guy."

I stayed down by the fence and watched the kids tackle each other until after the game on the field was over. When Peter came back to where I was standing, he was sweaty and he was smiling. He didn't mention it, but I was pretty sure he wanted me to notice that his lip was a little swollen and his shirt was torn.

I wanted to hug him, but I didn't. I just asked him if I'd missed anything by not playing. His answer came a lot faster than I'd ever seen him move. "Smear the Queer is *awesome*. You should've played."

I found Hill before I left. I wanted to let him know how proud I was of what he'd done, but I could feel myself getting emotional. I ended up telling him a little about going into *Peach Blossom* and seeing the initials on the window glass and finding the bullet, and how it could've been lost by some boy back in the early 1800s. Then I reached into my pocket and handed him the bullet.

He looked surprised when I said I wanted him to keep it. I was pretty sure that any of the other kids on my team would've just taken it and not said anything. He was trying to understand why I wanted him to have it. "But you're the one who found it."

"Something tells me that if a kid lost it, he'd want somebody around his age – somebody like you – to end up with it."

He looked at me and put it in his pocket, and then he ran off to find his friends.

October 7, 1967 – It's Saturday night and I'm in North Nashville with Don Ballenger, Richie Hooper, and Alan Doerner. We all coach in the same football league. We're about to watch a college game between Grambling and Tennessee A&I. None of us has ever seen two all-black teams play football. There are only a few other white people around. We were a little nervous about coming, but Vanderbilt is pretty bad this year, as usual, and we want to see a decent game.

All of us have heard how much better Tennessee A&I games are. We're waiting in line to buy our tickets when somebody behind us says, "Kill the white devils." It probably isn't a good idea, but I turn around. Everybody else in line heard it, too, but nobody is looking at us. I wonder if they all feel the same way.

Tennessee A&I was even better than we thought they'd be. Both teams were big and fast and explosive, and we'd never seen that much hitting. And we'd never seen or heard anything like the A&I band. We were used to the Vanderbilt band, which usually played music that belonged on *The Lawrence Welk Show*. When they played their geriatric songs and marched around in their black uniforms, they could've passed for a band of constipated morticians practicing for a funeral.

But the A&I band was something else. They took up an entire section of the stands, and they danced and moved the whole time they were playing. And when they started playing *Get on Up*, the students went crazy. They all started dancing and singing, and their singing was so precise it sounded more like twenty people were singing than a couple of thousand. A&I lost, but it was a great game.

Being in that part of the city was like being in another country. On the way home the streets were crowded. I could feel the tension when people noticed us going by. I smiled, but almost nobody smiled back.

Back in the summer Edwina Ferrell, a black lady who'd been coming to our house on Thursdays for twelve years to do laundry and clean, told Mother she was getting too old to be a maid anymore and that she was retiring.

Edwina was friendly and we talked a lot, and I could tell how much she liked me. If I was around when she was ready to leave, I took her home instead of dropping her off at the bus stop. She only lived about a mile from Tennessee A&I, but the streets in her neighborhood were usually empty on Thursday afternoons.

Mother ended up making a few calls, and one of her friends had a maid who was looking for more work. Her friend, who was fairly rich, said the maid was a good worker, but there was a complication. She paid the lady two dollars and fifty cents an hour, and if Mother offered her more than that, her friend would have to start paying that much, too. Mother promised to only pay two-fifty an hour, and her friend gave her the lady's telephone number.

Mother had paid Edwina more than that, and it didn't take her long to figure out how she could keep her promise and still pay Alene Brown, the new maid, what seemed fair. Alene, who was cordial but not nearly as friendly as Edwina was, got the extra money as a Christmas bonus. Alene pretty much kept to herself, and she never wanted me to drive her home.

The next time I saw Mike Higgins, I told him about going up

into North Nashville. The first thing he asked me was how I liked being in the racial minority. Then I let him know about the "kill the white devils" remark.

He said that every white person should know what it was like to feel that vulnerable. He said I needed to understand how vulnerable most black people felt. That I should think about how I'd feel about having the police and the courts and all sorts of other public institutions see me as a threat to society. What it would be like if the schools I went to were always short on funding? And if there were all sorts of barriers to keep me from living the life I wanted to live?

Chapter 23

Along with race and Vietnam and all the other issues there were, my nonexistent social life was on my mind a lot. Yancey Walsh had gone back to her college, but a freshman girl named Trish Craig came to Peabody that fall. If Trish wore shorter skirts and flexed her thigh muscles a few times, it would've been close to an even trade. Part of me wanted to go up to her and start talking, but all I did was look at her.

I hadn't noticed it before, but there was something about fall that made me want to have a girlfriend. I started thinking about what it would be like to go to Warner Park on a windy day in late October and catch falling leaves with a girl I liked, and who liked me. By the middle of October I was thinking about it every day. I felt like a coward for not trying to get something started with Trish Craig.

All I needed to do was introduce myself and tell her how much I wanted to get to know her, but I started coming up with all the things that could go wrong if I did. She might've already been dating somebody, or maybe she wouldn't want some guy to just walk up to her and ask her out.

But the biggest problem was that I never saw Trish when she was by herself. She was always with other girls. I couldn't see myself walking up and asking her out unless she was by herself.

I knew what Palani would've said if he was watching. He would've smiled and said something like, "Hey Kaimi, if you're gonna be a seeker of truth, it might be a good idea to start *telling* the truth. Just tell the girl what's on your mind." I still hadn't found the card with his phone number.

Mike Higgins noticed that I stared at Trish whenever she walked through the student center. After the third or fourth time, he said, "Oh for Christ's sake! Just go ahead and ask the damn girl out!"

On days when I knew I'd see her, I promised myself that I would at least talk to her. But there was always a flock of girls around and I never said anything. The leaves were starting to turn, and I finally decided that if I didn't do anything by the end of the week, I'd put the whole thing out of my mind.

On Thursday, the day before my self-imposed deadline, I was still trying to come up with a plan. What I finally thought of came from what happened the year before with the Princess of Khartoum. Helping a girl get into her locker wasn't all that different from changing a girl's flat tire.

Trish lived at home. She drove to school every day. My plan was to let the air out of one of her tires, and while she was standing next to her car, I'd walk up and change it for her. We'd have time to talk while I was changing the tire, and if things went okay, I'd ask her out. And at some point – after I got to know her well enough – I'd tell her what I'd done. I knew it was a crazy idea, but it was the only way I could think of to get her alone.

I cut a class and went down to where she parked her car, but I couldn't make myself do it. It was too crazy. I decided I'd just go home, but when I got to my car, my right rear tire was completely flat. I took it as a message from God. There wasn't much time before she got out of class, and I ran back to her car. I crouched down and unscrewed the cap on the valve of her right rear tire. It wasn't long before it was nearly flat. Then I went inside the closest building and looked out through the window of an empty classroom. And waited.

I saw Trish walk up to her car, but when I left the classroom, the hall was full of students. She must not have looked at her tire, and by the time I got outside, she was driving away. I knew she couldn't get far and I ran to my car.

I changed my tire as fast as I could, and then I drove along the route I was pretty sure she took. She got as far as a service station just south of the Peabody campus. Her tire was already being changed, and I just kept going.

A couple of weeks later I sent her an anonymous Thanksgiving card with $15 inside. At least she came out ahead on the deal. And at least she didn't get hit by a car when she got out to look at her tire.

November 10, 1967 – It's Friday afternoon and I'm standing by myself on the big field out in front of West High School. It's a half hour before we start football practice. Tomorrow morning we'll have our last game of the season on this same field. I think it'll give us a little more confidence if we practice here first. Our record is 4-4. If we come out on top tomorrow, we'll have a winning season. If we lose, we won't. It'll be tough to win. One of our best linemen is going out of town for a family wedding, which means School Zone Johnson will be starting at right defensive tackle. He's gotten a lot better, but he still has a long way to go.

West was about a mile away from Montgomery Bell Academy. Sometimes on Friday nights when I was little, when both West and Montgomery Bell had home games, and if the wind was right, I'd heard the cheering from both fields. It had already been announced that at the end of the school year, thirty years after it first opened and fourteen years after the retirement of Doc Scarborough, West would stop being a high school. The school board decided that West would become a junior high school, but at least the building would still be there.

West End High School was a beautifully designed building. My father had brought me to play on the grass in front of the school when I was three or four, and I remembered watching the ROTC units from West marching back and forth across the same place where we would be playing our game.

My parents lived in an apartment across the street from West right after they married, and my father told me about watching cadets march in front of the school not long after the start of World War II. He said most of those same boys ended up fighting in Europe or in the Pacific, and that some of them hadn't made it back home.

When I got to our game the next morning, I realized that it was the second anniversary of when I got kicked out of NROTC for wearing the green tie. By halftime, I thought there might be an Armistice Day curse.

We were playing a terrible game. Hill didn't have any blocking and we weren't doing anything on offense. The other team was dominating us, but they kept getting penalties and they fumbled a couple of times. It was still 0-0.

Even though their halfback was pretty good, he fumbled again at the end of the third quarter, and after that, they had more penalties. But late in the game, they finally started moving the ball. By then our defense was worn out.

The clock was running down, and when there was only time for one more play, their coach called timeout. The ball was on our seven-yard line. He'd been setting us up for a reverse, and I went out onto the field and reminded our defensive ends that if the play started off going away from them, to expect a handoff and wait for the ball to come back in their direction.

I tried to sound confident, but I didn't think we'd be able to stop them. I was already going over what I'd say to console Hill, who blamed himself every time we lost. They snapped the ball, and their quarterback ran to his left. It looked like a sweep, but he handed it off to their flanker, who took it back the other way. We were in a pretty good position to make the tackle, but it was a double-reverse. When the flanker handed it off to their halfback, both our right defensive end and our right cornerback had already taken off across the field. They were totally out of position.

The only player with a chance to stop their halfback was School Zone Johnson. He hadn't gone anywhere. He'd never played defensive end before, but when the other guys took off, he moved out to where our defensive end should've been. Then instead of waiting to see whether the halfback would cut to the inside, or fake to the inside and then go around him, Peter ran directly at him. Peter lowered his head and shoulders like he was going in for a tackle, but as soon as the halfback cut inside, Peter made a quick move to his left and managed to get his arms around one of the halfback's legs.

But the kid was big and strong and he stayed on his feet, and he started dragging Peter toward the end zone. Then Hill came in at full speed and leveled him. It was only a tie, but we celebrated.

When I got the kids together after the game, I asked Peter how he'd been able to get his hands on a player who was so much faster than he was. He looked around at everybody and smiled. "Oh, it's just a little move I picked up playing Smear the Queer."

When he was an old man, I was pretty sure Peter would still remember that tackle. And I was pretty sure he learned something about himself that he didn't know before. I wanted there to be moments like that for every player I coached.

Chapter 24

November 22, 1967 – I'm sitting on my bed and holding a letter from the Selective Service. It was waiting for me when I got home from school. I'm afraid to open it. My pulse is beating fast. I feel weak and a little cold. I've been a sitting duck ever since I flunked out of Vanderbilt. Whether I end up in Vietnam probably depends on a letter our family doctor wrote to the draft board a couple of months ago. I found the letter in the den next to my father's chair. My parents wouldn't have wanted me to read it.

Our doctor wrote that I'd been sick a lot when I was younger, and then he went into my problems with anxiety and how I went to see Dr. Burke. I didn't like reading about how messed up I was. The worst part was at the end of the letter. "During World War II, I sat on several discharge boards. I spent a good many hours discharging men who never should have been inducted in the first place. It is my considered opinion that this young man would not last three months in the army without having to be discharged."

If anything was going to keep me from going to Vietnam, it was what my doctor wrote. I thought it might bring me luck if I could open the envelope without tearing it, but it tore. I pulled out a folded form letter. Partway down the page there were two boxes. One box was labeled, "Not Acceptable." But the box that was marked with a big X said, "Fully Acceptable." I needed to go to practice and be around kids, but basketball hadn't started yet.

There was a coaches meeting the next week at the YMCA. A

couple of fathers were there, but most of the coaches looked like they were college students. There was a new league supervisor named Ralph Benson, and he'd stapled together several mimeographed sheets of paper. He referred to it as his *Coaches Bible*. After he handed out a copy to each coach, he started going through it page by page.

It included a long list of useless drills and some plays that would never work, and it also contained several prayers – Christian prayers. The prayers sounded phony, but he told us we were required to pray with our team before and after every practice and every game.

I was pretty sure I wouldn't get around to saying any of the prayers. I was coaching a few Jewish kids, and the prayers would've made them feel like outsiders. If I was going to pray with my team, the prayers were going to come from me.

The worst thing about the *Coaches Bible* was a section called "The Commandments of Coaching." I agreed with some of the commandments, like one that said, "A coach shalt not yell at referees." But a few of them could get me in trouble.

One said, "A coach shalt not use bad language in the presence of his players." I tried to keep myself under control, but there were times when I broke that particular commandment. Another one was, "A coach shalt not allow his players to use bad language." I didn't do very well with that one either. I didn't let kids get away with cussing if they were just showing off, but if somebody got hurt and turned loose with some profanity, I didn't say anything about it.

But the commandment that would've sent me straight to YMCA hell was, "A coach shalt not befriend his players." Supervisor Benson had been commenting on each commandment, but after he read that one, he put his shoulders back and looked around the room. "If you get too close to the boys you coach, your team won't have any discipline. You aren't there to be their buddy. You're there to be their *coach*. You can't be both. If you want a buddy, get a dog."

There was an increasing tone of arrogance in the way he was talking to us. He was letting everybody know that he was in charge, and that if we were going to coach, we'd coach the way he wanted us to coach. The longer he talked, the more he reminded me of Mr. Peters back at Battle Ground Academy.

I'd only planned to take the two sixth-grade teams from Woodmont, but a couple of guys backed out after Benson's performance at the coaches meeting, and I ended up with four teams. I didn't mind. If coaching two teams was part of what I was supposed to be doing, coaching four teams would be even better.

It would take more time, but I didn't think it would be that much more work if I coached two teams together at every practice. I wouldn't be studying anyway. I was squeaking by academically, but I would've been squeaking by even if I wasn't coaching.

Along with going to school and coaching basketball, I started having a weekly session with a psychiatrist. After I got the letter from the draft board, Mother called our neighbor, Martha Graves – the social worker who had told me about the Children's Home needing volunteers.

Martha knew a psychiatrist on the staff of Meharry Medical College who might be able to help me. He would supposedly write a letter to the draft board if he was seeing a patient who seemed unsuitable for military service. I wondered if he'd think I was as defective as our family doctor thought I was.

Meharry was the first medical school in the South to train black physicians, and it was located near Tennessee A&I. It only took 15 or 20 minutes to get to Meharry from my house, but I felt like a foreigner as soon as I drove into North Nashville.

I was nervous, but the college was in a pretty nice neighborhood and there was a place to park right next to where I was supposed to go. The name of the psychiatrist was Dr. Jordan Harrelson, and he seemed like a pretty nice guy.

He asked questions and I talked, and the hour went by pretty fast. I didn't go out of my way to sound crazy, but I didn't hold back when I was telling him why I didn't want to end up in Vietnam. The only thing that seemed strange was that he nodded off and fell asleep toward the end of our session.

My basketball teams started practicing, Christmas came and went, and on New Year's Eve, I went to a party at Richie Hooper's house. I'd been trying to think of a way to change my luck. I wanted 1968 to be a better year than 1967 was, and just before the stroke of the New Year I went into an empty bedroom and closed the door. I thought it might help if I did something creative, and I ended up standing on my head and propping myself up against a wall while the people in the rest of the house were counting off the last ten seconds of the old year.

February 2, 1968 – It's Friday morning and Mike Higgins is in his usual spot in the corner of the student center. Sean Metzger is sitting on the other side of the table, and they're talking about the Tet Offensive. Sean is especially animated. "Maybe this'll put a stop to all the Pentagon bullshit about how we're winning the war. Maybe America will finally wake up."

Mike looked at him and shook his head. "Well don't hold your breath. The war won't be ending anytime soon. Even if the public finally starts to figure things out, the defense corporations are making way too much money. Read up on what the Nye Committee turned up in the 1930s – back when Congress was investigating all the things the munitions manufacturers did to get America into World War One.

"And corporations are a lot more powerful than they were back then. They'll keep the war going as long as they can. They'll just hire more lobbyists and put a few more politicians on their payroll. They'll let Congress start an investigation or two, but then they'll start dragging their feet. They won't end up doing a damn thing."

A few minutes later I made the mistake of asking Mike if he thought Lyndon Johnson would end up serving another term. That set him off. "Johnson doesn't have a fucking prayer of being re-elected – not after South Vietnam just blew up in his face.

There's no way he'll get elected again. He's done, and if he doesn't know he's done, he's a damn fool."

When I asked him if he thought Senator McCarthy could end up being president, he didn't give me a direct answer. "I don't know about McCarthy. But Bobby Kennedy... I'm pretty sure he could win." Mike had a look on his face I hadn't seen before.

After a while, Sean stood up and put on his coat. "Well when it comes to Vietnam, if I get drafted I plan on being long gone by the time they come looking for me. I hate cold weather, but I'll go to Canada if I have to. Or maybe I'll just take off to Mexico. Good luck finding me down there."

After Sean left, Mike stared at me across the table. "For now, I'll just say that I hope Bobby doesn't end up running. If you want to sharpen your understanding of politics a little bit, go over to the library. Read what President Eisenhower said about the military-industrial complex right before he left office. Take a look at that and then if Bobby decides to run, we'll have a little talk."

I couldn't get away from hearing about Vietnam. It was always on television and there was story after story in the newspapers and magazines. The war hung over the Peabody campus like smoke. It was in the hallways and in the classrooms and out on the lawn, and it was all over the student center. I spent a lot of time picturing myself creeping through the jungle, and walking into villages that were too quiet.

I kept telling myself that as long as I was coaching kids and making a contribution, I was justified in staying home. I kept telling myself that I shouldn't go because of my problems with anxiety. But then I told myself that those were just excuses to get out of having to advance on real breastworks – not the symbolic ones I'd been imagining since I graduated from Battle Ground Academy.

A lot of guys who went into the service thought the war was stupid and corrupt and wrong. A lot of guys who were serving in Vietnam were making contributions when they left home. A lot of guys who were never going to walk again or see again – or who were going to live the rest of their lives in mental hospitals, or coming back to America in body bags – had gone through times when they were anxious.

A lot of them felt the same way I felt, but they served anyway. They went through boot camp anyway. They shipped out across the Pacific anyway. They faced whatever they had to face anyway.

At night I prayed about what I should do, but I didn't want to just pray for myself. A lot of times I prayed for everybody who had Vietnam staring them in the face. I understood that all the worrying I did about being sent to Vietnam was selfish. I should've spent a lot more time thinking about the way society treated black people and women and homosexuals, but most of the time I just worried about going to Vietnam.

February 18, 1968 – It's Sunday night and I'm on my way home after seeing The Graduate. I sat through it twice, and I'll probably go back and see it again. I wasn't getting any schoolwork done, and I didn't want to spend another night in my room wondering how soon I'd be on a bus on my way to basic training. Spooky comes on the radio and when the saxophone solo starts, I pretend I'm playing it for Elaine Robinson, the girl in The Graduate. I imagine that she's sitting in the front row and I'm staring at her while I'm playing, and she can't take her eyes off of me.

After I got home, I kept thinking about how the plot would've unfolded if the movie was about me instead of about Benjamin Braddock. It could've been called *The Non-Graduate,* but there still could've been a party and somebody could've still told me to consider a career in plastics. But the plot would've changed a lot after that.

Even if I found a way to go out with a girl like Elaine Robinson, I would've been nervous and I would've probably said enough stupid things that there wouldn't have been a second date. The part about Mrs. Robinson could've happened, but there was no way I would've pursued Elaine after she went back to college, and there was *absolutely* no way I would've had the courage to crash her wedding and run away with her.

But I kept thinking about how great it would be to have a girlfriend like Elaine, and ride around with her in a red convertible with the sun shining down while we listened to Simon and Garfunkel.

Chapter 25

February 27, 1968 – It's almost 6 PM on Tuesday. I'm at home with my parents watching the end of the CBS News. I came home from basketball practice a few minutes ago, and right before that, I had another session with Dr. Harrelson. He fell asleep again. I like it better when he stays awake, but he can go into a coma every time I walk through the door if he ends up convincing the draft board not to take me.

I'm getting ready to go see the first round of the district tournament at West High School. Some kids from last year's team want to go with me, but it's a school night and they have to finish their homework and eat dinner first. I'm not picking them up until 6:30. It doesn't matter that we won't get there before halftime. We aren't going to watch the game – we're going to see the end of an era.

I sat with my parents in the den, and Walter Cronkite looked at us through the television screen. There was a troubled tone in his voice. "We have been too often disappointed by the optimism of the American leaders, both in Vietnam and in Washington, to have faith any longer in the silver linings they find in the darkest clouds."

My father's respect for Walter Cronkite came from the years Cronkite spent as a correspondent in Europe during World War Two. He watched him every night. "To say that we are closer to victory today is to believe, in the face of the evidence, the optimists who have been wrong in the past."

My father was staring at the television. "To say that we are mired in stalemate seems the only realistic, yet unsatisfactory, conclusion." My father's expression was as serious as the expression on Walter Cronkite's face.

"It is increasingly clear to this reporter that the only rational way out then will be to negotiate, not as victors, but as an honorable people who lived up to their pledge to defend democracy, and did the best they could." My father didn't say a word. He just got up and went into the kitchen and poured himself another drink.

Brooks McMillan, Hal March, Will Evans, and I got to the game at the start of the third quarter. Davey Austin would've come, too, but he'd been grounded for talking back to one of his teachers. Even though they were in seventh grade and had moved on from Woodmont, most of the kids who played together the year before still came to my sixth-grade basketball games.

They remembered what I told them about Doc Scarborough and the 1954 miracle team. When they heard me say that the first-round game of the district tournament might be the last game a West High basketball team would ever play, they wanted to be there to see it.

I thought we were going to see the school's final game, but the West players were emotional and inspired and they played better than they had all season. I told the kids that even though Doc Scarborough was dead, I hoped he was somewhere watching. The game ended up going into triple-overtime, and when West won it on a long last-second shot, their crowd went crazy and there were echoes from games that had been played across three decades.

February 27, 1968 – It's around 8:15 – just after the game. I'm walking to my car through the parking lot, and Brooks and Hal and Will are a few feet behind me. I'm opening my door when I hear what sounds like a slap, and then I hear a struggle. It's pretty dark but I see somebody slam Brooks against the opposite side of my car. Hal and Will are about twenty feet away and they're both getting hit, too. There are three attackers. They're a lot bigger than my kids. I had practice this afternoon and my whistle is still in my coat pocket. I pull it out and start blowing it as loud as I can.

When the guy who was trying to hit Brooks straightens up, I look past him and yell for people who aren't there to come help us. The other guys move back toward the gym, but a short, muscular black kid I hadn't seen runs over to where I am. He says, "You wan a piece of me?" I tell him I just want them all to go away. He shrugs and walks back toward where the other three are standing with a tall, skinny black guy who looks like he's at least thirty. It's obvious that he told them to attack us. I get everybody into the car and as I'm driving away, the older guy yells, "White mother fuckers!"

The kids were stunned and confused, and there was a red welt where Brooks had been hit in the face. They all had tears in their eyes, but they weren't as upset as I would've been when I was their age.

I wanted to say something that would make them feel better, but I didn't think they'd get too much out of hearing a half-baked sociological explanation about why three black teenagers who were probably in ninth or tenth grade attacked three white seventh-graders who were a lot smaller than they were.

I just told the kids that there were bad people in the world and how sorry I was for what they'd been through. I dropped them off one by one, and after I told their parents what happened, I apologized.

I didn't get any sleep that night. I was ashamed that I hadn't been able to protect my players, but I didn't know what else I could've done. If I'd tried to help one of the kids, it might've made things worse for the other two. Any one of the black kids could've had a knife, and ended up using it on one of my players.

I couldn't get the older skinny guy out of my mind. I didn't care what made him the way he was. I wanted to find him. I wanted to do something to him. He was probably there to see East High, which played in the late game. Except for East High, the schools that played at West on Tuesday night were mostly white. The only way I'd see him again was if he showed up on Thursday night when East had its next game.

While I was lying in bed, I pictured the same thing over and over. I would come up behind him in the parking lot and hit him in the ribs as hard as I could with the biggest baseball bat I had. And then I imagined beating him until he'd gotten what was coming to him. I knew I wouldn't do it, but it made me feel better to think about it. By around four in the morning, I'd come up with a different plan.

From time to time when I was a kid, my father took me to basketball games. A lot of times I'd ended up under the bleachers looking for coins that had rolled out of people's pockets. I hadn't ever been under the bleachers at West, but when we were at the game, I noticed that there were fairly wide horizontal gaps running along the footboards of each row.

I knew what I wanted to do, but the only way it would work was if the guy came to the next tournament game. If he came, I needed to make sure he sat in the lower part of the bleachers.

There was a pair of worn-out tennis shoes in the back of my closet. The next afternoon I got some lighter fluid and took the shoes out into the backyard. On my first try, I didn't squirt enough fluid, and the shoe I was using didn't even catch fire. Then I used too much fluid and the shoe burst into flames. I didn't want the guy to end up in intensive care. The third time I got it right.

I wanted there to be just enough of a flame for him to feel his feet getting hot. I was pretty sure he'd panic when he looked down and saw what was happening, and then he'd try to run out of the stands. That, along with the rest of what I was planning, would cause a lot of commotion. If everything went right, he'd end up having to deal with the police.

Later that afternoon I went to a military surplus store and bought a pair of ankle cuffs, and then I stopped by the grocery and got some dried oregano.

The next morning I had an English test that I couldn't afford to miss, and after class I went to the student center. As soon as Mike

Higgins saw how tired I looked, he shook his head. "Okay, why were you up all night?"

He didn't wait for an answer. "No, let me see what I can rule out. You couldn't have been studying or writing a paper. You don't care enough about school to do something like that. And I seriously doubt that a young lady could've been involved. You only want what you can't have, and since you don't want what you *can* have, it couldn't be that either. I guess it doesn't matter. I just hope you don't feel as bad as you look."

He needled me a little more before I finally told him about the 1954 West team and Doc Scarborough, and taking the kids to the game. And what happened in the parking lot. I didn't say anything about what I was planning to do if the skinny guy came to the next game.

He said blowing the whistle was probably the best thing I could've done, but he told me that if he'd been involved – after he got the kids home – he would've gone back and tried to find the skinny guy. "He would've had a *very* long couple of hours."

He read for a few minutes and then he looked up. "Some Saturday night after the weather warms up, I should take you to North Nashville. It might broaden your cultural horizons a little bit." He didn't tell me what he thought I'd experience in North Nashville. And I didn't tell him that I was getting pretty familiar with the part of North Nashville around Meharry Medical College.

I got to West early the next night. After a half-hour, the skinny guy still hadn't shown up. I started to think he wasn't coming, but then I saw him walking across the parking lot. I moved in his direction as quickly as I could, and he didn't see me.

As soon as I got behind him I stopped. "Hey man, did you drop this ticket?" When he turned around I was pretending to pick up the reserved seat ticket I'd already bought. He came back and took the ticket, but he didn't say anything. I paid attention to his shoes and his pants while he was walking up to the entrance of the gym.

I followed him inside and I watched him go to his seat on the fourth row of the bleachers in the section where the East High fans were sitting. West had lost the early game, but some of their fans were still around. I saw a kid wearing a West jacket. He looked like he was about to leave.

I pulled an envelope out of my coat pocket, and I gave him five dollars to take it to the other side of the gym and hand it to the skinny black guy wearing the mustard-colored pants. I asked him not to say anything, and to leave as soon as he handed over the envelope. Then I watched him deliver the envelope and walk away. The skinny guy looked a little puzzled and then he opened it and read what I'd typed. He looked around and read it again before he put it in his pocket.

February 29, 1968 – I'm underneath the bleachers and the East High fans are cheering right above me. It's early in the fourth quarter. I've already slipped in and back out a couple of times and nobody seemed to notice. Everybody is watching the game, including the skinny guy wearing the mustard-colored pants and the dirty tennis shoes. If I go through with it, it won't take me more than 10 seconds to get out through the narrow opening between the metal supports. By the time anybody figures out what's happened, I won't be anywhere close to the guy who was behind the attack on my kids.

I put on a pair of latex gloves and took two plastic bags out of the left pocket of my jacket. One of the bags was half-full of oregano and the other one contained some bath powder. They looked like bags of marijuana and cocaine, and I slid them close to his feet. After that, I got the container of lighter fluid out of my other pocket. I unscrewed the small red cap, and took another look at his pants. He didn't notice the fluid I was squeezing onto his shoes.

Then I pulled out the ankle cuffs and snapped one of the cuffs around a metal support under his seat. It wasn't long before East made a basket and the crowd stood up to cheer. As soon as Mustard Pants stood up and moved his left foot back toward the opening, I reached through and snapped the other cuff around his ankle.

It was too risky to use the lighter fluid. If his pants were made out of the wrong kind of fabric, they might've caught fire and turned into a torch.

I slipped out from under the bleachers, and by the time I found a seat on the opposite side of the gym, Mustard Pants wasn't watching the game anymore. He was reaching down and trying to figure out how to get out of the ankle cuff.

I kept watching him, and after the game a couple of policemen went over and started talking to him. One of them bent down to look at the cuff, and when he stood up he was holding both of the plastic bags. I wanted to stay and see what else would happen, but the gym was clearing out and I couldn't attract attention to myself.

The police would find a way to get Mustard Pants out of the ankle cuff, and I was pretty sure they'd also check to see if he had a criminal record, or any outstanding warrants. I suspected that he did. I wondered what they'd think when they read the note in his pocket.

I wanted the note I'd written to sound like it could've come from the Bible. "When you brought harm to those innocent children two nights ago, you brought shame upon yourself. When you have felt the heat of Hell, confess and repent and you may find forgiveness." When I wrote it I thought that his burning shoes would be part of the equation.

Chapter 26

March 16, 1968 – It's Saturday morning and I'm sitting at the table in the den. There's an article about Hall Guthrie on the front page of the newspaper. He died yesterday in New York City of a bullet wound in his head. The article explained how outstanding he was and how he initially planned on going to medical school, but after getting involved in photography and film, he changed his mind. I watched him play in a lot of football games during his career at Vanderbilt, but the last time I saw him up close was almost six years ago – on the day when I saw the girl in the blue bikini at Willow Plunge. I feel sick inside.

If I could've been like any guy at Battle Ground Academy, I would've wanted to be like Hall Guthrie. It was like somebody made him up. Even though I'd only been a little twerp and he didn't know my name, he always smiled and said something to me back when we were at Battle Ground.

The same day I read about Hall Guthrie, Bobby Kennedy announced that he was running for president. I should've been excited that he was a candidate, but I couldn't get Hall Guthrie off of my mind. That night I dreamed that I found him sitting by himself in a classroom at Battle Ground. I was standing in the doorway, and he looked up and tried to smile, but then he broke down. I wanted to do something or at least say something, but I just stayed where I was and he kept crying.

March 17, 1968 – It's Sunday afternoon and I'm in Franklin at Hall Guthrie's graveside service at Mount Hope Cemetery. I feel out of place, and I'm standing off by myself. Everybody here knew him better than I did. It isn't the right weather for a burial. It should be a cold, overcast day, but it's warm and sunny. I can hear somebody sobbing, and several people have tears rolling down their faces.

After I left the cemetery I went on to Battle Ground, and I took a walk on the football field. Around forty years after Confederate soldiers marched toward the Union breastworks over that same ground, the first football game was played there. And over fifty years after that, Hall Guthrie put on his blue and gold uniform and ran out onto the field for the first time on a Friday night.

When his last game was over, Hall continued to run ahead, leading his classmates into life. And a few years later, after charging through the barricades of college football and academic life, he died on the field of battle. The newspaper article wasn't clear on how he died. I kept wondering if he'd killed himself.

From there I made the short drive over to where Willow Plunge had been. A couple of years earlier, after learning that civil rights activists were planning demonstrations to integrate the facility, the family that owned Willow Plunge had closed it down. By 1968 it was growing up in weeds, but I found the place where Hall Guthrie stood when he was catching and throwing the football, back in the summer of 1962.

I was still thinking about Hall Guthrie that night when I went to the Peabody College Library. I was there to get a copy of the speech by President Eisenhower that Mike Higgins said I should read if Bobby Kennedy decided to run. I knew Mike was going to ask if I'd read it, and I was curious about why he thought it was so important.

I left home without my wallet and I didn't have any change to make a copy, but I had a little tape recorder in my car. I talked into it when I was scouting football teams we were going to play. Later on, I listened to whatever I'd said about the offensive formations and defensive alignments I saw. I brought it in from the car, and read Eisenhower's speech out loud.

"The conjunction of an immense military establishment and a large arms industry is new in the American experience. The total influence – economic, political, even spiritual – is felt in every city, every state house, every office of the Federal government. We recognize the imperative need for this development. Yet we must not fail to comprehend its grave implications. Our toil, resources, and livelihood are all involved; so is the very structure of our society."

President Eisenhower didn't warn the nation about communism or about the Russians. He warned about an internal threat to America. That seemed strange, and so did something else. Eisenhower must've been thinking about what he said for a long time before he said it. If what he referred to as the arms industry was that much of a danger to the nation, I didn't understand why he waited until his last few days in office before he brought it up.

I listened to the tape a few more times on my way home, and when I got in bed that night, I memorized part of the speech. Eisenhower was the first President I could remember. On the day of the 1952 presidential election, I held Mother's hand when we walked up to Woodmont School. She took me into the voting booth, and after she showed me which lever to pull, she let me cast her vote for General Eisenhower.

He was sworn into office the January before I started first grade. I lay in the dark and repeated what Eisenhower said when he was leaving office in 1961. By then I was halfway through eighth grade.

"In the councils of government, we must guard against the acquisition of unwarranted influence, whether sought or unsought, by the military-industrial complex. The potential for the disastrous rise of misplaced power exists and will persist. We must never allow the weight of this combination to endanger our liberties or democratic processes."

The next day Mike was in his usual spot in the student center, and when he saw me coming he put down the book he'd been reading. "I thought you might show up today. So did you read Eisenhower's speech yet?"

I still didn't see the connection between the military-industrial complex and Senator Kennedy running for President, but I recited the three sentences I memorized. He didn't look as impressed as I thought he'd be. He just nodded and said we should meet up the next day in one of the buildings across the campus and find an empty classroom.

He had an appointment somewhere, but before he left he handed me a folder. "Now that you've read Eisenhower's speech, here's another piece of the puzzle. See what you think about this, and we'll get into it tomorrow. Then we'll talk about Bobby Kennedy running for president."

Inside the folder there were five typed pages. The first page was titled, *President John F. Kennedy – Speech at American University, June 10, 1963*. I read it a couple of times after I got home, but I didn't know why Mike gave it to me. I wanted to be as prepared as possible for whatever he was going to tell me, and I read the whole speech into my tape recorder. After I got in bed that night, I listened to it until I got tired of trying to figure out what I was supposed to understand.

I turned off the tape recorder, but I couldn't fall asleep. In some ways it could've been 1962 instead of 1968. I was lying in my bed and staring out the window at the top of the cedar tree, and now and then a car went by and sent shadows and patterns of light sliding along the ceiling.

I listened to my father snoring. He was drinking more, but it had been a while since I'd heard any harsh words coming from my parents' bedroom. One night at dinner he told me about the pressure that came with owning a business. After that, I understood him a little better.

He said he didn't just have to provide for our family and make enough money to pay back the loan to the bank, he was also responsible for protecting the jobs of the workers. By then Mother was also involved in the business. She was the personnel manager, and both she and my father knew the name of every employee in the factory.

A dog started barking pretty close by, but after a few minutes it was quiet again. I thought about the dog that had haunted the earlier nights of my childhood. I couldn't remember the last time I heard it bark. I was pretty sure it was dead. It had only been five-and-a-half years since the missile crisis, but it seemed like a lot longer than that.

Chapter 27

The night wore on and I started thinking about President Kennedy, and how my image must have entered his brain when he stared at me as he rode by in his limousine. I was pretty sure he never thought about the ride he took to Vanderbilt again, but I wondered if what he saw that day could've been stored away somewhere – below the surface of his consciousness.

And I wondered about other images his brain might've stored away over the course of his life. Twenty years before the sunny spring day in 1963 when he saw me on his way to Vanderbilt, the small torpedo boat he commanded had been cut in two by the bow of a Japanese destroyer.

Twenty years before he saw the funny-looking kid in the green shirt grinning at him from the sidewalk, the sun beat down on him as he made his way toward land with the strap of a life preserver between his teeth, dragging an injured crewmate behind him through the water. Before rescue finally came six days later, he overcame hunger and fatigue, and made several long swims in shark-infested waters patrolled by the Japanese, trying to get help for his stranded crew.

I wondered what had been going through Kennedy's mind when I was walking through my neighborhood in 1962, on the night when it seemed like the world was about to end. I reached over and turned the tape recorder back on, and then I rolled over and listened to his speech again.

"First, let us examine our attitude toward peace itself. Too many of us think it is impossible, but that is a dangerous, defeatist belief. It leads to the conclusion that war is inevitable, that mankind is doomed, that we are gripped by forces we cannot control. We need not accept that view. Our problems are man-made, therefore they can be solved by man. As Americans, we find communism profoundly repugnant, but we can still hail the Russian people for their many achievements in science and space, in economic and industrial growth, in culture, in acts of courage. Should war ever break out again – no matter how – our two countries will be the primary target. All we have built, all we have worked for, would be destroyed in the first 24 hours."

He looked into my eyes only months after I tried to pray myself to sleep on the longest night of the missile crisis – when I was waiting to see the flash that would end civilization. On that May morning in 1963, I looked into the eyes of a man who had contemplated the world in the wake of nuclear war – the destruction of his family retreat in Hyannis Port, the devastation of Boston and New York and Washington D.C. The obliteration of major cities across America and Europe, and Russia and the Soviet Union in ruins.

"We are caught up in a vicious and dangerous cycle, with suspicion on one side breeding suspicion on the other, and new weapons begetting counter-weapons. Both the United States and its allies, and the Soviet Union and its allies, have a mutually deep interest in a just and genuine peace, and in halting the arms race. In the final analysis, our most basic common link is that we all inhabit this small planet. We all breathe the same air. We all cherish our children's future. And we are all mortal. We have been talking about measures to limit the intensity of the nuclear arms race and reduce the risk of accidental war. Our primary long range interest is general and complete disarmament."

I looked into the eyes of a man who had foreseen death on an incomprehensible scale – who had thought through the consequences of the collapse of civilization. I looked into his eyes without knowing how hard he might've been pushed to order an attack that could've ignited a nuclear war. When I was fifteen years old I had looked into the eyes of a man who might have saved his nation, and the world, from his own generals.

"I am taking this opportunity, therefore, to announce two important decisions. First, I have agreed that high-level discussions will shortly begin in Moscow, looking towards a comprehensive test ban treaty. Our hopes must be tempered with the caution of history, but with our hopes go the hopes of all mankind. Second, I now declare that the United States does not propose to conduct nuclear tests in the atmosphere so long as other states do not do so. We must labor on – not toward a strategy of annihilation, but towards a strategy of peace."

By the time I looked into his eyes, he understood how close civilization had come to being lost. By then he had already decided to do what he could to protect humanity from the actions of reckless men. A breath of wind came through and pushed at the top of the cedar tree outside my window. I said a prayer, but before I said amen, I gave thanks for the life of President Kennedy.

I saw Mike the next afternoon. We walked across the campus to an academic building and found an empty classroom. He sat on the edge of the teacher's desk, and I took a seat at a desk on the third row. He looked at me without saying anything, and then he raised his eyebrows. I told him I'd been through Eisenhower's speech and Kennedy's speech several times, but I still didn't know what the speeches had to do with Bobby Kennedy running for president.

I expected him to start telling me what he wanted to tell me, but he didn't say anything at first. He just stared at me for a couple of seconds and then he crossed his arms. "I said we'd have a little talk if Bobby decided to run – I didn't say I'd paint the whole picture for you.

"I could just say one-two-three here's how it is, but all you'd have is the way I see things. It'll be a lot better if you figure it out for yourself. And you're probably a lot closer to having an answer than you think you are. Go back to the part of the speech you memorized about the military-industrial complex."

He listened while I recited what Eisenhower said, and then he joined in for the last three sentences, "We must guard against the acquisition of unwarranted influence, whether sought or unsought, by the military-industrial complex. The potential for the disastrous rise of misplaced power exists and will persist. We must never allow the weight of this combination to endanger our liberties or democratic processes."

He leaned back on the desk. "I'm pretty sure you've already asked yourself why the President of the United States of America waited until just before he left office to warn the country about the threat it was facing."

When I didn't say anything, Mike tilted his head to one side. "Do you think he was worried about political fallout?" He answered his own question, "No, that couldn't be it. He was leaving office in three days. He didn't have to worry about politics anymore." He leaned forward and crossed his arms again. "Okay, this is where you jump in and say what he might've been afraid of."

It seemed pretty obvious. "I think Eisenhower was afraid of the military-industrial complex. But it's hard to see how the most powerful man on earth would feel threatened by guys in business suits."

Mike didn't say anything and then he took a deep breath. "It might've been hard to imagine something like that back in January of 1961 when Eisenhower was leaving office, but with what happened in Dallas in November of 1963..."

He was quiet for a few seconds. "Okay, let's just leave it like this. Eisenhower was worried enough about the combined influence of the defense industry and the military – and at some point, you'll probably understand that the CIA is a big part of what holds those two pieces together – that he gave the country a warning just before he left office. Now what did you get out of the speech Kennedy made at American University?"

"He saw how close the world came to blowing itself up. He wanted to make sure it didn't happen again."

Mike was staring at me. "Well no shit. I already know what he said. What I want to know is if you picked up on anything in his speech that lined up with what Eisenhower said when he was leaving office."

I was pretty sure I had the right answer. "The defense corporations didn't want nuclear testing to end. They would've fought against getting rid of nuclear weapons." That didn't prove that the military-industrial complex was behind the assassination, but I didn't say it.

Mike stood up and walked over to a window. "Okay. So one president warns the country about a potentially dangerous group of powerful men, and that same group hates just about everything the next president does. If they allow that president to keep moving toward peace and disarmament, the defense companies that make up the military-industrial complex will lose billions of dollars. But there's something you need to understand.

"There's a big difference between the military-industrial complex and the military. At the end of the day, the men who run the big defense corporations don't give a rat's ass about America. They talk a big game, but they really don't give a shit about the country.

"But the guys in the military – most of them do give a shit. They were the ones who took on Hitler and Japan in World War II, and they were the ones who had to deal with Stalin and the Chinese after that.

"There's no shortage of colonels and generals who keep one eye on the defense industry job they'll be getting after they retire from the military, but most of the higher-ups in the military aren't focused on the money they can make in the private sector. Most of them are focused on protecting America.

"But let's go back to the run-up to the Kennedy assassination. Some of the generals who wanted jobs with defense corporations weren't just being influenced by the guys in coats and ties, they were also tangled up with the CIA.

"They tried to get Kennedy to commit American forces to an invasion of Cuba, but he wouldn't do it and they blamed him for what happened at the Bay of Pigs in 1961. And although the news media never seemed to figure it out, the same guys were behind what happened in Berlin seven months later. It pissed off the generals when Kennedy didn't escalate the confrontation with the Russians, but he got through that one, too.

"Then they tried to push him into using combat troops in Laos, but he wouldn't do that either. And after that, Curtis Lemay and his other military advisers did everything they could to get the president to bomb the Russian missile sites in Cuba. But he went against what they told him, and the crisis got resolved.

"Then, after *everything else,* Kennedy gives a speech about making peace with the Soviet Union. Vietnam, the biggest financial windfall since World War II, was right around the corner, and the corporations were already lining up to make money from another war. *And what a coincidence* – five months after he gave his speech at American University, President John Fitzgerald Kennedy, the most powerful man on the planet, gets his brains blown out in Dallas, Texas."

Mike turned around and looked out the window. "I'm pretty sure that's what was behind the assassination, but what you end up believing is up to you. I'm trying to say that you should do a whole lot of thinking about what happened to Kennedy, because I'm pretty sure that what happened to Kennedy has a lot to do with what's going on in Vietnam.

"I worry when I see guys like you and Sean walking around the campus. Guys your age should have your eyes wide open when it comes to wars and the government and politics and corporations."

He turned around and looked at me. "So have you figured out why I'm worried about Bobby Kennedy running for president?"

I thought I knew. "I guess it's because he'll run as an anti-war candidate. And if he does that, he'll be as big a threat to the military-industrial complex as his brother was. And if the CIA or the generals or the defense corporations were behind the assassination of President Kennedy, then Bobby Kennedy is in danger, too."

Mike kept his back to the window. "And Bobby isn't the only one. Americans are starting to figure out that Vietnam is a lie. The more the public understands what's going on, the more the people behind the war will be pushed into a corner.

"When people that powerful get backed into a corner, any national leader who advocates for peace in Vietnam will be in a lot of danger. That means Bobby Kennedy and that means Eugene McCarthy and that means Martin Luther King, and it means anybody else in a position of influence who opposes the war."

Chapter 28

March 21, 1968 – It's Thursday night and I'm on the front row of the east end zone of the Vanderbilt gym. I've been here for two-and-a-half hours. I came an hour early so I could get a good seat, but Senator Kennedy is almost an hour and a half late. Even though the rain is pouring down outside, the gym is almost full. A country music singer has been trying to entertain the crowd, but people are ready to see Bobby Kennedy and hear what he has to say. Five days ago he announced that he's running for president. The crowd is expecting him to tear into President Johnson over Vietnam.

Don Braden, who was in my class at Battle Ground, is wearing his Army ROTC uniform and he's coming down the row and checking everybody for weapons. I've brought my tape recorder, and I show it to him when he gets to me. He's all business. He would've been all business even if we'd been friends, which we hadn't been. He's perfect for the military and I wonder what he'll think when Senator Kennedy starts criticizing the war in Vietnam. He finishes his security check, and before long I notice a stream of people moving in my direction along the front of the end zone bleachers.

The crowd started cheering before I saw Senator Kennedy. He was walking right toward me and there was a frozen look on his face. He wasn't looking at anybody. When he got to where I was, I reached down and grabbed his hand, but it was limp. He just kept moving.

The stage was on the other side of the gymnasium and it took him a while to get there. Then there were dignitaries to mention and the usual introductions to be made. When he finally started his speech, I turned on my tape recorder.

The crowd seemed unified and they kept cheering after the speech. I got the feeling that Senator Kennedy had a good chance to get elected, and that if he became president, he might actually be able to stop the war. It was warm and bright inside the gymnasium, but it was cold outside and the rain was still falling.

By the time I got home, I'd gone back to wondering what I'd do if I got drafted, and after I got in bed I started praying. I prayed that I'd find out what I was supposed to do. I didn't expect the clouds to part and for a bunch of angels to show up blowing trumpets. I just wanted to get a clear answer.

I listened to the rain outside and I imagined being in a bunker on the other side of the world. An artillery shell was coming right for me. I imagined that there was just enough time to ask myself why I was there. I kept picturing the final seconds of my life, and I wanted to stop thinking about it. I finally reached over and turned on the tape recorder. The voice of Robert Kennedy sounded a lot clearer than I thought it would.

"Who is it that is trying to divide the country? It is not those who call for change. It is those who make present policy, those who bear the responsibility for our present course. They are the ones... President Johnson – they are the ones, not the people that dissent from his policies."

I listened to Kennedy and after I thought about the victims of napalm attacks and bombs, I started imagining that I was in a hospital room somewhere, sitting in a wheelchair and looking out a window with the afternoon shadows falling across the blanket that was covering my lifeless legs. I imagined living my life in the shadows and visits from my parents. How we would all pretend to be cheerful in the face of a future that held only aging and death for them, and deterioration for me.

"We see all this and we ask, 'How does this serve the national interest?' I say that it does not. In what way does the war's present course advance the security of this country, the welfare of Vietnam, or the cause for peace in the world? I say that it does not. If I am elected president, this course will be changed."

And I imagined being in a uniform and flying home on an airplane, but that I'd lost who I used to be – and the chance to be who I'd hoped to become. I imagined looking down at the expanse of ocean and being too numb to mourn the death of the life I could've had.

"We know then that all this is our responsibility – yours and mine and millions like us – and that it is far too important a matter to be entrusted to remote generals and leaders. We sense that this is not what the American spirit is about. This election is not for the rule of America, but for the heart of America."

I went back to imagining that I was in a bunker on the other side of the world just before the shell that was coming blew up beside me. Regardless of whether I survived, the war would grind on for as long as it could be politically sustained. Just before the shell exploded, I'd know that if I died, or if I was permanently disabled and would spend the rest of my life looking out the window of a hospital room, it would've been for nothing.

Lying awake in bed that night, I knew that I would be an idiot to give control of my life to people who would never even know my name. That was about as close to seeing angels and hearing trumpets as I got, but it was close enough. Dr. Harrelson would either be able to keep me out of the military, or he wouldn't. Either way, I wasn't going to Vietnam.

I had to find a way to keep control of my future, but I didn't want to go to Canada or go to jail or do anything to shame my parents. And I didn't want to do anything that would keep me from coaching.

Mike Higgins was in the student center when I went to lunch the next Monday. I told him about going to see Senator Kennedy. When I told him how close I was to Bobby Kennedy and that I shook his hand, he just looked at me.

Dr. Harrelson was still falling asleep, and it was getting harder to imagine that he was capable of writing a convincing letter to the draft board. I was pretty sure that getting out of the draft would be up to me. I kept coming back to the same idea. If nothing else worked, I'd get in my car and roll up the windows, and then I'd run a hose inside from the exhaust pipe.

As soon as I got light-headed I'd roll down the windows and drive to the hospital. I'd tell the doctors that I'd tried to kill myself because I was depressed, and when they found carbon monoxide in my blood, there would be proof that I was suicidal. At that point, they'd know I was unfit for military service. Then they'd classify me as 4-F and that would be that.

I wasn't going to tell my parents, but Mother was getting more and more worn down from worrying about me. Every time she went to the mailbox she expected to see my draft notice. I finally went ahead and told her what I had in mind. Even though I kept saying that I had no intention of hurting myself – I repeated it several times – all she heard was "suicide." She saw my plan as a cry for help, and I started seeing Dr. Harrelson twice a week.

I didn't tell anybody about it, but I *had* wondered about suicide a few times back when I was in ninth grade. But I just thought about it as a concept – I wasn't going to do it. When I was at Vanderbilt I didn't think about it at all, and as far as Vietnam went, I wouldn't have killed myself even if I knew somebody was going to tie me up and throw me in the back of a plane to Saigon.

When Tom Hendrickson came back from boot camp, he talked about how he wasn't allowed to get enough sleep, and that he did a lot of marching and running, and that he'd been picked on and screamed at all the time by his sergeant. He said the idea was to break each individual down, and then build him back up into the type of soldier who would go out and do what he was told without thinking about it.

I didn't want to go through all that, but I wouldn't have killed myself to get out of it. I wouldn't have killed myself even if I knew I'd end up with a sergeant like Mr. Peters or Ralph Benson.

A week or so later my parents had a conference with Dr. Harrelson, and he managed to stay awake until they left. When my father came home that night, he told me that Dr. Harrelson made him a promise. If he thought I wasn't right for the military, he would write a letter that my father could take to the draft board.

Despite what Walter Cronkite said about the war, my father still thought America should be fighting in Vietnam. I wondered how hard Mother pushed him to go see Dr. Harrelson, and hear all about his psychologically-fragile son.

It went against a lot of what he believed in, but he was willing to stand up in front of the draft board and explain why his only son would be a liability for the war effort. It made me ashamed, and I wondered how I could ever make up for putting him in that position.

Dr. Harrelson seemed a little different after he met with my parents. He wanted me to tell him how I'd come up with the idea to fake a suicide. I did the best I could to let him know that I'd never been serious about killing myself. I wasn't going to tell Dr. Harrelson everything, but I wasn't going to tell him anything that wasn't true.

Once he understood that I didn't have any intention of killing myself, he got curious about my coaching and why I liked kids so much. He finally got around to asking me about girls. I talked about the Princess of Khartoum and Yancey Walsh, and when I told him about letting the air out of Trish Craig's tire, he stopped writing for a minute. I got the feeling he was trying to keep from laughing.

He kept asking questions and while I talked, he scribbled a lot in his notebook. I tried to figure out what he was thinking from the questions he asked, but the main thing I noticed was that he didn't seem to focus on my anxieties as much as I'd expected him to. At some point, I told him about the kids getting attacked at the basketball game, but I didn't say what I did to Mustard Pants.

Chapter 29

March 31, 1968 – It's Sunday night and I'm in my room trying to make an outline for a talk I have to give tomorrow. Public Speaking is an easy class, but I need a good grade to make up for the D or the F I'm pretty sure I'll make in Math. The TV is on and President Johnson is about to address the nation. It wouldn't surprise me if he announces that he's sending another 100,000 men over to fight in the war.

"Good evening, my fellow Americans. Tonight I want to speak to you of peace in Vietnam and Southeast Asia – blah, blah, blah." Has there ever been a president who was a worse public speaker than Lyndon Baines Johnson? "North Vietnam rushed their preparation for a savage attack – blah, blah, blah. Their attack, during the Tet holiday, failed to achieve its principal objectives – blah, blah, blah. The communists may resume their attack any day – blah, blah, blah. We and the other allied nations are contributing 600,000 fighting men to assist 700,000 South Vietnamese troops in defending their little country."

And if we can induct a certain guy from Tennessee who screwed up in college and has an anxiety disorder, we might be able to win this damn war after all. "Last week President Thieu ordered the mobilization of 135,000 additional Vietnamese." Well, that'll sure put the Fear of God into the North Vietnamese. "It is our fervent hope that North Vietnam, after years of fighting that have left the issue unresolved, will now cease its efforts to achieve a military victory." Because they weren't watching television when Walter Cronkite said America couldn't win the war, and they have absolutely no idea that all they have to do is keep fighting.

Hearing President Johnson so soon after listening to Bobby Kennedy was like hearing Ethel Merman sing right after Doris Day. I went back to working on my outline, but after his speech changed direction, I heard every word he said.

"I have concluded that I should not permit the presidency to be involved in the partisan divisions that are developing in this political year." I could sense what he was about to say, and then he said it. "I shall not seek, and I will not accept, the nomination of my party for another term as your president."

Monday was April Fools' Day. I'd come up with a pretty good joke to play on my baseball team, and I was planning to use it to introduce some of the finer points of the game. I got the kids together and we all sat down out in center field. A few of my players responded to the way I coached, but most of them were a lot harder to reach than the guys who'd been on my team the year before. I wondered if it was because of me. Because I was being suffocated by Vietnam.

Except for Hill Murray and Moe Hall and a couple of other kids, they didn't seem to have much heart. There were times when Davey Austin had a big mouth, but he backed it up with a lot of effort. The resident smart aleck on my second baseball team was a guy named Gary Mack. He had plenty of ability, but he just went through the motions. He was basically a spoiled rich kid, but I didn't want to give up on him.

I came up with a story about how I'd helped an elderly neighbor clean out his attic over the weekend, and I told them I found an old book about magic. I said the old man gave me the book, and I'd read about how to cast a spell on a baseball.

Gary started shaking his head when I was explaining how the book claimed that dandelion seeds contained magical powers. "C'mon. We *all* know it's April Fools' Day, okay? We aren't in first grade."

I didn't say anything for a few seconds. "Okay Gary, since

you're so skeptical about the magical power of dandelion seeds, maybe you'd be willing to test it out." He rolled his eyes and shrugged, but he was always looking for attention and he stood up.

That time of year yellow dandelions were growing close to the ground, and there were also lots of whitish-gray spheres of dandelion seeds on top of long stalks. The seeds would blow all over the place when it was windy enough. I asked Alex Levine to go pick a dandelion stem with a lot of seeds on it. Alex was a really good kid, but he was the worst player on the team.

Gary stood at home plate and after I gave him a ball, I ran out into left field. I told him to hit it as far as he could. He took a deep breath, tossed it up, and hit a long fly ball. I took a few steps back and made the catch. Nobody saw me replace the ball I caught with the ball in my back pocket.

I ran in and told Alex to start humming one long note, and then to wave the sphere of dandelion seeds over the ball. He moved his hand around and hummed, and the seeds filled the air. I told the kids that if the book was right about the power of dandelion seeds, Alex had just put a magic spell on every ball we had.

Gary was sure that the whole idea of a magic spell was nonsense, and he let everybody know it. I went out a little past shortstop and told him to hit the ball as far as he could. He tossed up the ball and took a pretty hard swing, but it only went halfway to where I was standing.

The other kids laughed and Gary looked a little confused. He picked up another ball and took a ferocious cut, but the ball still didn't get to me. He tried three more times with three different balls before he gave up. Most of the other kids tried it too, but nobody could get the ball to the outfield. Everybody was impressed but Gary.

I looked at him and smiled. "And you still don't believe in magic spells?"

He just stared at me.

"The book also mentioned that dandelion seeds could be used to find money. Are you willing to give that one a try?"

He looked bored, but he took the quarter I gave him. I told him to hide it somewhere on his body, and that I'd use the dandelion seeds and try to find it. Alex went and got another stem of seeds, and I turned away from Gary while he hid the quarter. I turned back around and Alex handed me the dandelion stalk. I went over and started moving it over Gary's torso, and along his arms and legs.

Then I held the stem in front of his mouth. "Okay, let's have a look." He smirked and when he opened his mouth, I pushed the stem in as far as I could. The seeds stuck to the back of his throat, and he wheezed and coughed and started spewing wet seeds out of his mouth. The other kids were laughing and Gary kept choking and coughing until he drank some water. He glared at me, but he didn't say anything.

I did my best to look innocent. "Well, I guess dandelion seeds aren't as good at finding quarters as they are at putting magic spells on baseballs."

While everybody but Gary was wondering if dandelion seeds were magic, I started talking about the art of deception in baseball. I told them that when they were on base they should act like they weren't paying attention, but to watch the way the catcher threw the ball back to the pitcher, and to notice where the pitcher was standing when he was waiting for the ball.

If the catcher just lobbed the ball back, and if the pitcher was standing close to the rubber, a kid with average speed, if he hadn't drawn attention to himself before he made his move, could take off just as the ball was leaving the catcher's hand and make it to the next base, or steal home, before there was time for the pitcher to make a throw and get the runner out.

I also told them about using deception when they were in the field. I showed them how, if a runner on first base came off far enough after a pitch, the right fielder could slip in behind him and the catcher could pick him off. And I told them how a runner with his back to the ball could be kept from taking an extra base. If the fielder pretended he was catching a throw and then went through the motion of making a tag, that usually made the runner slide and stay where he was.

Then I showed them the hidden ball play. Even though players couldn't lead off in our league, there were times when a runner wouldn't pay attention to what was going on between pitches, and he'd wander off the base. If the fielder could sneak the ball into his glove, and if the pitcher stood just off the rubber and pretended to be getting ready to pitch, the fielder could tag out the runner if he stepped off the base. I told them that being a good baseball player was more than pitching and catching and batting.

At the end of practice, I asked Gary if he wanted to see whether the spell on the balls had worn off. After he gave me a dirty look, he walked over and picked up a ball and a bat. He went over to home plate, tossed up the ball, and took a hard swing. The ball flew out into left field and rolled all the way to the fence. He looked puzzled, but then he went back to looking unimpressed.

I didn't tell the kids that a couple of things happen to a baseball when it's been kept overnight in a freezer. One is that even though the core is frozen, after a few minutes the outer surface of the ball doesn't feel cold. The other thing is that as long as the core stays frozen, the ball won't go very far no matter how hard it gets hit.

Chapter 30

April 4, 1968 – It's getting late on Thursday evening. Practice has been over for twenty minutes and the kids have all gone home. I'm in the front yard of a house across the street from the field. I'm feeling around in the weeds for a baseball that got fouled off during batting practice. It's getting colder and I could use a jacket, but I'm determined to find the ball. I get on my knees and reach down into some high grass, and my fingers brush the surface of something slimy. I pull out a heavy, water-logged baseball that was probably fouled off during one of our practices last year. I finally stop looking for the ball. It couldn't have just disappeared.

I was on my way to my car when I stopped in the middle of the road. The pavement sloped down for about 200 feet and leveled off near a large mailbox on the right. I was still holding the ball I found, and I wondered if I could roll it all the way down past the mailbox at the bottom of the hill.

I pretended that if I could get it that far, the course of the universe would suddenly change and things would start getting better. The weather would warm up and more of the kids on my team would start playing with heart and Gary Mack would stop acting like a brat and my grades would get better and I wouldn't get drafted and Bobby Kennedy would be elected president and get America out of Vietnam and there wouldn't be any more race riots and my father would ease up on his drinking and I'd find the dream girl I was still looking for.

I acted like I was bowling when I hurled the ball down the middle of the pavement. It bounced and rolled along the street and it looked like it had a chance to make it to the mailbox, but then it started curving to the right. It rolled into a drainage ditch, and just then there was a loud crack and a limb crashed to the ground near where the ball went. Right after that a couple of dogs started barking, but it was hard to tell where they were.

By the time I got home, dinner was almost ready and the local news was on. My father was in his chair polishing off his second or third scotch and water, and he was working his way through the big crossword puzzle in the National Observer. It didn't matter if he'd been drinking. It never took him long to finish a crossword puzzle.

A few minutes later we brought our plates from the kitchen into the den, and we sat down at the little table where we usually ate. Mother had noticed that the knees of my pants were wet, and I told her about looking for the lost baseball and how it must've traveled into another dimension. She said that must be what happened to the missing socks, and to all the other items that were always vanishing around our house.

When a news bulletin came on TV, we stopped eating. Martin Luther King had been killed in Memphis. Neither of my parents were big supporters of the Civil Rights Movement, but they didn't just look shocked – they looked hurt.

The last thing I wanted to do that night was stay at home. I wanted to be somewhere else. I thought about Mike Higgins. I knew where he lived, but I didn't belong there. He would've felt the loss of Dr. King a lot more deeply than I did. He would've known that I wasn't grieving as much as he was, and he might've resented it. I wondered what he'd be like right after somebody he admired was murdered. He was scary enough already.

I didn't know Sean Metzger all that well, but when I called him up he seemed to want company. Mother and my father weren't too thrilled that I was going out, but they didn't ask me to stay home. My father just said that a lot of angry black people would be hitting the streets, and not to go anywhere near North Nashville. I wondered what was happening in the area around Dr. Harrelson's office.

Sean's apartment was on Capers Avenue, right across from the Peabody campus. By then he was living by himself. I didn't know that he and his wife had separated. His television was on and the news reporters were trying to sort through the information that was coming in.

Sean asked me if I wanted a beer. I told him that my father did all the drinking in our family.

He looked at me and shrugged. "Well if what just happened doesn't get you started, I guess nothing will."

We both thought that even if Dr. King wasn't shot by somebody in the Klan, he'd been killed by some racist. Sean was from Alabama, and he started talking about the four little black girls who were killed in Birmingham back in 1963, when their church was bombed.

"It made almost everybody I knew sick. But there are always low-bred, chicken-shit racist thugs around. I guess it makes them feel important to bully black folks. If some children get murdered along the way, they could care less. And god damn George Wallace and all the other southern politicians for egging on the white trash. After the bombing, I couldn't stand it anymore. That's why I came up here to go to college."

Sean had a lot to say about Martin Luther King. "He'd probably been getting death threats ever since the Klan found out who he was. He was in danger every time he went out in public, but he kept on marching and he kept giving speeches. He must've known they'd catch up with him sooner or later. He must've known that his kids would grow up without a father."

He shook his head and then he looked at the floor. "This guy had all these gifts, and we'll probably find out he got murdered by some semi-literate moron."

Sean didn't say anything when I told him what Mike had said – that Dr. King and Bobby Kennedy and Eugene McCarthy and any other political figure who was against the war was in danger from the military-industrial complex. He went to the kitchen to get another beer, but he came back out as soon as he heard Senator Kennedy's voice. Kennedy was campaigning in Indiana, and he announced the assassination to a crowd of black supporters.

"I have some very sad news for all of you ... Martin Luther King was shot and killed tonight in Memphis, Tennessee. Martin Luther King dedicated his life to love and justice between fellow human beings. He died in the cause of that effort."

Sean was walking by the table where he had his telephone, and when the phone cord caught on his foot, the receiver clattered down onto the hardwood floor. He shook his foot free of the cord, and went over and stood by a chair. Kennedy continued to address the crowd.

"For those of you who are black and are tempted to be filled with hatred and mistrust because of the injustice of such an act, against all white people, I would only say that I can also feel in my own heart the same kind of feeling. I had a member of my family killed."

Then Kennedy recited a poem from Aeschylus.

"Even in our sleep
pain which cannot forget
falls drop by drop upon the heart
until in our own despair,
against our will,
comes wisdom
through the awful grace of God."

After a few seconds, Sean walked over and kicked the telephone receiver. That made a vase fall over, and then he kicked the table. The table collapsed and the vase shattered when it hit the floor. He kicked the table one more time, and then he went over and sat down on his couch.

I waited a few minutes before I said that until the awful grace of God brought us a little wisdom, at least we had the awful grace of Sean Metzger.

I helped him clean up the remains of the vase, and then I went home. I didn't want to stay out too late and worry my parents. After I got home, I sat with them in the den for a while and watched TV. An earlier film clip from Walter Cronkite was being replayed. He was summarizing the first reports of the shooting.

"Dr. Martin Luther King, the apostle of non-violence in the civil rights movement, has been shot to death in Memphis, Tennessee. Police have issued an all-points bulletin for a well-dressed young white man seen running from the scene. Officers also reportedly chased and fired upon a radio-equipped car containing two white men. Dr. King was standing on the balcony of the second-floor hotel room tonight when, according to a companion, a shot was fired from across the street. In the friend's words, 'The bullet exploded in his face.' Police, who have been keeping a close watch over the Nobel Peace Prize winner because of the turbulent racial situation, were on the scene almost immediately. They rushed the 39-year-old Negro leader to a hospital, where he died of a bullet wound in the neck."

I sat with them for a few more minutes and then I went back to my bedroom. I wanted to feel more emotion than I was feeling. It had been a year since Mike gave me a copy of Dr. King's speech about Vietnam, and I took it out of my desk. I tried to hear his voice while I was reading what he said.

He spoke about the promise of America, but he pointed out that the country had turned away from its founding principles. He talked about the military might of America, and how it was being used against the Vietnamese on behalf of Western investors and local politicians, and the financial elite. He talked about the continuing pattern of American military involvement in the world – in Vietnam and in Central and South America, and in Africa and in other parts of Asia.

I read through his speech twice and then I got in bed. I was too mad at myself to fall asleep. If I had bothered to look at what Mike gave me, I would've already known who Martin Luther King really was. I'd always thought of him as a political figure. I was embarrassed about how ignorant I was. At the core of everything, he was a man on a spiritual mission. I decided to record some of Dr. King's speech and listen to it in the dark. I turned on my tape recorder and started reading.

"I sometimes marvel at those who ask me why I am speaking against the war. Could it be that they do not know that the Good News was meant for all men – for communist and capitalist, for their children and ours, for black and for white, for revolutionary and conservative? Have they forgotten that my ministry is in obedience to the One who loved his enemies so fully that He died for them? What can I say to the Vietcong or to Castro or to Mao as a faithful minister of this One? Can I threaten them with death, or must I not share with them my life? ... I must be true to my conviction that I share with all men the calling to be a son of the living God."

I lay in bed thinking about how courageous and brilliant and eloquent Dr. King was. I kept picturing him lying on the balcony where he'd been shot, and then being in the ambulance as his oxygen-deprived brain was dying. I prayed that his spirit still existed somewhere.

Although there was violence that night and over the next few nights, Nashville was spared the death and the destruction that swept through cities like Washington and Baltimore and Chicago and Louisville and Kansas City. Shots were fired and rocks were thrown and police were attacked and a few buildings in Nashville were set on fire, but after the National Guard showed up, that was about it.

Eight days later I had another appointment with Dr. Harrelson. I wasn't sure how safe it would be, but my father said he thought I'd be okay. I got the feeling that he'd already driven there himself to see how things were. The area around Meharry looked the same way it had before the assassination. Dr. Harrelson seemed a little more distant than before, and he fell asleep a few minutes after I started talking.

He'd already dozed off when I said that Mike Higgins had predicted the assassination. He was snoring when I talked about how there would be a lunar eclipse that night, and that I wanted to try to write a poem in honor of Dr. King.

I got back to my neighborhood, and after baseball practice, I went home and had dinner. A couple of hours later I went back to Woodmont. Sometimes on clear nights when I was in high school, I'd go up on the roof of our house to look at the moon or the stars. Then the city put up streetlights all over the neighborhood. It was hard to see the stars after that, but out on the baseball field, there wasn't as much of a glow.

By the time I lay down in centerfield, the shadow of the earth had already begun to slide across the surface of the moon. It was close to midnight when I finally decided what I wanted to write.

Eclipse

As I watched,
The illumination
Of his spirit
Was extinguished
By a shadow,
And the moon
Became blood red.

Chapter 31

The day after the King assassination, Sean got in his car and started driving. He ended up in a little town in northern Mexico. He was there for a few days, and he said he would've stayed a lot longer if he knew enough Spanish to get a job.

Just before Sean got back, Mike Higgins told me he had gone to North Nashville on the night of the assassination. He and a few of his black friends walked through one of the most volatile neighborhoods in town and did what they could to keep the anger from exploding into violence. I didn't ask him about the assassination. There was still too much grief and anger in his eyes.

He didn't say anything about it until a week or two later when I sat down at his table to eat lunch. "Did you ever look at that copy of Dr. King's speech about Vietnam I gave you?" I told him that I'd read it on the night of the assassination, and how little I'd known about Dr. King before that.

"That's what happens when all your information comes from television and the local newspapers. And it won't be long before they fuck up the next part of the story. Somebody will get arrested and the authorities will say it was a lone assassin. Then the mush-brained TV commentators and the mush-brained newspaper columnists will repeat whatever they've been told about who was charged with pulling the trigger, and why the assassination happened. And guess what? The mush-brained American public will lap it all up like hungry kittens."

After he stared out the window for a few seconds, he looked

at me. "Okay, when you get home there's something you should read again. Look at what King said about what's really going on when American soldiers are sent into foreign countries. That's something you won't hear much about from our so-called journalists."

That night I listened to the part of the speech where Dr. King explained what happened in developing countries when peasants demanded things like land reform.

"During the past ten years, we have seen emerge a pattern of suppression which has now justified the presence of U.S. military advisers in Venezuela. The need to maintain social stability for our investments accounts for the counterrevolutionary action of American forces in Guatemala. It tells why American helicopters are being used against guerillas in Cambodia and why American napalm and Green Beret forces have already been active against rebels in Peru... The words of the late John F. Kennedy come back to haunt us. Five years ago he said, 'Those who make peaceful revolution impossible will make violent revolution inevitable.' This is the role our nation has taken – the role of those who make peaceful revolution impossible by refusing to give up the privileges and the pleasures that come from the immense profits of overseas investments."

Three weeks later, after practice, I was back in the yard across from the field looking for another lost baseball. I heard something moving underneath a bush. When I pushed back a cluster of small branches, a baby mockingbird was scratching around in some dry leaves.

I didn't see its mother, but I left it where it was. When I came back the next day it was still under the bush. There wasn't any sign of a mother bird, and I picked it up and put it in the box I brought along in case I needed to take it home.

I called a pet shop and asked about the best way to take care of a baby bird. The lady on the phone said to put small pieces of a peeled grape on the end of a toothpick, and feed the bird that way. It didn't sound like it would work, but after a few days, the mockingbird was strong enough to hop out of its box. When Alene showed up for work the next Thursday, I could tell she didn't like having a bird in the house.

May 3, 1968 – I just had an appointment with Dr. Harrelson and I've come home to change clothes before practice. I'm going to take the mockingbird to Woodmont and show it to the kids. It shouldn't be long before it starts flying. Alene is leaving and she glances at me as she walks out the back door. I start looking for the bird and I finally find it on the floor in the den, behind my father's chair. It's alive, but its body is twisted and it can only move its head a little.

I wasn't sure what had happened, but if the bird hopped too close to Alene, she might've kicked it or hit it with a broom. I went on to practice and it was dead by the time I got back home. I buried it in the backyard. When Alene came back the next week, she seemed defensive as soon as she saw me. I didn't say anything about the mockingbird.

The next week, Mother found what was left of a teacup she'd gotten as a wedding present. It was under a paper towel in the trash. Mother asked Alene if she might've accidentally knocked it over when she was dusting. Alene didn't say anything. She just walked out of the house and she never came back.

May 25, 1968 – It's Saturday afternoon and I'm almost to the corner of Twelfth Avenue South and Edgehill Avenue. I'm praying that the traffic light will stay green, but it changes just before I get there. I was an idiot to come this way. This isn't like the area around Meharry. The intersection is right next to a housing project. If I'd gone downtown and then come south on Eighth Avenue, I would've been pretty safe. But I was running late for our opening game, and now I'm someplace I don't need to be.

Black people are on porches and they're standing in yards and they're out on the sidewalks. I look straight ahead and hope nobody notices me.

Ever since the assassination, there have been sporadic reports of rocks being thrown at cars being driven by whites, and a couple of times people have been dragged out of their cars and beaten up.

The light finally changes and I don't look to the side until I'm pulling away. Two guys and a girl are staring at me. They're about the same age as I am. The girl is scowling. I get the feeling that she's daring me to do anything but look afraid and move on. I'm only a couple of minutes from the baseball fields beside Fort Negley – a Union fortification built by slaves and former slaves during the Civil War.

My heart was beating about twice as fast as it should've been beating, but it wasn't only because I had just come through the Edgehill Projects. Our first game was against a good team, and I was hoping we wouldn't get slaughtered. Their pitcher was a big blonde kid who looked like he could use a shave, and he threw really hard.

There was a big kid on my team, too. His name was Charlie Green. I'd been working with him all spring, and he could've been the best pitcher in our league. When he did what I told him to do, he threw hard and he threw strikes. But when he stopped concentrating he fell apart, and once he fell apart he couldn't get the ball over the plate from ten feet away.

Woodmont was in a mostly upper-middle-class area, but Charlie and his younger brother, Joey, lived in a small rented house in the only working-class part of the neighborhood. Their father was a mechanic in a garage, and one of my players who lived nearby said that Mr. Green beat up his wife sometimes.

Charlie and Joey reminded me of the kids at the Children's Home. I got the feeling that Charlie was shamed a lot, and I wouldn't have been surprised if Joey, who didn't smile very much and who'd been in trouble several times for fighting at school, had been beaten up by his father.

The game was pretty close until the fifth inning. Our starting pitcher was batting, and after he got hit in the hand by an inside pitch, I put in Charlie to finish the game. He struck out the first guy, but then he forgot everything I'd tried to teach him.

I went out and did my best to settle him down after he started throwing balls, but he didn't hear anything I told him. He ended up walking seven batters before we finally got out of the inning. His father had been standing by himself near our dugout, but he got disgusted and left before the inning was over. I ended up taking Charlie and Joey home.

June 5, 1968 – It's just after six on Wednesday morning. I'm still half-asleep, but I think I just heard my father say, "Oh no!" I don't hear anything else and I wonder if I was dreaming. I stayed up last night and watched the election returns from the California primary. I went to bed right after Bobby Kennedy made his victory speech. I remember the only other time I heard my father say "Oh no" like that. It was eight or nine years ago when he got a call after one of his best friends killed himself. I want to stay in bed and go back to sleep, but I finally get up and head to the den. Mother has gotten up, too. My father turns toward us. He looks stricken. "The country is falling apart. Bobby Kennedy was shot last night."

I was in summer school by then, and when I walked over to the student center, both Mike and Sean were sitting at the corner table. Mike looked drained. "Kennedy might live for a day or two, but he won't make it – you can't survive a gunshot in that part of your brain. That takes care of just about everybody but McCarthy. And so the bastards win again. God bless America."

Sean hadn't shaved. The orange and black button on his shirt said, 'Kill a Commie for Christ.' He looked like he'd been up all night. "I'm trying to decide whether I'm going to Canada, or if I should join the anti-war movement. Or maybe I should just stop giving a shit."

We practiced that afternoon. We were working on baserunning at the beginning of practice, and I noticed Gary Mack and Joey Green off to one side whispering to each other. A few minutes later, when I was working with our catcher, Gary eased around and got down on his hands and knees behind Alex Levine. Joey ran over and pushed Alex, who fell backward over Gary. He hit the ground pretty hard and hurt his shoulder. Alex tried to act like he was okay, but then he started crying.

Gary set the whole thing up, but he was standing off to the side like he didn't know what happened. I wanted to grab him by his hair and wear his butt out with the handle end of a baseball bat, but I didn't even yell. When I told them to start running laps Joey took off, but Gary wanted to know how many laps he had to run. Alex was calming down and I asked him how many laps he thought was fair. He said five.

Gary gave him a threatening look, but he knew how mad I was and he started running. He also knew he was supposed to run all the way around the field, but he thought I wasn't looking and he kept cutting corners. After he went around the field five times, I told him to run ten more, and to run them the way he was supposed to run them.

He was resentful. "I'm not running any more laps."

I pretended to be sympathetic. "Gosh Gary, I guess I owe you an apology. I should've already taught you the right way to run a lap."

Then I lifted him up by the back of his pants, and his feet never touched the ground while I ran him around the field. He was probably getting racked in the process, but he didn't say anything about it.

After we went around the field once, I stopped. "Should I help you with the rest of your laps, or do you think you can do it yourself?" He started running.

I expected to get a call that night from one of Gary's parents, but I didn't. After I got in bed I kept thinking about how I wasn't getting anywhere with him or with either of the Green brothers, and there were two or three other kids who weren't doing much better.

When I told them about Doc Scarborough and the 1954 West High basketball team, Hill Murray and Moe Hall and a few of the others focused on everything I said, but Gary and the Greens weren't listening. Most of the kids on the team seemed to be having a pretty good time and most of them were getting better, but there wasn't anywhere close to the same magic there was on my first team.

I kept wondering what else I could try, but I finally fell asleep. When I went out to the kitchen the next morning, my father told me that Bobby Kennedy was dead.

July 2, 1968 – It's Tuesday night I'm in the third base dugout of the field at Warner Park. The score is tied with two outs in the top of the last inning. The other team is at bat and they have a runner on third base. The kid on third is a chubby little guy with glasses. His coach put him in as a pinch runner. He seems to be as clueless as he looks. Gary Mack, who's playing third base, has definitely noticed. He goes over to our pitcher and I watch him sneak the game ball into his glove before he trots back to his position. He's a few feet from the chubby kid, who's standing on top of the base. Gary is trying to think of a way to get the kid to leave the base. It's like watching a snake waiting to kill its prey.

When our pitcher stepped away from the rubber and pretended to be getting himself ready for the next pitch, Gary moved closer to the kid on third. As soon as the kid looked at him, Gary flinched and drew back. He pointed at the kid's jersey and pretended to look scared. "Oh man, there's a *hornet* on your shirt." The kid lurched to one side, and just as he was coming off the base I called timeout.

Gary glared at me. He knew I called timeout on purpose, and he kept glaring. The next batter got a hit, and the chubby kid scored the go-ahead run. When we came in to bat, I told Gary that he'd come up with a really smart play and he'd done it at just the right time. But I told him that winning the game wasn't worth what it would've done to the kid he would've tagged out.

I said it would be okay to pull it on anybody else on the other team, but not on their worst player. I let Gary get away with refusing to look at me. The season was going to be over in three weeks anyway.

I needed something to take my mind off of Gary Mack and the Green brothers, and off Vietnam and the draft notice that could show up any day. And off assassinations and political lies and all the other problems that were staining America.

July 4, 1968 – It's around five in the afternoon. I've just watched 2001: A Space Odyssey. The credits stopped rolling a couple of minutes ago and the movie screen is blank, but I'm still sitting in my seat in the front section of Belle Meade Theater. I'm trying to understand what I've just seen. I'd stay and watch it again, but there isn't another showing until eight o'clock. My favorite part was in the introduction. An apelike prehuman had just used a leg bone from an animal as a weapon, and then he hurled it up in the air. The bone was moving in slow motion. It was rotating counterclockwise while it was going up, but just before it started back down, it changed to a clockwise rotation. What a brilliant way to express the beginning of humanity. There's no telling how much symbolism I missed. I can't remember the last time I felt this inspired.

Chapter 32

July 30, 1968 – It's Tuesday afternoon. Baseball season is finally over, and we're having our team party at the Belle Meade Country Club swimming pool. It's the most exclusive club in town, and we're here because Moe Hall's father is a member. We ended up winning twice as many games as we lost and I like most of my players, but there are only two or three guys I'll really miss.

Most of the kids are jumping off the diving boards. I'm sitting on the side of the pool with my feet in the water. There's a radio on nearby and Grazing in the Grass is playing. Hill Murray and Moe Hall are trying to sneak up on me. I'm pretty sure they'll try to grab my legs and pull me in, but before they get any closer, they stop moving.

They're staring off to my left and I glance over to see what they're looking at. Yancey Walsh is coming toward me. She's wearing a white bikini. She sees me just as I'm turning around. She smiles from behind her sunglasses and she stops walking. I smile back and as I'm getting up I notice her glance down at my chest. Thank God I look halfway decent with my shirt off, and that I have a little bit of a tan.

I said I was there with my baseball team, and she told me how much she liked kids. She said she taught swimming, and that she might end up teaching school, but she still wasn't sure what she'd do after she graduated. I tried to be respectful, but every time she looked away I took in as much of her body as I could. What I saw was pretty much perfect.

She was friendly and I wanted to ask her if she was dating

anybody, but most of my players had clustered together in the pool only a few feet away. They were gawking at her like a bunch of little seals. Yancey laughed and said it looked like they were ready for me to get back in the water.

I watched her as she walked away, and then I turned around and did a mocking impersonation of a wonder-struck twelve-year-old boy. Then Moe Hall, who had the best sense of humor on the team, started singing his version of *Hello, I Love You.* When he stopped singing I told him that at least he could understand why I dumped his mother.

After that, I found a chair in the shade and sat down. I hadn't ever smoked marijuana, but Sean had told me how it felt to get high. What he described was pretty much the way I felt. But I wasn't sure if it was from seeing Yancey Walsh in a bikini, or because I'd talked to her for a few minutes.

I just sat in the shade and *Dream a Little Dream of Me* and *This Guy's in Love With You* and *Turn Around, Look at Me* all came on the radio to mock me. I half-expected to hear *Dream Lover*, but they hardly ever played oldies on that station. For the rest of the day the world seemed to be moving a little slower than usual. Palani would've laughed at me for having yet another extreme reaction to things.

Summer school was winding down by then, and I was still going through the motions of being a student. There were a few decent-looking girls around, but I was already thinking about the freshmen girls who would be showing up in the fall. I was in the student center talking to Will Adair, who was a classmate at Battle Ground, and after a while, he asked me if I'd ever heard of Diane Smith.

There were always a few girls with the reputation of being easy, or loose, or fast, or any of the other euphemisms that meant a girl was sexually willing. In the summer of 1968, Diane Smith would've been right at the top of just about everybody's list of supposedly willing girls. After I said, "Of course, I've heard of

Diane Smith," he asked me if I wanted to go out with her. And he wasn't talking about having a date in a week or two – he was talking about *that* night.

Will had been trying to go out with a friend of hers, but the girl he liked wouldn't go unless Diane came along, too. I wanted to know what she looked like, but Will hadn't seen her either. I hadn't heard that she was ugly, and I told him I'd go.

Will's roommates were out of town, and when I got to his apartment the girls were already there. The other girl was definitely good-looking, and Diane was pretty, too. She looked like a normal girl, but the only time she smiled was right when we met.

July 26, 1968 – It's around eight-thirty on Friday night. Diane and I are sitting on a bed in the back bedroom. She has dark brown hair and a pretty face and a fairly good body. I wonder how many other times she's gone into a bedroom with a guy she just met. I'm still not sure what to expect. I think she might lean over and start kissing me, and I start imagining what might happen if she does.

But she just sits on the side of the bed and looks around the room. I get the feeling that she's waiting for me to make a move, but it doesn't feel natural to do anything. There's one light on behind us and there's an open window across the room. A light rain is falling outside and the curtains move every time there's any wind. When I ask her what she wants to do after college she seems relieved.

We kept talking and after a while, Diane told me what happened to her the night before. She went to a party at the house of a guy who was a year behind me at Battle Ground. She ended up back in his bedroom along with three other guys. It got harder and harder for her to talk about, and then she started crying. I didn't know what else to do, and I put my arm around her.

There were times when I couldn't make out what Diane was saying, but pretty soon I understood that they all had sex with her, and some of them went twice. It didn't sound like it was forcible.

It sounded like she ended up in a situation that she didn't know how to get out of. I wanted to say something to make her feel better, but all I kept hearing myself say was that it wasn't her fault. The guy from Battle Ground was in the Fellowship of Christian Athletes, and he always made a big deal about being a Christian.

We kept talking and Diane finally stopped crying. She'd been wiping her eyes and blowing her nose a lot, and there was a little mound of tissues on the floor next to the bed. Instead of picking up the wet tissues, I got a waste basket and laid it on its side, and when she saw me pushing the tissues into the waste basket with my foot, she laughed a little bit.

Diane seemed like a nice person and I thought about calling her again after that, but I never did. I liked her, but I knew what would eventually happen. I'd come on to her at some point, and when I did, she'd wonder if the only reason I was nice to her was so I could do the same thing that the guys at the party had done. I just ended up writing a poem about her in my journal.

The Shadows of Another Room

Sitting on the edge of a bed
In the fragile light,
She watches
The curtains moving
In the shadows
Of the unfamiliar room.
Her words ache
With the shame
Of the night before,
When she was in another room
And on another bed.
After knowing that shame,
How will it be when
She goes into the next room
And sees curtains blowing

As she sits at the edge
Of another bed?
Will she imagine something
Breathing in the night,
Just outside a half-open window?

August 2, 1968 – It's Friday afternoon and I'm walking up to the front entrance of the apartment building where Sean lives. I've had my last exam and summer school is finally over. His window is open and I can barely hear Bob Dylan. I go through the door, and when I get to the top of the stairs I hear Just Like a Woman coming from his apartment.

When Dylan was singing about ribbons falling from curls and the loss of innocence, it made me think about Diane Smith. That part of the song fit her pretty well, but what reminded me of her even more was the part about aching like a woman and breaking like a girl.

Sean's door was open and I could smell marijuana. It was like he wanted anybody who came down the hall to know he was smoking pot. I hoped he knew what he was doing. If somebody called the police, he'd probably end up in jail.

I stood outside the door and listened to the last part of the song. When Dylan sang about being hungry and the world belonging to somebody else, I didn't think of Diane as much as I thought of myself back when I was at Vanderbilt.

Sean was in the bathroom and I played *Just Like a Woman* again. When he came out he was rolling another joint. "So I guess Dylan has finally worked his way inside your brain."

I didn't say anything and he sat down on his sofa. "Well better late than never. And speaking of Dylan, here's a little quiz for you – something you'd never learn in summer school. Where do you think he recorded *Just Like a Woman?*"

When I guessed it was in some little studio in Greenwich Village, he shook his head. Then I guessed San Francisco.

"Nope. Dylan cut that song, and *I Want You*, and almost all of the other songs in *Blonde on Blonde*, less than a mile from right here. I know a guy who played guitar on the session. And if that doesn't impress the hell out of you, I might need to see if you have a pulse."

He didn't need to see if my heart was beating. We sat there and listened to the rest of the album. I didn't know how being high would alter the way he'd respond, but I went ahead and told him about the evening I'd spent with Diane Smith. All he said was that it would make a good Dylan song.

Later on, I started talking about how incompetent I was with girls. I told him I could probably walk into a whorehouse with a hundred dollar bill taped to my forehead and still walk out as a virgin. That made him laugh, and he leaned back on the sofa.

"This whole thing with you and girls – you make it *way* too complicated. Maybe it would help if you just looked at sex as a biological process. If you drink enough water, it won't be long before you need to get rid of some water. A day or two after you eat, you need to get rid of what started out as food. And it's the same with reproductive fluid. By the time guys get to be teenagers, they're running around with an excess supply.

"You've made sex into more than it is. It's basically excretion. You just need to find some girl who thinks you look alright and who likes you a little bit, and get it over with. If you want to turn it into a romantic event, then have at it, but it might be a while before you can pull it off."

He shook his head when I started laughing. "I might need to rephrase that."

I didn't say anything else, but I wanted sex to be more than just biology. I wanted it to mean something. I wanted it to be more than just an animal act.

Pretty soon we were talking about politics. Sean said that the Democratic Convention was in a couple of weeks, and that we should drive up to Chicago and see what was going on. He said that with all the hippie chicks who'd be running around loose, there was a chance I could get deflowered by a flower child. He thought that was pretty funny.

I was curious about what would happen in Chicago, but I couldn't go. I would've had to put off football practice for a week, and there wouldn't be enough time to get ready for our first game. Sean said it wouldn't be much fun if he went by himself, and he didn't go either.

I felt a little guilty about not going to the convention. I told Sean I'd be willing to go somewhere else as long as I could start practice when I needed to. Two days later he told me not to make any plans for the next Friday night. He wouldn't tell me where we were going.

I went to his apartment on Friday, and we walked down to a dive in Hillsboro Village. It was a run-down little bar called The Villager. We went inside and I kept myself from asking him why we were there. There was an empty booth in the back and Sean ordered a pitcher of beer and two mugs. He'd forgotten that I wasn't twenty-one yet. When I told him I didn't have a fake ID, he just shook his head. "I should've known."

I asked for a ginger ale, and then *Crazy* came on the jukebox.

He waited till the end of the song before he said anything. "Have you come up with any theories about why we're here?"

"I don't know. Maybe you wanted to watch me have my first beer."

"A beer would add to your overall experience, but I brought you here so I can help you broaden your musical horizons *again*. Now that you're turned on to Dylan, it's time you discovered country music. Some of it's as good as anything you'll hear. Living in Nashville and not experiencing good country music is like living across the street from the Louvre and not going inside to look at the art."

He hadn't mentioned country music before. I wasn't much on rhinestones and sequins and twanging guitars, but there had always been country songs I liked. I just liked rhythm and blues and rock and roll a whole lot more. But Sean was right. I hadn't really explored the music that came out of Nashville.

While he slowly drained the beer from the pitcher, he sat across from me with his eyes closed and *So Lonesome I Could Cry* and *I Walk the Line* and *I'm Sorry* and *She Thinks I Still Care* and *Mama Tried* drifted and wailed and throbbed across the bar.

Sean ordered another pitcher and *The End of the World* and *Don't Come Home A-Drinkin'* and *Skip A Rope* and *Don't Touch Me* and *Just Because I'm a Woman* washed over us song by song. But the song that got to me the most was *She's Got You*. I'd heard it before, but I hadn't ever listened to it.

I made sure nobody saw me studying the customers in the bar. A lot of them looked like they'd either been working construction all day, or they were between jobs. Before he got too drunk, Sean mentioned that a couple of years earlier he'd been sitting exactly where I was sitting when a guy named Kris Kristofferson gave him his first joint.

I asked him who Kristofferson was, but he didn't say anything. He just held up his hand and walked over to the jukebox. After a few minutes, the song he selected came on. I liked it. It was called *Jody and the Kid*, and the Kristofferson guy had written it.

I ended up seeing one person I recognized. Charlie and Joey Green's father walked in with a short blonde woman. It wasn't Mrs. Green. He didn't see me, and we waited until he went to the bathroom before we left.

August 28, 1968 – It's Wednesday night and I'm walking up the stairs to Sean's *apartment. I was at home watching the Democratic Convention, but after a couple of hours of seeing the Chicago police beat up protesters, I couldn't stand it anymore. His door is halfway open. I expect to hear a television reporter talking about the convention, but the apartment is quiet. I push the door all the way open and Sean is lying on his sofa. His television is screen-down on the floor, and some smoke is rising toward the ceiling.*

Senator Ribicoff had been up on the podium nominating George McGovern to be the Democratic presidential nominee. When Ribicoff said the police were acting like the Gestapo, Mayor Daley started booing. When Sean saw Daley booing, he picked up the television and slammed it into the floor.

Mike Higgins lived on the opposite side of the campus and we ended up going over to see him. He came to the door wearing a white bathrobe. He didn't invite us in. We thought there was probably a woman in his bedroom. We stood at the door and he talked to us for three or four minutes. Before we left he said, "So how do you boys like living in a police state?"

Chapter 33

October 4, 1968 – It's three o'clock on Friday afternoon. I'm in a long line waiting to buy a ticket to see a football game at Montgomery Bell Academy. The visiting team is Pearl High School. High school games are almost always played on Friday nights, but with an all-black team playing against an all-white team in a white neighborhood only five months after the King assassination, there's no way the game was going to be played after dark. If there's a problem, it'll supposedly be a lot easier for the police to get things under control if it's still light outside.

Until a couple of years ago, black schools only competed against black schools in games refereed by black officials, and white schools only competed against white schools in games refereed by white officials. Pearl is unbeaten. They were a traditional powerhouse up until black and white schools started playing each other. Montgomery Bell hasn't lost a game in three years. There is almost no conversation in the ticket line. The black people aren't talking to each other and neither are the white people.

The stands were full by the time I got inside. The Pearl fans sat on the east side of the field and the Montgomery Bell fans sat on the west side, but there was some racial intermingling where I was standing – along the fence at the north end zone. The players from Pearl were bigger and faster than the Montgomery Bell players, but they committed crucial penalties and had trouble moving the ball on offense. There were no incidents on the field or in the stands, and Pearl ended up losing the game 20-7.

I stood near an exit and watched the fans leaving the game. Nobody on either side was smiling and nobody on either side was frowning. Nobody was saying anything, but a lot would be said once they got in their cars.

The worst of the Montgomery Bell fans – the ones who only saw demeaning, politically-inspired stereotypes when they looked at black people – would claim that Pearl lost because their players lacked intelligence and character. And some of the Pearl fans would say the game was lost because of the racially mixed team of referees. Some would accuse the white referees of being racially biased and the black referees of being Uncle Toms. I wondered what else would be said as they made their way back toward North Nashville. I stayed until almost everybody was gone, and then I started walking home.

I thought about all the unsmiling and expressionless black faces and white faces I'd just seen, and how most of them were concealing what they really thought. Most of them were wearing masks. My mask was different, but it was still a mask. If people driving by in their cars noticed me, they wouldn't have thought that the young white guy walking home from a football game was seeing a black psychiatrist in North Nashville twice a week.

I was still going to Dr. Harrelson, but I didn't think he'd be able to keep me from getting drafted. He was back to dozing off during our sessions, and after a while, I started telling dirty jokes after he fell asleep. Then I started using foreign accents. I tried to sound British during one session, and during the next session, I'd do my best to sound French or Spanish. And one time I talked for twenty minutes using a black dialect.

Even though Dr. Harrelson was asleep most of the time, I ended up doing what a psychiatric patient was supposed to do – I talked about what was really on my mind. I wouldn't have been nearly as honest if he'd been awake. I talked about the two YMCA football teams I was coaching, and what I thought about the guy who was running the league.

Ralph Benson was back again. At the coaches meeting he handed out a revised version of his *Coaches Bible*. It contained more prayers than there were before. He said that a lot of coaches had defied him in the past. He told us that we were "By God" going to say prayers with our teams before and after every game, and that we were "By God" going to do things his way. A couple of times while he was ranting, he gave me a hard look.

I did the best I could to cover up the way I felt – which was that he was a complete idiot. But despite being an idiot, he'd figured out what I thought. One of the referees could've told him that I wasn't praying with my teams, or maybe there were times when he didn't like the expression on my face. One way or another, I needed to stay at least one step ahead of him if I wanted to keep coaching.

One afternoon after Dr. Harrelson fell asleep, I mentioned what Mike Higgins said about the Republican and Democratic parties. He thought they were both controlled by corporations, and that it might not matter who got elected. But as far as I was concerned, Hubert Humphrey was a lot more likely to end the war than Nixon.

George Wallace was also running for president. When I'd seen Mike Higgins at Peabody earlier that morning, he had plenty to say about Wallace. "He picks Curtis Lemay as his running mate? Wallace must have *really* been impressed with how hard Lemay tried to destroy the world back during the missile crisis. Or maybe Wallace is just trying to make himself look better by having a running mate who's even more fucked up than he is.

"But Wallace has a definite strategy. He thinks if he can carry the South, he might get enough electoral votes to keep Nixon or Humphrey from getting a majority. Then the election would be decided by the House of Representatives. That's where he might have a chance to get elected. If Wallace ends up being the president, this country will have a whole lot more to worry about than race relations and Vietnam."

My personal life was as messed up as the country was. I had just turned twenty-one, but I might as well have been in junior high school when it came to girls. Even though the Sexual Revolution was all over the place, I hadn't kissed a girl since 1966 when I was going out with the Princess of Khartoum. Things weren't that good at home, either. My father was working all the time to keep the business going and he was drinking more. And the more he drank, the more melancholy Mother was.

While most of my classmates from Battle Ground Academy were sweeping over the top of the defenses and starting their last year of college, I was wandering around miles away from the front lines. They would graduate the next spring and move on with their lives, and I'd still be a third-rate student in a second-rate college taking irrelevant courses and learning next to nothing.

October 26, 1968 – It's 2:05 on Saturday afternoon, and one of my football teams has just lost 7-6. On the last play of the game, we had a touchdown called back when one of the referees inadvertently blew his whistle before the play was over. It cost us the game, but I'm explaining to my players that if we hadn't played like a bunch of morons for three-and-a-half quarters, we would've won anyway. I can see Ralph Benson out of the corner of my eye. He's been glancing over at me ever since he got here.

I was pretty sure Benson was trying to catch me in the act of not praying. After the season he'd probably use it as an excuse to get rid of me. So after I finished talking, I got all the kids to close in around me and bow their heads. Benson was too far away to hear what I was saying.

Speaking as quietly as I could, I told them that one of the things for which we should all give thanks was humor. Then I told them a joke. I picked one that would've really bothered Benson. "Why do elephants have wrinkled knees?" Nobody knew and I whispered the answer. By the time they all said, "Amen," Ralph

Benson was on the way to his car. He didn't hear Jay Wilson yell out the joke to his big brother.

"Hey Sammy. You know why elephants have wrinkled knees? It's from humping mice!"

I never heard about the joke from any of the parents, and I didn't feel guilty about the way I defied Ralph Benson. I talked to the kids all the time about things that could've been turned into prayers.

Sometimes it would be about how to treat people, and other times it was about being thankful for the good things in our lives. Telling them about Doc Scarborough and West High School winning the state championship in basketball, was worth about twenty years of Benson's empty prayers.

November 5, 1968 – It's Election Day and I'm standing in line in the Woodmont School lunchroom. I'm waiting to vote. Kids are getting their food and taking their trays back to their classrooms to eat lunch. A few of my players spot me in line. They seem surprised to see me doing something that doesn't involve football or basketball or baseball.

Twelve years ago I was a fourth-grader carrying my tray of food back to my classroom. I remember looking over at the adults who were waiting to vote, and seeing one of our neighbors wearing an Adlai Stevenson button. Until then I thought that everybody I knew was for Eisenhower. I look up and down the line of duly registered voters. They're all white and most of them are fairly well-off. I'm pretty sure their big worry is communism, and I know they're sick of race riots and hearing about Black Power.

Richard Nixon's campaign was all about law and order. He must have loved what happened in Mexico City. Two sprinters on the U.S. Olympic team gave the Black Power salute during the medal ceremony while the national anthem was playing. That was just three weeks before Election Day, but I was pretty sure that most of the people waiting in line to vote at Woodmont had already made up their minds to vote Republican by then. I voted for Hubert Humphrey, but I was sorry that Eugene McCarthy wasn't on the ballot.

I was sick of all the political ads, and I was sick of hearing people repeat what they'd heard in campaign commercials, and then act like they knew what they were talking about. I'd heard enough idiotic comments to last until the next election.

I was starting to think that most people shouldn't be allowed anywhere near a voting booth, but I kept hearing the same public service announcements on TV. "No matter who you support, it is your duty as an American citizen to vote." My public service announcement would've been completely different. "If all you do is sit around and listen to campaign propaganda, stay the hell at home on Election Day."

A married couple that Sean knew had an election party that night. I met him at their apartment. Everybody there thought we'd know who won by nine or ten o'clock, but the outcome was still too close to call at 1 AM. I figured that Nixon would end up winning. Unfortunately I was right.

Although my father voted for Nixon, he said he was trying to look at the Vietnam War objectively. He said it would be a while before Nixon could do anything about the war, and that it was probably time to see if Dr. Harrelson was willing to write a letter to the draft board. A week after the election he told me that I needed to write a letter, too. I didn't think it would do any good, but I went ahead and wrote a letter requesting what was called a medical review.

Chapter 34

My football teams won a few games, but we were pretty mediocre. I was starting to wonder if I was as good at coaching kids as I thought I was. After every game I got the kids to crowd around me, but Ralph Benson still suspected that we weren't praying.

When he showed up for the last game of the season, he stood on our sideline. He was close enough to hear what I was saying, but he was trying to look like he was just there to watch the game. He finally got the chance he'd been waiting for in the third quarter. There was a pileup near midfield, and after Frankie Feldman punched a kid on the other team, the referee threw a flag.

Frankie came running over to me and he was crying. "That little shithead bit me!" He held up his arm and there was a bite mark near his left elbow. I was trying to calm him down when Benson stormed over to where Frankie and I were standing.

He was fuming. He called over the head official. "Mr. Referee, remove this boy from the game. He's through." Then he glared at me. "I won't tolerate cursing in my league. I don't know what you've been teaching your players, but there is no excuse for that kind of language. Straighten this boy out, and I mean right now!" Frankie looked stricken. Then Benson said, "I'm stopping the game until I hear an apology."

The best way to shut Benson up was to get Frankie away from him. Frankie looked at me and I gave him a wink. Once we were too far away for Benson to hear what I was saying, I started gesturing like I was giving him a lecture. "Frankie, I don't blame you for cussing or for hitting the kid who bit you." I shook my finger at him. "That guy who kicked you out of the game is a complete jackass, but I know a way to shut him up."

He didn't look as upset after I said that, and then I told him a joke. "Do you know why elephants paint their balls red?" Frankie's head was down, but he was listening. "They paint their balls red so they can hide in cherry trees."

He was still hanging his head, and I couldn't tell if I'd cheered him up. Then I asked him if he'd ever heard of a partial apology. He said he thought he had.

"No, you haven't. It's something I just made up, but here's how it works. Start off by saying, 'I'm sorry' out loud. But you need to say it like you're about to say something else."

I could tell that he didn't understand what I meant. "Okay, here's what I'm talking about." I looked down and tried to sound serious. "I'm sorry that football season is almost over and that I won't be coaching you anymore... *even though you're a terrible athlete and a total sissy.*"

I was shaking my finger at him a little less. "Just say 'I'm sorry' the way I said it, but don't say anything else. And keep thinking about what else you actually want to say." I also told him to keep hanging his head when he was apologizing. Benson had to think he was ashamed.

I was next to Frankie when he walked over to Benson. All he said was, "I'm really sorry..." He sounded pretty convincing, and he said it with just the right inflection. Benson waited for a few seconds before he nodded and walked away. After the game started back up, I asked Frankie what else he would've said.

He was still unhappy. "I don't think I should say it out loud." But after the game was over, he looked over at me and forced a smile. "I like having you as my coach... *even though my little sister knows more about football than you do.*"

Benson was either short on coaches, or he still didn't have

enough evidence to get rid of me. His secretary called a couple of weeks later to let me know about the coaches meeting at the YMCA for the upcoming season in basketball. The meeting was a few days before Christmas, and Benson said the same things I'd heard him say before.

He handed out his *Coaches Bible*, and then it was time for him to beat his chest and let everybody know that he was the boss. Benson found some young guy with long hair who hadn't coached before, and that's who he started staring at and trying to intimidate. I sat in the back row and did my best to blend in with everybody else.

It looked like I was going to get through without a problem, but just before the meeting was over, Benson announced that one of us would be giving a closing prayer. He looked around the room like he was trying to decide who would give the prayer, and then he stopped and pointed at me. "Give it a try... *coach.*" From the way he paused and the way he said the word, coach, it was an obvious insult. Most of the other guys in the room probably picked up on it.

But I stood up like I had been expecting to be called on. I was holding my notepad and I turned to a blank page, and then I pretended to read a prayer I'd written for the occasion. I gave thanks for the privilege of working with kids, and I prayed that all the boys in our league would be better people, and go on to live better lives because of what they would experience during the coming season. At that point, I should've just said "amen" and sat down. If I had, the meeting would've been over and I would've gone home, and that would've been that.

The other coaches still had their heads bowed, and Benson was giving me a look of contempt. What he'd done to Frankie boiled up, but I probably wouldn't have said anything if I didn't have Vietnam breathing down my neck.

I was pretty sure I'd be getting drafted in the next few weeks anyway, and I didn't think I had too much to lose. I did the best I could to sound calm. It was almost like somebody else was talking.

I nodded at him as though I was finished, but as soon as he said, "You'll only have a few practices before ..." I interrupted him and continued with my prayer.

"And I pray that *everybody in this room* will be careful about what we say and what we do when we get frustrated with the children under our care. Please help us remember that the main reason we work with kids is to build them up."

Then I started staring at Benson. "And God, I pray that if *any of us* ever shames a child, the next thing we do is get down on our knees and ask you to forgive us." I said, "Amen," and after I nodded at Benson, I sat down. His face was red and I wondered if anybody else could tell how angry he was.

He mentioned, in an off-handed way, that he wanted to see me after the meeting, and after everybody else was gone he closed the door. When he turned toward me his fists were clenched and he was shaking. I thought he might try to hit me, but he just started screaming. He said that I'd always had a bad attitude, and he'd make sure I never coached kids again – at the YMCA or anywhere else.

I felt like there was a hole in my stomach, but I kept telling myself that I probably wouldn't have gotten to finish the season anyway. He kept yelling, but I was mostly thinking about how much I'd miss the kids on my teams. As I was leaving I asked Benson who he'd get to coach my teams. He sputtered that they weren't my teams anymore, and then he said he'd coach them himself until he found somebody else.

It was like I'd gone back to standing in a shadow at the bottom of a hole. That night when I was lying in bed, I thought it might be time to go on and volunteer. I could join the Army like Tom Hendrickson had, and take my chances in Vietnam. If I wasn't coaching anymore it didn't really matter.

That night I spent some time praying, and I thanked God for giving me the chance to coach, and for letting me find out how much I loved kids. I thought back on some of the guys I should've done better with, and I asked forgiveness for all the mistakes I'd made.

The next day I started calling the parents of the kids on my teams to let them know that I wouldn't be coaching. A couple of the mothers kept asking questions and pushing for answers, but I didn't go into what happened. Almost everybody told me how much their kids liked having me as their coach, and how much they'd miss me. After I made a few more calls, I wanted to go back to bed.

But if I'd stayed at home it wouldn't have taken Mother long to figure out that something wasn't right, and over the next few days I went out like I was shopping for Christmas presents. I left home early and drove around listening to the radio, just like I had during the bad old days when I was at Vanderbilt. A few times I felt like making up lyrics to some of the songs that came on, but I didn't do it.

The weekend before Christmas I ended up in Franklin and stopped at Battle Ground Academy. Nobody was around, and I parked my car and took a walk around the campus. It seemed like more than three-and-a-half years since I graduated.

The gymnasium was unlocked and I went inside. There was enough light coming through the windows to see okay, and I found a basketball under the bleachers and started shooting. I couldn't hit a thing at first, but pretty soon I got hot. I still thought I was good enough to have made the team back when I was in high school.

I ended up making 47 straight free throws, and then I went back outside and walked across the football field where I saw Hall Guthrie have so many heroic Friday nights. I wondered if he'd ever come back and walked around on the field. After that, I went down past the academic building to the front part of the campus, where we circled the flag on the day we graduated.

None of my classmates had died since Jack Johnson, but some were pretty far into drugs, and along with Tom Hendrickson, three or four guys were over in Vietnam. If I wasn't already dead or wounded or in some psych ward by then, that's where I thought I'd be in another year. I imagined some Benson-like sergeant deciding that I was a troublemaker and singling me out. I looked up Columbia Pike to where the Union defenses were, and I wondered if going to Vietnam would amount to charging breastworks.

Chapter 35

On the Monday before Christmas, I really did go shopping. I was in Castner Knott, a department store in Green Hills, and it was as crowded as I'd ever seen it. I was standing in a line at a cash register when I saw Yancey Walsh coming down the escalator. She was wearing jeans and a light blue turtle neck sweater. Everybody around her seemed to disappear.

I waved at her, and she gave me a big smile as soon as she saw me. She started toward me when she got off the escalator, but there were a lot of people standing between us and she stopped. She stood there for a few seconds, and then she shrugged and smiled and waved goodbye. I hoped she'd look back as she was walking away, but she just kept going.

I wanted to tell her how much I lit up inside when I saw her, and let her know that it wasn't just because of the way she looked. It was also because of who she was.

I would've gone after her right then, but I was nearly up to the register and I didn't want to lose my place in line. As soon as I paid for the shirt I got for my father, I went looking for her, but the store was too jammed and I gave up after a few minutes. I was pretty sure that even if I found her, I wouldn't have said what I wanted to say. That night I kept thinking about Yancey, and how a light seemed to be shining on her as she came down the escalator.

December 24, 1968 – It's the morning before Christmas and I'm in the den. I've just started reading the paper. The phone rings and Mother picks up the receiver. I hear her say, "Oh" and "I'm so sorry." After that, she says, "Yes. Yes, he did – back when he was in high school." I hear death in the tone of her voice. She's still on the phone when I get up and go over to her. She glances at me and then she looks away. I'm waiting for her to hang up the phone. I know she has something to tell me.

She didn't say anything for a few seconds. Then she told me that Yancey Walsh and the boy she was with had been killed in a wreck early that morning. It happened right in front of Belle Meade Country Club. The police thought they must've died almost instantly.

I didn't want Mother to know how I felt. After a few minutes, I took my basketball to Woodmont and started shooting. I shot like I was back in sixth grade. I stayed for a while, but it was cold and I finally gave up. I drove around for the rest of the day with the radio off.

I was watching the local news on television that night, and one of the segments was about the wreck. There was some film footage that showed what was left of the car. A jealous, drunken husband had been chasing his wife, who was with another man in another car.

The car the wife was in hit the car Yancey was in, and spun it around in the middle of Belle Meade Boulevard. The husband's car was going at least 70 miles an hour when it hit Yancey's car. He walked away with just a few cuts and a broken collarbone.

The Christmas Eve carolers showed up right after dinner. When they sang *Joy to the World* I pretended to sing, too, but I just mouthed the words. Later on, I was watching TV with my parents and we saw the transmission from the Apollo 8 spacecraft. It showed the surface of the moon from the lunar module. While the astronauts glided above the moon, they read a passage from

Genesis. I imagined Yancey's spirit gliding above places that had meant something to her.

I did the best I could on Christmas morning. My parents could tell that something was bothering me. I was pretty sure they knew what it was, but neither one of them said anything. I went back to my room after we opened presents. I wanted to write a poem about the presents under the Walsh's Christmas tree, and what they'd do with the ones for Yancey. I didn't get anywhere. Then I tried to write a letter to her parents, but there wasn't anything I could say that would've helped.

Christmas night was even longer than Christmas day had been. There weren't any sirens slashing through the darkness, and there weren't any dogs barking in the distance. Two or three hours before dawn, after an outbound train rolled down the tracks beside Harding Road, I finally got up and turned on a light. I still wanted to write a poem about Yancey, but the words wouldn't come. I didn't fall asleep until it was getting light.

December 28, 1968 – It's dusk on Saturday afternoon. It's cold and overcast. I'm in a cemetery twenty-five miles from Nashville. I drove around until I saw a freshly dug grave and some flowers. Yancey doesn't have a marker yet, but I'm standing between two tombstones inscribed with the name Walsh. It's almost Saturday night. Yancey should be back at her house getting ready to go to a party. She shouldn't be under the ground in a cold empty graveyard. I don't know how religious she was, but I try to say a prayer for her. "Dear God, please hold Yancey's spirit close to you and help her find happiness and peace. Please..."

There was a lot to pray about, but my prayer sounded hollow and I just started talking to her. "Well, I hope everything happened so fast that you didn't feel anything. I probably shouldn't even be here.

"I didn't go to your funeral. Sometimes people go to funerals just to see who else shows up. They sing a couple of hymns. Listen to the eulogy. But they mostly end up worrying about their own mortality. I didn't want to do the same thing. Not with you."

There were wet clods of earth in the dead grass around her grave, and I started pushing them onto the rest of the dirt with the side of my foot. "Remember the date we had? The way I smelled? I'd sprayed peppermint all over myself. I really wanted you to have a good time. It would've been great to go out with you again, but I didn't deserve it. I didn't deserve *you*. I was just trying to make myself look better by being with you.

"I felt the same way when we had that class together at Peabody. You kept wearing mini-skirts. And it took me a while to get over seeing you at the Belle Meade swimming pool last summer.

"I wondered if you had a boyfriend. I wanted to ask you out right then, but I'm an idiot and I didn't say anything. I thought about you a lot more after that, and then I saw you in the store in Green Hills. There was a light all around you.

"Guys paid a lot of attention to you because you were beautiful. I did the same thing. But the more times I saw you, the more I could tell what a good person you were. I should've told you that, but I didn't. And there's something else that's worse. Sometimes when I think about how you've had your life taken away, I end up feeling sorry for myself."

Some rain had started to fall. If it had been just a little colder it would've snowed, but that would've been too poetic. It was getting dark and I knew my parents would be wondering where I was. I still hadn't said what I came to say.

"You'd still be alive if I'd just gotten out of line in the store and come over and talked to you. All I had to do was say how much I thought about you. It would've just taken a few minutes, and it would've changed the timing of everything else for the rest of that night.

"You would've left the store a few minutes later and gotten home a few minutes later, and you would've been ready for your date a few minutes later, and you and the guy you were with would've been somewhere else when those two cars came tearing down Belle Meade Boulevard. Right now you'd probably be at home putting on lipstick in front of your bedroom mirror."

I wanted to cry, but I couldn't even do that. After a few more minutes I walked back to my car and left.

When I was at home I tried to act like things were okay. There wasn't much to do, and for the next couple of days I just drove around a lot. When I opened up the morning paper on New Year's Eve, I saw a photograph that one of the astronauts took of the earth floating just above the horizon of the moon. I went back to my room and tried to write about the insignificance of my problems, but I couldn't do that either.

That night I went to a party at the house of a guy who went to Battle Ground. Several of my classmates showed up, and one of them said there was a rumor going around about Hall Guthrie. He'd heard that Hall shot himself playing Russian Roulette. I didn't say anything. I didn't know what to say.

I left early and drove around until my parents went to bed. I stayed up for a while thinking about Hall Guthrie and Yancey and everything else that had happened over the course of that year. The last twelve months were like an open wound. I wondered if the wound would ever heal. I finally came up with a poem, but it wasn't the one I'd meant to write.

1968

The blood that flowed
Inside the car
And onto the pavement
From the body
Of Yancey Walsh,
And Senator Kennedy's blood
On the floor
Of the hotel kitchen
In Los Angeles,
And Dr. King's blood

On the balcony
In Memphis,
And the blood that flowed
From the head of Hall Guthrie
Onto the floor
Of the room where he died
In New York,
And the blood
That continues
To spurt and splatter
All across Vietnam –
All that blood
Has drowned
So much,
So very much,
Of what might have been.

Chapter 36

It was a relief when school started back up in January. At least there was something to do. I went to the student center more, and I even spent a little time in the library. I went out of my way to keep from driving by Woodmont. I didn't want to see the kids practicing. Every afternoon when I came home, I expected to find my draft notice waiting on the counter by the back door.

January 11, 1969 – It's early on Saturday afternoon and I've just opened the mailbox. There's a letter from the Selective Service on top of the other mail. I take it into the house and put it on the table. There's a basketball game on television and I try to watch it, but after a few minutes, I go over and pick up the envelope. I hold it in my hand for a few seconds before I open it.

It's a one-page form letter. At first I don't notice what's on line eight, but then I see it. There's a checkmark right in the middle of the box labeled "Not Acceptable." I put down the letter and walk around the den before I pick it up and look at it again. I don't know what to do so I just sit down. I lean back and close my eyes.

When my parents got home I showed them the letter. Mother's eyes filled up with tears and she went back to the bedroom. My father just looked at me and nodded. I got the feeling that he wasn't surprised.

The next day I asked him what he thought about me being classified 4-F. He tried to be diplomatic. He said that I might be a better fit for the military when I was a little older. I had the feeling there was something he wasn't telling me, and that night I asked him if he'd done something I didn't know about.

He didn't say anything at first, and then he told me that a few days after Thanksgiving, he called up the head of the local draft board and they'd gone to lunch. He didn't give me any details and I didn't ask for any, but it sounded like he convinced the guy that I was a basket case. I could tell that he didn't want to talk about it, so I just thanked him.

I didn't have a sense of relief or feel any exhilaration. I didn't think I deserved to feel good about getting out of the military. I wasn't getting drafted, but some other guy would be going in my place. If that guy ended up getting killed or wounded, or if his soul ended up getting torn to pieces, it would be because I wasn't willing to go.

I kept wondering if I should do something to Ralph Benson. He'd just keep pushing people around, and some of those people were the kids I cared about. It wouldn't have been too hard to come up with a plan to mess him up, but he was the way he was for a reason. There were times when I told myself to just forgive him and move on. But in the end, I wasn't ready to move on.

The week after the letter came from the draft board, I got a phone call. It was from one of the mothers who was especially disappointed when I called and told her I wouldn't be coaching basketball. She said that she and a few of the other parents wanted to talk to me.

We got together at Moon's Drugstore. Most of the kids couldn't stand Benson, and several players had already quit. A lot of guys weren't showing up for practice, and the parents wanted to put pressure on the executive director of the YMCA to bring me back as the coach. I said it would probably be better if I just started working with whatever kids showed up at Woodmont on Saturday mornings. We'd play basketball and see what happened from there.

The parents got the word out, and twenty-six kids showed up

the next Saturday on the playground at Woodmont. I divided them up as evenly as I could into four teams. I'd coached most of them before, and they knew how to scrimmage without a referee. We had two games going at once, and I went back and forth, pretending I was an announcer doing a play-by-play of each game.

February 1, 1969 – It's the middle of Saturday afternoon. The kids have come back to Woodmont after lunch and we've started playing again. When Frankie Feldman picks up a loose ball near the goal, I use my announcer's voice. "Feldman is wide-open. He's all by himself. There's no way he can possibly miss from that close. He shoots and... OH MY GOD – IT'S NO GOOD! What an absolutely horrible shot – it might have been the worst shot in the history of basketball!"

Then I try to sound angry. "All right. Timeout. I said TIMEOUT! Stop the game!" I walk over and give an order to an imaginary official. "Mr. Referee, get this boy out of the game. Anybody who misses a shot like that shouldn't be allowed on the court. He's through for the day."

Some of the kids already knew I was imitating Benson. And since everybody there knew what had happened to Frankie in the football game, the rest of them caught on as soon as I said, "What's the matter, son? Did somebody bite you on the arm again?"

Frankie was smiling like he knew what was coming next.

I tried to stay in character. "Now apologize to your teammates for letting them down, and then apologize to everybody else for making them see such an *abysmal* shot. And I mean RIGHT NOW!" Frankie didn't miss a beat. "Coach Benson, I'm real sorry... *that you're such a big fat turd.*" It took a while for everybody to stop laughing.

It wasn't too long after that when one of the fathers let me know that Ralph Benson had been reassigned. I should've known it would turn out the way it did. He didn't realize that one of the young coaches he was picking on was the nephew of a major YMCA benefactor. He was being transferred to a YMCA in East

Tennessee. I was glad he was leaving, but I had some regret about not giving him the kind of sendoff he deserved.

It was a blessing to coach again, but the nightmare I avoided was still raging in Vietnam. Although there was a continuing stream of officially-sanctioned reports about how well the war was going, the numbers of dead and wounded American and South Vietnamese soldiers didn't square up with what the generals and the politicians were saying. Peace talks had started in Paris, and Nixon kept repeating the phrase, "Peace with Honor." Almost everybody I knew thought it was just a political slogan.

Mike Higgins had said that the war would go on as long as the defense industry could make it last. He said they would keep pulling strings as long as a significant percentage of the public could be persuaded that America was winning the war. I was waiting to see if that's what would happen.

There were attacks all across Vietnam at the end of February, and while I was out on the playground at Woodmont coaching basketball, American forces launched another major counter-offensive into the demilitarized zone.

March 15, 1969 – It's a cold Saturday morning on the baseball field behind Woodmont School. We just had our first practice. One of the new kids who showed up looks like he wants to be anywhere else but on a baseball field. His name is Jack Thomason. I threw with him to make sure he didn't get hit in the face when we were warming up. After that we did some fielding, and then I pitched a little batting practice. We're almost through and one of the mothers has gotten out of her car. She's standing over near the backstop.

She looks younger than the other parents. She might be pretty, but she's wearing sunglasses and a big coat, and it's hard to tell for sure. She looks sort of familiar, and after practice is over, she comes up and introduces herself. Her name doesn't ring a bell, but I know who she is as soon as she takes off her sunglasses. The Blonde Bombshell still looks good. Jack Thomason is her son.

Her first name turned out to be Carolyn, but she was still the Blonde Bombshell to me. She wasn't wearing a wedding ring. The next time she came to pick Jack up, I let her know that I'd lived across the street from her before she moved away, but I could tell she didn't remember me.

I knew how old Jack was from his registration form. She'd gotten pregnant right around the time she moved away, and I kept wondering if Jack was conceived on Clearview Drive, right outside my bedroom window.

A couple of weeks later she mentioned that she got divorced a couple of years after Jack was born, and she told me that she'd moved back into the neighborhood – not far from where she lived before. One afternoon a guy with a beard was in the car with her when she came to pick Jack up from practice, but when we had our first game she showed up with somebody else.

Jack was the second-youngest kid on the team. I saw the same sort of vague sadness in him that I'd seen in other kids I coached who didn't have a father around. He was a little below average as an athlete, but he turned out to have a lot of heart and he really listened. Before long, he started to like baseball.

He had a chance to become a pretty decent player, and I started working with him after practice. Some of the parents probably thought it was because his mother was good-looking. The way she looked didn't hurt, but I helped him because he said he wanted to get better.

The Blonde Bombshell was still in her twenties, but she sounded a lot older. Her voice was flat and hollow. It must've sounded different back when she and her boyfriend were outside my bedroom in his car, talking about the great lives they wouldn't end up having. There was a lifeless tone to everything she said, and it made me wonder what she'd gone through. She was nice enough, but something was missing inside her.

She probably grew up way too fast. While her friends were off at college – dating and going to dances and doing all the things she thought she'd be doing after high school, she was taking care of a child. She was up in the middle of the night changing diapers and arguing with her drunken teenage husband. Who didn't stick around for long. She looked a little depressed sometimes, and I wondered how much she mourned the loss of her youth.

Even though I wasn't living in the shadow of the draft, I was still going to see Dr. Harrelson. He was still falling asleep. If he could've stayed awake, he would've heard me talking about how I needed to be a better coach. He would've heard me say that if I was the best coach I could be, maybe that would make up, at least a little, for staying out of the military. But I was still doing a lot of the same stupid things I'd always done. There were too many times when I yelled at kids when they messed up, and I still cared too much about winning.

One night I came home from practice, and the news on TV was all about a battle in Vietnam at a place called Hamburger Hill. It had been going on for days, and there were hundreds of casualties. There hadn't been enough time for whoever was drafted in my place to make it from basic training to Hamburger Hill, but I stayed up late that night and wrote a poem.

About Face

I slipped out of line
And another took my place,
And while he marched away
To face the enemy,
I lay in my room
In the dark,
Wrapped up
In the blanket
Of my childhood,
Trying to dream myself back
To a time
Before I knew
Who I was.
And who I was not.

July 5, 1969 – It's Saturday night and we're behind by one run in the last inning of a game against a team that beat us like a drum earlier in the season. I'm coaching third base, and Phil Skinner is on second. There are two outs and Jack Thomason steps into the batter's box. He's facing a good pitcher and he looks stiff. The first pitch is a shoulder-high fastball. It's almost in the catcher's mitt before he gets his bat around.

The next pitch is another fastball. He swings and misses again, but he's around a little quicker this time. It's no balls and two strikes, and he steps out of the box and looks at me. I can tell that he's nervous, but he doesn't look like he's afraid. He's already choked up on the bat, and he knows to swing at anything close to the strike zone. But he's like most kids – if he makes the last out, no matter what I say, he'll think it was his fault that we lost the game. The next pitch is a fastball at his knees. It's on the outside corner, but he fouls it off. At least he won't strike out on three pitches.

The pitcher looked confident and focused. He wound up and threw another fastball, but it was too far inside and it hit Jack pretty hard on the side of his front knee. He was probably as glad as I was that he didn't strike out, and he limped down to first base. Our leadoff batter was up next and a base hit would tie the game up. On the second pitch, he hit a line drive into the gap in right-center field.

Phil was on his way to third base and Jack was limping as fast as he could toward second, and their center fielder was still running after the ball. By the time he picked it up, Phil had roared by me on his way to tie the game, and Jack was closing in on third base. I took a chance and waved him home.

He limped by me when the throw from the center fielder was on the way to the relay man. The throw home was a little weak, and Jack and the ball got to the catcher at the same time. There was a collision and when the catcher dropped the ball, our whole team ran out and mobbed Jack.

After I talked to the kids, I walked over to the Blonde

Bombshell. She smiled, but she didn't say anything about what Jack had done. "Well, I guess I'd better get him home and put an ice pack on his knee." Her voice sounded empty and matter-of-fact – like she had a sink full of dishes she didn't want to deal with. I told her that what just happened could change the way Jack saw himself, but all she said was, "Well I guess we'll see you at the next practice."

I wasn't in summer school, but I had a couple of part-time jobs and I did a lot of driving. The car radio was always on. I'd be in my car thinking about the Blonde Bombshell, and *Spinning Wheel* would lead into *One*, and *One* would lead into *My Cherie Amour*.

I was pretty sure that I was on her mind, too. One day after practice I was standing next to a car, talking to one of the fathers. The Blonde Bombshell was behind me and I could see her in his driver's-side mirror. She was looking at me the same way I looked at her when she wasn't watching. A couple of times when I heard *What Does It Take,* the saxophone solo would start, and I'd pretend I was playing and that the Blonde Bombshell was eating me up with her eyes.

We had our last baseball game in the middle of July. Our team party was the next Saturday, and the Blonde Bombshell came over and started talking to me. After a few minutes, she mentioned that Jack would be leaving the next night to spend some time with his grandparents.

Then she touched my arm and invited me to come by her house and see if the astronauts could make it down onto the surface of the moon. I managed to accept her invitation without saying anything too stupid, and then she asked me if I liked peach daiquiris. I said I had no idea what a peach daiquiri tasted like, but that I couldn't *wait* to find out. She told me that Jack wouldn't be leaving until late afternoon, and to come by sometime after seven o'clock.

Chapter 37

July 20, 1969 – It's around eight o'clock on Sunday night. When I knocked on the Blonde Bombshell's side door about thirty minutes ago, the lunar module has been on the surface of the moon for over four hours. We talked a little, and then I followed her into the kitchen and she poured me a peach daiquiri. It wasn't as bad as I thought it would be. A few minutes later she handed me another one and we walked into her den.

I still haven't thought of how to get the ball rolling. If this turns out to be my first time, I don't want it to be awkward. We talk some more, but we don't say a word about Jack. I still can't think of a way to make a move that doesn't seem unnatural, and we just keep watching the moon landing. She looks bored, and then she goes from looking bored to looking irritated.

Things weren't moving any faster up on the moon. The world was still waiting for Neil Armstrong to climb out of the capsule and start walking around on the lunar surface. I was starting on my third peach daiquiri when I finally figured out a way to make my move.

I got down on the floor and I told her that instead of being on a carpet in Nashville, I imagined that I was lying on a beach somewhere out in the South Pacific, and nobody else was around. I said something about the warmth of the breeze, and before I could say anything else, she laid down next to me and we started kissing. I was somewhat drunk by then, and I kept telling myself to remember what a passionate kisser she was.

After I fumbled around with her clothes, she got up and turned off the volume on the television. Then she switched off all the lights. The Blonde Bombshell stood in the glow of the TV screen with her shirt half-open and slowly pulled off her jeans.

I was looking at her through a fog of daiquiris. I tried to think away the alcohol in my brain while I watched her take off the rest of her clothes. I'd been trying to imagine the way her body looked since I was thirteen, and even though it was eight years later, and even though Jack had left behind a few stretch marks, she looked good.

I could barely hear the television. Neil Armstrong was still getting ready to make his moonwalk. She got back down beside me and she took off my clothes. Feeling her skin against my skin drew me further into the moment, but I wasn't as absorbed as I thought I'd be.

I started imagining myself running naked around second base. The Blonde Bombshell was coaching at third and waving me home, and she was only wearing a baseball cap. It was hard to keep from laughing.

It wasn't long before I really was on my way to third base, and even though I hadn't been anywhere close to that far before, I knew I needed to do more than just sprint for home. I didn't want her to remember me as a guy who had no idea what he was doing.

I went head-first into third, and after I'd been there a while, I heard the TV reporter say that Neil Armstrong was opening the hatch of the capsule and that he was climbing out onto the ladder. I thought about trying to time my slide into home just as he was setting foot on the moon, but it would've been too staged and the Blonde Bombshell wasn't quite ready for me to score.

I was pretty sure the daiquiris were why I felt like I was watching myself in a movie. At some point, I started imagining that I was thirteen again and the Blonde Bombshell was still the way she was back when she lived across the street – back before her voice lost its music.

Her breathing got fast and then it slowed down, and then came back even faster. Around the time she was pulling away, I heard Neil Armstrong manage to mess up the one line he had to deliver, "That's one small step for man, and one... giant leap for mankind." As though man and mankind weren't the same thing.

It was just about time for me to score my run, and I reminded myself that I didn't need to set a world record for the least time ever spent on home plate. I didn't want her shaking her head about that either. I didn't need to worry.

Along with the distraction of the reporter on TV, I was experiencing the cumulative effect of several daiquiris. I was able to stay on home plate long enough to score two runs before I went back to the dugout.

By then Buzz Aldrin was out collecting moon rocks with Armstrong, and by the time I went home, Armstrong and Aldrin had been back in the lunar module for a while.

I went over and saw the Blonde Bombshell again a few nights later. Things were okay until I told her that what happened between us on the night of the moon landing was my first time. She seemed to be offended, but I didn't know why. Then she said I was lying, and she said it in her usual flat, disillusioned tone of voice, and with a touch of harshness.

I could've taken it as a compliment, but I didn't like the way she said it. I didn't know what to say and I just kept quiet. Before long we were down on the floor and she was breathing hard again. I didn't know what she was thinking about, or if she was thinking about anything, but I was pretending she was the girl in the blue bikini I'd seen at Willow Plunge back in 1962.

A couple of days later I ran into one of my friends from Battle Ground who'd been sort of a ladies man, and he asked me if I was dating anybody. I wanted to let him know that I wasn't a total loser anymore. It was stupid and I shouldn't have done it, but I told him a little too much about the Blonde Bombshell.

She called me up the next day and let me know that some guy

she didn't know, and who said he was a friend of mine, had asked her out. She'd already figured out what happened, but she asked me if I'd told anybody that I'd been seeing her. When I told her I had, she hung up before I could apologize. I felt bad about it, but I was surprised I didn't feel worse. And that was that.

I didn't go inside her house again, but I saw the Blonde Bombshell one more time that summer. She called me up after she backed over Jack's puppy. She needed me to help her put it in her car so she could take it to a veterinarian. It didn't take me long to get there. There wasn't a lot of blood, but his intestines had come out of his butt and I didn't think he was going to live.

He was whimpering and while I was sliding him onto a board I found in her garage, the Blonde Bombshell stood beside the car and told the puppy how stupid he was for getting under her car. She wasn't yelling. She was talking like she'd broken a glass or spilled something on the floor. She was probably a lot different when she was younger, but by then there wasn't much light in her spirit.

After I put the puppy in the car, she drove off. The next time I saw Jack was a few weeks later. When I asked him what he'd done since baseball season, he said he'd been to Georgia to visit his grandparents, but that his puppy ran away while he was gone.

Sean Metzger had graduated from Peabody in May. He was going to teach high school English in the fall, and he wanted to have one more adventure before he started working. He tried to talk me into driving up with him to New York City in August. He said we could stay with some friends of his.

There was supposed to be a big music festival somewhere up in New York State, and there would be girls all over the place. He promised that we'd get back before I started coaching football, and before school started up again.

I wanted to go, but then I started thinking about having to camp out at the festival. I wouldn't be able to take a shower the whole time I was there. Sean probably knew I wouldn't end up going, but he didn't let me off easy. He told me that at some point I needed to loosen up and start taking some risks.

I didn't see him again for three weeks. When he got back he looked worn out. After he told me about the festival and everything he'd done, I was surprised he looked as good as he did. Until I saw the movie, *Woodstock*, the next spring, I didn't know how much I screwed up by not going.

Not long after that, Sean's life turned upside down. We were planning to see *Easy Rider* the next weekend, but then he found out that the best friend he had growing up was dead. He had been killed in Vietnam. He went down to Alabama for the funeral, and it was another week before he came back to Nashville.

I didn't know if he wanted to talk about it, or what I'd say if he did. When I went by to see him, his apartment was dark. He was leaning back on his sofa. "Ricky lived right across the street from me when we were kids. We did everything together."

He started looking out the window. "He was a great guy – you would've really liked him. I was telling him about you the last time I was home. He was a helicopter pilot and he died trying to evacuate some Rangers."

His voice was trailing off. "So while I was up in New York listening to music and getting high and getting laid, Ricky was serving his country and getting killed." He reached over and picked up a bottle of beer from the table. "How in the hell can I ever live with that?"

Sean kept talking about Ricky and all the trouble they'd gotten into when they were kids, and he even laughed a few times. I didn't need to do anything but listen. Then he said what I was afraid he would say – that he was enlisting in the Army.

Trying to talk him out of it wouldn't have done any good. When I was leaving, I just told him that I'd see him when he got back from basic training. I ended up seeing *Easy Rider* by myself.

Football practice started and I had two teams again. The guy running the league was my age, and he'd coached for a couple of years. He was a huge improvement over Ralph Benson. He didn't talk about praying, so I made it a point to get the kids together after every game. We gave thanks for everybody being healthy and safe, and for the time we were spending together.

Peabody had started by then. I kept wondering if what had happened with the Blonde Bombshell would change the way I was around girls.

Chapter 38

October 14, 1969 – It's a little past noon on Tuesday and it's a perfect autumn day. I've just gotten out of history class and I'm walking across the Peabody campus. I'm thinking about trying out a new defense this afternoon in practice, and then there's a gust of wind. I look over at the way the shadow of a tree branch is moving on the grass, and I glance up. A girl is coming toward me on the sidewalk. She has auburn hair and it's shining in the sun and she's looking into my eyes. She's smiling like she knows something I don't know, but it happens too fast and I don't say anything. I smile at her as she walks by, and I just keep walking.

I'd been waiting for a girl to smile at me that way ever since my hormones kicked into gear. I should've stopped as soon as I saw her on the sidewalk, but all I did was walk past her like an embarrassed ninth-grade boy. I just went on to the student center, sat by myself, and ate lunch.

I could've said something like, "I've been waiting for this to happen, and I want to say the right thing. Nothing I can say will come close to what you said to me when you smiled, but I *really* want to get to know you."

That's what I should've said, but since I was a fourteen-year-old in a twenty-two-year-old body, all I did was roll up into an emotional ball and not say anything at all. I found out that her name was Bethany Brussard. She was a freshman from some little town in northern New Jersey. I didn't want to make the same mistake with her that I'd made with Trish Craig. I gave myself a deadline to talk to Trish, and all I did was let the air out of one of her tires.

I decided that I wouldn't say anything to Bethany until it felt natural. I'd wait until I ran into her on the sidewalk again, or saw her sitting alone in the student center, and I'd talk to her then. I'd ask her if she wanted to do something unusual – like maybe go to a park on the next windy day and try to catch some falling leaves. Then she'd smile at me the same way she did the first time I saw her, and things would take off from there.

It was another week before I saw Bethany again, but she was with a bunch of other girls. I couldn't just walk up to her and start talking. It wasn't long before I figured out when she went to the cafeteria. After that, I saw her a lot more, but she was always with her roommate, and there were usually two or three other girls tagging along, too.

At that point, it was November. My fantasy about being with Bethany in some secluded autumn meadow under a cloudless blue sky was as dead as the uncaught leaves that had fallen to the ground. By then she might've run away if I tried to talk to her.

I was pretty sure she noticed that I was around more than I should've been. Her roommate stayed with her like a bodyguard, but I kept telling myself that as soon as she was by herself, I would explain what was going on.

It seemed like Bethany was always just out of reach. There were times when I wondered if God was letting me experience a little pain to make up for what I was missing in Vietnam. And I wondered if I might've been allowed to have my fling with the Blonde Bombshell as punishment – just to let me know how things could be with a girl like Bethany.

There was a light shining on Bethany when I passed her on the sidewalk, but it wasn't the same kind of light that was around

Yancey when I saw her on Christmas Eve. Bethany was on my mind a lot, but I hadn't stopped thinking about Yancey Walsh.

I was frustrated about not having another chance to talk to Bethany, but I kept things in perspective. At least I wasn't on the far side of the world fighting in a war. I was living at home and wearing clean clothes and showering every day and going to college and coaching kids in the afternoon and eating whenever I was hungry and sleeping in a comfortable bed every night. And there weren't people all over the place trying to kill me.

In the middle of November, the news broke about a mass killing that had taken place in Vietnam over a year and a half earlier. Around the time that Hall Guthrie died, American soldiers massacred over 300 Vietnamese – including women, children, and infants – at a village called My Lai. The odds were about a thousand to one against the guy who was drafted in my place being there, but I still thought about it.

Football season went okay and Jack Thomason did all right, but the Blonde Bombshell and I only talked a couple of times. The season hadn't been over for very long when she got a job in Atlanta, and she and Jack moved away.

I took a couple of decent courses at Peabody that semester, but I missed sitting in the student center and hearing Sean and Mike talk about politics and religion. All I knew about Mike was that he was off somewhere working on his dissertation.

Sean wrote me a couple of letters from basic training. He made some cracks about the stupidity of the rules, but he told me he was still holding on to his individuality. When Thanksgiving rolled around, I gave thanks for how much better my life had gotten, and I prayed for Sean and for whoever went over to Vietnam to serve in my place.

Things got busy after basketball started up. I was coaching six teams, which meant practicing every day after school on the playground at Woodmont, having dinner at home, and then going back out to practice in a gym.

Once our season started, I coached all day long on Saturdays. And unless the weather was bad, I'd go over to Woodmont on Sunday afternoons and scrimmage with the kids who showed up. A lot of the guys came, and some of them were turning into pretty good basketball players.

December 14, 1969 – It's Sunday afternoon. Rusty Willis is feeling way too full of himself again. I'm standing next to the basket closest to the water fountain. I've been launching basketballs toward the far goal, and I try another full-court shot. The ball hits the backboard and bounces away.

Rusty is tired of watching me miss shots. "C'mon, let's choose up and play another game." I have a hopeful look on my face. "Something tells me I'm gonna make the next shot I take." He rolls his eyes. I look at him for a few seconds before I say anything. "You don't think I can make one from here?" He shakes his head. "Duh. You can try it all day long and you're just gonna keep missing."

I make a throwing motion and stare at the far goal. "Well, I bet I'll make the next shot I take." He looks interested. "Oh yeah? How much?" I shake my head. "Come up with something instead of money and we'll bet on that."

He's quiet for a few seconds and then he starts laughing. "Okay, if you miss you'll have to take off your pants and run five laps around the playground in your underwear." All the other kids start laughing, too, but I surprise them. "Okay, if I miss the next shot, I'll take off my pants and run around the playground five times in my underwear. But if I make it you'll have to do the same thing." Rusty nods and we shake on it.

Artie Horner and a couple of other kids were already smiling. They didn't know exactly what was about to happen, but they knew I'd set Rusty up. I looked down at the far goal and acted like I was about to make a long throw, and then I turned around and made an easy little bank shot on the goal I was standing right next to.

Rusty started to complain, but I repeated what everybody had just heard me say – that the bet was whether I'd hit the next shot. Everybody agreed that I didn't say anything about it being a full-court shot.

Rusty looked disgusted, but he didn't want the other kids to start calling him a welsher. After he made sure there weren't any girls or mothers around, he took off his pants and started running. Just before he got through, somebody took off with his pants. There was a brief game of keep-away, but he got his pants back before he hit anybody.

Chapter 39

December 31, 1969 – Sean Metzger is back from basic training, complete with his military haircut. We're at a New Year's Eve party in Mike Higgins' apartment. Sean is already drunk and he's in the kitchen with some woman he just met. I'm sitting on the sofa talking to Mike. He's making progress on his dissertation, but he says he won't talk about it until it's done. He's had a few beers and he's a little buzzed. He finally asks me what I'm going to do with my life.

I want to give him a good answer, but I'm on my third lime daiquiri. I start by saying that sometimes I see myself as a soldier who doesn't have the guts to go into battle. I tell him about my imaginary battlefield retreat, but that I might have found a way to contribute to the world. I say I'm pretty good at working with kids, and that maybe I'm supposed to help the guys I coach get ready for whatever they'll have to march off and face when they grow up.

Mike looked at me for a few seconds before he said anything. "It doesn't surprise me that you're good with kids. But there's something you aren't gonna like hearing. Right now you're in college, and coaching kids isn't a problem.

"But what about later on? The older you get, the harder it'll be for kids to relate to you the way they do now. And the older you get, the more their parents will wonder why you don't get married and have kids of your own."

He didn't say anything that I hadn't thought about lots of times before, and I'd also thought about what he said next.

"Maybe you should finally get serious about school and go ahead and get a teaching degree. But if you do, there's something you need to know. You might be able to act like a big brother when you're a volunteer coach, but you can't do that when you're a teacher. "

I was really starting to feel the alcohol. *And When I Die* was playing, but it sounded slower than it usually did. After Mike finished off his beer and put his bottle on the table, he leaned back on the sofa.

He glanced over and caught me looking at the scar next to his eye. "I got it in Korea. The Chinese were moving in on our outpost. A wave of those fuckers started coming at us from behind a formation of rocks. A grenade exploded and I got hit by a piece of shrapnel."

I hoped he would keep talking.

"One guy was almost on top of me and I shot him in the throat, and then our radio man opened up on the rest of them with an M2 and that was the end of it. The guy I shot was still alive, but he kept choking and coughing up blood. Our sergeant got tired of hearing him gagging and gurgling, and he ended up putting a round in his head."

He picked up his empty beer bottle, but instead of going to the kitchen, he stayed where he was. "You don't see yourself as a warrior, but I'll let you in on a secret. There are different kinds of soldiers.

"I knew this dumbass lieutenant back in Indochina. He was green and he couldn't wait to grab a flag and lead a charge. He kept telling everybody he wanted to win the Medal of Honor. He finally got his chance to be a hero, and he was dead in less than an hour. Most of the soldiers I knew didn't want to be heroes. Most of us wanted to be survivors. We were just trying to protect our buddies and get back home in one piece.

"You might've been surprised at how things would've gone for you in Nam. You remind me of this guy in my unit when I was in counter-intelligence at Bien Hoa. He thought about things all the time, too. If somebody had stuck him in formation and given him an order, he wouldn't have been worth a damn. But he was great at doing shit on his own.

"All we had to do was tell him what we wanted to know, and we'd turn him loose. We wouldn't hear from him for a while, but when he showed up again, he'd usually have the information we needed. He was hell on wheels. And he kept thinking up ways to fuck up the enemy. He was as good at that as anybody I ever saw. What I'm saying is that even if you aren't cut out to lead a charge, there were other things you could've done."

I was trying to take in what Mike was saying, but I was starting to feel like I was watching myself listen to him. *God Bless the Child* was playing, and I was trying to shut out the voices of the other people at the party. The daiquiris were taking control. I thought I'd wait a while before I had another one, but when I went into the kitchen there was a fresh batch in the blender and I filled up my glass again.

Pretty soon a bunch of people who'd been to a wedding showed up. They were mostly from out of town, and one of them was a good-looking teenage girl who was a cousin of the bride. She'd come all the way from the Netherlands to be in the wedding.

She and I were talking and the lights were getting turned off. Somebody said it was almost midnight. I looked around and Mike and Sean were both dancing with women from the wedding party and everybody was dancing and almost all of the lights were out and *Hey Jude* was playing in slow motion and I felt like I was in a dream and then I was dancing with the girl from the Netherlands and we were both laughing and we were holding each other and her body felt good and I wondered who the Blonde Bombshell was with and I knew Bethany thought I was an idiot and she was right and Yancey was off to one side and I was trying not to think about her and the girl from the Netherlands was every girl I'd ever dreamed about dancing with back when I was in high school and Yancey came up and cut in. As the 1960s faded away, I imagined I was dancing with a girl who'd been torn away from time. And *Hey Jude* just went on and on and on.

After the Christmas holidays, I swapped an English class for a class in Special Education. I hadn't developed a sudden interest in Special Ed. The class was almost all girls, and one of them was Bethany Brussard.

At our first seminar, everybody was supposed to talk about the area of Special Education that interested them. Some students wanted to work with kids who were blind or deaf, and some wanted to work with kids who were mentally challenged. Bethany and three other girls said they were interested in autistic kids.

I'd learned enough about myself at the Metro Children's Home to know that I didn't want to spend my life teaching handicapped kids to tie their shoes. I was glad people were willing to devote their lives to that kind of work, but I wasn't one of them. Luckily there was a program that focused on gifted students. That's what I signed up for, but I was still required to take other Special Ed courses.

It wasn't long before we started taking field trips. The first place we visited was called Clover Bottom, which was basically a nursing home for the mentally handicapped. Most of the wards weren't too bad, but then the lady leading our tour took us down a long corridor to some other rooms. I was standing right behind her when she unlocked the door of the ward that housed kids who were also deaf and blind.

The click of the lock must've caused a vibration, or maybe there was a change in air pressure when she opened the door. There were about fifteen kids in the room, and before we got inside they started coming toward us. There was a strong smell of feces, and they were moving their arms back and forth like zombies. One of the boys was coming right toward me, and it looked like his clothes were stained with waste.

I managed to sidestep him at the last second, but as soon as his hand grazed the girl behind me, he got her in a determined hug. Three more kids were right behind him, and one of them was filthy. They had me hemmed in, but at the last minute I jumped up and grabbed the top of the door. I pulled myself up, and the one who needed a bath went right underneath me.

I stayed where I was and pretty soon Bethany, and just about everybody in my class, was in the grasp of an affectionate but more-or-less-soiled child. I didn't get any hard looks from my classmates, and none of the teachers said anything. They either hadn't noticed, or they didn't blame me for taking evasive action.

I got away intact, but there was still one more ward to visit. We were taken to an unlocked room at the end of the corridor. It was lined with the beds of hydrocephalic children. The lady showing us around said they pretty much spent their entire lives in their beds. Some had enormous heads, and just about all of them had broomstick-sized arms and legs. I didn't know that children could look that way. That afternoon when I got back to Woodmont for basketball practice, I kept looking at my players. They were so full of possibilities.

The next week my Special Ed class went to a daycare center for autistic kids. It was called Cumberland House, and ten or twelve teenage boys were all together in one big room. We stood behind a long two-way mirror. After I saw what was going on, I wondered if Cumberland House would ever consider selling tickets.

One of the kids was hitting himself in the head with his hands, and a couple of other boys were banging their heads against whatever was nearby. But most of the guys were busy masturbating. I glanced over at Bethany a couple of times, but she didn't react to what she was seeing.

Standing around with a bunch of college girls while they were watching a room full of autistic boys pleasuring themselves was fairly awkward, and it seemed like a good time for some comic relief. I came up with what I thought was a pretty good line, but nobody laughed. All I said was, "Does anybody know who's winning?"

Chapter 40

February 28, 1970 – It's close to noon on Saturday at the Ensworth School gymnasium. Basketball season is winding down. One of my fifth-grade teams is blowing out the team we're playing. I'm trying to keep the score from getting any worse. My three highest scorers are on the bench, but we don't have any bad players. We're sagging back on defense and giving the other team open shots, and when we have the ball, we aren't shooting from less than twenty feet out.

It's been a really good season and I want to remember the way things are. Parents and grandparents and brothers and sisters are scattered in the bleachers on the other side of the court, and the stage at the south end of the gym is jammed with kids from Woodmont. A lot of guys stuck around after their games, and girls from various grades have shown up like they do every Saturday. At halftime and between games, they all run out onto the court and start shooting.

There was an hour break before the next game, but instead of going to lunch, I stayed at the gym. The boys were playing a pick-up game at the goal in front of the stage, and a few girls were shooting on the opposite end of the court.

An athletic-looking girl with blonde hair was making most of the shots she took. After a while, I saw Rusty Willis sneaking up behind her. He darted in and blocked her next shot, and then he ran away with her ball. He was trying to make it outside, but she ran him down before he got to the door.

Rusty was a fairly tough kid and the girl was about the same size as he was, but she got him in a headlock and threw him on the floor. Then she looked down at him like she was daring him to get up. She didn't say a word the whole time.

After that, she just walked away and got her ball, and started shooting again. Rusty sat up and grinned before he went back to playing with the boys. A little later I asked one of my players who the girl was. He said her name was Callie Lee, and that she was the fastest runner in the fifth grade. From what I could tell, she was as good an athlete as any of the boys I was coaching.

The spring semester was half over by then. I liked my Special Ed class pretty well, but I wasn't too interested in the other courses I was taking. Mike Higgins was back at the student center, holding court at the corner table, and we both wondered how Sean was doing. He was a month into his tour in Vietnam. Mike kept saying that if he followed orders and used his head, there was a good chance that he'd make it back okay.

I'd seen Bethany Brussard a few times, but even when she wasn't surrounded by her entourage, she was with her roommate. By that point, I'd waited too long to ask her out. And I still hadn't stopped thinking about Yancey Walsh. Sometimes I wondered how her face looked after the wreck, or what the impact did to her body. I went out to her grave a couple of times, but I never felt like I belonged there.

If Bethany was the one who was killed, I wondered if I would've made some dramatic pilgrimage all the way up to New Jersey, and stood beside her grave and said some of the things I said at Yancey's grave. If Bethany died and Yancey had lived, I wondered how much time I would've spent thinking about Yancey.

March 7, 1970 – It's the last day of basketball season and I'm standing in front of the Ensworth gym. It's close to noon and the solar eclipse has been going on for a while. It looks more like early morning than the middle of the day. Just about everybody has come outside, and a few kids from Woodmont are standing together across the parking lot. They've been taking turns looking at the sun through a piece of smoked glass. Callie Lee, the fastest runner in the fifth grade, is squinting up at the eclipse through the glass.

I walk up and Rusty Willis is telling her that if she stares at the sun for too long she could go blind. I tell Rusty that if she does go blind, he might be able to beat her in a game of one-on-one. She just lowers the glass and looks at me. The other kids have gotten tired of the eclipse, and nobody else is waiting for a turn. Callie Lee doesn't say anything, but she reaches out and offers me the darkened glass. I take it. When I look up, I see how the intervening moon has turned the sun into a crescent.

Baseball season came around again and I had a pretty bad team. Our pitchers couldn't pitch and our hitters couldn't hit. It would take a lot of work before we could even be decent, but it was a good group of kids, and they were trying to get better.

Vietnam was still raging and there were all the other usual problems, but the world didn't seem as crazy as it was the year before. Then, in the middle of April, an oxygen tank exploded on Apollo 13. It was widely reported that even if the astronauts could get most of the way back from the moon, their capsule was likely to burn up as soon as it reentered the Earth's atmosphere. Three days later, the night before they tried their reentry, I went to Woodmont to pray for them.

The moon was around three-quarters full and there were some clouds, but at times it was fully in view. I lay down in centerfield and I thought about the same thing that millions of other people were thinking about – what it was like to be one of the astronauts.

They were trying to get back home, but they knew they were probably experiencing the last few hours of their lives. If I was in the same situation, I was pretty sure I would've pointed the capsule out into space and put it on automatic pilot. I would've probably chosen to die looking out at the stars, and then just drift on out into space.

Sometimes I wondered if the Earth would end up that way – just a dead planet drifting away. I sat up and looked at the darkened windows of the school. It had been over seven years since the worst night of the missile crisis.

By the time we had baseball practice the next afternoon, the astronauts had made it back alive. The following Monday I noticed some posters on the Peabody campus that included the photograph of the Earth in the distance, just above the horizon of the moon. There was going to be an event on campus, but it didn't turn out to be about the space program, or about the Apollo 13 astronauts coming home.

The posters announced that Peabody, along with a lot of other colleges, was observing a celebration of the planet. It was called Earth Day, and interested students were invited to come to the auditorium and hear speeches about the environment.

If it wasn't for the photograph on the poster, I wouldn't have known about Earth Day. I went, and Bethany Brussard showed up, too. She sat a couple of rows in front of me with several other girls. I glanced over at her a few times, but I mostly listened to the speeches.

A scientist from some college I'd never heard of gave a talk about carbon dioxide. He said that if the amount of carbon in the atmosphere continued to rise, the temperature of the Earth would keep increasing. Within a half-century, there would be all sorts of problems – from melting ice in the Antarctic and rising sea levels, to unprecedented droughts and fires, to flooding and much more severe storms. And along with species going extinct, there would be all sorts of other catastrophic problems.

Then an older woman gave a talk about overpopulation. She had a decade-by-decade chart that began with how many people were living in the United States when the first census was taken in 1790. Only four million people were living in the country back then, but by the time my grandfather came over from Scotland in 1883 – less than a century later – the population was fifty million. As Earth Day was being celebrated – less than ninety years after that – there were over two hundred million Americans.

The woman said that by the end of the century, there might be three hundred million people living in the United States. By then the population of the Earth could be over seven billion – more than double the number of people who were on the planet when the students in the audience were born.

There was also a population boom in the neighborhood around Woodmont School. When I was growing up, it was pretty unusual to see a home under construction, but that had changed. Drastically. After the houses were built on Herbert's Field and all the condominiums went up at Regency Park, it seemed like something was getting built all the time.

Two weeks after Earth Day there was another event on the Peabody campus. President Nixon announced that American forces had been sent into Cambodia, and there were protests on college campuses all across the country. When four students were killed and several more were wounded by a unit from the Ohio National Guard during a protest at Kent State University, things went to a whole different level.

I wondered what Sean thought when he heard about it, and I wondered the same thing a couple of weeks later when two more students were killed at Jackson State, in Mississippi. Classes at Peabody were suspended after the Kent State killings, and a memorial service was held out on the mall.

I sat on the grass in the middle of the crowd, but I didn't feel like I belonged there. I wanted to be as angry as everybody else was about the students getting shot, but all I felt was some sorrow. A balcony of one of the women's dormitories overlooked the mall, and I saw Bethany sitting there by herself, listening to the speeches. By then I'd heard that she was transferring to another school.

I'd been thinking about how she'd remember me when she looked back on her time at Peabody, and the more I thought about it, the more it bothered me. I told myself that if she was still there when the speeches were over, I'd go over and talk to her. I was pretty sure she'd be gone by then, but she was still there when the crowd was breaking up.

I walked through the grass and stopped when I got to the sidewalk. The balcony was about ten feet above where I was standing, and she was reading. She didn't notice me until I cleared my throat. She looked down at me and I started talking. I told her the way I felt the first time I saw her, and what I should've said. And how much I wanted to run into her when she was by herself. Then I talked about everything else I should've done differently.

Sometimes she looked at me and sometimes she looked down at her book. I saw her smile a couple of times, but I couldn't tell if it was because she liked what I was saying, or if she was trying not to laugh. She never said a word.

Chapter 41

By the time I got through exams, baseball season had been going on for a while. My team was as bad as I thought we were. We kept working on our batting, but we still couldn't hit. And neither one of our pitchers threw hard enough to strike anybody out. It took a while, but I finally got them to where they could at least throw strikes. But the guys liked coming to practice.

At least we were decent on defense. Our outfielders were pretty good, and the better they got, the more I challenged them. I bought a fungo bat and I could hit some really high fly balls. I'd tell them that the bases were loaded with two outs in the last inning of a game, and our team was ahead by one run. I'd say that if the next ball I hit was caught, we'd win the game, and if it wasn't, we'd lose.

After a while, I started making up elaborate stories about what would happen if they missed the ball and made us lose the imaginary game. One of the scenarios was that if a kid didn't catch the ball, his father would be so ashamed that he'd start drinking, and after he got fired from his job for being a drunk, the family would lose their house and end up living in a homeless shelter. All because their inadequate son couldn't catch a routine fly ball.

But one afternoon after we'd lost a couple of games in a row, I came up with what turned out to be their favorite story. Charley Northern lived just a couple of houses down from Woodmont, and he'd show up at practice with his beagle, Hershel.

Charley was playing left field and I pointed over to Hershel.

"Okay, it's the bottom of the last inning and a guy in the mafia has made a big bet on our team. He says if anybody misses a ball and makes him lose his bet, he's gonna kill that kid's dog. So Charley, you *really* need to catch the next ball I hit.

"The mafia guy's name is Tony Two-Toes and he has a hundred grand on our team to win this game. If you screw up he's gonna take it out on Hershel. Now Hershel is a really good dog and it'll be a darn shame if something happens to him. He loves you and he's depending on you not to screw up.

"And you might as well know exactly what's gonna happen if you don't make the catch. Tony Two-Toes and a couple of his mafia thugs have a wood chipper, and they're waiting right around the corner. If you miss the ball, they're gonna get Hershel and push him *very slowly* into the spinning blades of the chipper."

I made a whirring sound like a chipping machine, including the way the pitch would change when its blades came in contact with Hershel, and then I improvised an imitation of Hershel's final whimper. When Charley was laughing hard enough, I hit the ball as high as I could. He misjudged it, but he made a last-minute lunge and Hershel was saved from his imaginary execution.

One day we were having a morning practice and hitting high fly balls led to more than a story. The kids were below average when it came to baseball, but a couple of them were especially bright.

I'd been talking about Apollo 11, and I asked them a question. "If I can hit a ball 150 feet in the air when I'm standing here on the field at Woodmont, how high could I hit it if I was standing on the surface of the moon?"

A couple of guys already knew that the moon only had one-sixth the gravity of the Earth, but they let everybody else guess before they said anything. After that, they proudly told their less-informed teammates that the answer was somewhere around 900 feet.

Then Artie Horner, who always liked being a skeptic, looked at me and smiled. "But there's *no way* you can hit a ball 150 feet in the air."

I told him I was pretty sure I could hit it that high because the big ash tree just beyond the left field fence looked like it was around 75 feet tall, and the highest balls I could hit were at least twice as high as the tree. Artie was shaking his head. "And there's *no way* that tree is 75 feet tall."

The next time we took a water break, John McMillan, who was a fourth-grader, went out into left field. He was even quieter than his older brother, Brooks, who'd been on my basketball and baseball teams the first year I coached. Maybe if John had talked more, I would've known there was a genius on my team.

It was a sunny day and he stood in the shade of the ash tree for a couple of minutes. Then he came back in and picked up the fungo bat. He looked like he was trying to figure something out, and I asked him what he was doing. "Well, I think I know how to find out how tall that tree is." The kids were milling around and a couple of guys started making fun of him. But John's best friend, Stephen Robbins, seemed pretty confident that John knew what he was talking about.

John pointed to the number – 36 – on the bottom of the bat handle. "See, this means the bat is 36 inches long." Artie said, "Duh John," and a few kids laughed. Then John held up the bat and pointed at the shadow. "All we need to know is how long the shadow is."

Then he went over and touched home plate with his foot. "See these two sides that come together at the back of the plate? They're both 12 inches long. That makes it easy to measure the shadow of the bat." I didn't know the dimensions of home plate, and I had no idea how John knew.

He handed the bat to Stephen, who held it perpendicular to the ground with the barrel end touching the dirt. Then John picked up home plate and used one of the 12-inch sides to measure the shadow. After that he said, "Okay, the shadow is about 24 inches and the bat is 36 inches." Artie was starting to nod.

John sounded like a reluctant teacher. "So 24 is two-thirds of 36, which means the shadow of the bat is two-thirds as long as the bat, and *that* means that the shadow of the tree is two-thirds of the height of the tree." By then most of the kids got it. They looked somewhere between surprised and impressed. He'd reasoned everything out on his own.

I just started clapping. Everybody else started clapping, too, and then John carried home plate out into left field to measure the shadow of the ash tree. The shadow turned out to be right at 48 feet long, which meant that the ash was about 72 feet tall.

Then the kids wanted to see how high I could hit a ball. They thought we could use the shadow of the ball the same way John used the shadow of the tree. Artie got a ball and started throwing it as high as he could, but nobody could see its shadow while it was moving. It was almost time for practice to be over, and I said that if anybody came up with a way to measure how high I could hit a ball, we could try it the next day.

Almost all the kids got there a little earlier than usual the following morning. John McMillan didn't say anything until I asked him if he'd figured it out. He looked a little uncomfortable, but he reached into his pocket and pulled out two spools of thread and a popsicle stick.

"Well, it might work if we pull out a little more than 150 feet of thread and tie one end to a ball and tie the other end to this popsicle stick. Then if the stick pops up off the ground when you hit it, we'll know the ball went at least 150 feet."

After I paced off 150 feet, I unraveled 152 feet of thread. I tied one end of the thread as securely as I could around a ball, and John tied the other end around the popsicle stick. On my first three tries the stick stayed where it was, but on the fourth try I really cut loose and I hit the ball as hard as I could. It went straight up and the stick went two or three feet off the ground.

I made a gesture of acknowledgment to John, but before I pitched batting practice I told the kids I had a question. I asked them how far the ball would've gone if there wasn't any gravity holding it back.

I expected somebody to throw out an answer, but nobody said

anything. John stayed quiet at first. I wasn't sure if he was thinking, or if he was just being humble. He finally understood that the other kids were waiting for him to say something.

"Well if there wasn't any gravity and if the ball didn't hit anything, it would just keep on going." He glanced up into the sky above the baseball field. "It would just keep on going forever."

There were days when storm clouds moved in while we were practicing. The western sky out beyond the school got dark and the wind rushed in, and by the time the thunder was rolling across the field, the kids and I would've run to the covered walkway that connected the front and back sections of the school.

I always worried about one of my players getting struck by lightning. I imagined a kid lying unconscious on the ground in the rain and watching him turn blue and then trying to resuscitate him and the ambulance coming too late and being with the bereaved family and seeing the article in the newspaper the next day and going to the funeral and watching the burial and spending the rest of my life saying how sorry I was for letting one of the kids on my team get killed. But during the 1970 season, at least while we were practicing at Woodmont, the storms stayed away.

I took two courses at Peabody that summer. Sean was five months into his tour, but sometimes I saw Mike at lunch. I came in one day in the middle of July and it looked like he was waiting for me. The morning newspaper was folded in front of him. I thought he'd launch into one of his tirades about Nixon or Vietnam, but there was something else on his mind.

He pointed to a story on the front page. "Did you see this?"

A federal judge had made a ruling in a case that was filed against the local School Board. I'd skimmed through the article that morning. After thirteen years of delaying tactics, the judge ordered the school board to submit a plan that would desegregate the local schools. Mike didn't look happy, and I asked him why he wasn't celebrating.

He started frowning. "Because they'll just come up with a quick fix. Black kids will get sent to schools in white neighborhoods, and white kids will get sent to schools in black neighborhoods, but it won't be long before private schools will spring up all over the place. That's where white families who can afford tuition will start sending their children. And as soon as that happens, public schools will start going downhill."

He shook his head. "The only thing busing will do is cripple public schools. It's the educational version of Ben Tre."

I must've looked lost. "Don't you remember that military spokesman from two or three years ago? He said that the only way to save a Vietnamese village we bombed into oblivion was to destroy it. That was Ben Tre. It was near Saigon. It was supposed to be full of Viet Cong, and we bombed it until it wasn't there anymore.

"Destroying neighborhood schools in the name of racial equality is like destroying a village in order to save it. And if that happens, guess what the big shots who run things in Nashville will do? They'll blame the judges and the civil rights activists. They've been dragging their feet since 1957, and now the only way to desegregate the schools is to ruin the whole educational system."

He'd been pretty calm at first, but he was getting mad. "Almost every city in the country has a small group of men who run everything. They stand behind the curtain and pull all the strings. If there's a more incompetent set of dumbasses in America than the morons who run things in Nashville, I'd like to know who they are.

"They work through the Chamber of Commerce, and they swagger around and congratulate each other about how civic-minded they are. They mobilized the business community to push for the consolidation of local government, and a few years later they pulled out all the stops and pushed through the referendum that legalized the sale of liquor by the drink. But they just kept turning their backs on the school system."

I'd met a couple of the men Mike was talking about. One of them did seem like a jerk, but the other guy was pretty nice.

Mike was on a roll. "If you believe in all that *noblesse oblige* bullshit they always try to project, then you aren't paying attention. It's been sixteen years, *sixteen years* since the Supreme Court ruled – *unanimously* – that separate but equal schools are unconstitutional.

"They had all that time to work with local black leaders and give the schools in those communities the same resources the white schools have always had. They could've gotten the black schools up to par, but our wise and benevolent city fathers just dug in their heels.

"They would've made things happen in a hurry if there was some money to be made in desegregation, but they stayed on the sidelines and the school system of the city they say they love so much is about to get turned upside down. Of course, their darling little children and their darling little grandchildren go to Ensworth and Oak Hill and Montgomery Bell Academy and Harpeth Hall, so they don't really give a shit.

"But somebody will give a shit in another forty or fifty years. If our city fathers had any vision, they would understand that a broken school system will eventually lead to a broken city."

I should've cared more than I did about what lousy schools would mean to the future, but I was focused on what would happen to Woodmont. The court case was on my mind from then on, and it bothered me every time I thought about it.

There was already a black kid in the fourth grade at Woodmont. I hoped that would make a difference. And I hoped that the only schools covered by the court order would be the ones close to the inner city. All I could do was keep on coaching and wait to see what happened.

Our baseball team lost more games than we won, but we had

a good season. A few of the parents said they were surprised at how much the kids had improved. I could tell that one of the divorced mothers really liked me, and a few weeks after the end of the season I saw her at the grocery. We talked for a while and then she told me her kids were with their father. I went to her house that night and I didn't leave till the next morning. Although she didn't look quite as good as the Blonde Bombshell, she was pretty and she was a whole lot nicer.

On the morning after Labor Day, I went up to Woodmont and watched the kids showing up for their first day of school. From wide-eyed first graders holding their mothers' hands to self-assured sixth graders, the kids paraded toward the front door. They went inside and after the bell rang, I went in, too. I followed the same route down the hall I'd taken with Mother on my first day at Woodmont.

The school looked a lot smaller than it did back then. I went down to my first-grade classroom and my old teacher, Miss Powell, was having her students count together to ten. I stayed out in the hall and listened. I was pretty sure we did the same thing on our first day.

When they got to ten, she told them to count back down from ten to one, but only a few of the kids could do it. I closed my eyes and pretended that when they got all the way down to one, there would be a flash of light and it would be 1953, and I'd be back in first grade again.

Chapter 42

Football season came and went, and on the night of the Woodmont Spaghetti Supper, I got away from all the kids and parents in the cafeteria and slipped down to the library. I found a few of the books I'd read when I went to school there, and I finally ran across the one I was looking for. It was called *The Little Shepherd of Kingdom Come.* I read it in fourth grade, and my name was still on the check-out slip inside the front cover.

I went into the building and walked around whenever I could, but I didn't know how much longer I'd be able to do it. There was a Thanksgiving play and a pageant before the Christmas holidays, and both times I ended up sitting by myself in one of my old classrooms. I kept looking for things that hadn't changed.

Miss Shay had retired, but the abacus my classmates and I made out of red and yellow-painted spools was still hanging above the blackboard in my second-grade classroom, and the same aquarium was beside her desk. And even though Mrs. Dickson had been dead since 1961, the old globe was still in the corner and the same maps were on the wall of the room where I'd spent fifth grade.

I coached seven teams in basketball that winter. We won just about every game we played, but I never stopped worrying about what would happen to the school. Until the court case came up, I had assumed that Woodmont would be around for another hundred years.

April 30, 1971 – It's four o'clock on Friday afternoon and I'm standing in the hallway at Woodmont. My neighbors, Mr. and Mrs. Crandall, are at the far end of the hall, standing in front of the trophy case. They're looking at a photograph of their son. His name was Ben Crandall and he grew up in the house where his parents still live – right down Clearview Drive from my house. He was killed in the Pacific during World War Two, just a few years after he was a student at Woodmont.

Mrs. Crandall had given me old newspapers and coat hangers when I came by every year for the paper drive, and she always bought Spaghetti Supper tickets in the fall and Carnival tickets in the spring. I remember Mother telling me that Mr. and Mrs. Crandall showed up at the Carnival every year, but that they never stayed very long. They just came inside and looked at the picture of their son in the trophy case, and at the photograph of the football team he played on when he was in eighth grade.

I walked outside and stood near the elm tree between the school and the baseball field. It was sunny and cool – perfect weather for a grammar school carnival. The cakewalk was underway up on the basketball courts, and kids were walking around the perimeter of a big circle painted on the asphalt.

It's Too Late was playing on the school's loudspeaker. The outer part of the circle was divided into numbered sections, and when the music stopped, whoever was on the winning space went over and took one of the homemade cakes or pies that were displayed on a couple of nearby tables.

Volunteers from the Men's Club and the PTA were running the various booths that were set up behind the school. Kids were buying snow cones and popcorn and cotton candy, and they were tossing rings and beanbags and throwing darts at balloons. And along with a Bingo game, there was an auction going on in the cafeteria. Donated items were piled on and around the stage, and being sold off one by one.

The Woodmont Carnival was the big event of the year for the school. Almost every family in the area had kids who were either going to Woodmont, or who went there when they were younger. The school had tied the community together since it was built during the early part of the Depression.

There were plenty of smiles and handshakes and hugs between people who might not have seen each other since the last carnival. Members of the local fire station showed up in the same firetruck they always brought, and younger children waited for a ride while their mothers and fathers talked nearby.

Twenty or thirty of my players had already lined up in front of the dunking machine. They were waiting for the tank to fill up with water. They'd done a whole lot of talking about how many times I'd get dunked.

The kids were still wearing the clothes they wore during Field Day, and the top finishers in the various events had the blue, red, and white ribbons they won pinned to their shorts or their T-shirts. One of my grammar school dreams had been to get a ribbon on Field Day, and then parade around at the carnival with it pinned to my shirt. I never came close to winning one.

After the dunking machine finally got full, I climbed up behind the protective wire screen and sat above the water on a single wooden plank. The kids got to stand behind a line about twenty-five feet away, and throw baseballs at the circular metal target on the front of the tank. They each got three throws. If they hit the target, the plank would collapse and I'd fall into the water.

A bunch of the guys in line were sixth-graders, and the first one was Rusty Willis. He had blue ribbons all over his shirt. He wanted the honor of being the first one to get me wet, and he was good enough to do it three times in a row.

My only hope was to distract him. *Mr. Big Stuff* was playing on the loudspeaker, and I pretended to be a broadcaster. "Ladies and gentlemen, our first participant will be Rusty Willis, and the song we're hearing could've been written with Rusty in mind." He laughed along with everybody else, and then he got ready to throw.

I just kept talking. "And *yes*, we're all aware of Rusty's long and tragic struggle with bedwetting. But despite that unfortunate condition, he has a *tremendously* high opinion of himself. His urinary ordeal has been heartbreaking to watch. But I'm told that his mother still thinks that the day might *eventually* come when she'll be able to get rid of his rubber mattress cover."

I didn't let up. "Well, the crowd is getting restless. They must be wondering if he's *ever* going to throw the ball. Maybe being around water is making it hard for little Rusty to focus. If he even *thinks* about water when it's this close to bedtime, there's likely to be an overnight flood in the Willis home." When he finally took his turn he was laughing, and he missed all three times he threw.

Page Whitney was up next. He threw sidearm and I told him that since he couldn't throw normally and since he wasn't any better than Rusty, there was no way he was going to hit anything either. He didn't come close, and neither did Artie Horner or Ezra Lyle, but Johnny Wilkins barely missed on two of his throws.

When Ben and Andy Mayer came up to take their turns, I started calling out the punchlines of inappropriate jokes I'd already told them. I got them laughing so hard that their little brother Josh, who was only nine, came as close to hitting the target as they did.

Then I changed my approach. Whichever kid was throwing got to hear about some tackle he'd missed or about a dumb penalty he'd gotten in football, or a wide-open layup he'd blown, or a fly ball he should've caught. A few more kids took their turns, but they were all laughing before they picked up a ball. Pretty soon there were a lot more kids around the dunking machine, and being surrounded by a crowd put extra pressure on whoever was throwing.

It finally got to where only two or three kids still hadn't thrown. "Well folks, I know it's unbelievable, but so far the sixth-grade boys have *utterly* failed to get me wet. There was a whole lot of big talk going around about how I needed to wear a life preserver, and that I needed to bring plenty of towels to the carnival. But here I am – still *completely* dry. What a humiliating failure by the sixth-grade boys at Woodmont School."

Four girls were standing off to the side. One of them was Callie Lee. She was a lot taller than she was the last time I saw her.

I kept on talking. "And what a disappointment for those girls over there. I wonder how it feels to come to school *every single day* knowing that the boys in your grade are all *complete losers*. There isn't one guy – *not one guy in the whole class* – who's been able to do something as simple as throw a ball from twenty-five feet away and hit a target."

The other girls were laughing and they started whispering to Callie Lee. There was a little more whispering and then she walked up to the front of the line.

What's Going On was playing on the loudspeaker. Brian Burroughs was the next kid in line, and he gave Callie the ball he was holding.

I said, "Will this girl save her class from complete disgrace?" Before I could say anything else, she fired a fastball that barely missed the target.

I shouldn't have been surprised by how hard she could throw. Brian handed her another ball and she threw again. The ball came in a little too high and it slammed off the tank and bounced down toward the baseball field. I waved at her so she'd look at me, and then I exaggerated a yawn like I was tired of watching everybody miss. I saw her focus on the target and step back, and the next thing I knew I was in the water.

Most of the kids who missed on their first turn got back in line. They were a lot more accurate the second time around. They were harder to distract and I lost count of how many times I got dunked. The crowd finally thinned out when it started getting dark.

I was cold and I went into the boy's bathroom and changed into some dry clothes. But before I left for home, I went down to the trophy case and looked at Ben Crandall's picture in his military uniform. He didn't look like he'd started shaving yet.

Along with Ben Crandall, there were photographs of several other soldiers who had gone to Woodmont. I started thinking about Sean. I'd written him a few letters, but he only wrote back once. He just mentioned how bored he was, and how much cheaper and more potent the marijuana was in Vietnam.

There was another photograph on display in the trophy case. It was of a boy named Steve Thomas who went to Woodmont after the war. He ended up being a football star at Hillsboro High School. I remembered when he died. I was in third grade.

Chapter 43

June 6, 1971 – It's Sunday afternoon. We finished baseball practice a few minutes ago, but three of the kids – along with Ezra Lyle who lives across the street – have volunteered to stay late. I'm taking a class in summer school about how to identify gifted students, and I'm giving the kids a creativity test as part of a paper I have to write.

Ezra and Johnny Wilkins and Page Whitney and John McMillan are all out in left field, and they're taking their tests near the big ash tree. I've tried to picture myself teaching during the day and coaching in the afternoon. I'm pretty sure I could be a good teacher, but it's hard to see how I'd ever get hired.

The kids seemed to enjoy taking the test. The biggest section was made up of forty identical circles. The idea was to include the circles in a series of drawings and then come up with a title for each one. The more detail there was, the more creative the kid supposedly was. If they just used the circle as a head and drew in two eyes and a nose and a mouth, they'd get a pretty low score. But if they drew a face that had more features – like eyebrows and hair and teeth and some extra lines – they'd get a higher score.

Ezra scored pretty high on one of his drawings. After he made the circle look like a roll of toilet paper, he drew a stick figure on top. He got extra points because he called it, "Being on a Roll." Johnny made a circle look like the moon, and on the surface, he drew what looked like an astronaut holding an American flag.

And Page turned a circle into what looked like a vortex. He called it "Falling."

Those were three of the best ones, but they weren't anywhere close to what John McMillan came up with. My professor said it was so far off the charts that he didn't know how to evaluate it.

Instead of completing forty individual drawings, John combined everything into one big picture. He couldn't draw all that well, but it didn't matter. He drew a big cross that divided the page into quadrants, and he turned the circles in the two bottom quadrants into people.

He used the circles as heads, and along with eyes and noses, he added arms and legs. He had them all looking up at the figures in the top two quadrants. The figures in those quadrants had human faces, too, but instead of giving them arms and legs, he'd surrounded them with a bunch of straight lines radiating out – the way kids draw light coming from the sun. And those faces were all looking up, too.

Above all the figures in the quadrants made by the cross, John drew another set of circles. They were faces, but they looked different from the faces looking up at them. Each one had two eyes and they were surrounded by wavy radiating lines, and they were also looking up. John called his picture "Worshipers." When I asked him what it meant, he said that the people at the bottom were worshiping gods. And the gods they were worshiping might have gods of their own, and those gods could have gods, too.

June 29, 1971 – It's Tuesday morning and I'm sitting on my bed. A couple of weeks ago I couldn't wait to get the newspaper and read the latest details about the Pentagon Papers, but I don't want to look at the story on the front page of today's newspaper. The Federal judge in the Nashville desegregation case has issued a sweeping ruling that will put an end to almost every local neighborhood school – including Woodmont. The school won't be closed, but it'll lose its fifth grade and its sixth grade. And while neighborhood children will be bused to inner city schools, students from other areas will be bused in to attend Woodmont. I wish there was something I could do about it, but there isn't.

Woodmont School opened in 1931. It turned what had been a geographical area into a neighborhood. The school and the neighborhood became intertwined, and in the 1950s I experienced some of what had been taking place for over twenty years.

We learned to read and write and do arithmetic, and we learned about history and geography and science. But because we grew up in a neighborhood where most of the children knew each other, we learned a lot more than that.

It was a little different for girls, but I knew how it was for boys. Before we started school, most first-grade boys didn't know each other. But after being in class and playing together at recess, friendships were made and we started going home with each other in the afternoon. It wasn't long before we were spending the night at each other's houses.

A lot of us eventually played on the same baseball and football and basketball teams, and we were Cub Scouts and Boy Scouts together, and we went trick-or-treating on Halloween, and sledding with each other when it snowed. We occasionally fished with each other on summer days, and sometimes on summer nights we played kick-the-can and spotlight, or camped out together. We went to each other's birthday parties, and to Belle Meade Theater to see movies, and there were times when we met up at Montgomery Bell Academy or Vanderbilt when there was a football game.

Woodmont was our school, and the surrounding neighborhood expanded our education. We learned a lot when we were away from our parents and our teachers. Some guys would climb all the way into the tops of trees or ride their bicycles too fast, but there were hardly ever any broken bones. There were a few fistfights and rock fights, but there were just a few black eyes or bloody noses or cut heads. We gradually learned which risks to take and which ones to avoid, and how to settle our differences.

And along the way, in addition to the chances we took, we exchanged information – from our preferences in rock and roll to what we'd heard about sex. School brought us together, and we got to know each other out in the neighborhood.

With busing, some of the kids from Woodmont would be sent across town and some would go to private schools. It wouldn't be long before most of the children in the area didn't know each other. Schools were what tied neighborhoods together, but what was being lost by putting an end to neighborhood schools was never mentioned by those who had engineered busing.

When I went to Woodmont for baseball practice that afternoon, I tried to cover up the way I felt. Page Whitney finally asked me if we'd keep practicing at the school. I told him it was stupid and wrong to put an end to a great neighborhood school, but the teams I coached would still be neighborhood teams. I told him we'd keep practicing at Woodmont just like we always had. I started pitching batting practice, and pretty soon I was thinking about a poem I wanted to write. I worked on it that night and I finished it a few days later.

The Color of Loss

A child climbs down
From a bus
And the school bell rings
And there are lessons
And questions and answers
And recess and lunch,
And then more
Answers and questions
Until the bell rings again
And the child climbs
Back on the bus
For the long trip home.
After looking out the window
At strangers

And at the houses of strangers
And at unfamiliar streets,
The child sees
A bus moving by
In the opposite direction.
As the black child
And the white child
Make their way home,
They ride by schools
That have been severed from
The neighborhoods
In which they were built.
And as the connection between
The schools and their communities
Bleeds away,
Each amputated school
And each diminished neighborhood
Is left with a complexion
That is without color.

I passed both of the classes I took that summer. There wouldn't be another graduation ceremony until the following spring, but I had enough hours to graduate. One night I went over to Peabody to return an overdue book to the library, and I ended up standing on the lawn where I would receive my diploma the next year. As long as I was there, I thought I might as well give a commencement address of my own.

"Ten years ago tonight I was away at summer camp. I was going to start high school a few weeks later, and I was pretty sure I was ready. I was confident that I had my life and America and the world and God all figured out. Once I got to high school I'd make good grades and play on the basketball team and have a girlfriend. Then I'd go off to college and graduate in four years.

"After that, I'd get a job doing something I liked and get married and have kids. That's what everybody did. I thought God was watching over me, and if I was a good person I'd end up in heaven. But by the time I graduated from high school, most of that had fallen apart.

"Ten years ago I thought that America was the guiding light of humanity. I still love America, but after the killing of President Kennedy and the killing of Martin Luther King and the killing of Bobby Kennedy, and with the war in Vietnam and all the racial turmoil and the killing of the college students last year, I think America might be losing its greatness.

"A lot of the way I feel about America is tied up with the love I have for the Earth. And the love I have for my neighborhood. I love the way the wind sounds at night when it moves through the trees outside my bedroom window. It's become part of me, and so has the sound of thunder when it rolls in from the west. I love the sound of katydids on summer nights, and windy days in late October when leaves blow down from the trees along Clearview Drive. And I love the way everything looks after a big snow and the smell of mowed grass and honeysuckle in the spring.

"When I think about America, those things are at the heart of the way I feel. But they come from nature. They all come from the Earth. I still love America, but after seeing what happened to Herbert's Field and what's happening to Woodmont School and with all the new houses being built everywhere, my love for America has changed. It doesn't feel like the same country anymore.

"And as for the world, after going through the Cuban Missile Crisis and with the population growing out of control, I'm starting to wonder if humanity will survive. When it comes to God I'm still a believer, but I have a lot more questions than I used to have.

"So here I am. I'm almost twenty-four. Next year I'll finally be graduating from college. I still feel like I'm lost, but I keep thinking that there's something I'm supposed to do."

Chapter 44

June 21, 1973 – It's around four in the afternoon and I'm on Westmont Avenue. I've just driven between Tom Hendrickson's basketball court and what used to be Herbert's Field. Billy Preston is singing Will It Go Round in Circles on the radio, and up ahead three girls are talking to each other across from the stop sign at Lynnbrook Road. I pull up to the intersection. There's a big tree on the side of the road, and two of the girls are standing in the shade. I remember them from a couple of years ago when they were sixth graders at Woodmont.

The third girl is in a patch of sunlight. She looks a couple of years older than the other two. She has blonde hair and an athletic physique, and she's wearing faded denim shorts and a bikini top. She looks at me for two or three seconds before I finally recognize Callie Lee. I want to say something about the dunking machine, but I don't have anything to say to the other girls, so I keep quiet.

A wave of wind pushes through the trees and bushes. It moves like an unseen hand across the uncut grass of a house across the street. I just wave at the girls and drive off. I look into the rearview mirror too late to see if Callie Lee was watching when I drove away. It seems like time is slowing down.

I drove to the place where I was house-sitting, and I ended up on a swing on the back porch. I was down on myself. The last time I saw Callie Lee, I'd seen her the way I was supposed to see her. A twelve-year-old with a whole lot of athletic ability. At twenty five I wasn't supposed to look at a fourteen-year-old girl and see a woman, but that's what I'd seen. I felt like I might as well have been wearing a trench coat and lurking at the edge of a schoolyard.

I'd seen good looking girls that age before, but they'd never made me feel like I needed to go somewhere and sit down. Up until then, the way I'd seen younger girls was always pretty normal. I knew how the world looked at older guys who saw younger girls the way I'd just seen Callie Lee. They were solitary losers who couldn't relate to women their own age.

There had been a time when I was a solitary loser, but I wasn't nearly as much of a loser as I used to be, and I definitely wasn't solitary. The Blonde Bombshell was still on my mind, and now and then I'd get together with a divorced or divorcing mother of a kid I was coaching. She would flirt with me or I'd flirt with her, and it usually wasn't too long before things got physical.

Most of the time they were lonely or bored, and they probably just wanted somebody around who thought they were still attractive. There were a few times when one of them wanted a more serious relationship, but it wasn't long before she understood, or seemed to understand, that I didn't want to get any more involved than I already was.

I was still living at home, but I did a lot of house-sitting, and I had jobs that ranged from working as a security guard to umpiring and refereeing games. My father's business was doing pretty well, but as soon as he walked in the door from work, he fixed himself a drink. And he didn't sit down in his chair in the den until he finished that drink and poured himself another one. He had another one before dinner, and after we ate he had one or two more.

Part of why he drank as much as he did might've been because of how hard he worked, but there was more to it than that. He worked hard and he was successful, but he hadn't wanted to be a businessman.

He'd wanted to follow in his father's footsteps and be a doctor.

But his mother blamed the death of his father on his work as a physician, and she didn't allow him to study medicine. And if being immersed in a vocation he didn't enjoy wasn't enough to account for his drinking, there were plenty of other contributing factors.

I didn't understand what he was up against when I was younger, but I eventually figured it out. He didn't fit into Nashville society. He and Mother were invited to parties sometimes, and they went out with other couples to dinner now and then. But it was because Mother was a friend of the hostess, or a friend of the wife in the other couple.

Men could talk to each other about politics or sex or about whatever subject they wanted, but social etiquette limited the appropriate topics of conversation when both men and women were present. It was okay to talk about moving into a new house, or share details about a party or a vacation, or talk superficially about business, or mention the achievements of children, or share opinions about Vanderbilt's football or basketball teams. Some light gossip was also permissible, but that was about it.

My father was especially intelligent and highly knowledgeable about a wide range of subjects, but he was intellectually isolated. The part of Nashville where we lived wasn't exactly a mecca for people with minds of his caliber.

And my father was an extrovert. If he was out at dinner and there was a piano player, there was a good chance that he would walk over to the piano and start singing. He had a really good voice, but that sort of spontaneity tended to make members of local society uncomfortable.

If he liked somebody he met, he would be open with his feelings, but what he saw as being friendly was often regarded as being overly familiar. He hadn't grown up in Nashville – he'd grown up in Manila. He was a large round peg in a small square hole.

But even if the rest of his life was perfect, I gave him all the motivation he needed to drink too much. What he wanted more than anything else was for me to come to the factory and work with him. His dream was to teach me everything he knew about running the business. It would've been an answer to his prayers for us to work together, and for me to take over when he was ready to retire.

But the factory was gloomy and gray, and hearing the clatter of sewing machines made me feel like I was inside a giant engine. And I was pretty sure it seemed like a prison to the people who worked there. They would've been somewhere else if there was a better way to feed their families. My father was used to it, but there were probably times when it felt like a prison to him, too.

A lot would've changed if I did what my father wanted. I might've been able to keep coaching for a while, but I couldn't have done it for long. I was pretty sure that being imprisoned all day at the factory would end up poisoning who I really was. I wondered if I'd end up in one of my anxiety pits. Or maybe I'd just end up drinking myself into a semi-stupor every night. I knew it was hypocritical to benefit from the money that came from the factory, but I wasn't sure what I could do about it.

Mother seemed to understand that I wasn't cut out to be a business executive. She just wanted me to find a way to make a living so I could get married. She was afraid that I'd spend my whole life in isolation and end up dying alone. She was loving and compassionate, and if there was a way to ease her mind without ruining my life, I would've done it.

She didn't drink as much as my father did, but just about every night she had some wine and faded into a blurry wistful mood that made her seem like she was somebody else. I cleaned up the kitchen after dinner, and then I usually headed out the door – whether I had anywhere to go or not.

I didn't expect God to whisper in my ear and tell me a way that I could be happy and make my parents happy, too, but I did a lot of praying anyway. And I started taking Mother to church on Sunday again. Dr. Rowe, who'd been our preacher since the 1940s, was retiring, and she wanted to be there while he was closing out his career.

He was an engaging speaker and he had always been especially kind to me. I didn't like thinking about it, but he hardly ever preached about poor people or black people, or about how Jesus would've wanted those people to be treated. I liked Dr. Rowe, but his sermons sounded like they were written so they wouldn't offend the wealthiest members of the church.

After a few months, Dr. Rowe was replaced by Reverend Carter Cortez, who was apparently hired because of his dynamic personality and because he was good at delivering sermons. He was a commanding figure when he was standing in the pulpit, but the committee that hired him either didn't ask him enough questions, or he hadn't told them what he actually believed.

Carter Cortez turned out to be a rigid evangelical. Just about everything he said seemed to imply that the only real Christians were people who interpreted scripture the same way he did. My mother and I listened to Reverend Cortez convey his dark version of Jesus Christ for as long as we could, but we finally heard enough about Christianity according to the Book of Revelation.

The last straw for me was a particular sermon when he started railing against science. He kept referring to scientists, and to people who accepted the accuracy of science, as secular humanists. He claimed that those who accepted science were worshiping man instead of God. That accepting the findings of science was turning away from God. I saw that as a completely warped view of Christianity. I looked at the people sitting around me, but nobody else seemed to hear what he was saying.

After we stopped going to church, I did most of my praying on long walks I started taking around the neighborhood at night. Being alone in the dark made me feel like I was invisible. I liked feeling invisible. Sometimes I prayed while I walked, but I did a lot more thinking than praying. There was plenty to think about. The Watergate hearings had been going on since spring, and the more information that came out, the more I wondered about what else was going on in the shadows of government.

It would've been entertaining to have Sean and Mike around and hear them blast Nixon. But it had been a while since I'd heard from Sean, and Mike was supposed to be somewhere in South America doing research for a book he was planning to write.

It had been over a year since details of the Watergate burglary started trickling out. The story had been getting wider and deeper and darker ever since. The first account was that thieves broke into the Democratic Party Headquarters at the Watergate office complex in Washington.

Then it was discovered that one of the burglars had CIA connections, and one of the other burglars was a security official for the Republican Party. After that, a big check written to the Nixon campaign turned up in the bank account of one of the burglars, and from there the Attorney General was implicated.

Nixon was re-elected, but both of his two top aides resigned the following spring, along with his Attorney General. Then he fired his White House Counsel. Not long after that, along with millions of other Americans, I started watching the Senate Watergate Committee investigate Nixon on television. I was watching when it was revealed that all of Nixon's Oval Office conversations were secretly recorded. By then I was pretty sure that administration officials had done a lot of lying.

And when I walked around the neighborhood after dark, I also thought about Vietnam. There was finally a ceasefire, but it was obvious that North Vietnam was in the final stages of winning the war.

Almost 60,000 American soldiers were dead and over 300,000 were wounded. More than a million Vietnamese had been killed, and hundreds of billions of dollars had been spent on the military. America was divided and being rocked with turmoil, but President Nixon and the politicians who claimed that America was winning the war in Southeast Asia were still saying there would be peace with honor. I hadn't stopped wondering what happened to the guy who went to Vietnam in my place.

The racial situation wasn't getting any better, and with the ruling of the Supreme Court in Roe versus Wade, there was more and more conflict around women's rights. I worried about America, and I worried about what was left of the place where I'd grown up.

There had already been a lot of change in the neighborhood by the time busing started, and things kept getting worse. Two different times I was walking along in the dark and I came up on a bulldozer or a backhoe parked in front of a big tree-filled yard where some distinctive older home had stood for decades. Within a few days, the house would be gone and most of the trees would've been cut down so that a bunch of look-alike houses could be built.

One night I walked over as far as Harding Road, which ran along the northern and western edge of the neighborhood. More and more businesses and apartments were being built there, and they were starting to press in on the houses and yards and quiet streets nearby. And there were rumors that developers were negotiating to buy both Woodmont Country Club and Richland Country Club, which contained the last large sections of open land in the neighborhood.

But at least Woodmont School was still there, and at least I was still coaching football, basketball, and baseball. We were the youngest baseball team in our league that summer, but we won just about every game we played. We didn't have any bad players. Even our bat girl, Ann Tracey, was good. She lived down the street from the school, and I'd coached her three older brothers. She let everybody know that she was our bat girl – not our bat *boy*.

Ann was nine, but she could hit and field like she was a couple of years older. She had a good arm, and if the league had allowed girls, she would've been on the team to begin with. I let her practice along with everybody else, and she got to play in a few of our scrimmages. About halfway through the season, we had a game against a team coached by a friend of mine. He said he didn't care if she played, and I gave her a spare uniform and put her in right field for a couple of innings.

She caught both balls that were hit to her, and she got a hit and stole two bases. She should've been playing earlier. It was my fault for not pushing it. The only games Ann sat out for the rest of the season were when the other coach wouldn't let her play because she wasn't on the official roster. When that happened, I let my team know why she wasn't in the lineup, and we'd usually have some extra fire once the game got started.

Then I got a call from a newspaper reporter. He said it was the first time he'd heard of a girl playing on a team with boys in Nashville. He said that with all the controversy about the Equal Rights Amendment and Title IX and Roe vs. Wade, and with the popularity of the tennis match between Margaret Court and Bobby Riggs, it would make a good story. I didn't say anything about politics when I asked Ann if she wanted to be in the paper. She thought about it, and at the end of practice, she said she didn't want to be famous. She said she just wanted to play baseball.

Chapter 45

One day I was walking beside the school and I noticed that the door to the basement was cracked open. I closed it, but it was still unlocked when I checked after practice a few days later. Nobody was ever there that late on summer afternoons. I went inside and after I walked down through the basement and up the steps into the lunchroom, I started wandering around.

The door stayed unlocked all summer, and I went in a lot after that. At first, I'd sit in my old classrooms, but then I started spending more time in the library.

There was a book in the history section that was big and heavy, and I remembered seeing it back when I was in the fourth or fifth grade. It was the *History of Davidson County, Tennessee*, which is the county where Nashville is located. I hadn't ever taken it down from the shelf, but I remembered wondering how there could be enough history about Nashville to fill up a book that thick.

I looked through it and I eventually came to a section called the *Recollections of Willoughby Williams*. He was eighty-two years old when the book came out in 1880, and along with writing about the way Nashville was back in the early 1800s, he wrote about people who lived outside of town. What really caught my attention was what he wrote about the area south and east of Harding Road – the land that eventually became the Woodmont neighborhood.

Further back in the book I found a picture of Willoughby Williams and an account of his life. Along with his land in Davidson County, he owned a big plantation in Arkansas and lots of slaves, and he'd been president of a bank and was a friend of both Andrew Jackson and Sam Houston. He lived on Harding Road for over half a century, and I kept wondering where his house was.

It wasn't long before I went to the county courthouse and looked up the deed to our house. My parents bought it at the end of 1945, and I traced earlier deeds to the property back into the 1800s. Establishing the ownership of the surrounding land got pretty complicated, but I eventually found out who owned property in the neighborhood all the way back into the late 1700s, when the area was first settled by white people and their slaves.

I was pretty sure that our house was built on land that was part of an old plantation, and I had a suspicion that the plantation might've been owned by old Willoughby Williams himself. I turned out to be right. There was a time when he owned the whole western part of the neighborhood. His property not only owned the land where our house was and where Moon's Drugstore and Belle Meade Theater had been built beside Harding Road, Woodmont School was on the eastern part of what was once his plantation.

And I was in for a surprise. I had no idea that the house where he lived most of his life was still standing. It was right on Woodmont Boulevard. I'd been going by it for as long as I could remember. It was the house everybody avoided on Halloween because the woman who lived there was supposed to be so scary. And crazy.

I wanted to know more about the history of the neighborhood, and I started going downtown to the State Library and Archives. I'd spend the whole day looking through old newspapers and manuscript collections and census records, and after a while, I felt like I was on a journey.

At some point, it occurred to me that working with kids was also like being on a journey. I was in my seventh year of coaching. I was a lot better than I was when I started, but I still had a long way to go. The better I got at teaching kids how to tackle and block and shoot layups and play defense and hit and catch and throw, the more I wanted them to reach their potential. But pushing kids to get better could cause problems.

One of the players on my baseball team that summer was Allen Earnshaw. Even though he hadn't played before, he was pretty good. He had heart and he was really intelligent, but he had a problem when it came to hitting. Once he had two strikes, he froze up. He wouldn't swing his bat. When there are two strikes, a batter needs to swing at anything close to the strike zone, but Allen just stood there with his bat on his shoulder. He kept letting good pitches go by for strike three no matter what I said.

He loved baseball, and it was something he had to get past if he was going to play at a higher level. We worked on it in practice, but it didn't help. I finally decided to try taking him out of the game when it happened. I explained what I was doing, and he seemed to understand that I was trying to help him get better. But in the very next game, he took a called third strike in the second inning, and after I took him out he sat at the end of the bench and cried.

Allen was a good kid, but his father, who was a professor at Vanderbilt, was aloof and unfriendly. He never said anything to me, and he didn't sit with the other parents at our games. He seemed to think that being there was a waste of time.

Allen was still upset after the game was over, and Dr. Earnshaw came over and gave me a condescending look. "I'd like to hear your explanation of why Allen was taken out of the game."

As soon as I started talking he broke eye contact and looked past me. I told him about the problem Allen had with striking out with the bat on his shoulder. I explained that nothing else had worked and that I was trying to make sure Allen could keep playing baseball when he got older.

He didn't seem to be listening. Dr. Earnshaw was shorter than I was, but he lifted his chin like he was trying to look down at me. His arms were crossed and his face was tense and his lips were pushed together.

He spoke like he was giving a lecture. "It should be apparent that humiliating Allen will *not* help him work through this problem that you say he has."

I started to tell him that what I was trying with Allen had worked with other kids, but he interrupted me.

"You seem to see yourself as omniscient. Is *omniscient* a word with which you have any familiarity?"

I didn't want him to see that he was making me mad, and I didn't want him to know I was worried. I didn't think Allen would ever play baseball again if his father took him off the team, and that's what I was afraid he might be leading up to. I hoped that after he was through putting me in my place – after he cooled down – that he'd eventually understand the approach I was taking.

He was still speaking slowly, but there was anger behind every word he said. "I not only have a doctorate in psychology – I'm the Vice-Chairman of my department at Vanderbilt. Do you know what I see when I watch you coaching your team? I see a young man whose *entire identity* depends on whether or not he wins games in the arena of children's athletics."

He stared at me and shook his head. "But what is even more troubling is how you react when a child fails to perform at what you consider to be a sufficiently high level. In that case, you are more than willing to destroy that child's self-esteem in order to win a game."

He stopped talking for a few seconds, but he kept staring at me with a look of contempt. I was going to stay quiet as long as there was a chance he'd let Allen stay on the team.

Then he got around to saying what he'd been waiting to say. "I had hoped that playing baseball would be a positive experience for Allen, but his experience has been anything but positive. That being the case, he will no longer be a member of this team. You will have to maintain your sense of identity at the expense of someone else's child."

I made sure I didn't talk too fast. "Do you know what *I* see?"

He was still staring at me. "No. I have absolutely no interest in hearing anything that you have to say." He turned around and started to walk away.

He wasn't going to change his mind, and there wasn't any reason to hold back. "Isn't that exactly what a megalomaniac would say?"

He spun around and I could tell that he was furious, but he didn't say anything. I tried to imitate his speaking cadence and his dismissive tone of voice. "Wouldn't a megalomaniac be convinced of his own *omniscience*, regardless of how little he bothered to learn about a given situation?"

Then I got in another question. "And isn't it true that a megalomaniac would never see himself as a megalomaniac? I mean couldn't a man, even a pompous professor, go through his whole life and never understand what he really was?" He was fuming, but he just turned around and walked to his car.

I hated to lose Allen. I was pretty sure that by the end of the season, he would've been swinging with two strikes. And I would've told him what I always told kids after they overcame a problem. How proud of him I was, and that the next time a problem came up in his life, he'd probably be able to work his way through that challenge, too.

But there was something else. Even though Dr. Earnshaw was a jerk, there was enough truth in what he said that I had a hollow feeling in my chest for a while. It was true that when the kids on my team looked bad, I felt like it made me look bad. And when they looked good, I looked good, too. It was also true that too much of the way I saw myself was tied up in how well I coached. I'd been aware of that for a long time.

When I went to bed that night, I dredged up every mistake I could think of that I'd made with kids. The mistake that cast the darkest shadow involved what happened with a kid named Timmy Hunley. He'd been on my basketball team a year earlier.

He was a nice kid, but he seemed more like a five-year-old than a fifth-grader. There's a big difference between a wonderment-filled child and a boy. Timmy would show up at practice, and half the time he just ran around like he was at a birthday party. The other kids didn't pick on him, but they thought he was a joke.

He was never going to make a junior high school basketball team, but in a couple of years, he'd be in junior high school. If he was still acting like he was in kindergarten by then, it would be a disaster.

But there was another reason I'd wanted to get Timmy to start acting at least a little closer to his age. At times he diminished the season for the rest of the kids on his team. He consistently messed up our practices. And when I put him in a game, it was like putting a flat tire on a car. He was the only player I had who never worked on his shooting and dribbling when he was at home. As far as I could tell, he didn't do anything to try and get better.

And he wouldn't take off his shirt when we scrimmaged. One team would take off their shirts so the teams could tell each other apart, but he was shy and the team he was on always had to wear their shirts.

I thought if I could get Timmy over his problem with shyness, I could give him some praise, and then I might be able to help him change in some other ways. At the next practice, I let him be one of the captains when the teams were being chosen. After that, I gave him the ball and told him to shoot a free throw. If he made it, his team would be shirts. If he missed, they would be skins.

He missed and I told him he was a skin, but then he gave me his childish little grin and shook his head. I was frustrated and I could feel myself getting mad. He was standing by the wall in the gym, and I told him again to take off his shirt. He still wouldn't do it, and I threw a basketball and it slammed against the wall about four feet above his head.

He thought I was trying to hit him. His eyes got big and he took off his shirt as fast as he could. He fit in a little better after that, but he didn't smile much anymore and he didn't play on my team again.

I felt like I'd killed his childhood, and I never stopped feeling bad about what I did. It was probably my biggest mistake as a coach. There were times when I went too far, but most of the time – almost all of the time – things worked out okay. But I never stopped thinking that I destroyed Timmy Hunley's childhood.

Chapter 46

July 6, 1973 – It's Friday afternoon and I'm at baseball practice. Chris Carpenter just made a head-first slide into third base, and he's torn up the side of his face. He's bleeding from two or three different places, and he's doing everything he can to keep from crying. He's sprawled in the dirt, and Teddy Wilson, Nate Wheeler, and Ann Tracey are propping him up. When the rest of the team gathers around him, it reminds me of the portrait of the Death of General Wolfe at Quebec.

Chris was about to break down, but I tried to distract him. "I want to ask you something."

He looked at me, but he didn't say anything. He couldn't understand why I'd ask him a question while his nose and the left side of his face were bleeding.

I tried to sound clinical. "Have you ever thought about what pain is?" I kept talking while I was helping him up. "Look at what you're experiencing right now. All those nerve cells are transmitting messages to your brain."

A couple of the kids were looking at me like I was crazy.

Chris was gritting his teeth. He was still fighting back his tears and there was anger in his voice. "I *know*."

I walked with him to the water fountain, and everybody else tagged along. I kept trying to distract him. "Zillions of cells are firing messages, and the messages are going up into your brain at a zillion miles an hour. Your brain is creating the sensation you're feeling right now. So what is pain? I mean isn't it really just an illusion?"

I had a first aid kit in my car, and after a few minutes, I started cleaning him up. He was staring at me. He still looked irritated. "*What is pain?* I can't believe you asked me that."

I shrugged. "Well, I guess I could've just stood around and watched you bleeding in the dirt."

Once I got everybody back together, I said we might as well rate his injury on a scale of one to ten. Teddy Wilson was Chris's best friend and he gave it a ten.

Nate Wheeler, the team smart aleck, had an immediate objection. "There's *no way* that was a ten. Look at his face. One side doesn't even have a scratch. To get a ten, *both sides* of his face should be messed up. And he's almost stopped bleeding. He probably won't even need stitches."

Chris was starting to smile. Nate gave the injury an 8.5 and everybody else started booing. He raised his arms and taunted the rest of the teammates. "That's right, keep on booing. Only a bunch of complete *idiots* would think that was a ten. And he didn't even cry. He was lucky to get an eight-and-a-half."

Ted glanced over at me. "Well he was *about* to cry, but then *somebody* asked him about pain."

The kids all looked at me.

I just shrugged. "So I shouldn't have tried to take his mind off how much he was suffering? You should all be telling me how impressed you are. I not only kept Chris from worrying about being disfigured for life, I turned it into a learning experience."

I took my turn at taunting the crowd. "But I guess it isn't your fault that you aren't bright enough to follow what I was saying."

The booing died down after a few seconds. "I just wish John McMillan was still on the team. He would've understood *exactly* what I've been talking about." I looked at them one by one like I was searching for somebody who was at least marginally intelligent. Then I let out a long sigh and gazed up at the sky again.

"Every time I try to tell them about anything that doesn't involve sports, they act bored."

I looked at them again. "Okay, even though you won't understand what I'm about to say, I'm going to say it anyway."

They probably thought I was about to take another stab at explaining that a thousand years earlier, Indian children had played all over that part of the neighborhood, or that frontiersmen and slaves and Civil War soldiers once walked across the land that became their backyards. Most of them already had expressions of amused defiance.

But instead of talking about history, I repeated what I'd said about pain being an illusion. Then I told them how important it was to understand the way their senses worked. I pointed out that even though they thought they were seeing me, all they were seeing was an image created in their brains. All they were seeing was their own matter.

I tried to explain that light was bouncing off what they saw as my body, and then coming into their eyes and activating their retinas. From there I went into how the light set off a chain reaction that traveled along their optic nerves, and on to the parts of their brains where the image of what they thought they saw was created.

And I told them that instead of hearing the sound of my voice, all they really heard was their own brain matter reacting to waves that were moving through the air and coming in contact with their eardrums. I tried to explain that the vibration of their eardrums triggered reactions deep in their brains, where they interpreted the sound of my voice. Then I told them that what they touched and smelled and tasted were also just interpretations created in their brains.

I didn't say anything else for a few seconds. There were a few blank stares and some daydreaming was going on, but a few of the kids seemed to be taking in what I said. I went ahead and told them a little more. "I'm fairly sure that particles of light don't have color and that sound waves don't make any noise, and I'm positive that individual molecules don't have any smell."

Charlie Edwards couldn't help himself. "Then I guess it's really true. He who smelt it dealt it."

I had a little more to say, and I waited for the laughter to die down. "We never experience anything except our own senses. The world might be exactly the way it seems to be, but what if it isn't? How can we be sure that what we sense isn't just a dream?"

If they were older I might've said a little more about awareness. I'd never stopped wondering what awareness was. As far as I knew, the part of the human brain where awareness was located had never been identified. I wasn't sure that awareness ended up in our brains. Sometimes I thought human beings might just be receptors. It seemed possible that what we experienced could be transmitted to a higher consciousness.

I wondered if that could be our function – to live our lives and transmit our experiences. If that was the way it was, maybe our awareness didn't die with our bodies. And there were other possibilities I didn't tell them about.

The kids had gotten pretty quiet, and I was trying to think of something funny to say. But before I came up with anything, Nate stood up. He was gesturing and moving his mouth like he was talking, but he wasn't making a sound. Then he started walking around like he couldn't see, even though his eyes were open.

He acted like he couldn't hear the other kids laughing. He kept moving around like he was a prisoner of his senses, and then the other kids started doing it, too. They didn't look all that different from the deaf and blind kids I'd seen at Clover Bottom back when I was in college. I watched my players moving back and forth across the infield, and they kept wandering around until they finally got bored.

That night, before I fell asleep, I thought about the kids on my team acting like zombies. I wondered which ones were portraying the adults they'd eventually become. I told myself that if I was teaching them in school – if I had them in class every day – I'd have a better chance of keeping them from growing up to live the lives of the walking dead.

Sometimes I tried to imagine what it would be like to teach at a school like Woodmont had been, back before busing. It wouldn't take me too long to go back to Peabody and get certified, but even if I got hired somewhere, I'd have to change the way I did things. I still didn't think I'd be very good with kids if I couldn't be myself.

I wanted to find a respectable career where I could be myself. A job would give my parents some peace of mind, and it would get my friends off my back. Sometimes when we got together they'd look at me, and then they'd look at each other and start singing the old rock and roll song, *Get a Job*.

They were always on me about being unemployed, but I acted like it didn't bother me. I said that as far as I could tell, society already had enough bankers and lawyers and businessmen and accountants and insurance salesmen. I told them if they knew of a job that wasn't being done, to let me know what it was and maybe I'd give it a shot.

It wouldn't have done any good to mention that I was spending at least as much time researching my neighborhood as they spent doing their jobs. But the way my friends and my parents and the rest of society saw it, if something didn't involve getting a paycheck, it didn't qualify as work.

At least I was learning a lot. By the summer of 1973, I'd learned the boundaries of each of the five farms that once covered what became the Woodmont neighborhood. Some of the property lines from back before the Civil War ran along current streets, and a few lines were still marked by rows of old trees that had started growing up in fence rows back in the 1800s.

But I mostly focused on Willoughby Williams. He'd lived on his land for sixty years. I pictured him riding across what became my backyard, or across what ended up being the baseball field behind Woodmont School. I kept slipping into the school after baseball practice, and sometimes I looked out the windows and thought about the slaves who had lived and worked and died on the Williams Place.

The soil around the site of Woodmont School was too shallow for crops. I was pretty sure the school was built on what had been a pasture. When I tried to picture what happened there back before the Civil War, I kept imagining a black man tending a herd of cows. I imagined him wearing ragged clothes and an old wide-brimmed hat, and walking past what was then a small ash tree when he was on his way to get a drink from the little creek a few feet away.

Chapter 47

We ended up winning our league championship, and we came in third in the City Tournament. When we had our team party, there was still a nasty-looking scab beside Chris Carpenter's nose, but by the time football practice came around, his face had healed.

I had the best football team I'd ever coached. We practiced on the big field out in front of West End Junior High School, and an all-black team from a different league practiced there, too. Most of the kids on my team had been bused to an elementary school in North Nashville in 1972, and they knew some of the guys on the other team.

Things were a little rough the year before, in the initial period of busing. During their first week of school, a few of the black kids decided to show the white kids who was in charge of the fifth grade, and some of the meeker kids got roughed up at recess.

Nate Wheeler was able to talk his way out of an altercation in the boy's bathroom, but Teddy Wilson wasn't much of a talker. He knocked down a kid who took a swing at him on the playground. Charlie Edwards was a talker, but he turned out to be even more of a fighter, and he gave the guy who came at him a bloody nose. There weren't as many problems after that.

They were the toughest group I'd ever coached and it was a good thing they were. The other coach and I made friends pretty fast, and it wasn't long before our teams were scrimmaging against each other. His team was fast and really physical, but we were almost as good as they were. After we'd played against them for a couple of weeks, we were a little better.

Depending on whether their families could afford to send them to a private school, and depending on what kind of students they were, when they got to seventh grade most of my ex-players went to either Montgomery Bell Academy or to West End Junior High School. Some of the guys who had played for me were on West's football team, and I wanted to see them play a game or two during the season.

September 27, 1973 – It's Thursday after practice and I'm walking up to the West football field. It's been a while since I've seen a Junior High School game. Most of the players are pretty awkward and slow. I wonder if I would've been able to play if I'd gone to a school like West instead of Battle Ground Academy. Surely to God, I was better than some of the guys stumbling around out on the field. Dan Thorne is standing beside the fence watching his son, Danny, who was on my team three years ago. I don't know whether I should go over and talk to him. He likes me and he's a nice guy, but he might rather be by himself.

Dan had played football at West back in the 1950s. When I was coaching Danny, he told me about his senior year. West had a home game against Hillsboro on a Friday night, and he tackled Steve Thomas, who was a star halfback at Hillsboro.

Thomas groaned when Dan hit him, and Thomas didn't get up right away. He was finally able to walk over to the sideline, but a few minutes later he collapsed while he was sitting on the bench. He was rushed to the hospital, and he died two days later. He never regained consciousness.

It turned out that Steve Thomas had taken a really hard hit to the side of his head a few games earlier in the season. That was when most of the damage was done. When Dan told me about it, I was pretty sure he was worried that the same thing could happen to his son. The day I saw him at West, it looked like he was watching Danny's game, but he might've been thinking about that Friday night back in 1955.

I knew about Steve Thomas before Dan told me about him, and I'd known about him before I saw his photograph in the trophy case at Woodmont. I remembered hearing my parents talk about his death right after it happened. I kept wondering what he experienced when he was losing consciousness. I wondered if everything just melted together when the world was going black.

I was on my way over to say something to Dan Thorne when I saw Callie Lee about fifty feet away. My heart picked up about half a beat as soon as I saw her. She was standing with some other girls. The rest of the girls were talking to each other, but she was watching the game. I didn't expect to see her at West. I thought she went to Harpeth Hall, the private school where a lot of Woodmont girls went after sixth grade.

I stayed where I was and went through all the reasons why I shouldn't look over at her. I kept watching the game, but I wasn't paying much attention to what was going on. I was trying to figure out why I was reacting to her like I was a ninth-grade boy. I didn't leave until the game was over, and by then she was already gone. I was pretty sure she didn't see me.

West had another home game the next week and I walked up after practice and saw most of the second half. I looked around from time to time, but there was no sign of Callie Lee. I kept telling myself I was glad she wasn't there. Dan Thorne was standing beside the fence again, and I went over and stood with him.

I finally mentioned Steve Thomas. Dan said he thought about what happened every day of his life. He went through the whole story again, and I finally asked him where Steve was sitting when he fell off the bench. After the game, we walked over and he pointed to the place where he collapsed, but he didn't go near the bench. I went home and wrote a poem about it.

The pain...
Diminishing,
The sounds
Of the band
And the cheerleaders
And the whistles of the referees...
Blending together,
The sounds
Of the people in the stands...
Fading into a distant murmur,
The stadium lights...
Swirling into the sky
Like a whirlwind of stars,
Friday night...
Receding into a dream.

I read through the poem a couple of times, but my mind kept drifting away from 1955. Callie Lee had been wearing a gray T-shirt and faded jeans, and I kept picturing the way she looked.

I didn't want to be drawn to her just because she was beautiful. If I had to be drawn to her, I also wanted it to be because of whatever set her apart from the girls she was with. She seemed completely detached from everybody else when she was standing by the fence watching the game. I wondered what made her seem so different.

It reminded me a little of the way things had been with Yancey Walsh, but the way I felt when I saw Callie Lee was more intense than how I felt when Yancey was walking up to me at the swimming pool at Belle Meade Club.

The feeling was also more intense than when I saw Bethany Brussard for the first time, and it was completely different from the way it was with the Blonde Bombshell, or with any of the divorced mothers I visited when they had a house all to themselves. Callie was probably stirring up plenty of lust, but it seemed to be pretty well bottled up.

I was trying to figure out what was going on. The only explanation I had was that I might finally be having the feelings I should've experienced when I was a teenager. Back then, when guys saw Yancey Walsh, I wondered if they felt the same way I felt when I looked at Callie. I kept thinking back to 1963. When I was singing Dream Lover. When I wouldn't let myself crawl out of my bedroom window and go to the party down the street. When I screamed into my pillow. When I ached for a girl like Callie Lee.

Ten years later, the God of Rock and Roll was taunting me. Hearing *Let's Get It On* was bad enough, but *Here I Am, Come and Take Me* was worse. It got to the point where I started laughing when either one of those songs came on the radio. I laughed, but there were times when I felt like I was standing in quicksand. There were times I felt like a pervert.

But I found a little refuge when I heard *Higher Ground*, which I was trying to find by staying away from West End Junior High football games. I started settling down after a while, and I kept asking myself how I could get turned upside-down by a ninth-grade girl. I told myself to stop thinking about her, but then I'd hear *Who's That Lady?* The wailing guitar reminded me of Callie Lee every time it came on the radio.

It seemed like history was mocking me, too. Just about every marriage I ran across when I was researching the neighborhood was between a groom in his twenties or thirties and a bride who was in her teens.

West Junior High was on land that had been owned by Joseph Erwin, the builder of *Peach Blossom*, where I'd found the bullet back in 1967. Erwin's daughter, Jane, was fourteen when she married. Her husband, Charles Dickinson, who was killed by Andrew Jackson in the duel, was almost twenty-three at the time.

After Erwin moved to Louisiana, the same land passed to Charles Bosley. When Bosley was forty-one, he married a girl who was nineteen. Jesse Wharton, who owned an adjoining farm, was twenty-nine and his wife was seventeen when they got married. And Willoughby Williams was twenty-five years old when he married in 1823. His bride was sixteen.

All the rationalizing I did made me feel a little better, but then I reminded myself that if Callie Lee and I were both around in the early 1800s, she would've been courted by the handsome son of a rich plantation owner, or by some war hero. I kept thinking that if I'd been alive back then, I would've probably ended up with the buck-toothed daughter of a struggling merchant, or the overweight daughter of a preacher, or with some other desperate young woman teetering on the brink of spinsterhood.

Chapter 48

October 17, 1973 – It's a sunny Wednesday afternoon. The field in front of West is alive with kids in football uniforms. The air is light and warm, and the wind is blowing from the south. Leaves are drifting down from the trees and dancing across the grass. A photographer showed up a few minutes ago and he has my team arranged into three rows. He's looking through the viewfinder of his camera.

Instead of saying cheese, he tells us to say champions, but Nate Wheeler says "pussies" and the kids are all laughing when the first photograph is taken. The photographer smiles at Nate and asks a question. "Is that your team nickname?" Then there's more laughter until I get everybody settled down. He takes another photograph and he says it looks good, but he takes a couple more just in case.

The camera captured a team of fifth and sixth-grade boys in football uniforms on an autumn afternoon. A few minutes later, while the kids were running through their plays, I wondered how many of them would eventually show the photograph to their own kids. And I wondered how much they'd remember about the season that was coming to a close.

They probably wouldn't forget that they won every game they played, and they might remember a few big touchdowns. I hoped they'd also remember the fun they had at practice and how it felt to get up on Saturday mornings and put on their uniforms and go to the games, and the way the grass smelled on warm October days and how much they liked being with each other.

I was pretty sure they'd also remember some of the things we did that didn't involve football. Early in the season, I recruited three or four fathers and a couple of older brothers, and we drove west for an hour and a half and took a canoe trip down the Buffalo River.

A few weeks after that we went east to the Cumberland Plateau and hiked through a gorge that connected two waterfalls. When we were walking up a creek, Sam Howell, who was a gritty little fifth-grader, spotted a rattlesnake. Then he found a forked stick and kept the snake's head pinned against a rock while everybody else went by. That would probably be right at the top of what the kids would remember about our season.

I tried to memorize everything I could about that particular afternoon. I looked across Bowling Avenue at the six-unit apartment building where my parents lived right after they were married.

They were on the top floor, and on the Sunday morning when news of the attack on Pearl Harbor came over the radio, they were in bed. I wondered what they were like back when they were in their twenties, and how many times they looked out at the field where I was standing.

The kids ran through the rest of our plays, and after we went over a new defense, I asked them what they wanted to do next. I already knew they wanted to play Smear the Queer. I divided them up into several equal teams, and they clobbered each other until they finally got tired. After that, they sat down and I started talking about our game on Saturday.

It was our last game, and I was telling them how much the season meant to me. At first they seemed to be listening about as much as they usually did, but then I noticed that some of them were gazing off in the distance. I thought that what I was saying must really be hitting home, but then I turned around.

Callie Lee and a girl I didn't know were standing about fifty feet away. After I smiled and nodded at them, I started talking to my team again, but I could tell that the girls were still back there.

Charlie Edwards and Teddy Wilson, who were already falling into the clutches of puberty, kept staring past me and they had especially intense looks on their faces. None of the other guys on the team had lost as much focus as Teddy and Charlie, but they were all distracted. After a couple of minutes, I said practice was over, but only three or four kids got up to leave.

The girls seemed to be waiting for me, and I walked back to see what they wanted. I was trying to think of something to say that wouldn't sound stupid. And I reminded myself not to stare at Callie Lee, and not to ignore her friend.

Before I got to them the other girl spoke up. "Would you like to buy a raffle ticket and help West End Junior High? The tickets are just a dollar each." She must've known that she sounded like she was in a bad commercial, and she started laughing.

Callie Lee shook her head and then she gave me a long look. "This is Claire. I got sick of hearing her bitch about all the raffle tickets she hasn't sold, so I brought her down here. But I wouldn't buy one if I were you." Claire gave her a half-shove and started laughing again, and Callie Lee shoved her back.

I pretended to be curious. "What's getting raffled off?"

Claire was still laughing. "It's... It's a car."

Callie Lee elaborated. "It's a crappy VW Beetle with about 400,000 miles on it."

Claire tried to shove her. "Shut up, Callie."

Callie Lee pushed her away again. "And it probably won't even start."

I reached into my pocket and pulled out a couple of dollars. "Well, I could *really* use a broken-down car that won't start, so I'll take two tickets." I looked at Callie Lee. "And I guess it wouldn't hurt to improve my odds a little bit. Are you selling tickets, too?" She said she had some at home. The drawing wasn't until the next day – at halftime of West's homecoming game. She said if I was coming to the game, and if I got there in time, I could buy them from her then.

The girls headed back up toward the school. Callie Lee looked every bit as good walking away as she had when she was looking at me with the sun and the wind in her hair. When I finally turned around, five or six of my players were still there. They were sitting in awestruck reverence. They reminded me of the way my baseball team had looked when I was talking to Yancey Walsh beside the pool at Belle Meade Club. They were curious about the girls, but they were trying to be cool about it.

Charlie finally spoke up. "Okay, what's the story?"

I acted like I wasn't sure what he was talking about. "You mean those girls? What about them?"

I was trying to guess what was coming next. Charlie was doing his best not to smile. "Well, we were wondering if they were prostitutes. I mean you gave one of them some money. How much would Miss Universe cost – a hundred bucks?"

The other kids were grinning and doing their best to look worldly. Nate Wheeler piped up. "A hundred? How about a *thousand*."

I pretended to look confused. "Are you guys talking about the girl in the sweatpants?"

Ted and Charlie didn't bother to respond, but everybody else was shaking their heads. When Nate finally spoke up, he used as facetious a tone as he could. "No, we mean the *other* one."

I acted like I was trying to picture Callie Lee. "You mean the blonde girl wearing the jeans?"

They all started nodding.

I shrugged and tried to look surprised. "It's funny that you mentioned her. She said she wanted to earn a little extra money. She came down here to ask if I knew of any families that might need a babysitter. But don't worry. I told her that when it came to babysitters, I was pretty sure none of you would want to spend half the night alone in your house with some teenage girl." Even Andy Pickard, who was a fairly wholesome fifth-grader, looked crestfallen.

We didn't have practice the next day and I made it to the West game just in time for the kickoff. Callie Lee didn't show up until the second quarter. Several men were staring at her when she was walking in. I couldn't tell if they were fathers or teachers. She came over to where I was and held out the tickets. "You still want to waste your money?"

"Sure. Why not?"

"Cause you ain't gonna win that crappy car."

I handed her four dollars. "Maybe I'll get lucky. Maybe I'll get as lucky as you were back in sixth grade when you threw that last baseball at the Woodmont Carnival."

She gave me a dismissive look before she went off to turn in my tickets. Her friend, Claire, was standing nearby and she walked over and gave me a big smile. "Hey, remember me?"

"How could I forget somebody resourceful enough to sell raffle tickets during a football practice?"

She kept smiling. "That was Callie's idea. A few weeks ago we saw you at a game, and she said you used to coach some of the guys we know. Then yesterday my teacher got mad at me 'cause I hadn't sold any tickets. Callie said you were out in front of the school just about every day coaching your team, and that you might buy one."

I was surprised that Callie knew so much about me. I felt like I was going over the top of a roller coaster. I told Claire I was glad they came by, but before I said anything else the winner of the drawing was announced over the loudspeaker. While a significantly overweight woman in her forties was hurrying out onto the field to claim her prize, Callie walked up and gave me a light punch on my right arm. "Well, better luck next time." I tightened up my bicep just in time.

I didn't have a reason to be at West once football was over, but I went to the first home basketball game under the pretext that I was there to watch Rusty Willis, who was one of the best players on their team. I would've gone to see him play at some point anyway, but it wouldn't have been that early in the season.

I spotted Dan Thorne, and I went over and sat with him. At

some point, he mentioned how bad West's girls' team was. Then he said that one of the best athletes in the school was a girl, but she wasn't playing. I was pretty sure I knew who he was talking about, but I didn't say anything. I let him point out Callie across the gym, and then I asked him why she wasn't playing.

Dan's son, Danny, knew her pretty well. He said that Callie liked sports, but she didn't like being on teams. He said that she used to live in Texas, but after her parents split up, Callie and her mother moved to Tennessee.

Sometimes I had practice, but I went to as many West games as I could. I usually saw Callie out in the lobby before the game, or at halftime. We'd talk a little, but that was about it.

A few of the guys I'd coached at Woodmont showed up at the games, too. Along with keeping up with them, I got to know Claire and a couple of Callie's other friends. I tried to treat Callie the same way I treated everybody else, but sometimes I had the feeling that she knew why I kept showing up. If she did know, she didn't seem to mind.

Chapter 49

March 12, 1974 – It's one o'clock on Tuesday afternoon, and I'm in the corridor outside the hearing room of the Nashville Board of Zoning Appeals. I've been waiting since nine this morning with about fifty other long-time residents of the Woodmont neighborhood. We've come to oppose the expansion of a condominium development that will be built near what used to be Herbert's Field. The developer is trying to get permission to build twice as many housing units as the zoning ordinances allow. The developer, followed by a lawyer and an architect and a traffic engineer, shows up and walks past us. A couple of minutes after they go inside, we are told that we can go in, too.

The room is crowded. The architectural drawings of the development are displayed on easels. Old Mrs. Hill gets up first. She says that she's lived in the same place since 1910. Her house is right across the street from the development. She tries to explain that putting so many houses on such a small piece of land will change the character of the neighborhood. The members of the board are sitting behind a long desk, but they aren't listening. And they aren't listening when other neighbors get up and talk about all the additional traffic, and about the destruction of the beautiful old trees that cover the property.

I was one of the last speakers. By the time I got to the podium, it was pretty obvious that the members of the Board of Zoning Appeals were there to serve the interests of the developer, whose name was Cyrus Wolff.

The staff attorney, Lonny East, treated Mr. Wolff and his

attorney like they were members of his family. His principal function seemed to be hurrying along the people who got up to speak. Lonny East was standing to one side of where the board members were sitting, and he and Mr. Wolfe kept whispering to each other.

I started off talking about how I grew up in the neighborhood, and that I'd been coaching neighborhood boys since the mid-1960s. I said that from what I'd seen, there was already too much development and it was detrimental to the kids I was coaching.

Something close to a scowl came over Lonny East's face, but then he shook his head and pretended to laugh. "And how does *that* happen?"

I ignored his sarcasm. "It happens all sorts of ways. When I was the same age as the kids I coach, there wasn't much traffic and everybody pretty much knew everybody else. Parents didn't worry about their children being safe, and kids could roam all over the neighborhood. There was a big field where we played baseball and football, and we rode our bicycles to Richland Creek and went fishing. Growing up that way taught us to rely on ourselves."

He crossed his arms in front of his chest. "Now let me guess – that's *all* changed because of development." He raised his eyebrows and looked over at Mr. Wolff and his lawyer.

"That's exactly what happened. The field where my friends and I played ball has houses on it, and after a supermarket was built right next to the creek, pollution started draining from the parking lot and killed off the fish. And you don't see many kids riding around the neighborhood on bicycles anymore. There are too many cars on the roads, and the people living in all the new houses are mostly strangers."

Lonny East looked at his watch, but I kept talking. "The more development there is, the less independent kids are going to be. Kids used to play outside together all the time. Now there usually has to be an adult around to supervise everything."

When Mr. Wolff looked at his watch, Lonny East interrupted

me. "Well if we made decisions based on things like that, we wouldn't have much of a city."

I jumped in before he could say anything else. "But we'd have a great town."

When some of the people from the neighborhood started clapping, he held up his hand. "Folks, if this turns into a pep rally we'll be here all day. Does anybody *else* have anything to say?" Nobody else from the neighborhood spoke, and the vote was taken. The board voted unanimously in favor of doubling the number of units in Mr. Wolff's development. As we were filing out, Mr. Wolff and Lonny East were having a conversation at the back of the room.

I was angry. The hearing was a sham and I didn't understand how zoning rules could be ignored in the face of so much neighborhood opposition. The whole way home I was mad at myself for not saying more than I had.

I hadn't said a word about how the next developer who came along would also want permission to build extra units, and if that kept happening it wouldn't take long to destroy what was left of the neighborhood. I should've pointed out how wrong it was to keep treating neighborhoods like they were nothing more than business opportunities for outside speculators.

And there was something else I didn't say. I should've confronted the big lie that was brought up every time a development was questioned. Whenever developers were pushed to justify what they were doing, they said that if a city didn't grow it would die.

I understood that Mr. Wolff and his beady-eyed, smirking lawyer wouldn't have listened, and neither would a pawn like Lonny East. But I should've pointed out that the area a city could occupy was finite. If it was true that a city *really* died when it stopped growing, then it should only be allowed to grow very slowly.

A bulldozer was brought to the property three weeks later. The oaks and beeches and poplars and walnuts and maples were just beginning to get their leaves. I stood by with a few other people from the neighborhood as the trees were leveled one by one and pushed into a pile to be burned. The last tree to go was a huge oak.

I closed my eyes for a few seconds when the blade of the bulldozer slashed into its bark. It didn't budge at first, but then the cleats of the dozer dug in and the operator started rocking his machine up and back. The tree shook and began to lean, and its roots started popping up before there was a final crack and it crashed to the ground.

An official from the State Division of Forestry came by and took a core sample from the big tree, which he identified as a Bur Oak. Then it was pushed into the pile and burned. When I called the Forestry Division a few days later, the official told me the tree had probably been standing since the late 1600s. He said it was healthy and there was no telling how much longer it could've lived.

But a man with more money than he knew what to do with decided that he needed to be even richer. I ended up writing a poem about it.

A Dark Wind

The sapling escaped
The trampling hooves
Of the buffalo and elk
And deer,
And it survived
Wallowing bears
And falling trees,
And there were blizzards
And ice storms,
But the sapling
Grew up strong and straight.
Men who hunted
Came and went

Until the bear
And the elk and the buffalo
Were gone,
And when light-skinned farmers
Came to settle,
A cabin was built nearby.
People with dark skin
Worked in the fields
And the farm
Became a plantation,
And after men in uniforms
Began to pass back and forth
Beneath the branches
Of the massive tree,
A great battle was fought
And the land was a farm again.
The farm eventually
Became a neighborhood,
And the tree remained
Until a dark wind
Blew from the empty hearts
Of shallow men
And the tree was destroyed
To make room for yet another house.

The men on the Board of Zoning Appeals were not the impartial individuals they pretended to be. Before long it occurred to me that when it came to Callie, I wasn't who I seemed to be either. I'd go to games like I was there to watch my old players, and when I talked to her I acted like she was still just another kid who'd gone to Woodmont.

Sometimes I wondered what would happen if I just came out and told her the truth. But I wasn't sure what the truth was. If I went back to see Dr. Harrelson – if he injected me with a big dose of truth serum and asked me what was going on – I couldn't have told him.

I kept my eyes off Callie as much as I could when I was around her. My lust was still bottled up inside my guilt, but lust was only part of what drew me to her. I was also drawn to her independence. There were times when it was like she was in some other dimension. It seemed strange, but sometimes I felt like she was older than I was.

I kept telling myself that in five years – when she was twenty – I'd only be thirty-one. I kept telling myself that I might need to wait till then before I could be honest with her. In the meantime, I thought the best I could do was stay at the edge of her life and try to figure out why she had such a hold on me.

Chapter 50

May 13, 1974 – It's late on Monday afternoon. Baseball practice is over, but Charlie Edwards and Teddy Wilson are still hanging around. All the teachers have left for the day and the school is empty. I'm waiting to go in through the basement door. I've brought along a new book by James Michener. It's called Centennial – which is the name of the fictional Colorado town where the story takes place. The book traces the history of the town and the surrounding area. It starts in the age of the dinosaurs and comes all the way up into modern times. I was planning to start reading it in the Woodmont library, but Charlie and Teddy seem like they want to talk to me.

I was rearranging the equipment in the trunk of my car when they finally walked over. Charlie had a serious look on his face. "Well, it happened." There was a touch of pride in his voice. "And Teddy did it, too."

"Am I supposed to know what you're talking about?"

Teddy smiled. "It shouldn't be all that hard to guess."

I looked at Teddy and then I looked at Charlie. "Let's see. You've done something you seem to be proud of, but you won't just come out and say it. So what did you guys do – kiss a girl?"

Charlie looked over at Teddy and laughed. "Like it would be *really big news* if we kissed a girl."

I was afraid I knew what they were trying to tell me, but I hoped I was wrong. "So if your big secret *isn't* that you kissed a girl ..." I let my voice trail off and then I acted like I'd suddenly figured it out. "Oh, I know. You kissed a *boy!* No, wait you ... *you kissed each other!*"

Charlie jumped in before I could say anything else. "We did it with a girl."

I knew that the way I reacted was important, but I wasn't sure what I should say. "Okay, what happened."

After they got home from our game on Saturday, they rode their bikes down to Moon's Drugstore to look at comic books and get some candy. They ran into a seventh-grade girl they knew and then they all went up into a field behind the parking lot. They already knew the girl was wild, and it wasn't long before they found out just how wild she was. There was no way that either one of them had used protection.

I tried to be analytical. "So what are you going to do now?"

"Nothing I guess," Charlie said.

Teddy looked puzzled. "Is there something we're *supposed* to do?"

I did my best to sound neutral. "I mean are you just going to wait around till she finds out if she's pregnant?" I could tell that they weren't following what I was saying and I tried again. "What do you think she'll do if she's pregnant?"

They seemed to be thinking about it, but neither one of them said anything.

I stayed matter-of-fact. "See if this sounds right. If she *is* pregnant, the first thing she'll do is tell her mother. Then her mother will tell her father. And after that, her parents will be making a phone call to your parents."

They didn't seem as worried as they should've been, and I started to think they might've exaggerated what happened. "So have you thought about telling your parents before that happens? I mean if she *is* pregnant you ..."

Then Charlie started talking. It turned out that their acts were closer to *attempted* acts, and the more I heard about what they didn't quite do, the harder it was to keep from laughing.

A few minutes after they went home, I was reading in the library. The more I read about Michener's fictional history of Centennial, Colorado, the more I thought about the actual history of the Woodmont neighborhood.

Sometimes at night I'd lie in bed and try to picture the people who had lived on the land where I was living. The entire north side of the neighborhood, including the campuses of both West Junior High and Montgomery Bell Academy, once belonged to Charles Bosley, who'd been an Indian fighter and a slave trader. He died there at the age of ninety-three.

The eastern part of the neighborhood, all the way over to Hillsboro Road, was owned by Jesse Wharton. He was a United States Senator, and before he had a nervous breakdown and died in the wake of a financial disaster, he was a close political ally of Andrew Jackson.

The southern edge of the Woodmont neighborhood belonged to Henry Compton. He fathered several children by a mulatto slave woman, and had several other children by his white wife. The middle part of the neighborhood, including the sites of Herbert's Field and Tom Hendrickson's basketball court, was a small farm owned by an old man named William Owen, who outlived four of his wives.

But it was still Willoughby Williams, the individual whose plantation comprised the whole western side of what became the Woodmont neighborhood, who intrigued me the most.

I was learning about the history of the neighborhood and coaching my teams, and even though I'd only seen her once since the end of West's basketball season, I thought about Callie Lee all the time. When I finally ran into her at Moon's Drugstore at the end of May, she seemed a little guarded. It wasn't the first time that I wondered if she knew what I was trying to hide.

I didn't like staying in the shadows. I kept telling myself that if she was picking up on the feelings I had, I should tell her what was going on. I wanted more than a friendship, but I told myself that if a friendship was as far as things would eventually go, then a friendship would be enough.

But there was a lot more to think about than coaching and neighborhood history and an underage girl. I'd been out of college for three years and I still didn't have a full-time job. It was harder and harder for my parents to disguise how disappointed and worried they were. They wanted me to have a career and to start making a living, but I was just coaching kids for free. And there were still plenty of jokes from my friends about how I was unemployed and living at home.

It wouldn't have been so bad if I thought my parents were wrong. But I was pretty sure they were right. Mike Higgins had said it over four years earlier. Unless something changed, all anybody would see after a while was an unmarried guy who worked at odd jobs, and who lived with his mother and father. I didn't know how much longer I could keep doing what I was doing.

But things could've been a lot worse. I could've been Richard Nixon. Watching the Watergate investigation was like watching an avalanche in slow motion. Nixon's own Attorney General had appointed a Special Prosecutor, but Nixon refused to surrender the tapes of conversations that had been recorded in the Oval Office. After he fired the Special Prosecutor, I didn't see how he could stick around for much longer.

July 25, 1974 – It's Thursday night and I'm hitting infield to my team just before the start of our game in the semifinals of the city baseball tournament. We're playing the Kappa Tomcats, who've won the tournament two years in a row. They'll probably win it again this year. Fifteen or twenty older black guys are standing beside the fence on the first base line, and they're heckling my players. I went to the Tomcats game last night and the same group of guys did the same thing to an all-black team from East Nashville. When a kid on the other team missed a ball or made a bad throw, they rode him until somebody else messed up. Some of the men look as young as twenty, but a few are probably forty.

Teams were supposed to get their players from inside a limited area. Every kid on my team lived less than a mile from Woodmont School, but the Tomcats players were drawn from all across the city. We were basically playing a black all-star team. Nothing had been done about the recruiting the Tomcats did, and nothing had been done about the Tomcats crowd – despite their reputation for getting out of line. League officials didn't want to be called racists.

We were taking infield and I hit a ball to Jimmy Franklin. It took a bad hop, and a guy who looked half-drunk yelled out, "C'*mon* Third Base, you gotta have more than *that*." And the man next to him was even louder. "Hey little man, if you that scared of the ball, take you little butt back on home to Mama."

That got a few laughs and they stood around waiting for their next victim. I had tried to prepare my kids for what might happen, but most of them looked somewhere between uncomfortable and scared.

I got the team together out at the pitchers mound. I asked them if they wanted to shake up the jackasses standing along the fence. They looked like I was about to tell them how to escape from the Alamo. They listened to what I told them, and then they went back out to their positions. Nothing happened until after I'd hit them a few more balls.

Charlie Edwards was playing first base and Chris Carpenter, who had a really good arm, was playing shortstop. When I hit the ball to Chris, he picked it up and threw it as hard as he could toward first. It really had some heat behind it. Charlie jumped up like he was trying to catch it, but it went about five feet over his head.

The ball cleared the fence and went into the crowd. It hit a chubby guy in a Tomcats T-shirt in the thigh, and there was a lot of laughter from the rest of the hecklers when he started hobbling around. The kids didn't seem as scared after that.

The home plate umpire was a black guy named Dorris Armfield. He'd called my games before, and we knew each other pretty well. He looked over at me as he was walking past our dugout. He was trying not to laugh. "Looks like big man had a little trouble gettin out the way. Tell your shortstop to put a little more on it next time."

When we were about to take the field in the top of the first inning, I was still trying to decide whether I should go ahead and even things up. I'd put some balls in the freezer the night before, and I brought them along in a cooler just in case. I didn't feel good about doing it, but "just in case" came when the heckling started up again.

Teddy Wilson was pitching. He had no idea the balls were frozen on the inside. They felt the same way they always felt. It was the third inning before what I'd done made any difference.

The Tomcats' best player, a big strong kid named Jerome, was batting and one of Teddy's pitches came in a little high and right down the middle of the plate. Jerome crushed it. It would've gone over the center field fence and maybe over a light pole, but Nate Wheeler came in a few steps and made a routine catch to end the inning.

The Tomcat coach broke the rules and some of the fans were sorry excuses for human beings, but Jerome was just a kid playing baseball and I'd taken something away from him. He would've probably remembered the monster home run he should've hit for the rest of his life. After that, I put the frozen balls away.

Even though we were using regular balls, Teddy had only allowed two base runners by the time we started the last inning. We scored a run in the top of the seventh, but Jerome came up again with one out and a runner on base in the bottom of the inning.

I almost put in Chris to finish up, but Teddy wanted to stay in the game. The second ball he threw was a pretty good pitch, but Jerome hit a long home run to left field that barely stayed fair, and we lost 2-1. After the game, when I shook Jerome's hand and congratulated him, he looked me in the eye and smiled. He seemed like a really good kid.

The day before our game with the Tomcats, the Supreme Court ruled that President Nixon had to surrender all recordings of White House conversations to investigators. Two days after the game, Nixon was cited for obstruction of justice. He resigned from the presidency two weeks later.

My father didn't think that Nixon should've been impeached, and he didn't think he should've resigned. Sometimes when he dug in on something, it was hard to reason with him.

I didn't want to argue with him about Nixon. Our relationship was under enough pressure as it was. When he was my age, he was married and he owned a small business. When he was my age he was training to go overseas and fight in World War II.

One night we were sitting in the den and he looked over at me. "I love you so much that sometimes it hurts." I was pretty sure I understood. He worried about me a lot. The longer I kept doing what I was doing, the less likely I was to find a decent job and get married and have a family. He thought it would be too late at some point, and I was pretty sure that Mother felt the same way. I had never stopped feeling guilty about disappointing them.

Chapter 51

September 6, 1974 – Hillsboro High School is playing a home game against East Ridge High from Chattanooga. It's halftime and the Hillsboro band is taking the field to a cadence being tapped out on the metal frames of several snare drums. I coached three of the seniors who play for Hillsboro. A few years ago they were little kids on the sidelines playing Smear the Queer during Friday night football games. Now they look like men. A couple of the sixth-graders I'm coaching have come to the game. They're watching every move the high school players make.

I'm standing down by the fence, and I finally spot Callie and Claire up in the stands. Claire nudges Callie when she sees me. While they're making their way down through the crowd, the band begins its version of Tell Me Something Good. Claire starts dancing. Callie shakes her head and tries to ignore her.

Claire got sidetracked by some girls, and I watched Callie walking toward me. I hadn't seen her over the summer. She looked like she could be in college. Most of the boys stopped talking as soon as they saw her, and they turned around and stared at her after she went by. She didn't do anything to advertise herself. She didn't even wear makeup. I couldn't tell how she felt about the way she looked. I wondered if she even liked being beautiful.

She seemed a little distant when she got to me, but she made a joke. "Want to buy some raffle tickets?"

"What's the prize this time?"

"It'll probably be another crappy car, but with less miles."

"How's high school going?

She shrugged. "It's okay for now, but before long I'll hate it." Then she gave me a look that lasted a little longer than usual. "I guess you thought high school was great."

I started telling her a little about how broken and lost I was in ninth and tenth grade, but I saw a frown cross her face. "Sorry. Sometimes I say more than I should."

I'd gotten into uncomfortable territory. She was a lot more at ease when Claire was around. It was a few seconds before she said anything else. "I don't think the guys you coached know any of that stuff."

"Well, it isn't a big secret. But unless a kid looks like he's going through the same things I went through, I don't talk about it much. I tell my players a lot, but there's a lot they don't know."

She glanced at me and looked away. "Like what?"

The band was playing a rendition of *Show and Tell.* It was perfect timing and I kept myself from smiling. "Well let's see... what wouldn't they know? They probably don't know whether I'm a kid or a grown-up."

She seemed a little less guarded. "I'm pretty sure they've already got that one figured out."

"Which one do they think I am?"

She hesitated before she said anything. "They think you're both. At least that's what they used to think."

I was beginning to see an opportunity. "They were probably right. Well here's something I bet they don't know. I write poetry – or at least I try to."

Callie didn't say anything.

I smiled at her. "Let me guess. You don't like poetry."

"It's more like I *hate* poetry. It's a boring waste of time."

"I used to feel the same way – at least about most of the poems I had to read for school. But maybe you wouldn't hate some of the poems I've written."

She looked unconvinced.

I was trying to think of what to say next when Claire walked up. The band started playing *The Joker*, and Claire was dancing again. She smiled at me and then she looked at Callie. "What have I missed so far?"

When Callie told her that I wrote poetry, Claire pretended to gag, but after a while they let me tell them about Steve Thomas and what I wrote about his death. They finally said to bring the poem to a game sometime, and they'd tell me what they thought.

The next week Hillsboro had a home game against Montgomery Bell Academy. There was a really big crowd. I saw Callie from a distance. She'd been absorbed by a small group of girls and a couple of attentive boys. Claire wasn't around.

It was close to the end of the game when Callie finally came over to where I was standing. "Well Claire has mono and she hasn't been in school all week." She seemed to be in a hurry. She looked down at the folder I was holding. "Is that the poem about the guy who died?"

I nodded and I pulled an envelope out of my back pocket. I'd written another poem. I promised myself that at some point I'd give it to Callie, but I didn't expect it to happen that soon. Friday the thirteenth was the last day I would've picked, but I took Claire's absence as a sign. I wouldn't have given it to Callie if Claire was around. I held up the envelope. "You might not want to read this one. It's just ... I don't know."

She looked at me. "Is it real long?"

"No. It's pretty short."

She held out her hand and I gave her the folder and the envelope. "What's it about?"

She didn't get a straight answer. "One of the things it's about is not knowing how something will turn out. And it's also about how the present will eventually become a long time ago." I should've just said the poem was about her. I should've said that I wrote it because there was something I needed to tell her, and I didn't know a better way to say it.

She slipped the envelope inside the folder.

"But if you don't like the first one, you'll definitely hate the second one, so don't even read it." I wanted to change the subject. "I have a message for Claire. Tell her that there'll be a whole lot of talk going around if half the boys at Hillsboro suddenly come down with mono."

That made her smile. She'd probably read both poems by the time the game was over. I kept thinking about all the reasons I shouldn't have given her the second one. When I got home I read through it again.

The Girl

He was old
When he had his stroke,
But he can still picture the girl.
After more than sixty years
He remembers
Once upon a time
When he was too old
And she was too young.
She was strong
And independent
And beautiful,
But there are days
When he struggles
To remember
More about her.
Now and then,
Alone in his room,
He rocks back and forth
In his chair and wonders
How much he told her –
And how much
She already knew.

We had our first football game of the season the next day. We weren't very good, and there weren't nearly as many kids on my team as there were the year before.

It could've been because after riding all the way home from North Nashville on the bus, some guys didn't have enough time to change into their uniforms and get to practice. Or it might've been because they didn't know who their teammates would be. It wasn't a neighborhood team anymore, and it wasn't a school team.

And it was harder to get the word out. When all my players were at Woodmont, I just went to a school assembly and announced when practice would be. But I couldn't show up and make an announcement at the school in North Nashville. It had kids from several different neighborhoods, and boys needed to be on teams that practiced close to where they lived.

With all the new houses being built, there should've been plenty of new kids moving into the old Woodmont neighborhood, but if they were around, they must've stayed inside most of the time.

A guy I knew pretty well coached the team we played in our first game. He was a good coach and I thought his team would kill us, but they were as bad as we were.

We ended up beating them, and after the game he told me that he was in the same boat I was in. He said it was hard to get the word out, and since a lot of his players didn't go to school together, there wasn't much chemistry.

I was surprised that we won the game that morning, but I was in for a much bigger surprise. When I got to my car there was an envelope on the front seat.

There was a short note inside. "It's been a while since I told you about the scar on my face. If you're interested in seeing me, be standing in the parking lot behind Belle Meade Theater at 8:30. A black guy in a Cadillac will be there to pick you up. I'll explain everything then. But if you don't make it, I'll understand."

At first I was surprised and curious, and then I was nervous.

Mike wouldn't have contacted me the way he did unless something was wrong. But I knew I'd be in the parking lot at 8:30. I would've felt like a total coward if I hadn't gone. It was a few minutes before I started wondering how he knew where I was.

Chapter 52

September 14, 1974 – It's Saturday night and I'm sitting in the back seat of an older-model Cadillac being driven by a black guy who says his name is Fats. I parked next to the gym at Ensworth. It only took me a couple of minutes to walk down to the theater. When he picked me up I started to open the front door on the passenger side, but he smiled and said we'd get less attention if I rode in the back.

We turn right on Harding Road and head toward town. Fats is friendly, but he doesn't have much to say. Maybe he isn't supposed to say much. I want to ask him where we're going and if he knows Mike, but I just look out the window. It isn't long before he turns left, and after we drive along the western edge of Centennial Park, we're almost to North Nashville.

It's a warm night and there are people all over the place. The farther we go, the more people there are. It's like there's a festival going on. Fats drives up a street in what was probably a white working-class neighborhood thirty or forty years ago. We pull up in front of a modest brick house. There's a small yard, and an old hackberry tree is beside a walkway that leads up to a porch. A couple of black men are beside the front door and they're smoking cigars.

I asked Fats what I owed him and he shook his head. "Naw man. It's all took care of." Then he smiled. "I'll be aroun back when you ready to go. Tiny know how to get me."

The windows of the house were open. When I was walking up to the porch I could hear *Can't Get Enough of Your Love, Babe*. The men with the cigars stopped talking as soon as they saw me. The closest one turned back to whoever was just inside the door. "Tell Tiny he got a vistuh." They went back to talking. It was like I wasn't there, and I tried not to look as awkward as I felt.

The last time I felt so conspicuously white was when somebody I never saw called me and my friends white devils when we were standing in the ticket line at the Tennessee A & I football game back in 1967. I listened to *Papa Don't Take No Mess* and *You Haven't Done Nothin'* before a big black guy finally pushed open the door. "Welcome to Tiny's Lounge. C'mon, I'll take you to Big Mike. He been spectin' you."

I walked into a large room where some mostly middle-aged black men were standing around and talking. The inside of Tiny's Lounge looked like a regular house, except that there was a bar on the right side of the front room. A few card tables were set up, but nobody was playing cards – at least not in the front part of the house. There was some cigarette and cigar smoke in the air, but it wasn't too thick.

We went to the left of a staircase and down a narrow hall past a restroom and three other rooms. The third door on the left was open. On the wall, there were big framed photographs of Muhammad Ali and the boxing promoter, Don King. Ten or twelve men were standing around a pool table that was doubling as a craps table.

On the right, behind the stairs, there was a kitchen that was also used as an office. Mike was sitting across a table from a small black man in a three-piece suit. I thought the big guy at the front door was Tiny, but Tiny was the man in the suit. Mike introduced me to Tiny, and after we shook hands, Tiny excused himself and went up toward the front of the house.

Mike was more relaxed than I thought he'd be. He leaned back and smiled. "I thought you'd show up, but I wasn't sure. So have you figured out why we're at Tiny's Lounge instead of in the land of the Caucasians?"

I resisted the temptation to call him Big Mike. "I think I know, but I wouldn't bet on it."

He motioned for me to sit where Tiny had been sitting. "Let's hear it."

I stepped around the table and sat down. The seat was still warm. "Well, maybe you don't want anybody to know where you are."

Mike nodded.

There was one more thing I was pretty sure about. "And we're in a place where there aren't any other white people, so I'm guessing that whoever you're trying to avoid must be white."

He looked like he was waiting for me to say something else, and then he nodded again. "Not bad. The reason I'm being so careful is so nobody will be able to connect you with me. But I need to explain a couple of things. First off there's Tiny. I've known him since back when I worked the door at *The Baron*. It was one of the first integrated nightclubs in the South. We go way back. I'd trust him with my life."

Mike shifted around in his chair. "Even though I haven't known you as long as I've known Tiny, I trust you. But before I tell you anything else, you need to understand that you can walk away from this whenever you want to. I won't think any less of you."

"I understand."

He leaned back in his chair. "When was the last time we saw each other?"

"It was the summer after you had the New Year's Eve party at your apartment. We were in the student center at Peabody."

Mike nodded. "That would make it the summer of 1970. Yeah, that sounds about right. You've gotta be wondering what I've been doing the last four years."

"I heard that you went down to South America to research a book you were going to write."

"Well, the book was just a cover. But I did go to South America, so I guess that's accurate enough." He didn't say anything for several seconds. "I remember telling you a little about the time

I spent in counter-intelligence, and what I thought about the assassination of President Kennedy."

I nodded. "Yeah, back in the early part of 1968 you said there had been a conspiracy. And you said Dr. King and Bobby Kennedy were both in danger."

Mike's face tensed up and there was a different look in his eyes. I wondered if he had the same expression when he was fighting for his life in Korea.

He started talking very slowly. "Yeah, I was always pretty sure the Kennedy killing was a professional hit. And if I'd gone ahead and tried to find out who was behind it... If I'd done something... maybe the next two killings wouldn't have happened. But I didn't do a goddamn thing."

He was opening and closing his right hand, and he was holding onto the side of the table with his left hand. He looked toward a window and the tone of his voice changed.

"I finally decided to start turning over a few rocks. I got to know some damn good intelligence officers when I was in Korea and Vietnam. And a couple of guys I trusted still worked for the Company. It took me a while, but I finally tracked down the guy I trusted the most. I'll just call him Lou. I flew down to see him in Chile right after the election of Salvador Allende.

"I laughed when Lou told me he was there to support our embassy, and he laughed when I told him I was there to research a book. We sat around and shot the shit for a while, and then I asked him if he remembered the first time we heard about the plan to overthrow the President of Guatemala, Jacobo Arbenz. He remembered it as well as I did.

"Lou and I were operating around Dien Bien Phu. One of the liaison officers had a really big mouth, and we made a game out of seeing how much we could get him to tell us. We'd take him out and get him drunk, and then we acted like he was too fucking stupid to know anything important.

"He eventually told us about CIA operations going all the way back to Syria and Iran. We already knew a lot of what he was telling us, but then he said that Allen Dulles, who was running the CIA, was getting rid of President Arbenz.

"If you're curious about how the world actually works, and why so many people in the third world hate America, read up on that little episode. Dulles was all tied up with the United Fruit Company. It was the strongest economic force in Guatemala.

"Dulles was United's corporate attorney back when he was a Wall Street lawyer, and after that, he was on its board of directors. He'd been on United's payroll for years. President Arbenz was trying to redistribute some unused land to poor farmers, so Dulles got rid of him.

"Anyway, Lou and I kept talking about Dulles. He did everything he could to manipulate Kennedy into invading Cuba. From there it was a pretty short step to November 22, 1963. Lou saw the assassination the same way I did. At that point, I went ahead and told him what I was trying to do.

"Lou was stationed in Washington at the time of the assassination. He said that what got his attention, along with the way Kennedy was killed and how easy it was to kill Oswald, was how many agents in the DC office were transferred out of town right after the killing. Somebody went to a lot of trouble to make sure that certain agents couldn't sit around and compare notes.

"Lou ended up at a station in Afghanistan. He didn't tell anybody what he thought. He just kept his head down. We talked some more and he finally said he was willing to do a little poking around. He was a smart guy and he knew at least as much as I did about how to stay under the radar.

"He said there was another guy he trusted who was still working for the Company, and he got him involved, too. He didn't tell me who the other guy was, and he didn't tell the other guy about me. They both sniffed around for a year or so, but when the other guy went dark, Lou got spooked. He got word to me that he was going to lie low for a while, and a few weeks later I found a package in my car. Inside the package was all the information he and the other guy had put together.

"They found out some really bad shit, and I'd come up with some really bad shit on my own. At that point, I decided to back off for a while. I needed to make sure I stayed invisible. By then I knew I hadn't been imagining things. By then I had a pretty good idea about how things were connected. But there was a lot more I needed to find out, and I started easing back into it a few months ago.

"Here's what I have in mind. The information I'm holding has got to stay safe while I figure out what to do with it. I'm doing everything I can to stay out of sight, but if something ends up happening to me, the information has to get to the right people. I've made copies of everything I have, and I've handed off those copies to a few people I trust – people who would be next-to-impossible for anybody to connect to me.

"You're one of those people. Even though we were at Peabody at the same time, somebody would have to turn over a whole lot of rocks to figure out that we even knew each other. The precautions I'm taking are to make sure things stay that way.

"What I need is pretty easy. Unless you did something stupid, you wouldn't be running much of a risk. If you tell me you're in, I'll give you a sealed packet. But you'll need to give me your word that you won't open it and that you won't tell anybody what you're doing. And I'll say this one more time. Don't get involved unless you want to be involved. If you walk away I'll trust you to keep your mouth shut, and we'll still be friends."

Chapter 53

I had been taking in everything Mike Higgins said. There was finally a way to start redeeming myself for not going to Vietnam. And for causing some other guy to go in my place. I told him I wanted to help, and he reached across the table and we shook hands. Then he gave me an index card with a phone number.

I was supposed to call once a month. He told me I should never call the number from home. He said the further from home I was when I called the better, and that calling when I was out of town was an especially good idea. He said I should try to use a pay phone, not to call from the same phone twice, and not to stay on the line for longer than thirty seconds.

Every time I called, I was supposed to ask to speak to a girl. It didn't matter who I asked for – it just had to be a girl's name. If I was told she wasn't home, that meant everything was alright. But if I was told to call back at a specific time, I needed to make the call, but from a different location.

If there was something wrong on my end – if I thought I was being watched or if there was some other problem – I was to ask for a girl and say that she was breaking my heart. Then I'd receive further instructions.

Mike said he was the only one who would know what he had given me. He said that if he needed to give me more information, I might get a letter in the mail or a note in my car with directions about when and where to make a pick-up. He told me it would always be signed, "Uncle Fred" or "Uncle" somebody.

Then he reached back behind his chair and picked up a medium-sized cardboard packet. He put it down on the table. It was completely wrapped in cellophane tape.

I picked up the packet. "I have two questions."

Mike nodded. "What's question number one?"

"If I call the number and nobody answers – or if the phone's been disconnected – what should I do?"

"What do you think you should do?"

"I should probably wait for somebody to contact me."

"That's right. And after two or three years, if you haven't been contacted, you should destroy what you have. Like I said, there are other copies. What's question number two?"

"Should I write a note to my parents in case something happens to me? If I got hit by a bus, would you want the packet destroyed or should they keep it?"

He thought for several seconds. "If you're reasonably sure they'd do what you told them to do, go ahead and write them a letter. You should tell them that after two years, if nobody shows up and asks for the packet, they should get rid of it." He looked at me and nodded. "You asked the right questions. But there's something else we need to talk about."

I thought we'd covered everything. "What's that?"

His hands were on top of the table. "This morning you were coaching kids in a football game. Now you're someplace you've never been before and you're listening to a guy you haven't seen in four years, and he's telling you that he's been snooping around in the shadows of the CIA.

"I guess I should be flattered that you trust me so much. But I wonder what you'll be thinking when you're on your way home tonight. I wonder what you'll think tomorrow morning when you wake up, or next week, or next year. Right now you believe what I'm telling you, but sometimes you'll probably wonder if I'm lying. Or if I'm crazy."

I didn't know what to say.

"It's okay to be skeptical as long as you can keep an open mind.

That means recognizing at least the *possibility* that what you see going on in the world – what's happening out in front of the curtain – is different from what's going on *behind* the curtain. I wasn't planning to say any more than I've already said, but I should probably give you an example of what I'm talking about. How closely did you follow Watergate?"

"I watched the hearings. And a lot of the time I was trying to guess what you were saying about Nixon."

Mike just nodded. "Well, what the public was told – what was going on in front of the curtain – is that there was a break-in at the headquarters of the Democratic National Committee. The public knows that some of the money found on the burglars was traced to the Committee to Re-Elect the President, and that individuals close to Nixon were involved. The public also knows there was a cover-up and about all the laws that were broken in the process, and that Nixon was involved the whole time."

Mike looked down at his hands. "That was all true, but a lot more than that was going on. The public has no idea that during the presidential campaign of 1968, Nixon engineered the sabotage of the Paris Peace Talks.

"If President Johnson had managed to end the Vietnam War before the election – and it almost happened – Nixon wouldn't have become president. The evidence of what Nixon did was presented to Johnson, but Johnson didn't expose Nixon. Nixon committed treason, and he knew that if the evidence was ever exposed, his presidency would be destroyed.

"Right after Nixon took office, Hoover told him about FBI wiretaps and the surveillance that was conducted, and he told Nixon that evidence had been collected about his sabotaging of the peace talks. After that Nixon ordered his closest aides to find the evidence, but they didn't turn anything up. Then the story about the Pentagon Papers hit the front page, and Nixon got deeply concerned.

"The evidence was floating around somewhere, and Nixon knew it would torpedo his re-election – and that he would be disgraced – if the Democrats had it. The CIA burglars who were arrested in the Watergate break-in had several objectives, but the most important item on their list was to find out if the Democrats had the evidence of Nixon's treason."

Mike looked at me from across the table. "It'll probably be decades before any of that comes out, but that's what was going on. And it might be decades after that before the public understands the connection between Watergate and Vietnam and a whole lot of other things."

I must've looked lost, and Mike gave me a little more background.

"Look, Nixon destroyed the peace talks by getting word to President Thieu of South Vietnam that he shouldn't go to Paris and negotiate with the North Vietnamese. The presidential campaign could've gone either way, and if the war ended before the election took place, Humphrey would be president instead of Nixon. Nixon let Thieu know that he'd get a much better deal from his administration than he'd get from Humphrey. That's why Thieu stayed home, and that's what killed the negotiations.

"By prolonging the war, Nixon and Henry Kissinger and a few other traitors caused the loss of tens of thousands of additional American lives, and millions of Vietnamese and Cambodian lives, and they wasted hundreds of billions of dollars."

Mike looked down at the table. "And that's just some of what goes on behind the curtain. Anyway, now that Nixon is gone, I'm pretty sure there will be investigations into all sorts of things, including the assassinations back in the 1960s.

"I'm going to uncover as much information as I can, and once the investigations get underway, I'm planning to give them what Lou found and what I've found." I was watching his eyes the whole time he was talking. I was convinced that he believed everything he was telling me.

He reached over and touched the packet, and then he looked at me. "Take care of this. And take care of yourself."

The big guy who brought me to see Mike took me out a side

door, and then he led me through Tiny's backyard and across a lot to another street. Fats was waiting in the Cadillac. Before I got in, I reached into my pocket and felt the edge of the index card with the telephone number Mike had given me.

By then it was after eleven, but when we got to the next street there were as many people walking around as there were before. I wanted to ask Fats if it was always that way in North Nashville on warm Saturday nights, but I didn't say anything.

There weren't many cars behind Belle Meade Theater when Fats dropped me off. After I walked up to Ensworth, I went back and sat on the steps in front of the gym. I balanced the packet in my right hand. It weighed a couple of pounds and I wondered what was inside.

I felt like I was starting another chapter in the scenario I'd been imagining since I graduated from high school. While the rest of my classmates were throwing themselves at the various defenses that stood in their way, I had been selected for a secret mission. Because I wouldn't be suspected, I was chosen to conceal a potentially crucial intelligence report.

I wasn't tempted to open what Mike gave me. I was going to do what he wanted me to do, and I was going to do it the way he wanted it done. He said there would be times when I might not believe what he had told me. I thought about that for a while. What Mike said was either true or it was false. Even if it was false, I didn't see any harm in holding on to the packet.

But I was almost positive that what he told me was true. I didn't think he was crazy, and I didn't see what he had to gain by making up such a complicated story. I kept going back to when he told me about the danger both Dr. King and Robert Kennedy were in right before they were killed. I just sat in the dark and thought for a while.

Chapter 54

September 28, 1974 – It's Saturday morning and the game clock is winding down. We're losing 23-0 to the Eagles. All their players go to the same private school, and they're the best team in our league. I dislike the other coach, but it isn't because we're losing and it isn't because we aren't going to score. None of the teams the Eagles have beaten have come close to scoring either. The Eagles coach has let everybody know that his team will get through the season without giving up any points. He has six assistant coaches and they're all wearing black and silver baseball caps, and black T-shirts with silver trim.

His team is hyper-organized and he calls his kids by their last names and yells at the referees. But what I really can't stand is that instead of playing his substitutes and holding down the score, he plays his starters the whole time. Every time they score he pumps his fist in the air like he's done something a lot more significant than run up the score on a bunch of kids. And he ends every game by running a trick play and trying to score a touchdown. He's done it three games in a row. It's become his trademark.

We would've beaten the Eagles every time we played if I had Ted and Charlie and Chris and Nate and the rest of my team from the year before. The team I had in 1974 could've played them twenty times and never come close to winning. But I'd been doing a little scouting. On the last play of their first game, their coach had called a double-reverse pass that went for a touchdown, and he used the same play to close out their third game.

On the last play of their second game, he called a toss-sweep that started to the right. Then the running back threw the ball back to the quarterback. He was wide open and went sixty-five yards to the end zone. The Eagles coach had called the same play at the end of game one and game three. There was a chance he'd go back to the play he called at the end of game two, and we'd worked on how to stop it.

With eight seconds left, they had the ball on their thirty-five-yard line, and their coach called timeout. I had one kid who really liked to hit. His name was Marty Burke. He looked over at me and lined up as the cornerback on the right side.

Sure enough, their quarterback pitched it to their running back who took off in the opposite direction from Marty. Then the running back stopped and threw a perfect pass back to their quarterback who was running toward Marty's side of the field. The quarterback caught the ball and just as he was turning around, Marty hit him going full speed.

Ken Downing was coming up, and the ball was on the ground when he picked it up on the run. Ken nearly got away before one of the Eagles players grabbed him by the back of his jersey, and just before he went down he lateraled the ball to his best friend, Hank Harvey. It looked like Hank had a chance to make it to the end zone, but he was pretty slow and he got pulled down at the five-yard line.

The other coach ran across the field to see about his quarterback, who was rolling around in the grass and trying to get some air back into his lungs. I was tempted to get the coach's attention and let loose with a fist pump, but I didn't do it.

October 4, 1974 – It's Friday night and I'm standing beside the fence at the Hillwood High School football field. I haven't seen Callie in three weeks. The last two Hillsboro games were on the other side of town, and since I was pretty sure she wouldn't show up, I didn't go. But Hillwood is a Hillsboro rival and the schools are only three or four miles apart. I'm still kicking myself for giving her the poem.

If she comes to the game and looks uncomfortable when she sees me, I'll leave as fast as I can and try to make sure she never sees me again. I feel like I'm on trial and waiting for a verdict. I tell myself for the umpteenth time that relationships between guys my age and girls her age were normal back in the 1800s, and for the umpteenth time, I tell myself that the 1800s ended over seventy years ago.

When she hadn't shown up by the start of the second quarter, I was pretty sure I wouldn't see her. A few minutes later I was watching the game, and somebody came up behind me and put a hand over each of my eyes. I knew it wasn't Callie. Playing *Guess Who?* wasn't her style.

I pretended to be thinking. "Let's see. Have you recently been quarantined to prevent the spread of an illness that's often associated with unsanitary kissing techniques?"

I heard a girl stifle a laugh. She didn't say anything and her hands stayed over my eyes. I kept pretending I didn't know who it was.

"Well, maybe you aren't familiar with the term, 'unsanitary kissing.' It means kissing with your mouth open. The saliva from your mouth gets into the mouth of the other person, and the other person's saliva gets into your mouth, along with all kinds of nasty germs."

She tried to suppress another laugh.

"Let me explain it a different way. A boy and a girl are kissing and she pulls away. She says, 'Oh I'm sorry – I think I just swallowed your gum.' Then the boy says, 'No, I just cleared my throat.'"

Claire took her hands away when she started laughing. "That is so *totally* gross."

I thought that Callie might've been standing beside her, but when I turned around she wasn't there. I waited for Claire to stop laughing before I said anything. "I sure hope I can't get mononucleosis from your hands."

"I think you'll be okay. I just washed up. No wait. Maybe that was *yesterday*. Anyhow, there are lots of ways to get mono besides kissing." Then she gave me an intentionally playful look. "But you're probably wondering where *Callie* is."

All I could do was try to be funny. "Callie? Callie who?"

"Callie, the girl who showed me those poems you wrote."

"Oh, *that* Callie.

"Yeah, *that* Callie."

I felt like I was doing a reasonably good job of covering up how awkward I felt. "So how is ole Callie getting along these days?"

Claire was enjoying the game we were playing. "Oh except for getting caught cutting school and being grounded, *ole Callie* is just fine. But the strangest thing happened."

"What's that?"

"It seems like she doesn't hate poetry anymore. She doesn't like talking about personal stuff, so you don't need to say anything about it, but I could tell how much she liked the poem – I mean the *poems*."

I was trying to think of what to say next when a couple of boys walked by and got Claire's attention. She went off with them for a few minutes, and when she came back her eyes were a little bloodshot and I could smell marijuana smoke on her clothes.

She took up where she left off, but she was talking a little slower. "Anyway, about the poem... Both of us were wondering if you were ever going to say anything."

"Say anything about what?"

"You know, about you liking her."

I wanted to admit it, but I stayed quiet.

Claire smiled and shook her head. "You didn't think we knew?"

I still didn't say anything.

She looked like she was holding back a laugh. "Oh my *God*, she's not stupid. And neither am I."

I tried to take refuge behind some humor. "Okay, let's suppose there might be a *molecule* of truth in what you're saying. And let's suppose that... What was her name again?"

"Callie."

"Oh yeah, Callie. Alright, suppose Callie thought somebody who was *clearly* too old for her admitted that he might *'like her.'* I'd hate for her to feel weird about it."

"You should've thought about that before you gave her the poem. But I wouldn't worry about it. Like I said, she already knew." She looked around at the kids in the stands. "We haven't told anybody else, but it wouldn't matter if we did. It's not like you're gonna be asking her to the prom."

She was right. Even though I mostly saw a woman when I looked at Callie, the thought of going on a date with her made me more than uncomfortable. I wanted her to have boyfriends and go through all the other experiences that were part of high school. I didn't want to interfere with any of that. I just wanted to be around when she wasn't too young for me anymore.

Claire finally drifted back toward the student section, and I stayed where I was and watched the rest of the game. I was glad that Callie liked the poem, but I still felt uneasy about it. That's when the God of Music decided to send me another message. The last song the Hillsboro band played at halftime was "*Don't You Worry 'Bout a Thing.*"

I was usually open with my friends, but I didn't tell them anything about Callie Lee. If they'd known what was going on, there would've been all kinds of jokes. They would've asked me if I read to her on our dates. They would've asked if we played with Barbies and had tea parties and watched Sesame Street together. And I was pretty sure somebody would've told me that if my relationship with Callie didn't work out, there were plenty of girls in kindergarten who weren't dating anybody.

We went back and forth at each other all the time, but I'd noticed that some things had changed. There was a little more condemnation behind their jokes when it came to how I still didn't have what they called "a real job."

I cared a lot more about what my father thought. The harder he worked to build his business, the guiltier I felt about not putting on a coat and tie and helping him. While I was doing what I enjoyed – researching the history of the neighborhood and coaching – there were times when he came home from work looking exhausted.

He put me through college, but I was still unemployed. Now and then he said how much he wanted grandchildren, but he always tried to say it in a humorous way. He seemed to be drinking more, and I was sure I was part of the reason.

Mother was about to turn sixty, and most of her friends were grandmothers. Sometimes I saw her wrapping a baby gift for a recently-born grandchild of one of her friends. She never said anything about it, but she knew she might not have grandchildren of her own. She was drinking a little more, too. I didn't blame her.

Sometimes I told myself that I should just let go ahead and make everybody happy. All I had to do was go to work with my father. Then I could move into my own place, and I'd be one step closer to having a family. That would be the biggest gift I could give my parents.

I told myself that if I cut down on the number of teams I was coaching, I'd probably be able to work at the factory and keep coaching for a while. And I told myself that I might still be able to do some research on the neighborhood from time to time.

But I knew that something else could happen. If I couldn't stand working at the factory, or later on if I forced myself into a marriage that didn't work out, I might start drowning the same way I had back when I was in school. It would crush my parents to watch me fall apart at that point in my life.

November 28, 1974 – I ate a big Thanksgiving meal with my parents, and then I walked to Montgomery Bell Academy. I'm standing out on the football field. Guys show up every year on Thanksgiving afternoon to play in a touch football game that has come to be known as the Turkey Bowl. It's sunny and cool, and there's a pretty good turnout. Twenty guys are standing on the field and ten are former Montgomery Bell players.

Three of them, including Phil Andrews, the guy who kicked me in the side on Herbert's Field back when we were in school at Woodmont, played football in college. Phil was an end at Florida. He's been married for a couple of years, and he hasn't stayed in very good shape. We decide that the Montgomery Bell guys should be on the same team and take on everybody else. We line up for the kickoff and I get in the middle of the field, about twenty yards across from where Phil is standing.

When Don Ballenger kicked off, I started running as fast as I could. I was looking up the field like I was watching the guy who caught the ball, but instead of going around Phil when he tried to block me, I got low at the last second and gave him a forearm. We had a solid collision, but I was moving pretty fast and I didn't feel much of the impact. He went down and I kept going.

I thought he'd get mad, but he didn't say anything and he didn't try to retaliate later on. It bordered on being a cheap shot and I should've regretted doing it, but it felt good to win a small victory for my ten-year-old self.

By the time I got back home, one of Mother's friends had dropped by with her husband. They were drinking with my parents. I didn't want to spend the rest of the night there, and I ended up going by myself to see *The Odessa File* at Green Hills Theater.

I thought that my involvement with Mike Higgins would make the movie seem more intense, but I was distracted. I kept thinking about the way my parents and my friends looked at me, and about the way I saw myself.

I was half-watching the movie, and pretty soon I was thinking about Callie. She had a boyfriend. I was a little envious, but I wasn't jealous. I gave the kid a lot of credit. A lot of guys at Hillsboro had their eyes on her, but he was the only one with enough guts to ask her out.

It didn't bother me that she was dating, but having to hide the way I felt about her did bother me. I wasn't sure why it came to me while I was sitting in the movie theater, but that's where I was when I started thinking that I should meet Callie's mother. The longer I thought about it, the more I wanted to do it.

The next time I saw Callie, I told her. I said that since her mother was bound to find out about me sooner or later anyway, I should probably go ahead and meet her.

I expected her to hate the idea, but she just shrugged. "If that's what you need to do, then go ahead and do it. I don't really care."

I would have rather been the forbidden fruit.

Chapter 55

December 20, 1974 – It's one o'clock on Friday afternoon and I'm in a Chinese restaurant in Green Hills called the House of Canton. I'm sitting in a booth across the table from Cheryl Lee, Callie's mother. She looks like she's around forty. She's still pretty and I keep trying to picture how she looked when she was Callie's age. She stares at me while I try to explain the way I feel about her daughter. I tell her about the first time I noticed Callie – back when she came to watch the boys from her grade play basketball on Saturday mornings at Ensworth.

Then I tell her about when I stopped seeing Callie as a little girl. I tell her how hard I tried to put Callie out of my mind, and about all the time I've spent trying to convince myself that the difference in our ages won't end up mattering. I even tell her about the poem. I was ready for Mrs. Lee to be angry or disgusted or afraid, but she just sits and listens. When I'm through saying what I came to say, she smiles at me.

She slid over to the side of the booth next to the wall and turned sideways. Then she leaned back and put her legs on the seat. "How did you think I was going to react to what you told me?"

"I don't know – maybe that you'd be worried. Or that you'd get mad."

"Do you know why I'm not worried or mad?"

I shook my head.

"A few weeks ago I found the poems you wrote. They were on top of Callie's dresser. I was pretty sure they didn't have anything to do with schoolwork. The last things I expected to find in her room were a couple of poems. I don't like poetry any more than she does, but I went ahead and read the first one.

"I couldn't understand why she'd have a poem about somebody who died at a football game. Then I read the other one. When I got to the part about the girl being too young, I was pretty sure it was about Callie.

"I didn't say anything about it at first. I didn't want her yelling at me about snooping around in her room. But the poem was on her bed a few days later. I thought she might've left it there because she wanted me to ask her about it, so I went ahead and said something. All she did was give me one of her looks."

Mrs. Lee smiled. "But I'm pretty sure she wanted me to know about it. That's probably why she didn't bite off my head. She eventually told me about the poems, and then she told me a little about you. Not that I hadn't already heard about you. Somebody said you've coached half the boys on this side of town.

"The thought that you had feelings for her worried me at first. And... well I can't say it doesn't bother me some now. I wish you were ten years younger. Even five years younger would help. But it sounds like you're... I don't know, trying to be mindful of Callie.

"If you can keep doing that, it might be good for her. She doesn't see her father much, and maybe if she had a friendship with an older guy who was looking out for her a little bit... "

There was a knife on the table and she reached over and started to push the blade around in a circle with her index finger. "And with the way she looks... I mean I'm not blind. I know you're... I understand the way boys – and men – see her. I try to be a realist most of the time. I don't think she's ready for all that yet, but I remember when I was her age. She's almost sixteen, and once she has a serious boyfriend...

"But I need to say this. If you find out that you... if you start losing your perspective, you might need to back away."

I was already nodding. "I understand." I almost went into how guilty I'd feel if I kept Callie from having a normal high school experience, but I didn't say anything.

She stopped the knife with her finger and then she started twirling it in the opposite direction. "And you should... well you should know that things probably won't work out the way you hope they will. Getting to know Callie isn't easy.

"I'm surprised she's let you get as close as she has. She has her boundaries. She's a lot like her father that way. But if she does let you get closer, and if you're still close in a few years... well who knows? There's also... she's been through some things that you should probably know about."

Just about all I knew was what Dan Thorne told me at the basketball game. We sat in the booth for another hour and Mrs. Lee told me how her home life had come apart. By the time she finished talking, there were lines in her face I hadn't noticed before.

Her husband's name was Jim and he was a captain in the Marine Corps. He was several years older than she was, and they married right after she graduated from high school. When she told me that, she looked at me and smiled. They moved around depending on where he was stationed. By the time he went to Vietnam, they were living in Texas and they had three daughters – twin girls named Tina and Dana, and Callie, who was six years younger.

Captain Lee was nearly killed when a land mine exploded and some debris hit him in the head. He was in two different military hospitals before he could go home. He received a medical discharge, and although he fought to stay in the Marines, he lost his appeal. He threw his Purple Heart and his other medals in the trash, but Mrs. Lee found them and put them away in a box.

Captain Lee had always been religious, but after he left the Marines he joined a Pentecostal congregation that sounded more like a cult than a church. He started seeing everything as being either black or white. Callie was pretty young at the time, but he was strict with his two older girls.

"Tina tried to do everything her father told her to do, but Dana was much harder to handle than Tina was. Dana ran away from home a couple of times, and when she was in eighth grade she started using drugs.

"One Sunday morning when Callie was in third grade... I was fixing breakfast. Jim told her to go and make sure that Dana was getting ready for church. Callie was still gone by the time I was putting the food on the table. Jim was waiting to say the blessing, and he was getting impatient.

"I went back and Callie was lying on the bed with her arms around Dana. Dana had died of an overdose during the night. She and Callie were so close... But Callie wasn't crying. She was just holding Dana. She... didn't want to let her go."

I didn't know what to say. I wanted to reach across the table and touch her hand, but I just told her I was sorry. She was quiet for a little while, and then she started talking about how her marriage came apart.

"Jim is a good man and he tried to be a good father. He always read the Bible and prayed a lot, but after he was wounded... the longer he was in the hospital the more convinced he was about what God wanted him to do.

"Back when Dana started getting in trouble... well, he was sure that God wanted him to be strict with her. A couple of days after her funeral, Jim was sitting in his chair. It was after dinner and he'd been reading the Bible."

Mrs. Lee shifted back around in her seat and put her feet on the floor. "That's when he said that it must have been God's will for Dana to die. I wanted to scream at him. I knew I had to get away from him."

But Captain Lee didn't believe in divorce. He wouldn't discuss it. Tina was devoted to her father and she wouldn't leave, but Mrs. Lee and Callie drove to Nashville the summer before Callie started fourth grade at Woodmont. She didn't tell me much after that.

Along with coaching kids and having a crush on Callie, I was paying a lot of attention to the news. Mike Higgins probably wasn't surprised by a big story that came out near the end of the year. Just before Christmas, a *New York Times* reporter named Seymour Hersh wrote about a huge intelligence operation that was run by the CIA during the Nixon administration. The program included spying on American citizens for political reasons. I already believed what Mike had told me at Tiny's place, and after the Hersh revelations, I believed it even more.

December 24, 1974 – It's the middle of the afternoon on Christmas Eve, and it's warm and windy. It's been raining off and on. I didn't think anybody was home and I was going to leave Callie's present at the front door, but she must've seen me through the window and she opens the door. She seems surprised that I've come by, and I wonder if it bothers her that I showed up unannounced.

Mrs. Lee isn't home. I tell Callie I'm just there to drop off her present. She looks at what I'm holding and she smiles. I went by a nursery and bought a one-foot-tall fir tree, and then I took it home and decorated it. It turned out pretty well and she seems to like it. She says she knows where she'll plant it. I tell her Merry Christmas, but she says not to leave yet. She half-closes the door and disappears inside.

After a couple of minutes, she came to the door again. She was holding an envelope. She looked uncomfortable. "It isn't really finished and it isn't any good, but... well here."

I took the envelope and started to thank her, but she cut me off.

"And I don't want to talk about it later on. I can't believe I'm giving this to you."

Chapter 56

When I drove away from Callie's house, I still had to deliver the poinsettias that Mother had asked me to take to her friends. After they were all dropped off, I went to Woodmont to meet some of the guys on my basketball team. It was still raining a little, and only a few kids showed up. For a couple of years, I'd wanted to get my players together and take them out to sing Christmas carols.

There was a party going on at the first house we visited. Half the people were drunk and we kept singing after they gathered near the front door. We ended up singing all of our songs twice. The $95 we got from that one house, and all the other money we collected afterward, went to the Fannie Battle Day Home, the local children's center that sponsored caroling every year.

One of the reasons I'd been looking forward to caroling was because Maurice Hawliczak would be singing. He came to Nashville from Poland when he was nine. He was a great kid and a pretty good athlete, but in addition to his thick accent, he had trouble pronouncing the letter r.

That made him the natural choice to sing, "And a partridge in a pear tree," when we sang *The Twelve Days of Christmas*. Understanding Maurice wasn't easy to begin with, and he was almost unintelligible when he sang his part. He seemed to take a measure of pride from the looks he got when his turn came around, which was 24 times at the first house.

But the main reason I was looking forward to caroling that night was because one of the houses where we'd sing was the old mansion where Willoughby Williams had lived from the 1820s until well after the Civil War. There were still rumors going around about the old lady who lived in the house.

The most widely-known story – from back when I was going to Woodmont – was that a couple of trick-or-treaters had disappeared on a Halloween night in the 1930s, and they'd never been seen again. Their bodies were supposedly buried in her cellar. I never really believed it, but some kids did.

The two-story mansion was big and dark and mysterious, and at night it wasn't hard to imagine that it could conceal the remains of two long-missing children. The more I learned about Willoughby Williams, the more I wanted to know about his house. I finally figured out that a good way to get a look inside was to take the kids there to sing carols.

December 24, 1974 – It's around 8 o'clock on Christmas Eve night. It's windy and there's a little rain, and I'm walking through the side yard of the old Williams Mansion. The kids are behind me and they're already singing. I can tell they're uneasy from the way their voices sound.

We've been to thirty-two houses so far and the kids were their usual uninhibited selves, but the closer they get to the front door of the old Williams place, the quieter they sing. Even Maurice seems nervous. I told them that this is the last place we'll stop, but it took a bribe to get them to follow me up to the house. I've promised that after we get through, I'll take them to the Krispy Kreme on West End, and they can have as many doughnuts as they want.

We walk up to the front door singing Silent Night and I ring the bell. We keep singing, but nobody comes to the door. We finish Silent Night and start Good King Wenceslas. We sing louder, but the house seems dead. They keep singing and I move up and look in through a window. A lamp is on in the corner of the front room. I can see a lot of old furniture and there are portraits on the walls, and there's a big bookcase that runs from the floor nearly to the ceiling. Light is coming from an interior room, but I don't see anybody.

The kids were relieved when we left. They were getting rambunctious by the time we got back to the road, but it was a long dark walk back to Woodmont School. When I finally started talking, I tried to sound troubled. "Do you know why we didn't hang around and sing *The Twelve Days of Christmas?*"

Nobody said anything.

"When I was looking in through the window, the front room... It was pretty dark, but I could see into another room. There was an old lady sitting in a rocking chair. You were all singing and I glanced back at you for a second. When I looked around again, the rocking chair was still moving, but the old lady was gone."

I swallowed and drew in a deep breath. "Well, I... kept staring back toward the room where she'd been. I thought I might be able to see her moving around. Then... then her face was right in front of me – right on the other side of the glass. She was just staring at me." I was behind the kids. Nobody saw me bend down and pick up a small branch from the edge of a yard we were cutting across.

I tried to sound scared. "There was a crazy look in her eyes and she had rotten-looking teeth, and there was some drool coming out of her mouth."

I started talking more slowly and my voice dropped to just above a whisper. "And then she was... she was saying something I couldn't hear. Her eyes looked even crazier, and she held up her right hand and started motioning for me to come inside. But I didn't move and after a few seconds, she let out what looked like a hiss.

"Then she started scratching at me with her fingers like she wanted to claw out my eyes. After that, she moved her face closer to the window and hissed again, and when she did, her breath fogged up the glass."

I pretended to shudder. "I've never seen eyes like that before."

Shannon Martin and Timmy James and Paul Foreman were all major league skeptics. After a couple of seconds Paul said, "You're full of it." But he didn't sound too convincing.

By then they were behind me and I started to say something

else, but I stopped. We were in front of a house with a big yard, and we were next to a bush.

I tried to sound scared. "Did you hear that?"

I looked toward the Williams Mansion, and when they looked back, I tossed the branch I'd picked up into the bush. It sounded like something was right beside us, and I let out a quick moan and started running toward the school.

Paul and Shannon and Maurice passed me, and Bart Williams and Timmy James were right behind them. They sprinted the whole way to Woodmont. When I came up, Shannon and Paul were yanking on the locked doors of my car. I started searching through my pockets, and I tried to look confused. "I think I... C'mon. We've gotta go back. We need to... I've lost my keys."

When I saw the looks on their faces, I couldn't keep myself from laughing. And when I saw the anger on Paul's face, I started laughing harder. He just shook his head. "You're such a *butt-hole*." Then I did my impression of a crazy old lady scratching at the air, and I hissed at him like a cat.

Judging from the number of doughnuts they consumed before I dropped them off, they all recovered. I went home after that and watched some television with my parents. I didn't open the envelope from Callie until after they went to bed. Her gift was an untitled poem she'd written.

Outside her window
The rain drizzles.
Inside her room
Thoughts are raining in her head.
There is mist in her eyes
Before a tear builds up
And runs down her cheek,
And then splashes on her toe.
The rain stops
But another tear
Slides down her cheek
And falls on her jeans.

But the sun finally comes out,
And as reflections
Shine through her window,
She starts to smile.
She opens her window
And laughing as the wind blows,
She climbs out
And runs after the wind.

The next time I saw Callie was at a Hillsboro basketball game. I wasn't going to mention her poem unless she gave me an opening, and there wasn't an opening. I would've told her how good it was and that she should think about keeping a journal.

I would've also told her how well she used words and how much writing might mean to her, but I stayed quiet. I ended up talking a lot more to Claire than to Callie, and another basketball game came and went. Mrs. Lee told me how hard it would be to get to know her daughter, but at least I'd been able to look through a crack in her wall.

On the first Sunday morning in February, a deep shadow moved across the neighborhood. A girl who went to Woodmont when I first started coaching was murdered in her apartment near Vanderbilt. Sally DePriest was in the same grade as Davey Austin and Brooks McMillan, and I'd coached two of her brothers. She grew up right across the street from the school.

I remembered her smile and how friendly she was. Sally was supposedly the victim of a single unknown killer, but crime was accelerating as the population of the area increased. She wasn't just the victim of whoever killed her, I thought she was the victim of the big city Nashville was being pushed to become.

With Watergate over and Nixon out of office, and with the war in Vietnam winding down, the country seemed to be emerging from some of its darkness. But I kept wondering what was happening behind the curtain Mike Higgins had talked about. I thought about him every day and sometimes I thought about him every hour.

I kept going back to how he'd predicted the assassinations of both Dr. King and Bobby Kennedy, and at the end of January, I found out he was right about something else. It was announced that the United States Senate would open an investigation into federal intelligence operations.

Chapter 57

February 14, 1975 – It's my father's fifty-ninth birthday and I'm sitting with him in the den while Mother fixes dinner. The business is going pretty well, and he's in a good mood. The book I gave him is on the floor next to his chair. He picks up his half-empty glass of scotch and takes another drink. It's as hard for him to talk to me as it is for me to talk to him, but I can tell he's about to give it another try.

"I think you know how much I love you, and that I want you to have the best life you can have. I don't say this enough, but I'm proud of you. I hear all the time about how well you work with the boys on your teams. But I'm concerned about your life. I'm concerned about the way things will be for you a few years from now if nothing changes."

I was doing the best I could not to look uncomfortable. He stopped talking for a few seconds before he tried again. "Sometimes I imagine you with a family. Nothing makes me happier than thinking about you sharing a home with a wife who loves you, and with children who love you. But as long as you're living with us and as long as you don't have a job, that can't happen.

"Coaching boys is fine and doing historical research is fine, but if you don't do more than that – if you don't make enough money to support a family... Well at the end of the day, I don't see how you can have much of a life unless you make some changes."

He was trying to say the right thing. "This morning I was thinking about how things were for me. I was thinking about how my life might've turned out if I'd stayed in the Philippines instead of coming to Vanderbilt. Going halfway around the world let me see myself from a different angle. I had to leave home to find my path in life.

"This... this is your home for as long as you want to stay, but have you thought about how things will be when you get older? Can you imagine yourself at thirty, or even at thirty-five, and still living here with us?"

I told him that I'd thought about it lots of times, and that I'd also thought about going somewhere else and trying to figure everything out. His face brightened up when I said that, and he got up and came over to me.

He leaned down and hugged me. "Just keep thinking about what you want to do. And let's keep talking about it." He put his hand on my shoulder and smiled. "Next year I'll be sixty. Maybe by the time I'm sixty-five I'll be a little closer to having a grandchild."

A few days later there was a basketball game at Montgomery Bell Academy. I had an idea that probably wouldn't work out, but I needed to give it a try. I was still thinking about the sadness on my father's face when he was talking to me about my future.

I'd gotten to know the assistant headmaster, Drake Michaels, pretty well by then. A good number of the guys I coached went on to Montgomery Bell, and the first time I met him, I mentioned that I'd coached Frank Minton. Then I asked him how Frank was doing. I'd expected him to be struggling, and he was.

I ended up telling Drake about Frank's alcoholic father and his depressed mother, and how there were a lot of times when he had to be a parent to his little brother. I explained that I'd given Frank a lot of extra encouragement, and that he eventually opened up about how things were for him at home.

There were times when I saw Montgomery Bell Academy as a prep school version of Vanderbilt, but Drake Michaels really cared about the kids who went there. We got to know each other kid by kid, and sometimes he'd call me up and ask if I knew anything about some boy who was having problems.

It was a long shot, but it seemed like there was a chance that I could get a job at Montgomery Bell – working with kids who were having a hard time. Drake was in his usual spot in the stands and I went over and sat with him. After a couple of minutes, I made myself tell him what I was thinking.

He did a lot of nodding while I was talking, but he didn't say anything at first. "Well Montgomery Bell doesn't have much of a guidance office, but we need one. If I was the headmaster I'd hire you in a second, but I'm not sure how my boss will see things. He's a good man, but he's pretty old-school. I don't know how he'll respond, but I'll be glad to talk to him. I'd love to have you over here."

He was pretty encouraging and I went ahead and made an appointment with the headmaster, but I tried to keep my hopes under control. The teachers I knew at Montgomery Bell all fit a certain profile. Most of them were pretty good guys, but they kept kids at a distance a lot more than I did. I didn't know if that was what I'd be expected to do, and if it was, I didn't know if I could do it.

Before I talked to the headmaster, another shadow fell across the area. A nine-year-old girl named Martha Tindall went missing from her neighborhood. She only lived a mile to the south of Woodmont School.

March 3, 1975 – It's Monday morning and Edward Francis, the headmaster of Montgomery Bell Academy, is looking at me from the other side of his desk. I've seen him plenty of times before, but I've never met him. The first thing I notice when we shake hands is how tired he looks. The second thing is his neck. There's a mass of fat bulging out over the top of his collar, and every time he talks, the bulge starts to undulate. For some reason, I'm not very nervous.

I keep reminding myself to just relax and see what happens. He tells me he's familiar with the coaching I've been doing, and that Drake Michaels has told him good things about me. I start talking about some of the Montgomery Bell students I've coached, and after a few minutes, Mr. Francis asks how I know so much about the guys who played on my teams. I start my answer by telling him about some of the problems I had when I was a kid, and how much it would've helped if some of my teachers or coaches had known me a little better.

I could've just had a superficial meeting with Mr. Francis. I could've just touched on a few vague details, but I went ahead and let him know that my players called me by my first name and that I told them jokes. I said I tried to do more than just coach them, and I described some of the hikes and canoe trips we'd taken.

Then I told him about taking the kids caroling on Christmas Eve, and about the joke I'd played after we left the old Williams place. I expected him to laugh, but he didn't even smile. He just leaned back in his chair. Then he coughed and his jowls wobbled like gelatin on a plate. "So these boys were running through yards in the dark?

"What would've happened if one of them had stepped in a hole and broken his ankle, or hit a spigot and split open his foot? What would you have told the boy's parents, or said to a lawyer if they decided to sue? And what if you were off somewhere and there was an automobile accident? Or if somebody drowned on one of those canoe trips?"

His face had taken on a red tinge and he shook his head. "Those sorts of activities... they need to be very closely supervised – at least they do when they're conducted in connection with a school. I'm beginning to understand how you become so close to your players. I believe you are well-motivated, but your methods are... Well, that certainly isn't the way we'd ever do things here."

I'd made him uncomfortable, but he was trying to be polite. There was a question I wanted to ask, but I was afraid he would take it the wrong way. I wanted to ask him about a kid who graduated from Montgomery Bell a year earlier. The kid committed suicide over the summer.

I wondered if anybody from the school had ever really gotten to know the guy. It might've made a difference if there was somebody for the kid to talk to – somebody he felt close to.

By then it was pretty obvious that Mr. Francis wouldn't consider what I had in mind. It would've meant taking some chances and exposing the school to some unpleasant phone calls, and maybe the possibility of a lawsuit now and then.

I didn't mention the boy who killed himself. I didn't want him to think that I was blaming the school. The kid might've killed himself no matter what the school did.

Mr. Francis ended up offering me a job, but it was probably just his way of saying no gracefully. He started talking about the boys in the Junior School who hadn't made a school team, and he asked if I would be interested in working with younger students in the intramural program. It didn't pay very much, but he said if that went well, it might eventually lead to a regular teaching job.

I thanked him for seeing me and I said I'd think it over. But by then I understood that he wouldn't like the way I did things, and supervising boys in intramurals wouldn't sound like a real job to my parents. Two days later I called him back. I thanked him again, but I told him I should probably just keep doing what I was already doing.

Turning down the offer from Mr. Francis seemed like the right thing to do, but I would've loved working with those kids. I was pretty sure I would've done a good job. I thought that working at Montgomery Bell might be the best opportunity I'd get. I was a little depressed after dinner and I went to bed early, but I couldn't fall asleep.

The Abraham Zapruder film, the home movie that captured the moment of President Kennedy's assassination, was going to be shown that night on television. It was the first time the public would be able to see it. One part of me didn't want to watch it, but I was curious and I finally got up and turned on *Good Night America.*

When the first bullet hit the president, he was probably looking at somebody the same way he'd been looking at me when he was on his way to speak at Vanderbilt. He was riding along in the sunlight, waving at people and smiling, and a few seconds later, after the first bullet hit him from behind, another bullet blew his head backward as it tore through his brain. It was horrible.

I turned off the television before they showed it again. After seeing his head get knocked back that violently, I wondered how anybody could still believe that the second shot came from behind him. I don't know when I finally fell asleep.

I coached six basketball teams that season and we won most of our games. I was a fairly good coach, but I wasn't nearly as good as my record made me look. I'd been coaching for nine seasons by then. I'd learned how to teach kids to shoot layups and rebound and play defense, and I knew what to work on in practice and what not to work on. Coaching kids, at least coaching kids well, was a lot more complicated than it looked. It was a craft, and most of the guys I coached against on Saturdays weren't very experienced.

Chapter 58

After basketball season was over, a lot of the kids I coached went out of town on spring break. I had always felt a little sorry for the guys who stayed home, and in 1975 I borrowed a van and took a few of them on a road trip to Gatlinburg, in East Tennessee. It was only a four-hour drive and we took a couple of hikes and spent a night in a cheap motel.

Edward Francis would've probably had a stroke, but instead of herding the kids all over Gatlinburg, I just divided them into pairs and told them to be back at the motel by 11 PM. They were all in the room by 10.

Before they came back, I went out and found a pay phone and dialed the number Mike Higgins had given me. I expected a man to pick up the phone, but a woman answered. I thought about making up a ridiculous name, but I played it straight and asked to speak to Anna.

The only thing the woman said was, "Anna isn't home," and then she hung up. I wondered where Mike was and what he was up to. I imagined him in some faraway bar having a beer with a guy who might have a piece to the puzzle Mike was trying to put together.

That night I asked the kids if they were imaginative enough to write letters to themselves when they were thirty. There were a couple of groans, but they all ended up doing it. I did it, too, but I wrote to myself when I was forty.

I didn't mention Callie. I just wrote that I hoped to God I was married by then, and that my wife and I loved each other. And that we had at least one child, and I wasn't trapped in some job I hated. I brought along a metal box that had a pretty tight seal when it was shut. After we put all our letters into the box, I closed it.

The next morning we started on a long hike. We ran into a ranger after we'd gone a mile or so, and Bart Williams and Shannon Martin asked him if we'd see any bears. He told us there weren't many bears where we were going, but that some wild boars had been spotted in the area a couple of days earlier. We kept going up the trail and I told the kids that I'd a whole lot rather run into a bear than a wild boar. I said I'd never seen a wild boar, but when I was around the same age they were, a huge hog had tried to kill me.

The summer after seventh grade I went with Gordon Lowe, a classmate from Battle Ground, to his grandfather's farm way out in the country. We ended up standing beside a fenced-in field that contained a 350-pound hog. Gordon told me how dangerous the hog was, and that the year before, a couple of his cousins had dared each other to run all the way across the field to the opposite fence. After a while, Gordon said that he'd do it if I would.

I wouldn't do it, but Gordon said he was going anyway. The hog was in the shade at the corner of the field, and he seemed to be ignoring us. When Gordon climbed over the fence and took off, the hog let out a snort and made a halfhearted charge, but Gordon had a pretty good head start and he got over the opposite fence with no problem.

We kept walking and the kids stayed close to me so they could hear what else happened with the hog. Then I told them about Gordon taunting me from across the field – how he'd put his thumbs in his armpits and started flapping his elbows and clucking like a chicken.

"The hog was over to my right, and his snout was down in the mud. He didn't look up when I was easing over the fence, but as soon as I started to run he bolted out of the shadows like a rocket and headed right for me."

There was a large dead tree on the trail, and the kids and I stopped walking. They wanted me to finish the story before we climbed over the tree.

"I was running as fast as I could. The hog was closing in on me, but he had to go through some mud. As soon as he was in the mud, I cut to the right. He cut too, but he slid and I gained a little distance before he closed in on me again.

"The hog was right behind me when I jumped up and grabbed the top of the fence. He tried to bite me as I was scrambling over the top, but all he did was hit me with his snout. When I looked down, there was pig slobber on the right leg of my pants. Gordon was almost as scared as I was."

We got past the tree and after a while we left the trail. Then we walked along a ridge to where another big tree had fallen over. We got some sticks and made a hole where the tree was uprooted, and then I got everybody to guess where they thought they'd go to college and what they'd end up doing for a living and how old they'd be if they got married. There were a few snide remarks and there was some laughing, but I could tell they enjoyed going through that ritual together. After we buried the box, we started back.

The kids were twenty or thirty yards in front of me when they got back to the tree we'd crawled over before. They climbed over to the other side, and when I got to the tree I was still thinking about the predictions they came up with. I held onto a small branch and I was trying to put my foot onto a limb on the far side of the tree when there was a loud snort right behind me. I lurched forward and lost my balance, and I crashed into some brush at the base of the tree.

Before I got up I heard Paul Foreman laughing from the other side of the tree. He'd slipped behind me while the other kids went ahead. They were all in on it, and they were snorting and laughing as they ran back toward the tree. Paul made sure I didn't look mad before he climbed over. Then he smiled at me, scratched at the air, and gave me a retaliatory hiss.

The body of Martha Tindall, who'd gone missing back in February, was found a few days after we got back from Gatlinburg. The police were looking for her killer, but there was no mention of a connection between her murder and the way Nashville was changing.

Saigon fell a month later. I thought about all the soldiers who fought in Vietnam, and about the families of soldiers who died. I wondered what they were thinking when they watched the news and saw the lines of people trying to get on helicopters at the American Embassy while the city was being overrun by the North Vietnamese.

May 10, 1975 – I'm walking through some trees and it's springtime, but there are only shades of gray and brown. I don't know that I'm dreaming. I come to an open area and Callie is sitting by herself in a patch of dead-looking grass. She glances up at me and then she looks away. I keep walking. There's more and more brush to get through, and thorns are scratching my skin. Then I'm in a swamp. My feet are sinking into the mud, and I lose one of my shoes.

There are ripples all around me. I think huge snakes must be swimming just beneath the surface of the water. The trees disappear and the swamp becomes the surface of a swimming pool and I'm standing behind Yancey Walsh. I can feel the skin of her back against my chest, but it isn't Yancey who turns around. It's Callie, and she looks betrayed.

I woke up in my bed on Saturday morning in the wake of a dream I didn't want to have. My dreams were usually light. They blew away like dry leaves in the wind. But after the dream about Callie, it took a few minutes for the way I felt to start withering. If I hadn't had a baseball game to coach that morning, I would've probably stayed in bed for another hour feeling guilty. When I was on my way to the field, I tried to give myself credit for all the things I hadn't done.

I liked to look at Callie, but I kept myself from fantasizing about her body. Now and then I'd run across a woman, or a woman had run across me, and there had been a physical relationship. Although other women drifted in and out of my imagination as an experience unfolded, the image of Callie Lee had never been part of the experience. I thought my lust was under control, but it had gotten strong enough to penetrate my sleep, and I was afraid it would get stronger.

We were about to have our first baseball game of the season and Ann Tracey was my starting pitcher. She played point guard on my basketball team and she had lots of athletic ability, but I could tell she was nervous. She was one of the first girls in Nashville to play on a team with boys, and she knew that people would be judging her. It was a lot of pressure for an eleven-year-old.

Ann had a good arm and she was smart and competitive, but she was just starting to develop some confidence in her pitching. For the first two weeks of practice, she was pretty wild, but after I got her to keep her elbow up and move her face straight down toward the catcher's mitt when she was pushing off the rubber, she started throwing strikes.

She'd been warming up for a couple of minutes with our catcher, Mark Windrow when a couple of players on the other team figured out that our pitcher was a girl. Pretty soon their whole team was looking at her and whispering, and not long after that they were laughing at her. I'd coached Ann's older brothers and I'd known her since she was four. She was a lot like a little sister, and I was pretty sure I knew what she needed to hear.

She was behind the third-base dugout, which was just an enclosure surrounded by a chain link fence. I got the catcher's mitt from Mark, and I went around the fence to where she was standing. "Is your arm okay?"

"Yeah."

I stepped off forty-five feet, and then I turned around and got down on one knee. I gave her a target and she threw a fastball that would've been outside. I threw the ball back. "If zero means you aren't nervous and a hundred means you want to go home and hide in your room..."

She didn't need me to finish explaining the scoring system. "Probably about a seventy." She threw another outside fastball. "I'll be okay."

"I'm surprised it's only a seventy."

"Why should I be more nervous than I already am?"

"You really don't know?"

She didn't say anything. Her next pitch was a change-up. She let it go too soon, and it came in high.

"Well, you've become a national symbol. That's gotta be... I don't know, a little bit intimidating."

Ann didn't say anything. She knew I was up to something. She threw a fastball, but it was in the dirt.

"I can see the newspaper headline now – 'Former Bat Girl Falls Apart in Opening Game Humiliation.' And there'll be a photograph of you standing on the mound with your hands over your face.

"But the worst part will be the story. Little Ann Tracey, for whom the Women's Movement had such high hopes, embarrassed herself and females all across the nation on Saturday. After walking her tenth consecutive batter without throwing a single strike, she burst into tears, left the field in shame, and took refuge in the family car. Her parents are agonizing over how to help their daughter who, despite having received the best coaching available, somehow managed to throw forty consecutive balls. Some onlookers attributed her awful performance to the behavior of the opposing team, who openly ridiculed little Ann with insulting imitations...

I paused until she started her wind-up. "...which included placing baseballs under their jerseys..."

She stopped before she threw the ball. She was doing her best to keep from laughing, and she started her wind-up again. "'Placing baseballs under their jerseys to create the appearance of... *hooters*."

She started laughing, and I stood up. Then I did an impression of a boy leaning back and pretending to enthusiastically shake imaginary breasts.

After that, she got focused and started bearing down. By the time she took the mound, she was throwing the ball where she wanted to throw it. The kids on the other team were still laughing and rolling their eyes and telling each other about all the home runs they were about to hit when she threw her last warm-up pitch. She threw it as hard as she could. It went about three feet over Mark's head and rattled the backstop.

The leadoff batter stopped smiling when he saw that, and he was nervous when he stepped into the batter's box. Ann struck him out on three pitches. She ended up throwing a two-hit shutout, and she had twelve strikeouts. None of the boys on the other team were laughing when the teams were shaking hands after the game. All Ann said was, "Good game." I hadn't told her to throw the ball into the backstop – she came up with that on her own.

On my way home after the game, I went back and forth between thinking about how well Ann did, and thinking about the dream I had about Callie. I didn't know if I'd be able to do it, but I told myself that if I had any more dreams like that, I might need to start backing away from her. I couldn't imagine her having a dream like that about me. I'd never seen any sign that I appealed to her physically. I hoped she'd feel that way at some point, but if it ever happened, I didn't think it would be any time soon.

Chapter 59

June 9, 1975 – It's late on Monday morning and I'm standing outside my father's room at St. Joseph's Hospital in Atlanta. I haven't gone in yet. I've been trying to prepare myself for what I'm about to see. An old man is teetering down the corridor behind his walker, and an orderly is coming in the opposite direction pushing a food cart.

I hate the way the hospital smells and I hate the way fluorescent lights make everything look. It's like an antiseptic mausoleum. I picture my father lying in his bed with an intravenous tube in his arm and a catheter coming out from underneath his sheet. I expect him to be pale and weak. I don't know if he'll be conscious. There's a chance that he could be a breathing corpse. I take a deep breath, push open the door, and go inside.

I was at home on Sunday night when Mother got the phone call from Atlanta. My father was there on a business trip, and he collapsed in a restaurant while he was having dinner. The next morning I took the first plane I could get to Atlanta. Mother had a stomach virus, and I went by myself. I would've driven down right after we found out, but I needed to bring his car back to Nashville.

He looked better than I expected. He was pale, but except for his catheter, there weren't any tubes. He was propped up in his bed and his eyes were closed. He looked up at me as soon as I went over to him. Before I could give him a kiss, he held out his hand. He wanted to show me how strong his grip still was.

He told me a little about the weight he'd felt in his chest and how he could barely breathe. He said he remembered thinking that he didn't want to die on the floor of a restaurant with a bunch of strangers gawking at him. The next thing he knew, he was waking up in the emergency room.

He didn't say it, but he must've been scared. He'd already gone through a lot, and the next few days and weeks would be filled with uncertainty. I didn't ask him if he'd been told how much his heart was damaged. I wondered how long a man typically lived after having a major heart attack at the age of 59. I wanted to focus on him, but I was also trying to protect myself from feeling too much.

I kept wondering if I'd be back in time for our game on Saturday afternoon. I hadn't missed a game since I started coaching. We were playing a pretty good team, and Davey Austin was covering for me in case I wasn't there in time. He was back from college for the summer. I knew he'd be good at coaching kids.

The cardiologist wanted my father to stay where he was for at least another week, but three days later he signed a waiver and he was discharged on the condition that he'd check into Baptist Hospital as soon as I got him back to Nashville. When I was helping him get in the car, he smiled at me and winked. He said he'd do his best to stay alive at least until we made it back home. He leaned his seat back, and he looked pretty comfortable when we were driving away from the hospital.

The tube in his nose was connected to a portable oxygen dispenser on the floor between his feet. I was pretty sure that he'd sleep most of the time, but when we were leaving Atlanta he sat up and started looking out the window. Before long he told me more about what happened.

At first he thought it might have been indigestion. He was about to call a taxi, but then he felt like a vise was tightening inside his chest. He said he thought he might be dying, but there wasn't enough time to be afraid.

He was quiet for a few minutes, and then he said he was having a lot of the same feelings he had when he was on his way up from

New Guinea to take part in the invasion of Leyte back in 1944. That whatever was going to happen, was going to happen. He said that all he could do was try to get through it.

He never said much about what he did and saw in the war, but when we were coming back from Atlanta, the war was on his mind. He started talking about landing in Australia, and about going on to New Guinea before he left for the Philippines.

"Traveling in a convoy was quite an experience. The sea was calm and I spent as much time on deck as I could during the day. I'd forgotten how blue and immense the ocean was. I remember having mixed emotions. I wouldn't have wanted to miss what I was about to see – what I was about to be part of. I didn't want to die, but I knew if I didn't face up to my responsibility, I wouldn't have been worthy of the life I wanted to have. I had to defend my country."

He stopped talking for a few seconds and I looked over at him. His eyes were closed and I thought he was about to fall asleep, but then he made a gesture with his left hand.

"It's one thing to suddenly be in danger, but we were about to be in a battle and we had a few days to think about it. However bad things got, I wanted to do what I was supposed to do. I didn't know how I'd react under fire, but I remember thinking that I'd rather get killed than be a coward.

"It was almost a relief when we finally got to Leyte. It was quite a show – quite a spectacle – to see the bombardment by the warships, and then approach the beach with all the other assault craft. It wasn't too tough when we landed, but I was in an intelligence unit and before long we moved up to a forward position.

"There was a lot of sniper fire and we had to deal with a couple of Banzai charges. Some of our guys said they weren't sure if the Japanese soldiers were brave or if they were just crazy. They came running toward us and we'd just mow them down. I never thought they were crazy. It took a lot of guts to make a charge like that, knowing they were going to die."

He was quiet for a while. His eyes were still closed, and the expression on his face was changing. We went a few more miles before he said anything else.

"When I was on my way up from New Guinea, I'm glad I didn't know what we'd run into after we came ashore on Leyte. I didn't know what it was like to stand guard at night. Or to sit in a foot of mud at the bottom of a foxhole – trying to get some sleep. And smelling the stench of rotting Japanese corpses a few yards away.

"That's how things ended up and I got through it, but none of that meant I was brave. It... just meant that I put up with the fear and the filth and all the rest of it. I kept going one day at a time, just like everybody else."

There was fatigue in his voice and it wasn't long before he fell asleep. He didn't wake up until we were going over Monteagle Mountain. I thought he'd nod off again, but he looked over at me and straightened up in his seat.

"I know we talked about this a few weeks ago, but now... there's a little more I want to say before we get back." He sounded a little groggy. I'd hoped that we could get back to Nashville without having to go back over how messed up I was, but there wasn't much I could do about it.

"With all the times I've told you how to live your life... well it might not have sounded like it, but in a lot of ways I admire the way you've stayed on the path you're on. I know it hasn't been easy. And you haven't ever been defiant or rebellious or anything like that. I want you to know that I've finally figured something out. I need to trust you. I'll still worry about you, but I need to keep reminding myself that the time will come when you'll decide what you want, and then you'll go after whatever it is.

"When we were talking in the den – back on my birthday... with what's happened... well this doesn't change anything. If it's time for you to head out and see the world, don't worry about me. I'll be fine. I'll be up and around and back to work in a few days. Your mother and I cherish you and we love having you around, but if you decide it's time to try something new, then go ahead and try something new."

When we got to Nashville, he asked me to drive him past the factory before we went to the hospital. He stared at the building as we went by. He wanted to go inside, but he didn't say anything. I stopped at a pay phone and called Mother.

She met us at Baptist Hospital and I took off for my game. I got there right after it was over. I was less indispensable than I thought I was. The team we played was just about as good as we were, but we beat them 8 to 1. Davey was great with the kids, and I could see how much they liked him.

I went back to the hospital, and then Mother and I had dinner. She looked tired, but she didn't seem depressed. I was afraid that she might've been crying herself to sleep at night, and it really bothered me. I thought about the relationship she had with my father. I wondered what things between them were really like.

They got married when they were both twenty-four – around the same time most of the other couples they knew were marrying. Mother and her friends were in each other's weddings, and after the war, they all stayed at home and raised their children. They got babysitters and went to each other's houses with their husbands on Saturday nights. They'd have drinks before dinner, and their husbands would wind up in another room, drinking the way they had back when they were in college.

I wondered what the men who were married to my mother's friends were like from nine till five on Monday through Friday. Back when I was younger, I saw them a couple of times a year when they came to our house. They must've been a whole lot more interesting and intelligent when their eyes weren't bleary, and when they weren't spouting off about politics.

If their wives saw their husbands the same way I did, most of them would've been divorced. But almost all of them had stayed together, and I was pretty sure I was missing something. My father was right in there with the other husbands on those Saturday nights. I hoped that Mother and her friends talked about their marriages with each other, but they probably didn't.

My father always watched *Lawrence Welk* on Saturday night, but after we got back from dinner, Mother and I started half-watching a show called *Emergency.* I felt awkward about saying anything, but I wanted to be sure she had somebody to talk to. I waited until there was a commercial. "How hard has this been for you?"

She looked at me, but she didn't say anything at first. I had a feeling that she wanted to tell me something, but she wasn't letting herself say it. "Well, it hasn't been as hard as being in a hospital."

I stayed quiet.

She probably thought the silence was awkward, and she said a little more. "I'm fine. I'm just not sure where things will go from here. There's... there are just a lot of question marks. I guess we'll have to do the best we can." She didn't want to have the conversation she might need to have, and she shifted the focus to me. "How difficult has this been for *you?*"

I let her play it safe. "Like you said, it hasn't been as hard as being in a hospital. But I think he'll be okay."

Then the phone rang. One of her friends was calling. Instead of waiting around and making another halfhearted try to get her to open up, I kissed her and left. I still didn't know how she felt about what happened to my father, or about her marriage, or about her life. Maybe she felt devastated by what happened, or maybe she didn't feel devastated enough.

And there were plenty of other things she wouldn't have talked about. She wouldn't have talked about how his drinking probably caused his heart attack, or that I was part of the reason he drank, or that if I went away for a while it might take away some of his burden.

Chapter 60

June 10, 1975 – It's Saturday night and I'm at a side table in the lounge of a restaurant in Green Hills called the Jolly Ox. It's only eight or ten minutes from my house, but tonight it seems like home is a thousand miles away. This would be a good night to get drunk if I still drank.

I want to forget about the feeling I've had in my stomach since the call came about my father's heart attack. I want to forget the people with strained faces in the hospital, and I want to stop thinking about coffins and church services and cemetery plots and grief. I order my usual – cranberry juice with lemon. I'm really tired. Marcy Chaffin is singing and she sounds even better than usual. She didn't notice when I came in and sat down, but she finally sees me. I get a different smile from the one I usually get.

I'd been coming to the Jolly Ox for a couple of years. It was a restaurant, but I came for the music. Marcy played there all the time, and after a while, she started coming over and sitting with me between sets. We'd gotten to know each other pretty well.

Sometimes the other customers thought we were a couple. She was smart and I liked the way she looked. She was a good singer and guitar player, and she mostly performed her own songs. I'd kissed her once out in the parking lot. She was a great kisser, but that was as far as things went.

It would've been different if it wasn't for Callie. It was one thing to go home with a divorced mother when I knew that we were just going to have a good time. But it was different with somebody like

Marcy. With Marcy it seemed like a long-term relationship might be possible.

She knew how much I loved coaching kids, and at some point, I'd told her how much it bothered my parents and my friends that I didn't have a job. It set her off when I said it. We were at one of the front tables and she said, "That is such total *bullshit*!"

People at a few of the other tables looked around. "You do have a job. *Coaching* is your job. How many hours a week do you spend with the kids on your team? If you throw in all the time it takes to draw up plays and keep up with equipment and go to coaches meetings and deal with parents, it's probably fifty hours a week."

After she settled down, she said the reason she'd gotten mad was because I'd acted like I was wrong to still be coaching. "Nobody would say anything if you were getting paid. Everything always has to be about money."

A couple of months before my father's heart attack, Marcy had asked me why we hadn't slept together. She started laughing when I said something about how it might mess up our friendship. "What in the *hell* are you talking about? Sex is a great way to find out if there even *is* a friendship."

I told her she was probably right, but I wasn't sure she was.

Marcy kept singing, and I drank my cranberry juice. I remembered the way she smiled at me that night. And I remembered what she said next. "Why do I get the feeling that there's something you aren't telling me?" I didn't know how she'd react, but I went ahead and told her about Callie Lee.

Marcy didn't say anything when I told her how young Callie was. I started to tell her more about why I'd only kissed her in the parking lot, but Marcy held up her hand. "Hey, I get it. You're emotionally monogamous." She grinned and shook her head. "I knew there was a reason you kept turning away from having a life-changing relationship with such an *alluring* rock and roller."

Then I found out why she'd shrugged off the age difference between Callie and me. She told me about the physical relationship she ended up having with her guitar teacher back when she was in high school. She touched me on the arm. "And you know what? We're still *really* good friends."

The set Marcy was playing lasted longer than usual. When I saw her adjust the microphone, I was back to thinking about how my father looked when he was lying in his hospital bed. Then she gave me a mischievous smile. She said there was a James Taylor song she hadn't sung in a while, and she was dedicating it to a friend. She started singing *Long Ago and Far Away,* and while she sang about a young man playing a waiting game and things not meant to be, she stared into my eyes.

Marcy had loved needling me about Callie. When she came over and sat down after her set, she gave me a playful look. "I hope you liked my little song, and if you didn't like it I hope that I'm forgiven."

"Of course I liked it."

Marcy looked at me a little more closely and then she picked up my glass and took a drink. "Still sticking with cranberry juice? I thought you might've branched out into alcoholic beverages."

"Does it seem like I've been drinking?"

She was studying me. "I don't know. You just seem a little different tonight."

"Is it good different, or bad different?"

"I'm not sure. I'd like to think it was my song, but... I don't know."

Before I said anything about my father, I held up my right hand. "There are two phrases I don't want to hear when I tell you what I'm about to tell you. One is, 'I'm sorry' and the other one is, 'Do you want to talk about it?'"

She understood. "That's the way I felt when my mother died."

I told her about the heart attack and she just listened. I waited a few seconds before I said anything else. It wasn't till then that I realized how much had changed since my dream about Callie. "And now I have a question for you."

"Okay."

I looked into her eyes. "Are you a mind reader?"

She stared back at me. "I think I am right now." She looked at me for a little longer. "I think you're reconsidering the limits of your emotional monogamy."

I nodded and it was a few seconds before I said anything. "So what do you think?"

She smiled and started shaking her head. "I think you have *the worst* timing in the world. I think that two weeks ago I started seeing somebody. I think that my new boyfriend *would not* understand how much I want to take you home with me tonight. And I think that even though he's playing a gig this weekend in, of all places, Atlanta, I'll have to do the honorable thing and just go home with my guitar and a sense of regret. But at least my *honor* will be intact."

I smiled at her. "So do you think we can still end up being *really* good friends?"

Marcy laughed. "I guess so. Just keep me posted on how things go with Lolita. Maybe by the time I get back on the market, I won't have to be in somebody else's shadow. And maybe by then you'll have a little more *carpe* in your *diem*."

A couple of nights later I had another dream about Callie, and Yancey was nowhere around. We were beside a swimming pool again and I was standing behind her again. Just before I woke up, I was moving my fingertips across her stomach.

My father stayed in Baptist Hospital for three days and he went back to work the following week. He was supposed to come home at noon and then gradually phase back into a full-time schedule. He only did that for a couple of days, but going back to his old routine didn't seem to do him any harm.

It wasn't long before he was playing golf on the weekends, and after that, things were pretty much back to the way they were before his heart attack. Then he started drinking again. I took that, and the second dream I had about Callie, as signs that I needed to go away.

And I knew it didn't qualify as a sign, but there was another reason to leave. My tenth high school reunion was going to be that fall. At least eight of the guys in my graduating class had served in Vietnam, and four of my classmates were doctors. Over half of the guys were married, and some of them already had children. The last thing I wanted to do was show up and let everybody know that I was an unemployed kids' coach living with my parents.

Then the roof fell in. Mother and I were in the kitchen. I was unloading the dishwasher, and she was reading the morning paper. She'd stopped reading and I saw her look at me.

I looked back at her. "Well, I hope you're about to tell me whatever it is that you don't want to tell me."

"There's an article about Woodmont. It's closing. The school board has decided it isn't cost-effective to keep it open anymore."

It was like hearing that a friend was in a coma. As long as it stayed open, there was a chance it could go back to being a neighborhood school. I didn't want to be around in September and drive past a vacant school building. I didn't want to see a place that had been so full of life for so many years, standing empty and defunct.

I wanted to go to the Philippines. I could drive to California and leave my car somewhere, and then fly on to Manila. After I saw the place where my father grew up, I might be able to figure out where he'd come ashore on Leyte. And then I could go all the way over to Culion, where my grandfather ran the leper colony back at the beginning of the century. And maybe at some point along the way, the heavens would open up and I'd figure out what to do with the rest of my life.

I didn't see how I could keep coaching much longer. Mike Higgins had been right. The older I got, the stranger an unmarried guy coaching kids would look to people. It didn't make sense to keep coaching until things turned bad.

I hated the thought of leaving Callie behind, but I didn't want to have another dream I'd have to conceal. I didn't want to leave the neighborhood or leave my parents, but if I left, it might give my father some hope that my life was moving in the right direction. There were some goodbyes I had to say.

A couple of days later I was pitching batting practice at Woodmont, and Callie drove by in her mother's car. Claire was with her and they just kept going. I didn't get a very good look at Callie, but they came by again a few minutes later.

She had on sunglasses and her window was down and her hair was blowing back in the wind. She looked like a model in a car commercial. I'd only seen her once during the summer, but she called a couple of times. Between having a boyfriend and two part-time jobs, she stayed pretty busy.

They didn't stop that time either, but I was leaning against my car when they drove up after practice was over. Callie was wearing shorts and a cutoff tee shirt. I kept myself from staring at her when she and Claire were walking up. Her boyfriend was out of town and she didn't have to work that day.

Claire came up to me and she threw out her arms. "Ta-da!"

All I did was look at her.

She was impatient. "Well, don't you notice anything different about me?"

She looked the way she usually did, but after a few seconds, I pretended to have noticed a change. "Oh my *God*! I should've seen it as soon as you got out of the car. And I think it makes you look so... *distinctive*."

Claire gave me an odd look. "What? What are you..."

I clapped my hands together and gestured toward her chest. "You've had one of your breasts enlarged! What a *unique* look!"

Claire was fairly well-endowed, and she usually dressed in a way that showed how much she liked being fairly well-endowed. She looked puzzled, but then Callie started laughing. A big grin came over Claire's face. When she took a step toward me and tried to hit me on the arm, I moved back and she missed. All she said was, "What a butt."

I turned halfway around and stuck out one hip. "Thanks, Claire. And all this time I thought you hadn't noticed."

"*I hadn't* noticed. But now that you mention it, I guess it is a halfway decent butt *for somebody your age*." She enjoyed her comeback for a few seconds. "Now do you want to hear what Callie brought me over here to tell you?"

"I'm all ears."

"After a whole year of watching high school guys fall all over themselves about Raquel Welch over there, I finally have a boyfriend. He gave me this necklace that you didn't notice."

She told me he was a year ahead of her in school, and that he'd just bought a car with money he made from working at a gas station. Then she described the way they met and how they flirted with each other, and all the details leading up to when he finally asked her out. Claire was great. She didn't know how pretty she was getting to be, or how smart she was. The guy she was dating didn't sound like he was good enough for her.

Callie was listening off to the side. After Claire finished telling me about her boyfriend, it was a good time to let them know I was leaving town. I did my best to sound sappy and overly nostalgic. "It seems like it was just yesterday when two shy young girls, unsure of themselves but hoping to sell a few raffle tickets, came down to one of my football practices."

Claire was smiling and Callie stared at me like she was waiting for a punchline. "Now here they are less than two years later, and they're driving and they both have boyfriends. It's so important to have somebody older to talk to – somebody to tell them about boys and dating and about all the other things teenage girls need to understand. And now, just when they need me the most, I won't be around. I'm going away for a while, and I feel like I'm abandoning these two innocent, *vulnerable* girls."

Claire looked sad, but Callie cut to the chase. "Where are you going?"

"Well, I plan to drive out to California, and from there I'll probably fly on to the Philippines. I don't know where I'll go after that, or when I'll be back."

Callie's expression didn't change. "What about all your teams?"

"I'll have to find somebody who wants to coach football. And maybe whoever it is will take over basketball and baseball, too."

Callie looked at me with her behind-the-wall expression. "Sounds like you could be gone for a while."

I didn't want there to be an awkward silence. "Yeah and since I won't be around, I thought I should go ahead and give both of you some advice."

Callie looked indifferent. "Okay, let's hear it."

I straightened up and cleared my throat. "There's one thing you should always remember about boys." I paused for dramatic effect. "They're all sex-crazed monsters and if you let them, they will completely ruin your lives." Claire laughed and Callie smiled.

It would've been great if Davey could've taken over my teams, but he was going back for his junior year at Ole Miss. He mentioned that two of his friends had talked about wanting to coach kids. Both of them were high school athletes, and they'd just graduated from college. Davey said they were nice guys, and when I called them they said they'd take my kids.

I called my fifth and sixth-grade football players, and I let them know what I was doing. Some of the parents wanted to put together a going away party, but I talked them out of it. I didn't think I'd be able to get through it.

By then I'd already told Mother and my father that I was going to the Philippines. Mother put on a brave face and hugged me. My father started smiling. He brightened up even more when I told him that I wanted to go to his father's grave and maybe see if the leper colony was still in existence, and then visit some of the places he'd gone during the war.

I probably sounded like I was twelve, but he kept nodding. I could tell that they thought it was a good idea for me to be someplace else. They didn't ask many questions about what I'd do once I got to the other side of the world.

After Mother went back to her bedroom, my father looked at me. "There are some things I need to tell you about. Things you should know before you leave."

Chapter 61

July 20, 1975 – It's Sunday morning. I'm in the car with my father and he's driving. I'll be leaving in a few days, and I'm about to find out what he wants to tell me. We cross the Broad Street viaduct and he pulls up beside Union Station. He points down toward where he first set foot in Nashville. "I was nineteen. I'd never been away from home before, but there were plenty of uncles and aunts and cousins waiting to meet me when I got here. I got off the train right down there. It's hard to believe it was forty years ago."

I think we're going on into town, but he drives back to the west. "This is the way we came after they loaded my suitcases into the trunk of the car." He's retracing the exact route he took that day. He remembers every turn, and he shows me the house on State Street where he lived until he graduated. We drive closer to the Vanderbilt campus, and after he shows me his old fraternity house, he heads for some of his college haunts.

He drove me out to Nine Mile Hill where his favorite nightspot, Hettie Ray's, was when he was back in college. "I won a trophy there in 1938 dancing the Big Apple." Then he took me back toward town and showed me where the Wagon Wheel used to be. "That's where I danced with your mother for the first time."

We got on Harding Road again, and it wasn't long before we drove past the little office on Church Street where he opened his first business. "The hardest thing was getting people to pay their bills." Then he showed me where his favorite restaurant was. "Kleeman's had the best apple pie I ever tasted."

And after that, we stopped in front of the Hermitage Hotel. "When I was in my senior year at Vanderbilt, I had too much to drink at our spring formal. Somebody bet me two dollars that I couldn't do a folk dance called the Hopak.

"We went into the men's room, and after I got down like a catcher in baseball, I started bouncing up and down and kicking out my legs. I thought I was doing okay, but I was going backward the whole time. I hit the back of my head on a urinal and it knocked me out cold." It took him a couple of minutes to stop smiling.

From there we drove out toward Calvary Cemetery. I didn't know that's where we were going until we went through the gate. The cemetery had been established in the 1860s. The rolling terrain was covered with big trees, and there were lots of shadows.

The roadways were narrow, and moving past all the gravestones and statues and monuments was like going through a maze. I wasn't sure my father knew where we were, but he finally stopped the car under a big oak tree. After we got out of the car, I followed him up the slope to where his grandparents were buried.

He stopped when he got to the family plot. "I don't know the last time I was here. I guess it was right around when you were born." Weeds were growing along the edge of his grandfather's gravestone, and he leaned down and started pulling them out by their roots. "It seems strange that I can remember my grandfather and not have any memory of my father. I was only two when he died, but my grandfather lived until I was fourteen.

"He was in Manila when my father died, and he came back out for another visit at the end of the 1920s. I think he was around eighty-five by then, but he didn't seem that old. Even though he walked with a cane, his mind was sharp and he stood up pretty straight. He lived with us for a year. He was eighteen when the Civil War broke out. He was living in Kentucky. Two of his brothers fought for the Union and one joined the Confederacy. He told me he didn't want to be a soldier, so instead of enlisting he went north and started teaching school."

I glanced over at him and smiled. "Maybe the way I felt about Vietnam was genetic."

He just shrugged. "Maybe so." He moved over to his grandmother's grave. "She died back before I was born, but my grandfather talked about how musical she was. He said she could play the piano and the guitar and the mandolin and two or three other instruments, but I've forgotten which ones they were. Anyway, they had five sons and my father was the oldest."

He ran the tip of his shoe across the veil of dried dirt that ran along the edge of her gravestone. It left a mark. "I should've brought you out here a long time ago." A breath of wind grazed the trees. "I think this is a good place to tell you more about what happened when I was in the Philippines – when I went back during the war. I'm not sure I'll get into all of it today, but if you make it all the way over there... well, it's time you knew.

"I've already told you about landing on Leyte. The first time I almost got killed was right after that. Now and then a Jap plane would come over and strafe us, and one morning I was driving a jeep along a muddy stretch of road when this bastard showed up out of nowhere. He was right on top of me and he opened up with his machine gun. Rounds started splattering in the mud behind the jeep, and I dove out and hit the ground. I heard the bullets whining and I could smell the tracers.

"I scrambled around and got behind a tree and I thought the plane was gone, but the pilot circled around and made another run along the road. I hadn't been going very fast when I bailed out, and the jeep ended up against a tree about a hundred feet away. When he came back around, he fired another burst from his machine gun and shot up the jeep.

"I got a look at the pilot. His cockpit was open and he had on goggles, and he was wearing a white scarf that trailed behind him in the wind. He turned his head a little when he went by. Even though I'm pretty sure he saw me, he didn't come back. I didn't have enough time to be afraid, but it wasn't too long before my legs got pretty weak."

Then he told me how a patrol boat dropped him off behind Japanese lines a few days later to gather intelligence about enemy activity in the area. "There were two enlisted men with me, and we went up through Carigara Bay and around past Biliran Island to the northwestern part of Leyte. We spent several days finding out as much as we could about enemy positions. We saw a couple of Japanese patrols, but they never knew we were there.

"The guerillas got word to us about three stranded American airmen from a downed B-25 that crashed in the Visayan Sea. They were a little banged up when they made it to shore, and the guerillas brought them to the plantation house of this Spaniard. His name was Don Felix Miertegui, and he was the biggest landowner in the region.

"Miertegui made me look like a hero when I brought the information he gave me back to headquarters. He knew the size of the Japanese garrisons at Valencia and Palompon, and how many enemy troops there were on nearby islands like Masbate. He not only gave me specific instructions about where our pilots should land if they couldn't make it back to base, he told me where they needed to go to avoid being captured.

"He showed me where the Japs had concealed some landing barges along the shore at Villaba, and said there were also barges hidden out on Poro Island. They were planning to use the barges in night attacks against our forces. Anyway, when we were evacuated we brought the guys from the B-25 back with us, and I'm pretty sure the intelligence we got saved some lives when our forces landed at Ormoc Bay a few days later."

My father didn't say anything else for a minute or two. I got the feeling he was remembering something he didn't want to talk about.

"I moved with my team and we kept advancing until we were closing in on Manila. We expected the Japanese to retreat. I thought we'd be in the city in a few days, and then I'd try to find Mama and Alicia.

"But the Japs dug in and the fight for Manila went on for nearly a month. I got there with my unit on the third day of the battle. I ah... I'll try to describe the way it was. The roar of artillery would go on for hours. Streets were blocked with rubble. The city south of the river was burning. Sometimes the smoke was so thick it blocked out the sun. Refugees were everywhere. And they just kept coming."

He took a deep breath. "We finally crossed the river. What was left of Manila was a nightmare. We didn't realize it at first, but the Japs were massacring civilians. They raped women. They raped girls – including little girls. They killed some of the females after they were raped. They even bayoneted babies. People were starving. The dying begged for help, and mutilated corpses were in the streets. Some had been beheaded. The dead were being piled up and the dying and the wounded were all over the place. The stench of death stayed in my nose, and I could taste it in my mouth."

He was quiet for a few seconds before he changed the subject. "Mama's sister, my Aunt Marina, was married to a Swiss businessman named Otto Weiss. Switzerland stayed neutral in the war, and I knew there was a chance that they hadn't been put into an internment camp. Their house was on the outskirts of Manila, outside Japanese lines, and I went looking for them as soon as I could. Otto and my aunt were out on their front porch when I got there."

"Otto was a character – a real wheeler-dealer. He made a fortune running an import-export business. After the Japs came in, he got involved in the black market with a Japanese general he'd known before the war. The general became his silent partner and kept him out of trouble, and the general also arranged for Mama and Alicia to keep living at home.

"Mama had been married to an American, but she was still a Spanish citizen and Spain was a neutral nation. The general took care of things from there. Otto said he hadn't seen Mama or Alicia since the week before the beginning of the American bombardment. He thought there was a chance they were still at our house. He didn't he thought they were alive.

"I'd been gone for ten years, but I still knew my way around Manila. Our neighborhood was south of the river. There was no way I could get home. I kept checking intelligence reports at headquarters, but nobody knew how long it would be before our lines moved up near the house. When I wasn't on duty, I went everywhere I could think of, looking for somebody who might've seen Alicia or Mama.

"One afternoon I got a jeep and drove up to Clark Field. That's where my father is buried. The cemetery had been shelled, and it took me a while to find his grave. His tombstone was cracked, but it was still legible."

Chapter 62

My father ran the tip of his shoe along the edge of his grandmother's gravestone again. He finally took a deep breath. The way he exhaled reminded me of the way I had exhaled just before I opened the door of his hospital room in Atlanta.

"American lines kept advancing. After a few more days, I went out and found a unit that had moved up to the edge of my old neighborhood. Some of the area was destroyed, but our house looked like it was still in pretty good shape. It was between American lines and the Japs. I started talking to this sergeant named Dutch. He was a really good guy. He was showing me the best way to get to the house, and he took a sniper round in the head. I never heard the shot.

"His brains hit me in the face. I helped a couple of his buddies move his body. We put him behind a jeep and covered him up. A friend of mine had been killed the same way a few days earlier. I was pretty numb by then.

"I needed to check the house to see if Mama's and Alicia's bodies were there. I was carrying a Thompson and I had my pistol, and I worked my way close to the house. One corner was partly caved in, and there was a hole in the roof. I didn't see any signs of life. I was shielded by the house, but there were still mortars and artillery shells to worry about.

"I got to the back porch as fast as I could, and then I went inside. There was less damage than I expected. The furniture was where it was when I left in 1935, and when I went upstairs, Mama's and

Alicia's clothes were still in the closets. I went through all the rooms and checked under the house. They weren't there.

"Otto told me what would happen after the Japs pulled back. He said that any abandoned houses that weren't already looted by the Japanese were almost sure to be looted by Filipinos. He said they were hungry and they didn't have anything, and they'd be looking for whatever they could find.

"I found my father's stamp collection and took it up to my old bedroom. I had just put it behind a stack of boxes in the closet when I heard somebody walking around downstairs.

"I assumed it was a man, and I listened to him move from room to room. I didn't know if he was a Jap soldier or a Filipino, but I thought he was a looter. I stayed in the closet, and I left the door partially open so I could see into the bedroom."

My father was looking at the ground and I noticed a change in the tone of his voice. "There was something slimy against the side of my throat. I reached down and part of Dutch's brain was on the collar of my shirt. I threw it on the floor. After two or three minutes I heard the guy walking up the steps, and then he came into the bedroom.

"He wasn't a Japanese soldier and he didn't look a Filipino. I couldn't tell if he had a gun. I watched him go over and look at himself in the mirror over the bureau. My Thompson was pointed at the middle of his back, and when he turned around to leave I said, 'No te muevas!'"

My father's voice was getting softer and he was speaking more slowly. "He... the guy was holding a pistol and I yelled at him. 'Caer su pistola!' But he didn't drop it. He couldn't see me, but he pointed the pistol in my direction.

"I don't remember pulling the trigger, but I must've fired three or four rounds. He staggered toward the hall and he went down in the doorway. He was hit in the chest, but he was still conscious. His pistol was on the floor. After I came out of the closet, I kicked it away from him.

"He tried to talk, but I couldn't understand him. He kept...

looking at me. He was trying to tell me something. I knelt down, but he couldn't talk. He knew he was dying. He stared at me and there was this... *sadness* in his eyes. I wanted to say something to him, but he turned his face away from me and died."

My father was still staring at the ground. He was pale and he looked smaller than I'd ever seen him look. "The guy was probably in his twenties. He looked Mediterranean. He wasn't a looter. He was just trying to make it over to American lines. I felt... I couldn't leave him in the house and I couldn't just dump his body outside.

"I rolled him over onto his back and lay down on top of him. My back was against his stomach and I held his arms in front of me. Then I rolled over and he was on my back. He wasn't very big. I got up and took him out through the back door. Our lines were fairly close, and I laid him down next to Dutch."

It sounded like it was the first time my father had ever talked about what happened. The wind came through the trees, but he didn't notice it.

"I got back to Otto's place, and one of their friends came by and said that Mama and Alicia had made it across to American lines. He'd seen them at what was left of Saint Luke's Hospital. When I made it to the hospital, I saw a guy I remembered from school. He'd seen me crossing a street the day before, and a couple of hours before I got to the hospital, he'd told Alicia I was in Manila. She left Mama in the least-damaged part of the hospital, and went out to find me. Mama was safe where she was, and I went looking for Alicia.

"It wasn't long before I ran into one of our old neighbors. He'd seen Alicia walking toward San Lazaro Racetrack. I found her not long after I got to the racetrack. She'd been hit in the back by some shrapnel and she was bloody, but she was okay. It had been days since she had anything to eat. She wanted to go back to the hospital and see Mama, but I took her to Otto's house.

"Alicia was walking behind me after we got out of the jeep. She said there was blood all over the back of my shirt. I got some water and then I left for the hospital. The streets were jammed with people and I felt like I was in a dream.

"Saint Luke's was chaotic and Mama wasn't where Alicia had left her. I was afraid I wouldn't be able to find her. I picked my way down to the far end of a corridor. I didn't see her at first, but she was lying in an opening under a staircase. I carried her outside and started looking for a medic.

"Mama had developed diabetes during the war and she needed insulin. A medical unit was set up a few hundred yards away, and after the medic gave her a shot, he handed me a bag of needles and a few vials of insulin. Then I took her to Otto's and put her in bed."

I noticed that his voice was trailing off. "Alicia was eating when I told her what happened at the house... what I'd done. She had a look on her face that I'd never seen before. She looked frozen. When I described the guy I killed, her hands started to shake.

"She told me his name was Ramon. His father was Italian and his mother was Spanish. They lived down the street from our house." My father closed his eyes. "Later on Otto said that he must've gone there to see if our place had been looted."

My father didn't say anything for several seconds, and then he opened his eyes. "Alicia and Ramon worked together in the underground. They had feelings for each other. Alicia just sat there at Otto's dining room table. She didn't cry. She didn't say anything. And she never went back home.

Mama finally told me that they'd talked about getting married after the war. Alicia never got over what happened to Ramon. She died in a plane crash when you were little. You were too young to remember her. There's a lot more you should know about Alicia... but I don't want to talk about this anymore."

I remembered her. I remembered sitting in her lap on our living room sofa while she read to me one Christmas. She was reading *The Three Little Pigs*, and every time she pretended to be the big bad wolf, I'd start laughing and that made her start laughing, too.

On the way home from the cemetery, my father drove back

through downtown and we went past Union Station again. My mother met him there in the summer of 1945 when he came home on leave. The night after he got back, he collapsed and was rushed to Thayer Hospital. He had jungle malaria.

"I was stuck in the hospital until a month or so after VJ Day. The melody of the war lingered on for me, but I was in a lot better shape than most of the guys in my ward."

A few days before I left, Callie and I took a long ride together. I drove into the countryside south of Nashville. She wanted to see if we could get lost. Every time we saw a side road we took it, and we ended up going through a little place I'd never heard of.

There was an old one-story frame building that looked like it could've been a general store a decade or two earlier. If there hadn't been a sign nailed to the side of the structure, we wouldn't have known we were going through Rudderville. It was raining a little and when we came over the top of a hill, not too long after we passed the store, we saw a rainbow out in front of us. It went most of the way across the sky. I knew it was probably a coincidence, but I took it as a sign.

We kept riding down back roads. Callie looked out the window most of the time, and I wondered what was happening on the other side of her wall. We didn't get back to civilization until it was almost dark. She never asked me why I was leaving. She told me to write her a letter if I wanted to, and then she got out of the car. She looked at me before she closed the door. All she said was, "Well, bye."

When I left in 1966, my parents stood in the cold and watched me drive away. It was different the second time. My father was going on a business trip. Mother fixed us breakfast that morning. He wanted to get on the road and beat the traffic, but before he said goodbye he looked at me for a long time. It was like he thought he might not see me again.

Then he walked over and picked up an office-size envelope. "You should read this at some point before you get to Manila. I wrote it about Alicia not long after she died. I wanted there to be a record of what she did during the war, and what she went through during the recapture of Manila."

After he handed me the envelope, he gave me a hug that lasted longer than our hugs usually lasted. I walked out with him to his car, and I watched him until he drove out of sight. I almost opened the envelope, but I decided to wait until I got at least as far as California.

I stuck around for another couple of days, and then I packed up and got ready to go. I wondered if Mother was going to break down the way she had before, but when I hugged her and kissed her goodbye, she held herself together – at least until I was gone.

Instead of going past Callie's house, I went by Woodmont and drove through the neighborhood on my way out of town. And that was it. Just before I got to the Interstate, *Holding On to Yesterday* came on the radio, right on cue.

Before long the miles were flying and West Tennessee shot by until I was in Arkansas and I was floating through my house like a ghost and my parents were old and they were staring at my portrait and then they were young and I was a dream my mother was describing to my father and I was lying in my bed and trying not to drown and something was pulsing through me and I felt like I was on fire and I was afraid that the world was ending and President Kennedy was looking into my eyes and Arkansas passed into Oklahoma and smoke and fire were roaring from the breastworks between Battle Ground Academy and the future and I was crawling away from the fear and the pain and the death of battle and I was lost and then I was back at Woodmont playing with kids and my father was shaking his head as I turned away from Vietnam and Mother was playing bridge with her friends and trying to think of what to say the next time somebody asked where I was working and I drifted and swirled through ten years of coaching kids and what I remembered seemed like the fragments of an illusion and I wondered if I was in New Mexico or if I'd already drifted into Arizona and Yancey Walsh was smiling at me before she walked away in the store on Christmas Eve and I climbed out my bedroom window and walked down the street to the party and my dream girl was standing in the shadows but she was hard to see and the band was playing *Hey Little Girl* and I was dancing with Callie and the highway seemed to go on forever and another afternoon drifted into another night and the darkness drifted back into light and the cars and the trucks and the towns went by and *Send In the Clowns* and *I'm Not in Love* and *At Seventeen* and *Carry On* faded in and out and Mike Higgins was in the backroom at Tiny's telling me what was behind the curtain and the miles and time flew past my window and thoughts and images and memories kept swirling around me as I drove on toward California.

Chapter 63

I was driving through California and the windows of my car were down and my father was wading ashore at Leyte and machine gun fire was slashing toward him as he drove his jeep along a narrow, muddy road and he was watching for Japanese patrols as he moved behind enemy lines and he was searching for his mother and his sister and the wind kept blowing past my open window and after taking a life he was haunted by his sister's loss and swallowed by her pain and he was in the military hospital with Mother standing beside him and the wind kept rushing by and he became a father and grew a business, and as he grew older he kept subduing his memories of the war, night by night and drink by drink.

I wasn't sure where I wanted to go. I hadn't seen Sean Metzger in years. I didn't have his address or his telephone number, but earlier in the summer I ran into a guy I knew back at Peabody. He told me that Sean was living out in San Francisco, and he knew the phone number of the record store where Sean was working.

I wondered if my cousin Wes was still in California. He served a few years for his manslaughter conviction, and then he was released on probation. Nobody in our family knew where he was, but they hadn't looked for him. There was always a chance that he'd changed. I didn't want to just write him off.

And my mother was still in touch with Ann Woodmore. She was living in some little town up on the Oregon coast. I didn't know if I'd call her, but at least I had her telephone number. I remembered the fear on her face the last time I saw her. I didn't realize it at the time, but the way she looked during the missile crisis was the way I felt. I hadn't ever stopped thinking about her, and at some point, I wanted to thank her for helping me.

I finally decided that I'd go to Newport Beach. I could see how Ronny and Susan were, and I could look for Palani. I'd never found his telephone number. I hoped he was alive. If he was alive, there was a chance he still went to the pier at night.

August 18, 1975 – It's two o'clock on Monday morning, and I'm pulling into the parking lot beside the Newport Beach Pier. I hear the ocean and breathe in its fragrance. I think about taking a walk along the beach in the dark, but I go up onto the pier instead. I don't expect to find Palani, but I might as well take a look. The pier hasn't changed since the last time I was here.

The people who fish at night are still sitting and standing along the railing, and they're illuminated by the same dim lights. It's quiet except for the sound of the waves. Then a woman catches a mackerel. The fish draws a couple of comments while it flops around next to her bench. Palani isn't here. I almost ask a guy if he knows him, but I just walk back down the pier and get in my car.

I tilted back my seat and slept for two or three hours. After the sun came up, I walked over and sat on a bench outside a little restaurant that was about to open for breakfast. I wanted to catch up on the news, and I got an *LA Times* from the rack.

It had been one thing after another since the congressional investigations got underway. Even though there were charges that the investigations could be part of a cover-up, reports issued by the Rockefeller Commission in June disclosed that the CIA had violated its charter. The agency had engaged in all sorts of illegal activities – from spying and conducting drug experiments on private citizens, to making political donations to preferred candidates.

And more came out after that. In July, the day after a source disclosed that the White House staff had been infiltrated by the CIA, its director, Richard Helms, swore that the CIA had not operated any death squads. Then a highly decorated former Army colonel publicly announced that Helms was lying.

After an older couple came by walking their dog, I started reading a story about an appearance Senator Church had made the day before on *Meet the Press*. The senator didn't mention the CIA or the NSA by name. He didn't have to.

"The United States government has perfected a technological capability that enables us to monitor the messages that go through the air... that capability at any time could be turned around on the American people, and no American would have any privacy left: such is the capability to monitor everything – telephone conversations, telegrams – it doesn't matter. There would be no place to hide.

"If this government ever became a tyranny, if a dictator ever took charge in this country, the technological capacity that the intelligence community has given the government could enable it to impose total tyranny, and there would be no way to fight back because the most careful effort to combine together in resistance to the government, no matter how privately it was done, is within the reach of the government...

"I know the capacity that is there to make tyranny total in America, and we must see to it that this agency, and all agencies that possess this technology, operate within the law and under proper supervision so that we never cross over that abyss. That is the abyss from which there is no return."

After a couple of days, I got together with Ronny and Susan. When I went to their apartment for dinner I didn't know what to expect. They had two daughters and they seemed to be getting along pretty well on Ronny's engineering salary, but they both looked tired and I could feel the tension in their relationship.

They were having problems and I wondered if they would stay together.

I came to the pier for three more weeks before I asked about Palani. I would've probably done it sooner, but I was afraid I might find out he was dead. It wasn't long before I picked out a guy who was there almost every night.

He answered without looking up. "Palani? No. What's he look like?"

I told him how old Palani was, and described his Hawaiian shirts with the sleeves cut off and his big arms, and that he liked to use squid for bait.

The guy kept staring out toward the water. "That sounds like Preacher. He comes around sometimes, but it's been a while since I've seen him."

A woman sitting a few feet away overheard my description of Palani. "Your friend... does he like to save souls?"

The guy I was talking to started smiling. "Yeah, Preacher has been known to try and save a soul now and then."

I was pretty sure that Preacher and Palani were the same person. I was relieved. I thought about giving the guy my name and Ronny's phone number in case Preacher came by, but I didn't.

I told myself that if he didn't show up by the time I left for Manila, then I might be able to look for him again when I came back through on my way to Nashville. I'd brought my copy of *Centennial* from home. I still hadn't finished it, and I started reading on nights when I came to the pier.

I liked being there at night. I usually waited till a couple of hours after dark, and I'd walk down to the end and find an empty bench under one of the lights. The later it got, the more time seemed to slow down. When I read about the fictional events that unfolded in Centennial, Colorado, I usually ended up wondering about what had happened in my neighborhood.

I still saw Ronny and Susan from time to time, and it wasn't long before Ronny's mother invited me to stay with her. She said she liked having me around the last time I was there, and it didn't make sense for me to keep staying in a motel.

September 11, 1975 – The pier is quiet. I'm holding the envelope my father gave me before I left. I've been mulling over what he told me when we were in the cemetery, and I keep thinking about my aunt. I haven't stopped wondering what else she went through during the war. I want to write a poem about the loving woman who doubled over with laughter while she was reading The Three Little Pigs. Only a few years earlier, she'd been a bloody, grief-stricken survivor in the wake of a devastating battle. I'd planned to be somewhere over the Pacific Ocean when I read what was in the envelope, but I don't want to wait that long.

My father's account was concise and well-written. Before the Japanese marched into Manila, Alicia destroyed all the records of her employment with the United States Army. Her uncle, Otto Weiss, explained to the authorities that Alicia, who was a fairly accomplished musician, was merely a young Spanish woman who taught piano and lived with her mother. That was enough to keep her from being sent to the prison camp that had been established at the University of Santo Tomas.

Although he was staunchly pro-American, Otto Weiss represented himself as a neutral Swiss businessman. He was a partner in a rock quarry, and he had concealed a large supply of nitroglycerin and dynamite in a small cave on the back part of his property.

Because Alicia had students in various parts of the city, she was able to go all across Manila without attracting suspicion. It wasn't long before she became an intermediary between her uncle and members of the underground. They were part of a network involved in transporting explosives and other supplies to Filipino guerillas fighting the Japanese in the mountains of central Luzon.

Alicia became more and more active in working with the guerillas, and her group included Ramon, the young man who had been killed by my father. One member of her network was captured, but he managed to kill himself before he was tortured. Then, Otto Weiss distributed cyanide tablets. Their network kept sending explosives to the guerillas, and there were indications that Japanese investigators were closing in on the group when American troops reached the outskirts of Manila.

Not long after the shelling started, Japanese soldiers had started killing civilians. Alicia and my grandmother hid during the day, and spent seven nights making their way toward American lines. They hid in the ruins of bombed-out houses, and spent one night in the grease pit of a garage. One morning they took refuge in a church, but it was strewn with the decomposing corpses of priests and nuns, and with the disemboweled remains of the men, women, and children who had been hiding there when they were discovered by the Japanese.

Squads of Japanese soldiers continued killing civilians. Bodies were lying in the streets. She and her mother were in the ruins of a house when an artillery shell exploded, and Alicia was hit by shrapnel. They had almost no food and just a little water while they were trying to escape.

Alicia weighed less than ninety-five pounds by then, but after two or three days she had to carry her exhausted mother on her back. At one point, they took refuge in a partially destroyed apartment building not far from American lines. My aunt was looking through the blinds of a second-floor apartment when she saw thirty-five or forty children coming up the street. They were being escorted by Red Cross nurses, and she watched Japanese soldiers open fire from a machine gun emplacement and shoot them all down.

Just before dawn on the morning when my father killed Ramon, my aunt maneuvered my grandmother through a final barrier of barbed wire. But before they reached safety, Alicia had to float her mother across the Pasig River on a wooden door. Not too long after that, she ran into a neighbor and found out that my father had come for them.

My father wrote about how they found each other at the

racetrack, and a little about her life in the years after the war. But he didn't end his account there. "I did what I thought I was supposed to do. But if I hadn't gone to the house to look for Mama and Alicia, Dutch wouldn't have been killed. I was scared, but if I hadn't been aiming at his chest when I pulled the trigger, Ramon wouldn't have died. When I killed Ramon, I killed my sister."

Chapter 64

The next day I walked down to the Wedge and back to the pier. I kept thinking about my trip to the Philippines. I wondered if any of the places my father had told me about, or mentioned in what he wrote about my Aunt Alicia, were still there. I wanted to see Palani, but I didn't know how much longer I'd stay in Newport Beach. I finally decided that I'd wait until it was too cold to body surf, and then I'd go on up to San Francisco and try to see Sean before I left for Manila.

There was a school down the street from where Ronny's mother lived. I saw a kids' football team practicing there just about every afternoon when I was on my way back from the beach. They looked like fifth and sixth graders. I mostly wanted to see kids practicing football, but I was also curious about whether the boys in California were any different from the guys I'd coached back in Tennessee. One day I got there before any of the players showed up. There was a track around the field, and I watched their practice while I was jogging.

Unfortunately for the kids, they were being coached by a couple of fathers who didn't know what they were doing. They knew how to blow a whistle and that was about it. Some of the players looked pretty athletic when they were messing around before practice, but they were sloppy when they warmed up, and their huddles were a mess.

Only a couple of offensive linemen knew how to get in a decent stance, and when the offense started running plays against the defense, almost nobody went full speed. The fathers were getting frustrated and I wondered if they'd give up and leave. I pictured myself going over and getting the kids on the right track, but the two dads stuck around and I finally left.

I still loved being in the ocean and swimming along the bottom and feeling the water rushing around me when a big wave came in, but the water seemed colder than it was before. I spent a lot of time walking on the beach.

There were good-looking girls and good-looking women all over the place, and there were times when it was hard to tell the difference. I'd walk along the edge of the water and tell myself that if I ran into somebody who could give Callie a run for her money, it might break the spell I was under. Then maybe I wouldn't be obsessed with her anymore. But nobody came close.

I was pretty sure that she didn't like being beautiful. That she saw the way she looked as a burden.

I thought about writing her a letter, but I didn't think she'd want to hear about how I was reading a book on the pier at night, or watching a marriage going bad. But not too long after that, something came along that seemed like it might be worth telling her about.

The surf was usually around two or three feet, and once in a while it would get up to seven or eight feet, which was right at my limit. But toward the end of September, some much bigger waves were on their way.

An unusually powerful storm was somewhere off New Zealand, and it was predicted to generate powerful surf all along the coast of Southern California. I'd been knocked upside down and sideways a few times by six-foot waves, and the waves that were on their way were supposed to be twelve to fifteen feet, and maybe bigger.

I hadn't ever been around waves that massive. A few times I was in the water when a nine or ten-foot wave moved in. I'd start swimming like I was going to catch it, but I always bailed out at the last minute. When waves were that big, I always ended up watching other guys take the risks I wasn't willing to take.

But mountains of water were rolling toward the California coast, and it was time to finally make myself go after a wave I was scared of. I kept reminding myself about how courageous my father was in the Philippines – back when he was my age. Taking on a big wave wasn't anywhere close to fighting in a war, but I kept telling myself that I should tackle a big wave at least once in my life. I was pretty sure that Callie would go after the first wave she saw.

September 24, 1975 – I hear the waves breaking as soon as I turn off Balboa Boulevard. They're exploding like bombs. There are a lot more cars than usual, but I finally find a place to park three blocks away from the ocean. People are walking toward the sound of the surf, and I follow them up past the end of 40th Street and out onto the sand. The swells are rolling in, and there's a red flag blowing on top of the lifeguard platform. The beach is crowded, but there aren't many surfers in the water. A wave thunders over the far end of the jetty where I kept the kid from climbing up on the rocks the last time I was in California. These waves are a whole lot bigger than they were back then.

I put on my fins and backed into the ocean, but I stopped when the water got halfway up my thighs. Frigid water had been churned up to the surface. I'd never been in water that cold. Watching the waves break while I was standing on the sand was one thing. Feeling the force of that much rushing water was something else. The closer a wave was, the bigger it looked, and I wanted to walk back up onto the sand.

But I stayed where I was. I made myself think about all the times I'd seen guys on my team take chances they didn't want to take. I thought about kids who made themselves tackle guys who were a lot bigger than they were. Kids who made themselves get in the batter's box even though the pitcher they were facing had just hit a batter with a fastball. Kids who got in front of another ground ball right after being hit by a bad hop. And I kept thinking about other quiet acts of bravery I'd seen since I started coaching.

I made myself go further out, but after ten or fifteen minutes I still hadn't gotten very far. I'd make it a few yards and a wave would roar in and sweep me back toward the beach. But there was finally enough of a lull for me to get out past the break line. There were ten or twelve other guys just down from me, but they all had boards and all of them were wearing wetsuits. I was the only body surfer.

I looked in at the people lining the beach. There were a good number of photographers, and they were waiting with their cameras and their oversized lenses to capture whatever images they could capture. I hoped somebody would photograph me when I was going over the falls, or if I got lucky, when I was riding the shoulder of a wave.

Getting out where I was took a lot out of me, and I needed to rest. After a few minutes, a big swell rolled underneath me, and I could see a huge set coming in. The other guys had been taking off on the second or third wave, and I decided to take the first wave and get it over with.

I got in position and took some deep breaths. When the wave got close I started swimming, but my arms felt heavy. I couldn't get where I had to be to catch it, and I almost got sucked over the falls. Looking over the edge was like looking down from the roof of a two-story building.

I was really cold and I couldn't feel my toes, but I didn't get scared until I started having trouble moving my arms. I could've asked one of the board surfers for help, but I was pretty sure I could make it back in on my own. After the next big set came through, I took off. My arms and legs were really sluggish, but I was most of the way in when a monster wave broke behind me.

I got one good breath before I went under. An avalanche of water tore through and ripped the fins off my feet and dragged me along the bottom. I don't know how long it was before I got back to the surface. I swallowed some water and I came up coughing, but I was close enough to get back to the beach.

The right side of my face was scraped up and both my elbows were bleeding. I felt shaky and I wanted to lie down on the sand, but people were staring at me and I started walking along the edge of the water. I tried not to look as bad as I felt. I spent a few minutes pretending to look for my fins before I went back to my car. I was shivering and I rolled up the windows and turned on the heater as high as it would go, and I drove around until I warmed up.

So much for my rendezvous with a giant wave that had been created by a distant storm. So much for proving something to myself. And so much for doing something worth writing about to Callie.

I got a letter from her four days later. Her boyfriend managed to graduate in the spring, but he wasn't going to college. He joined the Navy instead. "On Sunday I was more or less depressed and I ended up driving around and I started crying. After that I drove out into the country and went looking for Rudderville, but I couldn't find it. And then there's school – God how I hate it..."

She seemed like a different person when she wrote. It probably didn't matter that her boyfriend was leaving. It wouldn't be long before she had another one. I hoped the next guy would be better than the last one.

It looked like Palani might not show up, and I went ahead and tried to locate Wes. I went to the Newport Beach Library and looked through the telephone books that covered Los Angeles and the surrounding cities. There were eleven listings with last names and first names or initials that could've been Wes, and I started calling the numbers I'd written down.

On the fifth call, I heard his voice, but I was surprised to find him and I started stammering. Before I could tell him who I was, he cut me off. "Learn how to talk, asshole." He hung up on me. I didn't call him back.

Chapter 65

October 11, 1975 – It's about 11 PM on Saturday, and I'm at the end of the Newport Beach Pier. I'm making another run at writing a poem about my father and my aunt during the Battle of Manila, but I'm not getting anywhere. I hear a whistle. I look up and Palani is walking right toward me. There's a big smile on his face. He's a little heavier than he was, but he looks strong and healthy. I get up and start to shake his hand, but he stops me. After he leans his pole against the railing and puts down his bait bucket and his tackle box, he gives me a bear hug. "The prodigal friend has finally returned." A couple of people look around before they go back to fishing. He stares into my eyes for a few seconds. "Yep, I can still see Kaimi. I'm glad he hasn't disappeared."

Palani sat down beside me on the bench and ran his hook through a squid. "When I showed up last night, Miguel told me that a young guy with some kind of an accent was looking for me. But he said the guy didn't know me as Preacher.

"He couldn't tell me what you looked like, but I knew it was you when he said you read the whole time you were here. I'm just glad you stuck around long enough for me to see you."

He laughed when I told him about losing his phone number. "The same thing happened to me."

I'd forgotten that I told him how to get in touch with me.

"I kept thinking I'd hear from you, and after a while I decided to give you a call. But I couldn't find where I'd put your number. I thought it would turn up, but it never did. There were times when I was afraid you might've gone over to Vietnam and gotten yourself killed."

He reached back and threw his line out into the darkness. "It's just like old times, Kaimi. It's just like old times."

I was about to start asking him questions, but he spoke up first. "Some things have happened since... since the last time you were here. I want to catch up on you, but I should probably get my stuff out of the way first. That way I'll be able to listen to you without wondering how I'm going to explain everything."

The first thing Palani told me was why the people on the pier called him Preacher. "It was after I lost my oldest granddaughter. She had leukemia. It was... I don't know, about a year after you left. She was so smart and so good. When she died... well it didn't make any sense. I spent a few weeks screaming at God, just in case he could hear me. I didn't leave my house much, and one of my neighbors thought I was going crazy. She was probably right.

"It wasn't long before she showed up with the minister from her church. He was ten or fifteen years older than I was. If he'd been younger I might've just thrown him through a window. And if he'd told me that my granddaughter dying was part of God's plan, I might've thrown him through the window anyway. But all he did was ask about her and listen.

"After I told him that she had a brother and a sister, he said a couple of things... Well, what he told me got my attention. He said what happened to my granddaughter would change the lives of everybody who loved her. He said there are times when a journey can begin in the shadows and end up in the light.

"I wasn't sure what he meant, and I just kept listening. He said that my other grandchildren... they were on a journey, and that the direction of each one of their journeys was changed by their sister's death.

"He said that from then on, more and more of the decisions my grandkids made, and more and more of the friends they had, would be different than if their sister hadn't died. He said who they ended up marrying would be different, and the children they'd eventually have and love would be different, too. He told me that both of my grandchildren would probably hold a baby in their arms someday, and at that point, they might realize that the child in their arms wouldn't have been born without the loss of their sister."

Palani was trying to keep from getting emotional and he didn't say anything for a while. A few minutes later he caught a halibut, and after he put it in his bucket, he glanced over at me. "I had some other talks with that minister. The more I got to know him, the more I could see how wise he was. He made me think about this guy I ran into on Iwo Jima.

"It was three or four days after the landing, and the major told me to take a lieutenant named Jarvis out to a hospital ship. He and his men got cut off behind enemy lines, and he had the shakes.

"I found Jarvis sitting in his foxhole and he was praying. His voice was calm, but his legs were trembling and his hands were shaking. He looked like he was holding onto a jackhammer. I told him why I was there, and he said he wasn't leaving.

"He kept shaking and I asked him why he didn't want to be evacuated. He said he wouldn't ever be worth a damn if he went back to the ship. He said he wasn't going to live the rest of his life thinking he didn't do his duty. Then he asked me if it would help if he could get himself to stop shaking. I'd seen soldiers with the shakes before. I'd never heard about anybody being able to stop.

"I didn't see any harm in giving him a chance, but I stuck around to make sure he didn't run off. I sat on the side of the foxhole and he started praying again. He was talking to Jesus and then he started singing *Amazing Grace*. He kept singing it over and over and it took a while, but little by little he calmed down.

"By the time I stood back up I had... I don't know... I guess I had a whole lot of respect for the power of what he believed. And when I was taking him to HQ to see the major, we ran into a guy who was curled up into a ball. He was lying on the ground behind some sandbags.

"He was crying and Jarvis went over and started singing

Amazing Grace again. Then he started stroking the guy's hair, and after that, he put his hands on either side of the guy's face and started praying. I don't remember what he said, but his voice was really soothing. It was like he was somebody else.

"Pretty soon the other guy settled down, and he was up walking around by the time we left. I told Jarvis that I'd take care of things with the major. But before he headed back to his foxhole, I asked him to pray for me. When he did I could feel his prayer... it was like it was glowing inside me. I wanted to hold on to whatever it was that he'd given me, but I thought it was gone until I talked to that minister.

"I ended up going to the minister's church and then I started reading the Bible, and before long I was reading the Bible all the time. I felt like I was finally closing in on the truth, and I wanted to help other people find it, too.

"I started coming out here to fish again, and if somebody looked like they had a problem, I'd talk to them. I left them alone if they said they didn't want to talk, but most of the time they told me what was wrong. Every once in a while, I said something that helped. Anyway, that's why people around here started calling me Preacher.

"I committed myself to try to do God's will, and things went along pretty well for a while. But then the minister got sick and moved away, and the new minister... it was like he didn't have any... any grace. I kept hoping things would change, but one Sunday he preached a whole sermon condemning Earth Day. It was the first time I ever heard of Earth Day.

"He stood up in the pulpit and preached about how God gave mankind dominion over nature. After that, he said the environmental movement was ungodly. I've always cared about nature and I've always loved the ocean, and damn if he didn't end up condemning the people who were trying to save whales. I wanted to walk out right then, but I just sat there.

"Later on I asked him why having dominion over nature made it okay to destroy what God had created. He never answered my question. He just stood there and frowned at me. The guy just picked something out of the Bible and started using it like a weapon. And he used it against people who were trying to do what they thought was right."

Palani stopped talking and then he looked over at me and shook his head. "I've already talked you half to death, and I haven't even gotten around to what I wanted to say."

He hadn't caught anything for a while. He'd cast and slowly reel in his line, and while he was reeling it in he moved the tip of his rod up and back. Palani looked pretty much the way he looked before, but how he saw the world had changed.

I was thinking about my father when Palani told me how different he was after the death of his granddaughter. My father was a little different after his heart attack, and I wondered how much more he'd change.

Palani reached back and made another long cast. "Well, I tried a few different churches and I met some good people, but it seemed like a lot of the Christians I ran into were all about feeling morally superior. They weren't too worried about how they treated other people. When they said they accepted Jesus as their savior, it was like they were saying something they'd memorized. Sometimes they made being a Christian sound like it was an insurance policy they'd bought to make sure they didn't end up in hell.

"I kept wondering what would happen if the heavens opened up and God Almighty appeared and said that everything people believed was true except for the part about heaven and hell. If that happened, I was pretty sure there would've been a stampede out of every church and temple and mosque on the planet.

"I thought people should want to do God's work whether they got anything out of it or not. I really got tired of seeing Christians treat their relationship with God like it was a business transaction.

"I couldn't understand the way a lot of them prayed for things. They asked God for a new car or more money or a better house, but I didn't hear many folks offer to help God when they prayed.

I didn't hear them ask God how they could help other people. That's what I thought the New Testament was about – helping God by helping each other.

"Anyway, I told myself I must be missing something. After that, I spent even more time reading the Bible. Sometimes I read until the words started running together.

"But there were a few things I couldn't make myself believe. I really had a hard time when it came to hell. I never believed that a benevolent and all-powerful God would torture somebody's soul forever. Not even the worst human being on Earth would do that. I refused to believe that God is morally inferior to the people he created.

"And sometimes scripture seemed to be saying two different things. There were an awful lot of contradictions. I went down one dead end after another, but I kept on praying about it.

"One night I was out here fishing and I was thinking about how many different interpretations of the Bible there are, and how many different Christian denominations there are. That's when something came to me. It seemed to me that if the Bible really did come straight from God, there wouldn't be so much disagreement about what had been written.

"I still thought the Bible was a way to find God, but there was another way, and the preachers were ignoring it. Christians always say they believe that God created the heavens and the earth, but they don't pay much attention to the heavens and the earth that God created. Most people of faith just ignore nature. Why isn't having reverence for what God has created... Why isn't that a way to show reverence for God?

"I finally decided that God gave man the ability to understand nature for a reason. But the preacher who condemned Earth Day never said anything about that. He just kept saying that accepting science was going against God."

He shook his head and he was quiet for a couple of minutes. Then he handed me his pole and got up, and he walked down the pier toward the restroom. I stood up and leaned against the railing, and I looked down at the water. The surface of the ocean was dark and gentle.

When he came back he started talking before he sat down. "Was it Einstein who asked why God would've given him a brain if he wasn't supposed to use it? Whoever said it... Well, that's right. I think God gave us our brains for a reason."

I handed him back his pole.

"Couldn't God have given us the ability to develop science for a reason? Why wouldn't he want us to use science to understand what he created? I think it's wrong not to use our abilities. Maybe that's what the parable of the talents is about. I think turning our backs on what God has given us... That's the same as turning our backs on God. I... I wish I was explaining this better. It's real clear to me when I think about it, but it doesn't sound that way when I hear myself say it."

It sounded pretty clear to me. "You're explaining it fine."

"Well I don't know how you could follow any of that, but good for you if you did." Palani reached into his pocket and pulled out a plastic bag. "Here – you'll like this. I might not be much of a philosopher or whatever it is I've turned into, but I do know how to make brownies."

We sat on the pier and ate brownies, and after a while, he went a little farther down the road he'd been on. "I have a lot of admiration for Galileo. He damn sure used the brain he was given.

"Galileo studied what God created, and he found out that the Church had it all wrong. He discovered that the sun didn't revolve around the Earth – it was the other way around. Galileo got in trouble for telling the truth, but I believe he did what God wanted him to do."

Palani stretched and smiled. "Remember that verse you told me about before? The one about whatsoever is true and honest and just and pure? After I started going to church again, I looked it up in the Bible. It's a verse from Paul's letter to the Philippians. It still makes a lot of sense to me. I think that truth and honesty and justice and purity all lead to God, but right now I want to talk about truth.

"Whether it comes from you or me or Galileo or Einstein or anybody else, I've come to believe that what is true leads to God, and what is untrue leads away from God. I believe that God gave us brains so we can figure out what is true and what isn't true. I believe he gave us brains so we can know him through what he has created. The more I pray about it, the more I believe that God gave us brains so we can find him.

"I also believe that God wants us to protect what he's created. I can't stand it when I hear some Christian talk about how it's okay if some habitat is destroyed, or if a species that God created goes extinct. There's nothing okay about defiling nature and killing off God's creations." Palani was talking louder than he meant to, and the woman on the next bench smiled at him.

He nodded at her. "Sorry, Mary." Then he arched his back and stretched again. He reached up with his left hand and rubbed his right shoulder, and he looked over at me. "Next time I start blabbering just give me an elbow and tell me to pipe down." He was quiet for a few seconds. "There's a lot more I want to tell you, but it'll keep. Now I'm ready to hear what you've been up to."

Chapter 66

I'd wanted to tell Palani about my life for a long time. There were plenty of times when I pictured us talking together on the pier, but I was finally there and I didn't know where to start. I was stammering my way through telling him about college when he asked me a question. He wanted to know the most important thing I'd learned since the last time I saw him.

I was trying to come up with some piece of wisdom I picked up along the way, and I started stammering again. "You mean something like... like I learned in school?"

Palani shrugged. "In school or wherever. Learning is learning."

"Well, I guess the biggest thing is that I love kids." Then I told him about coaching at Woodmont and how smart and brave and complicated kids could be. And how honest they usually were and how their lives were full of possibilities. And that my life seemed to slow down when I was showing them how to catch a fly ball or shoot a layup or get in a three-point stance. And what it was like to be lost in the magic of an afternoon practice and watch some kid who was crying start to smile and what it was like to see fear turn into confidence. And I told him about all the color kids had brought into my life and how great it was when a relationship with a player – a relationship that started on a baseball diamond or a football field or a basketball court – turned into a friendship.

I realized that I was talking faster and faster, and I looked over at Palani. He was smiling and I shook my head. "Next time just give me an elbow and tell me to pipe down."

"Piping down is the last thing I want you to do. At first – right after you left – I kept hoping that you'd figure out who you really are. And later on, hoping turned into praying. When you were out here before, you kept beating yourself up. Like I said before, I was afraid you might beat yourself up all the way over to Vietnam. It sounds like when you discovered the way you felt about kids... When that happened, you discovered the light that you needed to find. It sounds like finding kids might've saved you."

Then I went ahead and told him how I got out of going into the military, and how guilty I felt that somebody else went in my place.

Palani held up his hand. "Okay, and the guy who took your place had to make the same decision that you made. He had to decide whether to go in or stay out. Maybe for you, it all came down to who was going to control your life. Was it the government – and with Vietnam that meant the politicians – or was it you?

"And for all you know, the guy who ended up going might've *wanted* to be a soldier. He could've been all gung-ho about the war. You can go around and around and worry about it for the rest of your life, but it won't get you anywhere.

"Maybe the path you were born to follow just wasn't supposed to go through Southeast Asia. It sounds like the kids you were coaching needed you a whole lot more than the army did."

Then I told Palani about imagining myself marching off into the future from Battle Ground Academy. I told him how I didn't charge into all the smoke and gunfire and climb over the top of the imaginary barricade, and about ending up back at Woodmont School. I told him that I wanted the kids on my teams to be more than I was – and more than they would've been if I hadn't come along.

I looked over at Palani. He wouldn't like the next thing I was going to tell him. When I tried to explain that my path was moving away from working with kids, he started shifting around like he couldn't get comfortable.

I told him how much I'd disappointed my parents and the way

my friends saw me, and how I didn't see any way I could keep doing what I'd been doing. Then I told him I was on my way to the Philippines, and how it might be a while before I went back home.

From there, I tried to explain that reading *Centennial* made me want to write a book about my neighborhood. I said it could be a nonfiction version of what James Michener had written, and it could end with what busing and all the development did to the place where I grew up. I stopped talking. I just sat there for a while and waited for Palani to catch another fish.

He finally stood up and handed me his pole. He took a few steps in the direction of the restroom, but then he came back. "False alarm." He took back his pole and reeled in his line. The bait was gone and he reached into his bucket for another squid. I couldn't tell him about Mike Higgins, but I didn't want to conceal anything else.

I wasn't sure how much he wanted to know about my history with girls, but I went ahead and told him. He'd been slouching, but he sat up a little straighter when I started talking about the Blonde Bombshell.

I told him what happened to Yancey, about a few of the divorced mothers and about Bethany, and I even told him about Diane Smith. I had a feeling that I was taking him back to his younger days. Then I told him about Callie Lee. I expected him to start shaking his head, or for his posture to deflate back into a slouch, but I didn't see any change.

I explained the way things unfolded from the time when Callie was a kid. I told him about trying to break through the wall that was around her, and how guilty I felt about the dreams I had, and how I couldn't make myself stop thinking about her.

He finally stood up and reeled in his line. His bait hadn't been touched and he made another cast. "Well, I don't guess anybody will ever accuse you of doing things the easy way."

He gestured for me to hand him a beer from his cooler. "I guess it would've been better if you hadn't seen her the way you did, but that's the way you saw her. It sounds like you tried to hold back on your feelings, and at least you were honest about it. I mean you even talked to her mother." He smiled. "I'm surprised she didn't faint."

Palani was about to say something else when the tip of his fishing rod started to bend. He jerked back on his line, and started reeling in a fish. He could tell that it would be too small to keep.

"A girl bowled me over like that back during the war. She might've been out of high school, but I couldn't tell for sure. It was right before I shipped out the second time." He lifted a small mackerel over the side of the railing. He unhooked it and dropped it back into the ocean.

"There was a dance and a friend of mine had a date with this girl. *Man* was she beautiful. She made me feel like I was in a dream. It was the first time anybody ever made me feel that way. I didn't do anything about it, and a couple of weeks later I was on my way to Honolulu on a troop ship.

"I thought about her the whole time I was in the service. I never saw her again, but I still think about her sometimes." He looked off into the darkness. "Have you ever heard about the green flash?"

"The Green Flash? It sounds like a comic book character."

Palani laughed. "No, a green flash is... It's sort of an optical event. At sunset, when you're on the beach or out in a boat and if the conditions are just right – when the air and the light are a certain way and when the top edge of the sun is just disappearing on the horizon – sometimes, for a split second, there'll be a burst of green light at the edge of the ocean.

"It's there, and just like that it's gone. That's the way I ended up thinking about the girl at the dance.

"I told myself that the reason she seemed to glow was because I was seeing her when she was more beautiful than she'd ever been, and more beautiful than she'd ever be again. I told myself that what I'd seen was her green flash. She was probably a knockout for years after that, but not the way she was that night. On that night she was magic."

After a while, he reeled in his line and threw another undersized mackerel off the side of the pier. I was thinking about the way Callie looked when I saw her standing beside the road in the patch of sunlight. I was about to get up and walk around when Palani smiled at me. "So you think you could've been blinded by the green flash?"

"If there was a flash with Callie, it was probably golden. And instead of going blind, it was more like I went crazy."

Palani laughed. "Yeah. Going blind would've probably taken care of the problem."

He was about to say something else, but his rod lurched down and hit the top of the railing. He pulled back as fast as he could and tried to set the hook, but whatever hit the bait was gone.

He started reeling in his line. "I don't know what that was, but it was *big*. The same thing happened three or four years ago. It ripped my rod right out of my hands. First time I ever lost a rod."

Mary started laughing. "Yeah, and he did a whole lot of cussing. *Especially* for a preacher."

Palani grinned. "Well, it was my favorite rod." He reeled in his line the rest of the way. His hook was bent to one side. After he cut it off, he reached down and opened his tackle box. He pulled out a larger hook and tied it onto his line. Then he ran the hook through another squid and made another long cast from the pier.

He was quiet for two or three minutes before he said anything else. "You've told me something that makes me want to stand up and dance across the pier. It's the way you feel about kids. I think that's a gift from God. But there's something else that I need to be honest about.

"Hearing you talk about turning your back on your coaching... That makes me want to lean down and bang my head against this rail. You have a gift. I hope you can find a way to keep on working with kids."

He reeled in his line more slowly than he had before. "And

about the girl... I understand why you'd want to wait a few years and see what happens. But a girl that age... you're gonna have to wait a *long* time. Spending the next few years of your life while you see how things turn out – that's taking a pretty big risk.

"It would be a shame if the right woman came along while you're giving all your attention to somebody else." He looked over at me. "That's probably more than you wanted to hear, but there's something else I want to tell you – I mean if you can stand to hear it."

"Go ahead. I need all the help I can get."

"Well, it's just an observation. There was something I said when you were out here before. It was the first time I called you Kaimi. I said that things seemed to hit you a lot harder than they hit most people. Back then it was the missile crisis and how bad you felt about flunking out of school. Now it's how much you love kids, and how you're coaching more teams than anybody else.

"And I think it's the same with the girl. She's beautiful and I'm sure a lot of other guys have been infatuated with her, but it sounds like you're the only one who can't turn around and walk away. But here's what I want to say about the girl. Maybe you're more in love with who you think she could end up being, than with who she is."

We were quiet until he was reeling in another fish. "Well Kaimi, this is it. I think it's time to call it a night. There's a lot more to say, but I'm all talked out."

He was leaving to visit his grandchildren in three days, and we decided to meet back at the pier before he left town. I stayed for a while and got out my journal, and after I got through writing about seeing Palani again, I started a poem. It was the first one I'd written in a while, but it came pretty easily.

We met on the pier a couple of nights later. I told him about some of the kids I'd coached and what was happening to my neighborhood and more about the book I wanted to write. And the way my parents saw me and about my father's time in the Philippines, and then I said a little more about Callie Lee.

He described growing up in Hawaii, and then he talked about working for the union. He said the union was on his mind a lot since Jimmy Hoffa of the Teamsters Union had disappeared back in late July. He told me a lot more than he ever had about his wife and how deeply he still loved her, and then he went back to telling me how much he missed his granddaughter and how much closer he wanted to be to God.

He was closing his tackle box when I let him know I planned to come back through Newport Beach on my way home from the Philippines. The sky was getting light when we walked down the pier to the parking lot. After he got in his car, I gave him a copy of the poem I'd written.

The Fisherman

Sensing that truth
Is somewhere out
Beneath the black water,
He comes back
Year after year
And casts his line
Into the darkness.
Then, after so many nights
Of gazing beyond
The illumination
Of the pier,
A night comes
When he finally sees it,
Shining and glowing
In the distance.
He watches it
Make a long, slow turn
And begin to glide

Toward him,
And as it rises
Near the surface,
Its tail moving slowly
Back and forth
In an elegant sweep,
He wonders if
It will lead him
Closer to God.

Chapter 67

I wanted to find Sean, and the next day I called the record store in San Francisco. He still worked there, but he was taking some time off. I got his home number, and a woman answered when I called.

She told me he wasn't home. She seemed a little wary until I told her who I was. He'd told her about me and she said he'd want to see me. She also said there was an extra room where I could stay. That night I told Susan and Ronny and his mother goodbye.

The next morning I took off up the Coast Highway. Southern California was more homogenized than ever. There were signs beside the highway that showed where one city ended and the next one began, but the cities were more like jurisdictions. The whole place was just one huge metropolis. I wondered if Nashville would be the same way in another hundred years. I was pretty far north of Los Angeles when I finally got away from the sprawl.

There were times when I could smell the ocean, and after a while, I found a good radio station. It wasn't long before the air was coming through the window and blowing the songs around, and I was imagining what the Philippines would be like and wondering if my father was okay and if Callie already had another boyfriend and how Claire was doing and if the kids I would've been coaching were having fun and if my old players at Montgomery Bell and Hillsboro were glad they were still playing football and how far the Woodmont neighborhood had faded into autumn, and I wondered if Sean still recited poetry and if he'd met

Lawrence Ferlinghetti, and what my father was thinking about in 1944 when he stared out at the Pacific Ocean on his way to war.

October 18, 1975 – It's a little after eleven on Saturday night and I'm driving into San Francisco. The streets are full of people. It's at least as crowded as the neighborhood around Tiny's place when I was in North Nashville. I find the old townhouse where Sean and his girlfriend live in part of the upstairs. I park around the corner on a dead end. After I walk up to the third floor, I go to the end of the hallway. The woman who opens the door is named Valerie. She's probably around my age, but she looks older. She looks tired. She says that Sean is asleep in the bedroom. She isn't sure she should wake him up.

It had been a long drive up from Newport Beach, and I told Valerie that I could see Sean in the morning. I talked to her for a few minutes and then I went into the spare room and fell asleep on a water bed.

I slept late. Valerie was reading when I came into the kitchen, and we started talking. At some point, I asked her if she liked poetry as much as Sean did. She was quiet for a few seconds. She started to say something, but then she looked away.

Before I could ask her if everything was okay, Sean came out of the bedroom. He'd been in the bedroom all night, but he looked like he hadn't slept. He walked over and hugged me. He told me how glad he was to see me, but he was forcing himself to smile. Then he said he wanted to take me out and show me the city.

He went to get dressed, but he ended up taking a forty-five-minute shower. While I was waiting for him, Valerie let me know that he'd been struggling for several months.

"He'll be okay for a while, but then he starts losing it. He's either way up or way down. Right now it's hard to even get him to go outside, but a couple of weeks ago he was talking about taking me down to Mexico. Things have been that way since spring. He had some problems last year, but this is a lot worse. He hasn't been to work for a week. I've been trying to leave, but he can't take care of himself."

Valerie wrote out a short list of things for us to pick up at the neighborhood grocery while we were out. It was another hour before Sean was ready to go. He was trying to be friendly, but he seemed sad and a little confused. He couldn't decide what he wanted to show me. We finally walked to Golden Gate Park and we ended up in the Botanical Garden. He was tired and we sat down on a bench beside a pond.

He was leaning forward and his eyes were closed, and I was watching a one-legged duck hop along the edge of the water. I went back and forth between wondering what I could do to help Sean, and wishing I was someplace else. I felt bad about wanting to leave, but he wasn't the same person I knew back in college. He was more like a stranger I felt sorry for.

Sean had been moving his hands along the underside of the bench, and he finally looked up. "You might not be able to tell, but... I'm glad you're here. I was a lot better a couple... couple of days ago. I... I'm still in here. I'm just trying to hold on." He glanced over and tried to smile.

I looked back at him. "I know. I see you."

It wasn't exactly a lie. I did see a few flickers of the old Sean, and I pretended I was talking to the old Sean. I told him about some of the kids I'd coached, and he started smiling when I got up and did my imitation of the way Huey, Dewey, and Louie had waddled when they ran.

And I told him about tricking Gary Mack with the dandelion and the frozen baseball, and about John McMillan figuring out how to measure the height of the ash tree in left field. He seemed to be feeling a little better, and I was still telling him stories about kids when we started back.

He stopped as we were leaving the park. "I'll be better in a few days. Then I could show you around. Could... Can you come back next week? Or maybe in a couple of weeks?"

He was ashamed that I'd seen him the way he was. He wanted

me to see him when he wasn't struggling, but I was already looking for an excuse to keep from coming back. I told him I was planning to drive up the coast to see a lady who had helped me when I was in high school.

He reached out and put his hand on my arm. "But… promise me you'll come back. There's this party. I want you to go to a party with Valerie and me." He squeezed my arm and looked into my eyes again. "It's on Halloween. It won't be as good as Woodstock was, but it'll… be really good." He squeezed my arm again. "Do you promise?"

I nodded. "Sure."

I was a little curious about what kind of party it was, but I was mostly thinking about how to get out of staying for another night. I wondered how long it would take him to start getting back to normal. We were close to a little grocery store when we heard the sound of screeching tires behind us.

A woman had been walking her puppy, but the puppy got away and was hit when it ran out in front of a taxi. The dog was squealing in the middle of the street and the woman was crying. The taxi driver slowed down, but then he drove away.

I would've kept on walking, but Sean ran out into the street to keep the puppy from getting hit again. The woman lived a couple of buildings away, and I went out and stood beside Sean while she went to get her car. The puppy was bleeding, and Sean was on his knees stroking its fur and trying to calm it down.

The woman finally drove up and Sean picked up the puppy and put it in the back seat. He offered to go with her to the veterinary clinic, but the woman shook her head and took off.

Sean looked weak and he went over and sat down on the curb. He didn't say anything. He just stared at the blood on his hands. When he started shivering, I said we should probably go back to his apartment. He didn't say anything when he stood up. He started walking down the sidewalk, and then he went into the grocery.

After a few minutes, I went in to look for him. He was sitting in the aisle near the back of the store. He was holding two jars of peanut butter and he was crying. Sean looked up when he saw me. "I don't know which one to get."

An elderly man with a shopping basket came up. He stared at Sean and then he moved to another aisle.

I tried to think of what to say. "I have an idea. Why don't we get both jars and let Valerie decide? I'll take the one she doesn't want. What's a road trip to Oregon without a little peanut butter along the way?"

I didn't like treating him like a five-year-old, but that's what I did. He tried to stop crying, and when he wiped away his tears with the back of his hand, he left some of the puppy's blood on his face. Then he reached over and put one of the jars back on the shelf.

After a few seconds, he looked up at me and started reciting *Buffalo Bill's Defunct*, by E. E. Cummings. When we were in college it had been one of his favorite poems. He was reminding me that some of the old Sean was still left. His eyes were glowing when he got to the end.

"How do you like your blueeyed boy
Mister Death"

Sean started crying again before I got him home. I told Valerie what happened, and she cleaned him up and put him to bed. When I offered to go out and pick up some food so she wouldn't have to cook dinner, she said that Sean would probably just stay in bed. She said she couldn't eat when he was the way he was.

I told her that the last thing she needed was a stranger hanging around. I said I'd see her again if I came back for the party on Halloween. She was glad I was leaving, and I couldn't wait to get away.

When I started across the Golden Gate Bridge I decided to see how far I could drive without thinking about the look on Valerie's face when I left, or about Sean crying in the grocery, or about how I wasn't any better than the cab driver who took off because I would've walked away from the puppy in the street if Sean hadn't gotten involved. By the time I got to the far end of the bridge, I'd thought about it all.

I stopped at San Rafael, and that night I called Ann. She said she'd love to see me, and that she had plenty of room if I wanted to stay for a few days and look around. I was tired and the next morning I overslept. After breakfast, I went to a pay phone and called the number I'd gotten from Mike Higgins. A woman picked up the phone and I asked for Jane.

All she said was, "Jane isn't here," and she hung up.

The farther north I went, the fewer people there were. A lot of Southern California was like the future, but Northern California was more like the past. My radio picked up a few small-town stations, but they came and went. A lot of the time there wasn't much to listen to. I kept going back to the way I responded to Sean and the puppy, and how I tried to protect myself instead of doing what I should've done.

I finally found a good local station on the radio. It came in pretty well for thirty or forty miles. The songs were all from an album by Joni Mitchell. *Woodstock* came on after *Big Yellow Taxi*, but it wasn't till I heard *The Circle Game* that I thought God was sending me a message.

The chorus was about the passage of time and looking back on the past, and I was wiping away tears by the end of the song. I was twenty-eight and I wondered how much longer I'd be going around in circles. I kept thinking about being a captive on the carousel of time, but after a while I was thinking about Palani and what I'd see in the Philippines. And about Callie and how long my parents would live. And the kids I'd coached and if Woodmont School was already being torn down. And finding the bullet in the old house and looking through the window of the old Williams place on Christmas Eve.

Then I let myself think about what Vietnam had done to Sean. While I was driving up the coast, I came up with a poem. I knew what I wanted to say by the time I stopped in Eureka, and I wrote it down in my journal.

Honor

He begged him
To stay home,
But his friend stood up
And marched out
To face the beast.
He told his friend
He would never
Follow him into battle,
But after seeing
The flag-draped coffin,
He stood up
And marched away.
He said he was honoring
His friend
And honoring
His forbearers,
But after he got back home –
After the beast
Had slashed him
And left his spirit bleeding
Like an injured dog
In the street –
He did not speak again
About honor.

Chapter 68

October 20, 1975 – It's Monday afternoon and I'm looking at the ocean through the picture window in the front room of Ann Woodmore's cottage in Waldport, Oregon. I'm not all that hungry, but she's gone into the kitchen to make us a late lunch. She gave me a long hug right after she opened the door. Then she took me by the shoulders and did the same thing that Palani did – she stared into my eyes. I didn't expect her to be so affectionate. I haven't seen her in thirteen years.

Her eyes look even bigger than they looked the last time I saw her. The lenses of her glasses must be thicker than they were back then, but except for her glasses, she's pretty much the way I remember her. I don't know if she can see all the way to the ocean, but she must see pretty well up close. There's a painting of an owl on her easel. There are also several other framed paintings of birds hanging in her front room, but I keep looking at the owl.

I brought in my suitcase and put it in her guest bedroom, and then I went into the kitchen. She'd made chicken salad sandwiches.

I didn't know what she wanted to talk about. "My mother put the portrait you did of me in our living room. I'm still trying to figure out how you got my eyes to look that way."

She shifted in her chair. "I think I remember telling you this before. I just painted what I saw. And your eyes look the same way they did then."

I started to tell her about my trip to the Philippines, but Mother had already let her know what I was doing. I wondered if Ann was going to start asking me questions – the way she did back when I was fourteen. That made me think about Dr. Harrelson, and I pictured the way he looked when he fell asleep in his chair, with his head off to one side and his mouth half-open.

Ann was watching me. "Are you going to let me in on why you're smiling?"

"I was just thinking about this narcoleptic psychiatrist I used to see."

That made her smile. "And now I'm wondering what made you think about your narcoleptic psychiatrist."

"Well you're a psychologist, and when I was trying to stay out of the military – out of Vietnam – I went to see this doctor in North Nashville."

Ann seemed to be thinking about what she wanted to say next. "I guess I can understand why you'd connect me with a psychiatrist. Our relationship started that way, but that isn't the way it ended up. I was trying to help your mother understand you, but *you* ended up helping *me*.

"When I was working on your portrait, back during the missile crisis... Well, seeing you turned out to be my therapy. Your mother wouldn't have asked for my help if she'd known how much I was struggling. I was barely holding on. I can go into all that later if you want to hear about it. But for now, I want you to know that you helped me through a very dark time."

I wasn't sure what to say. "I remember you telling me how scared you were."

"I probably should've kept that to myself."

"I'm glad you didn't. I needed to know that things were as bad as I thought they were."

She took off her glasses and started wiping the lenses with her napkin. "There's something I've always wondered about. I'm curious about what your mother... what she told you about me."

"It wasn't very much. I just knew you'd been friends for a long time. I can't remember when I found out that you were a psychologist."

She put her glasses back on and she looked at me. "Your mother and I have known each other since we were in grammar school. She was… she has always been so *compassionate*. She helped me through the worst part of what became an extremely unhappy marriage."

If Mother ever told me that Ann had been married, I'd forgotten about it. I assumed that she was always single.

"I wasn't sure I could help you, but I wanted to try. It was her idea to let you think you were just having your portrait painted. She said it would hurt your self-image if you knew that your parents thought you had problems. I was pretty sure you'd see through what was going on. I kept waiting for you to bring it up, but you never did."

"I don't remember when I finally figured it out. But it doesn't matter. I liked going to see you. And you helped me."

She smiled again. "Then I guess we needed each other. I had been in therapy for years by then. I was barely keeping my head above water when you started coming by. I always looked forward to seeing you. After you opened up, I looked forward to your visits even more.

"The time we spent together was just about the only light I could see sometimes. As long as you were telling me about your life, I didn't have to think about *my* life. Except for your visits, there didn't seem to be much of a point to anything. And then it looked like there might be a nuclear war."

She picked up her glass and took a drink of water. "I hope I'm not telling you more than you want to hear."

"You aren't. And there's something I should probably tell you. It's about the day you gave me my portrait. Maybe it would've cheered you up a little."

She looked curious. "Well, what was it?"

"I thought you were depressed because you were disappointed in me. Right before I saw how sad you were, I told you about a girl who used to live across the street, and how I thought about her all the time. You might've thought that was funny."

Ann started smiling. "I remember when you told me about her. She had a nickname, but I can't..."

"I called her the Blonde Bombshell."

Ann was nodding. "Well, you're right. If I'd known *that* was why you thought I was depressed, it might've been enough to make me smile – even with the world on the edge of a nuclear abyss."

She took another drink of water and then she put down her glass and pushed it away. "I've had an idea I want to tell you about. How would you feel if I started another portrait of you? It sounds as though you might not see your mother for a while. If the portrait isn't ready when you leave, I could finish it up after you're gone. She could have it in time for Christmas."

I'd only meant to stay a night or two, but I wanted to do it. It was going to be Mother's first Christmas when I wasn't at home. "That would... it would mean a lot to her."

Ann was smiling. "Good. We can get started as soon as you want. But if you'd like to take a walk while it's still light, there's a beautiful beach just down the hill."

I shook my head. "That's okay. I'll just go in the morning."

We went out to her front room. I sat down on the sofa with my back to the picture window. After she moved the painting of the owl and put a new canvas on her easel, she sat down and started squeezing tubes of paint onto her palette.

"This might be a good time for me to tell you what I've been doing since the last time you saw me. If I'd just driven here from San Francisco, I think I would rather listen than talk."

I wasn't that tired, but I wanted to know more about her.

She looked up from the palette. "The last time you saw me I was falling apart. I thought I'd be okay after the missile crisis was over – when the world settled down – but I didn't get better. My sister lived in a little house on Sanibel Island, off the Gulf Coast of southern Florida. That's where I went."

She picked up one of her brushes. "I spent the next year collecting shells and painting. I kept trying to understand what had happened to me. I didn't know anybody else who reacted to the crisis the way I did. Nobody I knew was forced to choose between leaving home and having a nervous breakdown.

"I took long walks on the beach and I did a lot of thinking. At some point, I realized that if a nuclear war *had* destroyed humanity, there wouldn't have been a point to anything that had ever happened.

"It took eons for primitive cultures to become civilizations. It took thousands of years of suffering and sacrifice before humanity finally began to understand itself. Billions of acts of grace led the way to civilization. But none of that would've mattered if we had destroyed ourselves. Until then I hadn't seen how fragile everything is."

After she moved her face a little closer to the canvas, she began to paint.

"The time came when I thought I was ready to go back to Nashville, and the week before Thanksgiving I was on the beach finishing a seascape. My sister came out and said that President Kennedy had been shot. I followed her inside and we were listening to the radio when his death was announced. He saved his crew back during the war, and two decades later he saved the entire world. He was so heroic..." She didn't say anything for a few seconds. "I ah... I couldn't stop crying. I didn't get out of bed for two days.

"And then Oswald was killed. Things got clearer after that. From then on, I knew that powerful people must have been behind the president's death. The most important assassin in American history could not have been killed, while he was in custody, without a lot of coordination. It couldn't have happened unless powerful people were involved.

"I didn't need to know which secret group of self-serving men was responsible. Whoever they were, they had committed murder for the same reason self-serving men always murder. They diminished the world for the same reason such men always diminish the world. For money and for power and for prestige."

She reached into the pocket of her sweater and pulled out a handkerchief, and then she took off her glasses and wiped her eyes. "I wanted to do something to honor President Kennedy, but I knew I'd never do anything if I let myself sink down into another emotional pit.

"And I'd never do anything if I kept hiding from life in my sister's beach cottage. My brother lived in San Diego and I ended up moving there. I rented an apartment and went back to practicing psychology.

"I was around your age when I started my first practice. It was just before the end of World War Two. It's hard to believe it was over thirty years ago. I was in the same office until 1960, but my marriage finally got so bad that I had to stop seeing patients. I didn't realize how much I missed it until I opened my practice in San Diego.

"I had been working for nearly four years when Dr. King and Bobby Kennedy were murdered. They were both heroic men. They must have known they were endangering their lives when they took the stands they took. And whether they were killed by twisted men in powerful groups, or by twisted men working alone, they died at the hands of the same sort of twisted men who killed President Kennedy."

She didn't say anything for a few seconds. "I still wanted to do something in memory of President Kennedy, and after those killings, I also wanted to do something for his brother and for Dr. King. Hearing myself say that... well it sounds so idealistic. But I didn't want to sit around feeling helpless again. I wanted to dedicate something to them. I just didn't know what it was."

Chapter 69

Ann brought her face even closer to the canvas. "One of the first patients I saw after the assassinations of Dr. King and Senator Kennedy was a man who was ordered to see me. He was driving on the Coast Highway, and the car in front of him had a bumper sticker of a political candidate he despised. He thought the car was going too slow. After the man started honking his horn, the first car slowed down even more. My patient lost his temper and pulled around the other driver, and then he ran him off the road. A policeman saw it happen and arrested him.

"The judge gave him a choice. He could either go to jail, or he could go into therapy. The man was fairly intelligent, but he was completely entrenched in his view of politics. He came out of college with an idealized view of how the world was going to be, but his marriage was a struggle and he resented his wife. He had a job he didn't like and he resented his supervisor. He seemed to resent the whole world.

"He worked as a volunteer in the Nixon campaign, and after the 1968 election, he got involved with a right-wing group. He read some articles and one or two books, and it wasn't long before he was expressing a deep contempt for war protesters and civil rights workers and hippies and black people and immigrants and people on welfare. He said they were all ruining the country. He had found a narrative, and he was sure it was all true."

Mr. Godshaw had some of the same beliefs, but he wouldn't have run anybody off the road.

"And a month or two after that, I started seeing another patient. He was displaying the same sort of behavior. He would go to a restaurant or a bar and start talking about politics. And he made sure he was loud enough to be overheard. He waited for somebody to give him a dirty look or argue or tell him to be quiet. When that happened he got belligerent, and sometimes he got into fights.

"He wasn't well-educated, but he was bright. He dropped out of high school after his father lost his job, and he ended up working in a factory. He worked the night shift and got married when he was twenty. Pretty soon there were children to support. He was forced to get a second job. He worked hard, but he felt like a failure.

"A couple of his co-workers were especially radical, and it wasn't long before he was sure that America's entire economic system had been rigged to exploit workers and enrich the upper class. It wasn't long before he was convinced that the rich were all parasites living off the working class, and that God and religion were only lies used to manipulate the masses into accepting diminished lives.

"When it came to politics, one man was on the extreme right and the other was on the extreme left, but they acted the same way. That really got my attention. And I finally realized that I had other patients with the same profiles.

"My brother's wife – my sister-in-law – had a younger sister who developed a religious obsession. My sister-in-law gave me a lot of insight into how she and her sister grew up. After their father abandoned the family, their mother became less loving and more and more controlling. The younger sister had nightmares and there were bed-wetting incidents. She was terrified of death, but she gradually seemed to work through everything.

"She went away to college and married, and she eventually had two children. Then she found out that her husband was having an affair. There was a divorce. And it wasn't long before she joined a fundamentalist Christian church. Her personality changed so radically that her family pressured her to see me. She was intelligent enough, but she wasn't very analytical. She didn't respond well to ambiguity.

"She finally told me that her church was the only church that worshiped the true God. That her beliefs were the only true beliefs. She believed that evolution was a lie created by Satan. She also believed that Satan had concealed fossils and dinosaur bones in the ground, so that humanity would be deceived about the age of the Earth. She said that was how Satan tried to undermine belief in the Bible. She ended up withdrawing from her family because of what they believed. She didn't even go to her mother's funeral."

I wondered how the woman would've felt about Reverend Carter Cortez.

Ann moved her face close to the canvas again. "The church gave her a narrative that answered her emotional needs. She had been abandoned, but God would never abandon her. Her mother and her husband both withdrew their love, but God would always love her. She was afraid of dying, but God would allow her to live forever. The narrative gave her what she needed, and she accepted every belief that came with it.

"All of those patients were convinced they were right. None of them had any interest in other points of view. They were resentful and frustrated and angry and scared. They wanted a simple explanation for what they didn't understand about the world. The narratives they picked up gave them groups to join and enemies to hate and a way to feel intellectually and morally superior.

"They were like most human beings. They had an inherent need to be part of something larger than themselves.

"And from time to time I had other patients with the same profile. I eventually put together a list of my patients who saw everything as being either black or white. I identified eight men and five women who were all certain that everything they believed was true."

The difference between the patients she was describing and

other people, was like the difference between alcoholics and casual drinkers.

"No rational person believes they are right all the time. The symptoms of those patients were especially pronounced. I thought I might have stumbled across a psychological condition. I wrote an article about what I thought I had identified. I called it Propaganda Vulnerability Syndrome, and I was planning to submit it to a psychology journal.

"But then a friend of mine read it. She said there were already studies that explained how emotionally vulnerable people were drawn to simple narratives. Even though she was very diplomatic, she let me know that I was way behind the curve.

"But I didn't give up on honoring the men I wanted to honor. At first, I wasn't sure I could do it and it's taken me a while, but I've been writing a novel. It's about what could happen to America if enough people are captured by a false narrative. I don't know how good it is, but I'm nearly finished.

"The novel is set a few decades in the future. The lies told by the government about Vietnam and Watergate have been followed by additional lies until the public doesn't know what to believe. There was a time when primitive people were handicapped by limited information. My book is set during a period when people are handicapped by *conflicting* information.

"The book takes place when the world is changing faster than it has ever changed before. Life has become increasingly complex. People are finding it much more difficult to understand why things are the way they are. The population of the country continues to rise by millions of people every year, and there is more and more social friction. The friction causes frustration and resentment, which are spiraling into anger and fear.

"The climate of anger and fear has created an opportunity for the worst of those seeking more money and more power. Technology has made it easy to manufacture believable lies, and propagandists have become bolder in spreading the false narratives they create. The complexity of the truth is being overwhelmed by the simplicity of the lie, and the more hate and fear the propagandists stir up, the larger their audience becomes. And the larger their audience, the more money and power the propagandists have.

"The book is set in a time when large numbers of people have clustered around a single highly-polished false narrative. Gullibility has metastasized into a national cult of aggressive ignorance. When a demagogue runs for the president, he attracts enough of the angry and the poorly-informed to be elected.

"Once he takes office, he addresses complex problems with the same simple solutions that brought about his election. And America falls further and further into the darkness of political partisanship. By appealing to the worst aspects of human nature, he soon surrounds himself with an army of rabid and violent followers. Like other demagogues, he becomes a dictator. I have a couple of different ideas, but I'm still not sure how the book ends."

It almost sounded like Ann was writing an updated version of *Nineteen Eighty-Four*.

"I'd love to write as well as Rachel Carson did, or as well as Harper Lee. But at the end of the day, I'll be satisfied if it turns out to be a fitting tribute to President Kennedy, and to Dr. King and Senator Kennedy."

Chapter 70

Ann stared at the painting and picked up a small brush with a fine tip. I wondered if she'd already painted my eyes. After a while, she asked me what I did on the night of the Missile Crisis – after I left her house. I told her about sitting in my sixth-grade classroom at Woodmont and walking around the neighborhood, and I didn't stop talking.

I told her about my date with Yancey Walsh and Mr. Peters falling down the stairs. I told her about seeing President Kennedy and how I felt when he was killed, and watching Jack Johnson dying beside the creek. And about my first trip to California and body surfing. And going to Tijuana with Wes and seeing the bullfight. And I told her about imagining I was marching into battle after I graduated from Battle Ground Academy. She asked me a few questions, but most of the time she just sat and painted. There were times when it seemed like we were back in her house in Nashville, and it was 1962 again.

Ann kept painting, and after three or four hours, we went to a café just down the road and had dinner. She did most of the talking while we were eating dinner. She talked about Waldport and some of her neighbors, and how much she loved taking walks on the beach when it was warm and sunny. I was pretty tired when we got back to her house, but we stayed up past midnight.

I tried to explain about Vanderbilt and the professors who didn't have much passion for teaching. And the students with even less passion for learning, and the emptiness of the fraternities and not being able to concentrate. And wearing the wrong tie on the day the admiral showed up and flunking out of school and going to see Dr. Burke and volunteering at the Children's Home. And how much I hurt my parents. I was starting to tell her about going back to California when we both ran out of steam.

The next morning I was still tired, but I made myself get up. Ann was asleep and I put on a jacket and went for a run on the beach. When I was driving up the day before, I'd noticed the waves. Along most of the Pacific coast, there were only one or two break lines offshore. But in that part of Oregon, there were at least five or six lines of breaking waves, and sometimes there were nine or ten. It was beautiful.

I ran pretty far and I did a lot of thinking about Sean and his depression. I went back and forth between trying to come up with an excuse to keep from going back to San Francisco, and feeling guilty about abandoning him. I finally got tired of thinking about it. I stopped for a few minutes at what was left of a huge log that had washed up onto the sand. I looked out at the lines of breaking waves, and pretty soon I was imagining what it would be like if Callie was with me on the beach.

On the way back I thought a lot about my father and Alicia and what they went through during the war. It occurred to me that the beach and the coastline and the ocean hadn't changed much in thirty years. Instead of 1975, it could've been 1945. I watched the waves washing up onto the sand, and I imagined my father on the other side of the Pacific, trudging through the water during the landing on Leyte.

I pictured myself walking up onto the beach at Leyte, and I wondered how hard it would be to move around when I got to Manila. If I could find the house where my father grew up, maybe whoever lived there would let me see the room where he killed Ramon.

Ann was fixing breakfast when I came back. I put up the dishes after we ate, and we picked up where we left off the night before. I sat on the sofa, and she sat down in her chair and started painting again.

She glanced up from time to time while she was working, and sometimes she stopped painting and stared at me. At first, I thought she was studying some facial feature she was trying to capture. But I finally remembered that she'd stopped before – back when I was a teenager – because of something I said.

The first time she put down her brush and stared at me with her magnified eyes was when I told her about wanting to punish myself by going to Vietnam. She peered at me the same way when I told her about praying that I'd figure out what I should be doing with my life. And she put down her brush when I was telling her about the kids on my teams, and the way they listened when I was telling them about Doc Scarborough.

She stared at me when I talked about the letter my doctor wrote to the draft board and Ralph Benson waving around his *Coaches Bible,* and my father standing by me when the draft board was trying to take control of my life. And she smiled when I told her about sitting across from Dr. Harrelson. Waiting until he was asleep before I said what I really wanted to say.

For the next few days, I got up and took morning runs on the beach. After I went back and ate breakfast, Ann sat in front of her easel and painted until lunch. We'd have another session that lasted until dinner, and after dinner we kept going until we both got tired. Whenever she leaned forward and moved her face close to the canvas, I stayed quiet. When she focused that way, she was usually holding the smallest brush she had. I kept wondering what part of the painting she was working on.

I would daydream, and I spent a lot of time staring at her other paintings. They looked like photographs of dreams. On the wall to the left of where I was sitting was a painting of an eagle landing on a big piece of driftwood, with the sea in the background. And on the same wall, along with paintings of some other seabirds I couldn't name, was a painting of an osprey flying along the shore with the tip of one wing grazing the water.

They all had the same dreamlike quality, but the one I stared at the most was the painting of the owl that had been on her easel. It was propped up against a table. The owl was perched on the weathered wreckage of an overturned boat that was half-buried in the sand. There was a bank of low clouds above the ocean, and the owl was looking down the deserted beach. It looked like a storm was moving in.

But when I wasn't daydreaming or staring at her paintings, I was usually talking. I kept thinking she'd get bored, and I finally asked if I was telling her more than she wanted to know.

She shook her head. "The more you tell me, the more of you I'll be able to capture."

I wondered how many other artists listened to the people they were painting, and worked what they heard into their paintings.

I didn't go into any physical details and it was a little awkward at times, but I went ahead and told her about my encounters with the Blonde Bombshell and the divorced mothers. And that same afternoon, when we were walking on the beach, I told her about Callie Lee.

I expected her to wait a while before she told me what she thought, but she stopped walking and looked out toward the ocean. "I don't know how much you want me to respond, or if you want me to respond at all."

"I guess I'd like to hear whatever you want to tell me."

Ann smiled. "Well, that could go on past Christmas, so I'll try to limit myself." She was quiet for several seconds. "You said you didn't think you would've been so drawn to Callie if you hadn't been so introverted in high school. You could be right about that. It makes sense that you'd try to pick up some of what you missed when you were a teenager.

"But there are one or two things you should think about. You are drawn to who Callie is and to the way she looks, but do you actually have a friendship? Do you make each other laugh? Do you want to tell each other things you've never told anybody else?"

I didn't like the answer I had to give her. "Well, we don't have that yet. Right now she doesn't laugh all that much, at least not when she's around me, and she doesn't like talking about things that are personal. But I'm pretty sure she likes me. I think her feelings could grow into a friendship... and maybe into something a lot deeper."

Ann started walking again. "And that might happen, but from what you've said... I'm sure you must've thought about the consequences of waiting to see what happens. In two or three years you'll be thirty. How old will she be?"

"When I'm thirty she'll be nineteen."

"No matter how much her feelings for you have grown by then, she'll still be a teenager. You'll be in your mid-thirties before she really starts getting to know herself. How many other relationships – relationships that could help you understand what you're looking for in a woman *and* help you understand yourself better – how many of those relationships will you have missed by then?

"Do you see a connection between the experiences you missed in high school, and the experiences you could miss over the next few years? I wonder if you could be devoting yourself to Callie to protect yourself from experiencing a real relationship."

I'd thought about that a few times, and it sounded true when she said it.

She looked like she was trying to decide what else she should say. "And I know that Callie must be flattered to have you take an interest in her. But knowing that you're waiting for her to grow up – that's a lot of pressure. I'm sure she's aware that she might end up disappointing you, and that can complicate the way she feels."

She started to say something else, but she caught herself. "There's more I could say, but I'm getting tired of hearing myself talk. I'd rather listen to the ocean for a while."

When I ran the next morning I kept thinking about Callie and Sean and the Philippines, and what was going on at home. And I kept wondering about Ann. I wanted to know about her husband

and what had turned their marriage bad and if she'd ever wanted children, but I was pretty sure I wouldn't say anything.

I finally got through telling her the rest of my story. The only thing I didn't go into was what I was doing for Mike Higgins. I waited for her to start asking questions again, but she painted for another half-hour before she put down her brush and looked at me.

"One of the positive things about being sixty years old is that I've experienced long sweeps of time. Fifty years ago I knew your grandmother. I spent the night with your mother all the time back then – back when we were little girls. Your mother and I would sit in the parlor for hours listening to your grandmother play the piano. I'll never forget how talented she was and how much grace she had.

"I remember when she died. My parents took me over so I could say how sorry I was. Your mother couldn't stop crying. She loved her mother so much, and to lose her so suddenly... I don't think she's ever stopped crying.

"Your mother inherited her mother's grace. She continued her mother's journey, just as her mother had continued *her* mother's journey. It's the same with your father. He is on a journey, too. I visited him when he was in the military hospital, but until you told me about it a few days ago, I never knew what he went through in the Philippines. And I remember Alicia. She seemed to have a lot of... I guess it was inner strength. I didn't know what happened to her during the war either.

"But what I started to say is that the older I get, the more I understand how connected lives can be. Seeing the same grace in you that I saw in your grandmother, and that I've always seen in your mother, well... those sorts of things almost make being sixty years old worthwhile. *Almost,* but not quite.

"You told me something when I was painting your first portrait. I've never stopped thinking about it. You told me you were praying and that a current entered your body. You said that whatever it was, it gave you something that wasn't there before.

"But I knew you before that happened. There has been something inside you *all along*. Maybe the current just made what was already there get brighter." She moved her face even closer to the canvas. "Anyway, some people have a light inside of them. And I've always thought you were one of those people.

"You probably didn't need to hear my advice about Callie. She's part of your journey and you're part of her journey. But I've been thinking about another part of your journey a lot more."

Ann looked over toward her front window. "I keep thinking about you walking away from working with children. How many people have your ability to touch lives? It makes me sad to think about you turning away from that.

"One of my biggest regrets was that I didn't continue to embrace a gift that I had. I loved sculpting. I eventually fell back on painting, but working with stone was my first love. After college, I went to study at an art institute in Paris. My professor... well he was a very manipulative man. I shouldn't have allowed that to stop me, but it did stop me. I tried to go back to sculpture a few years later, but by then I'd lost something. And whatever it was – it never came back."

She moved her right hand across her face like she was brushing away a shadow. "You have an unusual gift, and the more unusual a gift is, the more difficult the surrounding terrain can be. You will always have to deal with what other people think about you – with what they *say* about you."

She shook her head. "You said it the other day. There are already more than enough lawyers and accountants and bankers and businessmen in the world. What you didn't say is that there aren't many people with a gift for touching lives.

"And I suspect that you have other gifts. You sounded so passionate when you told me what you've discovered about the history of your neighborhood. I can see how curious you are about the past – how driven you are to learn more. I've come to believe that wherever there is passion, there's a gift. I just hope that you'll eventually find a way to use the gifts you've been given."

She made me sound like I had more abilities than I had. I didn't tell her that I was good with kids because *I was* a kid. And I didn't say that if I had an inner light, then a lot of other people had inner lights, too.

She stopped talking and then she laughed. "I guess I sound more like a motivational speaker than a therapist." She looked at me and smiled. "Do you have a preference?"

"I'd say it's a tie."

I wanted to write a poem about Ann and give it to her before I left. The last couple of mornings I'd tried to come up with an idea while I was running on the beach, but nothing came into focus.

She went back over and sat down in front of the canvas. "I just need to do a little more touching up on your portrait." She moved her face closer to the easel, and after she added a few more bits of color, she pushed back her chair and stood up. "Well, I think that should do it."

October 29, 1975 – It's past midnight. Ann went to bed a couple of hours ago. I'm in front of the picture window, looking out toward the ocean. I can see a light in the darkness. I think I've finished the poem for Ann, but I need to read through it one more time. I walk over and stand in front of the easel. My portrait has the same dreamlike style as her paintings of the birds, but it isn't what I expected. In one way it's like the portrait she did when I was fifteen. She's painted me the way I wish I was. I look confident.

What surprised me is the way she painted it. The right side of my face is behind a shadow. It changes the way I look. At some point, she added a fleck of white pigment to my right eye, and it's shining through the shadow. The more I look at the painting, the more I like it.

I slept late the next morning. I could tell that Ann didn't want me to leave. Two different times during breakfast she mentioned that she'd ship the portrait to my mother, and two other times she told me to be careful in the Philippines.

She walked outside with me when I went to my car. She said she hoped she wouldn't be an old lady the next time she saw me, and she hugged me. I gave her the poem right before I left. It was pretty close to the way I wanted it.

The Owl

Her eyes flash open
And she drops,
Silent as a falling feather,
Into the night.
She glides through the darkness
And when a glimmer of light
Escapes from a shadow
On the forest floor,
She swoops onto a perch
And stares down
At a single illuminated life.
After a time she soars away,
And circling higher and higher
Into the deepening darkness,
She is aware of the stars.
But she never loses sight
Of the life
Shining up at her
From the dark terrain below.

Chapter 71

I hadn't gone two miles before I was wondering how I could get out of going back to see Sean. I came up with some pretty convincing excuses, but soon I was thinking about how the beach at Leyte would look and what else I should've told Ann about Callie and whether I'd ever coach kids again and if I could find the leper colony where my grandfather worked and what it would be like to be in the closet where my father was standing when he shot Ramon and if there was a way I could ever get my father to stop drinking.

Driving down the winding road and moving along the coastline and seeing the motion of the sea and feeling the rush of the air was hypnotic, and after a while, my mind drifted back home. I knew how the neighborhood would look. By the time I was ten, I'd noticed the signs that winter was coming.

There was a thick growth of tickseed along the fringes of our backyard, and when the bright yellow flowers started to die, it meant that August was nearly over. By the end of September, the yellow flowers and the lightning bugs would all be gone, and the katydids that had pulsed with the rhythm of a beating heart back during the summer would be gone as well. The trees would be full of red and yellow and orange leaves by the last part of October, and then November would come. It only took one storm to strip the remaining color from the trees, and bring autumn to an end.

I drove down the coast, and looking out at the ocean I pictured the last warm afternoon when grade school kids practiced football out in front of West End Junior High School and the last games of the season at Montgomery Bell Academy and Hillsboro. And then I imagined leaves floating down all across the Woodmont neighborhood.

October 28, 1975 – It might as well be Halloween night in San Francisco. I'm standing in the lobby of the Hyatt Regency Hotel with Sean and Valerie. I assumed we were going to a party at somebody's apartment, but it turned out to be a big deal called the Coyote Ball. There must be over a thousand people here. Sean and Valerie smoked some marijuana in the car. That's when Valerie told me that the ball is an event to raise money for Coyote.

Coyote stands for "call off your old tired ethics." It's an organization trying to legalize prostitution. It took a while before Valerie told me that there would be a lot of prostitutes at the party. Then she mentioned that there would also be a lot of gay men and lesbians there. She never got around to letting me know that it was a costume ball. Except for a naked guy who's standing about twenty feet away, I think I'm the only person who isn't wearing a costume. The naked guy, who Sean thinks is supposed to be Apollo, is spray-painted gold from his feet to the top of his head.

I didn't know that Sean and Valerie were wearing costumes until they took off their coats. They've written, "Putting the Cheek in Chique," in chartreuse letters on their matching lime-green tee shirts. I don't catch on at first, but then they turn around. They've both cut away the back pockets of their jeans, and they each have one bare butt cheek on full display.

Thanks to Apollo, who was able to maintain himself at what appeared to be something more than half-staff, nobody seemed to notice the areas of skin that Sean and Valerie had revealed. And I didn't think anybody noticed me in my blue jeans, my blue sweatshirt, and my tennis shoes. Sean wasn't the way he used to be, but he was a whole lot better than he was a couple of weeks earlier. Neither one of us mentioned his breakdown in the grocery, or said anything about the puppy.

He was pretty calm, and he and Valerie smiled at each other a couple of times after we got to the party. There were at least three open bars, and they spent a good bit of time waiting in the closest line for their next drink. There was also plenty of pot being passed around. Every time a joint came their way, Sean and Valerie took a hit. They got less and less coherent, and after they ran into a couple of their friends, I faded into the background. It wasn't long before I went off on my own.

The music was loud and *When Will I Be Loved* faded into *Killer Queen* which faded into *The Hustle* which faded into *Lady Marmalade.* I kept squeezing past people in costumes and moving through indistinguishable conversations while *Fire* and *Fame* and *Dance With Me* and *Get Down Tonight* and *Bungle in the Jungle* and *Pick Up the Pieces* ebbed and flowed under a low haze of cigarette smoke tinged with the scent of marijuana.

I'd always thought of homosexual men and lesbians as being injured and sad and isolated, but there were plenty of men holding hands with men, and there were even more women holding hands with women. Then I saw a couple of guys dressed as unicorns – one was pink and the other one was purple.

Every time the unicorns pretended to mount each other, they got a big laugh. And an overweight blonde woman was walking around by herself. All she had on was a pair of orange Bermuda shorts and a Viking helmet.

With all the costumes, it was hard to tell how old people were. Some guys looked like they were in their early twenties, and I saw two men who might've been in their eighties with their arms around each other. But most people were probably somewhere between twenty-five and forty.

I couldn't tell the lesbians from the prostitutes, and I couldn't always tell the women from the men. I was walking past what I thought was a good-looking woman when I heard her clearly masculine voice. At first, the crowd seemed bizarre, but it wasn't long before I got used to it.

I hoped that not being in a costume would make me invisible, but I got a few stares. The first time it was from a shirtless guy dressed like a fireman, and the next time it was from a guy in a turban. I wasn't sure if the looks meant, "Can I buy you a drink?" or whether it was more like, "What in the hell are you doing here?"

After I'd been walking around for a while, I saw another naked guy who was spray-painted. He was standing at the edge of a crowd. He was completely silver. I thought he might've been Mercury.

If I'd known what I was getting into, I wouldn't have guzzled down a big glass of water right before we left Sean's apartment. I finally walked over and stood across from a bathroom just off the main lobby. A lot more guys were going in than coming out, and I decided to look for a more isolated facility.

I roamed around until I found a corridor with bathrooms down at the far end. The only person I saw was a woman standing outside the door of the ladies room. She was dressed to look like an old-time prostitute.

Along with a lot of makeup, she was wearing what looked like vintage lingerie. She had on dark stockings and a garter belt, and there was a flimsy red shawl around her shoulders. She started to say something, but I just gave her a quick smile and went on into the bathroom.

I interrupted a climactic moment between a middle-aged white man in a toga and a young black guy wearing a grass skirt and a couple of leis made out of flowers. I got back out into the hallway as fast as I could.

The woman in the lingerie was laughing. "Well, I guess what they say must be true."

The moment felt less awkward than I would've thought. "What do they say?"

"That three's a crowd."

From what I could tell she was pretty, and I wanted to say something that was at least halfway clever. "There's something else they should say."

She had a playful look on her face. "And what might that be?"

"If a Roman takes on a hula girl, the hula girl will come out on top. So to speak."

She looked at me and smiled. "I'm starting to suspect that I just won ten bucks."

I waited for her to tell me what she'd bet on.

"When Albert saw you, he looked at your costume and said you were gay. I said I didn't think so, and we put ten dollars on it."

I was confused. "But I'm not wearing a costume."

She was still smiling. "Well, Albert thinks you are. He's the hula girl in the bathroom by the way. When he saw you walking through the lobby, he went around trying to find out if anybody knew the cute guy who showed up dressed like a straight person."

She stood there for a few seconds before she said anything else. "But you need to confirm that you're straight, or Albert won't pay me."

"What if I have lesbian tendencies?"

She almost laughed. "That doesn't count."

"Okay, then I'd say he owes you ten dollars."

"So what brings an unescorted straight guy to the Coyote Ball?"

"You want the short answer or the long answer?"

She pretended to think. "How about the real answer?"

I said I was from Nashville and that I'd come with Valerie and Sean, and then I told her a little about who he used to be and who he'd become. She didn't ask any questions, but she was listening. I wanted to know who she was. And why she'd come to the Coyote Ball dressed up in old-fashioned lingerie. I finally just said, "Sooo... "

She looked at me and curtsied. "Sooo tonight I'm Belle Cora. I've decided to spend an evening away from my bordello, and I've transported myself here from back in the 1850s." I was getting ready to ask her who she was when she wasn't in a costume. But the restroom door opened and Albert came out rearranging his grass skirt. He was followed by the Roman, who was adjusting his toga.

The Roman kept walking, but Albert looked at me and stopped. He seemed a little disappointed when Belle told him that he owed her ten dollars. I thought he might ask me for verification, but he just looked at Belle. "I can't pay you till Monday. My skirt doesn't seem to have any pockets."

"That's okay," she said. "You can just stick it in the mail."

"*Oh my.*" Albert started fanning himself and gave me a flirtatious wink. "Well, I'm certainly willing if he is."

She shook her head. "Isn't there a luau going on in another bathroom somewhere?"

Albert turned to me and shrugged. "I appear to have been dismissed." He winked at me again. "Well have fun, Sweetie." He started back up the corridor, but then he stopped and turned around. "And if things work out with Liza, make her give you a ten-dollar discount."

I got the feeling that he'd answered one of my questions about her, but I wasn't sure. I smiled at her again. "Sooo... "

"Do you want the long version or the short version?"

"Either one."

Liza nodded. "About what Albert said... about giving you a discount. I'm not here on business, but I *am* in that business, at least I am sometimes. But I don't think of myself as a prostitute when I'm not on the job. Tonight I'm just a girl dressed up like a San Francisco whore from back during the gold rush."

I liked Liza. "I'd love to hear the long version of your story, but before the next eager couple shows up looking for some privacy, I need to visit the restroom."

She gave me a big smile. "Just be careful where you step."

Liza was smart and easy to talk to, and while I was in the restroom I had to keep reminding myself that she was a hooker. I wasn't sure if she'd stick around, but she was still there when

I came back out. We ended up walking down to the end of the corridor and sitting on a table.

She told me a little about her family and her hometown in Colorado and where she'd gone to school, and she even talked about her first boyfriend. By the time we'd been there a half-hour, I had a pretty good idea of who she'd been before she came to San Francisco.

I could tell she liked being away from the crowd. The more she told me, the harder it was to imagine her showing up somewhere at night and knocking on a door, and then going inside to be with a guy she'd never met.

At some point, she started talking about a telescope she had when she was a kid, and how much she had loved taking it out behind her house and looking at the stars. Then she was quiet for a few seconds. "You know what would *really* be cool? It would be cool if we could go somewhere tonight and look at the stars."

By then I'd learned just about everything I was going to learn from being at the Coyote Ball. I was open to whatever Liza had in mind, and for once I wasn't worried about how things might end up.

Chapter 72

It took a while, but I finally found Sean and Valerie. They were both pretty drunk and pretty stoned. I said I was leaving, but I wasn't sure they'd remember I was gone. Liza and I took a taxi to get my car and then we drove to her apartment. I waited in her front room while she changed out of her costume.

When she came out of her bedroom she looked like a different person. I'd thought she was older than I was, but without her makeup, she looked like she could've just graduated from college. She was even prettier than I thought she was.

She reached inside her closet and when she turned around she was holding a pair of binoculars. "This is the best I can do. I *knew* I should've brought my telescope when I came out here."

Liza said there was a place where she'd seen more stars in the night sky than any place she'd ever been. It was just outside of Yosemite Park, and there was a cabin where we could spend the night. She told me it would take about three hours to get there. She sounded like she was serious. If it wasn't for missing Woodstock, I probably wouldn't have gone. I didn't ask her who owned the cabin.

We started driving and Liza picked up where she left off when we were at the party. She said her parents were nice, average people, who took her to church every Sunday when she was growing up. She went off to college, but she didn't go back home after she dropped out. She ended up working as a receptionist. All she said about being a hooker was that she started doing it so she could afford a better place to live.

There were a lot of questions I didn't ask. I kept wondering how often she had normal conversations with a guy.

After a while, she looked over at me. "Okay, now I want to hear about your life. And you can give me any version you want as long as none of it's bullshit."

I told her about high school, and all she said was that the girls who seemed like they were out of my league were probably just as insecure as I was. From there, I went into my time at college and how I'd tried to stay away from Vietnam, and I told her about coaching. I talked about some of the kids on my teams. The story she liked the most was about Ann Tracey striking out the boys who'd been laughing at her.

I told her a few more coaching stories, and then I got into how much I'd disappointed my parents and the way my friends saw me, and that I was on my way to the Philippines. I told her about the Blonde Bombshell and Yancey Walsh and the divorced mothers, and after that, I tried to explain about Callie.

She didn't say anything at first. There was just enough light coming from the dashboard for me to see the outline of her body. She'd shifted around and brought her left leg under her right leg. Her back was against the door. "And this girl – she's sixteen?"

"She is now."

She didn't say anything else for another minute or two. "So how do you feel about being on the way to Yosemite with a part-time hooker?"

I wasn't sure what I should say. "You want the real story?"

"Yep."

"Well, I guess I feel like I'm... sort of on an adventure. A few hours ago I thought I was on my way to somebody's apartment, and I ended up at a big costume party on the corner of Sodom Boulevard and Gomorrah Lane, and then I was talking to a girl wearing nineteenth-century lingerie and now it's the middle of the night and..." I wasn't sure how much I should say.

She shifted again on the seat. "And... ?"

"And now we're going to some cabin out in the middle of nowhere to look at the stars."

She clapped her hands together. "Cut! I think we need to shoot that scene again. Try it again, and this time don't play it so damn safe. Come on. This could be one of the best talks you've ever had with a girl. Tell me what you're thinking about – what you're *really* thinking about – right now."

I still didn't know how honest I wanted to be. "Well, I'm on my way to look at the stars with this girl, and she's really pretty and smart and funny, and I'm wondering who she... who you are. I'm also wondering what's about to happen, or what's not about to happen, and I'm wondering how you feel about your life."

"You mean about being a hooker."

"Well, yeah I guess that's... that's part of it."

She clapped her hands again. "Cut! You hesitated. Let's try it one more time."

I made myself say it. "Okay. How do you feel about being a hooker?"

"How do you think I feel?"

I didn't want her to clap her hands again. "I don't think you like it."

"What makes you think I don't like it?"

"Back before... well there was a different tone in your voice when you were talking about it."

She got quiet, and after a few seconds she still hadn't said anything. I waited for a car to come toward us so there would be enough light to see her face. I glanced over just as a pickup truck blew by. She was staring straight ahead. She looked serious, but she wasn't frowning.

The pickup was out of sight before she said anything. "Well, it's not like I'm a drug addict who turns tricks in somebody's back seat so I can pay for my next fix. I started out stripping at fraternity parties and then at bachelor parties. That's... that's how I got my first clients. And I haven't been doing it that long. The last time was two weeks ago. A guy was getting married and his groomsmen wanted him to have one last fling."

I imagined letting go of the steering wheel just long enough to clap my hands. I wanted to say, "Cut! The tone in your voice is too flat. Try it again." But I just kept driving.

We'd gone another mile before Liza said anything else. "You're right though. Sometimes I don't like the way it makes me feel. And I *really* don't like the way it's making me feel right now."

When the next car went by I glanced over again. Her eyes were closed. Before I could think of something to say, she let out a sigh. "Look, we don't have to do this. Sometimes I'll think of something and it'll seem like a great idea, and then it doesn't turn out right."

I went ahead and clapped. "Hold on a minute. Timeout. I need some context. What are you thinking about? What... What's going on?"

"I just... One minute we were riding down the highway and I was thinking about all the stars we'd see, but then I started thinking about what'll happen after we look at the stars. At some point, you're either going to put a big move on me, or you aren't.

"If you make a move, I'll wonder if the only reason you left the party with me was so you could get laid. Which you probably think is a sure thing since I'm a hooker. And if you don't do anything – if all we do is look at the stars – I'll wonder if it's because you're afraid of getting VD. So either way it goes, it'll be messed up. *Shit!*"

I went ahead and told her what I wanted to say. "Well, I don't think you should give up on the original script."

She seemed surprised that I said anything. "Oh yeah? Well if you've got a better version, I'd love to hear it."

"Okay, here it is. Two people who've just met each other, and who obviously like each other, drive off into the night to look at the stars. The girl starts worrying about what the guy is thinking, but the guy thinks he has a solution – no pun intended."

When I didn't say anything else, Liza spoke up. "I guess this is where I'm supposed to say, 'Okay... what's the solution?'"

"And this is where I say, 'It's a surprise.' But I'll let you in on this much. There's at least one scenario you haven't thought about. And pretty soon you'll understand that coming to look at the stars was a *really* good idea."

She glanced at the clock on the dashboard. "Well we're over halfway there, so I guess we might as well keep going."

She seemed so confident when she was dressed up as Belle Cora. She almost seemed proud to be a hooker. I should've known that things were more complicated than they looked.

We went another ten miles and Liza still hadn't said anything. I finally broke the silence. "Are you trying to figure out my brilliant solution?"

"Nope. I'm just over here beating myself up."

"About what?"

She didn't say anything for a few seconds. "Oh what the hell. Here's a little *context*."

Liza started telling me about her first sexual experience. She was in ninth grade. "Once I got past the first time, I liked it. I decided that I'd do it when I wanted to do it, but it wasn't like I was out of control. A couple of my girlfriends were a whole lot wilder than I was.

"They'd go to parties and a few times they ended up in a bedroom with two or three guys. But they were just using sex to get attention. I'm pretty sure they didn't even like it that much. Anyway, having them around gave me some cover. And I got away with a lot. It wasn't long before other girls were getting wild, too, and I stayed under the radar – at least for a while."

Then she told me about when she thought she was pregnant during her senior year. "It turned out to be a false alarm, but I'd already told my mother by then and she went crazy. She grounded me for two months. After I graduated, my parents sent me to a religious college in Utah. I was there for a year. I kept hearing that the only time sex was okay was if you were married and trying to get pregnant. I think the general idea was for the wife to lie there and grit her teeth and say Bible verses in her head until her husband was done."

There was some frustration in her voice. "And then one of my teachers gave a lecture and said that the devil was always lurking in the shadows, waiting to use sexual desire to undermine God. That was it for me. I left for San Francisco as soon as the semester was over.

"I understand why my mother and those idiots in Utah would hate what I'm doing. I get that. But what pisses me off is that *I'm* not okay with what I'm doing. So how's that for context?"

I wasn't sure she was looking for an answer. "Have you figured out why it bothers you?"

"Maybe it's the way people look at me when they find out. Even if I stopped today, it wouldn't matter. All I'll ever be is an ex-hooker."

"Some people would see it that way. But plenty of people would just chalk it up to something you did when you were young."

"So you think I should quit?"

"I guess it depends on how it makes you feel. If you don't feel good about doing it, you should probably do something different." I didn't know enough to be giving her advice, and I didn't say anything else about it. Neither did she.

A few miles later we were passing an all-night service station, and I saw her look over at me. "Later on tonight... I just don't want things to get awkward."

I started nodding. "I know what you mean. Some of those constellations can be pretty embarrassing."

She knew something else was coming. "Okay. Why are constellations embarrassing?"

I tried to sound troubled. "Well... you know how the Big Dipper is... well it's inside of the Ursa... I mean Ursa Major. And the Little Dipper is... it's inside Ursa Minor." She didn't say anything and I couldn't see her, but I hoped she was smiling.

November 1, 1975 – It's after three in the morning and I'm out in a field behind a cabin somewhere west of Yosemite Park. I'm leaning back against a boulder and Liza is in front of me. My arms are around her and we're looking up at the stars. I'm freezing, but neither one of us is ready to go back to the cabin. I've never seen so many stars and I've never seen so many meteors. Every minute or two another streak of light slashes across the sky.

We've been talking about infinity and how many galaxies there might be. Neither one of us thinks there was a beginning to existence. She sees it pretty much the same way I do. Because something exists, and because something can't come from nothing, then something must have always existed.

Liza didn't say anything on our way back down to the cabin. Heat from the fire I'd built was radiating from the hearth. We were both cold, but after we sat in front of the fire and warmed up for a few minutes, the energy started flowing between us. I was about to tell her what I had in mind, but she brought it up first.

"Okay, so what's your secret solution."

I managed to tell her without sounding too awkward. The interior of the cabin seemed to be glowing, and she stood up and started taking off her clothes. I felt like I was in a dream. The shadows were moving on the walls and the ceiling, and the firelight was playing off of her skin.

She lay down and it wasn't long before she caught fire and sent off sparks two or three different times. She finally said she couldn't take it anymore, but I started back up and there were more sparks. She kept whispering for me to let myself go, but the only way she'd know I wasn't there for myself was if I held back.

I fell asleep after a while, and when I woke up she was standing by a window and looking outside. A little bit of light was coming into the sky by then. It was cool in the cabin and she'd put on her sweater. When she saw that I was awake, she walked over to the fireplace. She put more wood on the fire and pushed at the bottom log with the poker.

She looked at me, but it was a few seconds before she said anything. "There's something I want to make sure I understand."

"Okay."

"You pretty well proved that you aren't worried about VD, and that you didn't drive all the way out here to get laid. What I want to know is how much your high school obsession had to do with last night."

"She didn't have anything to do with it."

"You sure about that?"

I waited a few seconds before I answered her. "Yeah. It might have mattered a few months ago, but I don't think it does anymore."

"You know why I'm curious?"

"Yeah. If I'd taken some vow of celibacy because of Callie, last night would've meant something different. But if you could've been reading my mind, you'd know it wasn't a factor. And if you could read my mind right now, you'd know how glad I am to be here with you."

After I stood up, I walked over and put my arms around her. "So what if I go blind and end up living in a mental institution because of all the diseases I just caught?"

She took a deep breath and then she started laughing. "You are *such* an ass."

We got some sleep and there were more sparks, and it was mid-afternoon before we started back to San Francisco. After a while, she looked over at me. "You know, your quest to win the heart of young Callie might make a pretty good movie. An older guy and an underage girl – there are just *so* many possibilities."

"It wouldn't get much of an audience."

Liza looked amused. "Oh I don't know, *Lolita* did pretty well."

"But like I said, the version of *Lolita* starring Callie is rated G."

She shook her head. "That's too bad. Sex is a pretty good way to get to know somebody."

I didn't say anything and she kept talking.

"I don't see how anything will change until you find out who she is. Right now you have her up on a pedestal, and the pedestal she's on is locked inside a glass case. You're waiting around to see if she grows up to be your soulmate, but you aren't getting to know her and she's not getting to know you.

"And it isn't just the sex, it's what you talk about afterward – all the things you didn't talk about before. Glass cases and pedestals don't last very long once sex is involved."

She was quiet for a few seconds. "This won't be a surprise, but I had an older guy in my life when I was her age. I'd already been fooling around by then, and it wasn't long before we got together. And I was the one who made all the moves. Who knows, maybe one of these days Callie will jump down from her pedestal. Maybe she'll be the one who breaks through the glass."

"Well, I won't hold my breath."

"Then it won't happen. Not with the way you can hold yourself back."

It was a few miles before I looked over at Liza. "You feel okay about last night?"

She didn't answer me at first. "Well as I'm sure you recall, I did see *a whole lot* of stars."

When we were about an hour from San Francisco, we stopped at a gas station. I went inside to pay, and when Liza came back from the restroom, I got her to drive. I'd been thinking about what I wanted to write since we left the cabin.

After we got to her apartment, I didn't mention the way I felt about telling her goodbye. I was pretty sure she felt the same way I did. I wanted to believe that I might see her again. I almost told her that I'd try to stop by on my way back from the Philippines, but I was pretty sure I wouldn't.

I didn't know how having a girlfriend in California would work when I was back in Nashville. I was afraid of getting in too deep. I was protecting myself again. I was running away from life again.

Liza gave me a long hug. When I handed her the poem, I said

the only thing I could think to say. "Don't read this till I'm gone. And there's something I want you to promise me."

"What's that?"

"Promise that you won't forget what a complete idiot I am."

She gave me a half-smile. I was pretty sure she knew that we'd never see each other again. "How could I *ever* forget a thing like that?"

Sparks

She watched the sparks
Swirling up into the darkness
From the tree of life,
But does she imagine the sparks
Forming into a constellation?
Will she ever find her own image
In the night sky?
Will she, in time,
Come to see herself
As she really is –
Glimmering, not tarnished,
Not diminished, but vibrant?

It was close to sunset when I went by to let Sean and Valerie know I was leaving. Valerie came to the door. She was in her pajamas and wearing a hangover. Sean was still in bed. I asked her to tell him goodbye for me and I left.

I was pretty tired, but I wanted to drive at least part of the way to Los Angeles. Then I'd stop somewhere and get some sleep, and the next day, after I dropped off my car at a storage lot, I'd head for the Philippines.

Chapter 73

It had been a while since I called my parents, and I stopped at a phone booth on the outskirts of San Francisco. It was Saturday night and I wasn't sure they'd be there, but my father answered the phone. I was glad I got to talk to him first. I told him about the portrait Ann was sending, and that she was shipping it to his office so Mother wouldn't know about it. Then I told him I was about to leave for Manila.

I kept waiting for him to tell Mother to get on the other phone. He didn't sound the way he usually did. He was subdued. It was almost like somebody was pointing a gun at him and he couldn't tell me about it.

I finally said, "Is everything okay?"

He didn't say, "Everything is fine." What he said was, "Well I think things will turn out okay. Everything will work out."

Ten days earlier Mother had found a small lump on the side of her right breast. It was malignant. She was scheduled for a mastectomy on Tuesday. He said he knew that I wanted to talk to her, but she went to bed early and I should call back the next morning. He said I didn't need to come home. Mother had already told him there was nothing for me to do. They had discussed it and they wanted me to go ahead with my trip.

They talked about whether they should even tell me. I could've guessed everything she said. She would be fine. It would bother her if I came back. I should just go on to the Philippines and everything would be back to normal by the time I got home. I told my father that I'd be there by Tuesday afternoon at the latest. He didn't tell me not to come.

I went north until I got to I-80. It was the closest interstate going east. I was tired, but I had a long way to go and I wanted to get as far as I could before I stopped driving.

Howling shadows were closing in on me, and I turned up the radio and started saying the 23rd Psalm. But I kept seeing the scalpel cutting into Mother and then I thought about her suffering in a hospital bed and I imagined her disfigured body beneath her bandages. The howling got louder, and the shadows finally swarmed in and started devouring what was left of the light.

I got something to eat in Reno. I wasn't sure, but the waitress seemed to be flirting when she said there weren't many motels between there and Elko. By the time I started driving again, there were only a few cars and trucks on the road. After a while, I felt like I was in a trance, and then it was like I was flying. I cut off my lights once, but when I looked up I couldn't see any stars.

Now and then I passed an exit to some little town, but instead of turning off the highway and looking for a vacancy sign, I kept driving. The night wore on and by the time I went past Elko, most of the shadows had eaten their fill. I wanted to pull over and rest for a few minutes, but I was afraid I'd end up sleeping till morning.

I tried to think about kids I'd coached and Callie and my neighborhood and body surfing and Liza and Ann and Palani and Sean and Mike Higgins and where I would've gone in the Philippines, but Mother was in the background of every thought I had. I kept driving and after pieces of her life floated around for a while, they started coming together.

I pictured her back when she was a sensitive little girl with four older brothers. I remembered her saying, just about every time she talked about her childhood, how loving her mother had been. And I remembered her telling me about having her first menstruation.

Her mother had been dead for a year by then, and when she

started to bleed there wasn't anybody to tell her what was happening. She had been sure that she was dying, too. She never stopped mourning for her mother, and even though she smiled all the way through high school, there was always a touch of sadness just beneath the surface.

She never forgot how quickly life could fall apart, but she was pretty and popular and she went away to college. And after she graduated from Hollins, she went to Europe and heard lectures at Cambridge and danced in London with Leslie Howard, the movie star, and received love letters from two or three different British admirers, and kept scrapbooks about the art she discovered while she was living in Florence.

She came home and got a job as a social worker, and in her spare time, she did volunteer work with crippled children. And rather than play it safe when it came to choosing a husband – instead of embracing one of the privileged young men from well-regarded families who were there for the taking – she chose to go through life with an outsider.

He was intelligent and hard-working and likely to be successful, but she raised a number of eyebrows by accepting the proposal of a young man with the reputation of being overly familiar in certain situations. It was whispered that he could be, on occasion, socially off-key.

After their first year together, she had a miscarriage and the war came, and when her husband left for the Pacific there was separation and there was fear. On his return, there was his illness, but then they bought the small home where they expected to raise their family. There were two more miscarriages and the growing fear of childlessness, before the long-awaited birth and the glow of motherhood.

Many years later, along with the slowly unfolding sadness of trying to encourage a son who couldn't seem to thrive, there was the sadness that came in the wake of harsh words spoken late in the night. And then there was a mass of malignant tissue.

I let myself remember how she sobbed over the open grave of her father while she stood beside the long-closed grave of her mother.

I almost stopped in Wendover, Nevada, but it was getting light by then and I decided to go on to Salt Lake City before I got a room. I turned on the radio and found a classical station playing a cello suite. It was nearly dawn when I drove out onto the desert, but it looked like I was moving across the surface of a flat empty sea.

I was flying and the cello mourned, and when I passed a car or a truck, the slow wisps of blowing dust moved in harmony with the mood of the music. The cello was hypnotic and the sun began to rise above the eastern horizon and illuminate the desert. Muted tints of red and gold filled the sky, and the terrain started glowing. I didn't know if it was a sign from God or a coincidence of nature. It was a few minutes before the color faded away, and then the cello eased into silence.

I found a cheap motel just outside of Salt Lake City. I fell asleep thinking about a poem I wanted to write for Mother. I didn't wake up until after dark on Sunday night. I showered and ate a quick dinner, and I was back on the road a little before midnight.

It was around seven o'clock on Monday morning when I got to Denver. By then I knew what I wanted to write. I wrote it in my journal when I stopped for lunch in Hays, Kansas.

The Queen

Her father
Ruled the kingdom,
And while her four older brothers
Became powerful princes,
Her mother –
So loving and gracious and noble –
Would smile at her
And call her a princess.
But the little girl

Knew who she was.
And then her mother was gone
And as the little girl wept,
She drew in a sense of solitude
That would remain
Throughout the years when
Others would smile at her
With deep admiration.
They saw a princess,
But when she gazed into the mirror
All she saw,
All she ever saw,
Was a sad little girl.
After her husband
Went away and after
He returned from the war,
After she saw him through
His illness,
And many years after
Having wept in solitude
Longing for a child
She could not seem to have,
She stood in the snow
Bravely holding back her tears
As the son
She had finally been given
Drove away.
And he continued to drive
Away and away and away
On his troubled journey.
And she stood by
Again and again and again,
Fearful and holding back tears,
Always courageous,
Always loving,

Always gracious,
Always noble,
And always and always
And always a queen.

It was a long haul across the rest of Kansas, but I was flying. The wind was blowing in through the windows and the radio was on and the stations faded in and out most of the way to Missouri. It was late on Monday afternoon when I stopped somewhere between St. Louis and Kansas City.

I slept past midnight, but I was still tired when I got back on the road. Missouri became Illinois and Illinois became Kentucky, and the closer I got to home, the more I felt like I was dreaming. It was dark and the lights were off in our house when I pulled into the driveway. They would be up soon, and I sat on the patio and waited.

November 4, 1975 – The light comes on in the kitchen and I walk up to the back door. I expect to see my father making a cup of coffee, but it's Mother. Her back is toward me and she's wearing her light blue robe and standing beside the sink. Even though she can't eat because of the surgery she's about to have, she's gotten up to fix my father some breakfast. She opens the same cabinet she's opened for the last thirty years, and she reaches for the same dark green mixing bowl she always uses.

She turns on the front eye of the stove and then she opens the refrigerator and gets a carton of milk and a couple of eggs. If I could see her face, I'd probably know if she's thinking about going to the hospital, or if she's just trying not to think. After she breaks two eggs into the bowl, she picks up a fork and whisks the yolks and whites together. She adds a little milk before she empties the bowl into the skillet she's been using for as long as I can remember. After I watch her put two slices of bread into the toaster, I tap on the glass. She stops moving, and then she begins to turn around. She has a smile on her face before she sees me.

She opened the door and I gave her a long hug. My father heard the door close, and when he came into the kitchen we hugged, too. Mother didn't complain that I'd come home. I didn't say anything about her cancer or the surgery. They just wanted to hear about my trip.

I talked about Palani and about staying with Ann, and just about the only things I left out were how Sean had fallen apart and being at the Coyote Ball, and about going to Yosemite with Liza.

My father and I waited in the lounge while Mother was in surgery. He finally started talking about the Philippines, and along with going back through a lot of what he told me at the cemetery and what he told me on the way home from Atlanta after his heart attack, he repeated some of what he'd written about his sister.

Mother was still unconscious when they brought her to her room. My father talked some about business, but then his voice trailed off. Mother didn't say much after she woke up, and she had a hard time staying awake. We finally left, and as soon as we got home, I went to my room and fell asleep.

Chapter 74

November 5, 1975 – It's a little after 4 PM. I'm sitting in a booth near the lunch counter in Moon's Drugstore. I remember sitting here in 1958. I'd just gotten out of fifth grade and I was playing on a baseball team made up of kids from Woodmont. We all came to the drugstore after our game. Our regular third baseman went out of town, and I ended up having to take his place. The pitcher on the other team was really good. I hadn't wanted to get hit by one of his fastballs, but I'd been a lot more afraid of dropping a pop-up or having a ball go through my legs or striking out with the bases loaded, and losing the game for my team.

I told my parents I was sick, but they made me put on my uniform and go to the game. I was nervous and I struck out the first time I was up, but I didn't make any errors and I ended up getting a couple of base hits. The last one was just a dinky infield hit, but we had a runner on third base and it drove in the winning run. We came to the drugstore to celebrate, and I was sitting just about where I'm sitting now. It doesn't look all that different from the way it did back then. People made a big deal out of the way I'd played, and even Jamie Reed, our best player, came over and said, "Good game." It doesn't seem like that long ago.

Callie doesn't see me when she shows up. I watch her walk behind the counter and put on an apron. A man sits down and orders. She doesn't spot me until she's serving him his sandwich. She gets to me as fast as she can. I'm still sitting in the booth when she bends down and kisses me on the side of my face. She starts to hug me, but then I feel her put on the brakes. She pulls away, but she's still smiling at me.

The man sitting at the counter finished his sandwich and left, and Callie had some time to talk. After I told her why I came back and how Mother was doing, she told me about a guy she liked. She said they hadn't gone out yet, but she was pretty sure they would. Then she said that even though she and Claire both hated school, they showed up every day and neither one of them was failing anything.

When I was telling her what I did while I was gone, she didn't seem too interested until I told her about the Coyote Ball. I didn't go into what happened in the restroom between the Roman and Albert in his hula skirt, or anything about my brief adventure with Liza, but I told her just about everything else.

Claire showed up, and as soon as she saw me she ran over and got me in a bear hug and gave me a big kiss on the lips. "We thought you were in the Philippines. How come you're back already?"

Callie was shaking her head. "Well, you won't get a lot of answers if you squeeze him to death."

When I was telling Claire about Mother, I saw fatigue in her eyes. She looked like she'd been up all night. "What about you and the guy you told me about before I left? Is he still..."

Callie cut me off. "He's history. Hey Claire, you've gotta hear about this party he went to in San Francisco. Naked guys were walking around, and there was weed all over the place."

I told her about the party, and when I described the two unicorns, Claire was laughing so hard it looked like she might fall on the floor. A woman came in with her kids, and Callie went back behind the counter to make cheeseburgers. Claire and I talked for a little while longer, but I didn't ask about her boyfriend.

I went to the hospital after that. Mother was in pain, but she didn't say anything about it. Her surgeon came by while I was there. He talked about the lymph nodes he removed, and he said he would know the results of the biopsies within a few days. As soon as the doctor left, I went back to telling her about what Ann remembered from when they were girls.

We brought her home from the hospital on Friday. That night she was lying in bed, and she told me that some of the nodes that were removed during her surgery were malignant. She hadn't let my father tell me because she didn't want me to start worrying any sooner than I had to. She didn't know if she'd have to go through chemotherapy, but she was starting radiation in a few weeks. She looked up at me and smiled. "So at least I'll get to keep my hair for a while."

She was scheduled for physical therapy before her radiation treatments started, and the doctor said it shouldn't be too long before her life started getting back to normal. My father kept saying he was pretty sure she'd be okay, but the night after she came home, after she was in bed, we were standing in the kitchen. He looked troubled and he said we'd just have to hope for the best.

Callie had called me the night after I went by the drugstore. She and her mother wanted me to come to their house for dinner on Sunday. But she called me again three nights later and said we had to put off the dinner. She'd slipped out and gone to a party on Friday night. It was raided by the police after some neighbors complained about underage drinking, and she ended up in juvenile detention. After her mother went to pick her up, she went through Callie's room and found some marijuana. Callie was grounded for six weeks.

She was only allowed to go to school and to work, and the only visitor she could have was Claire. And that was only on weekends. Her mother was standing next to her when she called to tell me what happened. She said making the call with her mother there was part of her punishment. Her voice was as flat as the desert in western Utah. She said she couldn't talk to anybody on the phone, and not to come by the drugstore.

Her mother called me a few days later while Callie was at school. She said it would be okay if I wanted to write Callie a letter or two. I could tell how worried she was. For people like Sean, drugs and alcohol were like putting sharp knives in a baby crib, but I didn't see that with Callie.

Claire only called once. She didn't sound much like herself and I got the feeling she was bored. She said she'd call again in a few days, but I didn't hear from her for a while.

I couldn't just sit around the house, and after a couple of days, I went back to researching the neighborhood. Just before I left for California I found out that there was a lot of historical information in the old lawsuit case files that were stored on the top floor of the Davidson County courthouse. I went downtown and talked to one of the clerks in Chancery Court. He looked surprised when I told him I wanted to see the records. He said they were up on the seventh floor, and that it had been a while since anybody went up there.

He laughed when he gave me the key. "Just watch out for critters."

I got on a back elevator and rode up to where the county jail had been located until sometime in the 1950s or 60s. There wasn't much light and it was dirty and musty, and I kept hearing something scurrying around. It could've been mice, but it sounded more like rats. Court records were scattered all over the place.

I poked around for an hour before I found the docket books from Chancery Court stacked up in one of the cells. They were heavy, oversized volumes and each one had a long index of plaintiffs and defendants. It took a few hours, but I went through all the books from the 1800s, and I made a list of the court cases that involved the early landowners in my neighborhood. The cases all had numbers, and I found a few files with the same numbers before I ran out of time.

I went back the next morning and after four or five hours I found just about everything on my list. The files were stored in boxes, and most of the boxes were jammed into jail cells. Each file was folded into thirds and tied with a length of old ribbon. They were all coated with grime. They were full of information about land disputes and slaves and events that took place back when the Woodmont neighborhood was farmland.

When I was looking through the files, I forgot that I was on the top floor of the courthouse. I read through a lawsuit concerning a tract of land owned by Jesse Wharton, and I felt like it was 1821 – 142 years before the night when I walked across the same tract of land and knocked on the front door of the house where Yancey Walsh was waiting inside.

I read about a boundary dispute that involved the farm where Joseph Erwin built *Peach Blossom*, and where Charles Dickinson was buried after being killed by Andrew Jackson. There were times it felt like it could've been 1809 – 164 years before I stood where one of Erwin's cornfields had been and looked over at Callie Lee while she was watching a football game.

It didn't seem like 1975 when I found a document that mentioned three of the slaves who lived on the Owen farm. They were named Albert and David and Henry, and they worked the land that would include Tom Hendrickson's basketball court and Herbert's Field.

And it didn't seem like 1975 when I was reading a lawsuit about the property where Charles Bosley built his mansion on the site of an old frontier fort – a century before Montgomery Bell Academy was established on a rise just across a creek. It seemed more like 1817 – 150 years before the boys on my football team played Smear the Queer there on a Friday night.

But I didn't look through three of the largest files. Each one was at least two inches thick and they all involved Colonel Willoughby Williams, who owned the land where both my house and Woodmont School were eventually built. I got the files I wanted and took them down to the clerk's office, and I spent the rest of the day making copies.

That night I went back to my room. I stayed up till daybreak reading and making notes about what I brought home. One document contained a list of all the land that Colonel Williams owned. He had tens of thousands of acres, and I didn't understand how he could afford so much property. Up until then, I thought I knew a lot about the history of the neighborhood. By morning I understood how much more there was to know. Every time I learned something, there were more questions.

The oldest file involved John Nichols, the father-in-law of Colonel Williams. He was a slave trader and he made enough money buying and selling slaves to purchase the land that became the western part of the Woodmont neighborhood. He had been sued by his partner in the slave trade, who claimed that Nichols cheated him.

The pages and pages of testimony gave details about the slaves the partnership bought and sold, and there was a good deal of information about a light-skinned sixteen-year-old slave girl named Easter. Nichols had removed her from the partnership for purposes that were not explained. Other documents listed additional slaves, and I kept wondering where they lived and how they were treated.

The most compelling document I found was a map that was drawn in 1829. It showed the entire western section of the neighborhood, with all the fields and pastures and streams and woods. I wondered how much more information I'd be able to turn up.

I kept thinking about all the information that had been dumped on the top floor of the courthouse, and I started to wonder why Woodmont School wouldn't be a good place to store and preserve those records. A few days later I called our councilman, but he wasn't interested in the city having an archive. And I didn't get anywhere when I tried to make an appointment to see the mayor.

Chapter 75

November 21, 1975 – It's Friday night. I'm a little hesitant about walking into the Montgomery Bell Academy gym. I'm about to see a lot of kids I'd love to be coaching. They'll want to know if they can be on my team again, but it's too late. When I called the guy who runs the YMCA league, he told me the teams already had coaches, and that the kids had already been put on teams.

Five of my old players are on the Montgomery Bell varsity. They're out on the court warming up. John Wilkins and Ben Mayer look over when I walk into the gym. Ezra Lyle and Hal North don't see me, but Page Whitney shakes his head and smiles when I stagger and look shocked that he made the varsity.

I go up to the top row of the bleachers. It isn't long before several of my ex-players are sitting with me. I catch up on how school is going, and I tease them about how they couldn't possibly have girlfriends and about what terrible athletes they'd always been. After a few minutes, it doesn't seem like I've even been gone.

At the start of the second half Inman Roberts, the athletic director at Ensworth, comes over and sits down. We've coached against each other for seven or eight years and we're pretty good friends. We talk some and after I tell him why I'm not coaching, he looks at me and starts smiling. "I think there's something you and I need to talk about."

Inman said that the two fourth-grade teams at Ensworth needed a coach. "I had a couple of young guys all lined up. Then they came in and talked to my headmaster, and they both backed out. Our old headmaster loved sports, but the guy who took his place thinks children's athletics are a waste of time."

He shook his head. "He isn't a bad guy, but if it was up to him, he'd probably get rid of school sports altogether. He interviews anybody who volunteers to coach our kids. I guess he wants to talk about all the ways that athletics can be harmful to children."

Ensworth was almost as close to my house as Woodmont, and after the start of busing, several of my players went there and played for Inman. I took in everything he was telling me. "So I'd need to talk to the headmaster?"

Inman nodded. "Yep. But there's something I need to warn you about."

"What's that?"

He sounded apologetic. "There are some... Most of the parents at Ensworth are good people, but there are a few... well they can be pretty hard to deal with. They're used to getting their way."

I'd encountered overly involved parents from time to time, and I could see how a school like Ensworth would have more than its share of what my coaching friends and I called "crazies."

The way I looked at it, the children of unstable parents tended to be insecure, and insecure kids tended to struggle when it came to sports. And as soon as an insecure kid started to struggle, it was a fairly good bet that his coach would be hearing complaints from a least one of the insecure kid's crazy, insecure parents. There might be a few problems, but I didn't see how Ensworth could have anybody worse than Dr. Earnshaw, who'd pulled his son off my baseball team a couple of summers back.

A good number of my ex-players were students at Montgomery Bell, and more of them came up to see me before the end of the game. By the time I left, I'd caught up on what went on while I was away. Along with some drunk driving arrests and quite a bit of drug use in the school, one of their schoolmates had tried to kill himself a few weeks earlier. When I was leaving I passed Mr. Francis, the headmaster. He looked at me and nodded when I said hello, but it was hard to tell if he remembered me.

December 1, 1975 – It's Monday afternoon and I've been shown into the office of the head of school at Ensworth. Donald Grayson is behind his desk, and he's leaning back in his chair and talking on the phone. I want to get back to coaching kids, but after what Inman Roberts told me about Mr. Grayson, I'm not getting my hopes up.

There are a couple of diplomas hanging on the wall behind his desk. They're too far away for me to see where he went to school. He has what sounds like a New England accent. He's laughing a lot and trying to turn on the charm. He must be talking to some rich donor. He finally hangs up and his expression changes. There's just a hint of a frown when he looks at me, but he covers it up with a smile. It disappears almost as quickly as the frown did.

Donald Grayson got straight to the point. "Mr. Roberts tells me that you and he have talked, and that you may be interested in coaching two of our school teams. Before we go any further I ought to tell you that I'm not entirely convinced that schools should be directly involved in athletics.

"In my opinion, athletics should be conducted as an outside activity. But school teams are ingrained in the culture at Ensworth, so..." I thought he would shake his head, but he didn't.

"At any rate, I am in the process of refining our mission statement and one of the areas that needs clarification is the proper role of athletics in the lives of our students." He stopped talking, and instead of asking if I had any questions, he raised his eyebrows.

I just nodded and waited to hear what he'd say next.

"I've had a pair of meetings with our faculty committee, and we've come up with a preliminary draft. It's still a work in progress, but our revised school policy will call for athletic programs at Ensworth to be conducted in such a way – and I'm paraphrasing here – as to foster health and confidence, as well as a sense of belonging, for all participating students."

He stopped talking and raised his eyebrows again. When I

didn't say anything, he asked me a question. "If I recall correctly, Mr. Roberts said you have been coaching children for several years. Would you mind talking about what you hope to accomplish through your... coaching?"

I noticed the way he paused. "I asked myself that question back when I first started working with kids, and I don't think my answer has changed very much."

I was reading the expression on his face. He was probably expecting to hear some vague statement, and then he would enlighten me about the proper role of sports in the lives of children.

"I want the experiences a kid has while he's on my team to have a positive influence on the arc of his life." He was expecting me to elaborate, but I wanted to see how he'd respond if I just raised my eyebrows.

He seemed a little off balance. "That... I would be interested to hear a bit more about how you achieve that."

Two types of people ran schools – educators and administrators. Nothing was more important to educators than helping students become better people. Administrators would never admit it, but they mostly focused on avoiding and managing conflict. I wondered how Mr. Grayson saw himself.

I didn't mention how crucial it was to get to know kids. And I didn't mention that it was a lot easier to have an impact on children's lives if they had a close relationship with their coaches. I just said something safe. "Almost every situation that comes up in coaching is an opportunity to change a kid's life."

That morning I'd read the Ensworth mission statement in the school handbook I borrowed from Inman Roberts. Instead of using the same didactic tone Mr. Grayson used, I tried to talk like we were just having a conversation.

"Your mission statement says that the school's athletic program should promote health. Kids get plenty of exercise when they play on a team. It's also important to look at their future health.

Smoking and drinking and drugs will all be coming at them in a few years, and I try to prepare them for that."

Even though it probably wouldn't have helped my case, I was ready to tell him about the unflattering impressions I did of drunken, chain-smoking drug addicts doing everything from missing shots in basketball to not being able to catch a baseball. But he didn't ask me how I turned kids against alcohol and drugs and tobacco. He just sat behind his desk and looked at me.

I didn't mention all the times I did those impressions, and I didn't go into how I avoided using positive reinforcement unless there was something positive to reinforce. I just said how important it was for kids to develop a genuine sense of confidence.

Since at least the early 1970s psychologists had insisted that coaches should only use praise when they were working with kids. They seemed to think that if a fly ball was hit to center field, and if the center fielder wet his pants while he was running away from the ball, the coach should congratulate him for not running away any faster than he had, and for not completely emptying his bladder.

It didn't take kids long to figure out when they were being lied to. It wasn't all that hard to just go ahead and teach them to catch a fly ball. Kids knew the difference between accomplishing something they could be proud of, and getting a false pat on the back and a trophy at the end of the season just for showing up.

But I didn't go into any of that with Mr. Grayson. All I did was tell him that I couldn't count how many times I'd seen a boy develop confidence after he overcame a challenge. I didn't mention Smear the Queer, but I spent three or four minutes telling him about Peter Johnson. I wanted him to understand that what Peter did back in 1967 had probably changed his life. Mr. Grayson didn't have much of a response. There was a lot more I wanted to say about how sports could build confidence, but I didn't think he would take it in.

Then I started talking about how important it was for kids

to feel like they were part of something. That being on a team brought about a sense of belonging. He seemed to pay more attention when I was telling him about some of the times I'd been left out when I was a kid. I had the feeling that Donald Grayson was picked on a lot when he was a boy. I would've bet that he was usually the last kid chosen at recess.

It wasn't long before he looked at his watch. "I have another meeting in a few minutes, and I'm afraid I need to cut this short. I'll just tell you what I told two young men who were in last week. We'll treat this season as a trial arrangement. Then we'll get together again after the season and talk about how things went."

I could see why the other guys decided not to coach at Ensworth. Mr. Grayson was a nice enough guy, but he seemed to think he was doing me a favor by allowing me to volunteer my time.

December 9, 1975 – We're halfway through our first practice, and eighteen sweaty fourth graders are running for the water fountain at the south end of the Ensworth gym. A couple of the kids are fairly good, five or six are pretty bad, and the rest are somewhere in between. Most of them seem like regular kids, but there are a few whiners. I wonder if I'll end up being as close to these guys as I was to the kids at Woodmont.

There's one boy I already like a lot, but I don't know his name. I get the feeling this is the first time he's ever played a sport. Even though he has a hard time dribbling, and even though he can't get the ball up to the basket, he hasn't stopped smiling since we started practice. He's chubby and short and slow, but he's been listening to everything I say and he's trying as hard as he can.

He seems to have a great little spirit, but something else makes him stand out even more. I wonder how long it'll be before he starts getting teased about how effeminate he is. After he gets some water he prances back out onto the court and picks up a ball, and then he starts trying to dribble again. I go over and check through my roster. His name is Whiting Caswell.

Two fathers had been standing over by the side door of the gym with their arms crossed. They came up after we finished and introduced themselves. They were the fathers of the two best players I had. When they asked me if I needed any assistant coaches, I tried to be tactful. I said I'd let them know if I did. I hoped they weren't planning on showing up for every practice.

Ensworth played in a league that had one division for strong players and a separate division for weak players. That meant I was supposed to put the best players on a good team and the weak players on a bad team. It was a stupid idea. There was no reason to tell fourth-grade boys that they were already second-class players.

Ability would matter when they got to high school, but for the next two or three years it would mostly come down to who liked basketball and who didn't. The kids who liked to play would end up practicing more on their own and trying harder. Every year I coached, there were kids with average ability who did better than kids who were bigger and faster and stronger.

We were going to have equal teams, and both groups would play in the strong division. The kids would have the whole season to show what kind of players they were. They liked the idea of equal teams, but when the two fathers heard me announce what I was doing, one of them gave me a look of disgust and they both left shaking their heads.

When I asked Inman Roberts what the problem was, he didn't say anything at first. "Well first off, I think having equal teams is a good idea. But whatever you do around here – somebody isn't gonna like it.

"Both those guys think their sons are superstars, and they don't want their boys to be on losing teams. But the one you need to watch out for is Jones Colbert. He's a big-time real estate developer and he doesn't mind running over people. And his wife is as bad as he is."

Mr. Big-Time Developer should've already figured out that his son would be a lot better if he practiced against somebody as good as he was. And it was the same with the teams. I was pretty sure we'd struggle at first, but two equal teams playing against each other in practice would improve a lot more over the course of a season than two unequal teams. Most of the parents were nice to me, but after I divided the teams, a few people started treating me like I was contagious.

I couldn't tell what Whiting Caswell's mother thought. She was the opposite of Whiting. She was tall and slender and aloof. When the other mothers spoke to Mrs. Caswell, she usually just nodded and they moved on. Several of the women who had kids on my team looked like they went to the beauty parlor every day. When they came by to pick up their kids at the end of practice, they looked like they were on their way to a party. Mrs. Caswell didn't look like she was trying to impress anybody.

After a few practices, I went over and told her how much I thought of her son. She looked at me for two or three seconds before she said anything "Well, Whiting does seem to be enjoying himself." She kept looking at me, but she never smiled.

I got to our next practice a few minutes early so I could ask Inman Roberts about Whiting and his mother. He was sitting in his office trying to fix a basketball pump. He told me that Mrs. Caswell's father had been one of the richest men in Nashville, and Whiting was her only child. Her husband wasn't around, and Inman wasn't sure whether he'd left her or if she'd thrown him out.

When I mentioned how the other parents acted around her, he just shrugged. "They're afraid of her."

"Because she's rich?"

"Well a lot of it is her money and the influence she has, but it's also because she knows a lot about the other rich folks in Belle Meade. Our last headmaster told me about an Ensworth board meeting when one of the other board members got on her wrong side.

"She finally looked at the guy and told him if he said another word, he'd regret it. The guy was the president of a bank, but after that, he just sat there and he didn't say anything."

"And what's your take on Whiting?"

Inman leaned back. "That boy never stops smiling. And he'd try to run through a wall if you told him to. It wouldn't do anything to the wall, but he'd still try to run through it."

I hoped he'd say something about how effeminate Whiting was, but he didn't. I wanted to know if he'd had other kids like Whiting, and how boys like that were treated at Ensworth once they got to sixth or seventh grade. I'd coached a few guys like that before, but none of them stood out as much as Whiting did.

I wrote two letters to Callie, but I didn't have much to tell her. In the second letter, I pretended that she was the imprisoned mastermind of a huge marijuana ring. I caught her up on the various members of her fictional gang and threw in a few funny lines, but it would've been a lot better if I hadn't thought that her mother would read it, too. She wrote back and told me that if she wasn't about to be paroled, she'd be looking for a way to escape.

Around the time I got Callie's letter, Claire called me up and said she wanted me to meet her at the next Hillsboro basketball game. We sat together the whole time. She talked about how bored she was, but she never said anything about her boyfriend. I thought about asking her why she looked so tired, but I didn't say anything.

Chapter 76

I spent my days researching neighborhood history, and the more I learned, the more obsessed I was with the Williams house. Along with the map I found in the Chancery Court files, I ran across an aerial photograph of the neighborhood from the 1930s at the State Library. From the photo, I figured out where the meadows and fields and woods and old roads had been back in the early 1800s.

But I still didn't know where the slave cabins were, or what Willoughby Williams was like as a person, and there were a thousand questions in between. Sometimes I'd lie awake at night and imagine the plantation in the decades before the Civil War. And I never stopped thinking about what I'd seen through the window of the old Williams mansion on Christmas Eve.

I finally got around to finding out about the woman who lived in the house. Her name was Miss Delores Young, and she'd lived in the old Williams mansion since her father bought the place in the 1920s. It shouldn't have taken me as long as it did to come up with a way to approach her.

I was pretty sure she'd want to know as much as she could about the place where she'd been living for over half a century, and I put together a brief history of the Williams plantation. It ended up being eleven pages long. After I wrote her a letter asking if I could meet her, I put the history and the letter in an envelope and left it in her mailbox. Four days later I got a note saying she'd love to see anything I'd found.

December 18, 1975 – It's a cold Thursday afternoon, and I'm standing at the front door of what was once the Williams mansion. I hear footsteps coming from inside, but a truck speeds by on Woodmont Boulevard, and I don't hear the click of the lock. The door opens and I get a good look at Miss Delores Young.

She is short and plump and she's wearing a pink dress that she's probably had since back before World War Two. I can't help thinking about the decades of neighborhood children who convinced each other that the woman who lived alone in the old house had kidnapped and murdered small children. She squints and shields her eyes from the afternoon glare, and then she touches me on the arm and asks me to come inside.

The swathe of sunlight on the carpet narrows into a sliver and disappears when she closes the door. The air inside smells old. The only sounds are our footsteps and the slow ticking of the grandfather clock in the corner of the room. My eyes adjust to the dimness and I follow her past an array of antique furniture, and past several portraits and a massive bookcase. She stops outside the door of the next room. I feel like I've walked into the 1920s.

She looked down at the two folders I was holding. "I can't wait to see what you've brought, but first I should tell you a little about this house. It has seen *a whole heap* of living. It was right at a hundred years old when Poppa bought it in 1922. Poppa called this room where we're standing the front parlor. It was his favorite room. It has hardly changed since we moved in."

She pointed to a large leather chair. "Poppa died right over there. He was reading the newspaper. We thought he was asleep. He was ninety-three. He and Mama had been married for sixty-eight years by then. She passed on just a few months after he did."

I was wondering if I should say I was sorry, but she kept talking. "The first thing I want to tell you is that Poppa knew Willoughby Williams. When Poppa was a boy Colonel Williams must've been around eighty. Poppa always called him Old Colonel Williams.

"My grandfather had a blacksmith shop on Harding Pike, about halfway into town from here. Colonel Williams was one of his best customers. Poppa grew up working in the shop, and he would see Colonel Williams every now and again. Poppa used to tell about one particular time when he rode out here on his horse.

"He was delivering a message, and Colonel Williams was back in this room behind me. It was his study. Poppa went in and Colonel Williams ended up telling him about one time when General Jackson and Sam Houston were passing through the neighborhood. It was in the 1820s – back before Jackson was president. When Houston was Governor of Tennessee. They stopped off when a storm was coming up, and they ended up spending the night.

"They stayed up late talking about politics or horses or whatever they were talking about, and then they finally went to bed. Colonel Williams told Poppa that Houston was snoring so loud that nobody in that part of the house could get any sleep. General Jackson came downstairs and laid down right here in the parlor, but he could still hear Houston snoring. The study was quieter and he finally went in there and slept on the floor."

I would've written down what she was saying, but I didn't want to distract her by rummaging around for my pen.

She glanced down again at the folders I was holding. "My eyes have been giving me some trouble, but I got through a good bit of what you wrote. There was a lot I didn't know anything about."

It was a few seconds before she said anything else. "It means so much to me that you have an interest in this place. The house is pretty run down and I... Well, I assume that's why people aren't very curious about it. Now and again I think about writing as much as I know, but I'm not much of a writer." Then she put her hands together and smiled. "Well, I have quite a surprise for you."

Miss Young opened the door of the room I'd seen the year before on Christmas Eve, when I looked in through the window.

"This is the study. This was where Colonel Williams told Poppa the story about Sam Houston snoring, and where General Jackson ended up going to sleep."

A fire was burning in the fireplace. The study was much smaller than the parlor, and a lot warmer. There was a rocking chair in front of the fireplace, and an antique writing desk and a table and a couple of other chairs were across the room. But what drew most of my attention was the bookshelf that covered one of the walls, and an old wooden trunk in the corner.

Miss Young noticed me staring at the rows of old books. "Well, those books are part of what I want to show you. They belonged to the Williams family. Colonel Williams died somewhere in the early 1880s, and after his son, John Henry, died in the 1890s, the place was sold and the family left behind all these books. And they left a lot more than just books."

She pointed toward the corner. "They also left that trunk. It's full of old papers. When the Kenners moved in, they carted off all sorts of clothes from the attic and things from the kitchen, but Mr. Kenner decided to leave this room the way it was. And after Poppa bought the place, he left it alone, too. I grew up with Evelina Kenner, and it looks the same way it did back when we played in here as little girls."

It seemed like Willoughby Williams could've just walked out of the study. There was a pretty good chance that Miss Young was going to let me look through the trunk. My mind was running wild.

"Every three or four years Poppa would come in here and open the trunk and start poking around. He pulled out letters and old deeds and tried to read through them, but after an hour or two he put everything back and closed the lid.

"If I'm making Poppa sound lazy, I don't mean to. It's just that Willoughby Williams' handwriting is so... well it's just about *impossible* to read." She gave me a big smile. "I'd love to know what you're thinking right now. You look a little thunderstruck."

I told myself not to talk too fast. "I'm way past thunderstruck. I don't know if there's a word for wanting to jump up and down and run around the room and turn flips, but that's what I feel like doing." I went ahead and said it. "I sure hope you'll let me see what's in the trunk."

She was already nodding. "You can get started whenever you'd like. I'd love to see you write a longer history of this house. I'll be eighty years old before I know it, and it would mean so much to see this place get the recognition it deserves. But if Colonel Williams' scrawl turns out to be too much, I'll understand."

Before I opened up the trunk, I showed her what I'd brought. She sat down and tried to look through the folders, but her eyesight was a problem. Sometimes she'd hold what she was trying to read close to her face, and other times she moved it a little to one side or the other. I ended up telling her what I'd found out about the Williams slaves and the land purchases, and about John Nichols being a slave trader.

After a while, she sat back in her chair. "Well I could sit here all day listening to you, but I need to go upstairs and freshen up before my niece comes by to get me. I've been invited to a holiday dinner. But that doesn't mean you should leave. You're welcome to stay and look through the trunk for as long as you'd like."

I hoped she wasn't just being polite. "Are you sure?"

"Yes, dear. I hope you're still here when I get home. I'll be curious to hear what you find. But if you have to leave, just pull the door to. And you can come back whenever you want to. I'm here most of the time." She started to leave, but she stopped at the door. "Oh, and if you want to pull anything out of the trunk, there are empty boxes in the back of the pantry."

After she left I walked over to the trunk and lifted the heavy wooden lid. It was packed with old documents. At the top, there were bundles of letters tied up with string, and it looked like there could be five or six more layers underneath.

I could see where Mr. Young had looked through a few stacks of letters. He'd tied them back up in a bow – like he was tying a shoe, but the other bundles were tied with square knots. It looked like they hadn't been opened since back in the 1800s.

I untied one of the bundles that had already been examined. I could see why Miss Young and her father, and probably Mr. Kenner, didn't go through much of what was in the trunk. The first letter I read had been written by Willoughby Williams to his son in 1852.

His handwriting was especially hard to decipher, and it took me a while to get through the first page. There were a few words I couldn't figure out, but I finally got the gist of the letter. I wanted to see what else was in the trunk, and I went and got several boxes from Miss Young's pantry.

I kept pulling out letters and documents, but a couple of times I made myself stop and think about where I was and what I was being allowed to do. Then I looked around the room and tried to imagine Andrew Jackson asleep on the floor.

The bundles of letters from the two upper layers filled five boxes. It took twelve more boxes to hold the rest of the letters and loose papers I pulled out. Under everything else there were four large leather-bound ledgers, and between the ledgers and one side of the trunk were several more bundles of letters. But those letters looked different from the letters at the top of the trunk. The paper looked older and they were tied with twine instead of string.

Chapter 77

December 24, 1975 – Callie is opening the front door of her house late on Christmas Eve morning. I called her mother and she said it would be okay if I dropped off a Christmas present. It's another living Christmas tree, but this time I've decorated it with little brass ornaments. I can see that she likes it. She seems to be glad I'm there. Her mother isn't home and Callie invites me inside. I don't think she wants to hear about my basketball teams or about what I've found in the trunk. I start to tell her about talking to Claire at the basketball game, but she looks away. All she says is, "Yeah, I know."

We talked for a while and then she surprised me. She asked me when I noticed her for the first time. I said I was watching from the bleachers when she threw Rusty Willis down on the floor of the Ensworth gym. Then I talked about seeing her look through a piece of smoked glass during the solar eclipse, and what I remembered from being in the dunking machine at the Woodmont Carnival when she threw the baseball that put me in the water.

She gave me a different kind of smile than I'd seen before. "Yeah, I remember that stuff, too."

And then I went ahead and told her how I felt a couple of years later when I saw her standing beside the road with her friends. Too much of me – most of me – hoped that she'd look into my eyes and glance at my lips, and that her eyes would move across my face and down to my neck and my shoulders.

I wanted a current to start moving between us. I thought I might've felt something once or twice, but I wasn't sure. By the time her mother came home, Callie was talking about a college guy who lived down the street, and who wanted to ask her out.

December 25, 1975 – It's Christmas morning and it's raining outside. My parents are sitting on the living room sofa and I'm handing Mother a present from my father. It's been seven weeks since her surgery. Every day I wonder what's happening inside her body.

I try to tell myself that her cancer cells are all dead, but sometimes I imagine them inside her, growing wherever they can take root. She probably thinks about the same thing, but she hasn't mentioned it and she never complains. I look at her while she opens her gift. She seems frail and I wonder if she looks that way to my father. He doesn't look too good either. He's gone back to playing a little golf and she's walking around the neighborhood again, but that doesn't mean they're okay.

Thirty years ago they were having their first Christmas in this house – right in this room. They were only a little older than I am now. There's one more present for Mother. I pull it out from behind the tree, and she gives me a funny look when I prop it up against the sofa. I watch her face as I pull the wrapping paper away from Ann's painting. She doesn't say anything, but there are tears in her eyes.

I wasn't sure if Mother would like the portrait. I thought having part of my face shaded by a shadow might be a little too unusual, but she wanted me to hang it on the wall next to the one Ann finished when I was fifteen.

Callie had gone off to Texas to visit her father, and with Ensworth out for Christmas break, I had plenty of time to dig through what was in the trunk. I spent New Year's Eve with Miss Young. I built a fire in the fireplace in the study, and she sat in her rocker and read.

I told her what I was finding, and from time to time I read something I thought she might enjoy. She went to bed, but I stayed up reading letters till after four in the morning. By then I was pretty good at deciphering Colonel Williams' handwriting.

He owned a lot more land than I thought. And along with all his property in Tennessee and his big plantation in Arkansas, he had stock in all sorts of businesses. In the 1840s he'd been president of the largest bank in the state. His letters were almost always about money, but I still hoped to find out how he treated his slaves.

There were usually between fifty and ninety slaves on his home plantation, but there were several hundred more on his plantation in Arkansas. Colonel Williams owned around five hundred people at the beginning of the Civil War. I kept looking for something in the trunk that would explain how he had enough money to own so much land and so many slaves.

January 10, 1976 – It's the first Saturday morning of basketball season. The kids are out on the court warming up. Mrs. Caswell is sitting by herself, three rows behind our bench. Her son, Whiting, has been trying to get a rebound. After several tries, he finally gets his hands on a ball that rolled off to the side of the court. He has his usual smile, and he keeps smiling when his shot hits the underside of the rim and bounces away.

Jones Colbert and a couple of other fathers are sitting together on the top row of the bleachers. In a few more minutes they'll have a lot to shake their heads about. We aren't ready to play anybody, much less Oak Hill, which is supposed to be the best team in the league. They're running through a series of drills on the other end of the court. They've been practicing since the middle of November and it shows. We didn't get started till the week before the kids got out of school for Christmas. Oak Hill would beat us even if all my best players were on the same team.

My other team had already lost. It would've been a slaughter, but the other coach didn't know what he was doing. The game against Oak Hill went worse than I expected. They ran a really structured offense, but even though they beat us by twenty-four points, I saw where they might be vulnerable.

I was frustrated, but I stayed positive and most of the kids didn't seem too upset about getting clobbered. When I got the team together after the game, I went through what each kid had done well – that part didn't take too long – and then I talked about what needed improvement.

When I got around to Whiting I said he needed to keep working on dribbling and shooting, but when I told him he was improving on defense, his smile got even wider than it was before.

Jake Colbert scored almost all of our points. He played hard and he hated to lose. After I told him how much I respected his effort, I let him know that we'd be getting a lot better. I just hoped his father wouldn't poison the well in the meantime.

Mr. Colbert looked at me when he was leaving the gym. All he did was frown and look disgusted. I couldn't tell what Mrs. Caswell thought. I spoke to her, but all she did was nod.

I went home from the gym and spent the next two or three hours drawing up a full-court zone press. It would take a few weeks before we could execute it, but I thought we should be able to run it pretty well by the end of the season.

The next week at practice Jake Colbert handed me a sealed envelope from his father. There was a note inside. All it said was, "If you want to score some points and maybe win a game or two this season, you might want to take a look at this offense." It was a copy of an article on how to run a 3-2 offense. He'd eventually see a 3-2, but it wouldn't be the one he had in mind.

Basketball wasn't much fun if kids didn't get to run and shoot. If all they did was set up and try to run a motion offense, they wouldn't learn many skills. By the time my players were in high school, the dominant players wouldn't be white guys who played on private school teams that ran pattern offenses. The dominant players would be guys who'd gone out on the playground and played in pickup games from the time they were little kids. The dominant players would be black guys who grew up doing a whole lot of running and gunning.

Chapter 78

January 16, 1976 – It's Friday night, and it's halftime of the basketball game between Montgomery Bell Academy and Hillsboro. The Hillsboro gym is crowded. Callie isn't grounded anymore, but she and Claire haven't shown up yet. I'm standing near the court and I'm talking to some of the guys I used to coach. One of them is Brian Burroughs. He was on my football and basketball teams for three years, and he was in Callie's grade at Woodmont.

He's an especially good-hearted kid. The second half is about to start and the other guys go back to their seats. But Brian stays where he is. He stares at me for a couple of seconds. "There's something I need to tell you." It's loud where we are and we move toward the back corner of the gym. He has a serious expression on his face. "You know Callie's friend Claire? Well, she's... she has a bun in the oven."

It wasn't unusual to hear about some high school girl getting pregnant, but it hadn't ever been somebody I knew. Brian usually had a smile on his face, but he looked worried. "She's knocked up, but she's acting like everything is okay."

I had a lot of questions. "How did you find out?"

"I have a cousin who works at the public health center. She took down Claire's information when she showed up. When she found out how old Claire was and that she went to Hillsboro, she figured that I probably knew her. But she didn't say anything until Claire didn't show up for her appointment. My cousin said it's bad when a pregnant teenager misses an appointment.

"She was worried that Claire might not know what she should do, and she asked me about Claire's parents. There's no way she would've told her parents. They're... well, they're really hard on her. I think she's probably been talking to Callie about it, but there's a chance that even Callie doesn't know."

The buzzer went off and the second half was about to start, but Brian had more to say. "I've thought about calling Callie up and asking her if she knows about Claire being pregnant, but she'd go ballistic over something like that. She'd make me tell her how I found out, and I can't get my cousin in trouble."

It was hard to picture Callie getting that angry. "Do you know how far along Claire is?"

"She's at least a couple of months."

"Is the guy who got her pregnant the same guy she was going out with?"

He was nodding. "I don't think it could be anybody else. But now he's in the army. guess it happened when he came home after basic training."

Brian kept staring at me. "And she probably hasn't told him. The only person she would've told is Callie, and like I said, I'm not even sure about that. I thought there might be a way you could help her. Just don't tell Callie or anybody else that you heard it from me."

Claire and Callie never made it to the game. I hoped they were together somewhere, and that they were talking about what Claire was going to do.

I didn't sleep for more than an hour or two that night. The temperature was falling, and from time to time one of the wooden joints in the walls of the house would pop. I should've known that something was wrong when Claire and I were sitting together at the game earlier in the season. I lay in bed and kept going from one dark thought to another.

I'd always liked Claire, and I should've taken more of an interest in her life. I didn't even know she had problems with her parents.

I kept picturing her going into her second trimester while she was still trying to decide whether to have the baby or have an abortion. She seemed like a boat drifting toward the rocks during a storm.

From the way she avoided the subject of Claire's boyfriend, it was obvious that Callie knew about the pregnancy. And it was obvious that she didn't want me to be involved. Callie and I were getting closer, and I didn't want that going up in smoke.

But I couldn't turn my back on Claire if she needed help. The only choice I had was to tell Callie what I knew, and let her know that I'd do what I could to help Claire. I kept trying to think of how I should explain things.

I slipped in and out of a succession of half-dreams, but after a while, my thoughts drifted to Callie and what it would be like to lose her. And then I was asleep and I was sitting next to her and we were alone in her house like we'd been on Christmas Eve morning. She was staring at me and we were moving closer to each other, but as soon as she touched me, the vision evaporated. I tried to bring it back, but I was a boy again and I was alone in the darkness and somebody was crying, and I didn't know who it was.

I saw Callie the next day at the drugstore. I got there in the middle of the afternoon when she wouldn't be too busy. She stayed behind the counter and I sat down on one of the stools while she made me a grilled cheese sandwich. She kept smiling at me, but her look turned cold as soon as I said that I knew Claire was pregnant.

Then I told her I was going to write Claire a letter. She kept staring into my eyes. It was a few seconds before she said anything. "How did you find out? Claire didn't tell you. She wasn't going to tell anybody."

"I found out from a friend of a friend who works at the health center."

She looked skeptical. "Why would somebody tell *you* about it?"

"Maybe it's because of all the kids I know. Claire missed an appointment and they were worried about her."

She was staring right through me. "Well you can't tell *anybody*. And you can't write her a letter. You can't say *anything* to her."

The drugstore counter seemed to be getting wider. I looked back at her. "I wish it was that simple."

She was defensive. "It *is* that simple. It's none of your business. It's *Claire's* business. You know what'll happen if you talk to her or write her a letter? I'll lose her as a friend. There's no way she'll believe that I didn't tell you."

I could see the anger in Callie's eyes. She hadn't moved from where she was standing, but she seemed a lot farther away than she'd been. I just asked her a question. "Don't you think she needs help?"

She didn't say anything. She just kept staring at me.

I tried to stay calm. "Look, I have to write her a letter. I'm not going to tell her what to do. It's not my place to tell her what to do. But she needs to make a decision while she still has a decision to make."

There was no softness in the tone of her voice. "She already knows her options. That's what she's been doing. She's been trying to decide what to do."

I waited a few seconds before I said it. "So she still hasn't made up her mind?"

I saw Callie's face getting flushed. "She probably has. But I'm not... it's been a while since we talked to each other."

I didn't want to sound like an adult making a point. "Well if she still hasn't decided, she's running out of time. Pretty soon she'll be facing a whole different situation. Do you understand what I'm saying?"

I could tell she was trying not to lose her temper. "*Yes. I know.* After three months everything gets harder. She'll be in her second trimester. I get it."

I tried to speak gently, but not too gently. "It'll be harder – physically and emotionally." I wanted to confirm what Brian had told me about Claire's parents. "What about her mother and her father? Is there any way they..."

She cut me off. "She and her parents don't get along. She's adopted and they're both religious fanatics, okay? I don't even think they love her. If they do, you'd never know it."

"Well is there anybody she can talk to?"

It was a few seconds before Callie said anything. "I don't know. Am *I* anybody?" It seemed like the counter was ten yards wide. "How about this? I'll tell you what we talked about, and then you tell me if I'm anybody. So let's see. We talked about what'll happen if she doesn't get an abortion.

"We talked about what her parents will do if they find out. One time they threw her out of the house just for sneaking off and going to a party. She stayed with me for a week before my Mom got her parents to let her come back home.

"And we talked about how everybody at school would know about it and that girls would call her a slut. How she'd have to leave Hillsboro and figure out how to take care of a baby, and how nobody would want to go out with a girl who has a kid. And that she couldn't go to college, or ever find a halfway decent guy who'd want to marry her."

She didn't give me a chance to say anything. "And we talked about whether she should have an abortion. She said her real mother could've had an abortion, but she didn't. She said having an abortion wasn't natural and it didn't seem right, and if she had one it would eat at her for the rest of her life.

"And yeah, we talked about how she could have the baby and let somebody adopt it. But she said she wasn't going to do it – not when there was a chance her baby could end up with crappy parents like the ones she has." There was resentment in her voice. "And let's see what else... Oh yeah, she did a lot of puking and she cried most of the time, and last week she said she wasn't going to talk about it anymore."

I wasn't sure what I should say next. "Well, I don't think anybody could've handled things any better than you did."

She didn't say anything and the expression on her face didn't change.

I needed as much information as I could get. "Why wouldn't she talk about it?"

Callie gave me a look that was somewhere between angry and exasperated. "*Because all she did is cry.*" She stopped looking at me. "And the last time she wasn't just crying. She was freaking out. That doesn't need to happen again.

"There's no point. She's probably decided by now anyway. And there isn't anything you can write in some *letter* that she hasn't thought about already. She's gonna do what she's gonna do." She turned around and picked up a wash rag. "If you send her a letter..."

I felt empty inside. Leaving right then would've been more than awkward. I went ahead and finished my sandwich, but I couldn't taste it. While she was wiping down the far end of the counter, I was thinking about what I should say in the letter I was going to write. I finally got up and told Callie goodbye, but she didn't even look up.

Chapter 79

January 23, 1976 – It's late on Friday morning. I'm pulling up across the street from the obstetrician's office. Claire just shakes her head when I ask if she wants me to go in with her. She releases a long breath and gets out of the car. She crosses the street and she doesn't look back. I watch her walk up the steps to the office and go through the door. I don't know how long the procedure will take. I turn on the radio and try to think.

Hillsboro students are taking their mid-term exams. The only one Claire had today was English. She got through at ten and I was waiting in the parking lot when she left school. She looked stricken and numb when she was getting in the car, and her expression hadn't changed by the time she went in to see the doctor. I am mourning for Claire. She's really kind and smart and brave. I reach back and get my journal, and I start writing.

On Saturday, just before I left Callie wiping the counter in the drugstore, it hit me that one of two things was true. Either Claire had already decided what she was going to do, or she hadn't.

If she hadn't decided, she might've changed her mind about wanting somebody to talk to. And if she had decided, she probably wouldn't be as emotional as she was the last time she was with Callie. Either way, she might welcome some support.

If she wanted to have the baby, she would need somebody to be with her when she told her parents. If her parents were as bad as Brian and Callie thought they were – if they were just going to throw Claire out – she'd need all the help she could get while she was deciding what to do next. Our neighbor, Martha Graves, was a social worker, and I asked her about the social services available to pregnant unmarried teenage girls.

In the letter I wrote to Claire, I told her I knew the situation she was in. I said I wanted to help her no matter what she decided to do. I couldn't leave the letter in her mailbox, so I waited around and handed it to her when she was coming out of school on Monday afternoon.

She called me that night and told me she was getting an abortion. She'd already found a doctor and she had an appointment for that Friday. When I told her I could help her pay for the doctor, she said she had enough money saved up to pay him herself. She was planning to take a cab, but when I offered to drive she sounded relieved.

It was a couple of hours before she came back outside. She looked like she was walking away from a plane crash. She didn't want to go home, and we drove around for a while. She held herself together as long as she could, but she finally broke down.

I pulled into a church parking lot and I held her while she was gasping between waves of tears. I was pretty sure she hadn't slept the night before, and after fifteen or twenty minutes of sobbing, she was worn out. She was too tired to cry anymore, but she kept holding me until she got her breathing under control.

She needed to eat and we went to an out-of-the-way little meat-and-three place a few miles west of downtown. I finally got her to take a few bites of a yeast roll. She leaned back in the booth and closed her eyes. Her voice wasn't much more than a whisper. "I don't know how I... can get through what I've done."

I didn't say anything at first. "I don't know either, but you will."

She opened her eyes, but she didn't say anything.

She needed some hope. "Even though you won't forget about this, you won't end up seeing it the way you see it right now."

Claire closed her eyes again. "But what I've done won't ever change. It won't be any different when I'm seventy. Something inside me was..." A tear welled up in the corner of her right eye and rolled down her cheek. She struggled to say what she had to say. "Another life was growing inside me and I just *ended* it. That's the way it is, and it'll always be that way."

I stopped myself from saying anything. I'd made a copy of the poem I wrote. I pulled it out of my journal and handed it to her, but after a few seconds, she put it on the table. "I'll... look at this later on."

The Cradle of Grief

Her grief cut her
To the bone
And she continued
To bear its scar,
But after a time
Her grief faded
Into sorrow.
It was years
Before she understood
That a blessing
Was cradled in
What she first saw
As a curse.
It was years
Before she saw
That all the pain
And all the sadness
Had brought her
The man she loved.
It was years
Before she saw
That the darkness
She endured
Helped give her
The infant in her arms.

It was years
Before she finally understood
That an unrealized life
Allowed her to have
The child she adored.

I was pretty sure I wouldn't hear from Claire for a while, and I didn't think I'd hear from Callie at all. I wondered if she would use what happened as an excuse to get away from me. She could've been having misgivings about me all along. She might've needed to escape. I hated the idea that I might've been diminishing her life.

Along with thinking about Callie, I thought a lot about Mother. She would go out and take walks when the weather was good, and at first, she seemed to be getting stronger. But there were days when she looked weak and unsteady. I tried not to think about clumps of cancer cells floating through her bloodstream and multiplying inside her body.

And I tried not to think about how much more my father had been drinking since her diagnosis. I could tell how worried they both were, and it took me longer than it should have to come up with something that might make things a little better.

January 25, 1976 – It's Sunday afternoon and I'm in the den with my parents. My father is sitting in his chair and Mother is across the room on the sofa. I clip the microphone to his shirt and turn on the tape recorder. After I give the date and introduce him, I ask my first question. "Who's the oldest member of your family you can remember?"

He looks toward the kitchen. It's like he's looking into the past. "I can remember my grandfather." He's still gazing into the kitchen, and he tilts his head a little to one side. "He was a school teacher. He was around seventy-five when my father died, so he was born in the 1840s. The first thing I remember about him is sitting on his lap on the front porch of our house in Manila. I had fallen off my rocking horse and hurt my knee."

After I thought for a while about what questions I wanted to ask, I went out and bought a new cassette recorder and a box of tapes. Mother would've been reluctant to let me interview her even if she was healthy, so I started with my father. All I did was turn on the recorder and ask a question. He took it from there.

We sat down for about an hour every night, and he covered lots of ground. He went into detail about growing up in Manila and coming to Vanderbilt and getting married and about his time in the military, and he talked a lot about his business career.

Mother was listening to everything he said. I could tell there were details about his intelligence work that she'd never heard, and she probably hadn't known how much danger he was in. She didn't move when he was talking about killing Ramon. "The way he looked at me... I can still see his eyes... He was staring up at me. I'm still trying to forgive myself."

And I wondered what she was thinking as she listened to his version of their years together. "The first time I danced with your mother was at the Wagon Wheel. She was on a date with my cousin. At the end of the dance, I told her I was going to marry her." He closed his eyes. "Francis Craig's orchestra was playing *Begin the Beguine*. Sometimes I can still hear it in my head."

When I couldn't think of any more questions to ask, and after it seemed like he'd said everything he wanted to say, I asked Mother if I could interview her. She was reluctant, but she went ahead and did it. She'd probably been preparing herself the whole time she was listening to my father. I didn't expect her to say much about her mother, but after she talked about how affectionate she was, she passed along some details I'd never heard before.

"It was the last day of June and I was outside playing. Father came to the front door and yelled that she was awake. A blood vessel in her brain had ruptured and she'd been unconscious for three days. I ran inside, but I didn't want to make any noise. I remember tiptoeing up the stairs.

"She looked like she was just waking up from a nap. I went over and put my head on her shoulder. She smiled and ran her fingers along the side of my face, and then she started stroking my hair. Her bedroom was pretty warm and she asked me to get her a bowl of ice cream.

"I ran down to the kitchen and got the ice cream – it was strawberry – out of the ice box. I thought she'd like me to brush her hair while she ate her ice cream. But by the time I got back up to her room, she was unconscious again."

Her words came much more slowly. "Her breathing kept getting weaker and I didn't want to be there anymore. I went to my room and got on my bed, and when I heard my brothers crying, I went outside. She died right after the sun went down."

I was surprised that she said so much about her mother. And she remembered a few things her mother said about my great-great-grandfather, who came to Nashville in the 1830s. "It was a pretty small town back then, and even though he was just a carriage maker, my great-grandfather knew Andrew Jackson." He probably knew Willoughby Williams, too.

Recording my parents worked out pretty well. Mother seemed to be a little more relaxed for a while. It might've been my imagination, but I didn't think my father was drinking quite as much.

January 27, 1976 – It's Tuesday morning. Miss Young is in her rocking chair and I'm standing beside the trunk. The room is getting cold, and I walk over and put a little more wood on the fire. She's been looking at a wedding invitation from the 1840s, but she puts it on her lap and looks over at me. "Every time I watch you pick up a letter or start reading through a document, I can't wait to hear what you've found. I swear, it's better than watching television.

"With everything you've already told me, and with whatever else you'll find, it won't be long before I could sit down with the ghost of old Willoughby Williams himself and hold up my end of the conversation." There's a touch of wood smoke in the air and it blends with the fragrance of antiquity. The fire crackles and I slowly untie the twine from around

a bundle of letters I found at the bottom of the trunk. They aren't in the handwriting of Willoughby Williams.

The letters were all from Joseph Erwin, the builder of *Peach Blossom*, to John Nichols, the father-in-law of Willoughby Williams. In 1821 Erwin's son, Isaac, had married Nichols' daughter, Mary. After reading through the first nine or ten letters, I could put together a lot of what happened. Within a few years the marriage fell apart, and a deep bitterness had developed between their fathers.

By then Joseph Erwin was living in Louisiana, and the letters he wrote to Nichols reflected the animosity he felt. In one letter Erwin claimed that Nichols had swindled him in a land purchase, and in another, he condemned Nichols for being a drunkard. He accused Nichols of everything from not maintaining his fences to having appropriated missing livestock. But I was blindsided by what I read in the last letter Erwin wrote to Nichols.

> Sir – I am in receipt of yours of the 20th instant,
> in which you not only impugn the character of my son,
> Isaac, and of myself, but you dare to assail the character
> of my deceased son-in-law Mr. Dickinson, who was slain
> in so cowardly a manner by Mr. Jackson.
> Your dissipation appears to have inflamed the lowest
> elements of your character. The nature of your supposed
> character first came to my notice some years ago when I
> inquired of you as to the whereabouts of the ball that
> took Mr. Dickinson's life. Although it was last in the
> possession of your daughter, Mary, you feigned ignorance.
> I remain convinced that she removed it from my home in
> order to spite me, but for what imagined offense I know not.
> Such seems to be the character of the entire Nichols family.
> Sir, I shall ever regret having suffered the misfortune of
> our acquaintance...

I read it through two more times and my mind was still racing.

There was no proof that the ball I'd found at *Peach Blossom* was the same ball Joseph Erwin mentioned in his letter, but the letter made it easier to believe that it was.

I'd found it in a room that had the initials *I E* etched into the glass of one of its windows, and Mary Nichols, who was suspected of having taken the bullet, had been married to Isaac Erwin. After I read the letter to Miss Young, I told her about finding the ball and giving it to Hill Murray. She just sat in her rocker and smiled.

The next day I went downtown to the State Library and did more research on the duel. I learned a lot, but I only ran across one account that had anything to do with the ball. A man who saw the corpse of Charles Dickinson observed that after passing through his body, the ball ended up just below the surface of his skin. There was no mention of the ball being cut away, but it was clear from Joseph Erwin's letter that it had been removed.

And a few days after that I found out why Willoughby Williams was so wealthy. At the bottom of the trunk, there was a small ledger with a record of all the land he inherited from his father.

Before Willoughby Williams was born, his father brought his wife and several slaves west across the mountains. His father was in possession of a large number of North Carolina warrants – warrants that established his rights to an enormous quantity of land. Separate records in the ledger revealed how his father came to have so many warrants.

Willoughby Williams' grandfather had been the Secretary of State of North Carolina, and his father was a senior official in the same office. The Secretary of State oversaw millions of acres of public lands, and both men were principal figures in a widespread conspiracy involving the part of North Carolina that later became Tennessee.

They were ultimately tried and convicted of their crimes, but even after his conviction, Willoughby Williams' father remained in possession of a number of the illegally obtained land warrants – warrants that would establish his son's financial position. It wasn't hard to see a connection between how Willoughby Williams had gotten his land, and what was happening to the neighborhood that was built on his farm. They both involved corruption.

Ever since Herbert's Field had become a real estate transaction in the mid-1960s, the bulldozers never stopped rolling. Apartments and condominiums and look-alike houses kept springing up everywhere. The people who lived in the neighborhood showed up time and again and asked the Planning Commission and the Board of Zoning Appeals to impose some moderation, but those institutions were controlled by developers. I was still trying to understand how developers had been able to maintain their power for so long.

One afternoon before basketball practice, I drove around and tried to count the number of housing units that had been built within a mile of my house since I'd started coaching at Woodmont. I lost count at 1500. I couldn't see much difference between the land speculators of the 1780s and 1790s who worked in the shadows to illegally accumulate vast amounts of land, and the shadowy developers who were devouring my neighborhood like a swarm of locusts.

Chapter 80

January 29, 1976 –My players are sitting along the edge of the stage at the south end of the Ensworth gymnasium. I know exactly what I want to say. "Most people would stand here and all they'd see is a bunch of goofy-looking little kids with their legs dangling off the end of a stage. I see the same thing, but I also see kids who don't seem to understand the concept of keeping score. Both of our teams have played three games. Do you know how many of those games we've won?" Nobody said anything. I put my hands over my face like I finally understand that they're all morons.

I look off to one side and pretend I'm talking to some imaginary presence. "Good God, they don't understand the difference between winning and losing." Most of them have started smiling. I take an exaggerated breath and talk to them like they're three-year-olds. "Okay, I'll try to explain this in a way you'll understand. The numbers on the scoreboard show how many points each team has. The idea is for our team to end up with more points than the other team. Now let me ask you again. How many games have we won?"

Whiting was giggling. "None."

I put my hands over my heart. "Ah, the sound of a child's innocent laughter. Well, now that you guys understand the concept of winning and losing, I have another question. *Why* haven't we won any games?"

Jake started to say something, but he stopped himself.

"Come on, Jake. Don't be shy."

"We're losing because of how you divided up the teams."

I pretended to think about what he'd said. "I suppose that *is* a possibility, but I have another explanation." I was pretty sure they'd like what I was about to tell them, but I didn't know how it would go over with their parents.

"After our game last Saturday, if we'd all gotten on a bus and gone up into North Nashville and ridden around, guess what we would've seen? Playgrounds full of black kids playing basketball.

"When we watched them playing defense, they wouldn't have been standing around like statues on the lawn of some mansion. They would've been staying low and overplaying and trying to steal the ball. When one of them got a rebound, he wouldn't have stood there like he was waiting for his Mommy to give him his allowance. He would've run up the court as fast as he could, trying to find somebody to pass to. And after a missed shot, you wouldn't have seen even *one* kid looking around like he was waiting for his butler to run over and get him the ball.

"They would've been doing two things that you guys don't seem to know anything about – *jumping* and *rebounding*. They would've gone up as high as they could and tried to grab the ball. If the ball rolled away, they wouldn't have worried about scraping their elbows or bruising their knees – they would've gone after the ball.

"And if somebody did skin his elbow or bump his knee, he wouldn't have laid there like he was waiting for his nanny to call an ambulance. He would've gotten his little butt up and kept playing. You might *actually* be able to win a few games if you stopped playing basketball like a bunch of rich little white kids."

Whiting started laughing. "But we *are* a bunch of rich little white kids."

"But you don't have to play like you are. What if you pretended you were somebody else while you were playing basketball? What if you started pretending you were black kids from North Nashville? You don't have to do it if you don't want to, but if you'd like to give it a try..."

I held up a handful of index cards. "See these? There's a name on each card. If you don't like the name you get, feel free to come up with a name on your own." I went down the row and each kid drew a random card. It didn't take them long to get excited.

Once I'd gotten them to quiet down, we had formal introductions. One by one they hopped down from the stage and handed me their card. After using my best African-American accent to introduce Otis and Tyrone and Cedric and Ronell and Earl and everybody else, I got around to Jake and Whiting. Jake seemed pleased to be Tarique and I finished up with Whiting.

"And let me introduce our final athlete, Jaquez."

Whiting hopped down from the stage and ran over to me. "I don't want to be Jaquez. I want to be *Jermaine*."

"Okay *Jermaine*, but excuse me for just a second." I went over and opened one of the doors on the side of the gym. I put my hand to my ear. "Can anybody hear that?"

Whiting and some of the other kids shook their heads.

"That's the sound of every guy in North Nashville named Jaquez breathing a sigh of relief." I started walking back toward the stage, but I stopped and went back and opened the door again. "And *that's* all the guys in America named Jermaine screaming, *NOOO!* at the top of their lungs."

When Whiting did his impression of Jermaine strutting back to the stage, everybody cracked up. I thought they'd like having basketball names, but I didn't expect them to be as proud of their new names as they were.

I used their North Nashville names when I pretended to broadcast their scrimmages. "Oscar moves up the court and he's closely guarded by Tarique. Oscar passes to Cedric and he's wide open, but *OH NO!* Instead of driving in for a wide-open lay-up, Cedric has suddenly turned into J. Thomas Worthington. He doesn't look like a basketball player. He looks like he's trying to find a badminton partner at the country club."

From then on, anybody who played like a rich white kid or who didn't hustle became J. Thomas Worthington. And after I told them I'd be handing out the J. Thomas Worthington trophy at the end of the season, they really picked up the pace.

When it came to the way I coached, the Ensworth kids reacted pretty much the same way the Woodmont kids always had. Their favorite part of practice was when I imitated them screwing up.

It wasn't long before Mr. Marling, the assistant headmaster, showed up at practice. It was obvious that he was there to check on what was going on. He stood near the stage and he did everything but take notes. I'd planned to work on our press, but I wanted him to see what he came to see.

I took on my role as sportscaster and we had an especially long scrimmage. He got to hear all the new names, and there were several mentions of J. Thomas Worthington. He stayed the whole time, and he left without saying anything.

Inman Roberts stopped by our next practice. He had a smile on his face. "Well, you sure know how to shake things up. Mr. Grayson has gotten calls from some of the parents. He told me that the first one was from Mary Ann Colbert. She said the other boys were calling Jake names at practice. There were two more calls like that, but it didn't take Mr. Grayson long to figure out what was going on."

It was pretty obvious. "Let me guess. The parents who called were friends of the Colberts."

"That's right."

"And the assistant headmaster came by to monitor our practice?"

"Yep. He was making sure there wasn't any name-calling, and that nobody was getting picked on." His face turned more serious. "Just watch out for the Colberts. Jake's a good boy, but his parents are trouble."

When I was coaching, my mind was on the kids and basketball, and when I was reading old letters in Miss Young's study, I was back in the 1800s. But I still spent a lot of time thinking about Callie. For the first two or three weeks I felt some anticipation when the telephone rang, but after a while, my anticipation had pretty much faded away. I kept expecting to hear from Claire, but she didn't call either.

February 7, 1976 – It's Saturday morning and it's my second game of the day. We're playing a pretty weak team and we're ahead by eight points with less than a minute left. I've taken out my best players and Jake is sitting beside me on the bench. We're on defense and Whiting is trying to guard the kid with the ball. Jake yells to him, "Sag left! Sag left!" When the kid with the ball starts backing in toward the goal, Jake yells, "Hands up!" and both of Whiting's hands go up.

The kid keeps backing in and Whiting tries to hold his ground. He adds in some drama when he finally falls back onto the floor. The referee blows his whistle and calls a charge on the kid with the ball. While Whiting is walking down to the other end of the floor and thinking about the free throw he's about to shoot, Jake and the other guys on the bench are cheering. Whiting is smiling even more than usual.

Everybody quiets down when Whiting steps to the foul line to shoot the front end of a one-and-one. The referee hands him the ball and he bounces it the way he's seen other kids bounce it. He heaves it toward the basket, and it hits the backboard at least a foot to the right of the rim. Whiting stomps his foot the way he's seen other kids stomp their feet after a missed shot, but he's still smiling.

I didn't think he'd get it all the way to the goal, and he probably didn't, either. I looked around the gym after the game. Our other team won the earlier game, and they all stuck around. Both teams had gotten better since the start of the season.

I wondered what Jones Colbert and the other parents in his gang were saying to each other. And I wondered what they would've been saying if we'd used our press. We could've had a winning record by then, but I was saving the press for the tournament.

I didn't see Jones Colbert when I looked around the gym, but I saw somebody else. My father was on the top row of the bleachers with his back against the gym wall. My first thought was that he was there to give me some bad news about Mother.

I went up and sat beside him, and he shook my hand. "Congratulations. And tell me about the little boy who took the last free throw. I've never seen anybody look that happy about missing a shot."

"His name is Whiting Caswell and..."

"Whiting *Caswell*? Well, I'm certainly familiar with the family."

He told me about a couple of Whiting's ancestors, and how they'd made their money in railroads and banking and real estate. Then he got around to telling me why he was there. "This morning your mother and I were eating breakfast, and we were talking about how much you love coaching.

"She asked me why it meant so much to you. When I told her I didn't know, it bothered me. I thought if I saw a game or two, I might be able to answer that question. She would've come with me, but she wasn't quite up to it."

There was a time when I wouldn't have wanted him there. "Well, I'm glad you came. What do you think?"

"Now that I've seen you in action, I have a better sense of why you like it so much. You have quite a connection with the boys on your team." The next game was about to start, and he looked down at a cluster of kids gathering around their coach. I got the feeling there was something else he wanted to say.

"You know I... I've said this before, but I haven't said it enough. I'm proud of the work you do. Coaching doesn't make you any money, but it's still work. You've been working with children and I'm sure you've changed some lives, but I'm afraid there were times when I acted like the work you're doing isn't important.

"You'll eventually need to balance it with something that will give you an income, but you should be working with kids. I guess it's like a ministry. Anyway, I want you to know that I'm proud of you. I'm proud that you've been doing this with your life."

I didn't know how to respond. Instead of just sitting next to him and feeling good about what he said, I wondered why he told me how he felt. I wondered if he was still reassessing things because of his heart attack. I wanted to change the subject. I'd been meaning to catch him up on the research I was doing, and it seemed like a good time to tell him about what I'd found in Miss Young's trunk.

I talked about the letters and the maps and the slave records. I told him that I had enough material to write a pretty good local history book. I wasn't sure he understood why anybody who didn't live there would want to read about our neighborhood, and I told him about *Centennial.* I said that James Michener told the story of a fictional locale through time, and that a non-fictional version could show that a lot of American neighborhoods had histories that were worth exploring.

He didn't say much, but he kept nodding. I probably ended up telling him more than he wanted to know, but he seemed to be listening.

One of the things going through my head that night before I fell asleep was how Jake had pulled for Whiting. It reminded me of how Hill Murray helped Peter Johnson – back when I had my first football team. It wasn't the first time that a kid I was coaching made me think about some kid I used to coach. There were times when I felt like I was standing beside a carousel watching guys I coached several years back, and guys I was still coaching, going around and around and around.

Chapter 81

I knew it was a long shot, but I still thought that a Nashville government archive should be established at what had been Woodmont School. I knew a man named Ken Robbins. He was a prominent banker, and I'd coached his son, Stephen. It hadn't been long since I saw a photograph of him in the newspaper, standing beside Mayor Richardson.

I was pretty sure he liked me, and when I called him up he said he'd be glad to talk to me. I went to his office early the next week. I told him about the records on the top floor of the courthouse, and then I talked about how much Nashville needed an archive. And that Woodmont could be turned into a history center. He said he didn't see anything wrong with the idea, and he told me he'd check into it and "find out if there are any roadblocks."

Mr. Robbins called me three days later. He didn't have good news. He'd talked to the mayor's chief deputy. A group of investors were working behind the scenes to acquire the Woodmont property. After the school building was torn down, a condominium development would be built on the site. Two or three of the investors involved in the condominium were big contributors to the mayor's campaign, and he supported the project.

Mr. Robbins said that even if the mayor was neutral, there wouldn't have been a way to pull off what I had in mind. "For an archive to be established, the mayor would have to propose it and then the city council would have to fund it, and having an archive isn't anywhere close to being a priority. It probably should be, but it isn't."

I'd pictured Woodmont being torn down ever since it closed. That was bad enough, but the thought of condominium units being built on the baseball field and on the basketball courts and the playground, and covering up the site of the school building, was a lot worse.

I started to thank him for what he'd done, but he interrupted me. "I have something else to tell you, but I need your word that you won't repeat this part of our conversation. I know the men in the development group fairly well, and I don't like creating problems for myself."

He spoke very slowly. "You can't save the school building, but there might be a way to keep all those condos from getting built. From what I understand, the councilman who represents the neighborhood doesn't get along all that well with Mayor Richardson.

"If enough people from the neighborhood were to start making noise about turning over public property to developers, the councilman might listen. He might see the political benefit of finding some public use for the property.

"I know it's not what you're after, but it might make a nice park. The school building and the land are still under the control of the school board, but it won't be that way for long. The developers are pushing for the Board of Education to declare it as surplus property and turn it over to General Services. Once that happens it'll be too late to do anything. General Services will put it out for bids, and the developers will buy it."

I hated to think about the school building getting torn down, but everything else could stay the same if it ended up being a park. At least it wouldn't end up like Herbert's Field. I asked him who was trying to develop the property.

"Well, the lead developer is a guy named Jones Colbert. I can't prove it, but it wouldn't surprise me if he had something to do with the decision to close the school. He has a good bit of influence and that would be right in line with the way he does things. Anyway, once the property gets turned over to General Services, he's got the politics all lined up.

"Like I said, the only way to stop it – and it won't be easy – is for people to raise holy hell about it. People from the neighborhood need to call the councilman and show up at the next Park Board meeting and demand that the property gets used as a park.

"But you shouldn't get your hopes up. The developers put Mayor Richardson in office and he knows it. It'll take a whole lot of pressure for him to back off. And in case you're wondering why I'm telling you so much, I don't have much use for guys like Colbert."

It was probably just a coincidence that Jones Colbert was the dark force behind the destruction of Woodmont School. But when something was especially coincidental, like when a song on the radio seemed to be mocking me, I wondered if God might be trying to tell me something.

I wanted to finish going through Miss Young's trunk, but I had to let people in the neighborhood know what was about to happen to the Woodmont property. I'd coached a lot of kids who lived near the school, and I was pretty sure that some of their parents would be willing to go on the warpath.

I planned to go from house to house, but after I made some calls, word got around fast. Within a few days, a petition was being circulated demanding the creation of Woodmont Park. Whenever I saw somebody from the neighborhood, I brought up the school and the condominiums, but most of the people I talked to had already signed the petition.

It wasn't long before there was a story in the morning newspaper about neighborhood opposition to the development. The next day I got a call from a reporter at Channel 4, one of the three main television stations in Nashville. The guy said he wanted to interview a few people who opposed the development. I would've rather let somebody else do it, but I agreed to talk to him. I didn't ask him how he got my name.

I met the reporter and his cameraman out in front of the school the next afternoon. The reporter asked me how I felt about the school property becoming a condominium development. I said it was wrong to surrender public land to private interests when the land was needed for the good of the public. Then he asked me if I knew how much the condominiums would add to the tax base.

I gave him an honest answer. "Even if the condominiums generated a million dollars a year in taxes, it wouldn't be relevant."

The reporter didn't expect me to say that. "A million dollars wouldn't be relevant?"

I felt the camera zooming in on me. "That's right, it wouldn't be relevant. The population of this neighborhood has tripled in the last ten years. More and more kids are moving in, and they need a place to play. That doesn't translate very well into dollars and cents."

I said a little more about all the open space that was being lost, and I asked where neighborhood kids would play, and where the kids I coached were supposed to practice baseball. I thought I'd done okay, but when the story came on the news that night, the only part of my interview that was broadcast was when I said that the tax revenues were irrelevant.

I got the feeling that Jones Colbert or somebody working with him gave the reporter the questions he asked. It was obvious that Colbert had plenty of pull at Channel 4, and his influence didn't stop at television. Before long there was an article in the afternoon newspaper. It was written by the executive director of the Chamber of Commerce. The article was about the opposition of the Woodmont neighborhood to the project.

The article said that there should be a partnership between the people of Nashville and the development community, because growth was good for everybody. It ended up making the usual claim – that if a city didn't grow, it would die.

I decided to go ahead and write a letter to the editor. I tried to make the point that I didn't make after the Board of Zoning Appeals rubber-stamped the development where the old Bur Oak had been pushed down and burned. I wrote that a city couldn't grow indefinitely, and if it was true that a city died as soon as it stopped growing, it should be obvious that growth ought to take place as slowly as possible.

My letter didn't get into the newspaper, but there was an article about how development held down taxes by adding to the tax base, and that growth made the city a better place to live.

Then there was another story describing the benefits of condominium units. It focused on how senior citizens, who usually didn't want to keep up a big house and a big yard, would be able to stay in the same neighborhood after their children grew up.

After that, a petition in support of the development started circulating in the neighborhood. I was slow to figure it out, but I finally understood that a whole lot more people than Jones Colbert wanted the development to be built. I kept wondering who they were.

Chapter 82

I didn't know much about putting together a grassroots campaign, but I had some experience when it came to coaching basketball. My teams had kept getting better.

We started scrimmaging against the Ensworth fifth graders. They were bigger and faster and a year older, but they had a hard time breaking our press. I put Whiting over on the right side of the court, and even though he was slow, he was smart and dependable. He did a pretty good job of cutting off anybody who tried to dribble between him and the sideline.

Mrs. Caswell never spoke to me, but she always nodded when I spoke to her. I got even more dirty looks from the Colberts after I spoke up on TV against the development. The handful of parents who always sat with them shunned me like I was a sinner in a country church, but the other parents were friendly enough.

There was a mystery woman who always brought Sam Brown to our games. She didn't look old enough to be his mother, but she seemed too old to be his sister. I wondered if she could be his nanny. She was pretty and I guessed she was in her early thirties. I would've said something to her, but I saw her talking to Jones Colbert a couple of times and I thought she might be one of his acolytes.

The Saturday after Whiting missed his free throw, I was up at the top of the stands getting ready to scout a team we would play in a couple of weeks. The mystery woman was standing near the scorer's table and I saw her look around at me. Then she started walking up to where I was sitting. She stopped right in front of me, one row down from my seat.

She looked like she was trying to keep from laughing. "Well I've been waiting for *somebody* to introduce us, but that hasn't happened. And I was hoping that you might introduce yourself at some point, but that hasn't happened either.

"This is me pretending to be forlorn." She put the back of her right hand against her forehead and gazed off into the distance. Then she looked at me again. "So now I'm forced to overcome my *intensely* shy nature and introduce myself." She stuck out her hand. "I'm Carla Thompson. I'm Sam Brown's divorced aunt."

I could tell she was enjoying her performance. I didn't know what to say.

She was smiling. "Have I already mentioned how shy I am?"

I decided that I might as well play along. I pretended to go over what she'd said. "You know, I think you *did* mention something about that."

She nodded. "In that case you must know how *awkward* I feel, just standing here like this."

I wanted to say, "Glad to meet you. I'm Sam's unmarried basketball coach. Are you trying to seduce me?" But I just invited her to sit down.

Carla's older sister was Sam's mother. Carla lived in the Thompson's guest house, and she did things like take Sam to school and pick him up, and take him to basketball practice and his games.

Her eyes moved across my face and down to my mouth. "My sister isn't exactly the world's most involved mother, and her husband is even less involved than she is. But at least you didn't have to hear how unhappy my brother-in-law was when Sam came home and announced that his new name was *Ladarius*. When he came out with that at dinner, I cracked up."

She didn't say anything else about being divorced, but at some point, she said she'd been sober for five years. Carla looked athletic, and she eventually told me that she had played on her college tennis team. She said how much she liked coming to Sam's games. After a while, she started talking about the parents of some of the kids I was coaching. She barely mentioned Jones and Mary Ann Colbert. I was pretty sure she knew they didn't like me.

I finally said that I'd wondered if she was part of their group, and she rolled her eyes. "I'll have to fill you in on Jones Colbert and his insane wife later on. But right now I have something else in mind. Could I interest you in a cup of coffee?"

I looked at her and tried not to smile. "Sorry, I don't drink coffee."

She didn't miss a beat. "Then how about a little me... I mean tea."

February 14, 1976 – It's Saturday afternoon and I'm sitting in a booth across from Carla Thompson in the Shoney's restaurant in Belle Meade. She orders a coffee, and when I ask for some tea, she tries to look serious. "Perhaps you forgot what I said earlier – that it was either me or the tea." She puts her foot against my ankle. She slowly moves it up to my calf, and I feel my face getting red. She starts smiling. "Oh, you're blushing. How boyish. And how... fetching." She moves her foot further up my leg. "I know what you're thinking. You don't deserve me. And I was only kidding. Go ahead and enjoy your tea. You can save me for later."

My inner voice kept warning me to stay away from her. I was ignoring it. One part of me thought that anybody who was that direct might be psychotic. It was also possible that she was lonely and she'd end up sticking to me like tar. I went through all my usual hesitations, but she looked good and I'd never met anybody like her before.

"So there you were, minding your own business at a basketball game, and an hour later you're sitting with a woman you've just met and she's rubbing your leg with her foot. You must have *a lot* of questions." She pulled her foot away and leaned back in the booth. "So what do you want to know?"

I made myself look into her eyes. "I... I guess why me and why today?"

"Cutting right to the chase. I like that. Okay – why you? Well first of all, you're *awfully* cute. And second of all, I felt sorry for you. You had no idea what you were getting into – coaching at Ensworth and having Jones and Mary Ann Colbert as part of the equation.

"I kept thinking you'd roll over and let him run the show the way he usually does. But you basically told him to take a hike, and after that, you threw some salt on the wound."

"How did I do that?"

"He told anybody who'd listen that you didn't know what you were doing. And when it became obvious that you knew *exactly* what you're doing, it made him look bad. Not that he wanted to coach the team. He just wanted to *control* it. Anyway, I like the way you put him in his place, and I *love* the way you are with kids.

"Sam wasn't sure about playing basketball. Now he wants me to go out and shoot with him all the time. And in case you've forgotten how cute I think you are, this is my impression of a flirtatious schoolgirl." She looked into my eyes and ran her fingers through her hair.

"And the other thing you wanted to know was, 'Why now?' Let's just say a girl shouldn't spend Valentine's Day alone unless she wants to. And I don't want to. There's another piece to the 'Why Now?' puzzle, but I can get into that later on."

The waitress brought her coffee and my tea. I watched the steam rising out of her cup, and I kept wondering what I was getting myself into.

She didn't say anything for a few seconds and then she started smiling. "Because you must be *dying* to know all about me, I'm going to give you a crash course." She laughed and then she took a deep breath. "Carla was a shy, *studious* girl. She loved to draw and she loved to read. Her family was wealthy, and *so of course* she had lots of playmates, but her playmates were never as interesting as the children she read about in books.

"Her physical development came rather late in high school, and it wasn't until she was in college that she started getting attention because of the way she looked. That was around the same time when her *natural urges* began to announce themselves. She didn't see herself as a beauty, and yet there was *something* about her that young men, and men, found attractive.

"Carla still didn't know much about sex, and so *of course* she married the first man she slept with. He was twenty-seven and he kept telling her how sensuous she was. She was nineteen, and she thought he was *quite* a catch.

"But it didn't take long for that to change. She was already getting tired of him by the time she figured out that he liked her father's money considerably more than he liked her. And then she found out the *damnedest* thing. Not only had he started seeing another woman after they were engaged, he was *still* seeing her.

"Her family tried to console her. They said, 'Poor Carla – you must be *devastated*.' When she didn't act devastated, they thought she was being brave. The truth was that Poor Carla didn't give a damn. She was mad at herself for being stupid, but that didn't last very long.

"Her husband spent four years trying to get her pregnant. He'd been trying to *seal the deal*, don't you know. At some point, she started wondering why she had never been *with child*. Two different gynecologists checked her out, and children were not in the cards for Carla.

"She did some traveling and after she took a couple of what she likes to call rehabilitation sabbaticals, she ended up living in a commune out in New Mexico. That's when she became *considerably* more comfortable with her own sexuality. If her parents hadn't *persuaded* her to come back home and help with Sam, she'd still be out there."

I took a drink of tea. I was thirstier than I thought.

Carla took a sip of her coffee. "So here she is. Thirty-three and *looking pretty damn good* all things considered, and there's usually a man around she can put up with. And truth be known, now and then a woman will show up and capture her fancy. She hates insincerity and she can't stand liars, which is somewhat redundant. And her aversion to mendacity might be somewhat difficult to understand, considering that she lives in *glorious* Belle Meade. One thing I can say is this – there's nothing like a few years in a commune to change one's perspective.

"Although Carla has become something of a social heretic, she tries to be discrete. But her family has been prominent for six generations and they have *lots and lots* of money. That means she has the luxury of not having to worry about what people think.

"Anyway, every now and then, she runs across somebody she wants to be with. At the moment that somebody happens to be *you*. And the best news of all, at least from a male point of view, is that she *can't stand* the idea of obligations. Friends are fine, but she doesn't want a boyfriend *or* a girlfriend. Carla *really* likes her freedom."

She picked up her cup with both hands and smiled. "Okay, now it's your turn."

I wondered what it would be like to describe myself in the third person the way she had, but I was pretty sure I'd screw it up if I tried to do it that way. Although I didn't go into too many details, I told her about the way I'd been in high school and how long I'd felt like a loser. I told her a little about coaching kids and feeling like a loser again. And what my father did during the war and that I wanted to go to the Philippines, and how I came back because of Mother.

I could tell that Carla was waiting to hear about my romantic history. I told her about Yancey Walsh and Bethany Brussard, and even though they didn't qualify as romantic encounters, I explained about the Blonde Bombshell and the divorced mothers.

The waitress came by and after she poured Carla another cup of coffee, I went ahead and told her about Callie. Before I was finished, she leaned back in the booth and started fanning herself. "An underage girl. How *scandalous*. And you haven't even kissed her?"

Then she looked at me and shook her head. "I probably shouldn't tell you this, but just because she's in high school doesn't mean she's all that innocent – especially these days. She might be able to teach you at least as much as you could teach her."

She seemed to be studying me. "Well... I'd say that, all-in-all, you've been a pretty good boy. If I'd known about your *tremendous* powers of self-restraint, I might not have been so confident when I came up to you after Sam's game. Now I'm surprised that you came here with me."

I finished my tea and put down the glass. "I wasn't about to go through the rest of my life wondering what I missed."

It was almost sunset when we pulled up to the Thompson's guest house. I didn't want Sam to know I was there. When I asked Carla what I should say if he showed up, she smiled.

"That won't be a problem. Sam doesn't roam around the property if it's anywhere close to dark. He's *somehow* gotten the idea that there's a monster living in the woods behind the house, and that it only comes out at night."

I sat on her sofa and she turned off all the lights and lit a candle. She sat across from me and at first we just talked. But after a while, she told me about an erotic experience she had, and she ended up describing one of her fantasies. She seemed to be saying whatever came into her mind, and by the time she came over and sat next to me on the sofa, I was pretty well lost in the images she was describing.

Things got going and she was passionate and uninhibited. I didn't keep up with her all that well, but she seemed to enjoy herself. I got the feeling that she always enjoyed herself. I wondered if I'd ever be able to shut off my brain and surrender to my body the way she surrendered to hers. When it was almost daylight, I got ready to leave.

She held onto me at the door. "Do you remember when I said there was another reason I came up to you today?"

"Yep."

"And do you remember when I said I had something to tell you about Jones and Mary Ann Colbert?"

"Yeah." The last thing I wanted to think about was the Colberts.

"I might as well just come out with it. Mary Ann has been whispering to some of her friends that you're... how shall I say this? She has told a few of her friends that you're a homosexual. She and Jones probably talked it over and decided that starting a good juicy rumor would be the best way to keep you from coming back to Ensworth and coaching again."

Carla must have sensed how empty and cold I felt. She put her hands on the sides of my face. "But here's the good news. I know *exactly* how to take care of their little smear campaign. I'm planning to start a little gossip of my own.

"I know four or five different women who've never heard a secret they could keep. I'll probably wait for a few days, but word is about to get out that I'm having a fling with my nephew's basketball coach. When they hear how much *fun* you are, the news will be all over Belle Meade within forty-eight hours."

"Won't that hurt your reputation?"

She moved her hands down to my shoulders. "My reputation? I'm an unattached thirty-three-year-old Belle Meade divorcee. And *everything* that implies. The only way I could shock anybody would be if I suddenly became celibate."

I had another question. "How much does all this have to do with what just happened?"

"You mean did I seduce you to see whether you're gay?"

I nodded.

"That isn't why I hit on you. I've had my eye on you ever since the first game. I was going to wait till the season was over. All the

Colberts did was speed things up a little." She slipped her index finger into one of my belt loops and pulled. "I'm just sorry I waited as long as I did. And this better not be the last time I see you."

I was almost too tired to say anything. "It sounds like I'm *obligated.*"

Chapter 83

February 20, 1976 – It's Friday afternoon and I'm limping along Valley Brook Road. My knees and my elbows are bleeding, but I don't think I'll need any stitches. The front tire of my bike is wobbling and I'm trying to push it back home. The rim of the wheel is bent and the tire is flat. My bicycle had been in the basement since high school, but I took it to a shop a few weeks ago and got it fixed up. I wanted to start riding it when the weather got warm.

It felt like spring this morning, and I got on the bike and took off. I was looking at a big oak tree while I was coasting down a hill, and I hit a pretty deep pothole. I almost went over the handlebars. I was lucky to get off with just bloody knees and elbows. I'm trying to keep the bicycle moving in a straight line, but the front wheel isn't cooperating. I know a few families that live nearby, but I'm pretty sure I can make it home okay. I'm on the left side of the road and I hear a car slowing down as it comes up behind me on the right. I know who it is as soon as I hear her voice. "Are... are you okay? What happened?"

Claire pulled up beside me and stared at my bloody elbows, and at the blood soaking through the knees of my jeans. "Well hold on a minute."

After she pulled into the next driveway, she got out and opened the trunk of her car. The bike barely fit. I got in her car and she kept looking at the blood on my forearms.

"Should I take you to the emergency room at Vanderbilt?"

I told her it looked worse than it was, and then I asked if there was someplace she needed to be. She said she was just out riding around. I told her that instead of going straight home, I might as well drop my bike off and get it fixed. I could've done it later, but the bicycle shop was three or four miles away and I wanted some time to talk.

It had only been a month since I'd seen her, but she looked different. She'd lost weight. Her face was leaner and so was her body. Her jeans looked like they were at least one size too big.

I wasn't sure why I hadn't heard from her. It might've been because she didn't want to talk about the abortion, but it could've had something to do with Callie. I was about to say how much I'd been thinking about her, but she spoke up first.

"I've almost called you about a thousand times. I wanted to talk about what happened and about the poem. But you just quit coming around. We used to see you all the time. You just don't show up anymore. Callie says it's because you're mad at her. She told me what she said to you at the drugstore."

"I'm not mad at her. She was just trying to protect you. She's your friend. A friendship like the one you and Callie have is a gift."

Claire glanced over at me. "What about her friendship with you? Is that a gift?"

"I'd love to end up having a real friendship with Callie. Maybe it can still happen, but right now it seems pretty... complicated."

We got to the bicycle shop, and I went inside. I still hadn't figured out what I wanted to say by the time I got back in the car. "What if having me around is messing her up? I don't want to be the reason she misses out on something she needs to experience."

I didn't want her to misunderstand what I was trying to say. "Look, I'll always care about Callie. But if I don't give her enough room to figure out what she wants, I wouldn't deserve her friendship. And it isn't just Callie I care about. I want a friendship – a *real* friendship – with you."

Claire was quiet most of the way to my house. When we got

there I patted her arm and thanked her for picking me up. She gave me a long look, but she didn't say anything else.

I saw Carla the next day at our game. She was sitting with Mrs. Caswell. She noticed that I was limping, and she came over to me while the kids were out on the court warming up. "I thought that by now you would've recovered from our *tryst*. I mean it's been a whole week. This is me pretending to pity you." She tilted her head to one side and pushed out her lower lip. "I guess I'll need to take it easier on you next time."

I looked at her and tried to cross my eyes. "That would be a shame."

"So what happened?"

"Bicycle wreck."

Carla smiled. "I didn't realize that chasing school girls on bicycles could be so hazardous."

"I guess it's a lot more hazardous than climbing on top of some semi-conscious hippie in a commune."

She almost laughed. "Well at least you can get around. I guess tonight we'll just have to stay away from any activity that involves you being on your *knees*. Now as much as I'd like to stand here and flirt, you have a game to coach and I have the flames of a rumor to fan." After she checked to make sure none of the kids were looking in our direction, she put one arm around me and gave me a fairly long kiss on the lips.

Every time I got a chance to look back at what was going on in the bleachers, she was sitting with a different mother. Jones Colbert got there late and he was sitting on the top row of the bleachers. His wife wasn't around. He didn't see Carla kiss me and she knew it. I looked up during the third quarter and she was next to him. It looked like she was flirting.

She finally went down to sit with Mrs. Caswell. I couldn't wait to find out what Carla was saying, but it would be a while before I got to hear about it.

After the game, she asked me if I wanted to see a movie. She knew I'd go along with whatever she wanted to do. We sat down in the stands, and she handed me the movie section of the newspaper.

"See if you can guess what I want to see."

I scanned the entire page, but I didn't see any obvious candidates. "Well, assuming that you don't want to drag me to the Avant-Garde Cinema to see *Pornucopia*, I've narrowed it down to *Barry Lyndon* and *One Flew Over the Cuckoo's Nest*.

"*Barry Lyndon* looks like it involves the aristocracy in the 1800s, so it might be irresistible to a member of the ruling class. But I'm betting that you want to see *One Flew Over the Cuckoo's Nest*. I've read the book. It might be right down your alley."

"Bingo. I've read the book, too, and it *is* right down my alley, but that's not why I want to see it."

"Then what's the reason?"

Carla smiled wistfully and stared off into the distance. "This is me looking infatuated. I've always had *such* a crush on Jack Nicholson."

We went downtown and saw the afternoon matinee. She didn't say anything about what she'd been up to in the bleachers until we were having dinner at a little restaurant near the theater. After we ordered, she straightened up in her chair.

"This is Carla being pleased with herself." She put her hands together and smiled, and then she started moving her head like she was keeping time to a song. "When she was at the game today, Carla just *happened* to mention to a few of the ladies in attendance that she'd recently spent a rather *torrid* evening with a certain young basketball coach. Guess which women who have children at Ensworth are finding out what a stud you are?"

She knew that I wasn't anywhere close to being a stud. "I have no idea."

"All the ones who love gossip, which is most of them. And the more sexually frustrated women are, the bigger gossips they tend to be. *God*, it was fun to watch them getting all – how can I say this delicately – all *titillated*. But what was even more fun was toying with Jones Colbert. He's come on to me a couple of times in the past, but *God knows*, he's never gotten anywhere. Have I mentioned the way I feel about manipulative liars?"

"Yep."

"I'd be willing to bet that he's feeling pretty good about himself right about now. It wouldn't be all that surprising if Mary Ann gets lucky tonight, although having Jones Colbert and sexual intercourse occupy the same thought makes me feel a little queasy. Anyway, a few hours from now Jones might be displaying a little extra *vigor* within the *sacred* confines of his marital bed.

"And, *oh my*, I sure hope he doesn't get carried away while he's in the throes of passion. Wouldn't it be just *awful* if he accidentally called his wife Carla? This is me pretending to be worried." She put her hands on both sides of her face and furrowed her brow as she tilted her head to one side.

"But that's not even the best part. Now he thinks he has a chance to be with me. So if he ever sees the two of us together, and at some point, I'm *sure* he will, he'll have a hard time not thinking about what we're doing to each other when we're alone. The better his imagination is, the more it should sting." She rubbed her hands together and squinted. "This is Carla looking diabolical. And *sadistic*."

I waited a few seconds and then I put the tip of my index finger beside my chin and tried to look serious. "And this is me wondering what you and Mrs. Caswell were talking about at the game."

She gave me a confident smile. "I promise I'll tell you *all* about it, but not just yet."

She only made one reference to the movie we saw. It was a couple of hours later when we were lying on her bed. She was sitting up and she'd just finished telling me about another one of her fantasies. She was illuminated by a single candle.

"You know, even though I'm more obsessed with Jack Nicholson than I *ever* was before, I'd still take Sean Connery if I had to choose." She didn't say anything for a few seconds and then she lay back and looked at the ceiling. "Who would you pick?"

"Hmm… Nicholson or Connery – that's a tough one."

She elbowed me. "Which *actress*?"

"I'm not sure. It might be Cybill Shepherd. Or maybe Jennifer O'Neill."

Carla nodded. "Okay, but which one? Who would you want beside you? In a secluded beach house – *bathed* in the flickering light of a candle – with the sounds of waves crashing outside?"

"Probably Cybill."

"Okay. And what if you had to choose between Cybill Shepherd and your teenage heartthrob?"

"It's still… it's still Callie. But I wouldn't complain about Cybill or Jennifer."

Carla rolled over and propped herself up on her elbow, and then she ran the tips of her fingers along my arm. "And I wouldn't complain about Jack, or about Cybill or Jennifer for matter, and I'm certainly not complaining about you."

Chapter 84

Sometimes it was like a wave was breaking on top of me. I was getting to know Carla and wondering how I could keep up with her the next time we were together. I was trying to avoid being ambushed by Jones Colbert. I was getting my team ready for the tournament. I was doing what I could to keep the Woodmont School property from being turned into a condominium complex. I was wondering if I should talk to Claire about her abortion. I was pretty sure that I'd lost Callie, and I wondered if all the attention I'd given her had distorted her life. And I was worrying about Mother, and trying to figure out how to deepen my relationship with my father.

Although there were times when I felt like I was getting knocked around underwater, other times I felt like I was in the middle of a slow-motion tornado. The more things swirled around me, the more I looked forward to walking into Miss Young's study and losing myself in the 1800s.

I finally finished listing everything in the trunk. I'd filled up two legal tablets with the date, the writer, the recipient, and a brief description of the contents of each letter. I also included information about the deeds and legal documents and ledgers and slave records I found. There were also around four hundred old books in the bookcase. Most of them had belonged to Willoughby Williams.

I looked through all the books, and although I only came across two letters, one of them – which had been stuck between the pages of a well-worn volume on the bottom shelf of the bookcase – answered one of the biggest questions I had. It was written in 1854 by Colonel Williams to his son, John Henry Williams, who ran the farm near Nashville while the colonel was away at his plantation in Arkansas.

After passing along information about the size of the latest cotton crop and the state of the market in New Orleans, Colonel Williams gave his son advice on how to run a successful farming operation.

> *There should be a system for every part of the farm. The floors of the negro cabins should be eighteen inches above the ground so that the air can pass freely underneath. The cabins should all be united and should surround the pinnacle of a rise so that the filth, from which many diseases arise, will wash away. When arriving at the place where the slaves are at work, you should cast your eyes around to see if they are all at their tasks. A negro who must be told a second time to perform a task must be punished. Never threaten to chastise a negro. The act should always be immediate. One negro, like one mule or one steer, can destroy much more than they are worth unless attended to. They are creatures not to be credited.*

February 29, 1976 – It's early Sunday afternoon and it feels more like May than late winter. I tell Carla that we should be walking around in Percy Warner Park instead of going to lunch at Belle Meade Country Club. She says she has a surprise for me, but she won't tell me anything else. We see Jones Colbert standing outside the front door like a guard. He's with several other men, but he stops talking and glares at me.

Carla knows he's watching when she puts her arm around me, and we go on up the steps and into the foyer. On our way toward the dining room, she gets intercepted by two women in their thirties. They seem to know her fairly well. They look me up and down, and one of them gives me a knowing smile before she sticks out her hand. "I'm Felice. And you must be Carla's new... friend."

Carla got me away from the women as soon as she could, but she stopped before we went into the dining room. "The surprise is that we've been invited here by a friend of mine. And here's some advice you probably don't need. Just be yourself."

I did my best to look excited. "*Oh my God.* You never said you knew Cybill Shepherd!" Then I pretended to surreptitiously smell my underarms.

Mrs. Caswell was sitting at a table in the corner of the dining room. Only a few people were still eating. There were flower arrangements in the center of each table, and the sun was shining through the windows. It felt almost as much like spring as it did outside.

Mrs. Caswell looked bored and intimidating, as usual. I had no idea why we were having lunch with her. She extended her hand and welcomed me. She gestured at the nearly empty dining room. "I prefer to dine after the rush is over. It's so much quieter."

After she thanked me for coaching Whiting, she shifted in her chair. "It may be beneficial if you understand the nature of my relationship with Carla. Our families have known each other since well before the War Between the States.

"Our great-grandfathers were co-founders of a bank and several businesses, and our grandfathers were partners and served on a number of boards together. I am half a generation older than Carla, but both of us endured similar marital situations. I mention all this to underscore the fact that I have known her for a very long time. And that I trust her completely.

"I also want to comment on one particular point. Carla has made me aware of a rather unpleasant situation that has arisen, and it has arisen through no fault of yours. She is an unusual young woman and she has chosen to deal with the situation in an unusual way. I have offered my help, but it appears that my help may not be necessary.

"After our meal, I'll explain why I wanted us to get together. But for now, I want to acknowledge the impact you are having on Whiting. Aside from Inman Roberts, whom Whiting adores, my son does not have an adult male figure in his life. I deeply appreciate the attention you are giving to Whiting. He has developed a great deal of fondness and admiration for you, and it is my hope that you will continue your affiliation with Ensworth."

A light-complected black man with reddish hair and freckles came up to the table. I was pretty sure he was the head waiter. "The roast beef is *really* good today, Miz Caswell."

Mrs. Caswell gave him a brief smile. "We will each start with a Faucon Salad. And Red, I do hope you've saved us some especially good cuts of the roast beef."

Red smiled back at her. "Now Miz Caswell, you *know* that I have." I had the feeling that Red always waited on her, and that there was a similar exchange every time she ordered a meal.

For the next ten minutes, she asked me questions about my family. My father's uncle was wealthy and she was familiar with that line of my family, but she didn't know my parents. After that, she wanted to know what I did when I wasn't coaching.

She was more interested than I thought she'd be when I told her about my research on the Woodmont neighborhood. After a couple of minutes, she mentioned that Charles Bosley, the Indian fighter and slave trader who owned the two-thousand-acre plantation that adjoined the land of Willoughby Williams, was her great-great-great-grandfather.

I offered to give her copies of everything I'd discovered about him, and she told me that she had some of his papers. She said that she'd be glad to show them to me after she put them in some sort of order.

We finished our meal and she insisted that we have dessert. After Red came by with three large slices of chess pie, a different expression came over her face. "I know this isn't the proper time or the proper place, and I hope you will forgive me, but there is a particular matter I want to discuss. If there is another way to ask this, I don't know what it is."

She stared into my eyes. "You have been working with boys for several years. You must have coached other boys with the same characteristics that Whiting displays.

"He is a wonderful, loving child, but he is very effeminate. I worry about what will happen to him when he starts to become a teenager, and in the years after that. I assume that you have coached boys who turned out to be homosexual, and I am hoping you can help me prepare Whiting for what he might face if he *is* a homosexual."

I danced around her question. I said that I'd coached effeminate players before, and although I expected that most of them ended up being gay, I didn't think they all were. And I told her about Ty March, who was one of the best football players I'd ever coached. He'd been an all-city player at Montgomery Bell Academy. He was about as far from effeminate as a kid could be, but he opened up about his sexuality after he went off to college.

She knew I was holding back. "I understand that there's no way to be certain, but how likely do you think it is that Whiting will turn out to be a homosexual? I ask because I am trying to decide whether he should start seeing a therapist before his life becomes... more difficult. I am asking you to give me the most straightforward answer that you can."

I was going to tell her what she wanted to know, but I needed to ease into it. "There were a few guys who went to Battle Ground Academy with me who were different – different in the way that Whiting is different. They were called queers or fairies, along with a lot of other names. A few years ago I was at Moon's Drugstore, and I ran into one of my classmates.

"He said there was something he wanted to tell me. He was a little hesitant, but he finally told me he was gay. And he wasn't even one of the guys with a nickname. When I asked him how he'd survived at Battle Ground, he said he tried to stay invisible.

"Then he told me that four or five other guys in our class went through the same things he had. But nobody he mentioned was as effeminate as Whiting is, so I guess I'd be surprised if Whiting doesn't end up being gay."

Mrs. Caswell had been staring at me the entire time. I couldn't tell what she was thinking. I glanced over at Carla and she just raised her eyebrows. She could've been saying, "Is that all?" But I thought she might be saying, "If you have anything else to say about Whiting, now is the time."

I looked at the arrangement of tulips and roses in the vase at the center of the table, and then I looked back at Mrs. Caswell. "Whiting has... I haven't ever coached anybody with a better spirit than he has. He has this... this *purity*. He isn't embarrassed about being the worst basketball player we have.

"Sometimes when a kid knows he's the worst player on a team, he'll be ashamed. Or he might think there's something wrong with him. He might even start hating himself. Not Whiting. The first time we practiced, he realized how much better the other kids were. He came over to me – and of course, he was smiling. He asked me why he couldn't get the ball up to the basket, and why he was so bad at dribbling.

"I showed him a couple of things to work on and ever since then, every time he has a chance, he's practiced on his own. He hasn't caught up with the other kids, but he gets a little bit better every week. He isn't too bad at playing defense, and now and then he'll pick up a... rebound." I almost said loose ball.

Mrs. Caswell was still staring at me and the expression on her face hadn't changed. I thought I might've confused her.

"I'm trying to say that Whiting has already found a way to deal with being different. He isn't embarrassed and he doesn't hate himself because he struggles with basketball. If he turns out to be gay, I wouldn't be surprised if the same thing happens."

She shifted in her chair. "Are you advising me against getting psychological help for my son?"

"No. I think in a year or two it would make sense to get him ready for what might be coming. But I just hope he won't end up with... the wrong therapist. I hope that... Well, Whiting needs to understand that there isn't anything wrong with him. He needs to understand that there's something wrong with the world. I hope he'll eventually understand that he doesn't need to change. And I hope you can find somebody who will help protect his spirit."

Mrs. Caswell sat back, but she was still staring at me. "Thank you for your honesty. I have had those same thoughts for some time. And I agree that it is too soon to expose Whiting to such *adult* concerns. But I do intend to begin the process of locating a sympathetic psychologist, or perhaps a psychiatrist. And when I do locate one, I wonder if I might ask for your help. I hope you will be willing to share your perceptions of Whiting, as well as your concerns, with that individual."

"I'll do whatever I can to help Whiting."

She was still looking at me and she nodded. "And I have one other small request. Please call me Ellen."

"Well it won't be as easy, but I'll give it a shot."

She leaned back in her chair and gave me a little smile.

I had a lot of questions for Carla, but I waited until we were walking back to her car before I said anything. "Did you know she was going to ask me about Whiting?"

Carla shook her head. "Nope. But I'm not surprised that she did. You handled that *really* well. You might not know it, but you've made a new friend."

I was still curious about what Carla was trying to engineer. "How much does Mrs. Caswell know about us?"

"Everything except the details. I knew it wouldn't bother her. I told her at dinner one night, and I also told her about the nasty little rumor the Colberts are circulating, and what I'm doing about it."

"So is she going to help with the rumor?"

Carla stopped in the shade of a tree. "Like she said, I don't need her help."

"Okay, but you've already told me that you're up to something else that involves Mrs. Caswell. What's the other reason we came here for brunch?"

"There are two other reasons, but here's the only one I'll tell you about. I want you to keep coaching at Ensworth. You and Inman Roberts together... you two are exactly what those boys need. But if you're going to stick around, it will be especially helpful to have a friend like Ellen Caswell. I'll tell you the rest of it later on. I'm still not sure that everything will work out the way I want it to."

Chapter 85

March 6, 1976 – It's Saturday afternoon in the Oak Hill gym. We've made it to the finals of our league tournament. Jake and Whiting and the rest of my players are warming up with a rebounding and shooting game they invented on their own. It's their idea of what happens on the playgrounds of North Nashville. Sam, who prefers to be called Ladarius, shoots from just past the foul line.

If he makes it he gets to shoot again. He misses and everybody scrambles for the ball. Jake, who is imagining himself as Tarique, snags the rebound and puts up a quick shot before he gets swarmed by Tyrone and Cedric and Otis and Jermaine. They call their drill "Up and In." It's a little like Smear the Queer. They like it almost as much as scrimmaging.

I glance back at our section of the bleachers. Carla is wearing white jeans and a black sweatshirt and a black and orange baseball cap. I want to look at her a little longer, but I don't. Jones Colbert and his followers are sitting in a cluster several rows back. Along with the usual mothers and fathers and sisters and brothers, a few grandparents have showed up for our big game. And off to one side, sitting across the aisle from Inman Roberts and a couple of Ensworth teachers, are Mother and my father.

My two teams were in the same bracket, and after they both won in the first round, they played each other in the semifinals. The team with Jake and Whiting won by three points, which put them in the championship against Oak Hill.

Oak Hill didn't come close to losing a game all year. When we shook hands in the lobby before the game, the Oak Hill coach was somewhere between overconfident and serene. I acted like I expected my team to get embarrassed. His kids hadn't come up against a good full-court press all year, but that was about to change. I was pretty sure that Oak Hill was in for a long afternoon.

We were behind 4-0 after a couple of minutes, but Jake got a steal, went the length of the court, and made a layup. Then we set up our 3-2 zone press. The point guard from Oak Hill passed the ball to their other guard. He took a couple of dribbles before Sam and Jake moved in and trapped him. He couldn't go anywhere, and he stopped dribbling.

There were only a few more seconds for him to get the ball past half-court, and Sam and Jake were all over him. He did what most kids did in that situation – he tried to pass the ball upcourt to the last teammate he saw. My other players had already rotated over and cut off the passing lanes on that side of the court. Will was right where he was supposed to be. After he intercepted the ball, he hit Jake with a pass and we were off to the races.

Oak Hill was behind 8-4 and they still hadn't been able to get the ball across half-court when their coach finally got one of his players to call timeout. He tried to make some adjustments, but his team would've needed a couple of practices to learn how to counter what we were doing. Oak Hill was good at running their set offense, but it was hard to run a set offense when there wasn't a chance to set up.

We got all the offense we needed off of our press. We were ahead by eleven points at halftime, and we were up by fourteen when I called off the press at the end of the third quarter. Oak Hill cut our lead down to eight points, but that was as close as they could get. They kept fouling to stop the clock, and Whiting got knocked down near the end of the game.

It was an intentional foul, and he got two shots. He hadn't scored all season and the kids on our bench started chanting – "Jermaine. Jermaine." His first shot was an airball, but the second one hit the middle of the backboard right behind the rim. The ball rattled around a little before it went in.

Our kids were jumping up and down and yelling, and I glanced back at Ellen Caswell. She just nodded at me. Before I turned back around, I saw Jones Colbert. He looked at me right after I saw him. I could tell he was irritated, and I winked at him. It wasn't like we were ever going to be friends.

My parents left before I could introduce them to Mrs. Caswell. I thought about taking my team to Moon's Drugstore and getting them all milkshakes, but I didn't know if Callie was working. I didn't want to see her unless I knew she wanted to see me.

Basketball season was a blessing, and there were other blessings. I was thankful for everything I was learning about Willoughby Williams and the history of the neighborhood, and I was glad to have my hands full with Carla.

Those parts of my life helped me balance the fears I had about Mother's health and the emptiness I felt when I thought about Callie. And the stress of having to deal with Jones Colbert. He hadn't been able to run me out of Ensworth, but he was relentless in pursuing his condominium development.

The petition in favor of his project supposedly got quite a few signatures, and the councilman who represented the neighborhood finally released a statement saying that he would stay neutral on the project. The mayor gave it his public support, and there was another article in the newspaper praising the plan.

The article called attention to an upcoming meeting of the Park Board. After mentioning that a public display in support of a park on the former site of Woodmont School was anticipated, it announced that the developers, who were identified as the Colbert Group, would be hosting a reception on the school grounds prior to the Park Board meeting. There would be a large tent, refreshments and appetizers would be provided, and guests could see renderings of the project and ask questions.

April 6, 1976 – It's late on Tuesday afternoon and I'm in a hearing room, waiting to address the members of the Park Board. I've been standing in line for almost a half-hour listening to residents urge the board to formally request the Woodmont School property. Jones Colbert supposedly shook a lot of hands on Saturday, but the event he hosted didn't discourage people in the neighborhood from showing up at the hearing.

There are a lot of people I don't know, and I've seen several of my former schoolmates from Woodmont and a few of their parents. And along with thirty or so mothers and fathers of kids I've coached, I see a few of my ex-players. Almost everybody in the room is wearing blue and gold buttons that say, "Support Woodmont Park."

The lady in front of me has been talking about how crowded the neighborhood has become, and that the remaining open space should be preserved. I've been watching the board members. They haven't asked any questions, and most of the time they haven't been looking at the person who's speaking. There's applause when the lady sits down, and it's my turn to speak.

I didn't say anything until two of the board members who were talking to each other noticed the silence and looked up. I gave my name and said that I'd been living in the Woodmont neighborhood my whole life. I didn't say what I'd planned to say.

"When it comes to the site of Woodmont School, a lot has been going on in the shadows. Our councilman originally said he supported having the property become a park, but something made him change his mind. Maybe he got a call from the mayor. I wonder if the mayor has called any of you."

There were some murmurs from the audience, and the board members were all staring at me. "I think you already know how you're going to vote, so I'll just say a few things for the record. I don't know how much money the developers will make from their project, but I'm clear on what it'll cost the neighborhood.

"The field behind the school will be gone. Kids are out there playing all the time. For almost fifty years, kids have been going there to do all the things kids do when there's a place to play. The basketball courts and the playground will be gone. The nearest park is two miles away. The kids in the neighborhood can't walk or get there on their bikes. There's too much traffic. Maybe they'll be able to catch a ride with their parents now and then. Is that what you have in mind?

"The children in the Woodmont neighborhood *need a place to play*. It's wrong to allow public property to be sold to developers. It's *wrong* to take that away from the neighborhood so that a few rich men can get even richer. Please accept the Woodmont property and make it a park."

There was applause from the audience. A few other speakers addressed the board, and then the chairman polled the other members. There was a consensus. The chairman said he and the board appreciated the viewpoints expressed by members of the community, and he acknowledged that a park would be good for the neighborhood. But he went on to say that budget constraints had to be considered and that, "At this time, the Park Board cannot support another property."

Until the end of the meeting, I thought there was at least a chance to have a park. I should've known what would happen. Before I left I saw Jones Colbert. He was sitting alone in the back row. The expression on his face was somewhere between a sneer and a smirk. Before I looked away he half-opened his mouth and gave me a long, slow wink.

A reporter stopped me before I left and asked if I had a comment about the board's decision. I almost said that the fix was in. And that the developers had used their campaign contributions to buy themselves another payday. But I didn't want to make it easy for the guy to write a story about how the people who opposed the project were just angry.

What I said was in his article the next day. "The people who live in my neighborhood wanted a park, but a developer who lives in Belle Meade wanted to make money by building condominiums. Now we won't have any open public space. I have a question for the mayor and the councilmen and the Chamber of Commerce, and whoever else is running Nashville. Why do you keep allowing the neighborhoods of the city to be degraded by over-development?"

I'd gotten a call from Inman Roberts a few days earlier. He wanted to talk to me, and I went to see him the day after the meeting of the Park Board. He was down on the track showing some sixth-graders how to pole vault. He was a genius when it came to working with kids, and it was obvious how much they loved him. He grew up on a little farm outside of Franklin, and he brought all sorts of old-time rural values right into the heart of Belle Meade.

As soon as he got a break, we sat down and he gave me a big smile and slapped me on the knee. "Like I said before, you have really shaken this place *up*. Several of the parents got together and let the headmaster know that they want you here coaching their boys when football comes around next fall. You have fans around here that you don't even know about."

"So I guess that means they outnumber my enemies."

"Well, there are some of those, too. And of course, you've got one in particular."

I was curious about how the headmaster felt about me. "What about Mr. Grayson?"

"Oh, I think you make him nervous. He doesn't like getting phone calls from parents and he doesn't like sports. That means he *really* doesn't like getting phone calls from parents *about* sports. What makes him nervous is the way you do things. You already know about the calls he got when the boys came home with names like they were black kids from North Nashville."

He was still smiling. "Don Grayson is a good man, but he'll always worry about what you might come up with next. The main thing is that you've won over the kids, and that means you've won over most of the parents. So I'm supposed to find out if you'd be willing to coach our fifth and sixth-grade football team next fall."

Although I didn't like the thought of being around Jones Colbert again, I wanted to coach football. I was already wondering if Whiting would try to play. I wasn't sure if it was a good idea, but I thought he'd probably give it a shot. I needed to be there if he did. I didn't have to think it over. I went ahead and told Inman that I'd coach in the fall.

Chapter 86

I didn't want to go overboard with the way I saw Jones Colbert. I reminded myself that I was seeing him at his worst. He couldn't have raised a kid like Jake and been as awful as he seemed to be. I wanted to see him as he was, and I wanted to see Willoughby Williams the way he had been. There was probably another side to Colonel Williams. Reading through the letters he wrote toward the end of his life, I got the sense that he might have been mellowing.

When he was in his eighties, he wrote an account of the way Nashville and the surrounding countryside had been when he was young. His library, which contained a wide variety of books and journals devoted to agriculture, revealed a man with a great deal of knowledge about farming, and some of his letters showed that he had a deep connection to his land.

He had mastered the complexities of animal husbandry, and he was well-versed in everything from the science of crop rotation to the proper cultivation of vineyards. Sometimes I wondered what he would've thought about what was happening to his farm. And there were times when I wondered if his view of slavery might've eventually changed.

Land speculators like Willoughby Williams' father and grandfather, and developers like Jones Colbert, didn't seem too far removed from the dark figures that Mike Higgins was trying to identify.

Several congressional investigations were going on at the same time, and it seemed like there was a new revelation every week. In the middle of April, there were articles in both Nashville newspapers about the connection between a couple of Mafia figures, Sam Giancana and John Roselli, and the CIA and President Kennedy.

There had been a sexual relationship between Kennedy and a woman named Judith Exner, who was also involved with Giancana. Just before he was to testify before the Church Committee about Mafia involvement in a CIA plot to kill Fidel Castro, Sam Giancana was murdered. I wouldn't have been able to forget about what Mike Higgins was doing even if I'd wanted to.

I got a call from Claire at the end of April. I felt guilty that I hadn't called her first. She said she had a birthday coming up and there was something she wanted. I was pretty sure it wasn't a puppy or a box of candy.

"I've always wanted a surprise party." She sounded serious.

"Unless you're planning to get hypnotized, it won't be much of a surprise."

Claire had it all figured out. "Yeah it will. I'll only know that there's going to be a party and who's coming. The rest of it is the surprise."

"Okay, I'll give it a shot. How many guests do you have in mind?"

"There'll be three of us."

I was pretty sure I knew who else she was inviting. "Okay. When is it?"

"This Saturday."

It took me a while to come up with an idea I liked.

May 1, 1976 – It's the middle of Saturday morning and I'm walking up a trail that leads through the hills just south of Radnor Lake. Claire is behind me and Callie is behind Claire. We're less than fifteen minutes from Green Hills, but it seems like we're in the middle of nowhere. It's early spring and there isn't much undergrowth. A light brush of wind pushes through the trees and I lead them off the trail. Wherever Claire thought we might be going, it wasn't here.

I'm sure Callie is wondering where we'll end up, but she hasn't said anything. We come to a rise of level ground, and there's a canopy of black and silver streamers hanging from two overhead limbs. Underneath the streamers is a card table covered with a tablecloth, and there are three chairs. The table is set with plates and glass goblets and silverware and napkins, and there's a vase with seventeen red roses in the center of the table. The cake is in a box in front of the chair where the birthday girl will sit. Claire can't stop smiling, and Callie is smiling, too.

I'd never seen either one of them that dressed up. Callie was wearing khaki pants and a white shirt that was unbuttoned at the top. I told myself that I wasn't going to look at her the same way I'd been looking at her for the past three years. But she still killed me and it was probably obvious.

And it hadn't taken Claire long to blossom. She had on white shorts and a black tank top with spaghetti straps, and her arms and shoulders and legs were strong and her skin was tanned. Her baby fat had pretty much disappeared, along with a lot of her awkwardness. They probably thought we were going to a restaurant. We finally sat down, and Callie and I tried to sing *Happy Birthday*.

After we had some cake, Claire looked over at me. "Well, you really came through. I'm *totally* surprised." She nodded toward Callie. "You know what she gave me? She promised she'd go wherever I wanted and not ask any questions."

She ran one of her fingers across a smudge of icing at the edge of her plate. "Now there's one other thing I want, and it's from both of you." She looked at her icing-coated index finger, and then she licked it clean. "I can't stand to watch you guys drifting away from each other. It shouldn't be that way.

"No matter what else happens, or what else doesn't happen, you two have got to stay friends. And I don't mean just somebody-you-used-to-know friends. I mean *real* friends. Like..." Her eyes were watering up. "Like the kind of friends you were to me when I really needed you." She couldn't fight off her tears. "*Shit*. I wasn't gonna do this."

After she picked up her napkin and wiped her eyes, she looked over at Callie. Callie held back for two or three seconds before she started laughing.

Claire was staring at her. "What are laughing at, *bitch?*" As soon as she said it, she started laughing, too. Then she threw her napkin and hit Callie in the chest. Callie threw the napkin back and hit Claire in the face and they were teenage girls again.

Mayor Richardson, and whoever else was behind making sure that Jones Colbert got the Woodmont property, didn't waste much time after the Park Board meeting. It was turned over to General Services in the middle of May, and the sale was announced not long after that. Back in February, I'd planned to coach baseball, but then I decided not to. I didn't want to be out on the baseball field while the school was getting torn down.

After I finished making copies of everything I found in Miss Young's study, I went downtown almost every day and combed through obscure manuscript collections at the State Library and Archives. I hadn't stopped thinking about Mrs. Caswell, and what had come down to her from Charles Bosley.

Once or twice a week I would get a phone call from Carla inviting me to pay her a nighttime visit. But when she called a couple of weeks after Claire's party, she was especially animated. All she said was that we had a date for lunch the next day. She said I should wear something nicer than blue jeans and a T-shirt, and not to be late.

I met Carla at her house. She was still as happy as she'd sounded on the phone. We left in her car and after we went about a mile down Belle Meade Boulevard, she turned onto a side street with even bigger yards and bigger houses. I had an idea where we might be going, and I wasn't surprised when we turned into a long, gravel driveway between two large stone columns.

Chapter 87

We ate lunch in Mrs. Caswell's sunroom. She and Carla did most of the talking. I hoped she was going to show me the Bosley family information, but I wasn't sure that was why we were there.

After dessert, Mrs. Caswell took us into her library. There was a portrait of Whiting above the fireplace. There was a big smile on his face. The artist couldn't have captured his spirit any better. Mrs. Caswell pointed out which of the old portraits on the wall came from the Bosley mansion. As soon as she identified the individual in the last portrait she showed me, I must've nodded.

She stared at me before she said anything. "Are you familiar with his story?"

I kept looking at the portrait, and I told myself not to say too much. "He was Charles Bosley's oldest son. I'm glad to finally know what he looked like. He was disinherited by his father in the 1840s when he wouldn't end his relationship with a mulatto woman."

I saw a quick smile. "I suppose that some family scandals are simply too *salacious* to ever be forgotten."

After she told me a few things that I already knew about Charles Bosley, she talked about the final days of the Bosley mansion. Not long before World War One – and not long before the old home was razed, members of the family came and divided up the furnishings and all sorts of personal belongings. Mrs. Caswell's grandmother took a drawer full of letters and other documents that nobody else wanted.

She went over to a table and opened a metal box. Along with the rest of the papers, there were at least fifty old letters. She said a few were written by Charles Bosley, and that most of them involved his farm. But instead of inviting me to sit down and start reading, she handed me a large, sealed envelope. Copies of each letter were inside.

"Now this might be a good time to show off my garden."

Carla and I followed her out the backdoor. I'd glanced over at Carla a few times while we were inside and she'd looked a little bored, but she seemed to be getting excited.

Mrs. Caswell pointed to some chairs in the shade. "We'll sit out here under the Jessamine arbor."

In the middle of her garden was a small latticework structure covered with vines, and an abundance of yellow flowers were growing on the vines. I nearly sat down before Mrs. Caswell and Carla, but I remembered my manners at the last minute. The scent of the flowers was somewhere between buttercups and honeysuckle, but I seemed to remember that jessamine was poisonous.

Then they started talking about azaleas and roses and irises. I pretended to be paying attention, but I kept thinking about what was inside the envelope she gave me. I heard a buzzing sound. I thought it was from a carpenter bee, but there was a ruby-throated hummingbird about fifteen feet away, hovering under the arbor. The feathers on its throat kept changing color. It looked like a flying iridescent flower.

Mrs. Caswell kept turning away from Carla and looking at a bird feeder out on her lawn. A squirrel had climbed up the long metal pole, and it was perched on the wooden platform, eating birdseed. It was bothering her, and she finally stopped talking about flowers.

"That squirrel has become the bane of my existence. He gorges himself on birdseed and there's nothing left for the birds. He doesn't know it, but his days are numbered."

I wondered how she knew that the squirrel was a male.

Carla looked interested. “Are you going to do him in?”

Mrs. Caswell almost smiled. “Oh yes. I definitely have something in mind for Mr. Squirrel. It frustrates me that I have to wait, but Willie is off this week.”

Carla was amused. “Are you thinking poison?”

Mrs. Caswell was already sitting up straight, but she managed to sit up even straighter. “No, it’s a bit more subtle than poison. There are plenty of hawks in this neighborhood, and several days ago it occurred to me to put the feeder out in the middle of the lawn. I don’t know why I didn’t think of it sooner. As soon as a hawk flies over and sees Mr. Squirrel stuffing himself with birdseed, the nearest tree will be too far away for him to escape.

“When Willie gets back I’ll have him move the feeder away from the azaleas. I just hope I’m watching when a hawk swoops in and skewers him with her talons.”

Carla was grinning. “Are you willing to set aside etiquette long enough to allow one of your guests to fill in for Willie?”

After I pulled the pole out of the ground and moved the bird feeder out to where Mrs. Caswell wanted it, I went back under the arbor and sat down.

She thanked me and then she looked at her watch. It didn’t take her long to change gears. “I feel that I should add some perspective to what you are about to hear. After we had brunch at the club – after our conversation about Whiting’s nature – I had a greater understanding of what an important figure you are in my son’s life.

“That is when I told Carla that I wanted to express my appreciation. She and I have gone to lunch on two separate occasions and we have devised a plan. But I should explain that my motivation extends beyond acknowledging your role in the life of my son.”

She paused and raised her chin, and she started speaking more slowly. “When we were at brunch, I did not mention how offensive I found the nature of the rumor Mr. Colbert and his wife were attempting to perpetrate about you. That is the sort of mistreatment I expect Whiting to face later in his life." Her expression was the same, but her neck was flushed. "The financial success Mr. Colbert has achieved appears to have gone to his head. Carla and I both feel that he might need to be humbled.

"I have asked her to explain the details of what I have already put in motion. But before she does, I want to respond to the question you asked in an article I saw in the newspaper. It may be helpful if I explain the dynamics of the situation you encountered at the meeting of the Park Board. If what I read was accurate, you don't understand why the city does not protect its neighborhoods."

I didn't hear any defensiveness in the tone of her voice.

"What you should understand is that Nashville, along with every other city in America, is an economic enterprise. The value of our real estate and banks and newspapers and television stations, not to mention the value of any number of other local businesses, is not only tied to the rate of increase in the local population, it is also tied to the increase in the amount of capital coming into our city.

"Our Chamber of Commerce works to bring more people and more employment opportunities and more capital into Nashville by pursuing strategic initiatives. Those initiatives range from securing federal highway improvements to upgrading our airport to recruiting corporations from other cities. And because our population cannot rise unless people have additional places to live, land use policy is a crucial consideration.

"I am not defending the way things have been done. I am merely trying to answer the question you asked. As you are aware, Belle Meade and a few other enclaves have prohibitive zoning ordinances, which leaves neighborhoods like the one in which you grew up to absorb all the new housing.

"Developers like Mr. Colbert do the dirty work and, as you have surmised, the Planning Commission and the Board of Zoning Appeals both operate on behalf of developers. As Nashville has grown, those institutions have increasingly come under the control of those who directly benefit from growth.

"There should be a degree of balance, but there are times when balance is not achieved. It seems as though we might be experiencing one of those times. If I had grown up in your neighborhood, I suspect that I would feel precisely as you feel."

"She looked at her watch again. "Now I'm afraid that I must excuse myself. There is an event I am compelled to attend. I would much prefer to stay and hear Carla explain our plan. And even though I'm sure she will make this point, I will say it as well. It is *imperative* that you never repeat any part of what you are about to hear."

Carla and I sat back down after Mrs. Caswell left. I shifted to the front of my seat and put my knees together, and then I folded my hands on top of my lap. "This is me waiting patiently to hear what you and Mrs. Caswell have cooked up."

She leaned forward in her chair. "And this is me about to tell you. I didn't think Ellen would want you to know what was about to happen, but she said that if she could trust you with her son, she could trust your discretion. But she *does* believe in being careful."

Carla put her elbows on her knees. "This is so... perfect. Sometime in the next few days, Jones Colbert will get a telephone call from the attorney who oversees the Caswell family trusts. Ellen is the sole trustee. One of the trusts owns several large tracts of commercial property in downtown Nashville. Every decade or so, the trust redevelops a portion of its real estate, and then sells it and reinvests in other property.

"The attorney will inform Mr. Colbert that he is being strongly considered to redevelop an especially choice urban site. A few days after that, he will meet with the attorney and the property manager who jointly oversee what is owned by the trust.

"After he signs a confidentiality agreement, he will be thoroughly briefed on the project. Demolition on the property is scheduled to start this fall. When the attorney describes the scope of the development, he will make sure that the by-then-very-eager Jones Colbert understands that his full attention will be required. The attorney will make sure that Mr. Colbert understands that his continued involvement in the condominium project is a concern.

"At that point, the attorney will disclose to Mr. Colbert that the trust is in negotiation with the city regarding the exchange of several parcels of land. The attorney will explain that the trust would be open to purchasing the school property and including it with the parcels being conveyed to the city. He would let Mr. Colbert know that if his investors were willing to be bought out, they would make a small but reasonable profit on the transaction."

My head was spinning. "And you think he'll do it?"

"He'll be falling all over himself to do it. He'll see it as his chance to move into the big leagues. A high-profile urban project has a much larger payoff than developing condominiums out in the suburbs."

"But that's a lot of money. How can Mrs. Caswell..."

Carla cut me off. "The lawyers came up with an approach that involves using tax write-offs and working with the family's charitable foundation. Ellen didn't even try to explain it to me. All she said was that, in the end, buying the Woodmont property wouldn't end up costing a prohibitive amount of money.

"Anyway here's the big picture. The land will be transferred back to the city. The school building will still be torn down, but the land will become a park."

I was trying to get everything straight in my head. "And where does Jones Colbert learn his lesson in humility?"

"That, lover boy, is the most delicious part. He lives in a big house in Belle Meade and he has a mortgage and three kids at Ensworth. And he and Mary Ann both drive expensive cars and belong to the Club, and every year he goes on a golfing vacation to Europe.

"He isn't rich enough to live the way he's been living. He carries a lot of debt, and if something *unforeseen* should happen to his income stream – well things could get a little dicey."

She looked at me for three or four seconds. "Some real estate contracts are written to give the party of the first part the option of voiding a relationship if a developer's finances start looking shaky. There are circumstances under which the party of the first part has a *fiduciary responsibility* to sever that sort of relationship. Suffice it to say that unforeseen events occur from time to time, and sometimes people end up getting humbled."

Carla stopped talking and looked at me. "Of course, if some economic misfortune *should* happen to Jones Colbert along the way, it wouldn't surprise me if the trust gave him a smaller project – something that would at least let him keep his head above water. No one would want to see children punished for the misdeeds of their father."

The hummingbird reappeared a few feet away, and Carla sat back in her seat and closed her eyes. She was letting me absorb the moment. The squirrel had scampered away when I went out to move the feeder, but it was venturing back onto the lawn. It was sitting on its haunches, eyeing the relocated birdseed. The shadow of a hawk slid across the grass behind the squirrel, but there would be, at least for a time, no sudden descent.

That night, after I walked to Woodmont and stood on the baseball field for a while, I came back home and looked through the copies of what Ellen Caswell gave me. The letters contained plenty of information about the Bosley farm, and there were four separate newspaper advertisements offering rewards for Bosley slaves who had run away.

But the most important item was a highly detailed map of Charles Bosley's property. It showed every field and each structure, and it revealed the precise location of the place where Charles Dickinson was buried after his duel with Andrew Jackson.

Chapter 88

May 22, 1976 – It's Saturday morning and I'm standing at the edge of the Confederate Cemetery in Franklin with Callie. A few clouds are drifting above us. The rows of tombstones look like people in a sanctuary gazing up at a pulpit. She notices that cedar trees are growing up from several of the graves, and I tell her that I've always wondered if the trees contain molecules from the remains of southern soldiers. The tops of the cedars sway in the breeze, and as shadows slide back and forth across the limestone markers, Callie stops to read the inscription on a gravestone.

We promised Claire that we'd talk about what happened before the abortion, and I picked Callie up at her house. At first, she wanted to drive around and get lost again – the way we did when we found Rudderville, before I left for California. But when we were on our way out into the country, she noticed the sign for the cemetery. While we were walking around, I told her about the Battle of Franklin. When I reminded her that I went to school on the battlefield, she wanted to see the campus.

A few minutes later we were standing where my classmates and I circled the flagpole on the day we graduated in 1965 – one century after General Lee surrendered at Appomattox. I described how Confederate troops had surged toward the Union defenses, and I told her that we were in the place where some of the soldiers who were buried in the cemetery took the final steps of their lives.

I said that a good many of those soldiers had been around the same age she was. Callie seemed to be taking everything in. She wanted to see where the breastworks and the trenches were, and we started walking north up Columbia Pike.

It was time to say what I needed to say. The words didn't come easily. "When we were at the drugstore the last time... I understood that you were protecting Claire. I stayed away from you after that, but it wasn't because the way I felt was any different. I needed to give you some room. It was hard to turn my back on the way I felt – on the way I still feel – but I hadn't been thinking enough about what was right for you."

Callie looked like she could've been daydreaming, but I didn't think she was.

"I was always looming in the background, so I backed away. I'm still trying to figure out a couple of things, but it seemed like the right thing to do."

She glanced over at me. "What are you trying to figure out?"

"It's been three years since all this... since I started all this. I'm pretty sure your feelings haven't changed all that much. You liked me okay back then and I'm pretty sure you like me okay now, but that's about it. The last thing I'd want is for you to pretend to have feelings you don't have. Feelings are either there or they aren't."

We were almost to the place where the Union defenses had intersected the road, and I started walking more slowly.

Callie looked at me. "That's what you figured out?"

I wasn't sure how much more I should let myself say. "On Christmas Eve, when I came by your house and gave you the tree, you were... you seemed... different. I got the feeling that something might... you know, be about to happen between us. I don't know. Maybe I was just imagining it."

We stopped walking when we got to where the breastworks once stood. I was glad to change the subject. "Right around here, the Confederates were packed so close together that some of them couldn't even fall down when they were shot. Corpses were standing up the next morning."

Callie seemed to be picturing the way things looked after the battle. Then she stared back toward the Battle Ground campus.

"Well here's how it was on Christmas Eve. I'd been grounded for six weeks. When you showed up I'd been in my room smoking some weed. I was pretty high and it could've been perfect timing, but by then... I was pretty sure you wouldn't do anything.

"At first, when I knew you liked me, I wondered if you'd put a move on me. It wasn't like I was waiting around for it to happen, and I'm not saying I would've done anything if you had. I just thought about it sometimes. Then after a while, when nothing happened... I thought you felt too guilty. You'd already said that the way you felt about me wasn't my problem, and I finally just quit thinking about it."

I noticed how many times she was using the past tense.

She was quiet for a few seconds. "Claire said you think you might've messed up my life. I almost started laughing when she said it. Having you come around didn't make me miss out on anything – especially not when it came to high school. I don't know what it used to be like, but now it's a joke. High school isn't like *American Graffiti* anymore. You shouldn't feel bad about taking my mind off being stuck in a crap hole. I didn't mind when you showed up. Most of the time I liked it."

A big truck geared down and almost stopped. I couldn't see the driver, but he must've been taking a good long look at Callie.

She ignored the truck. "There's another thing you haven't figured out."

"What's that?"

She seemed a little hesitant. "When you came to the drugstore the last time, I... I'd been trying to get Claire to tell you she was pregnant. I told her you could help her, but she wouldn't talk about it. Then she finally broke down. She tried to make me swear that I wouldn't ever tell you what I'm about to tell you, but I wouldn't swear and she told me anyway."

Callie seemed to be going over what she wanted to say. "She told me how she felt about you. I should've known. She's been into you all along, but she just locked away her feelings. And that was before you took her to get her abortion and wrote her that poem and had the party for her out in the woods. She's a whole lot more into you now."

"And she knows you're telling me this?"

She nodded. "Yep. She didn't want me to, but I said I was telling you anyway. She says you don't see her that way, and even if you ever did, you'd just end up worrying about the same things that you worried about with me. She says it can't go anywhere."

Callie moved closer and gave me a push. "You look like your dog just died. Anyway, Claire's been on this kick of talking everything out, so I'm sure you'll both end up saying whatever you need to say."

She shook her head. "Ain't that a bitch? She's been into you all this time, while you've been waiting for me." It wasn't long before she started singing *You Can't Always Get What You Want.*

I was looking past her, but I saw her look at me. "That's my favorite Stones song. Every time I heard it I'd think about you. Now it makes me think about Claire."

Another truck slowed down and the driver gave a blast on his horn. I pointed to where General Strahl was killed a few yards inside the Union breastworks, and then we started back. Before we'd gone too far, I also showed her where General Cleburne and General Adams were killed, trying to lead their troops forward.

We kept walking and it struck me that Callie would probably end up marrying somebody like Mike Higgins or Hall Guthrie – somebody who'd charge over the top of breastworks during a battle.

I slowed down before we got to the car. "Do you have any advice about Claire?"

Callie shrugged. "You don't need any. You're friends. You'll talk and things'll be okay. Maybe you two should drive out into the country together and try to get lost. I'm the one who needs advice. When I tell her what I just sang to you, she might try to kill me."

The longer I waited to call Claire, the more awkward it would be, and I went ahead and called her that night. When she answered the phone I just said, "Wanna go for a ride in a big fast car?" I heard her groan and then she started laughing.

She drove my car and we went way out into the countryside southwest of Nashville. She finally got us lost, and by the time we found our way back, there wasn't much more to say. It was hard for her, but she told me how she felt about me and how much our friendship meant to her.

Then she took her turn at singing *You Can't Always Get What You Want*. But she didn't just sing the chorus – she sang the whole song. She had a really good voice, but of course, she didn't know it. I could feel the current flowing between our bodies, and I could tell that she felt it, too. Part of me wanted to tell her to pull off the road, but I understood all the reasons why I couldn't let anything happen.

Claire had no idea how good she looked, and I couldn't tell her.

Chapter 89

Carla came down with a cold. It was a few days before she called and said she was ready for some company. She was sitting out on her patio when I got to her house.

"Do I look like I've been under the weather?"

"You look great." I started raising my eyebrows up and down. "Are you still... *contagious?*"

She gave me a playful look. "Not any more than usual. And I'd love to have my way with you, but I'm determined to stay celibate until next week. We're going to have *so* much fun – at least I am. I just hope you're willing to indulge me."

I had no idea what I was about to hear.

"My plan is for you to take me to the premiere of *All the President's Men*. It's next Thursday at Belle Meade Theater. And guess who's going to be there?"

"I'm pretty sure it won't be Nixon."

"I'll give you a hint. It's somebody I might even choose over Sean Connery. And I'll give you another hint. Think about *Butch Cassidy and the Sundance Kid*."

"*Oh boy!* Is it Katherine Ross?"

She gave me an insincere smile. "No, smartass. And it isn't Paul Newman – although he's on my list, too. No, it's Robert Redford. I've always had a thing for him. It's one of my most *intimate* secrets. He's coming to the premiere and I suspect that as soon as he spots me in the crowd, he'll find me irresistibly attractive. We'll stare into each other's eyes, and after he does whatever he needs to do at the theater, we'll drive away together into the night."

I tried to act disappointed. "And you'd just ditch me?"

She looked amused. "*Of course,* I would. And I'd go by myself, but I don't think I should be without an escort when Mr. Redford sees me. I wouldn't want to look like I couldn't find a date, would I?"

I didn't mind taking her to the premiere. "I'll try not to fall apart – at least not until after you've driven away."

"This is Carla looking pleased." She smiled and tilted her head, and put the tips of her index fingers where her dimples would've been if she had dimples. "But there's always a chance that he will *somehow* be able to resist our natural chemistry and fail to whisk me away, which brings me to my next request. And if you don't want to do this, I'll understand.

"In the unlikely event that things don't work out at the premiere, I'll need *something* to help get me over my disappointment. This is Carla making sure she doesn't see you cringe." She turned her head and shielded her eyes with the back of her right hand. "The Swan Ball is only two days later, and *I can't tell you* how excited I'll be if you would consent to be my escort. I assume that you know all about the ball. And I also assume that you've never been."

The Swan Ball was the big social event of the year in Nashville. It was held at Cheekwood, which was once a large private estate at the edge of Belle Meade. It had been turned into gardens and a fine arts center. It was beautiful. The Swan Ball was Cheekwood's annual fundraising event. I wasn't wild about the idea of having to put on a tuxedo and spend several hours surrounded by a bunch of socialites, but I went ahead and told her I'd go. She'd done a lot for me, and I was also a little curious about the Swan Ball.

June 10, 1976 – It's Thursday evening and I'm sitting with Carla inside Belle Meade Theater. We're watching All the President's Men. Woodward and Bernstein are meeting with Deep Throat in the shadows of a parking garage. It reminds me of the way I felt when I was with Mike Higgins in North Nashville at Tiny's. Robert Redford is supposed to give a talk and answer some questions from the audience after the movie. He's probably killing time back in the manager's office.

When his limousine pulled up a couple of hours ago, a few hundred fans were gathered in front of the theater. Carla was positioned on the front row. I was standing beside her. I shouldn't have been surprised when Redford gave her a long look and a quick wink as he walked by. Between her perfect hair and the plunging neckline of her embroidered white blouse and the black lace choker around her throat, and with the way her skin was glowing, I should've expected it.

After the movie, Carla and I went outside and stopped on the sidewalk in front of the theater. I took her in my arms and pretended to console her. "I can only imagine how devastated you must be. I was sure that Redford would be waiting in the lobby, and then take you away in his limousine. Do you want to walk down to Moon's and smother your sorrows with a cheeseburger?"

She smiled and shook her head. "You know where I made my mistake? Bringing a date. If I'd been by myself he wouldn't have been able to hold himself back."

I took a deep breath and stuck out my chest. "Well, I guess that makes me the guy who ran off the Sundance Kid."

We were walking to her car and she glanced over at me. "I have a couple of things to tell you, but I wanted to wait till after the movie. You'll like the first one. I got a call from Ellen this morning. Your friend Jones Colbert and his partners were *very* happy to sell the school property to the trust. By the end of the summer, the city will own the land, and there's already a signed agreement with the city that it'll become a park. And around this time next year, Jones Colbert will start to learn his lesson."

Knowing that Ellen Caswell had done what she planned to do was a lot better than being told that she was planning to do it. I could feel my emotions building up. I'd already thanked Carla for what she'd done and I would've thanked her again, but she kept talking.

"And here's the second thing. In a couple of weeks, I'm going to Italy. I might be back by September, but I could be gone until at least Thanksgiving. I just find it *so difficult* to leave Tuscany in the fall."

I was disappointed, but she'd told me that she went off on long trips from time to time. I'd miss Carla as much as I'd miss her body, but I understood. She was a free spirit.

Ever since I was a teenager I'd kept my parents in the dark when it came to anything that involved girls. It was ridiculous. There were plenty of times when I came home late, or when I didn't come home at all. They had to know that I wasn't just sitting by myself in the dark somewhere.

I wanted to let them know that I was taking Carla to the Swan Ball. I probably couldn't have kept it a secret anyway. They had friends who would be there. I didn't want somebody calling Mother the next day, and telling her that they'd seen me. I decided that I'd let them know at dinner on Friday, the night before the ball.

They both tried to act casual when I told them. It was like I'd mentioned that I was going to a ballgame. It was my fault for having been neurotic for so long. They didn't feel like they could ask me any questions, so I told them a little about Carla and how I'd coached her nephew. They knew I was leaving out a lot of information. It was still light outside, and after a while, Mother went for a walk.

I kept thinking about how long I'd kept them in the dark. It was time to finally stop acting like I was fifteen. I went into the den and sat down on the sofa. My father was in his chair, reading the afternoon newspaper.

I made myself start talking. "I should probably apologize for never letting you or Mother know anything about... you know... my social life. I've always made everything so awkward."

I caught him off-guard, but he didn't look uncomfortable. He folded the paper and put it in his lap. "You don't need to apologize. You're just private about some things. Sometimes we wonder where you go at night, but we don't expect you to tell us where you've been. We want to know all about you, but it's okay to keep things to yourself."

"It wouldn't kill me to open up a little bit."

He smiled at me. "Is there something you want to say about who you're taking to the Swan Ball?

"No. She's just a friend. I mean she's... she's more than a friend, but it isn't romantic." I was trying not to get flustered, but I felt myself blushing.

My father was trying not to look amused. "I'd love to hear anything you want to tell me, but... You do things in your own way and you're on your own schedule. He didn't say anything for a few seconds. "Just stay on the path you're on. You'll get where you need to go."

At least it was a start. At least I'd opened the door a little bit.

Chapter 90

June 12, 1976 – It's a warm night and I'm walking into Cheekwood Mansion with Carla to attend the Swan Ball. The entrance hall is decorated with red, white, and blue bunting. There's an art exhibit from the collection of Dr. Armand Hammer on display, and Carla is trying to decide if we should go through the gallery first, or wait until later on. There aren't too many other couples here. She says she prefers to be fashionably early.

We go up the stairs to where part of the mansion has been transformed to look like an old saloon. A few guests are already in the saloon. Two of the couples look like they could've been around when Grant was president. The official theme of the ball is "A Salute to American Waterways." The saloon is supposed to be part of a river town in 1876, when America is celebrating its centennial. I didn't expect the Swan Ball to be this ritzy.

Carla decided that we should wait until we were leaving to look at the paintings. We went out the back of the mansion and walked through a garden to an enormous tent that spread across the lawn. A wooden floor had been installed under the tent. And there were tables covered with red satin tablecloths and decorated with gold-gilded candelabras and flower displays.

There were chandeliers overhead, and at the far end of the tent was the focal point of the ball – a large replica of a steamboat. It was trimmed in red-white-and-blue, and was named the *Golden Swan*. It was about twelve feet high and thirty feet long. It had upper and lower decks, an ornate railing, a rotating side wheel, and a smokestack that reached the top of the tent.

And between the tables and the steamboat was the red-white-and-blue dance floor. After dinner, Les Brown and His Band of Renown would set up in front of the steamboat, and the guests would go out and try to waltz or foxtrot. Or perform whatever dances they could remember from back in the days of their youth.

Carla got a glass of wine at one of the bars, and I followed her over to the edge of the tent. After we watched couples drift by for a few minutes, she pointed out an older man standing about twenty feet away.

"That guy was a *very close* associate of George Heran, who died a few years ago. The shadowy Mr. Heran liked to work behind the scenes. He was involved in all sorts of businesses and served on lots of boards. He appeared to be a respectable bachelor, but it seems that he was quite fond of young men. It was said that from time to time loans were arranged and careers were enhanced based on certain *non-monetary* considerations.

She pointed out another man a few feet away. "And the pompous-looking man over there is Pat Brosnan. His father was one of the men who founded the Consolidated Life Insurance Company. During the Jim Crow period, the company made millions of dollars every year selling overpriced insurance to black people all across the South. A white man would come by every Saturday, right after payday, and collect the premiums. Most black people didn't think they could say no if a white man in a business suit showed up at the door asking for a little money.

"The Brosnans act like royalty, but they never mention that they got their money by feeding off the poor. These days the Brosnan men put on their coats and ties every morning and go to their offices and pretend to work, but they spend a lot of their time drinking and taking vacations and having rendezvous with other men's wives."

I wanted to hear more stories, but one of her friends spotted Carla and walked up with her husband. Her name was Barbara and her husband looked like he'd been drinking since that morning.

He kept staring at Carla's body and he was being pretty obvious about it. She ignored him and his wife was ignoring him, too. Barbara was wearing what must've been a really expensive dress, and she had on a diamond necklace and matching earrings. I thought she was in her mid-fifties, but later on, Carla told me she was still in her early-forties.

Barbara seemed like a nice person and I felt sorry for her. It looked like she'd spent a good part of the afternoon at the beauty parlor, but it hadn't helped much. Her hair was dyed and sprayed and stiff and it didn't have any luster, and the color she'd chosen didn't quite match the tone of her skin. She was out of shape and it was probably a struggle when she was squeezing into her girdle. When she looked in the mirror I hoped she saw what she wanted to see.

While Barbara was dragging her drunken husband away, two more couples came up, and some other couples wandered over after that. I met a lot of people, but I didn't try to remember anybody's name. The women all told Carla how great she looked. They were right. She was wearing a backless silver evening gown, and her skin and her hair were shining.

She returned every compliment she got, and adjectives like *fabulous* and *gorgeous* and *stunning* were getting tossed around. I saw a few couples who were friends of my parents, but they were pretty far away and I couldn't tell if they saw me.

We finally got away from everybody, and I followed Carla to the bar where she got another glass of wine. We were on our way over to see the steamboat when I finally asked her what I'd been wondering ever since we got there. "This has to cost a fortune. How much were the tickets?"

I could tell she was trying not to laugh. "Oh *my*. How *gauche*. What an *egregious* breach of etiquette. Here I am, trying to expand your social horizons, and you have the *audacity* to ask how much money I spent on your ticket.

"This is the beautiful and stunning Carla looking awkward and distraught." She pretended to chew her fingernails, and then she put the back of her hand against her forehead and gazed up at the top of the tent. "But if you *must* know, the tickets were $100 each. And *yes*, it does cost a fortune to put on the Swan Ball, but most of the expense is covered by sponsors." She took my arm and we started walking. "And when might I expect your next faux pas?"

While we were strolling over to look at the steamboat, it occurred to me how comfortable Willoughby Williams would've been at the Swan Ball. Carla studied the replica for a minute or so, and then she turned around to look at the crowd. She moved a little closer to me. "So how do you feel about being here?"

"Well, I'm not all that thrilled about wearing a tuxedo."

She took a step back and looked me over. "But you clean up so well. You look so... *spiffy*."

I mimicked her tone. "But I feel so... *ridiculous*."

Carla gave me a patient smile. "Every once in a while, it doesn't hurt to put on anachronistic clothes and uncomfortable shoes, and show the world that you're a member of the ruling class. From time to time we need to remind ourselves, and everybody else, who's really in charge. Sometimes it isn't quite enough to own a big house and belong to an exclusive country club and have a stock portfolio as thick as a telephone book."

"Is that really the way it is for these people?"

She shook her head. "No. They're pretty much like everybody else. Most of them are nice. Most of them do things for other people. Sometimes they might be too concerned about the image they project – living in the right neighborhood and associating with the right families and sending their children to the right school and being members of the right country club and all that – but almost all of them are good people.

"But a few of them... they're the ones that I find so *fascinating*. They're almost like a separate species."

"You sound like a sociologist."

"Why thank you, lover boy."

The tent was starting to fill up. Carla was scanning the guests who were milling around on the opposite side of the dance floor. "Here's a crash course on the hard-core species in question. And like I said, I'm *only* talking about the most stereotypical segment of the Nashville aristocracy.

"They see everything in terms of their position in the world. They envy and resent anybody they think is superior to them. And they feel contempt toward everybody they think is beneath them. They are driven by the way they are seen by other members of the upper crust. Money is their lifeblood, but it's more complicated than who has the highest net worth. If it was just about money, they'd never give any away. But at times they can be very philanthropic."

I wasn't sure what she meant. "So unless they..."

"There are usually strings attached. The species-in-question makes sure those strings are tied to something they want. A lot of times it's prestige. They don't give away money out of benevolence. They want to *appear* benevolent, but they give money away so they can be well thought of, and that gives them more influence. What it boils down to is that nearly everything they do is done for their own benefit. And the nastiest ones seem to like hurting people along the way."

I was looking across at the crowd. "I just hope nobody is over there reading your lips."

She didn't say anything for a few seconds. "I guess there's nothing like living in a commune to turn an involuntary aristocrat into a heretic." She glanced away. "I'll be glad to tell you more about the subspecies I'm talking about, but it looks like somebody is making a grand entrance."

The crowd parted and the Governor of Tennessee, Roy Branton, and his wife, and Ambassador Milford Dunley and his wife, were walking toward the steamboat with a couple of African men who were each wearing a headdress and a robe. There were medals on both sides of Ambassador Dunley's tuxedo jacket. He was wearing a sash that looked like it should've been worn by some European king. Not by a retired insurance executive who raised a bunch of money for the Nixon campaign and then became an ambassador. But the ambassador certainly looked like an ambassador.

Governor Branton, on the other hand, did not look like a governor. He was a politician from a small town, and he still looked like a politician from a small town. He and Mrs. Branton looked like they could've accidentally wandered into the tent looking for a circus. But they didn't seem nearly as out-of-place as the two African men beside them.

I leaned over and put my mouth close to Carla's ear. "I seem to recall you saying that I was gauche. Well here's my next faux pas." I did my best to sound like a Belle Meade patrician. "Oh my *Gawd*! Those aren't waiters! Nigras have invaded the Swan Ball! How *outrageous*! This would *nevuh* be allowed at the Club."

She reached down and grabbed my hand. "Shhh!"

I ignored her. "But perhaps they are merely here to entertain us." I gestured toward the steamboat. "Perhaps they're here to sing "Old Man River."

She squeezed my hand harder. "Will you *please* shut up?" She was trying not to laugh. "I'd prefer that you *don't* cause a diplomatic incident. They're from Sudan. The short one is President Nimeiry. I think they're here for an international trade conference."

I switched to a rural accent. "What ur we gonna be a sendin over thar to Africa? I bet it's some moonshine, ain't it? And what in the *hell* are we gonna do with all the gall-durned camels they'll be sendin' over here to Tennessee?"

She was okay until I made a sound like a distressed camel. That pushed her over the edge. Ambassador Dunley spotted Carla right when she broke out laughing.

He came over and kissed her on the cheek. "Carla dear." He seemed especially glad to see her.

She put her arm around his back and hugged him. "Hello Milford." Then she turned to Mrs. Dunley. "Hi, Jean." She gave her a hug and a kiss. After I was introduced to the Dunleys, and after Carla and I were introduced to Governor and Mrs. Branton, we met the Africans, President Nimeiry, and his Minister of Education, Dr. Khalid.

The president was cordial, and Dr. Khalid was especially open and friendly. They both spoke English better than either the Governor or Mrs. Branton. After another minute or so, the ambassador led them over to look at the steamboat and meet some of the other guests.

Not too long after that, the mass of couples on the other side of the dance floor parted again. An older couple was with Mayor Richardson and his wife, and they were making their way through the crowd.

Carla was staring at the group. "And the Guest of Honor makes his grand entrance."

I was surprised. "*That's* Armand Hammer?" When I saw him on television a few months earlier, he looked like he wouldn't live more than three or four days. He'd already spent several weeks in the hospital by then. It was just before he was to be sentenced for making an illegal payment to the Nixon campaign.

He had been in a wheelchair when he arrived at the courthouse. The reason the judge didn't throw Dr. Hammer in prison was because his doctors testified that he had an incurable heart condition. They said that he was rapidly deteriorating. He looked pretty healthy to me.

Carla was thinking the same thing. "It looks like the old man has made a *miraculous* recovery." She started to say something else, but she stopped herself. "Oh. You have *got* to be kidding."

Dr. and Mrs. Hammer and Mayor Richardson and his wife were about to come over and look at the steamboat, but Jones Colbert, with Mary Ann right behind him, had moved along the edge of the dance floor and cut them off. It reminded me of the way Jack Ruby moved in on Lee Harvey Oswald in the basement of the Dallas police station. We watched Jones shake hands with the mayor, and then with Mrs. Richardson and with Dr. and Mrs. Hammer.

The photographer Jones almost certainly had paid to trail along behind him was getting in position. After he took pictures of the three couples and then of the three men, he took a picture of Jones Colbert and Dr. Hammer standing side by side like they were old friends.

The whole encounter took less than a minute, but Jones would have a photograph of himself standing with an international business tycoon and art collector. He'd probably have it enlarged and hang it on the wall of his office, and for the rest of his life, he'd use it to try to impress whoever he was trying to impress.

After the photos were taken, the entourage started for the steamboat, but they were intercepted by another couple who were lying in wait. Carla leaned toward me. "I wonder if he'll recognize me."

"You've met him?"

"I haven't just met him, he's tried to seduce me."

I pictured the old man with the big glasses and the oversized bow tie making advances on Carla, and I couldn't keep from laughing. She looked at me and smiled. "I'd love to know what's so funny, but there isn't time. I'm starting to think that a little caper I haven't told you about might actually work. If Dr. Hammer remembers me, just go along with whatever I do. I'll explain everything later."

Later that night she told me that Dr. Hammer had been a guest at the Swan Ball once before. She'd met him in 1973, when Cheekwood presented him with the Swan Award for his contributions to art. Receiving that honor led to part of his collection being loaned to Cheekwood.

During his visit three years earlier, Dr. Hammer gave Carla his private telephone number. And when he leaned over and whispered how much he wanted to show her Los Angeles, he had put his hand on her leg. He offered to fly her there, and asked her to call him. When she was telling me about it she shrugged. "Who knows? If he'd been a couple of decades younger I might've done it."

Dr. Hammer and Mayor Richardson and their wives came right toward us. Dr. Hammer moved like he was in his fifties. His eyes lit up when he saw Carla, but his wife was beside him and he didn't say anything. The mayor started to make the introduction, but right before he said Carla's name, she interrupted him. "Oh, Dr. Hammer, it is so nice to see you again."

Then Carla introduced me to everybody. The only one who didn't make eye contact and smile was Dr. Bigshot. He just gave me a perfunctory nod. Carla's hand stayed in his hand for longer than I would've expected.

The mayoral entourage fell in with the group being led by Ambassador Dunley, and Carla and I followed them over to the steamboat. We were soon joined by another member of Dr. Hammer's party – a tall woman in a black dress. She was attractive and had reddish hair, and she looked like she was in her late thirties. She was reserved but polite when she introduced herself. "I'm Martha Wade Kaufman. I'm the curator of the collection." She seemed intelligent and I was sorry I didn't know more about art.

While I was watching the dignitaries talking to each other, Carla was maneuvering closer and closer to Dr. Hammer. His wife was still beside him, and Carla gave me a quick look and tilted her head toward Mrs. Hammer. I started talking to Mrs. Hammer and I moved a little bit at a time until she finally had her back to her husband.

She couldn't see him without turning around, but I was looking right at him. He took Carla's hand again and she put her other hand over his. While Mrs. Hammer was going on and on about the replica of the steamboat and how beautiful everything was, Carla and Dr. Hammer finished their brief conversation.

Carla went over to talk to Martha Wade Kaufman, the curator, and Dr. Khalid walked over to Dr. Hammer. A couple of minutes later I saw Dr. Hammer looking around. As soon as he saw his curator, he tried to get her attention. She didn't see him at first. It didn't take him long to get frustrated. By the time she finally glanced over at him, he was glaring at her.

She quickly left Carla and went over to Dr. Hammer. I couldn't hear what he said, but his posture had turned stiff and one of his hands was balled into a fist. I saw some pain in Martha Wade Kaufman's eyes when she was walking away. I was fairly sure that I was the only one who saw what happened.

Chapter 91

I was pretty sure I understood what was going on. Dr. Hammer was a womanizer and he had a massive ego. His wife looked a lot older than he did, but his curator was a good-looking woman less than half his age. I understood why he'd have an affair, and I wondered how many of the people at the Swan Ball, both the men and the women, had done the same thing.

Dr. Hammer seemed to be a real bastard. He had made illegal contributions to the Nixon campaign. And it was obvious that staying in the hospital and showing up in court and being pushed around in a wheelchair and informing the judge that he was dying had all been an act. On top of all that, I was pretty sure he was a bully. He seemed like a king-sized version of Jones Colbert.

Carla was talking to Ambassador Dunley when I left to follow Martha Kaufman. I wanted to know what he had sent her off to do. She went straight to the bar and got two glasses of red wine. I waited for her to start back before I got a glass for Carla.

It took Martha a while to make her way through the crowd. I'd almost caught up to her when an overweight man she was passing suddenly wheeled around, and his elbow hit one of the glasses she was carrying. It flew out of her hand and broke on the floor, but she made a quick move and avoided getting wine on her dress.

She looked slightly flustered when I came up beside her. "If wine dodging was an Olympic event, that was at least a 9.5." I wasn't sure she recognized me, and I nodded toward the steamboat. "You met me over there. I'm..."

"Oh yes, you're... you're with Carla."

I handed her the wine I was holding. "Here. Take this one and I'll go back for reinforcements." She gave me a blank look, and then she thanked me and left.

Martha was standing with Carla and Dr. and Mrs. Hammer when I got back to the steamboat with Carla's wine. I didn't say anything about the broken glass, and it wasn't long before Martha started to excuse herself. "I really should go over and check on the collection."

Carla looked at Martha and put on an accent straight out of *Gone With the Wind*. "Why, Martha Wade Kaufman! In the South, it isn't *propuh* for an unescorted female *to go traipsing around* at a social event of this *magnitude* without a handsome young man at her side."

Dr. and Mrs. Hammer both smiled, and when Carla looked at me, I put my right arm against my stomach and bowed.

Whatever Carla was up to seemed to require Martha's absence. There wasn't much Martha could say, and I walked with her to the mansion. I felt sorry for her, but I didn't know what I could do to help.

She was quiet until we got to the gallery. "I should thank you for helping me after my mishap with the wine glass." She sounded tired. "If there's anything you'd like to ask about the collection, I'll be more than glad to tell you what I know."

"I wish I knew enough to ask an intelligent question, but I only made a B- when I took art appreciation in college."

She almost smiled. "I'm not sure that I believe you."

"Okay, it was a C+. I really am *profoundly* unsophisticated when it comes to art, and I'll swear to it on a stack of Norman Rockwell prints."

That made her smile. I could tell that she was trying to think of something to say. She half-turned to the paintings on the wall we were passing. "Well, you wouldn't need to have taken art appreciation to be drawn to some of the works in this collection."

I'd been scanning the paintings, and I slowed down when we got to what I was pretty sure was a Van Gogh. I liked the swirls of color in the sky and the way the trees seemed to be melting. "I think this one might be trying to speak to me."

Martha straightened up a little and smiled. "And you said you were unsophisticated. Are you familiar with his Saint-Remy Period?"

I smiled back at her and shook my head. "I must've skipped class that day."

She seemed to relax a little. "It's called *Hospital at Saint-Remy.* The long yellow building in the painting is the asylum where Van Gogh spent a year of his life. He was staying there when he painted *The Starry Night.* He left in the spring of 1890, and he was dead by the middle of that summer."

We both looked at the painting for a few seconds, and then she looked at me. "I enjoy hearing what people see when they take in a painting – particularly when they see it for the first time. May I ask what you see?"

I saw an opening. "I'll give it a try. The trees and the people and the hospital are the way they might look if they were being seen through a wave of heat rising off a road in the summer, or if they were being seen by somebody who was delirious with a fever. Or maybe by somebody who was crazy."

Martha didn't say anything and I kept talking. "And I do like Norman Rockwell. I think it's because his paintings tell stories. Some of his narratives can be a little sappy, but I remember one time when I spent about an hour looking at *Homecoming GI.* It's a painting of a young soldier who's just made it home to his family from World War Two. There are all sorts of stories in that painting."

Martha seemed to be listening. "Do you see a story in this Van Gogh?"

I was trying to think about how to set up what I wanted to say. "Well, I see the *beginnings* of a story. I'm looking at the woman holding the red parasol. She's at the edge of a pretty steep slope, but the painting doesn't show whether the ground levels out, or if it just keeps sloping downhill.

"Maybe it represents going toward a grave. And there's a man across from where she is. He's moving in her direction, but she isn't looking at him. She looks like she's gazing off into the distance.

"The woman with the parasol has her back to the hospital. Maybe she's turning away from the fear and the death she's just seen. The front door of the building looks like the mouth of somebody in pain. It makes the whole hospital look like it's in agony. And in the area where she's walking... I don't know, it seems washed-out and kind of depressing.

"But the colors above her are bright and rich. The trees and the sky are vibrant. Maybe that represents the difference between the physical world and the spiritual world. And there's something else about the sky."

Martha was staring at the painting. "What's that?"

"There's a blue sky. So the sun should be out, but it's hard to tell if there are any shadows. Maybe that's another indication that we aren't seeing the physical world."

I wanted to finish the story I was making up about the painting, but I didn't have enough time. One of the sponsors walked up and started talking to Martha, and before long she went back to check in with Dr. Hammer.

I stayed a little longer and I kept looking at the painting until I came up with something that might help her. I found a lady coming out of an office and she gave me an envelope and some Cheekwood stationary. After a few minutes, I'd written what I wanted to write.

Dinner was served and then the orchestra started playing. I would've been willing to dance if I could've taken off my shoes and if all the geezers had stayed in their seats and if Les Brown and his Band of Renown had played more songs from the second half of the Twentieth Century.

But Carla, who wasn't exactly sober, wanted to dance and she knew how to get what she wanted. She reached down and while she was groping me under the table, she said the only place she'd tell me what she was planning was out on the dance floor.

The band was playing *Sentimental Journey* when she told me that she was going to war with Mary Ann Colbert. "Well here's the gist of it, Lover Boy. On two occasions that I know of, Mary Ann has told her friends – one of whom is *much* closer to me than she is to Mary Ann – that I'm a lesbian and that you really *are* gay. And that you and I are pretending to have a physical relationship to conceal the *repugnant* nature of our respective sexual orientations. It made her look bad when we became an item, and she's invented another lie to cover her tracks."

Carla seemed glad to have a reason to unleash herself. "Anyway, here's what I'm cooking up. I wanted you to go with Martha to the gallery because she was a distraction. When I was talking to Dr. Hammer, he kept looking at her. It was like he was checking to see if she was watching him. I thought she'd be gone longer if you went with her.

"Dr. Hammer not only remembered me, he said he was hoping to see me tonight. I told him that I wanted to call him after the first time we met, but that I was still married at the time. I told him my husband had hired a private investigator and I was trying to be careful. Which, of course, is complete fiction.

"I knew he'd forgotten my name and he doesn't hear all that well, so right now he thinks my name is Marian Colbert and that I can't wait to fly out to LA and surrender myself to his *commanding* presence and his *wanton* desires.

"He's leaving for Russia tonight, but at the end of next week, I'll give him a call. That's when I'll set up the visit he's been anticipating for these three *long* years. Meanwhile, a dear friend of mine who lives in LA, and who *loves* being part of a good adventure, will play the part of Dr. Hammer's private secretary.

"She'll contact Jones Colbert and tell him that one of Dr. Hammer's businesses is opening a branch office in Nashville.

She'll say that there's a real estate opportunity Dr. Hammer would like to discuss with him. Without saying why, my friend will also convey Dr. Hammer's desire that Mrs. Colbert should accompany her husband to Los Angeles."

Sentimental Journey led into *Perfidia*. I looked around for Jones and Mary Ann, but I didn't see them. "Arrangements will be finalized and round-trip airline tickets will be sent to Mr. and Mrs. Colbert. When they land in LA they will be picked up by a limousine. Then they'll head for the Beverly Hilton, which is where Dr. Hammer thinks I'll be staying when I come out for our supposed rendezvous.

"I'll be in Italy by then, but I'll call Dr. Hammer on his private line right after I have supposedly landed. After I tell him what I'm about to do to him, he'll *really* be looking forward to my visit.

"He will have given me the hotel manager's name and his number, and I'll call the front desk to make sure that Jones and Mary Ann are expected. The bellhop will get their luggage as soon as they arrive, and they'll be taken up to the room they think Dr. Hammer has been generous enough to provide. I anticipate that there'll be a *wee bit* of confusion once he opens the door.

"From that point on, things become less predictable. But I don't see them all sitting down and trying to figure out why a married couple has shown up instead of the woman named Marian he just talked to on the telephone. I think he'll probably tell them to go away *well* before they get around to that.

"There's a slight chance that the Colberts will figure out that I was behind their little adventure, but I doubt they will. If they do figure it out, I'll be more than glad to tell them exactly why they had it coming.

"But I haven't gotten to the best part. The weekend before they leave for LA, their friends will throw Jones and Mary Ann a Bon Voyage Party at the Club. Photographs of the grand occasion will be in at least one of the newspapers, and while they're away, quite a few members of Nashville society will be waiting to hear *all about* what the Colberts experienced on their grand trip.

"The details will be hard to come by at first, but before long, word will *somehow* leak out that they were never shown around Los Angeles by Dr. Hammer. A lot of people will *somehow* get the impression that Mary Ann and Jones made the whole thing up, and they'll lose a lot of credibility.

"And things will get even worse next year when Jones has his *unfortunate* financial setback. Once that happens, I'm fairly sure that people won't be too interested in anything the Colberts have to say about you or me or anybody else."

Perfidia was coming to an end and the band started playing *Near You*. It was written back in the 1940s by Francis Craig, the local band leader my father told me about.

Carla took a deep breath. "And Ellen Caswell owes me five dollars. When I told her what I had in mind, she bet me that I couldn't pull it off. And there's one more thing." She pulled away from me, and then she threw her shoulders back and put her hands on her hips. "This is Carla looking triumphant."

Dr. and Mrs. Hammer got up to leave, and when Carla went over to tell them goodbye, I slipped an envelope into Martha's hand. I just said, "From now on, every time I see a Van Gogh I'll think about you."

Martha looked puzzled at first, but she took the envelope and smiled. She started to say something, but I heard Dr. Hammer's voice behind me. "Let's go, Martha. It's late."

I wondered where she'd be when she read it. And whether she'd think I was crazy.

Vincent's Whisper

As Vincent was capturing
Her image on his canvas,
The woman
Holding the red parasol
Was making her decision.
The world was
Melting around her,

And seeing the
The entrance
Of the asylum
Begin to scream,
She knew it was time
To set herself free.
The woman with the parasol
Looks out from the canvas
At the woman
In the black evening gown
Standing in the art gallery,
And seeing the irony,
A faint smile
Crosses her face.

It was after one-thirty when we got back to Carla's house. The Browns were in Nova Scotia. It was still pretty warm and we took a late swim in the pool. Carla was a wild woman. She tried to get me to spend the night, but I didn't want to show up at home on Sunday afternoon in my rumpled tuxedo, knowing what my parents were thinking.

The whole way home I thought about how uninhibited Carla was. It never took her long to lose herself in an experience. If we were musicians she would've just closed her eyes and played by ear. I would've been next to her, leaning forward and trying to read the notes. I couldn't imagine myself ever doing what she was able to do – be completely in the moment.

Chapter 92

June 13, 1976 – It's almost dawn when I pull into the driveway and get out of my car. The backdoor light is on. So is the light in the den. I'm carrying my tuxedo jacket. I can't wait to take off my shoes, get undressed, and go to bed. The backdoor is unlocked and I go inside. I walk into the den and my father is slumped forward in his reclining chair. I go over and lean him back. He looks gray. His chest is moving, but his breathing is shallow. The front of his shirt is soaked with saliva. I put the palms of my hands against his cheeks, but he doesn't respond. There isn't time for an ambulance.

I ran outside and pulled my car as close to the house as I could. I opened the passenger door and left the motor running, and I ran back into the house. He weighed more than I did, but I got his chair out to the patio. Then I pushed and dragged it the rest of the way to the car.

I was dripping with sweat by the time I tried to pull him out of the chair. I couldn't get him up at first, but I finally turned around and got on my knees in front of him. I put his arms over my shoulders, and I held him against my back while I stood up and pivoted around. He groaned when I was wrestling him into the car.

When I made it to Baptist Hospital less than twelve minutes later, he was still alive. After he was wheeled away by the trauma team, I went back home. Mother was just waking up. I was still wearing my shirt and my tuxedo pants. She probably thought I wanted to tell her about the Swan Ball. She was sixty and she'd known death since she was eleven, and I saw the sadness in her eyes when I told her what happened.

My father was still in the trauma unit when we got to the hospital. It was mid-morning before a doctor came out to talk to us. He said my father was in stable condition, and that the next seventy-two hours would be critical.

A couple of days later I was in his hospital room and he was sleeping. I was trying to block out the sound of his heart monitor. I watched him breathe, and while I was studying his face I saw the way he would look when he was lying in his casket. I was tired of thinking about how soon that could be, and I started writing.

The Pilot

Just before it shot into view,
He had heard it drone and rattle
Behind him,
And as two lines of bullets
Hissed toward his jeep,
He dove out
And scrambled behind a tree.
By the time it turned
And came for him again...
By then he was out of its path.
When the cockpit flashed by
He saw a streaming white scarf
And a pair of goggles,
And on the face of the pilot
Was an expression
He could not interpret.
He would hear the rattle again
As he moved through a war-ravaged city,
And when he lay in a sweltering hospital room,
And in the dreams and half-dreams

Of three more decades of living.
He sensed it circling above him
When his hair was turning gray,
And from time to time he has wondered
How long it would be
Before it made
Its final descent.
He has imagined seeing
It glide in for a landing,
And then watching as the pilot
Steps out onto the wing,
Adjusts his scarf,
And begins to remove his goggles.

The cardiologist wouldn't make a long-term prognosis. After nine days my father came back home. He was in good spirits, or at least he pretended to be. Mother didn't say anything, but I knew she wasn't only worrying about him – she was worrying about me. She was worrying about what I'd do when they both were gone. There were times when I thought about that, too.

A nurse stopped by every morning for a week, and then she gave him the go-ahead to start working half-days. Before long he was back to his old schedule, but he was still weak and I wondered how much stronger he'd get.

There wasn't any reason to stay at home, and I went back to doing research at the State Library. One day at the end of June I went into a little downtown market and called the number Mike Higgins gave me. When I asked for Melinda I expected to get the usual response – that she wasn't home. But the woman who answered said to call back the next day. Then she asked if I would be sleeping at home that night. As soon as I answered, she hung up.

The next afternoon I drove about forty miles west of Nashville.

I made my call from a gas station near a little town called Charlotte and asked for Lisa. All the woman said was, "under the front seat." Before I could ask if she meant the front seat of my car, she hung up.

I went back to my car and felt around under my seat, but all I found was a comb and the receipt from the motel where I'd stayed in San Raphael, when I was on my way up to see Ann. But when I reached under the seat on the passenger side, there was an envelope. There was a piece of paper inside. "At 7 PM on the Fourth of July, be where you were picked up the last time you saw me." The message was typed and it was signed, "Uncle Douglas."

July 4, 1976 – It's just before seven on Sunday evening. It isn't as hot as it usually is on the Fourth of July. It feels more like early May. Only a few cars are in the lot behind Belle Meade Theater. All the President's Men is still showing. It's the two-hundredth anniversary of the founding of the nation, and I wonder how many of the people watching the movie tonight came to make a political statement.

I have no idea what Mike is about to tell me. I've been running through all sorts of possibilities. It seems like more than two years since the last time I stood out here in the parking lot waiting to be picked up. An older car is coming toward me. I would've recognized Fats sooner if he'd been in his Cadillac. He gives me a big smile and nods toward the front seat. "Hey, man. Climb on in." I feel like I'm a character in a movie.

Even though the windows were down, there was the distinct smell of just-smoked marijuana in the car. Fats started driving toward town on Harding Road, but he was stoned and we were only going about twenty miles an hour. We passed three churches before we went a mile. Fats stared at each one we went by, and he finally spoke up. "Man, y'all sure got you some big-ass churches out in here."

The main Independence Day event in the city was taking place in Centennial Park, and before long we were in heavy traffic. I assumed we were going to Tiny's place, but instead of turning left toward Tiny's, Fats kept going straight. By then the traffic had almost come to a standstill.

The crowd was filling up the big grassy area in front of the replica of the Parthenon, and people were still streaming into the park. Even though the stage was pretty far from the street, we could hear the Nashville Symphony performing *It's a Grand Old Flag*. Fats turned up the radio until all we could hear was *Give Up the Funk*.

We got through the worst of the traffic, and Fats turned left and then he turned left again, which took us back toward the park. He pulled in behind an office building. After he turned off his engine, he reached down and handed me an envelope. "Tiny said give you this."

There was another typed note from Uncle Douglas inside. He wanted me to walk around the park until the fireworks display got going. Then I was supposed to go to the obelisk near the lake. A blue 1972 Impala would be parked nearby with a newspaper on the dashboard. I was to get in the front seat on the passenger side and wait. I put it back inside the envelope and opened the door.

When I asked if I owed him any money, Fats gave me a big grin. "Naw man. We still good. Tiny got it."

After I wandered around for a few minutes I saw Allen Charles, the guy who was the youth minister at my church back in the 1960s. He and his family were sitting on a big blanket in the grass. After he left the church, he went into the antique business. He seemed a lot happier than he was the last time I saw him. A few months back I'd read a story about him in the newspaper.

He started an educational foundation that was dedicated to preparing poor children for school. He was telling me about it, and then he smiled. He said that leaving the church made it a lot easier to lead a Christian life. I looked at Allen sitting on the blanket with his family. I wondered if I'd ever have a wife and a child or two, and what it would be like to sit in a park with my family and watch fireworks on the Fourth of July.

After a few minutes, I went over to the Parthenon. It was one of the best-known structures in Nashville. It was a replica of the monument to the goddess Athena in Athens, and it supposedly looked the way the original structure had looked during the height of Greek civilization. Generation after generation of city leaders, usually claiming to be great admirers of ancient Greek culture, insisted on referring to Nashville as "the Athens of the South."

As far as I was concerned, with the way the city kept tearing down historic buildings and destroying neighborhoods, what connected Nashville to Athens didn't have anything to do with culture. At some point, I wanted to write a letter to one of the newspapers and point out that the only real connection between Athens and Nashville was that they were both located near places called Sparta.

Chapter 93

I walked around the Parthenon a couple of times. When it was getting dark, I went down to Lake Watauga, which was a lot closer to being a pond than a lake. I saw the blue Impala, and a few minutes later the symphony started playing again. When the first rocket exploded, I went over and got in the car. The interior light didn't come on. The car was facing the Parthenon, and I had a pretty good view of the fireworks.

I listened to the *Battle Hymn of the Republic*, and after about five minutes the driver's side door opened and Mike Higgins got in. The flash of a rocket illuminated his face. He had a short beard and he'd lost some weight. All he said was, "Hold on a minute."

Mike stared into the rearview mirror like he was waiting for a signal. The symphony went into *Stars and Stripes Forever,* and every time a rocket went off, I caught a glimpse of his face. I saw the scar from the wound he'd gotten in Korea, and I saw his eyes. He looked tense. He must've finally seen whatever he was waiting for, and then he turned toward me.

He didn't ask me how I'd been doing. "I'll only be here until the fireworks are over. I need to leave with the crowd, so I'll get straight to the point. A lot has changed since I saw you at Tiny's. I'm going to tell you some things and you'll have to decide if you think I'm telling the truth and if I'm sane. And then you'll have to decide if you want to stay involved in this."

Mike put both hands on the steering wheel and stared through the windshield. "I'll start by telling you a little more about what's in the packet I gave you. It has copies of affidavits related to the conspiracy surrounding the Kennedy assassination. And now I have a lot more evidence. It'll take too long to explain the significance of everything in the packet and how it all fits together, but I'll give you an idea of what I've been working on."

I was looking at Mike most of the time, but I glanced up at the fireworks when they went off. There wasn't any wind and the smoke from the previous rocket was illuminated by the next rocket. I heard him exhale and he started speaking more slowly.

"Like I already told you, what happened in Dallas never smelled right. First, there was the president's Secret Service detail. Why didn't they secure the buildings along the route? Why were they operating with only a partial crew? And what about the president's head wound? Every doctor and every nurse in Parkland Hospital who saw Kennedy described the same injury – a massive *exit* wound in the *back* of his head.

"I've talked to a lot of those people. There are eleven sworn statements in the packet, and they all say that the wound in the president's head indicated that he was shot from the front. And I talked to a few witnesses who were close to the motorcade. They said the same thing – that at least some of the shots came from the front. That means that Oswald, even if he was a shooter, wasn't the only shooter."

He didn't say anything for a few seconds. *The 1812 Overture* was being played, and several rockets went up and exploded all at once. I looked out at the upturned faces of the people in the crowd.

"And most of the witnesses said something else. They said that the presidential limousine slowed down and stopped, or nearly stopped, when the shootings took place. And two days later an armed civilian was allowed to just walk up and kill the most notorious murder suspect in American history? I knew those things couldn't all be coincidental, and I was just scratching the surface. No notes were taken and no recordings were made during the interrogation of Lee Harvey Oswald. Why not?

"All those eyewitnesses in Dallas reported that there was a gaping wound in the back of the president's head, but the military doctors who conducted the autopsy in Washington swore that he'd been shot from the back. There turned out to be missing photographs and x-rays from the autopsy. And the windshield of the Presidential limousine was removed and destroyed before it could be examined.

"Somebody has to believe that *all* those things are coincidental to think that the assassination of President Kennedy wasn't engineered by officials at the highest levels of the government. And that's still just the tip of the iceberg. Other things would also have to be coincidental."

I saw Mike tense up. I looked in the mirror above the dashboard. A man was walking up behind the car, and he was moving pretty slowly. Mike didn't say anything until the man was gone. I noticed how cool it was getting.

"By the time I saw you at Tiny's, I'd gone to a lot of places besides Dallas. I went to Washington to see an old friend of mine who was an agent. I'll call him Hal. Hal wanted me to meet Frank O'Neill and Jim Sibert. They were in the room representing the FBI during the autopsy.

"O'Neill changed his mind at the last minute and canceled, but I talked to Sibert. Even though he showed up, Sibert didn't want to talk to me either. At first, he wouldn't say much, but he finally confirmed that Kennedy was shot from the front.

"He said the wound in Kennedy's throat was definitely an entry wound. But he'd been ordered to say it was an exit wound. He told me that before the doctors enlarged it, the hole wasn't any bigger than the circumference of a pencil. I asked him if he would come with me and make a notarized statement, but he wouldn't do it. Hal finally got him to agree to do something else.

"Hal wrote down what Sibert said he observed during the autopsy and what he was ordered to say. Sibert read through it and signed it, and then Hal and I signed it as witnesses. We both gave Jim our word that we wouldn't release it without his permission. A copy of that is in the packet, too.

"And when I saw you at Tiny's I'd already been to Chicago. I went there to see Abraham Bolden. He was a Secret Service agent. President Kennedy was scheduled to attend the Army-Navy football game at Soldier's Field on the first Saturday in November 1963, but an informant got word to the authorities that there was going to be an assassination attempt.

"Bolden had information that four snipers were in Chicago and that they were planning to shoot Kennedy at an overpass on the expressway while his motorcade was on the way from the airport to Soldier's Field. Bolden was one brave son-of-bitch. He was too honest to stay quiet. He ended up getting framed for a crime he didn't commit, and he spent some time in prison. He'd been discredited, and even though he was still in danger when I talked to him, we went to a notary. His affidavit is also in the packet."

I didn't want to believe what Mike was saying, but I believed him. He didn't go into how much planning there would've been, or how many people would've had to be involved. He didn't need to. The symphony was performing a medley of songs from the armed forces, and they were in the middle of the Marine Corps Hymn.

"I backed off for a while, and then last year the Zapruder film was shown on television. When the bullet hit – when I saw the president's head go straight back – I knew I had to get involved again. I'd been lying pretty low for a while, but I made another trip to Washington.

"I had another lead from Hal, and we went to see a guy named Dino Brugioni. He was an old Air Corps guy during World War Two, and after that he was in the CIA. We knew three or four of the same people. He ended up working for NPIC, the National Photographic Interpretation Center, which is a CIA operation.

"I'd already talked it over with Hal, and we both thought that with all the evidence tampering there was, the film might've been altered, too. Dino was a straight-up guy. He'd kept his mouth shut for all those years, but it was like he'd been waiting for somebody to ask him about what happened. It seemed like he was getting something off his chest.

"On the day after the assassination, a couple of Secret Service agents showed up with the film. Dino was the duty officer. He watched it three or four times before it was altered, and he was very clear on what he saw. He said that in the original version of the film, the limousine came to a stop. He also said that when part of the president's skull got blown away from the back of his head, it was clearly visible on the film."

The symphony started playing *the Star Spangled Banner* and a long salvo of rockets cut into the sky.

"Dino gave me an affidavit, but I promised to keep it private until he authorized me to release it. Dino knew, just like Jim Sibert had known, that if I went public without his permission I'd be cutting my own throat. If somebody kicked down either one of their doors in the middle of the night, it wouldn't be long before somebody kicked down my door, too."

The fireworks exploded in a grand finale above the Parthenon, and there was a long round of applause. Some people were already leaving the park, and Mike started talking faster. "Like I said, things have changed since the last time we talked. I have a lot more to tell you, but there isn't enough time to do it here."

I wanted to hear what else he had to say. "When do you want to do it?"

"It needs to be tonight."

"Are we going back to Tiny's place?"

There was enough light to see Mike shaking his head. "No. We need to go someplace I've never been. You'll understand when I tell you everything. They don't know where I am, and I'm going to keep it that way."

Chapter 94

July 5, 1976 – It's a little past midnight. I've been standing in the shadows by the basement door of Woodmont School since 10:30. I walked here from home after I got back from Centennial Park. The hedge between the southern side of the school and the house next door is at least twelve feet high, and the door can't be seen from the road.

I keep wondering what I've gotten myself into. The soldiers who ended up in the Confederate Cemetery in Franklin must've been wondering the same thing when they were moving toward the Union breastworks. The sounds of firecrackers and bottle rockets ricochet through the darkness, and a couple of neighborhood dogs start barking.

I wonder which way Mike will come to get here. I'm scared, but I'm more curious than afraid. I don't know what could have gotten him so spooked. The dogs finally quiet down and I start listening to the katydids. Their rhythm is supposed to slow down on cool nights, but they sound like they always sound. I see a shadow moving along the hedge. Mike must've come down the little creek that runs near the edge of the baseball field.

I opened the door and we went down through the basement and then up the steps and into the lunchroom. I'd already told him there wasn't an alarm. He wanted to be near some windows, and I took him around to my fifth-grade classroom. There were streetlights along the road in front of the school, and we could see each other pretty well. The furniture still hadn't been removed, and Mike sat down on the edge of the teacher's desk. I sat where I sat in fifth grade – in a desk on the right side of the second row.

He seemed to relax a little, but he glanced out the window every time a car went by. "Things are a lot more dangerous than they were. The month after I came back from talking to Dino Brugioni in Washington, I started to feel like I was being watched. It was just an instinct, but something didn't feel right.

"I looked around for bugs, and I finally found a tracking device attached to the frame of my car. It was next to the right engine mount. I left it there for a couple of months, and then I disappeared." Another car drove by and he stopped talking.

"Do you know who put it there?"

"I'll get to that in a minute. But first, you've got to know what you're involved in. Two years ago, when you and I were in the back room at Tiny's, I told you about the friend I called Lou, and how much I trusted him. After he'd been underground for a while, he came up for air. But then – after a few months – he went dark again.

"I still haven't heard from him. I don't know if he's hiding, or if he's a corpse. Right now you're still invisible. The best way for you to *stay* invisible is to shake hands with me and wish me luck, and then walk out of here and go home."

I was somewhere between nervous and scared.

"I've told you this before, but you need to understand, you *really* need to understand, that the world isn't the way it seems to be." He stood up and reached into his hip pocket. He pulled out a small flashlight and a photograph. We moved away from the window. He turned on the flashlight and shined it on the photograph. It was a picture of me and Martha Kaufman talking in front of the Van Gogh at the Swan Ball.

My mind was racing. I tried to slow down and think.

Mike was staring at me. "How do you think I got this?"

There were a few pieces I was trying to put together. "Well somebody was watching me. And whoever took the picture already knew I'd be at the ball, so unless Carla was involved, I guess my phone was bugged."

Mike was nodding. "It was me. I've been keeping tabs on you.

It had to be done. I needed to know if you were associating with anybody who would raise any red flags. I needed to know if you were under surveillance. There are a lot of ways to get on some agency's radar. I was pretty sure you weren't selling drugs or anything like that, but I had to know who you saw on a regular basis.

"A member of my team was already monitoring you, and then he started keeping tabs on your friend Carla Thompson. She had a marijuana bust in California and another one in New Mexico, and she's done a lot of international traveling. If she was on somebody's list when you showed up, you might've been put on the list, too. Anyway, that's how I found out you were going to the Swan Ball."

Another car went by and he watched until it disappeared over the rise. "Taking her to the Swan Ball wouldn't have been so bad, but damn if the illustrious Armand Hammer wasn't the guest of honor." He was shaking his head. "I couldn't believe it. He's on *everybody's* list.

"His father was one of the founders of the communist party in America. He's been working with the Russians for decades. I got briefings on him back when I was an operative. And after that, a few days after the party, your friend Carla called his office. He was out of town, but there's no way my people were the only ones listening in on that call.

"And then she left the country. I doubt if anybody was keeping up with her before, but they're watching her now."

"Does that mean I'm on a list, too?"

"You could be. But all you did was meet Hammer. And by the way, there's a chance that the woman with you in the photograph is a CIA agent."

I felt like an idiot.

Mike saw me shake my head. "What's wrong?"

"Leave it to me to write a poem to an undercover agent. I thought she needed help. You really think she's an agent?"

"I'm not sure, but wouldn't surprise me. At least I don't have to ask what was in the envelope you gave her." I was pretty sure I saw a quick smile. "You shouldn't be too hard on yourself. She probably appreciated the poem. And when it comes to your girl, Carla, they probably aren't too interested. They might poke around a little, but then they'll move on. Her name will end up in a report in a file cabinet somewhere, and that'll be it.

"The photograph was taken by a friend of mine. He was one of the waiters. He used to do undercover work for the police. I've known him since the old days in North Nashville. Anyway, I brought along the photograph to help you understand the way things are."

He was quiet for a few seconds before he took a deep breath. Then he slowly let it out. "I doubt you're on anybody's list. And like I said, if you want to keep it that way, you need to walk away now. If you need a little time ..."

I was already imagining myself slipping past sentries and making my way into enemy territory. "I don't need more time. A few hours ago, when we were at the park, you were talking about the assassination and all the evidence you've found about a conspiracy. You told me that was only the tip of the iceberg. I want to hear about the rest of the iceberg."

"Okay. And you'll still be able to change your mind – no questions asked."

Mike sat on the edge of the desk and what he told me spread out like ripples on the surface of a pond. "I hoped that the congressional investigations were going to blow the lid off everything. I got some of the evidence about the killing of President Kennedy to the Church Committee. I wanted to see if they were serious.

"I don't know if they followed up on what I sent or not. It might have seemed like a serious investigation, but it could've just been an extension of the cover-up. They mostly released information that couldn't have been concealed for too much longer anyway. And none of it exposed who was behind the assassination.

"I can't prove it, but I'd bet everything I have, including my life, that everything leads at least to the top of the CIA, which means to Allen Dulles. He was still running everything – even after Kennedy fired him. A cover-up that massive *couldn't* have been executed without Dulles. People whisper about Johnson being behind the assassination, or that Hoover was directly involved, but I doubt that they were.

"Read up on Dulles sometime. He was a power-hungry sociopath. Read about back when he was a Wall Street lawyer. It won't take you long to come across his relationship with the Nazis. And he ended up basically running the Warren Commission. Dulles was one sick bastard, and his inner circle – guys like David Phillips and Jim Angleton and Ed Lansdale – they were right in there with him."

He was staring out the window. "And I'm fairly sure the trail doesn't end with Dulles. He'd been serving the highest echelon of Wall Street financiers since back in the 1930s. I don't know if he was following orders or if he just had to get permission, but I'd really be surprised if he violated the chain of command.

"Nobody will ever prove where the trail actually leads, but by the time Lou resurfaced, he suspected that it led right into the inner circle of the Council on Foreign Relations. Even though the information only came from one source, Lou said the source was highly credible.

"The bigshots in the CFR were Nelson and David Rockefeller, along with Treasury Secretary Douglas Dillon and a few others. I'd heard of the CFR, but after Lou filled me in I spent about a month researching it. I'm not sure, but he might've been right – the Council on Foreign Relations could've been involved.

"According to Lou's source, an enormously valuable mineral deposit had been discovered in a remote part of Indonesia, and the Rockefellers were in position to take control of a massive amount of gold and copper and oil. But Kennedy was a big obstacle to what they were planning.

"Trying to make peace with the Soviet Union, and laying the groundwork to pull out of Vietnam, made Kennedy enough of a target. But the strategy that Dulles put together to give the Rockefellers control over all those Indonesian resources couldn't succeed if the faction Kennedy supported stayed in power."

Mike was trying to control his anger, but I could hear the emotion in his voice. "Things will keep trickling out over the next thirty or forty years. At some point, after they're all dead, maybe people will finally get to read all about how Dulles and his henchmen used the CIA to do things like murder Patrice Lumumba and Dag Hammarskjold.

"And they're just part of a long list. America should be a blessing for the world, but the Wall Street oligarchy, along with Dulles and all their other employees, has turned that blessing into a curse all across the world."

I went ahead and asked the obvious question. "Why did they do it?"

"For all the usual reasons. For Dulles it was power. For people like the Rockefellers – if they were involved – it was for more money and even more power. When corporations get big enough, they operate like empires and the men who run them act like kings.

"Remember when we were at Tiny's, and I told you about how the CIA overthrew President Arbenz in Guatemala? Like I think I said then, that was Guatemala being invaded and conquered by the United Fruit Company.

"The year before that, in 1953, Western oil interests used the CIA to conquer Iran. The Congo was conquered by Western mining interests in the same way in 1961. That's what happened in Indonesia in 1966. All Dulles ever had to do was claim that he was fighting communists. As soon as he said that, the politicians would just wag their tails and go lie down in the corner.

"And when Kennedy was murdered in 1963, it wasn't the CIA attacking another country – it was an element within the CIA attacking the United States of America. Dulles is dead, but Angleton and Phillips and Lansdale are still around. And so are plenty of other guys just like them – and they're still betraying the country. I don't know if it'll make any difference, but I have to fight back."

I didn't know what to say.

"When they killed Kennedy there was too much circumstantial evidence to cover everything up, but they did manage to wipe away their fingerprints. Individuals inside the CIA are still working for global corporations, but I think I might've found a way to slow them down.

"When he came out of hiding, Lou connected me with a former agent who was part of a bogus operation before he retired. The operation had been in place for years, and I'm almost positive it's still active.

"The agent was a surveillance officer, and he was assigned to monitor designated American scientists. He was told that he was part of a team working to keep sensitive information from being passed to the Soviets or the Chinese, or any other foreign government. Our secrets have been stolen plenty of times before. Foreign agents identify a leading scientist, and after they do something like set up a compromising sexual liaison, they follow it up with blackmail.

"Anyway, the CIA agent did things like record phone calls and read mail and plant bugs and listen in on conversations. One of the scientists he was monitoring was a young physicist named Robert Asberry, who was also a brilliant mathematician.

"Both of Asberry's parents were involved in the Manhattan Project, and he was working in the field of quantum physics. From his phone calls, it sounded like he might've made a breakthrough. The agent put that in his next report, and two months later Asberry was dead."

More fireworks crackled in the distance.

"The death seemed suspicious to the agent. And it seemed even more suspicious after he connected a few dots. Dr. Asberry lived alone out in the country, but his body was found in his bathroom with his feet against the door. And the door was closed.

"The first question the agent had was why the bugs he planted in the house all went dead a few days earlier. His second question was why a man would close the bathroom door when he was living all alone out in the middle of nowhere.

"While the agent was monitoring him, Dr. Asberry made several calls to a self-taught inventor named Kermit Anderson. Anderson had developed some new type of engine, and Asberry was talking about combining his technology with what Anderson invented. Right after Asberry died, Kermit Anderson disappeared. The agent had been listening in on Anderson for months. He didn't believe that he had just disappeared.

"The agent was suspicious, but before long he got a completely different assignment. A year or so later he found out that one of the other scientists he had been tracking was dead. The guy had been working on a synthetic fuel. He was attending a conference in Mexico City, and his body was found in the bathroom of his hotel room. With the door closed."

"The agent saw what was happening and he wanted to quit, but he was afraid of drawing attention to himself. So he just kept working."

I still didn't know what Mike wanted me to do.

He walked over to the window. "When I talked to the agent, he told me the name of his supervisor. I did some digging around, but I didn't get anywhere. Then Lou got on it. It took him a while, but not long before he went dark, he found out that the agent's supervisor answered directly to Jim Angleton. Lou and I both had the same thought.

"When a scientific breakthrough was identified that would cut into the profits of the wrong corporation, a team at the CIA – a cell of rogue agents – would be activated. Certain corporations have developed close relationships deep inside the CIA. There's nothing like a little irony. Jim Angleton was the Chief of Counter-Intelligence. What better choice than the Chief of Counter-Intelligence to order the killing of especially intelligent scientists from time to time?"

He kept looking out at the street. "Here's why I'm telling you all this. Kermit Anderson eventually turned up. He's just thirty miles from Nashville – in the psychiatric ward of the VA Hospital in Murfreesboro. He was there for several years, but three months ago he was moved out of the psych ward. He was put in a part of the hospital complex that's a cross between a retirement home and a nursing home. I don't know how they keep him from running away, but he isn't on a secure floor.

"They may have lost interest in him, but I doubt it. Maybe I set off an alarm when I went to see Dino Brugioni. It was right after I talked to him when things started feeling different. But Brugioni didn't have any connection to the scientists. I don't know who's tracking me, but I've ended up on somebody's list.

"Maybe there's a team keeping an eye on anybody trying to investigate the Kennedy assassination, or maybe it doesn't have anything to do with Kennedy. Maybe it's just about the operation that's been killing the scientists. But I think it could be both. Anyway, I keep having the same thought. The same operation behind killing the scientists, could've been behind killing President Kennedy.

"And I think whoever is running that operation could be setting a trap. I think they might be dangling Anderson out there to see if anybody bites. Why else would they suddenly make it so easy to get to him?" He looked at me and there was a change in the tone of his voice. "It would be taking a big risk, but somebody needs to talk to Kermit Anderson. You already know why it can't be me."

Chapter 95

Mike took a step away from the window. "I need somebody I trust. Somebody who can't be connected to me or Lou or anybody else who's been involved in any of this. I need somebody with a profile that's as far from espionage as possible. Somebody with a profile like yours. Never served in the military. Lives with his parents. Doesn't have a job. Coaches kids.

"Somebody needs to go to Murfreesboro and try to get information from Kermit Anderson. But our deal hasn't changed. Don't get involved unless it's something you're willing to do – unless it's something you feel like you *need* to do.

"And there's a chance he isn't even being monitored. There's a chance that he just happened to lose his mind within a few days of Dr. Asberry's death. It's possible that's why he was committed, but you'd have to assume that somebody is watching everything he does and listening to every word he says."

There was something I didn't understand. "What do you want to find out from this guy?"

"I'll get into that in a minute, but there are a couple of things you should understand first. There's a lot you don't need to know – things you're better off not knowing. I'll just say that I have connections inside the CIA. They've known that a smaller CIA has been working inside the CIA for a long time.

"My friends think it's a cancer, but they can't make any moves until they have enough information to work with. If they can identify the leaders of the cell, those leaders will be arrested and interrogated. Then, if it can be determined that they were behind both the killing of the scientists and the killing of President Kennedy, the whole conspiracy behind the assassination in Dallas might finally be uncovered.

"But there are always concerns about moles. My friends want as much done outside of the Agency as possible. That's where I come in.

"You asked me what I want to find out from Kermit Anderson. One thing is a statement about what happened to him. I also need information about his engine, and what he and Dr. Asberry were working on together.

"If their project was a major breakthrough, that would reveal a clear motive for the killing of Dr. Asberry and the kidnapping of Mr. Anderson, and it would make the connection between the CIA and any corporation that was involved easier to establish. The more information there is, the stronger the case against the cell will be.

"And if Anderson came up with a breakthrough invention, I want to get the information to DARPA or NASA or to wherever it needs to go. If he made a significant discovery, it shouldn't end up under the control of a corporation that murders American scientists."

I was already wondering how I could get to Kermit Anderson. "Do you think he'll talk?"

"He might if he wants to get back at the people who took away the last few years of his life. But it would take some time. I think the only way he'll open up is if there's a relationship."

I didn't quite understand. "But you talked about setting off alarms. Building up trust will mean making a lot of visits. If he's being watched and I start showing up all the time... Wouldn't alarms be going off all over the place?"

"Yeah. If they're watching him, you'll definitely show up on their radar. But then they'll check you out. They'll look at your school records and the records from your draft board and anything else they can find. You already know what they'll see. A guy who used a psychiatric evaluation to stay out of the military, and who coaches boys in sports. And like I said, lives with his parents.

"You're so off-profile that if you can come up with a believable cover story, there's a reasonably good chance they'll think you're just a coincidence. But even if they think you're a coincidence, they'll still tap your phone and read your mail and watch you – at least for a while.

He didn't say anything for several seconds. "If Kermit Anderson *is* being watched, his room at the hospital has already been bugged. I'll say this again. You'd have to assume that they're listening to everything you say.

"Every time you're in the hospital, and especially when you're with him in his room, you'd have to stay in character. When you're in his room you'll always have to be exactly who they think you are. You could never ask him about his invention.

"And at least one agent would be stationed inside the hospital. It might be a woman or it might be a man. I'd look for somebody who started working there around the time Anderson was transferred out of the psych ward.

"If you did pick up on somebody watching you, you'd know that Anderson is bait. But even if you thought you knew who it was, you couldn't relax. Sometimes they use decoys. Sometimes they make one agent easier to identify. That draws attention away from the lead agent."

A pack of firecrackers went off not very far away. Mike glanced outside and then he looked back at me. "The trickiest parts will be knowing when to let him know who you are and what you want, and then coming up with a way to get the information without anybody finding out.

"But you couldn't force it. In the end, he'll either be willing to tell you what he knows, or he won't. He'll probably ask you who I am. If he does, you can come up with a false name for me, but go ahead and give him as many answers as you need to give him."

He answered my next question before I asked it. "And you'll have to come up with your own cover story. It'll sink in a lot deeper if you create it yourself. It isn't as hard as it sounds. All you need is a good reason to start talking to him. It has to make sense, and the simpler it is the better. It just can't have anything to do with the work he was doing."

We heard voices from somewhere out in front of the school, and we saw five teenage boys walking up the road. We watched them stop and look back, and then they scrambled a few feet in our direction and hid behind the end of the hedge that ran along the side of the school.

A car was coming and the kids started laughing. One of them lit a match and tossed a large pack of firecrackers out into the street. The firecrackers started exploding right in front of the car, and there was more laughter when they ran back toward the baseball field.

Mike started talking a little faster. "I just have a few more things to tell you. You need to destroy the copies of the evidence I gave you when we were at Tiny's. The originals are in a secure place now. It might not happen for a while, but somebody could get inside your house and start looking around. Make sure you get rid of the packet."

"And there's something I need to make sure you understand. If things look like they're going south – if you get scared – you can't go to the police or the FBI. An hour after you showed up and reported what was going on, the CIA would know about it, too.

"The CIA is plugged into every law enforcement agency in America. The cell will be monitoring every report that comes in from the field. They have people waiting to catch a whiff of anything that could threaten their operation. Going to the authorities would blow up the operation and put a lot of people in danger. I wish I could tell you that the good guys will be waiting to come to the rescue, but they won't be."

He stood up beside the desk. “Are you sure you still want to go through with this?”

“Yes.”

I didn’t answer the question he’d asked. Mike asked me if I *wanted* to try and find out what Mr. Anderson knew. I didn’t *want* to. I was scared and I had no idea how I could pull it off. He should’ve just asked me if I was *going* to do it. That was the question I answered.

All he did was nod. “Then here’s this.” He reached into his pocket and handed me an envelope. “It’s everything the agent could tell me about Kermit Anderson. He’s been off the case for a few years, so there was a lot he couldn’t remember. It isn’t much, but it’s all the background I have. Once you have it memorized, get rid of it.”

Mike told me I should start calling in once a week. He said if everything was okay on my end, to ask for a woman. But if something was wrong, or if I needed to hand off any information, to ask for somebody with a male name.

“If nobody answers the phone, or if whoever answers says the person you asked for is in Mexico, that means there’s a problem on my end. It could mean I’ve gone completely underground, or that I’m being held somewhere. Or it could mean I’m dead.

“If that happens you need to pull the plug on whatever you’re doing with Kermit Anderson. You’ll need to hand off any information you have. You’ll have a telephone number. It’s on a card I’m about to give you. Memorize the number and get rid of the card.

“If you call the contact, use a pay phone. The individual you’d be calling lives in town, but he isn’t home all the time. The best time to call is in the middle of the night. Ask for the ticket office and he’ll know why you’re calling. He’ll set things up from there.

“I’m working with other people, but I’m the only one who knows what you’ll be doing with Kermit Anderson. I’ll be the only person who could give you up, and I don’t plan on letting myself get caught. But even if that happens, I've had a lot of counter-interrogation training. I'd do everything I can to protect you."

He thought that if we needed to meet again, it might as well be back at Woodmont, but I told him the school was scheduled to be torn down. He wanted me to think of another place. I mentioned the Confederate cemetery in Franklin, but he said the sheriff probably went by every night to run off teenagers or anybody else who wasn't supposed to be there.

Then I thought about Willow Plunge. I'd driven by the last time I was with Callie. It had been abandoned for ten years and it was grown up with weeds and underbrush. Mike asked a couple of questions about it, and he said it sounded okay.

We shook hands and I told him goodbye. He went back out through the basement, but I stayed in the school for a while. I walked around and I ended up in my sixth-grade classroom. It was already empty. I remembered too much. I finally went outside and closed the basement door. I was pretty sure I wouldn't be coming back.

It was late when I got home. I stayed up and read through the information the agent compiled on Kermit Anderson. He was born in 1917 near Bethesda, Tennessee. I'd heard of Bethesda. It was several miles outside of Franklin.

After high school, he went to work as a welder, and during World War Two he was a pilot in the Army Air Corps, flying bombers from California and delivering them in Australia. After the war, he was a machinist for a defense contractor, and he came up with his invention toward the end of the 1950s.

The agent only remembered a few details about what Mr. Anderson developed. He had installed his invention on a model helicopter, and when he flew it over an electrical substation, it created some sort of an electronic storm and knocked out the whole facility. That was how the government found out about him. He'd been monitored and agents broke into his apartment to take his invention, but they couldn't find it.

It wasn't a lot to go on. I read through the information a couple of times, and then I tore it up and flushed it down the toilet. I was worn out. I turned out the light, but I couldn't get to sleep. When I finally dozed off, I was thinking about how I could talk to Kermit Anderson without attracting any attention.

Chapter 96

I was tired when I woke up on Monday morning, but I went to the State Library and tried to do some research on Bethesda, and on the Anderson family. Bethesda was down in the southeast corner of Williamson County, about thirty miles from Nashville. The latest available census records were from 1900 – almost twenty years before Kermit Anderson was born.

Just about all I learned was that there were Andersons all over that part of the county. I couldn't get anywhere without knowing who Mr. Anderson's father was, but I poked around and spent several hours going through the microfilm of the Franklin newspaper, the *Review Appeal*. I finally gave up, and I was on my way home when I figured out what I should've been doing.

The next morning I drove to the library in Franklin and talked to the lady at the reference desk. I said I was looking for information about men from Williamson County who served in World War Two. She showed me a big scrapbook full of local newspaper articles from the 1940s. After about half an hour I found what I was looking for. It was an interview with Kermit Anderson's father at the end of 1942, just after his son graduated from flight school in Texas.

Knowing his father's name opened everything up. The courthouse was nearby, and after going through tax records for a few minutes, I found the location of the Anderson family farm. By noon I was a little south of Bethesda at a place called Cross Keys, and looking at the old house where Kermit Anderson grew up.

Over the next few days, I went back to the State Library and learned as much as I could about his family and the surrounding neighborhood. I was looking through a reel of microfilm when I got lucky. I ran across an old newspaper account that might give me a way to start talking to Mr. Anderson. In 1863 a young ex-Confederate soldier named Will Biggers had been killed by a small squad of Confederate cavalrymen. Will Biggers was a resident of Cross Keys.

The following Monday I made the hour drive to the Veterans Hospital in Murfreesboro. The building looked like a nursing home. Inside it smelled like a combination of disinfectant and urine. There was a general mustiness, but the place wasn't as depressing as it could've been.

The program director was a nice woman in her forties. She said she'd been working there for six years. Mike was probably right. Anybody monitoring Kermit Anderson wouldn't have been there that long.

I said I was hoping to do volunteer work with some of the patients, and I told her about the interviews I did with my father. When I was talking about the Battle of Manila, she said she had an uncle who was in the battle. I told her I was hoping to tape record the war experiences of some of the patients, and after I built up enough of an oral history collection, the tapes would be donated to the State Library.

The program director said some of the guys who served in Korea and Vietnam might not be ready to talk about what they'd been through, and that I should probably start with the older patients. Two days later she took me to meet a veteran who was willing to be interviewed. When we were on our way to his room, we went past the patient lounge on the lower floor. A couple of old men were watching the Democratic Convention, and the television was blaring.

The first guy I interviewed was a red-faced man in a wheelchair. His room was cramped and it looked like he hadn't shaved in a week. His name was Mel and he was from Chattanooga. When he was sixteen, he dropped out of high school and started working in a hardware store. The day before he left for boot camp in 1943, he went to work and put in ten hours checking the inventory and washing windows. He fought in North Africa, and he was wounded in Italy.

When Mel was talking about getting back home, I got pretty emotional. It was the middle of the morning when he got to Chattanooga. He went straight to the hardware and put on an apron, and then he filled up a bucket and started cleaning the windows. I kept thinking about how my father felt when he made it back – right before he got sick.

Mel was a nice guy and he told me how much he liked telling his story. Before I left he had me take him down the hall to see a friend of his named Eddie. Eddie fought all the way from the landing on D-Day until the surrender.

By the time I interviewed Eddie two days later, Jimmy Carter was the Democratic nominee. Carter seemed okay, but I had too much else to think about. I liked interviewing Eddie about as much as I liked interviewing Mel. And parts of Eddie's story made me as emotional as what Mel had told me. I felt a little guilty about having an ulterior motive for being there.

The next day I went back to the State Library to look for more information about Kermit Anderson and the area around Bethesda and Cross Keys. When I was going through some issues of the *Review Appeal* from 1959, I came across a photograph of Mr. Anderson and an article about his invention – the Magnetic Ion Motor. Everything seemed a lot more real after that. And even though it wasn't a very good picture, at least I'd gotten some idea of what he looked like.

I went back to the library a couple of days later, and I started talking to a guy who was sitting next to me at a microfilm reader. He worked for the Tennessee Division of Archaeology. His name was Stan Smithson and he was an historical archaeologist.

He was trying to learn about the diets of slaves in the Upper South by analyzing the animal bones around sites where slave cabins had stood. He'd already done excavations at the Hermitage, which was the plantation of Andrew Jackson, and at Belle Meade plantation, which ultimately became the city of Belle Meade.

Stan said that most of the animal bones he and his team recovered were from pigs and cows and sheep, and that the proportion of the bones they found was almost identical in each place. He was looking for a third plantation site to investigate. If the percentages of bones stayed the same, it would support his theory that in the upper South, slaves on large farms were provided with predetermined amounts of pork and beef and mutton. When I told him about the Williams plantation and all the research I'd done, he started smiling.

Three days later I took him to see Miss Young. She was excited about what Stan wanted to do. She gave him a tour of the house, and when we were in the study, I showed him what Willoughby Williams wrote about where slave cabins should be built. He had the same thought that I'd had – that Colonel Williams was describing where the cabins on his plantation stood.

Then we walked out to where Miss Young's backyard began to slope down toward Sugartree Creek. Stan pulled out the trowel he brought along, and squatted down and started scraping up small areas of ground. After a few minutes, he'd turned up several pieces of broken pottery, a couple of buttons, and some small bones. Stan said he found the same sort of debris on the sites of slave cabins at the Hermitage and at Belle Meade.

But he couldn't get started right away. There was a major report he had to finish, and he said it was better to wait for the weather to cool off a little.

It would be a while before the dig got going, and since football didn't open up until the end of August, I started going to the hospital in Murfreesboro almost every day. The more time I spent interviewing the other veterans, the less suspicious I'd look when I tried to talk to Mr. Anderson.

I usually worked in an extra question or two during my interviews. When I was talking to a guy named Morris who fought in Italy, I asked him if he knew of any patients who'd grown up in Middle Tennessee. He said he played cards with a guy who was from Columbia. Columbia wasn't all that far from Bethesda, and when I interviewed the man from Columbia, I asked him if anybody else at the hospital was from the same area.

He didn't say anything for a few seconds. "Well now, there is a guy up on the second floor. Hasn't been here long. Pretty much keeps to himself. Stays in his room most of the time. Seems like I heard he was from somewhere outside of Franklin and that he was in the Air Corps, but I'm not sure."

The next day I went back to see Mel. We talked for a while, and then he got around to telling me how Jesus helped him live through the nightmares he had after he got back from the war. When I was leaving, I said that somebody had told me about a patient who served in the Air Corps and who lived outside of Franklin. He started to nod. "Yeah. I believe his name is Anderson. He doesn't have a lot to say. He lives down at the end of my hall. It's the last room on the right."

On my way home I kept thinking that I should've asked Mel more about Jesus. I'd started praying again, but I didn't feel like my heart was right. There were times when I felt like I was just talking to myself. Sometimes I felt like I was alone. I didn't think I could do what I needed to do if I was alone.

My life was changing too fast. I was starting to feel like I was somebody else. When I told Mike Higgins that I'd go to Murfreesboro, it seemed like the right thing to do. It was a chance to make up for Vietnam, and do something for the country. During the day I thought I'd done the right thing, but at night it was different.

It was clear to me that Mike believed everything he told me, but I'd lie in bed and wonder if what he believed was true. I told myself that he could've made a false assumption along the way. I told myself that he could've reached the wrong conclusion.

I'd go over everything Mike had said. I always ended up thinking he was right, and then the anxiety would flow over me like an incoming tide. I'd lie in bed and worry that I'd back out, or that I'd end up getting thrown into a car and pushed down onto the floor. I imagined getting taken to a room somewhere and interrogated, and what it would be like to know that my life was about to end.

And sometimes when I lay in the dark, after I thought about dying, I thought about my life and what awareness was. I'd been thinking about awareness for as long as I could remember, and the older I got, the more I wondered about it. I had ideas that I hadn't read anywhere – and that I'd never heard anybody else talk about.

Even though I was pretty sure that somebody had already thought of everything I'd come up with, I wanted to write it all down just in case. I wanted to write everything down, but I wasn't sure I'd have time to get it finished.

Chapter 97

Lying awake at night had at least one benefit. It gave me time to plan my next move. I'd seen the same male nurse just about every time I went to the hospital. He smiled at me a couple of times when I passed him in the hall, and I noticed him joking around with the patients. I got the feeling that he'd been there for a while. I was pretty sure he wasn't an agent, but even if he was, it made sense to connect with him. Mel told me the guy's name was Buddy Swanson and that he'd been a corpsman in Vietnam.

When I went back the next time, I made sure I ran into him. I told him who I was and I told him about the oral history project. He knew about the interviews, and he offered to introduce me to several of the older veterans. He said he'd been working at the hospital for nearly five years, and that he'd learned a lot from talking to the men who lived there.

A few mornings later I saw him when he was on his way to lunch. I told him that I had an idea. I asked if I could interview him and record some of the stories he'd heard from veterans, back before they passed away. He got sort of excited, and at lunchtime, I met him in the break room. I spent half an hour recording what he'd heard from an old patient who died three or four months earlier. The guy was 96 and he fought during the Philippine Insurrection, right after the Spanish-American War.

The old man was on Leyte and he helped recover the body of a captured American soldier who'd been crucified upside down and disemboweled by Filipino fighters. After that, his unit went into the closest village they could find. They shot everybody they saw, including women and children, and burned down all the houses. Buddy said it sounded just like Vietnam.

Over the next couple of weeks, I did a few more interviews with Buddy in the break room. It wasn't long before we were telling each other dirty jokes, and we got to be pretty good friends. One Saturday we were talking in the cafeteria, and I saw a girl walking across the room.

Buddy turned around to see what was distracting me. "Oh, that's Elinor. She volunteers on the weekends. Guess how old she is?"

"I don't know – twenty?"

"Not even close. She's about to be a junior in high school. But don't feel bad, she fooled me too."

I just shrugged. God could've been toying with me again.

After I finished recording the stories he'd heard from deceased veterans, Buddy told me about his time in Vietnam. He didn't go into a lot of detail, but he said he was in the middle of a few firefights. He'd never been hit, but guys had died in his arms.

Then he told me about the closest he ever came to dying. A half-track backed over him while he was kneeling beside a wounded Marine. The ground was soft, and he almost suffocated before somebody pulled him up out of the mud.

He was shaking his head. "Getting a scratch from a piece of shrapnel would've gotten me a Purple Heart, but almost drowning in the mud didn't get me a damn thing."

I didn't hide what I did to stay out of the military. I told him about going to see Dr. Harrelson and all the rest of it. I let him know how much I respected what he'd done, and that there were times when I felt ashamed for not serving. He said if he'd known he could stay out of Vietnam by going to see a shrink, he would've done it, too.

He was married and he had a couple of kids, and he invited me to come to his apartment for dinner and meet his wife. It was the night President Ford made his speech at the Republican Convention. Ford was on the Warren Commission and he pardoned Nixon, and I didn't listen to much of what he had to say.

If an agent was there, I was pretty sure it would be somebody who worked close to Kermit Anderson. The most suspicious person I saw was a skinny orderly who wore glasses. He worked on the second floor, and he seemed to be out of place.

August 28, 1976 – It's eight o'clock on Saturday morning and I'm standing beside the Ensworth football field in the shadow of a big maple tree. It's the first day of practice. It's cool for late August. Only a few sixth graders have shown up so far. Inman Roberts called me last night. He let me know that Jones Colbert had been recruiting a few of the best athletes in the fifth grade, along with some of the best sixth graders, to play with Jake in another league.

I've been planning to put Jake at quarterback and safety, and I need a lot of the other kids to have a decent team. If they aren't playing, and it doesn't look like they are, it's going to be a long season. Whiting Caswell is standing next to me. He was the first one here and he's grinning.

Jones Colbert was like a villain in a movie. He was diabolical. Recruiting the best fifth-grade and sixth-grade athletes was a clever way to try and get rid of me. If the boys who played on my team lost every game, they probably wouldn't have a good experience, and that would put pressure on the headmaster to change things. But Jones had dug himself a deeper hole when it came to Ellen Caswell.

After practice, Whiting was out on the field trying to kick a football to Sam Brown. Ellen was sitting in her car and I walked up to say hello. She went straight to what was on her mind.

"I want you to understand that even if Whiting had been invited, he would *not* have played on the other team. He has been looking forward to being with you again ever since the end of basketball season. The issue, what *incenses* me, is that he and several of his classmates, as well as the unathletic sixth-graders, were left out.

"They were not even given the *opportunity* to be on a team with the rest of their schoolmates. They were essentially told they were not wanted." I watched her neck getting red and I could see the anger in her eyes. She had one more thing to say. "I know next to nothing about football, but I'm afraid that you will have very little talent on your team."

She was right. Most of the kids looked pretty soft. If I let my players tiptoe around and avoid contact, they'd get intimidated every time they played on Saturday. By the first game, I wanted them to like running into other kids. There wasn't much time to get them ready, but I had to make them more physical without turning our practices into nightmares.

I decided to use names from North Nashville again, but I thought they should earn their names by overcoming some challenges. Even though I wasn't sure what the challenge would be, I knew a good way to toughen them up while I figured it out. They'd be playing a lot of Smear the Queer. But out of deference to Whiting, I shortened the name of the game to Smear. It was a rough game, and I worried if he and a few of the other kids would be able to deal with the contact.

August 30, 1976 – It's late on Monday afternoon on the Ensworth field. I've divided the kids into teams of four players each, and I've given each team a number. It's our first game of Smear. I call two numbers, and after I kick the ball as far as I can, the kids take off after it. A team wins when one of its members brings the ball back and puts it in my hands. Whiting is running as fast as he can, but he can't keep up. He reminds me of Peter Johnson when he was on my team, but Whiting is even slower than Peter was.

John Stanley gets to the ball first, and just as he picks it up, he gets tackled from behind and the ball comes loose. Matt Knight picks up the ball and two kids from the other team pull him down and start trying to turn him over. Matt's three teammates jump in. They're all in a pile struggling to get the ball. Just about the only things that are illegal are kicking, biting, pinching, punching, clipping, kneeing, elbowing, and grabbing face masks. John finally rips the ball away, but somebody steps on his hand when he's trying to stand up.

A kid I'd never coached before ended up with the ball. His name was David Dobbins. John tried to catch him, but David was too fast. John was tired and frustrated, and it was obvious how angry he was from the way he was moving. Then he saw Whiting.

Whiting was on the other team, and he was standing straight up. Just before David gave me the ball, John crashed into Whiting as hard as he could. Whiting went down hard and started gasping.

His eyes were open twice as wide as they usually were. He was too afraid to cry. He'd never had the wind knocked out of him before, and he thought he was dying. The kids gathered around and I knelt down beside him. Then I put my hands on his helmet and looked up into the sky. I assumed that at least some of them had seen faith healers on television.

"Lord, I beseech you – even though Whiting *did not listen* when I told him not to stand straight up, and even though *I told him to pay attention* whenever somebody was running toward him, I pray that you will *heal* this stricken child! I *beseech* you, Lord, to restore the *breath-uh* to his *body*!" Two or three of the kids were smiling. Whiting looked at me like I was crazy, but by then his breath was coming back. When he sat up, I lifted my hands and let out an evangelical whoop. "It's a *miracle*!"

I gave them all a quick explanation about what happened to the air in Whiting's lungs when he got hit, and then they got back to playing Smear. After a half-hour they were tired and after an hour-and-a-half they were exhausted. But by then Whiting and the other more passive kids had started to figure out that the more aggressive they were, the less they got knocked around.

I was a little surprised when they all showed up at the next practice. I was also surprised that I hadn't gotten any calls from concerned parents. But I noticed Ellen Caswell sitting in her car.

She was at the upper end of the field keeping an eye on what was going on, and a couple of other mothers were watching from their cars, too. After the kids stretched and did their exercises and ran a lap, Whiting was one of the first ones who started chanting, "Smear! Smear! Smear!"

The more veterans I interviewed, the more I liked interviewing. I tried to keep my eyes wide open when I was there. I still thought the only one who seemed out of place was the thin orderly. I'd been up on the second floor plenty of times, but I still hadn't seen Kermit Anderson. There wasn't any reason to keep putting it off, and I decided to go ahead and try making contact with him.

I picked the next man I interviewed because he lived right across the hall from Mr. Anderson. He fought in World War One, but he looked almost old enough to have been at Gettysburg. We went out and sat on the sofa at the end of the corridor. We were only about ten feet from Kermit Anderson's door, and it wasn't long before I saw him.

When the old man was describing a truckload of French soldiers he saw a few hours after they were exposed to chlorine gas, Mr. Anderson came out into the hall on his way to lunch. He didn't look over at us. We were still there when he came back, and after he glanced at the man I was interviewing, he peered over at me.

Kermit Anderson looked a little like the Wizard of Oz would've looked if he didn't have a mustache. His eyes were intense, but he didn't look crazy. He was a lot shorter than he looked in the newspaper photograph. I guessed he was about five foot four.

The next day I was back in the same place, but I was interviewing a different veteran. I smiled at Mr. Anderson when he came back from lunch. He just looked away, went inside, and closed his door.

The day after that I was there again, and he looked at me and nodded as he was going into his room. When he nodded at me again a couple of days later, it was time to talk to him.

I was sitting by myself the following Monday when he came back down the hall after lunch. As soon as he got to his door, I stood up and said hello. He glanced at me when I told him my name, and then he looked away. He looked pretty uncomfortable, but he waited before he went into his room.

He finally decided to speak to me. "Name's Anderson." He spoke slowly and he had a rural accent. He pronounced his name like he'd had a shot of Novocaine in his tongue.

I didn't try to shake hands with him and I tried to sound relaxed. "I'm glad to meet you, Mr. Anderson."

He didn't say anything.

"I've been talking to some of the other men who live here."

He stared at the floor like he was looking for something.

"You've probably noticed me out here with my tape recorder. I've been recording their stories from back when they were in the service."

He shifted his weight but he still didn't go into his room. "I... I figgerd you for a social worker." He didn't sound like a brilliant inventor.

"Well, I guess there are worse things than looking like a social worker. At least you didn't think I was a lawyer." I almost said psychiatrist, but I caught myself just in time.

He glanced at me again and then he looked away. His face seemed a little more relaxed.

I kept talking. "My father was the first person who told me about the war. He was in the Army Air Corps."

Mr. Anderson didn't say anything, but he was listening.

"He ended up in the Philippines, but before that, he was over in Australia."

Mr. Anderson didn't say anything about the times he flew from Long Beach to Australia delivering bombers. He wasn't going through the door I had opened. I started answering questions I wanted him to ask. "I went to high school on the site of a Civil War battle. I've liked history ever since then."

He just kept staring at the floor. I glanced down the corridor a couple of times, but I didn't see anybody watching us.

"I remember wishing that somebody had gone around and talked to those soldiers. I wish somebody had interviewed them about what they went through at the Battle of Franklin."

Mr. Anderson straightened up a little and looked at me for a couple of seconds. I thought he was going to say something, but he stayed quiet.

I went ahead and took a chance. "Were you in World War Two?"

He shifted his feet and stuck his hands in his pockets. "I was just a ferry pilot." His drawl was even slower than before. "Took planes from Long Beach out to Brisbane, Australia. Never was in combat though."

I could tell he was ready to leave. It seemed like I was going down a dead-end road, but I kept going. "Do you remember what you were doing when you heard about Pearl Harbor?"

He gave me a hard look before he gave me an answer. "I expect I was somewhere out back. Prob'ly in the chicken house nailin' up a loose board, or somethin' like that. The news was comin' in on the radio and Daddy called me to the house."

Mr. Anderson turned to go into his room. I had pushed too hard. "Well thank you for talking to me."

He nodded and pushed open his door.

I had one more question. "Oh, I meant to ask you where you were living when the war broke out."

He stopped and looked back at me. There was a frown on his face. "We were out in the country – a little place called Cross Keys."

He made sure I didn't ask him anything else. He went into his room and closed the door behind him.

I sat down on the sofa at the end of the hall. I wanted to look like I was about to have another interview.

Three days later I was waiting for Mr. Anderson when he came back from lunch. I could tell he wasn't happy to see me.

I stood up and held out a copy of the article I'd found in the old newspaper about the Will Biggers killing in Cross Keys during the Civil War. "I ran across this a few weeks ago. I thought you might like to have it."

He didn't say anything. He just took it and went on into his room.

Chapter 98

September 14, 1976 – It's Tuesday morning and I'm with Stan Smithson in Miss Young's backyard. We're standing in the place where he picked up a couple of bones and some pottery and a few buttons the first time he was here. He's pretty sure there were slave cabins located all over this part of Miss Young's property. I watch him measure off a one-meter by one-meter square.

Two other people will be working on the dig. There's a girl from the Division of Archaeology named Karen Jackson, and a guy named Rogers Shaw from the Historical Commission. Karen is cute and has a good body. When she showed up I saw her give the woman who dropped her off a long kiss. Rogers is a nice guy who I've talked to a few times at the State Library. Karen and Rogers are laying out a separate square about twenty yards away, and a little further down the slope.

After Stan and I used shovels to lift sections of sod from the square, we laid them aside and he got to work. He picked up his trowel and began scraping away the dirt, a quarter-inch or so at a time. After he put any visible archaeological material into a plastic bag, he scooped the loose earth into a bucket.

When the bucket was full I took it over and dumped it onto a wire mesh screen that was laid on top of a wheelbarrow. Then I sat on a wooden box and started retrieving what was hidden in the dirt. I ran my trowel across what was on the screen, and the dirt passed through the mesh and dropped into the wheelbarrow.

It wasn't long before whatever was in the dirt was on top of the screen. Along with small rocks and roots and pebbles, and an occasional worm or a beetle, some human-related material would be exposed. It reminded me of fishing.

The first items I found were a nail and some broken pottery, and a small blue bead made out of glass. I put everything I picked up into a plastic bag. As soon as I got through with the bucket from Stan's square, I went over and got buckets from Karen and Rogers.

After an hour and a half, along with fragments of glass and pieces of broken pottery, I came across some bones, a lead ball, three more glass beads, and several pieces of what Stan identified as shards of Indian pottery. It wasn't long before he unearthed the upper torso of a small porcelain doll with both arms still attached.

Miss Young came outside from time to time to look at what we'd found. I offered her my trowel and my seat on the box, but she said her back wouldn't let her do anything but watch. Stan kept excavating and after a couple of feet, he reached the level where there weren't any more artifacts. While he was measuring off another square, I filled up the first square with the dirt that had been screened, and then I replaced the sod.

There weren't many things I would've rather been doing than sit beside the wheelbarrow and look for pieces of the past in the dirt. After the upper torso of the doll turned up, I kept thinking that it could've belonged to one of Willoughby Williams' daughters back before the Civil War. I imagined some wide-eyed little girl picking up her new doll for the first time on a long ago Christmas morning.

The doll was probably a cherished childhood possession, but at some point, it must have been broken, or maybe outgrown. It could've been given to a slave girl, or maybe it was salvaged after it was thrown away. I tried to picture a little black girl playing with the doll, and I wondered what stories she would've made up while she played.

I sat on the box, and while I was screening dirt I thought about what I was finding. And about the kids on my football team. And my parents. A few times I looked over at Karen, and then I'd start thinking about Callie or Claire. Or about Carla. But Kermit Anderson was never too far away. Most of the time he might as well have been sitting a few feet away on a box, watching me run my trowel across the dirt.

September 17, 1976 – It's 5:15 on Friday afternoon and we're having practice at Ensworth. The kids are laughing and talking while they put on the jerseys I've just handed out. The school photographer is waiting to take our team picture. It won't be long before he lines the boys up in rows, and then the shutter of the camera will click and one instant of their childhoods will be preserved. It could be another seventy or eighty years before the last living member of the team opens up his yearbook and looks at the photograph. Before he stares at the faces of boys he knew when he was young.

It was perfect weather for football. We needed to run through our plays and work on our kicking game, but the kids complained whenever they had to stop playing Smear. Our first game was the next morning. I was sure we'd lose, but I didn't think we'd get intimidated. We'd been physical even before I introduced the kids to the challenge they had to overcome before they earned their North Nashville names. The kids called it Crush.

It didn't take them long to get the hang of playing Crush. There were three squads of three blockers each. Their job was to keep a single rusher from getting through them and touching me with both hands. The kid who was trying to get to me had to break through each squad, one at a time. When he got through the first group, the next group would take over, and if the kid could make it through that group, they dropped off and the last group got their turn.

Going through the drill was voluntary, but every kid on the team gave it a try. Only David Dobbins got through on the first day. He just barreled through everybody who got in his way. The only kid who got shaken up was Whiting.

I wondered if the blockers would take it easy on him, and on some of the other kids who weren't very good, but they didn't. They'd been listening when I told them that if they made it less of a challenge, it wouldn't mean anything when a guy got to me.

One or two kids usually broke through every practice, and whoever made it either picked out one of the names I thought up, or came up with a name on his own. Whiting jumped in and took at least one turn every time we practiced, but he only made it past the first squad once. It was a little like watching the Paul Newman character in *Cool Hand Luke* keep getting knocked down during the fight scene.

I'd already told him that the only way he could get to me was to stay low and attack the blockers, and that he had to use his hands and arms and keep moving his feet. And I told him it would help if he went a little bit crazy. I said that unless he was suddenly able to move ten times faster than I'd ever seen him move before, trying to run around the blockers wouldn't work.

But he must've needed to find that out for himself. He started by circling to the right and then he tried to circle around to the left. The longer he went, the slower he moved, and the slower he moved, the more he stood up. It wasn't long before David Dobbins nailed Whiting with a full-speed block. Whiting ended up on his back trying to breathe, but he knew he wasn't dying and everybody clapped for him when he got up.

A couple of days later I went home after practice and ate dinner, and then I drove to Franklin to watch Battle Ground Academy play against Hillsboro. There was an outside chance that I'd see Callie and Claire, but they didn't show up.

I sat by myself on the top row of the stands. I hadn't been to a game at Battle Ground since I was a student, but I didn't pay much attention to the game.

I looked around at all the places where I'd done things, and where things had happened to me. But before long I was imagining the soldiers of Major General Brown's Division moving across the ground that had become the football field. I ended up thinking about my next mission to Murfreesboro, and a poem drifted in like a cloud. I wrote it down as soon as I got home.

The Soldier

The night before,
Moving silently through the darkness,
He was able to elude the pickets.
When morning came,
The sounds of battle
Roared down
From the breastworks
Like a flood.
He stands at the edge
Of the mist-shrouded creek,
And with the dark water
Sliding past him,
He steps back
And launches himself
Toward a sliver
Of exposed bedrock
Several feet out
In the current.
Throwing out his hands,
He comes down
Onto the uneven surface
And goes into a crouch.
He slowly stands up,
And as the shroud
Above the creek
Grows thicker,
He senses that
He is being followed.
He will be easy to track
If his feet touch the water,

And he stares further out
Into the stream,
Searching for the next expanse
Of dry rock.

Our game the next morning went pretty much the way I thought it would. Although the kids were a little unsure of themselves at first, they really started hitting in the second half. Whiting got clobbered a couple of times, but it didn't bother him. He'd been through a whole lot worse in practice. The other team won 25-0, but they looked like they were ready for the game to be over. My kids wanted to keep on playing.

After the game, I went back to Murfreesboro. When I counted the political signs I saw in front yards, there were a few more Jimmy Carter signs than Gerald Ford signs. I found Buddy in the cafeteria, and I sat with him while he was finishing lunch. Mr. Anderson was sitting by himself across the room.

I acted like I hadn't noticed him, but I made sure he saw me when I was leaving. I was relieved when he got up and started walking in my direction. I was going to let him catch up to me at the elevator, but when I walked out into the corridor I almost ran into the girl Buddy had told me about a couple of weeks earlier – the high school student who volunteered at the hospital on the weekends.

She didn't see me coming and she dropped some of the files she was carrying. She looked like she was somewhere between flustered and irritated.

I bent down and started picking up the files off the floor. I acted like I didn't know what they were. "*Oh my God!* These are *official* government records. You should *really* try to be more careful."

She gave me a cool look. "So you're saying it's *my* fault?"

I handed her the files. "Well if you hadn't cut the corner, there would've been more than enough room for me to get by. But I'm not complaining. I don't get too many chances to show off my cat-like reflexes."

She shook her head and looked away, but then she looked back at me. Even though she had a beautiful smile, I stopped myself from flirting with her any more than I already had. Then she told me what I already knew – that her name was Elinor and that she was a volunteer. She never got around to telling me she was still in high school. I would've talked to her a little longer, but Mr. Anderson was waiting for me a few feet away.

He came up as soon as she left.

"Hey, Mr. Anderson. It's good to see you again."

He was withdrawn before, but he started rocking back and forth on the balls of his feet, and his eyes were shining. "I've been wantin' to tell you... about the killin' in that old newspaper story you gave me." He was talking pretty fast, but he still sounded like his tongue was asleep. "Will Biggers he... he and my grandfather, they were first cousins.

"My grandfather died back before I was born, but my grandmother, she told me all about Will Biggers. If you wanta know about the Civil War, well a whole lot happened out there around Cross Keys."

"I want to hear anything you can tell me, but can I get what you're telling me on tape? I'd hate to miss something you said."

"You wanta tape record me?" He stared at me for a second or two. "Well, I guess that'll be alright."

I went out to my car and got my tape recorder, and I was on my way to Mr. Anderson's room when I saw the skinny orderly looking at me. I was pretty sure he was an agent. I thought I might seem a little less suspicious if I got to know him, but when I nodded and smiled, he looked away. I imagined him scurrying off somewhere to listen to what Mr. Anderson and I were about to say.

Chapter 99

Mr. Anderson's room had a bed, a dresser, a mirror, a reclining chair, and a television, and there was a small bathroom. If the hospital orderly was an agent, and if he was listening, all he heard was Kermit Anderson telling me how the Civil War unfolded around Cross Keys. Mr. Anderson must've remembered everything his grandmother ever told him.

He talked about how Nathan Bedford Forrest was born and raised just ten or twelve miles from Cross Keys, and that Forrest knew almost everybody in the neighborhood. Around the time he became a Confederate General, he visited the area and rounded up as many horses as he could for his troops. And there were times when he hid out in a small cave at the head of a hollow near the Anderson home.

I tried to pay attention to the pattern of his eye contact, and the nature of his body language while he was telling me what he knew about the Biggers killing.

"Will was a Confederate. He and his younger brother Lum – they were in the 24th Tennessee Infantry. Their unit was up in Kentucky, but Will got sick and they sent him home. After a year or so, he found out that his brother... Well, one of his brothers had joined up with the Yankees and his unit was over in Franklin. Will rode over to see him. They visited for a while, and then Will went on back home.

"It wasn't many days after that when some fellas from General Van Dorn's escort company showed up at the Biggers house. Van

Dorn had just been killed down in Spring Hill by Dr. Peters. Van Dorn was... you know, foolin' around with Mrs. Peters. Her husband, Dr. Peters... he shot General Van Dorn in the head, and Van Dorn's men went out looking for somebody to take it out on.

"They rode over to Cross Keys and found Will, and they took him up Pulltight Hill and shot him all to pieces. They claimed he was a spy because somebody saw him in Franklin talking to the Yankees. He was just twenty-two.

"His younger brother Lum was a Confederate, and even though Van Dorn's men were Confederates, Lum had a notion to find out who was in on killin' his brother. Then he'd start takin' care of 'em one at a time. But he knew that as soon as he got the first one or two, the rest would've been on him. They would've come and hunted him, and if they couldn't find him, they might've killed his family.

"A lot of people around Cross Keys and Bethesda were mad about what happened to Will. Well, Lum... what he did was join up with the Union. He ended up recruiting a mess of folks to fight for the Yankees. But that wasn't the end of it. My grandmother wasn't sure how he did it, but by the end of the war, Lum had found out who did the killin'. It took him awhile, but he ended up gettin' three or four of the men who murdered his brother."

When I gave the article to Mr. Anderson, I was trying to connect with him. I was just hoping he'd open his door a little bit. I didn't expect him to open it all the way. I hadn't thought that I'd end up sitting in his room for three hours. I got the feeling that it had been a long time since he talked to anybody.

My brain was spinning way too fast that Friday when I was on my way home. I kept watching a car in my rearview mirror. I was pretty sure it was following me. I felt like I was a character in a movie. It was like I was in a deserted old house, and I'd heard a noise behind me while I was walking up a creaking staircase. I wondered if Will Biggers thought somebody was following him back in 1863, when he was on his way home from visiting his brother in Franklin.

The car finally turned off onto a side road, but my imagination kept spinning around like a ride at the state fair. Mr. Anderson kept going by in a blur. Sometimes he was an old farmer and sometimes he was a wizard, and there were times when people without faces were standing behind him.

I still hadn't figured out how to get what I needed without getting caught, and I was tired of thinking about it. I was listening to the radio, and *Lowdown* and *Magic Man* and *Still the One* and *Play That Funky Music* and *Say You Love Me* swirled together, and I felt like I was hearing them from inside a tornado.

The tornado didn't slow down until I heard Buddy Holly singing *That'll Be the Day*. It had been a while since I thought about the plane crash that killed him and Richie Valens and the Big Bopper. I remembered when I heard about it. I was in the sixth grade at Woodmont, and I was eating in the lunchroom.

I was calmer by the time I got back to Nashville, but I couldn't fall asleep. I kept thinking about what could happen to me because of what I was doing in Murfreesboro. After a couple of hours, I turned on the light and got out of bed.

If anything happened to me, I wanted to leave something behind for my parents. I wanted to write something that would help them understand the way I saw the world. I sat there for five hours, but I only came up with a few disjointed sentences. It was like when I was a student back at Vanderbilt.

September 21, 1976 – It's Tuesday morning and I'm working in Miss Young's backyard. It rained yesterday, but the skies are clear and it feels like late October. Stan is talking to Miss Young, and I'm kneeling at the edge of his square. I scrape over a clump of dirt with my trowel, and I notice a shiny white surface. I expect that it's another piece of pottery, but it turns out to be the legs and the lower part of a porcelain doll. I go over and sort through the bags from last week. I find the one I'm looking for, and I take out the doll's torso. The two pieces of the doll came from squares that are twenty feet apart, but the pieces fit together perfectly.

A news van from Channel 5 showed up a few minutes after I went back to work. Stan thought one of the neighbors must've seen what we were doing and tipped off the station. He didn't look happy about it, but he got up and talked to the reporter. After a quick interview, the reporter and the cameraman started filming what we were doing.

If I was under surveillance, being interviewed at an archaeological dig and showing up on the news would help my cover story. The reporter looked like she was around my age and she was fairly good-looking. Karen stared at her when she was on her way over to talk to me.

The reporter wanted me to keep working while she was interviewing me, and the cameraman filmed me talking about Willoughby Williams and the house, and about some of the slaves. She seemed interested in what I was saying. I wondered if I should ask her out, but she was a lot less friendly when the camera stopped rolling.

She went over and started talking to Stan again. I noticed Karen grinning at me, and she started laughing when I gestured toward the reporter with both of my hands like it was her turn to take a shot.

I'd told Mr. Anderson when I was coming back, and on Wednesday morning he was waiting on the sofa at the end of the hall. He said there were a bunch of things he forgot to tell me. I saw the skinny orderly out of the corner of my eye when I followed Mr. Anderson into his room.

I turned on my tape recorder, and for the next hour, he gave me an even more detailed account of what his grandmother told him about life around Cross Keys during the Civil War. Then he started telling stories that went back into the 1830s, when his great-grandfather built a stone house not too far from Pulltight Hill.

I was trying to pay attention to his eyes and to the way he held himself while he was talking. I noticed a difference when he was talking about things that didn't involve his family. When he told me how Pulltight Hill got its name, he looked away more often and his face was more relaxed. He said that the road was steep, and that the leather straps on the horses and mules would tighten up and stretch while they were pulling wagons up to the top of the hill.

It was different when he told me about sleeping in the same bed with his grandmother when he was a boy. His face tensed up and he leaned forward in his chair. There was no electricity in rural Williamson County in the 1920s. Because he was afraid his grandmother would fall down when she went to the privy in the middle of the night, he ran a wire from an old car battery to a light bulb. It was his first invention. He was eight years old.

"My grandmother... well she was tickled to death with what I rigged up. After that, she kept tellin' people that I'd grow up to be a great inventor. She always encouraged me, but she did a lot more than that. She taught me things. She taught me all about astronomy. Sometimes in the summer, we'd sleep outside. We'd lie out in the pasture and make up stories about planets in other solar systems. We looked up at the stars and we'd talk till we fell asleep."

A short visit would've been easier to understand for whoever might've had us under surveillance, but I stayed so long that he almost missed lunch. Before I walked down to the cafeteria with him, I told him that I had an idea.

I said I'd like to put what he was telling me into a book about where he grew up. He started shaking his head. He said he wasn't interested in writing a book. But when I told him that all he had to do was talk and that he'd still be the author, he started smiling.

We were on our way to the elevator, but before we got there he went over to the nursing station. He said something to one of the nurses, and the nurse nodded. It looked like he had to let somebody know any time he left the second floor. I wondered if he'd been told that they'd take him back to the psych ward if he left the floor without permission.

I didn't go with him down to the cafeteria. I'd already decided that we should do all our talking when we were in his room. If his room was bugged, anybody who was listening could hear what we were saying. But if we were in the lounge or out in the hall or down in the cafeteria, anything we said – anything that couldn't be monitored – might look suspicious.

Chapter 100

September 24, 1976 – It's Friday morning and I'm behind the Williams mansion. The story about the dig was on Channel 5 on Tuesday night, and there was an article in the Nashville Banner the next afternoon. I keep telling myself that the publicity will be good for my cover story. Stan is reorganizing the bags of artifacts, and I'm running my trowel along the edge of the square. I pick up a large clump of earth and break it apart with the edge of my trowel. The dirt is encasing a circular piece of metal. As soon as I see what it is, I ask Stan to come over and take a look.

Stan knocked away a little more dirt. "Yep. This definitely makes the highlight reel. It's an iron foot shackle – a manacle. It's hand-forged. Probably from the early 1800s, but it's hard to tell for sure."

He walked back over to the artifact box and picked up a marker. After he wrote the necessary information on a plastic bag, he slid the manacle inside.

A few minutes later, when Karen came over and dumped another bucket of dirt onto the screen, I was thinking about how I'd put the ankle cuff on Mustard Pants during the basketball game at West High. She was walking away when she suddenly spun around. She knew I'd be checking her out. She pretended to be offended before she started laughing.

I just shrugged.

I was tired. I'd stayed up late the night before writing an account of the Will Biggers killing. I thought it could end up being one of the chapters in Mr. Anderson's book, and I wanted to give it to him as soon as I could.

I was fairly sure he'd like it. And if anybody snooped around in his room and read what I'd written, it would confirm that I was just there to record historical information. While I was writing, I came up with an idea about how to tell Mr. Anderson while I was really there. If everything fell into place, there was a decent chance that I could find out what I needed to know without anybody knowing about it.

I was looking at a rusted fork I'd just found when a muscular black guy came around the side of the Williams mansion. He looked like he was in his early forties and he moved like an athlete. He stopped and took off his sunglasses and looked around, and then he walked up to where I was sitting.

He had a quiet presence, and he looked like he could tear a phone book in half. There were tattoos on both of his forearms. He was fairly light-skinned, and it was easy to make out the tattoos. One said *Ahab* and the other one said *LRRP*. I knew what the second one meant. It explained the way he carried himself.

He smiled at me and nodded, and I smiled back. It seemed awkward to come right out and ask him who he was, so I just told him my name. When we were shaking hands he stared into my eyes like he was looking for something. I didn't expect his eyes to be hazel.

"I'm probably not supposed to walk up here like this, but a couple of nights ago I was watching the news on TV. And I saw the story about this dig." He spoke almost as slowly as Kermit Anderson did, but his voice was deeper and he pronounced his words a lot more clearly.

He glanced down at the fork I was holding. "You talked about how this was the old Williams place. It sounded like you knew a lot about the people – white and black – who lived here."

"Well I wish I knew about a hundred times more than I do, but I'm learning as much as I can."

If I'd been thinking, I wouldn't have just launched right into telling him about the dig. As soon as I went into how Stan was trying to learn about the diets of slaves, I started worrying that I'd say something the wrong way. I kept tiptoeing around race and slavery, and I finally stopped talking.

I wanted to start over. "And that's my impression of a lame white guy talking about slavery to a black man he just met."

He looked surprised and then he smiled. "So that wasn't you?"

"I'm afraid it was, but I'm working on it."

He was still smiling. "Well, I've heard a whole lot worse." He stuck out his hand and we shook hands again. "It'll probably help if I tell you who I am and why I'm here. My name is Edge Walton. I've been doing some research, and if I can find enough information, there's a book I'm hoping to write. I think you might be able to help me out."

His smile got a little wider. "And for what it's worth, I don't care if you use the term Negro or black. And if you have to go all the way back to colored, I'll forgive you." He looked over at the Williams mansion and then he looked back at me. "And how should I refer to those of *your* ethnicity?"

"Oh, I'm not all that particular. Cracker, Honkie, Ofay, Whitey – but I'd appreciate it if you could stay away from the term, White Devil."

That made him laugh. The book he wanted to write was a biography about an elderly couple in North Nashville. They'd been married in 1902 when they were both in their teens. He had interviewed them at great length about their lives, and he wanted to include as much as he could about the history of their families. He thought they might make it to their seventy-fifth anniversary, but the old man had gotten pneumonia and died back in January.

The old lady was in her nineties, but her mind was still sharp. She told Edge that her mother had been born and raised on the old Williams place on Harding Road. She didn't know, or she'd forgotten, that the house was still standing. He didn't know about the house until he saw the story about the dig on television. He wanted to know as much as I could tell him. He thought that if he could give the old lady some details, she might be able to remember more about what her mother had told her.

My heart rate had picked up. I took Edge to meet Stan and then we went over to where Karen and Rogers were removing the sod from another square. After that, I told him there was something in the house he needed to see. He looked curious, but he didn't ask any questions.

We went to the back door, and after I told Miss Young who he was and why he was there, we followed her inside. We went straight to the study, but before I could start telling him what he was about to see, the telephone rang and Miss Young excused herself.

Edge took a long look around the room. "The lady I'm writing about is named Addie Davis. Her father's name was Israel Compton. Addie doesn't know much about him, but she knows a little about her mother. Her name was Anna. She told Addie that she was a house servant, so I guess that means she worked in *this* house.

"Anna called her mistress Miss Lizzie. Anna told Addie that Miss Lizzie would slap her across the face sometimes. Anna said the woman was as mean as the devil, and that she'd hated Miss Lizzie with a vengeance. She also said the Williams place was strict. Addie is pretty sure she remembers her mother saying that the slaves got whipped sometimes, but she isn't sure."

Edge Walton was about to find out a whole lot more than he ever thought he would. I'd seen Anna's name in the slave records, and I knew who her mother was. And I knew who Miss Lizzie was. She was the wife of Colonel Williams' oldest son, John Henry Williams.

I hadn't seen any documents that mentioned slaves being whipped, but from what Willoughby Williams wrote in the letter to his son, I was pretty sure whippings weren't all that unusual on the Williams plantation. I didn't tell Edge what I knew. It would mean a lot more to him if he found things out the same way I had.

I went over and opened the trunk. I started pulling out the slave records that had been kept by Willoughby Williams. I handed them to Edge, and as soon as he saw what they were he let out a whistle. I noticed how carefully he handled each piece of paper, and how quickly he read through every page. I thought he'd have trouble with the handwriting, but it didn't seem to be a problem. I went over by the bookshelf and waited.

After two or three minutes he looked across the room at me. All he said was, "Damn." He was holding the sheet of paper on which Colonel Williams recorded the date when Addie's mother, Anna, was born, and that Anna's mother – Addie's grandmother – was named Sarah.

I brought him bills of sale from when slaves were bought, along with wills and lawsuits and mortgages involving slaves. I watched him read through the records from the trunk, and after a few minutes, he held up a small piece of parchment. "I can't believe this." Then he started reading.

"Received of John Nichols, eight hundred and fifty dollars in full consideration for three Negroes, to wit, one man named Manuel aged thirty years, one woman named Sarah aged twenty-eight, and one small girl named Sarah aged five years, which Negroes I warrant and defend from myself, my heirs, and all others, as witness my hand and seal this fifteenth day of August, 1809, signed William Smith."

He didn't say anything for a few seconds. "So the little girl was Addie's grandmother, and *her* mother and father were Addie's great-grandparents. I... well Addie's in for one hell of a surprise."

I could tell he was stunned. Then he looked at his watch and shook his head. "I hope that you're about to tell me that it's okay for me to come back. I have to take Addie to the dentist. I'd get out of it if I could, but I can't."

He said he'd be back the following Monday or Tuesday. I told him that in the meantime I'd make him copies of what he'd seen so far. He said he had a whole lot of questions for me, and he wanted to bring along a tape recorder when he came back so he wouldn't have to write everything down. When we were going back outside he put his hand on my shoulder. "Well, I sure owe you one." I was wondering what he'd think when I showed him the manacle.

Chapter 101

September 25, 1976 – It's five o'clock on Saturday morning. My window is open and I'm listening for a katydid, but all I hear is crickets. It'll be getting light before long. I still haven't slept. I'm bone tired, but I can't get my brain to slow down. It was just after midnight when I finished writing what I plan to give to Mr. Anderson. I hope it doesn't turn out to be my death warrant. I'm almost sure Mike Higgins is right about what's going on. If he is right, it'll be too late to get out of everything once I show Mr. Anderson what I've written.

I wouldn't have stayed up all night if Edge Walton hadn't dropped out of the sky. His tattoo, LRRP, means Long Range Reconnaissance Patrol. Mike Higgins mentioned the LRRPs to me back when we were at Peabody, and I eventually went to the library and got a book written by a guy who was a LRRP in Vietnam. Edge Walton was willing to sacrifice himself for his country – just like my father had been.

Having a warrior show up could be a coincidence, but I thought it might be a sign from God. For the thousandth time, I wonder if I'm putting myself in danger by talking to Mr. Anderson. And for the thousandth time, I tell myself that I probably am. I keep thinking about what it will do to my parents if something happens to me.

I took a shower and left for our game. I did a lousy job of coaching. The other team wasn't very good and we would've beaten them if I'd been thinking halfway straight. We lost 13-6, but we played pretty well on defense and the kids hit harder than they had the week before. I called the plays and tried a few things on defense, but I mostly zoned out. I watched Whiting on a few plays. I wondered if he knew how bad he was.

When he was in the game, I played him at nose guard on defense. He was learning to stay low, but he usually ended up on the ground. I didn't play him much on offense, but there were a few times when I put him at wide receiver as a decoy. He was pretty good at making it look like the quarterback was going to throw him the ball. After the game he was laughing because the other team double-teamed him a couple of times.

He was the only player on the team who still hadn't gotten to me when we played Crush. I could tell how much he wanted to be Jermaine again, but he never came close to getting through. I didn't think he'd be able to pull it off.

I went straight from the game to Murfreesboro. The closer I got to the hospital, the more I felt like it was the right time to open up to Mr. Anderson. The longer I waited, the harder it would be for him to trust me.

Elinor was waiting for the elevator when I got there, and we rode up to the second floor together. She was smart and friendly, and I wanted to get to know her better. I was drawn to her, but it was different from the way I'd been drawn to Callie. I was drawn to her, but I kept my foot on the brakes.

Mr. Anderson was sitting on the sofa outside his room. We went inside and he closed the door, and I gave him what I wrote about the killing of Will Biggers. He read at least as slowly as he talked.

He finally looked at me and nodded. "I see what you mean about it bein' my book. It's like I wrote it myself, but it sounds a lot better."

"They're all your words. I just put them in order."

"Well I expect there's more to it than that, but it does sound like me."

I made myself go ahead and jump off the edge of the bluff. I just hoped that I'd land in the water. I picked up the legal pad I'd brought along. "I've written some other things that involve Will Biggers – at least in a way they do." When I put my index finger against my lips, his face turned serious.

I handed him the pad and I kept talking. "I hope this makes sense."

He stayed quiet while he read what I'd written on the first page. 'I'm pretty sure somebody is listening to us. Please read the next four pages. And please don't say anything out loud unless we've already talked about it. If there's something we haven't already gone into, it needs to be written on this tablet. I'll take the tablet with me when I leave. That way there won't be anything to find if somebody searches your room.'

Mr. Anderson looked at me and nodded.

I handed him a pen. "Oh, and you might need this in case you want to make any corrections."

He turned to the next page. 'I really am interested in the history of Cross Keys. And I really do want to put together the book we've been talking about. I am who I've told you I am, but there's a lot I haven't told you yet. I hope you'll understand why I had to be careful.'

He looked at me before he went on to the next page. 'Your grandmother told you that by the time the war was over, Lum Biggers knew the names of his brother's killers. She didn't know how he figured it out, but I have an idea about what could've happened. He wouldn't have been able to just go around asking questions. Like you said, everybody would've known what he was up to.

"I think he found somebody he could trust, maybe somebody who couldn't be connected to him, and then that person found out what Lum wanted to know. I have a friend who is a lot like Lum Biggers. And I'm a lot like whoever might've helped Lum Biggers find out who killed his brother. The murder of Will Biggers is a lot like the murder of a physicist named Robert Asberry. I understand that you knew him.

'My friend thinks that Dr. Asberry was killed by a team of

government agents who were working for some large corporation. My friend thinks that Dr. Asberry was killed because he invented something that was a financial threat to that corporation. He believes that what happened to you was done for the same reason. My friend also thinks that you're being used as bait. He thinks you were moved into this room so the agents who kidnapped you can see if somebody tries to get information from you, or tries to take you away.

'He's been working with a small group of agents and former agents who want to put a stop to what's being done to American scientists. He wants to release the details of your invention, and the details of whatever Dr. Asberry invented, to the right people in the scientific community. He sent me here to find out if you'll tell me about your invention, and what Dr. Asberry was working on. He also wants to know what was done to you.'

It took a while for Mr. Anderson to turn to the next page. I didn't want the long silence to raise any suspicions. "I hope everything I wrote about Lum Biggers is accurate."

He didn't look at me and he didn't say anything. By then he was reading again. 'An agent who had you under surveillance figured out that scientists were being systematically killed. He kept quiet for a few years, but what he knew was eventually passed along to my friend. It had been a while since the agent monitored you, and I've written down all the information he could remember.'

Mr. Anderson tapped the pen against the tablet while he was reading about himself. He had a solemn look on his face. He looked at me again before he turned to the last page.

'Before we met I was trying to think of a way to approach you, and I did some research. I found an article about your father in an old issue of *The Review-Appeal*. That's how I learned that you were a pilot during the war, and it led me to the house in Cross Keys where you grew up. Later on, I found an article about the Magnetic Ion Engine.

'Everything I know about you was in the information that came from the agent, or from research I've done, or from what you've told me. You probably have a lot of questions. If you'll write them down, I'll bring back the answers as soon as I can. I hope that we can work together on this.'

We'd been quiet for too long and I asked him a question. "How do you think your grandmother would feel about what you've been reading?"

Mr. Anderson looked drained, but he nodded. "Oh, I believe she'd like it. I believe she'd like it just fine." He looked at me. "And I believe Lum Biggers would like it, too." He was quiet for more than a minute, and then he looked over at me. "You know there's... there's a piece of the story I still haven't talked about. I don't know if I should tell you about it, or just write it all down. Lemme think about it for a minute."

Then he put his index finger against his lips. He stood up and walked over to his bureau. He picked up a hand mirror and I followed him over to the entrance to his bathroom. He handed me the mirror and pointed to the top of the door frame. When I held up the mirror, I saw a horizontal pencil-sized metal object next to the wall. I assumed it was a microphone. I looked at him and he nodded.

He walked back over and sat down in his chair. "You know, I expect I'd better just write down the part of the story I left out."

I didn't want us to be as quiet as we'd been. While he was writing down his questions, I started reading my piece on Will Biggers out loud. I read as slowly as I could without sounding suspicious. By the time I finished reading, Mr. Anderson had put down his pen. He pointed to what he'd written on the first page and handed me the tablet. I expected his handwriting to be a wild scrawl, but it was fairly clear.

'At first I thought you were a government man. But you didn't act like a government man. You said you were some kind of a historian. I believed that at first. But they're still trying to find my motor. I went back to thinking you might be a government man.

'I expected them to listen in on me. There's two microphones in here. Maybe more. I don't know why they put me here, but your friend could be right. I might be willing to tell you some things. But you need to answer the questions I wrote down.'

I nodded, but I didn't look at his questions. "I'll make these changes when I get home. And if I have time, I'll get started on writing up what your grandmother told you about Cross Keys back before the Civil War."

I started to leave, but I stopped at the door. I pulled out the picture of my football team. "I almost forgot to show you this." It would help him understand that I was who I'd told him I was.

He took the photograph and looked at it for several seconds. "Yeah, I remember you tellin' me that you coached a ball team. We had a team at Bethesda when I was in grade school." He winked at me and smiled. "I was little, but I was pretty hard to catch. Lemme hold on to this for a couple of days. I wanta see if any of your boys are as small as I was."

I told him I had other copies of the team picture, and that he could keep it.

Things had gone as well as they could with Mr. Anderson, and I was still keyed up when I got home. I tried to act as normally as I could during dinner, but Mother could probably tell that something was going on. I went to my room and read over his questions.

He didn't ask me Mike's name, but he wanted to know a lot about his background. And he asked what I knew about Dr. Asberry. I was too tired to write down the answers. I just watched some television and went to bed early.

I was having a bad dream when I woke up on Sunday morning. I dreamed I was getting into my car when I was leaving the VA Hospital, and that men without faces were closing in on me. I tried to run away, but I was barely moving. I had a similar dream the next night, and when I woke up on Monday morning I was sweating.

It rained all day long on Monday. By then I'd already written down the answers to Mr. Anderson's questions. I wanted to work on what I was trying to write for my parents, but I couldn't get my thoughts to connect. My mind would drift, and I ended up wondering if some of the kids I'd coached might eventually want to read what I had to say.

For the rest of the day, I worried about what could happen to me, and what could happen to Mr. Anderson. I felt like I was standing on a tightrope a hundred feet above the ground and my legs were shaking. When I finally fell asleep that night, I dreamed that I was walking through Woodmont School. I dreamed that I was searching for somebody, but I couldn't find anybody. Nobody else was there.

Chapter 102

September 28, 1976 – It's eight-thirty on Tuesday morning and I've been looking at the oak tree in Miss Young's backyard. It must've already been pretty big when the Civil War started. I'm going back to see Mr. Anderson this afternoon, but I'm trying to put that out of my mind. Edge Walton should be here pretty soon.

I'll give him the copies I made of the slave records, and I want to make sure he has everything he needs from the trunk. I keep wondering what he'll think when I show him the manacle. It might be a coincidence that Edge showed up wanting to tape-record me right after I started recording Mr. Anderson, but I haven't stopped thinking that he could be a sign from God. But if it is a coincidence, I appreciate the irony.

I dump a bucket of dirt on top of the screen. Right after I pick up my trowel, Claire comes around the side of the house. Callie is right behind her. I feel my heart jump.

I tried to act the way I usually acted around them. "Oh my. It looks like somebody has decided to skip school. I thought that since you girls are seniors, you'd be throwing yourself into your studies."

Claire shrugged. "We're going back after second period." She looked around and then she looked at me. "Last week I was watching television, and I saw you were out here. We've never been to an archaeological dig before."

"Do you want a quick tour?" Callie still hadn't said anything.

I took Claire and Callie over to where Rogers and Karen were digging. Karen sounded detached and clinical when she was telling them about the dig, but she was gazing at them while they were walking over to where Stan kept the artifacts. I waited until Karen looked at me, and after I tilted my head, I started moving my index finger like I was warning her to behave.

I followed them over and showed them the manacle, and then Claire pushed Callie with her elbow. It was pretty obvious that there was something Claire wanted her to say, but Callie just picked up a bag that had part of the broken doll.

Then Claire cleared her throat in as obvious a way as she could, and stared at Callie. "If you don't tell him, I'll tell him."

Callie shrugged. "Go ahead and tell him. I don't care."

Claire seemed a little frustrated. "Well her parents are getting back together. Or at least they're going to give it a shot. She's going back to Texas on Saturday."

I said something about how it might be tough for her to leave a month into her senior year. I didn't know what else to say.

She looked indifferent. "I sure won't be losing any sleep about getting away from Hillsboro. And there's a certain annoying bitch I know who's promised to come out and visit as soon as she has enough money to get there. Things are gonna change after everybody graduates anyway. I'm just taking off a little early."

I wondered how she really felt about leaving. I started to ask her if she thought she'd come back, but I didn't. She put down the artifacts and looked at Claire. "We need to get back to school."

Callie looked at me for a couple of seconds. All she said was, "Well, bye."

She headed for the car, but Claire hung back. She gave me a long look before she said anything. "Are you okay?"

I looked back at her. "Yeah, I guess."

"I'm not talking about Callie." She was shaking her head. "There's... There's something else. I saw it in your eyes before you knew she was leaving." She kept looking at me. "It's still there."

I just said I wasn't getting enough sleep. I thought about telling her that I might be pregnant, but she could've taken it the wrong way. Callie started honking the horn.

Claire looked back at me as she was leaving. "Well I'm not blind. I know something's wrong."

I would've gone over and joked around with Karen about the way she'd been staring at Claire and Callie, but I just sat down on the box and started screening dirt. It would've been okay if Callie and I could wind up as friends, but I was pretty sure that even if she came back from Texas, we'd end up being strangers. My throat felt as hollow as my chest.

She didn't realize it, but she'd helped me get past whatever had been holding me back since I was fourteen. But instead of making a difference in *her* life – instead of helping her – I'd gotten obsessed with how I wanted things to turn out. I'd been selfish. We'd just keep drifting away from each other, and it was my fault.

I picked through the dirt on the screen. I thought back to the late summer night in 1963 when I was in my bedroom – when I could hear the music from the party that was just down the street. I remembered telling myself that my dream girl could be there. I remembered how much I'd ached to go to the party. How much I'd ached to turn myself loose and finally start dancing. There were times when I'd imagined that the girl at the party that night was Callie. I wondered if anybody else would ever come along and take her place.

Edge Walton showed up a few minutes later. He was carrying his tape recorder and there was a big smile on his face. "You know what Addie said when I told her that her grandmother's name was Sarah? She got excited and said, 'That's right. That *was* her name.' And when I told her that her great-grandmother's name was also Sarah and that her great-grandfather was named Manuel, tears came to her eyes.

"After a while, she remembered a couple of things that Anna had told her. She remembered Anna saying that her mother was a really good cook. Anna said the Williams family would go on and on about her mother's biscuits.

"And she remembered something about one of the Williams boys. His name was Andy. He taught her mother to read. It could've gotten both of them in a lot of trouble, but nobody ever found out."

He stopped talking and after a few seconds, I glanced at the house. "There might be a few more records in the trunk, but before we go inside there's something I want to show you."

We went over and I started showing him the artifacts. He picked up the beads and the bones and the broken parts of the doll. He handled them with the same reverence he'd handled the papers from the trunk in the study. Then I showed him the manacle.

I didn't count on how much impact it would have. I held it out to him, but at first he wouldn't take it. His hand hesitated a little before his fingers closed around the piece of iron that had likely shackled Williams family slaves from time to time.

After a few minutes, we went inside. Miss Young was away playing bridge, and Edge followed me into the study. I opened up the trunk and he turned on his tape recorder. For the next two hours, while he looked through more records, he asked me questions about Willoughby Williams and what I knew about life on the Williams plantation. He was a good interviewer.

By the time we went back outside, there were several buckets of dirt ready to be screened. I got another wheelbarrow and another screen and another box and another trowel, and Edge sat across from me while we got to work. He found a button and a glass bead within the first two or three minutes.

He asked a few questions about what he was finding, but before long he stopped talking. He ran the trowel across the screen like a surgeon. He looked like he could've been working on archaeological digs for years.

His mind seemed to be somewhere else, and then he looked at me. "This is the way I used to feel in church. I'd be sitting on the front row and my father would be preaching, and sometimes I got caught up in the Holy Spirit. Back then life could seem... I don't know, almost *magical*." His voice trailed off. "Then I grew up."

He pulled a small hinge out of the dirt. "But anyway, here I am. And now I definitely have enough information to write the book. I just hope I can do justice to Addie – and Langford. He was her husband." Edge scraped the dirt off the hinge and put it in a bag. "You remember the other day when I said I owe you one?"

I nodded.

"Well, now I owe you a lot more than one."

"You don't owe me anything."

I meant what I said, but it was the right time to let him know what I wanted to do. "But there is something I've been thinking about – I mean if you're willing to do it."

He stopped moving his trowel and he looked at me. "What've you got in mind?"

"I want to interview you just like you've been interviewing me." I told him about the veterans I was talking to in Murfreesboro, and what my father did in World War Two, and how I stayed out of Vietnam. I said it didn't make up for staying home while other guys my age put on their uniforms and served the country, but that recording the experiences of soldiers was at least something.

He was quiet at first. "I'll tell you as much as I can, but some of what happened... a lot of what happened... I'll just have to do the best I can with that. But I haven't said anything about being in the service. How did you know I was in Nam?"

I couldn't stop myself from smiling. "Well I *might* be a psychic, but having LRRP tattooed on one of your arms could have a little something to do with it."

Chapter 103

September 29, 1976 – It's Wednesday morning and I'm on my way down the hall to Mr. Anderson's room. I haven't seen him in four days. It might be my imagination, but something doesn't feel right. My heart is beating fast and the corridor seems longer and narrower than it was before. I'm looking for the skinny orderly, but I don't see him around. As soon as I knock, Mr. Anderson opens the door. He has a serious look on his face.

I stepped inside and he closed the door. He was staring at me. "Did you get a chance to write anything else about Cross Keys?"

"Yes sir." I reached into my tablet and handed him the answers to his questions.

He took what I wrote, and walked over to his chair and sat down. He read through everything, and then he went through it all again. He finally looked up at me and nodded. "Well, that looks alright."

He stood up and went over to his bureau. "I wrote down some more things I remember about Lum Biggers. It's turnin' into quite a story." He handed me at least twenty pages of notebook paper.

I sat down and started reading through what he'd written. 'Your friend is right about the government men using me for bait. Somebody was here on Sunday night. I was at supper. I'd put up a piece of tape. It ran from the top part of the door frame down to the top of the door.

'The hospital folks don't come in here on the weekend between four o'clock and six o'clock. But the tape was broken when I got back. They didn't find anything. The information I'm giving you was on me the whole time.

'Even if they got it, they couldn't figure out what it said. It's all in code. But they'd know we're up to something. They'd interrogate us and get rid of us. But they still wouldn't get what they're after. I'm pretty sure I didn't tell them anything before, and it'll go the same way if they try it again.'

I didn't let myself think about getting tortured. I just kept telling myself that we wouldn't get caught.

'I wrote down what they did to me, and what I remember about a couple of the doctors. There's also a summary of the Magnetic Ion Motor, and a little about what Bob Asberry was doing.

'It's been slow going, but I'll get the rest done as fast as I can. There might be a way I can get us a little more time. I think I can throw them off some. When you're through reading this, just turn on your tape recorder and start interviewing me.'

Mr. Anderson was staring at me. "Well, what do you think about Lum Biggers now?"

I looked back at him. "I'd say he was the wrong man to go up against." I glanced through the pages of notebook paper. They were full of numbers, front and back. I didn't see an explanation about how to decipher the code, but I was pretty sure he'd written it down somewhere. "If it's okay with you, I'd like to turn on my tape recorder and hear some more about Cross Keys."

He started telling me about his ancestor, Laban Hartley. Mr. Anderson grew up in the old Hartley home. It was built out of limestone slabs that were three feet thick, and it took seven years to build. There were orchards on the farm, and he talked about how Laban Hartley made peach brandy in huge vats down in his cellar. He said the brandy was famous across four counties.

I studied him while he was talking about old times in Cross Keys. He held his head at the same angle and looked around the same way he did back when he had told me about Pulltight Hill.

Then he nodded and glanced toward the microphone above the

door frame. "Now I'm goin' to tell you somethin' I haven't talked about yet. I didn't want you to think I was losin' my mind."

When he changed gears, his body language and his eye contact both changed. He leaned forward and stared into my eyes.

"When I was eleven years old, my grandmother died durin' the night. We slept in the same bed. When I woke up, she was lyin' on her back and she was as white as her nightgown. Her mouth was open and her eyes were open. She looked surprised."

Mr. Anderson kept staring at me. "I touched her face and it was still warm. Some of the neighbor ladies came by that afternoon to get her ready for her casket. They told me to go out and play. I went outside for a while, but it was real cold and I came back to the house. When I opened the bedroom door, my grandmother was laid out on the bed. They were cleanin' her neckid body with wet washrags. Her eyes were still open and I ran back outside. I ran outside and I just kept runnin'.

"I went up to a peach orchard that was on the side of a hill. The wind was comin' through the trees, and it kept blowin' and blowin' until it started to sound like whisperin'.

"It was gettin' colder and I walked down to the south pasture. There was a big sycamore tree growin' in the fence row, and all the upper branches were white. When they moved around in the wind they looked like the fingers of a skeleton. By then the sun was goin' down, but I stayed where I was till I heard this owl. It sounded like screamin'.

"I was too scared to stay where I was, and I ran back home. The women were out in the parlor standin' around the casket. Ole Miz Grigsby was combin' grandmother's hair. I went into the bedroom to get away from everybody. Somebody had changed the sheets, and I got under the covers and fell asleep. I woke up two or three times, and I could still hear people out in the parlor."

Mr. Anderson hadn't taken his eyes off me. "But the last time... well when I woke up I could hear my grandmother breathin'. She was lyin' next to me, but we weren't at home. It happened other times after that. It still happens. Sometimes I wake up and I'll be somewhere else, but she'll be right beside me. Sometimes she talks to me. Sometimes she *tells* me things.

"One time when it happened, she showed me an engine. It hadn't been invented yet, but it was right there in front of me. I saw how it worked. After I got back home, I started tryin' to figure out how to build it. I finished it a long time ago, but I've got it hidden."

I thought he was blowing my cover, but it was too late to cut him off.

"The other night she said the engine shouldn't stay where it is. She said it belongs to the whole world. She told me I should write down how it works. What do you think about that bein' in the book?" He shifted in his chair and he seemed to relax, and then he reached down and retied his left shoe.

By then I'd put myself in the place of whoever was listening. From the way Mr. Anderson told me about the engine, it should've been obvious that I didn't know anything about it. I wasn't sure, but maybe it wasn't as bad as it seemed to be at first.

And there was something else. He seemed to believe that he'd talked to his dead grandmother. Whether he believed it or not, whoever was listening must've thought they were getting pretty close to learning all about Mr. Anderson's invention.

I wanted to go somewhere and think, but I had to make my cover story look good. I stuck around and interviewed him for another hour. He told me about some of the old Civil War veterans and ex-slaves who lived around Cross Keys when he was a boy, and he went back to looking around the room while he was talking.

Before I left he pulled a folded piece of paper out of his shirt pocket. It explained the code. It was simple and it was brilliant. I only had to read through it twice. I gave it back to him and after he tore it up, he flushed it down the toilet.

When I left the hospital, the papers Mr. Anderson gave me were in my tablet. I wasn't nervous until I saw the skinny orderly. I was waiting for the elevator and he was standing near the nursing station next to some file cabinets. I was pretty sure he'd been looking at me.

I was by myself on the elevator. Nobody was waiting for me when the doors opened. I didn't look behind me when I was walking to my car, and nobody seemed to be following me when I drove back to Nashville. I wanted to go home and start deciphering the papers, but I had football practice.

September 29, 1976 – It's getting late on Wednesday afternoon. The trees that border the Ensworth football field are almost as green as they were when we had our first practice. Whiting has gotten more and more physical from playing Smear, but he hasn't come anywhere close to breaking through when we play Crush. His mother still shows up at every practice. She parks up at the far end of the field, and watches from her car. I've been expecting her to ask me to put an end to Crush, but she hasn't done it.

We're about to play again. Whiting raises his hand, as usual, to volunteer. His stance is better than it was, but he still looks awkward. He moves into the first squad of blockers, but he's up too high and he isn't very intense and they drive him back and knock him down. He gets up and walks around like he's dizzy, but he says he wants to go again.

Every kid who played Crush would start just across from the blockers on the line of scrimmage. But the next time Whiting lined up, he was three yards off the line. I should've known he was up to something when he started acting dizzy. His stance was a lot better, and he let out a scream when he launched himself toward the blockers.

He came in lower and faster than before. His extra momentum caught the first line by surprise, and he broke through before the second line was ready. Whiting looked like he was getting pushed from behind. He screamed again just as he got to the second group. He knifed past Jeff, who was one of our best players, and then he got away from Ken Robbins. He made it through the second line, but the last squad was ready for him.

Whiting let out a growl, but he was too high and David Dobbins put a solid lick on him and knocked him backward. That sent Whiting into his version of a frenzy. His eyes were big and angry and he ran at Matt, but at the last second, he suddenly veered to the right. John was a little out of position, and Whiting twisted and clawed his way past Matt. He broke through and just before he got to me I turned sideways to protect myself. I didn't want to take a helmet in the stomach, or worse.

He grabbed me with both hands and he was panting. I thought he might fall down, but he stayed on his feet. He looked around like he was waking up from a dream. The other kids were staring at him. Nobody said anything at first, but then Ken and Jeff and David started chanting, "Jermaine! Jermaine!" Whiting just stood there and grinned. I kept myself together, but just barely.

I gave them a water break, and while Whiting was reenacting his triumph, I went up to see Ellen. I wanted to make sure she understood what she'd just seen. She was already crying. I just patted her on the hand and went back down to the field.

That night after dinner, I went back to my room and got to work deciphering the papers I got from Mr. Anderson. He used the photograph of my football team to create his code. After he gave a particular number to each vowel, including the letter Y, he matched up the twenty players on the team with the twenty consonants in the alphabet. I was in the photograph, but I wasn't part of the code because I wasn't wearing a number.

Matt was on the left end of the back row. He was number 51. Fifty-one was used to represent the first consonant – the letter B. Sam was next to Matt and his number, 24, represented the letter C. David was the last of the seven kids in the top row, and his number, 69, represented the letter J. Whiting was on the right end of the middle row, directly in front of David. His number was K.

From there the key moved right to left, and at the end of that row, it dropped down to the bottom row and moved back left to right. John was on the right end of the front row, making him the twentieth kid, and his number represented the last consonant – the letter Z. Unless somebody had the photograph, they wouldn't be able to figure out his code. And Mr. Anderson made things more complicated by mixing in additional strings of numbers. They were all meaningless.

His handwriting was fairly small and there were twenty-one pages, front and back, to work through. The first night I only translated eight pages.

I thought about handing off the information to Mike, but I decided to wait until I decoded the summaries. I wasn't making much progress on what I was trying to write for my parents. I didn't mind getting away from spinning my wheels.

Chapter 104

September 30, 1976 – It's Thursday morning and Edge Walton is emptying a bucket of dirt onto the screen on top of his wheelbarrow. I can see the anticipation in his eyes as he picks up his trowel. I should probably be home decoding Mr. Anderson's papers, but I want to hear Edge tell his story. My tape recorder isn't running yet, but it's next to us on a box. I want to know as much as I can about the nightmare that he experienced. The nightmare I was able to avoid.

At first I wasn't sure it was the same for anybody else, but I've noticed that Stan and Karen and Rogers all change when Edge is around. I haven't stopped wondering if it's a coincidence that he showed up when he did. He's holding an object that's too caked with dirt to identify.

After Edge scraped away most of the dirt, he held up an old skeleton key. "And now I want to know what this unlocked and how it ended up where it did." He didn't say anything else for a couple of minutes. Then he nodded at the tape recorder. "Well, I guess I'm ready whenever you are."

We sat there and I listened to him for the rest of the morning. Edge was born in Central Kentucky. He'd already told me that his father was a preacher in the AME Church, and that was what brought the Walton family to Nashville.

He talked about how easily sports came to him and how much he liked competition. He played football and basketball and baseball at Pearl High School.

By the time we went to lunch, I had a pretty detailed account of his childhood and his teenage years. By then he'd found several more buttons, along with some nails and bones. He also uncovered the rusted blade of an old knife, a penny from 1840, and a broken comb made out of a tortoise shell. I didn't bring the tape recorder along when we went to lunch.

Moon's Drugstore was only three or four minutes away. Before we sat down I told him I'd do my best to protect him if anybody attacked him for sitting at the lunch counter. He just smiled and shook his head. As soon as we got back to Miss Young's, I turned the tape recorder back on.

"I was a little on the short side, but I had some offers to play college ball. Coach Gentry wanted me to play for him at Tennessee A&I, and both Grambling and Florida A&M recruited me. There were a few white schools up north after me, too. The NFL didn't have room for any five-foot-nine-inch linebackers. If I wasn't going to get a chance at pro ball, I didn't see the point of playing anymore.

"I decided to go to Fisk and focus on academics and get the best education I could. After that, I planned to go to graduate school and get my doctorate in English. I thought I'd end up on a university faculty and spend my summers writing. I had my life all planned out."

When I interviewed the old soldiers in Murfreesboro, I usually needed to ask a lot of follow-up questions. But Edge kept anticipating the next thing I wanted to know. Before I asked him if he'd been involved in the Civil Rights movement, he brought it up on his own.

"When I was a senior at Fisk, the sit-ins were going on in downtown Nashville. I believed in the cause – we all did – and my best friend and the girl I was going with kept pushing me to get involved. I'd been stopped on the street and hassled by white cops. And I'd been called nigger and all the rest of it, but nobody had ever put their hands on me.

"If I'd gone to Woolworth's and sat down at the lunch counter and had some cracker smack me upside the head... Well, I wasn't sure if I could keep myself from messing him up.

"The whole idea was to be non-violent. My father knew my temperament. He didn't want anything to happen that would keep me from getting hired by some university later on. He said it was one thing to get arrested trying to integrate a lunch counter. It was something else to go to jail for putting somebody in the hospital."

The expression on Edge's face was as calm as his voice. He kept running his trowel across the screen and picking items out of the dirt. He talked about how he worked for a couple of years and saved up enough money to move up to Washington, and about getting his master's degree at Howard University.

He reached down and put a bone into the bag. "I was committed to getting my Ph.D. I had a strong transcript and I got admitted to all three places I applied, but I didn't get enough financial aid to live on. I didn't want my grades getting pulled down by a part-time job, so I decided I'd go ahead and spend some time in the army. There weren't any wars going on, and when I got out I'd have some money saved up. And the GI Bill would pay my tuition.

"I could've gone through officer training, but being a black officer could get complicated. I didn't want complicated. I just wanted to serve for a few years and get out. I thought I'd probably end up being a clerk. I told myself that with a little luck, I'd get stationed in Europe. I thought I'd be out before I knew it."

He shook his head. "Then Vietnam heated up, and after basic I got sent to a base north of Saigon. And, of course, I ended up under a racist lieutenant from West Virginia. He put me on point every time we went out on patrol.

"I had to get away from him before he got me killed. By then I had a whole lot of aggression to get rid of, and I signed up for Recondo School at Nha Trang. Going through two-a-days in August when I played football at Pearl was pretty tough, but it was a joke compared to what went down at Nha Trang. It was jungle hell, but I got through it. A whole lot of guys didn't."

He was quiet for a few seconds. "Nha Trang took care of my aggression, but it wasn't long before I felt like I was disappearing. I wasn't who I'd been before. The war mattered some at first, but after a while, there were only two things I cared about. The guys on my team and the choppers that flew in to resupply us.

"Our whole team felt the same way. Vietnam didn't matter to us. Sometimes America seemed like it was just a place we'd end up going back to. And it's for damn sure that we didn't care about capitalists and communists.

"We always executed our mission, but the war had to take care of itself. We got very good at what we did. Since you know about LRRPs, you know the sorts of things we were doing."

I knew. Sometimes LRRPs stayed out for weeks at a time. They did everything from gathering intelligence to ambushing enemy units to killing specific individuals. Sometimes they were spies and sometimes they were assassins.

"We got to be like brothers. There were usually six men on our team. I was the only black guy. It was the first time in my life when that didn't make a damn bit of difference. I'm not saying that's how it was on every team, but that's how it was with us. Zero difference.

"We were like brothers, except we were probably closer than brothers. It finally got to the point where there was only *one* thing any of us cared about. *All* of us getting out alive. I could've come home in '67, but I stayed in and did a little more time. We'd decided that we were all coming home *together*."

Edge got quiet again. He looked like he was running something through his mind. "Well, that's what I was doing in Vietnam from a hundred thousand feet up. I wasn't sure about getting into anything else, but... You need to understand what it was like on the ground."

I didn't think I deserved to hear what I was hearing. The expression on my face must've given me away.

He looked at me. "You okay?"

"Yeah. It's just that... it's an honor that you're telling me this."

I was pretty sure he didn't understand what I meant, but he nodded. I noticed that his eyes looked different.

"One of our missions was in the Central Highlands just along the Cambodian border. We'd been out for three weeks watching part of the Ho Chi Minh Trail. We got to our extraction point – the LZ was in this bomb crater – but the NVA shot down our chopper as it was coming in.

"We knew the NVA was really close, and we didn't have long to get everybody out of the Huey. The pilot and the crew chief were dead. The co-pilot and the door gunner were hurt, but they could both walk. We loaded up a little food and some extra ammo, and then we booby-trapped the Huey and fell back."

He picked some dirt off of a large hand-wrought nail and put it in the bag. "We were four or five hundred yards away when the chopper blew up. It was getting dark and the NVA was on our tails. We'd change direction, and they stayed right with us. They'd have reinforcements by the next morning. The only way to get them off us was to make them pay.

"I was team leader and I stayed behind. I had a hollow metal spear I bought off another LRRP when he rotated out. It was in three sections and it was six feet long when it was screwed together. It had sharpened points on both ends. I practiced with it all the time, but I hadn't used it.

"I got into some brush next to the path where there wasn't much overgrowth, and I waited. I'd been watching NVA units for months. I knew how they moved. They had a point man same as us, and when I heard him coming I leaned back and held the spear with both hands – right above my head.

"There was a little bit of moonlight. As soon as I could see enough of a silhouette, I tried to drive the tip of the spear into the base of his skull. He twitched a little, but he didn't make much of a sound. I ran my fingers down the shaft to his head and pulled out the spear. It hit him just behind his right earlobe.

"The rest of his team was close, but I didn't know if they heard him fall. I moved back, and after I went about a half-mile down the trail, I rigged up a trip line and an explosive. Then I kept moving until I found another opening where the moonlight was coming through the canopy. I stayed where I was for a half-hour after I heard the blast. When the NVA didn't come, I took off after my team."

He saw me glance at his right forearm. His face relaxed but he didn't smile. "That's why I have Ahab tattooed on my arm." He was still looking at me, and he put down his trowel. His face hardened again. "I might as well go all the way through with this. What else do you want to know?"

I probably sounded like I was back in grade school. "Was there any sound... you know, when the spear hit him?"

Edge raised his chin and tightened his lips. "All I heard was a grunt and the air coming out his mouth. And when the spear came out there wasn't much suction. It sounded like pulling a stick out of the mud."

I glanced over at the tape recorder. The reels were spinning inside the cassette and there was still plenty of tape. "With what you went through in Vietnam... I mean are you still..."

"Yeah. I still carry it around. It'll never go away, but it's gotten better. After I got back, there wasn't anybody around who understood what I'd done. My team was scattered all over the place. I couldn't just sit down with my father and tell him about all the men I killed and the way I killed them. The anti-war movement was rolling and I decided to lie low. It would've been a real bad time for some kid to come up and spit in my face.

Edge looked at his watch. "That's probably as good a place as any to stop – at least for today. I should drop in on Addie. She loves hearing about what we're digging up, and maybe she'll remember something else."

Chapter 105

After I had football practice at Ensworth that afternoon, I went home. I could tell that Mother wanted to talk to me. Her doctor had run some tests a few days earlier, and I tried to brace myself for bad news.

But she said how tired I looked, and she wanted to know if anything was wrong. I told her I was spending a lot of time going to Murfreesboro and working on the dig at Miss Young's place, but that the dig wouldn't go on much longer and I'd have a break after football was over.

I wasn't sure she believed me, but she changed the subject and then she brightened up. She'd gotten back her test results and she was in remission. The doctor told her that the long-term odds were in her favor. He'd run more tests in six months, but he expected her to come through everything okay.

And she had another piece of news. She and my father were going to Spain and Italy and Greece. They'd be gone for at least a month. She lived in Florence for a while right after college, and she'd always talked about going back. They planned it before she got the news from her doctor. They hadn't known whether the trip would be a celebration or a farewell tour.

Stan had a scheduling conflict and we didn't work at Miss Young's house on Friday. The only thing I had to do was coach our game on Saturday morning. We beat a team that was as bad as we were, and my kids acted like they won the Super Bowl.

I went home after that and got back to work. While I was in

my bedroom converting numbers into words, I kept picturing Mr. Anderson sitting in his room, writing out row after row of coded information. On Sunday afternoon I finished deciphering his summary of the Magnetic Ion Engine, along with the rest of what he'd given me.

The key part of his engine was a convex lens made out of heat-treated basalt. All I knew about basalt was that it was volcanic rock. He had exposed the lens to radioactive sodium while it was being superheated in a kiln. The exposure created microscopic tunnels all through the lens. After that, he mounted the lens about an inch away from a radioactive source.

The ions from the source accelerated as they passed through the tunnels in the lens. When they came out the back side, they were concentrated by magnets into a stream of ions that drove an armature. That was the Magnetic Ion Engine. Mr. Anderson had gone to a hobby shop and bought a model helicopter, and attached the engine to the helicopter.

It only weighed about fourteen ounces, but when he flew it over an electrical substation, it was powerful enough to knock out the entire facility. The summary disclosed that barring some external event, the helicopter would've been able to operate continuously for the half-life of whatever radioactive material was being used to propel it. He had used radioactive sodium.

At first, I didn't understand why the Magnetic Ion Engine would attract the attention of some big energy corporation. Then I read his analysis of how much additional power would be generated if what was characterized as nuclear waste was used to fuel his engine.

An enormous amount of energy could be produced each year by using the spent fuel rods that were created in nuclear plants. And that was only one application of the technology. I wondered if somebody in the coal or oil or gas industry was trying to suppress Mr. Anderson's invention, or if somebody in the nuclear industry was trying to steal it.

I felt like my relationship with irony was getting deeper. I'd heard of uranium and cesium and thorium, but that was about it. I'd gone from being a student who avoided chemistry and physics like they were radioactive, to trying to make sense of radioactivity. And I was even less prepared for what I read about the work that brought about the killing of Dr. Asberry.

The only thing I knew about quantum physics came from an article I'd read in a magazine a few months earlier. Dr. Asberry had developed what he called an Electromagnetic Thrust System. From what I could understand, his invention came about because he discovered a mistake in a crucial equation that had been written by a renowned physicist named Paul Dirac.

Dirac's equations had established that there would be an absolute vacuum in space. But Dr. Asberry's analysis revealed that there was never an absence of particles.

I couldn't follow all the details, but the corrected versions of Dirac's equations indicated the existence of particles across the universe. The particles would continually appear without having an identifiable origin and then disappear. The Electromagnetic Thrust Engine used those temporary particles to create an electromagnetic field against which rocket power could propel a spacecraft.

Dr. Asberry's work also indicated that the Electromagnetic Thrust System made it theoretically possible to create a revolutionary type of engine that could operate within the Earth's atmosphere. I understood why that would get the attention of all sorts of giant corporations.

I wondered if Dr. Asberry was murdered because whoever wanted him dead had learned all the necessary details about what he had invented. And I wondered if the only reason Mr. Anderson was still alive was because they needed to know more about his engine.

When it came to what Dr. Asberry and Mr. Anderson were working on together, they were exploring how the Magnetic Ion Engine could be used to power space vehicles utilizing Dr. Asberry's thrust system. I spent some time trying to understand randomly appearing particles and the creation of electromagnetic fields, but I didn't get very far.

Then I decoded Mr. Anderson's account of what he went through. He was abducted when he was getting out of his car in front of his apartment. He tried to describe the places he'd been taken. Then he listed a few of the questions he was asked about his engine, and what he was working on with Dr. Asberry.

When he didn't cooperate, he was taken to what sounded like a private medical facility, where he was injected with drugs and interrogated. He wrote down what he could remember about the doctors, but he'd been put through a series of shock treatments, and the information was fairly vague. He had no idea how long he was there, but he said he didn't tell them anything.

From there they brought him to the psychiatric ward in Murfreesboro. What had been done to him was a horror story. A peaceful, solitary man – a man who had worked his entire life to develop his scientific gift – was held captive and tortured by corporate thugs who probably saw themselves as patriots.

It was time to hand off what I had. That afternoon I drove about forty miles northeast of Nashville to a place called Castalian Springs. I found a pay phone outside a little store, and called the number that Mike Higgins had given me. A woman answered and I asked for Ernest. She said to hang up and stay where I was. She called me back a few minutes later. All she said was, "Tonight around eleven."

Chapter 106

October 3, 1976 – It's after eleven-thirty on Sunday night. I've been here for over an hour. I made sure nobody followed me. I parked across the road and walked down the railroad tracks for a couple of hundred yards, and then I cut back to where Willow Plunge used to be. Now there's only brush from the road back to a line of trees. The day I spent here in the summer of 1962 is like a dream. I remember kids splashing around in the water, and the music playing. I go over to where I saw the girl in the blue bikini, and I look at the place where Hall Guthrie threw the football. It's like I imagined the whole thing.

The moon was over half full. After a few more minutes, I saw a figure come out of the trees across the road. I could tell it was Mike Higgins. I was standing under a big tree about a hundred feet from the road. I started walking in his direction. I put my tongue against the roof of my mouth and made a clicking sound. He didn't look up, but he changed direction and headed right toward me.

He came up to me and he was all business. I could hear the tension in his voice. "Why am I here?"

I handed him the envelope I brought. "I have Mr. Anderson's account of what happened to him. And there are summaries of the Magnetic Ion Engine and Dr. Asberry's Electromagnetic Thrust System. There's also an account of what they were working on together. I didn't think I should wait any longer to hand this off."

He took the envelope. He didn't say anything at first, but then he nodded. "It was a good call."

He pulled his flashlight out of his hip pocket and started looking at the numbers on the sheets I'd clipped together. After I handed him a photograph of my football team, I explained how the code worked. Then I gave him everything I wrote to Mr. Anderson, and what he wrote back to me. Mike had his back to the moon. I saw him nodding when I told him about my cover story, and how Mr. Anderson and I were operating.

He stayed focused. "What else do I need to know?"

"Mr. Anderson thinks it could take him a few more weeks to write down the rest of what he's giving us. But there's a problem. His room is bugged, and he isn't sure he'll have enough time to get finished." Then I told him about the story Mr. Anderson came up with to string along whoever was listening.

Mike was taking everything in. He didn't say anything for a few seconds. "Have you asked him where his engine is?"

"Not yet."

"Well don't worry about it. It would help to get the actual invention, but there must be a reason he hasn't already told you. Asking him about it could just delay things. What you're getting is more important. Now we need to talk about something else.

"When we met at the school, I told you that you'd be on their radar as soon as you started talking to Kermit Anderson. By now they're *really* watching you. They're trying to figure out if you're up to anything, but since you're still out walking around, they haven't figured it out."

A pickup truck came slowly up the road. It rattled when it went over the railroad tracks. The tone of his voice changed. "There's no way to tell when they might make their move, but they won't wait around forever. All you can do, other than shut things down between you and Mr. Anderson, is try to improve your odds. You need to cut way back on your visits.

"I'm working on a way for you to hand off whatever else you get without leaving the hospital. If I can set it up, I'll get word to you. I don't want you holding information when they pull the trigger.

"And don't spend any more time deciphering what he gives you. I have the code now. Hand it off as soon as you get it. I'll take it from there. Maybe it won't be too long before you can go back to being a civilian. And in case you don't already know this, what you've done – you're a natural."

I almost said something about fear being a great motivator.

That night I went home and took another shot at writing what I wanted to say to the world. All I did was wad up pieces of paper and throw them in the direction of the trashcan. I wanted to explain the way I'd started to see everything, but the harder I tried, the less I could concentrate.

The next morning I was back behind Miss Young's house screening dirt. I didn't know if Edge was coming, but I had my tape recorder just in case. It wasn't long before he showed up. He went right to work. We turned up the usual items, and after about an hour I found a brass thimble.

Five minutes later I found what looked like a child's ring carved out of bone, and then I found the bone handle of a brush. Edge had only found a few pieces of broken pottery. He was good-natured about it, but I could tell he was ready to find some artifacts himself.

I looked over at him and pretended to yawn. "You know, there are guys who actually *find* things – things like those records in the trunk, or all these artifacts I've turned up this morning. Then there are guys who have those things *shown* to them."

I kept talking. "But you shouldn't feel bad. I mean you *were* a star athlete and you *were* a scholar and you *were* a war hero. I'm sure you'll *eventually* get the hang of archaeology."

By then he was grinning. "It's good to be lucky, white boy, but being lucky don't make you any good."

A few minutes later he put down his trowel. He used his thumbnail to scrape away the dirt from what he was holding. He finally looked over at me. "I found this artifact a couple of minutes ago. Now that I have studied it for a while, I suppose I might as well show it to you." He held up the head of a doll. He tried to sound professorial. "I shall now go over and see if, as I suspect, it fits the rest of the doll."

It fit. It came from a square that was about thirty feet away from where the upper torso was found. Nobody had a theory about how the pieces ended up so far apart.

We had lunch and then he said he was ready to get back to the interview we'd started the week before. I set up the tape recorder and turned it on. After he told me about his last mission as a LRRP, I asked him about coming back home.

The first thing he told me was how hard it was to go from the life he'd been living in Vietnam, to living at home. He said he wasn't ready for a relationship when he came back from Vietnam. The only time he talked to women was in bars. The more he told me, the more serious he was, and then he got quiet.

After a while he looked at me. "I've done a lot of thinking about what else I want to tell you. Except for what happened after the chopper crashed, I've stayed up in the clouds. I don't want to do it, but I need to give you a little more detail. It's the only way you'll understand."

Chapter 107

Edge was quiet for a few seconds. He seemed to be going over something in his mind. I watched a monarch butterfly flutter by a few feet behind him. "I enlisted a few months after President Kennedy was assassinated.

"I was told I was fighting communists. What I finally figured out was that the Viet Cong and the NVA were mostly just guys who were willing to die to get us the hell out of their country. Sometimes I felt like we were the British and they were the Americans. I came back here and a few weeks later Dr. King was killed.

"I was in Vietnam in February. I was home in April, and armored personnel carriers were rolling through North Nashville. It looked like my house was in the middle of a war zone. By then I felt like the police and the soldiers in the National Guard were the British, and the folks in my neighborhood were American colonists.

"The night after the assassination I was standing out on the sidewalk and a couple of yokels from the Guard drove up in a jeep. They said there was a curfew. They told me to get my black ass off the street. You know what I did?"

I shook my head.

"I started laughing at them. It was probably the first time I'd laughed in two years. They looked at me like I was crazy. I *was* crazy. And when they looked at each other, that made me laugh even harder. They knew I was laughing at them, but they didn't know what to do about it. They finally just drove on up the street. I was mourning for Dr. King, but I felt better for a few minutes.

"After a while – I guess it was three or four days later – the soldiers had all left and the neighborhood got back to normal. I'd been thinking about applying to a couple of doctoral programs, but I wasn't ready. I'm still not ready. Before Vietnam, I was really into literature. I loved to read and I wanted to write. After Nam, and after Dr. King was murdered, literature seemed irrelevant. I couldn't imagine myself writing. I just bought an old car and took off.

"I went to see some of the guys who were on my team. Only one had a father and mother who were still together, and two of the guys didn't have anybody to go back to at all. I was a lot better off than they were, but I was thinking about killing myself. Even though I kept telling myself that I couldn't do that to my parents, I wasn't sure how much longer I could hang on. I was looking for a reason to stay alive.

"My father finally got me to sit down with him. He knew I was in trouble. He ended up talking about God. He said there were a lot of things we weren't meant to understand. He was trying to help me, but it didn't do any good. Not long after that, I heard about an old married couple. They'd been living in the neighborhood, in the same house, since around the turn of the century.

"I wasn't sure what led me to do it, but the next week I went to meet Addie and Langford. Knocking on their door might've saved my life. They were both very kind and very wise. They'd seen everything from the worst days of Jim Crow to the passage of the Civil Rights Act. I started going by and talking to them a couple of times a week. It took a while, but they helped me find my way back to who I was."

Edge pulled an unbroken knitting needle out of the dirt. It looked a lot like the one I found. Another monarch butterfly fluttered behind him and I wondered if any were behind me.

"I ended up loving Addie and Langford. They were such good

people, and so were most of our neighbors. I knew a lot of the kids on our street. It killed me that they had to live through Dr. King's murder. And some of the soldiers patrolling our neighborhood had treated them like they were the enemy.

"I wanted to know who or what the enemy *actually* was. I wanted to know what was poisoning America – and the world. I wanted to know what was going on back in the shadows. It occurred to me that trying to find the enemy was a good reason to stay alive. At first, I thought the enemy might be politics.

"Politics was behind the war in Vietnam and politics killed Dr. King, but I finally figured out that politics comes from people. Politics is just a reflection of humanity. The enemy had to be more than just a reflection of humanity. It had to be something *inside* of humanity."

Edge pulled another unbroken needle out of the dirt. Then he stretched and smiled. "If I'd known how good it feels to sit outside on a fall day and find artifacts, I would've had another reason to stick around."

I wanted to ask him how close he came to killing himself, but I didn't say anything.

He picked up his trowel again. "I didn't think I'd find the enemy until I understood things better, and I started talking to people about the way they saw the world. I heard a lot of opinions, but opinions didn't help me understand what was going on. I didn't get anywhere until I went back and reread the Declaration of Independence and the Constitution.

"One of the keys to finding the enemy was right there in the Declaration. 'We hold these truths to be self-evident, that all men are created equal, that they are endowed by their creator with certain unalienable Rights, that among these are Life, Liberty and the pursuit of Happiness.'

"And there was another key in the Preamble of the Constitution – 'We the people of the United States, in order to form a more perfect union, establish justice, insure domestic tranquility, provide for the common defense, promote the general welfare, and secure the blessings of liberty to ourselves and our posterity, do ordain and establish this Constitution for the United States of America.'

"That's when things started getting clearer. Those are supposed to be the principles at the heart of America. People in the United States hear those words on the Fourth of July and some people know them by heart, but almost nobody lives by them.

"Black folks have had a front-row seat on that contradiction for way too long. And right now I'm thinking about the people who used these knitting needles I just found. Right now I'm thinking about the people who lived here on the Williams place.

"I finally came around to thinking that the ideals behind the Declaration of Independence and the Constitution are on one side of a struggle that's been going on since the dawn of civilization. I think the struggle is between people who only care about themselves, and people who also care about others. The way I ended up seeing it, the enemy is selfishness. And selfishness covers both the lust for money and the lust for power.

"What Jefferson wrote in the Declaration of Independence and what Madison wrote in the Preamble of the Constitution were powerful and enlightened ideas. But as far as the people who lived on this place were concerned, those words were lies. 'All men are created equal?' What did that mean to the slaves who were living here?

"And the *unalienable* rights of life, liberty, and the pursuit of happiness? The people on the Williams place didn't have any rights. How many of them could've been doctors or scientists or writers or teachers? Just about all they were allowed to be were field hands and house servants. Maybe the slaves who had to knit all day were the lucky ones. But whatever they ended up doing, their lives were stolen from them."

A monarch floated in and landed behind Edge on the box of artifacts, and another one passed over his head.

"I keep thinking about all those slaves whose names are in the records over there in the house. Maybe he wouldn't have done it, but old Colonel Williams could've beaten any one of them to death whenever he wanted to. And he would've gotten away with it. Or he could've taken children away from their families, and just sold them down the river.

"So much for Life. So much for Liberty. So much for the Pursuit of Happiness. And so much for forming a more perfect union, or establishing justice, or ensuring domestic tranquility, or promoting the general welfare, or securing the blessings of liberty. People who say that America has lived up to the ideals on which it was founded are either stone-cold ignorant, or they're stone-cold lying."

The butterfly flew away from the box. "Slave owners like Willoughby Williams corrupted the dream of America. The Southern aristocracy was rich and powerful because of slavery, and men like the Colonel meant to keep it that way.

"And the aristocracy didn't just own slaves and land. They owned the banks and the railroads and the steamboats, and they owned the newspapers. They controlled society. No wonder they were able to get so many poor white Southerners to leave home and fight. To fight and die for them.

"Southern aristocrats turned the words in the Declaration of Independence and the Constitution into lies. Those words sounded a little closer to being true after slavery was over, but they were turned right back into lies during Jim Crow. They became lies every time there was a lynching. They were closer to being true after the Civil Rights Act became law, but they still get turned into lies. It happens every time a black church gets burned down, and every time somebody gets beaten up or killed by a racist cop for being black."

He picked up a clod of dirt and crushed it between his fingers. It fell in pieces onto the screen. "But I've gotten off course. Like I said, things came into focus after I read America's founding documents. I decided that the enemy was selfishness. The enemy was anybody who satisfied their greed and their thirst for power by preying on other people.

"It was an old story by the time America came along. Slaveowners were pretty much the same as royalty. Plantations like this one were small kingdoms, and the Williams family might as well have been royalty.

"Plantations and kingdoms were both economic machines. So were a lot of churches. Nuns and priests have done a world of good for people, but hasn't the hierarchy of the Roman Catholic Church always been an economic machine? And haven't a lot of the Protestant denominations that came along later turned into machines, too?"

A pair of butterflies drifted a few feet above his head.

"Plantations had a whole lot in common with factories in the north that paid next-to-nothing for labor, including child labor. And they were connected. How much of the cotton picked by slaves on southern plantations ended up being turned into textiles by workers in northern factories? Those factories were just a different kind of economic machine. Slaveholders and factory owners didn't think twice about destroying the lives of their workers as long as they could keep on getting richer. They kept feeding off the lives that were making them rich. It's never stopped.

"Modern corporations are just more complex economic machines. When it comes to a lot of the biggest corporations, if people get in the way of corporate profits, people can go straight to hell. And if it comes down to what's good for the country or what's good for the corporation, then the country can go to hell, too. I think that's what Vietnam was all about."

A monarch landed on the grass behind Edge, and then it fluttered away.

"Parts of our economic system have always been based on lies. In the old days, the plantation owners wanted free labor, and their lie was claiming that black people were less than human. At least they weren't living in the jungle back in Africa.

"Factory owners wanted cheap labor. Their lie was that the best option for poor children was to work all the time. At least they weren't starving to death. The lies have changed, but the lying is the same. And the lies go way beyond exploiting workers.

"Remember how hard the automotive industry fought against installing seatbelts? Putting in seatbelts would add to the cost of cars. The industry was afraid that more expensive cars would hurt their sales. So they invented the lie that seatbelts didn't save lives. To hell with the thousands of people who got killed every year when they could've lived. And to hell with all the people who got maimed for life."

I thought about Jack Johnson turning blue beside his overturned car in the creek, and about Yancey Walsh lying in her grave.

"The tobacco industry wants to sell more and more cigarettes, and it keeps claiming that cigarettes don't cause cancer. To hell with whoever dies in the process. And the chemical industry wants to make every dollar it possibly can. It keeps claiming that its products don't pollute the air or the water, or damage the environment, or cause cancer. To hell with the environment, and to hell with whoever gets sick.

"Their executives say whatever they need to say to keep selling poison, because as long as they keep selling poison, they keep on making money. They look like human beings, but they're more like economic robots in coats and ties. They got where they are because they conformed to the one thing that corporate machines are programmed to do – make as much money as possible."

Another monarch flew a few feet above his head.

"And the politicians they pay off all run little corporations of their own. I'm talking about politicians who use the power of their office to get rich, and they're both Republicans and Democrats.

"I'm talking about politicians who grab every corporate campaign contribution they can get their hands on. I'm talking about the ones who were always bellowing about how communists were on the verge of taking over the American government. And how all of Southeast Asia would fall to communism if Vietnam fell. They said what they said and they voted the way they voted because they were being paid to do it.

"What was good for corporations, was good for the individual bank accounts of politicians. Those kinds of politicians are the ones who led the fight against everything from tobacco legislation to seatbelt laws to environmental regulations. They keep fighting to protect industries that pollute the air and the water, and they fight like hell to keep all those government dollars flowing to the military-industrial complex."

Edge stood up and looked around. After he picked up the screen and laid it aside, he pushed the wheelbarrow over and tipped another load onto the growing mound of discarded dirt. Then he came back, put the screen on top of the wheelbarrow, and dumped another bucket of earth onto the screen.

Chapter 108

Edge sat back down on his box and looked at me. "But I'm only talking about the politicians and the corporations that hurt people and damage the country. I'm *not* talking about honest politicians and public servants and responsible corporations, and I'm *damn sure* not talking about small businesses.

"Small business has made America what it is. I had an uncle up in Kentucky. He borrowed a little money and bought an abandoned building. And after he spent a year's worth of nights and weekends fixing it up, he opened up a little country store. He worked hard and after a while, he was doing pretty well. He paid taxes. He gave a few people jobs. He donated to the community. He deserved every penny he made.

"There are people like my uncle selling goods or providing services all across the country. They treat people fairly and they charge fair prices. They're the fabric of America. But a lot of the giant corporations and the robots who run them and the politicians who protect them are like cancer. They undermine what America is supposed to be, and they're getting more powerful all the time. If something doesn't change, they'll end up destroying the country.

"But big corporations and self-serving politicians are just part of the problem. They need armies of political partisans to make their greed possible. Partisans are destroying the American dream, too. Look at what happened after President Johnson signed the Civil Rights Act. Forget about the nation's founding principles –

millions of white people were scared about blacks getting more political power. Scared white people were easy to manipulate, and the right wing got a flood of new partisan recruits.

"And they weren't just in the south. They were all over the country. The Republicans have been using race to prop up the right wing ever since. Every time an election comes around, they beat on their drum and talk about how they'll keep the economy strong and create jobs and fight communism. But that usually isn't enough, so they start talking about law and order. As soon as they mention that a few times, a whole lot of white folks run up to get in line.

"They know exactly which buttons to push. They're experts. But propaganda wouldn't be a problem if people weren't so gullible. It's just like religion. Do a good enough job of indoctrinating people and they'll believe just about anything.

"The best example of that is the film clip of President Kennedy being shot. His head gets blown backward, but millions of Americans still say he was shot from behind. It's right there in front of them, but they believe what they've been programmed to believe."

He found part of what looked like a rusted belt buckle, and he started scraping off the dirt with his trowel. A butterfly was floating several feet behind him.

"Then there's the left wing. It seems like they want the government to control just about everything. That didn't turn out too well in Russia. The workers in the USSR ended up being ruled by Stalin, and he started killing them off a million or two at a time. The Soviet Union turned out to be just another corporation. The Third Reich was a corporation, too. And look at the big labor unions. I'm not saying they aren't necessary – they are.

"At first the unions took on the big corporations. A lot of corporations don't care about their workers. Like I said – they're just machines. They pay as little as they can for labor, and they don't care about working conditions and benefits. Unions have done a lot of good, but how many of them ended up getting hijacked by the mafia? And the mafia is a big corporation, too. It sucks up as much money and as much power as it can."

Before he said anything else, we heard a helicopter flying somewhere off to the west. Edge listened for a few seconds, and then he put the blade of his trowel against the corner of the screen and scraped away some dirt.

"This is a little off the subject, but the left wing has a big weakness. It's the moral righteousness – the arrogance. I'm talking about war activists and it's personal. There was this really good kid on my LRRP team. His name was Jose Munoz. After he got home, a few of those morally superior left wingers found out that he was in Nam.

"He was barely holding on as it was, and then they started calling him a baby killer. One afternoon he stayed late at the garage where he was working. Then he blew off his head with a shotgun. The NVA couldn't kill him, but those peaceniks damn sure did. I understood being against the war. But I will *never* understand being against our soldiers."

Edge stopped talking. He was holding a clod of dirt. He cracked it open like an egg and the stem of a pipe fell onto the screen. He looked over at me and smiled. "Are you ready for me to shut up yet?"

I shook my head.

He swept his trowel across the dirt. "A lot of the time left wingers are incompetent and undisciplined, and God forbid that they would ever think all the way through a problem. Look at the War on Poverty. They supposedly have all this compassion for the poor, but they won't do what's necessary to resolve it.

"They refuse to talk about overpopulation. As long as the population keeps going up, there'll just be more and more poverty. And poverty steals more lives than slavery ever did. The left wing is always trying to fix problems, but those problems will just keep getting worse as long as the population is too high for the planet to sustain. It doesn't matter how much money gets thrown around.

"The population won't level off on its own. It'll just keep going up until there's a catastrophe. Like a worldwide epidemic or a massive famine or a full-scale nuclear war. And after something like that, it could take a thousand years for whatever is left of humanity to get back to where their ancestors have already been."

Edge stopped talking and straightened up. At first, I couldn't see what he'd found, but he finally held up what looked like a coin. He spit on it and wiped away more of the dirt. It turned out to be a fifty-cent piece from 1827. He kept staring at it and turning it over in his hand. "I'd love to know how this got lost. A half-dollar was a whole lot of money back then. Especially if it belonged to a slave."

He took it over and showed it to everybody, and when he came back I was putting a new tape in the recorder.

"Well, I'll take that as a sign that you still haven't heard enough." It was almost a minute before he said anything else. "From time to time, somebody will say that America is a beacon for humanity. I think that's what we're supposed to be. We're *supposed* to show the world that there's an alternative to kings and dictators – to selfishness and greed.

"How many hundreds of millions of lives are still being stolen by totalitarian governments? America should be shining a light on dictatorships and oligarchies, but our light is only as strong as our country is. Watching the promise of America being betrayed by politicians and corporate robots in coats and ties... well it breaks my heart. And it makes me angry.

"Millions of good, pure-hearted people have risked their lives, and hundreds of thousands of people have *sacrificed* their lives, for the dream of America. I saw it in Vietnam. The enemy of America – the enemy of humanity – is selfishness. I'd love to drive a spear right into the base of its skull."

"I remember watching Eisenhower give his farewell address about the military-industrial complex. I thought about that speech a lot when I was in Nam. It was obvious that the defense corporations were making billions of dollars off the war. Eisenhower never mentioned Boeing or Lockheed Martin or General Dynamics or Monsanto or Dow, but those were some of the corporations he was talking about."

Edge picked up another bucket of dirt and emptied it onto the screen. I watched a monarch gliding in. It seemed like it might land on his shoulder before it drifted away. "I think the bad guys are winning. And they're getting more powerful all the time. There was a lot I didn't like about the anti-war movement. But when all hell started breaking loose at the end of the sixties, I thought things might change.

"I'd been in Vietnam. The Pentagon Papers had been released. I'd watched the Watergate investigation. I understood that when it comes to politics, just about everything that's visible is a lie. And corporations are behind most of the lies. I also learned that lies are more powerful than the truth. The truth is usually complicated, but it doesn't take much to invent a lie that people will believe.

"The Viet Cong and the North Vietnamese were fighting for independence from foreign powers, but it was easy to claim that they were fighting for worldwide communist domination. That's what most people believed. Black people want life, liberty, and the pursuit of happiness. But it's easy to claim that we just want to live on welfare and take drugs and steal, and that's what most white people seem to believe.

"The world will just keep getting more complicated. And the more complicated it is, the easier it'll be for politicians and corporations to manipulate the public.

"They'll keep preying on the public and churning out lies. People will be more and more misinformed. 'Oh no, our product doesn't cause cancer.' 'Oh no, our industry doesn't pollute the rivers or the oceans or the air.' 'We have to go to war to protect the nation.' 'Everything we're doing is for the good of the country.'

"Lies are their main weapon, and they damn sure know how to lie. Sometimes I wonder how much longer democracy can last."

It sounded like he'd been talking to Ann. He glanced over at the tape recorder and then he looked at me. "Most people have no idea what's going on. They just swallow some story and that's that.

"Right-wing partisans and left-wing partisans are always sure their side is right. And they think that everybody on the other side is either evil or ignorant. Partisans spend a lot of time convincing themselves that the truth is on their side, but deep down they don't care about the truth. All they really care about is defending the beliefs of their group. Both sides need each other, but they don't know it.

"I would hate to end up living in a right-wing country or in a left-wing country. Either one would be a disaster.

"It wouldn't be long before a purely right-wing country replaced its democracy with a police state. Or turn America into a Christian nation. Either way, an oligarchy or a dictator would end up running everything. The masses would be exploited for the benefit of the few, and there would be a lot more peasants and a lot more prisons. It would be a medieval system. And a country under the total control of the right wing would be an environmental disaster.

"But a country absolutely controlled by the left wing would end up in chaos. No restraint on domestic spending. Inadequate military spending. And because solutions aren't always fair, a problem like overpopulation could never be fixed.

"The future of society would always be in danger of being sacrificed for some myopic view of fairness. The population would keep on increasing, and after the left-wing country fell apart, it would probably end up just like the right-wing country. It would be under the control of a dictator or an oligarchy.

"Political partisanship is a disease. The last thing America needs in the White House is a political partisan posing as a statesman, or political partisans in Congress posing as public servants, or political partisans in robes on the Supreme Court posing as jurists. But that's where I think we're heading. And there's something even worse than having the government run by political partisans. It's a government run by corporate operatives who manipulate political partisans to seize power.

"So that's my take on the world. Along with racism, greed born from selfishness is what killed Dr. King. Greed got us into Vietnam, and I think selfishness is behind what keeps poisoning the world."

He stopped screening and sat back, and then he looked at his watch. "I need to leave in a few minutes. I've got to go to the grocery and pick up a few things for Addie."

He looked down at the dirt in the next bucket. "But there's something else I want to say before I take off. I've told you about reading America's founding documents. Well, there was another source I went back to. When I was growing up, and especially when I got in trouble, my father would make me memorize passages from the Bible. A couple of the passages I memorized were about selfishness.

"I won't get the words just right, but I can come pretty close. 'For I was hungry, and you gave me meat. I was thirsty, and you gave me drink. I was a stranger, and you took me in. I was naked, and you clothed me. I was sick, and you visited me. I was in prison, and you came to me.

"'Then shall the righteous answer him, saying, Lord, when did we see you hungry, and feed you? Or thirsty, and give you drink? When did we see you a stranger, and take you in? Or naked, and clothe you? Or sick or in prison, and come to you?' And Jesus said, 'Verily I say unto you, inasmuch as you have done it unto one of the least of these my brethren, you have done it unto me.'

"That's from the book of Matthew. And this is from James. 'You rich men, behold the hire of the laborers who have reaped in your fields, and who you kept back by fraud. Behold, the cries of them who have reaped are entered into the ears of the Lord. You have lived in pleasure on the earth, and been wanton. You have condemned and killed the just, who do not resist you.' He looked down. "That part always makes me think about Dr. King."

It also made me think about Kermit Anderson and Dr. Asberry.

He smiled at me. "I didn't mean for this to turn into a church service." He glanced up at a butterfly floating over his head. "I guess I had to go through Vietnam and everything else for the Bible verses I've heard my whole life to get inside me. What I want to say is that those verses have a lot in common with the spirit of the Declaration of Independence. And with the preamble of the Constitution.

"I think the same spirit is behind 'Do unto others as you would have them do unto you' and a nation based on life, liberty, and the pursuit of happiness. It's my belief that the spirit behind 'Love thy neighbor as thyself' is the spirit behind a nation dedicated to justice, the general welfare, and the blessings of liberty.

"That spirit nurtures humanity, but plantation owners and factory owners, and kings and corporations and self-serving politicians keep poisoning the human spirit. They're the enemies of humanity, and they could end up being the *destroyers* of humanity."

He glanced over at two of the excavated squares and at the mound of dirt, and then he looked at the large box with the bags of artifacts. "So here I am. It took me a while, but thanks to my parents and Jesus Christ and Dr. King and Addie and Langford, and thanks to a woman named Inez who I haven't gotten around to telling you about, I feel like I've been delivered from the wilderness."

He shrugged. "I think I'm starting to know the truth. And who knows – maybe the truth will end up setting me free. I'll write my book about Addie and Langford. And maybe after that, I'll find a way to take a little bit of the fight to the bad guys."

Then he smiled. "Maybe the pen really can be as mighty as the sword – or the spear. And if it doesn't turn out that way, maybe I'll just take Inez on down to Mexico and start my life over."

Edge came by the next day and said he was going out of town. Addie had gotten a call that morning from an elderly first cousin living in Los Angeles. Edge found out that the cousin knew some details about slave times on the Williams place. Edge said a couple of guys who were with him in Vietnam lived on the West Coast, and there was a chance he wouldn't be back for two or three weeks.

He told everybody goodbye, and as he was leaving a monarch butterfly drifted in and briefly hovered just above his head.

Chapter 109

Three days later I drove my parents to the airport. It was going to be the longest trip they'd ever taken together. I made sure they couldn't tell how worried I was. With both of them gone, for the next several weeks I'd be coming back to an empty house at night. Even though Mother had cancer and my father had a bad heart, there was a chance they'd live longer than I would.

As soon as I got back from the airport, I went to work on the doors of our house. Thanks to Mr. Anderson, I knew how to make sure nobody was inside when I came home. I started with the back door.

I got our ladder and drove a small nail into the mortar between two of the bricks above the door. Then I stuck a thumbtack into the top of the door. I tied one end of a piece of thread around the tack, and looped the other end around the nail. The nail was almost too small to see, and the thread was the same color as the paint on the door. I went on and did the same thing to the rest of the doors in our house.

Every time I left home, all I had to do was loop the thread over the nail. If it wasn't broken when I got back home – and if none of the threads above the other doors were broken – I'd know the house was empty. I'd be sure that nobody had gone inside.

It would've been a lot easier if I could've just padlocked the doors. But I was supposed to be a guy who just happened to show up and talk to Mr. Anderson about history. A guy who just happened to show up wouldn't have any reason to padlock the doors of his house.

After I finished putting nails and tacks and threads above the other doors, including above the door to the basement, I tried to figure out what to do about the windows in my room. They were the only windows in our house that would open. The others had been painted shut for years.

I ended up drilling holes all the way through the top of the lower sashes and into the bottom of the upper sashes. Then I slid long nails into the holes. I did the same thing to the door that led from inside the house down to the basement, except that I drilled diagonally down into the floor through the basement side of the door.

If the thread above one of the outer doors was broken when I got home, and if the thread to the basement door wasn't broken, I could go in that way. I could listen for a while, and if I didn't hear anything I could pull out the nail and go upstairs.

The other thing I did was destroy the information I'd been holding for Mike Higgins. I took the packet out into the backyard, and after I doused it with lighter fluid, I burned it. I should've done it sooner.

By the next day, everything was finished. Before I left home, I loaded the .38 caliber pistol my father kept under his socks in his top drawer. It was the pistol he used in the war. I put it under the front seat of my car, and I planned to have it in my pocket every time I came home and checked the doors.

I decided to wait a couple of weeks before I went back to Murfreesboro. I thought I'd spend more time at Miss Young's, but the dig only lasted for two more days. Stan was apologetic, but he was forced to oversee an emergency salvage project. A highway construction crew was widening a road northeast of Nashville, and the site of a thousand-year-old Indian village had been uncovered.

Stan said it might be a blessing in disguise. Over the winter he could identify and interpret the bones and the artifacts we recovered, and he'd decide where else on the Williams place to look for cabin sites. With the dig on hold, I had more time to write what I was trying to write, but I didn't know if I'd get anywhere.

Part of what I wanted to say went back to something Palani had told me. He talked about finding God through his creations. It was clear to me that if God just wanted a void, he wouldn't have created the physical world. And it seemed clear that if God wanted there to be more than a void, he would want Earth and humanity and the rest of his creations to endure rather than just cease to be.

I was pretty sure that Palani was right about something else. He thought that God gave people logic and science in order to preserve humanity and the rest of his creations. Palani, and Edge, led me to see God and the teachings of Jesus in an expanded light. Loving thy neighbor and turning the other cheek were both in harmony with the perpetuation of humanity. Other parts of scripture were also in harmony with the continuation of humanity. Like being guided by what was true and honest and just and pure. I could've explained that much, but there was a lot more I wanted to say.

I kept praying that it wouldn't be long before Mr. Anderson finished putting everything into code. I hadn't stopped wondering if he actually believed he talked to his dead grandmother. And if he really had visions.

October 23, 1976 – It's Saturday morning and it's our last game of the season. I'm trying to take everything in. I want to remember as much as I can, but I'm not focusing very well. Being at the game doesn't feel the way it usually feels. We've gotten a lot better since the first practice, but the team we're playing should beat us. We might be able to give them a better game if all our players were here. A stomach virus has been going around and we're missing two of our starters. Whiting has always been a substitute, but today he'll have to start at nose-guard. It's a lot like nine years ago when Peter Johnson was in the starting lineup. Whiting is excited, but he won't be excited for long. I've been watching the other team warm up across the field. The guy playing center is big and strong.

Last night I stayed up late trying to write, and I'm really tired. I look around and do what I can to clear my head. The maple trees across the field have turned red and yellow. But they seem like trees in a photograph.

We were only a touchdown behind after the first half, but Whiting was getting dominated and the big center was rubbing it in. At first, Whiting wasn't staying low enough. He looked like he was on roller skates when he was being driven backward down the field.

But when he got lower, the center just pushed him down and jumped on top of him. Sometimes after the play was over, the kid would let everybody know how dominant he was. He put his hands on Whiting's helmet and pushed down on his head while he was getting up. He took his time, and Whiting was usually the last player on the field to get up off the ground.

I didn't know how embarrassed he was until halftime. "He keeps knocking me down, and I can't do anything about it. And he keeps laughing at me and calling me names." He was doing his best to hold back his tears.

I offered him a way out. "Do you want to move over to tackle?"

He looked at me like I'd asked him to quit. He just shook his head and walked back onto the field. David Dobbins came over and he was angry. He wanted to move from safety to nose guard, but when I told him that Whiting didn't want to change positions, he just nodded and walked away.

I hoped that the other coach would tell his center to tone it down, but as soon as they went on offense, the kid was back to humiliating Whiting. After a couple of minutes, I noticed David talking to Whiting between plays. We were still a touchdown behind with four minutes left in the third quarter.

When the other team lined up to punt, Whiting ran back and David whispered something to him again. Whiting lined up like he was playing safety and as soon as the punter yelled "Down," Whiting started trotting toward the line of scrimmage.

He moved like he was running through a field of daisies, but he was gaining speed when the punter got to "Set." The big center was still looking back through his legs when the punter yelled "Hut." Whiting counted on the ball being snapped on the first hut, and he timed it perfectly. The center snapped the ball and he was just starting to look up when Whiting crashed into him as hard as he could.

The center staggered back and fell on his butt and Whiting pounced on top of him. For the next three or four seconds Whiting looked like a bull rider trying to stay on a bull. When the play was over and the whistle finally blew, Whiting managed to get one of his hands on the kid's helmet when he was getting up.

The next time we went on defense was early in the fourth quarter. Whiting lined up at safety again, and he started trotting toward the line of scrimmage as soon as the quarterback yelled, "Down." The other team was in their regular formation and the center saw him coming. Whiting didn't slow down.

He guessed that the center would snap the ball on "Hut" and he was right again. All his games of Smear and Crush paid off. Whiting hit the center hard enough to knock him back a little, and he was able to get past him. He didn't get in on the tackle, but he came pretty close.

On the next play, he lined up at safety again. He ran in the same way he did before, but he stopped just before he got to the line. The center was distracted and he made a bad snap. They were deep in their own territory, and when they lined up to punt on fourth down, Whiting came charging in again.

Instead of looking back through his legs at the punter, the big center was looking at Whiting. When he snapped the ball, it hit the ground and bounced away from the punter. David recovered it in the end zone, and the game ended up in a tie.

When our guys were shaking hands with the other team, David stayed close to Whiting. The big center looked angry and he started toward Whiting. He stopped when he saw David. David was glaring at him and holding his helmet by the face mask like it was a weapon he couldn't wait to use. The big center took another look at Whiting, and then he turned around and went the other way. Whiting had no idea what had happened.

After the kids went home I stuck around for a while. I wanted to stay in that moment. I wanted to watch the leaves drifting down from the trees and feel the wind against my face. The next game started, and I was standing alone beside the end zone. I noticed a guy walking toward me. It was Hill Murray. I hadn't seen him since before he went off to college.

He smiled and we shook hands. "Another *tie*? Seems like by now you would've learned how to win the close ones. Remember that football game we played out in front of West?"

"Of course I remember. All I can say is thank God for Peter Johnson."

"*School Zone*?" He was still smiling. "Hey, *I* was the one who made that last tackle."

I did my best to look dismissive. "You were all the way over on the other side of the field. School Zone was the *only* guy on our team who was where he was supposed to be. But I do seem to recall that you ran over in time to *help him* knock down the ball carrier."

Hill was grinning. "Well, aren't you going to ask me who I'm here to see?"

"I was about to."

"One of my cousins is playing in the game that just started. I heard you were still coaching, but I didn't know you'd be here. I looked across the field and there you were."

He was in town for a long weekend. He was going to Duke. He was majoring in business, and he showed me a photograph of his girlfriend.

I was picturing the way he was when he was on my team. I looked into his eyes and I saw the same awareness I'd seen on that long ago Friday night at Montgomery Bell Academy.

There was something I'd wanted to tell him for a long time. "A lot happened that season, but I think about one thing more than anything else. And it wasn't that tackle you made."

He looked curious.

"It was what you did for Peter when you got him to play Smear the Queer at the football game."

At first he didn't know what I was talking about, but then his eyes lit up. "Oh yeah, I remember that. Didn't you make up some story? It was something about Peter getting fat and the stands collapsing and crushing some little kids."

I reminded him how Peter had been standing by himself that night, watching everybody else playing together. I told Hill that he was the only kid there who understood what to do. The muscles around my mouth started to betray me and I was trying to fight back my tears. I might've been able to get through what I wanted to say if I hadn't been so tired. Or if there wasn't already a knot in my throat from seeing what Whiting had done. Or if or if or if.

"I want you to know..." Then the tears came. "I want you to know that you opened a door for Peter that nobody else could've opened. That's why I wanted you to have the bullet. I would've told you how proud I was of you right then, but... this would've happened."

I would've felt more awkward, but Hill had tears in his eyes, too. He took a step toward me and touched my arm. Then he smiled at me. "I never understood why you gave me the bullet. It sort of became my good luck charm."

I wiped my eyes and tried to laugh. "Well judging from the girlfriend you have, it must be working."

He couldn't remember how I found the bullet, and I described the small upstairs bedroom at *Peach Blossom*. Then I told him about the duel between Andrew Jackson and Charles Dickinson, and about the letter from Joseph Erwin and how the bullet that killed Dickinson in 1806 had gone missing. I told Hill I'd never be able to prove it, but that the bullet I found could've come from Jackson's pistol.

We stood there for a few more minutes talking about the guys who were on his team. Peter Johnson had moved away, and we both wondered where he was. Hill kept glancing at my eyes, and he finally said he needed to watch a little of the game with his uncle.

But before he left, he reached into his hip pocket. He held out his hand and showed me the bullet from *Peach Blossom*. "I keep this with me all the time. But when it comes to who helped Peter, it wasn't just me.

"If I gave him something, so did you. That means this bullet belongs to both of us. It's *our* bullet and it's your turn to have it for a while." He didn't say anything else for a few seconds. "I can't guarantee it'll win you any games, but maybe you'll be able to use a little extra luck sometime."

I didn't want to take it, but I did. "Well, I guess I could *borrow* it for a while. But if your girlfriend suddenly dumps you and you start flunking out of school, or if you come down with some raging venereal disease and all your hair falls out, you have to *swear* that you'll let me give it back." We shook on it.

I stayed where I was, but I only half-watched the rest of the game. The clouds were getting thicker. It seemed like some rain was moving in. I let the breeze blow across my face and I watched the leaves falling, and I thought about how long Hill would wonder what was wrong with me.

Chapter 110

October 24, 1976 – It's a little after two on Sunday afternoon. I'm walking into the Veterans Hospital in Murfreesboro. My mouth is dry. I feel weak and I'm sweating. Buddy is in the cafeteria and I go over and say hello. The first thing he asks me is if I'm on my way to see Mr. Anderson. My chest gets tighter and my heart beats faster.

I get on the elevator and ride up to the second floor. Elinor is standing over by the nursing station. I might've had a dream about her last night, but I'm not sure. She waves at me and I wave back, but I keep walking. The skinny orderly is standing at the door of the supply closet. When I look at him, he looks away. It feels like everybody is watching me walk down the corridor to Mr. Anderson's room.

Mr. Anderson looked as tired as I felt, but he seemed glad to see me. When he stared into my eyes, he lifted his right hand and gave me an okay sign. He went over and sat down in his chair. "Well, I've been doin' some writin', but not as much as I wanted."

He nodded toward the microphone over the door frame, and then he sat forward in his chair. There was a slightly theatrical touch in the tone of his voice. "I haven't been feelin' too good. And I've been seein' my grandmother just about every night. She'll be layin' beside me and then I wake up. You remember that invention I told you about? She keeps sayin' it belongs to the world. I've decided to go ahead and write up the whole thing."

Mr. Anderson sounded like he believed everything he was saying. He picked up an envelope from the table beside him. "But I did make a few notes about the history of Cross Keys." He handed me the envelope and started telling me about an argument between his grandfather and General Forrest. It was over the price of a stallion.

There were several sheets of paper inside the envelope. The first one started the way I hoped it would. 'I'll be finished by next Sunday. The Asberry equations were taking too long. I just worked them into a story. My grandmother and I made it up back when I was a boy. I threw in some other equations, too. But his are the ones in paragraphs that begin with words at least eight letters long. Those are the only ones that matter.

'Once those equations get taken out, all you need is the football picture you gave me. Each equation matches a number on a jersey. Seventeen equations came from Bob Asberry. The first one links to the number of the boy on the left side of the top row. The second one goes with the number of the next boy and so on – from the left to the right on the top row, then from the right to the left of the middle row, and left to right on the bottom.

'After the equations are all matched up with numbers, the numbers need to be put in numerical order from the highest number down to the lowest. Then the equations will be in order. Somebody would have to go down a lot of holes before they'd know which equations were which. You need to take it with you today when you leave.'

My throat tightened up even more, but I nodded. I could be stopped when I was leaving the hospital, or when I was on my way home. But Dr. Asberry's equations might be as important as anything Mr. Anderson was going to give me. I was already thinking about how soon I could get them to Mike.

I glanced at the equations. They looked like hieroglyphics, and I went back to reading.

'I walk around in here talking to my grandmother. Sometimes I talk about my engine. I know they're tired of waiting to find out how it works. It'll be bad when they figure out they aren't getting what they want. That's when they'll come for me. They'll give me drugs. Question me again. Then they'll get rid of me. I'm evidence. I don't expect to get out of this alive.

'I'd like to keep living. But I'd rather be dead than let those son-of-a-bitches get what they're after. I'm pretty sure you'll make it out with the equations this time. And if you get out with everything else the next time, you'll have it all. I hope I have time to get finished. My engine could change the world. What Bob Asberry and I were working on together could change it even more.'

I went through the motions of asking more questions, but all I could think about was the drive home. It wasn't long before I put the papers under my shirt and left. Elinor stopped me before I got on the elevator. She had something to ask me. I wanted to get away from the hospital as fast as I could, but I saw the orderly out of the corner of my eye.

Elinor seemed a little nervous. "I know you've been interviewing some of the patients. And I... Well if I brought my father here to the hospital, would you interview him, too? I've tried to get him to sit down at home with a tape recorder and talk about World War Two, but he still hasn't done it."

I wanted the orderly to see me having a relaxed conversation. "And you think he'd talk to me?"

"I'm pretty sure he would – especially since it's part of a program for veterans. Buddy told me the tapes are going to the State Library. I want Daddy to be remembered for what he did during the war. He was a tank commander on Iwo Jima. He won a Silver Star."

The more I was around Elinor, the more I liked her. A lot. She was open and genuine, and I would've interviewed her father even if she didn't seem like the girl next door. Even if she didn't have such a good spirit and such a beautiful smile.

She already had a date in mind. "He's pretty flexible on Sunday afternoons. How about a week from today?"

If he was watching, the orderly only saw a brief conversation. I went out to my car and my heart was racing. Things looked the way they always looked. I just got in my car and drove away. Nobody was following me, but I didn't go straight home. I drove in the opposite direction until I stopped in a little town called Woodbury.

I called the number Mike gave me, but nobody answered. I needed to be sure I'd called the right number. I tried again, but there still wasn't an answer. I felt empty.

Mike had told me what it would mean if nobody picked up the phone. It would mean that the operation was compromised. It would mean that he was in hiding or that he was a prisoner. Or it might mean he was dead. He'd told me what to do. I had a number to call, and whoever answered would tell me where to take everything.

It was dark when I got back to my neighborhood. I didn't turn on the flashlight. They might've been watching the house. If they saw me checking the doors, they'd know I thought that I was being watched. I reached up and found each of the threads with my fingertips. They were all unbroken and I went inside.

I spent the rest of the night trying to figure out what to do. There was a chance Mike was dead, but I convinced myself that he was hiding somewhere. I went back and forth between deciding to pull the plug, and waiting until I could get the rest of the information from Mr. Anderson. I hated the idea of leaving something crucial behind.

They hadn't come into my house yet. The odds were pretty good that they still didn't know what I was doing. I kept telling myself that all I had to do was leave the hospital one more time without getting stopped. I just needed to go back one more time.

I didn't look at what I'd gotten from Mr. Anderson. I wouldn't have been able to focus. I was tired and I got in bed early, but I couldn't fall asleep. I kept thinking about the envelope, and I finally got up and pulled out what he had given me.

He'd disguised the equations as mathematical explanations for the advanced technologies that he worked into his story. It looked completely indecipherable. I ended up skipping over the equations, and I read through the story that Mr. Anderson wrote down.

I imagined him back in the 1920s, lying beside his grandmother in a field out in the country. Looking up at the stars. Sometimes the story was a little hard to follow, but it was essentially a fable about a civilization on a distant planet.

I read it twice before I got back in bed. I drifted off, and after half-dreaming about Mr. Anderson's fable, I fell into a nightmare.

I watched shadows swirl up into a column of air like the debris in the funnel of a tornado, and I was in a church and I was naked, and the people in the pews were dressed in glowing blue robes. They were all staring at me. I was trying to run away, but I couldn't move. Then the floor gave way and I was falling. I fell faster and faster and I thought I was going to die, and I started to pray.

I kept falling until I was in my room. And I was a boy again and I was praying that whatsoever was true and honest and just and pure would set me on fire and save me. I started falling again, and when I finally hit the ground there was no impact. I was in a place I'd never seen, but I felt like I'd always been there.

I was in some separate dimension, watching a civilization come into being. There were times when it was like watching a movie, and there were times when I was part of what was unfolding. I didn't want to leave, but I started fading back into my life. It was dark when I woke up. I wasn't sure that I'd been dreaming.

I got out of bed, went over to my desk, and turned on the light. I wrote down everything I could remember. By the time I got back in bed, I wondered if I could still be dreaming.

The first thing I did the next morning was go over and read through what I had written down the night before. Some of it fit in with what I was writing for my parents. It wasn't long before I saw how to put it into a fable of my own. Into a parable. And I saw something else. I saw how writing a parable might protect me. There were a lot of gaps to fill and it would take some work, but I had a sense of what I needed to do.

If the dream was a coincidence, it wasn't the only coincidence there was. Coming across the story about Will and Lum Biggers was the longest of long shots, and I couldn't have made a connection with Mr. Anderson without it.

It was hard to see Edge Walton as a coincidence. He'd come into my life out of the blue. It was like he'd been sent to teach me about duty. And there was something else. He saw the world pretty much the same way as Mike and Palani and Ann saw it. Along with that, having somebody as unlikely as Whiting teach me about courage was hard to explain away.

And there was Elinor. On the same day I was supposed to pick up the rest of the information from Mr. Anderson, she wanted me to interview her father. There was an easy way to get the information out of the hospital without being caught. All I had to do was take along a large envelope that was already addressed and stamped. Then I could slip in the information from Mr. Anderson.

Elinor wouldn't mind mailing it for me. I'd address it to somebody I trusted, and the first person I thought of was Claire. I could let her know it was coming, and she'd hold it for me until I picked it up. Then all I had to do was call the number Mike gave me and drop it off along with everything else.

There was also Hill Murray and the lead bullet from *Peach Blossom*. He said it was a good luck charm, but I kept wondering if the bullet might be a message. Ever since he gave it back to me I'd been reaching into my pocket and rolling it around between my fingertips. I finally pulled out all the research I'd done on *Peach Blossom*. I went back over the details of Andrew Jackson's duel with Charles Dickinson.

Jackson made powerful enemies during his rise to power. There had been rumors that the duel with Dickinson, who was regarded as the deadliest marksman in Tennessee, was instigated by Jackson's political foes in order to have Jackson killed.

Jackson and Dickinson would only be standing eight paces apart, and Dickinson was routinely able to shoot a suspended string in two from that distance. Jackson was no more than an average shot, and he went to an experienced duelist for advice. A strategy was soon devised. The duelist showed Jackson how to obscure the location of his heart, and he advised Jackson to let Dickinson take the first shot.

On the morning of the duel, Jackson put on an oversized topcoat. It was worn so that the line of its seam, at which Dickinson was expected to fire, would be slightly off-center instead of directly in front of Jackson's heart. When the duel commenced, Dickinson fired quickly and his bullet struck the seam, missing Jackson's heart by only a fraction of an inch. Jackson was badly wounded but he stayed on his feet. Then he took his shot. Dickinson was hit in the abdomen, and he died several hours later.

Andrew Jackson, whose death would've altered the arc of American history, took Dickinson's bullet with him to his grave. The bullet that Jackson fired – the lead ball I might be carrying in my right front pocket – was cut from just beneath Dickinson's flesh before he was buried.

When I reached down and touched the bullet, I told myself that Jackson was a lot less likely to survive his ordeal than I was to survive mine. His strategy saved him. He and his adviser had analyzed every detail of the situation he was in. It shouldn't have taken me as long as it did, but not long after I started going over the details of my own situation, I knew what I needed to do.

Chapter 111

I needed to go someplace where I couldn't be watched. After breakfast, I drove into town and parked on the upper level of a parking garage. Nobody was around and I got under my car and turned on my flashlight.

As soon as I shined the light at the right engine mount – where Mike had found his tracking device – I saw a small rectangular metal box attached to the frame. I didn't know much about cars, but it was obvious that the box didn't have anything to do with the engine. I left it where it was.

My heart was racing and I felt numb. I was too scared to go home. After a few minutes, I drove over to the State Library. I ended up sitting by myself in the back corner of the reading room. I did the best I could to settle down. It was hard to breathe.

I tried to read back through what I'd written when I woke up from my dream, but I kept picturing an agent putting the transmitter on my car. I wondered if it was the same guy who was tracking the places I went. I wondered if he had gone to any of my football games. Or if he'd parked in a driveway across Woodmont Boulevard and watched me screening dirt behind Miss Young's house. If the rogue agents figured out what I was doing, I wondered if he was the one who would kill me.

I wanted to start writing my parable, but people kept coming in and out of the reading room. Somebody could've been there to watch me.

I wasn't getting anything done, and then I heard the crash of metal hitting metal. It came from outside. Two sections of a train were being coupled on the tracks just down the hill from the library. After three or four minutes, the train started moving to the west – in the direction of my neighborhood. I started imagining that I was close enough to the tracks to run down and climb up into a boxcar through an open door. I listened until I couldn't hear the train anymore.

I was calming down when I noticed a middle-aged woman across the room. She kept looking at me. I could feel my throat tighten up. I breathed in as deeply as I could, but I could taste my fear. I kept trying to think of a place where I could hide. I glanced at the woman and she looked away. I felt like a hunted animal. I listened for another train. She was looking at me again, and I imagined making it to another train before it pulled away. She stared at me over the book she was pretending to read. I made myself breathe. I kept imagining how it would feel to escape into the darkness of the boxcar.

The woman finally left, and I started to calm down. After a while, I went back to thinking about the parable. If I could make myself seem like a prophet, they wouldn't see me as a spy. I knew what I wanted to write, and the words began to flow like they were coming from someplace else.

'We have traveled from Etharyos. Our planet once circled a star similar to the star being circled by your planet. Forests and an abundance of flowers covered much of Etharyos. Our vegetation had a feature not found in your world. Our plants changed color in response to changes in the atmosphere. When there was wind, the foliage of Etharyos displayed wave after wave of shimmering colors. Our storms were dazzling.'

I had to be more convincing. In my dream, I had been standing in a garden, watching plants change color as the wind flowed and ebbed and flowed again. I had breathed in exotic fragrances and lost myself in the beauty that surrounded me.

'Our planet was an iridescent garden, but as the population of Etharyos grew larger, more and more of our forest was felled to make way for fields and pastures.

'Towns became cities. Leaders became rulers and empires formed. Empire eventually warred against empire, and the victorious subjugated the vanquished. Civilizations rose and fell, and isolated superstitions became elaborate beliefs, each with its own set of rituals and stories.

I thought I might be more convincing if I sounded like a philosopher.

'Nearly all of the beings of Etharyos were troubled by the prospect of death, and most took refuge in what they believed. Along with providing lessons that guided believers during the course of their lives, each belief offered its own version of immortality.

'Although some on Etharyos were skeptical of belief, the majority were believers. Most had absolute confidence in the inerrancy of what they believed.

'Beliefs became more powerful, and believers went to war with each other. The fervor of warriors was seldom diminished by the knowledge that they were opposed by warriors who were equally fervent. Among those who waged war, few understood that they might be worshiping the same deity as their enemies worshipped.

'Nonbelievers were equally rigid. Rejecting all belief, they were convinced that existence was without purpose. They regarded deities as nothing more than the fantasies of the fearful.'

My mind began to drift, and then I heard the crash of another train being coupled together. I wanted to keep writing, but I had lost my focus. I was tired of thinking about the agent who was sitting in a room somewhere, tracking me wherever I went – trying to decide if I was who I seemed to be. I walked around for a few minutes, and it was a while before I was writing again.

'The innovations of science were used by the powerful to degrade our planet, but they also revealed the wonders of existence. Because scientific discoveries often contradicted the dogma of scripture, science came under increasing attack by believers. As the attacks continued, the scientists and poets and philosophers and historians of Etharyos came together to defend science. They formed what was called the Movement.

'The Movement coalesced around the understanding that Etharyos and its inhabitants were on a journey through a vast cosmos. There were billions of stars in the galaxy that contained Etharyos, and it was eventually understood that there were billions of other galaxies. It came to be accepted that all the matter in the universe had been brought about by an explosion called the Event of Origin."

To get whoever was listening to believe me, I had to go much deeper.

'For generations, the Event of Origin was regarded as the beginning of existence. But some within the Movement began to theorize that the explosion might have been something other than a beginning. Some theorized that it might have been a continuation.

'It was proposed that the Event of Origin could have been a collision of separate remnants of a prior universe coming together at the speed of light. Once the possibility of a single previous universe had been acknowledged, it was theorized that there could have been an infinite succession of prior universes.

'And after an infinite number of prior universes were theorized, it was proposed that the cosmos could contain an infinite number of simultaneously existing universes.

'Those within the Movement increasingly understood that

there might be no limit to space or time, or to existence. It was eventually understood that existence might be the natural state of the cosmos.'

I wanted to finish the first part of the parable, but I was worn out. When I was walking to my car, another train was moving west along the track. It was probably on its way to Memphis or Paducah. By the time it got to the Mississippi River, I hoped I'd be asleep. I ate at a restaurant in Green Hills, and then I drove around for a while.

It was dark when I got home. I stopped at the backdoor and reached up, and the thread was dangling in the darkness.

I could feel my father's pistol in my back pocket. I wasn't shaking, but I was scared. I kept telling myself that I shouldn't be surprised. I walked up into the backyard, and I stared at the house. There was no sign that anybody was inside.

I crossed the road and went through a narrow stretch of woods that ran along a neighbor's back property line. I slowly circled around and got as close as I could to the side of our house. After a few more minutes, I slipped into the yard. I went over and checked the thread above the outside door to the basement. It wasn't broken. Unless the door from the kitchen had been knocked down, nobody could be downstairs, waiting for me in the darkness.

It was hard to breathe. My hands felt cold. Once I was inside, I stood still and listened for somebody walking around upstairs. I thought about my father standing in the closet in Manila in 1945.

If somebody was there, I wondered if I could lure him down to the basement. I could hide under the stairs and shoot through one of the openings between the steps. I decided that they would just send somebody else to kill me.

I couldn't wait any longer. I went up the basement steps and pulled the nail out of the hole I'd drilled. I stayed as quiet as I could for several minutes. I didn't hear anything.

I opened the door and got on my hands and knees, and I started crawling from room to room. I was the only one in the house. I slipped back down into the basement, and put the nail into the hole before I went outside. After I looped the thread over the nail above the basement door, I walked around to the back of the house and went inside.

I went into the kitchen, and after a few minutes I got a mirror. I started going from room to room, looking for listening devices. At first I didn't find anything. But then I saw a microphone on the underside of the desk in my bedroom. It didn't matter how many more there were.

I kept telling myself that things weren't really any worse than they were before. Mike had warned me. He'd said that I'd wind up on their radar. But knowing I was under surveillance made me feel numb inside. It made everything seem cold. I told myself the same thing over and over. All I had to do was get through the next few days. All I had to do was get the rest of the information from Mr. Anderson.

I was too keyed up to go to bed. I stayed up and tried to finish the first part of the parable. Before I went back to pretending that I was a being from another planet, I tried to visualize whoever was listening.

'The predictions of science were repeatedly verified. As additional discoveries were made, there were more and more challenges to long-held assumptions.

'Awareness had long been perceived as having evolved from matter following the Event of Origin. But most within the Movement came to understand that if there were prior universes, there was another possibility to consider.'

I had been thinking about the implications of infinity for years, but I was struggling to write what I wanted to say. A breath of wind came through my window, and I looked out and watched the cedar tree stir and be still again.

'Most came to understand what it meant if both matter and awareness existed in an infinite succession of earlier epochs. If that was the case, the question of which gave rise to the other was meaningless. If that was the case, it was understood that either could have given rise to the other, and it was possible that awareness and matter might have always existed independently.

'It was a possibility that nonbelievers could not dismiss through logic. After acknowledging that an enduring intelligence could be a natural component of the cosmos, more and more of those who formerly denied the possibility of a deity fell silent. More and more nonbelievers turned from atheism to agnosticism.'

A light pulse of air flowed through the window, and the top of the cedar tree moved like the tip of a slowly beckoning finger. I went over and tried to look into the night sky. There was too much glow from streetlights to see any stars. I tried to imagine the cosmos as an ocean that never ended. I stared out at the top of the cedar tree for a while before I started writing again.

'The most orthodox among the believers continued to turn inward – still denouncing or dismissing scientific findings that challenged the doctrines they embraced. But a growing number of believers turned outward. A growing number began to see science as a gift from The One – whom many on your planet call God.

'For the first time, great numbers of the devout came to regard scientific revelations as part of divine truth. They came to regard the natural world as a sacred source of divine revelation, and science as a gift from The One.

'They came to understand that the creations of The One must be in harmony with The One. They saw that by understanding what was in harmony with The One, they could grow closer to The One, and in that way, the search for scientific truth became a central part of their faith.'

Chapter 112

October 31, 1976 – It's Sunday afternoon. I've been working on the parable, and I've only had a few hours of sleep since Friday. I'm walking up the sidewalk of the Veteran's Hospital in Murfreesboro. I feel like I'm looking at the hospital through the wrong end of a telescope. I know it hasn't moved, but it looks farther away than it was before. The entrance makes me think about the front door of the hospital in the Van Gogh painting. The hospital door isn't screaming, but it looks ominous. I keep telling myself to take everything one step at a time. I feel eyes all over me.

Buddy saw me as soon as I went inside. He gave me a wry smile. "Well, *Elinor* is pretty excited about you interviewing her father."

I knew what he was implying. I made myself say what I would normally say. "Hey, she asked me to do it."

He gave me a playful look. "Yeah, I bet I know how that went. She gave you one of her big smiles and you were ready to say yes to *whatever* she had in mind. I guess it's a good thing that all she wanted you to do was talk to her father."

I pretended to have been taken aback. "Here I am trying to do a favor for an *innocent* young girl, and you turn it into something lurid."

He stopped needling me. "Is there anything else on your interview schedule today? We're having lasagna tonight and you're invited for dinner."

I had an excuse. "Well I'd love to have some lasagna, but it's Halloween. I need to get back home before the little goblins start showing up for their candy. As soon as I say hello to Mr. Anderson and talk to Elinor's father, I'll be heading back."

Buddy gave me a long look. "I'm still trying to figure out how Kermit Anderson ended up being your favorite veteran. I have a hard time even getting him to say hello. All he's ever told me is that he was in the Air Corps."

I didn't want to miss a beat. "Yeah, he doesn't have much to say about World War Two. Most of the time we talk about the Civil War and the history of where he grew up. I'm trying to help him put together a little book about it."

That seemed to satisfy him. I didn't think Buddy was part of the cell, but he brought up Mr. Anderson two weeks in a row, and that made me suspicious. Then something else hit me. Mike had me under surveillance at the Swan Ball. Buddy might have been working with Mike.

By the time I got to the elevator, I was telling myself that I really couldn't be sure that Mike was who he said he was. He could be using me. He might be working for the Russians or the Chinese. Then I wondered if he could be working with the rogue agents.

Something else occurred to me when I was on the elevator. I would be a lot safer if Mike *was* working for Russians or the Chinese. Foreign agents might leave me alone after their operation was over. But if he was working for the corporations, I'd be another loose end they had to get rid of.

I had to reel myself in. I had to keep believing that Mike was who he said he was. It was too late to believe anything else. It was too late to do anything except get off the elevator and walk down the corridor to Mr. Anderson's room.

When he opened his door he looked drained and solemn. As soon as I was inside, he handed me forty or fifty pages of notebook paper. "I've been thinkin' about what I've told you about Cross Keys. I expect we'll end up havin' a pretty good book. I should be finished writin' about the invention in another three or four days." He looked into my eyes. "But I'm still not sure how it fits in with everything else."

I took an envelope out of my tablet and slipped in all his information. "I'll be glad to tell you what I think, but whatever you decide will be fine. It's your book."

He stared at me like he was looking for something. "Well, I guess we'll just have to see."

I put the envelope inside the tablet. I wasn't sure I'd see Mr. Anderson again and I shook his hand. It was the first time I ever touched him. I hadn't realized how small his hands were. There was only one more thing I needed them to hear me say. "I'm looking forward to reading about your invention. I'll see you in a few days."

I started out the door, but he had something else to tell me. "I've been wishin' that you could drive me out to Cross Keys sometime. I could show you the old house where I grew up, and take... take you down to the cellar." He was still staring into my eyes, and there was an expression on his face I hadn't seen before. "You might like seein' where old Laban Hartley made all that brandy."

Nobody was waiting in the corridor when I opened the door, and nobody stopped me on my way down to the break room. That's where I met Elinor and her father. He looked like an ex-Marine. He had a thick neck and broad shoulders and big forearms. He also had the same authentic smile as his daughter. I turned on the tape recorder, and I only ended up asking three or four questions. The rest of the time he just talked.

He said there wasn't any resistance to the landing on Iwo Jima, but things changed the next day. The three tanks he commanded were moving toward the middle of the island when they lost infantry support. They were almost a mile inside Japanese lines when two of the tanks were disabled by satchel charges.

He came up out of the turret of his tank, and shot a Japanese soldier who was running toward his tank with another charge. Then all three tanks came under machine gun fire. He climbed down and was able to move around behind the enemy position. I could tell that he didn't like talking about it, but he went ahead and described killing the men in the bunker with his submachine gun.

He was still haunted by what he did. He said the only thing he was proud of was getting all three of his tank crews back alive. I got the feeling it was the first time Elinor heard a lot of what she was hearing. I could see the deep love she had for her father. Her eyes were shining the whole time he was telling his story.

I changed my mind about asking her to mail the envelope containing Mr. Anderson's information. All she had to do was walk out of the hospital and put it in a mailbox on her way home, but there was always a chance that somebody was watching her. I couldn't put her in danger.

I shouldn't have even thought about involving her or Claire. I shook hands with her father and told Elinor goodbye. I felt like I'd known her for a long time.

The sun was getting low in the sky when I went out the front door. I started walking down the sidewalk toward the parking lot. I wasn't sweating, but my arms and legs felt weak. If anything was going to happen, it would be after I got away from the hospital.

I glanced around when I was getting in my car. I didn't see anybody, but they knew where I was. I kept telling myself that all I had to do was make it back to Nashville.

I assumed I was being followed while I drove down the interstate. My heart was already beating too fast. The closer I got to Nashville, the faster it beat. It was racing by the time I pulled into the parking lot beside the Vanderbilt Library.

I reached under my seat and pulled out the equations I'd already gotten from Mr. Anderson. Then I picked up my tablet and got out of the car. I tried not to walk too fast to the front entrance of the library. They were about to lose track of me.

They'd know my car was parked beside the library. They would assume I was there to do research. As soon as I got inside I found a pay phone. I went into the booth and pulled the door closed, and then I called the number I'd gotten from Mike.

He said to make my call in the middle of the night, but I wasn't going to wait that long. A guy picked up on the fourth ring. I asked for the ticket office, and at first he didn't say anything. Then he gave me a separate phone number. "Somebody will be there to take your call in twenty minutes."

After I hung up, I stayed in the booth and watched the students walking by. A couple of minutes later I thought about the envelope I hadn't given to Elinor. It had Claire's address on the front. I slid out the stack of papers I'd just gotten from Mr. Anderson. I put them with the equations, and I threw the envelope into a trash can.

When I called the guy back, he picked up on the first ring. "Are you calling from a pay phone?"

"Yes."

"Okay. I have two questions. Our friend told me that you'd be calling if he was unavailable, and if you needed to make a delivery. Is that the situation?"

"Yes, it is."

His next question made me a little nervous. "Where are you right now?"

"I'm at Vanderbilt."

"Okay, I'm pretty close to Green Hills. Should I come to you, or do you want to come to me?"

I didn't tell him that my car was being tracked. "I'll come to you."

He didn't say anything for a few seconds. "Do you know the area around Harpeth Hall?"

It was the next neighborhood south of Woodmont. "Yeah. I know it pretty well."

"Okay, I'll be on Sneed Road. It's the next street east of Estes. I'll be between Hobbs and Sneed Terrace."

The little girl who went missing the year before had lived just two streets over from there. Her body was found partway between that section of Sneed and her house. "I can be there in about forty-five minutes."

"Okay. Kids will be out trick-or-treating and I'll be walking by myself. I'll say 'Happy Ground Hog Day.' Does that sound okay?"

I went down the hallway and up the stairs, and I left through the back entrance of the library. It was dusk when I walked across the campus to the field where I'd stood in formation wearing the green tie when I was in NROTC. I waited there for a few minutes. When I convinced myself that nobody was watching me, I started jogging.

I ran through part of fraternity and sorority row before I turned south. There were three miles of back streets and yards between where I was and where I was going. Nobody would be able to follow me.

The glowering faces of pumpkins with candles inside were on front porches, and trick-or-treaters were everywhere. They seemed to be moving through the streets in slow motion. I felt a sense of exhilaration when I was knifing through the half-darkness of Halloween night. I might as well have been invisible. Neighborhood blended into neighborhood, and a few minutes after I ran past Woodmont School, I got to the north end of Sneed Road.

Halloween was the perfect time for a rendezvous. There were clusters of children all over the place. There were fathers pushing baby strollers, and mothers keeping their eyes on kids who could walk, but who weren't old enough to go off on their own.

I walked down Sneed. It wasn't long before I thought I saw somebody I recognized. I was pretty sure Joey Green was standing in a driveway. He had been on my baseball team eight or nine years earlier – back in the '60s. He was standing next to a little blonde girl who was dressed up like a princess. I wondered if she was his daughter.

Two or three minutes later I saw a guy coming in my direction. It wasn't long before he said, "Happy Ground Hog Day." He was carrying a pack over his right shoulder. He didn't look like a spy. I started walking with him, and when we were about halfway down the street I followed him into the driveway of a house with all its lights turned off.

I wanted to ask him if he knew whether Mike was okay, but I probably wasn't supposed to ask any questions. If either one of us got caught and interrogated, the less we knew the better. I handed him the information from Mr. Anderson.

He didn't look at anything I gave him. He just put it in his pack. I wondered if what I gave him would make any difference.

He straightened up after he closed the pack. "I don't know your name, but I know that this is your first operation. I need to make sure you understand a few things. Number one – your part in this operation will *never* be over."

I wasn't sure what he meant.

"Everything about this operation has to stay buried for the rest of your life. And I mean *everything*. If anything comes out over the next few months, the people we're after will scatter and disappear."

I hadn't thought that far ahead.

"And if anything comes out after that, the next time a cell crops up, they'll know the mistakes this group made and they'll be harder to root out. You can *never* disclose anything about the technology. You can *never* disclose anything about who you were working with. And like I said before, you can *never* disclose anything about your involvement in this."

That was all he said. We didn't shake hands. He just looked at me for two or three seconds and then he walked up the driveway. He went across the road and disappeared between two houses. After a couple of minutes, I left, too.

There were still plenty of trick-or-treaters around, but it wouldn't be long before they started thinning out. I wondered if teenagers would show up later on and smash pumpkins or heave rolls of unfurling toilet paper into the trees along that part of Sneed. I went through a sideyard and cut over to Estes Road before I started jogging. I ran until I got to Woodmont, and then I cut across the baseball field and walked the rest of the way back to Vanderbilt.

I had been exhilarated when I was on my way to deliver the information, but my exhilaration was gone. The group behind the killing of Dr. Asberry and the other scientists – the people who had both me and Mr. Anderson under surveillance – were still out there. The surveillance team thought they were just a week or so away from getting what they were after. Once they realized they'd been set up, they'd have both me and Mr. Anderson in their sights. I needed another plan, but I didn't have one. We were both sitting ducks.

When I got back to Vanderbilt I went in the rear entrance of the library, and then I walked down the stairs and left through the front door. I drove straight home. None of the threads above the doors were broken. I went in and took a shower, and I got in bed.

I was dead tired, but I knew I wouldn't be able to just turn off the light and fall asleep. When I finally dozed off I was trying to think of a way to protect myself without compromising the operation.

Chapter 113

It was still dark outside when I woke up. At some point, I'd had a dream about Elinor. We were standing on a beach at sunset and a line of four seagulls was flying just above the ocean. As the dream was ending she looked over and asked me how many children I thought we'd have.

I would've thought more about the dream, but I went back to wondering about the guy who was monitoring me. I wondered what he thought when he listened to me walking around the house or taking a shower or fixing something to eat. And I wondered if I talked in my sleep.

I was worn out by the time the sun was coming up, but I didn't want to stay in bed. I got dressed and went outside, and I got in my car. Then I started driving. I thought I might feel better if I tried to get lost.

I went west and south and west again before I started turning onto smaller and smaller roads. Being lost when I was driving around with Callie or Claire meant not knowing where I was, but being lost when I was alone was different. It almost made me feel invisible. The guy who was tracking me must've been wondering what I was up to.

I ended up on a one-lane gravel road in the middle of nowhere. Before long it changed from gravel to dirt, and after two or three miles I came to a creek that flowed across the road. The creek continued to the base of a nearby bluff, and from there it followed the contour of the bluff until it disappeared around a bend. It was a beautiful and secluded place.

I wasn't sure how deep the water was, and I got out of my car. I thought about turning around and going back, but I went over to the edge of the water and threw a rock out into the middle of the ford. I couldn't tell from the splash whether it was shallow enough to get across. The sun was out and it was fairly warm, and I took off my shoes and socks and rolled up my pants.

The creek didn't feel any colder than the Pacific Ocean felt when the surf was up. I waded out to the middle and the water came about halfway up to my knees. There probably wasn't anybody within two miles of where I was standing, and I melted into the feeling of isolation.

I hadn't been there before, but the creek seemed familiar. I was still standing out in the current when I figured out why. When I slipped away from camp on the morning after my grandmother died, I stood on a bluff and looked out at the Caney Fork River. I imagined paddling a canoe all the way up to where the river began – going as far as I could up the creek that formed its largest tributary. The creek where I was standing looked like the creek I had envisioned.

When I had been on the bluff, picturing the creek leading up to a distant spring, I was pretty sure the river didn't always originate in the underground channels that led to the spring. I remembered thinking that when it rained hard enough and long enough, the origin of the river extended beyond the water-glutted crevices that fed the spring, and went all the way up into the clouds.

I stood in the water, sliding the bottoms of my feet across the bedrock. I thought about the times when remnants of hurricanes would roll up from the south. When the rain extended as far as the ocean, the origin of the creek was a lot farther away than the clouds.

The water sweeping around me flowed on to the Duck River, and after a day or two it would join the Tennessee before moving into the Ohio and then the Mississippi on its journey down to the

Gulf of Mexico. I imagined sunlight shimmering on the surface of the Caribbean and evaporation rising into the clouds, and I was staring down at the water when something came to me. The origin of the creek, and its destination, might be the creek itself.

I watched a feather drift by on top of the water. Imagining the feather as a single life, I wondered if there were poems about lives being the tributaries of the human journey. But by the time the feather floated out of sight, I was back to wondering how long I'd be alive, and what being alive was.

I hadn't stopped thinking about awareness. I remembered talking to my baseball players about it, just before they started moving around the field at Woodmont like they were zombies. I still suspected that my sense of awareness might extend beyond my brain. Watching the water moving past me, I thought of my awareness flowing away and then flowing back to me from farther up the creek.

I decided that my car would probably make it across the water, and I drove to the other side. After I went several hundred yards, I came to another ridge. It looked like it should've been the end of the road, but it wasn't.

The road was steep and there were some ruts, and before I got to the top I had to get out and move a big limb that had fallen. I kept thinking I'd eventually have to stop and go back, but after I drove along the top of a ridge for another half-mile or so, the road dropped down into a valley.

There were more ruts to ease over and there was another creek to go through, and then I came to a deteriorating farmhouse. It looked like it hadn't been occupied for years. The front porch was falling in and the roof was sagging. In the front yard there was the rusted-out body of an old Packard surrounded by weeds. By then I'd gone miles without seeing anybody. It was how most of America would've looked if the missile crisis had ended with a nuclear war back in 1962.

I finally came to a frame house. I waved at a man who was

standing out beside his barn, but he just stared at me. After another mile the road got wider, and I passed two or three other rundown houses before I came to a paved road.

I turned onto the road and there was a small community a little further on. I stopped at a country store across from a brick schoolhouse. I went in and got a grilled bologna sandwich. I was going to eat while I was driving, but when I went outside, some kids were playing in the schoolyard across the road.

They looked like third or fourth graders, and they were over by a merry-go-round. Just about all their clothes looked like hand-me-downs, and most of them had homemade haircuts. The merry-go-round was homemade, too. It had six wooden boards that served as seats, and the seats surrounded a circular metal hub that came up about four feet out of the ground.

The section holding the seats was connected to the hub by rounded metal bars. In front of each seat, there was another bar for the kids to hold on to. But they weren't playing the way children usually played – going around and around while a couple of other kids stood beside the merry-go-round and gave it an occasional push.

There were four kids, three boys and a girl, pushing from down between the seats and the hub. The merry-go-round was picking up speed as the kids trudged around in a tight circle, pushing the bars in front of them. The kids on the seats were leaning forward, and the faster they spun, the tighter they held on.

They went faster and faster, and the centrifugal force started taking its toll. It looked like their arms were getting tired, and the inner edge of the seats must've been digging into the backs of their legs. One by one they let go. Most of them hit the ground without getting hurt, but there were a couple of hard falls.

There was finally just one boy left. His arms were wrapped around one of the curved vertical bars that separated the seats. Before long he was only holding on with his hands. His feet were behind him. He was almost as close to being horizontal as to being vertical. He looked like a flag in the wind. He went around two more times before he finally sailed off.

He landed hard on his side, but he rolled when he hit. After he brushed off his shirt, he reached down and started rubbing behind his knees. The merry-go-round stopped, and he climbed down next to the hub to help push. The other kids were still getting in their seats when the merry-go-round started moving again.

I watched them go through five more rounds before a bell rang and they all went back inside. I couldn't stop thinking about the difference between growing up in the country and growing up in the suburbs. And how anemic suburban childhoods had become.

Chapter 114

I ended up going back through Franklin. I drove up Columbia Pike and turned onto the street beside Battle Ground Academy. If there hadn't been students around, I would've walked up to the study hall and gone into some of my old classrooms. I just pulled over and parked.

I looked at the part of the campus where so many soldiers had advanced to their deaths. I thought back to when I walked around on the battlefield when I was a student, imagining myself as a seventeen-year-old Confederate soldier. It was twelve years later, and the way I looked at things had changed.

If I'd been a Southerner during the Civil War, I was sure I would've despised slavery a lot more at age twenty-nine than at seventeen. I still wondered how my family would've responded to slavery if we'd been around back in the 1850s.

I was pretty confident that my father wouldn't have bought any slaves. If slaves were inherited, I told myself that he and Mother might've taken them up north to a free state and emancipated them. And if the slaves didn't want to leave home, they might've been liberated and been given some land. Or there might've been another way for them to live where they wanted to live.

But even if my family did the best we could as slave owners, I knew where I would've probably been, as a twenty-nine-year-old Southerner, during the closing months of the Civil War.

Even though I was older, I still wouldn't have the courage to face all the shame and condemnation that would've come from not serving in the Confederate Army. And even if I did have that level of courage, I didn't see how I could've fought against so many people I loved, and who loved me.

There was always a chance I could've gone somewhere to wait out the war, but I would've probably joined up. If I was alive by the time of the Battle of Franklin, I still couldn't see myself advancing into all the smoke and death to attack the breastworks.

But at the age of twenty-nine, I wouldn't have cowered in the dirt. And I wouldn't have looked for a way to get back to the rear. At the age of twenty-nine, I would've done everything I could to become a spy.

I imagined showing up in Franklin wearing civilian clothes and hobbling around on a crutch I was pretending to use. While the rest of Hood's army was moving up to Spring Hill, I would've been blending in with people in town. I saw myself gathering as much intelligence as I could, and then slipping away and making my way south to deliver my report.

I would've told myself that I wasn't serving the Confederacy. I would've told myself that the information I was trying to collect might save the lives of friends and neighbors and relations who joined the Confederacy.

I left Battle Ground and turned north on Columbia Pike. I drove through the place where the Union defenses stood, but I didn't go straight home.

I stopped off at Mount Hope Cemetery and I walked over to where I'd stood eight years earlier, when Hall Guthrie was buried. If he'd been a Confederate soldier at Franklin in 1864, he would've been waving a battle flag and leading his unit straight into the Union breastworks. He would've ended up the way he ended up 104 years later – having lived a heroic life, and among the fallen.

Standing in the cemetery I saw the benefit, more than I ever had before, of bringing everything to a sudden end. Dying the quick death of a hero was a much better fate than being hunted down and killed as a spy.

The Civil War followed me home. I should've said more to Whiting and David and the rest of the kids about how Confederate units staggered into the outskirts of Nashville following the nightmare at Franklin.

I should've told them that Ensworth was built near the perimeter where a southern picket line was positioned. That our football team practiced on the same ground where retreating Confederates and advancing Union soldiers skirmished in December of 1864. It would've brought another dimension to their games of Smear and Crush.

I went home that night and got in bed early. I lay in the dark and thought about what the agents would do when I didn't show up the following Sunday. They would compare notes, and then they'd come for Mr. Anderson and take him away. The first time they interrogated him, they had made sure to keep him alive. The next time they wouldn't hold back.

I wasn't sure how much longer I'd be alive either, but I thought it would be at least another week before anything happened. I needed to finish the parable while there was still time. I got out of bed and turned on my light.

I read back over what I'd written about the Movement being established on Etharyos. And about the intellectual transformation that had begun to take place among its believers and its nonbelievers. Then I read what I'd written over the last couple of days. I needed to sound more like a philosopher.

'The connections between The One and science and the natural world had become clear. More and more believers understood the need to reconcile the pronouncements of ancient scripture with the observations of science, and what became known as the Reconciliation soon commenced.

'The Reconciliation was regarded as a sacred search for truth.

It was recognized that unlike some of the words contained in scripture, the works of The One were not in conflict with each other. Ancient texts that conflicted with the works of The One were gradually discredited, but texts in harmony with the works of The One gained new power.

'As more believers brought discernment to their religion, more non-believers began to moderate their earlier skepticism. Growing numbers of believers and non-believers considered the implications of infinity, and became aware of the journey of which they were a part.

'It was widely observed that the validated texts of the principal beliefs of Etharyos were profoundly similar. It was observed that there had always been, among the sacred scriptures of every religion, teachings to nourish the journey of the inhabitants of Etharyos. Teachings that condemned undermining the lives of the many for the benefit of the few.'

There was a ripple of wind and a dog started barking from somewhere down the street. After a couple of minutes, the air grew still and the night was quiet again.

'Despite the Reconciliation, some nonbelievers were still unable to see an ultimate purpose to their lives. While those were resigned to their eventual non-existence, many others saw another possibility.

'Acknowledging the limitations of their knowledge and questioning their assumptions, they saw that their existence might be more than a cosmic accident. Recognizing the connection between their lives and the journey of their planet, they began to understand that their lives drew meaning from the journey of Etharyos. They saw that the journey of their planet connected them to the cosmos.

'As their connection to the cosmos came more into focus, the inhabitants of Etharyos felt an increasing kinship with their planet. Most believers came to understand that the continuing degradation of their divinely-created planet, and the destruction of its divinely-created lifeforms, was profoundly wrong.

'Most believers came to see the stewardship of Etharyos as their spiritual obligation. Most who were without belief came to see protecting Etharyos as their moral obligation.'

I heard the distant whistle of a westbound train as it rolled toward the Woodmont neighborhood. I imagined that I was in an empty boxcar – looking out through the open door at the empty streets and empty yards and darkened houses.

'But by the time of the Reconciliation, the many were under the control of the greedy and powerful few. Seeing the threat posed by the Reconciliation, those who held political and military and economic power had joined forces. They formed what was known as the Hierarchy, and maintained control over Etharyos for many more generations.

'Although much of its ancient environment had been destroyed, a surviving section of luminescent forest continued to grow in one remote part of Etharyos. When an enormously valuable mineral deposit was discovered beneath the remaining forest, the Hierarchy was determined to reap the financial benefits of the discovery. The degradation of Etharyos had become a deep and burning issue, and the Movement rose in opposition and confronted the Hierarchy.

'It was understood that the self-serving actions of the Hierarchy not only threatened all of the lifeforms the ancient forest sustained, it endangered the journey of Etharyos as well. As soon as those who directed the Hierarchy were confronted, they began to defend their interests more aggressively.

'The Hierarchy had long been clever and disciplined in its use of propaganda. Determined to crush the Movement, it engaged in more and more bribery and violence and assassination. But being subjected to rational analysis by the Movement, the flaws in the narratives perpetrated by the Hierarchy were continually exposed and discredited.

'Having lost its legitimacy, the Hierarchy increased its use of force. But confronted by the unyielding will of the Movement, and increasingly opposed by those within its own ruling families, the Hierarchy consumed itself in the final stage of its collapse.'

Chapter 115

The next morning I got a phone call from Buddy. Mr. Anderson had disappeared during the night. Buddy wanted to know if I'd heard him say anything about wanting to run off. I almost asked if he was sure Mr. Anderson left on his own, but I caught myself. My phone was bugged. I would've given myself away if I suggested that he could've been kidnapped.

All I told him was that I was supposed to get together with Mr. Anderson in a couple of days. I wanted to believe that Buddy was who he said he was, and I wanted to believe that Mr. Anderson was able to slip past the staff while the rest of the patients were asleep. He knew what was coming and it made sense that he would try to escape. But it was just as likely that agents came in during the night and took him away.

I pictured the empty corridor and agents going into his room and sedating him. I pictured the skinny orderly and whoever he was working with getting Mr. Anderson outside without being noticed. I imagined Mr. Anderson waking up in a locked room somewhere – wishing he'd tried to escape. Wishing he'd killed himself when he had the chance.

I was still tired when Buddy called, and I got back in bed. I was glad it wasn't dark. I stared at the ceiling, and thought about the long nights of lying awake when I was younger. I let myself remember the tone of my father's snoring and the sound of the dog barking in the distance. I was more alone and more afraid at twenty-nine than I'd been at fifteen.

I reached over and got the bullet off the top of my bedside table. I was rolling it between my fingers when I fell back asleep. When I woke up I couldn't remember any dreams. I was hungry, but there wasn't much at home to eat. I was on my way out the door to get a sandwich, but when I ran my fingers over my right front pocket, the bullet wasn't there. I went back to my room, and I finally found it down where the sheet was tucked into the mattress.

I put it in my pocket, and while I was looping the thread over the nail above the back door, an idea came to me. It was like a bubble drifting up to the surface of a pond. There was another way I might be able to protect myself. There was another way to reinforce the idea that I was just a strange guy who happened to show up and start interviewing Mr. Anderson.

I spent most of the day at home, working on the parable. The next time I left the house was when I drove over to a school off White Bridge Road to vote. I almost voted for Jimmy Carter, but nostalgia won out. I voted the way I would've voted in 1968 if his name was on the ballot. Eugene McCarthy was a third-party candidate, and I gave him one of the 5000 votes he received in Tennessee.

Late that afternoon I left the television on in the den and walked to Woodmont. I wanted whoever was listening to think I was at home, getting ready to watch the election returns. I brought the parable and my tape recorder and a few blank tapes with me.

There was a bulldozer parked beside the main part of the school building. I didn't know when it had been hauled in and unloaded, but I knew why it was there. I wouldn't let myself think about what was going to happen.

I walked around to the side door and went in through the basement. I didn't think I'd ever be back inside the school again. I went up the steps and walked out into the lunchroom. The floor was covered with debris, and graffiti had been spray-painted on the walls.

I went over and stood where the voting booth had been when

my mother let me pull the lever for Eisenhower back in 1952. I looked around and then I went out through the double doors and into the hall. After I passed my fifth-grade classroom and the library, I walked around to the stairs and went up to the principal's office.

I sat on the floor and turned on my tape recorder. Then I started talking about coaching kids and the history of the neighborhood, and some of the people who had tried to teach me about life. It didn't seem all that different from when I talked to Dr. Harrelson after he fell asleep. It was time to read the parable, and I put another tape in the recorder.

I read about the luminescent plants and the development of religion on Etharyos. I had just finished reading about the triumph of the Movement over the Hierarchy when I heard the clicking of a train. It was approaching the far side of Bosley's Knob. I imagined that I was standing beside the track, waiting to make my escape. Looking down the track and waiting.

'With the victory of the Movement over the Hierarchy, a discourse took place across the planet. Most inhabitants of Etharyos, regardless of their spiritual perspective, had become dedicated to the journey of which they were a part. It was decided that there would be a global discussion regarding the destiny of the planet.

'The possibility that Etharyos might not endure was examined. For some, the death of the planet would mean the desecration of a sacred gift from The One. For others, it would mean that no heroic life ever lived, no sacrifice ever made, and no act of grace ever performed would have any ultimate meaning.

'Most eventually understood that if Etharyos ever ceased to be, all the beauty ever expressed through our art and music and literature, and all the knowledge accumulated during the existence of our planet would be without meaning. Most agreed that the death of Etharyos would signify that its existence, and our own, had been of no consequence.

'It was decided that the Movement must take control of the journey of Etharyos, which came to be called the Journey. It was recognized that our planet could not sustain the number of inhabitants it supported. Because Etharyos could not fulfill its destiny unless balance was achieved, it was decided that the size of our population would be brought under control.

'A major decision was also announced. The chemical poisoning of the planet would be brought to an end, and vast sections of forest would be replanted in a global ceremony of ecological reclamation.

I heard how slowly the train was moving. I imagined I was in the boxcar, standing at the open door and feeling the night air against my face.

'After more discourse and more deliberation, it was declared that Etharyos was an obscure sphere spinning in orbit around an obscure star, and that our star occupied an immense galaxy containing a swirling expanse of other stars and planets. It was declared that our galaxy was part of a vast universe containing a swirling expanse of other galaxies. And that our universe might occupy a cosmos swirling with an endless multitude of other universes.

'It was ultimately decided that all the institutions of the planet must operate in absolute harmony with the Journey. A declaration was eventually announced. It stated that Etharyos was a seed floating within a vast cosmos, and it would either grow and blossom, or wither and cease to be. The compact was dedicated to the perpetuation of the Journey, and to the blossoming of Etharyos.

The horn of the train blared and echoed across the neighborhood.

'The colonization of other life-sustaining planets was regarded as a crucial step in the blossoming of Etharyos. Preparations were made for the time when future generations would inhabit other solar systems within what was called the Sphere of Exploration.

'The movement anticipated that the colonies of Etharyos would continue to spread, and that another civilization would eventually be encountered. It was suspected that the infinite cosmos surrounding us likely contained an infinite number of other civilizations, which came to be called Omegas. It was decided that only when the civilization that sprang from Etharyos came into contact with another civilization – and only when harmony with that civilization was achieved – would the blossoming of Etharyos have been attained.'

The engineer gave another long blast from his horn. I stopped reading and paused the tape recorder. The train was picking up speed. It was entering Dutchman's Curve. I imagined leaning out of the open boxcar and trying to see the track ahead, where over 100 people had died in the catastrophic collision of 1918.

The train kept moving to the west, and a couple of minutes later I heard the horn in the distance. It was probably passing Belle Meade Mansion by then. It would keep picking up speed, and as it rolled out into the countryside, the illumination from the lights of Nashville would slowly fade from the night sky. I turned on the tape recorder and started reading again.

The agents had to believe that I was just an eccentric who came to Murfreesboro to record the stories of old soldiers. They had to believe that somebody who made up a parable wouldn't be involved in espionage. If they didn't believe it, they would be coming for me. I needed to barricade the doors. If I could hear them breaking in, I would still have a chance to get away.

Andrew Jackson had survived his duel by concealing where his heart was. If they came, I needed to conceal where *I* was. One of the tapes I made would be playing. They would hear my voice coming from my room, but I'd be down in the basement. As soon as I heard them upstairs, I'd escape through the basement door.

Unless somebody was waiting right outside, they wouldn't be able to stop me. I would run through yards until I got to the backyard of the Williams mansion. Then I'd go past where the slave cabins had been and move down across Sugartree Creek. From there it was less than a half-mile to the Belle Meade police station.

I would pretend to be catatonic, and I would be detained. I would spend the night in jail. I would act however I needed to act to get transferred to a psychiatric facility. I should be safe there, and I'd stay until Mother and my father came back from Europe.

When my parents showed up, I'd tell them as much as I could. There was at least a chance that everything would blow over after a few months. If the agents came to my house, it was the best option I had.

But if things went the way I hoped – I wouldn't have to act like I was crazy. After whoever was listening heard what I was about to say – after it was passed along to whoever else would hear it, they might conclude that I was way too much of an oddball to be involved in espionage. They'd eavesdrop for a few more days, or a few more weeks or months, and then they'd decide that I was nothing more than a coincidence.

It was around midnight when I got home. I went up into the attic and got the spare mattress. After I took it down to the basement, I got the telephone out of my parents' room and plugged it into the jack at the bottom of the basement steps. I put my father's gun on the floor next to me.

I went back up to my room and sat down at my desk. I knew what I wanted to say. I needed to come off as innocent and a little bit nervous. I pretended I was fifteen again, and I started to talk.

"Here's how I know you're listening to me. When I go out, I always leave my bedroom door open at a particular angle, and the angle had changed. It was something I started doing when I was a teenager. I wanted to know when my mother or my father went into my room. The angle of my closet door was different, too.

"The chair beside my desk had also been moved. But nothing had been taken. I didn't understand why an intruder would come into my bedroom and not take anything. Then I started looking around. That's when I found out you're listening to me. I knew it was a bug. I saw a picture of one not too long ago in a magazine article.

"I keep wondering who would want to listen in on me. I thought about calling the police, but they'd ask me who would have a reason to come into my house and bug my bedroom. I wouldn't be able to tell them anything.

"The police couldn't do anything without suspects or a motive, but they might make a follow-up call after my mother and father get home. My parents aren't in good health. There's no point in giving them anything else to worry about. I want this to be over by the time they get back.

"And I want it to be over before I go crazy. If that's what you're shooting for, it's working. I haven't been getting much sleep. If I've done something wrong, let me know what it is so I can apologize. I've wondered if you're a homicidal maniac, but I don't think a homicidal maniac would sneak into a house and bug somebody's bedroom. A homicidal maniac would just show up with an ax.

"If there's something you want to know, just call me up and I'll try to give you an answer. I guess that's about it. If I don't hear from you tonight, I'll talk to you again in the morning."

Chapter 116

November 3, 1976 – It's seven o'clock on Wednesday morning and I'm in the den. There's a bowl of oatmeal in front of me. I know I should eat something, but I'm not hungry. The air in the basement was stagnant and I didn't get any sleep last night. I kept hearing sounds, but I didn't hear anybody walking across the floor above me. The television is on and the news is about the election of Jimmy Carter. I'm too numb to care. I keep thinking about what else I should say to whoever is listening. I'm worried about saying the wrong thing and giving myself away. I can't concentrate anymore. I can't keep looking over my shoulder for much longer.

One of the reasons I made the recordings was to make them think I was upstairs. But I wasn't thinking straight. If the phone started ringing while they were listening to my voice on the tape, the story they had to believe would fall apart.

Being down in the basement, there wouldn't be enough time to get upstairs, turn off the recorder, and then answer the phone. I couldn't be downstairs and pick up the telephone. I couldn't start talking while they were hearing my voice on the tape. And I couldn't just let the phone keep ringing. The phone was bugged. They would know if it was disconnected, or if I'd taken it off the hook.

Everything they heard – everything I did – had to sound completely normal. My plan to be in the basement when they came was too risky.

I tried to think. I felt like I was drifting in and out of a fog. There was too much light coming in from outside, and I closed all the drapes. I seemed like I was somebody else when I was wedging the kitchen table between the back door and the counter beside the stove. After I moved furniture against the other upstairs doors in the house – and after I blocked off the basement door – I went back into my room.

I looked over at the tape recorder on my desk. I tried to visualize the agent who was listening to me. When I started talking, I wanted it to sound like we were having a conversation.

"Well, you didn't call last night. I've been trying to imagine what you look like. I'm picturing you sitting in a room somewhere, listening to me through headphones.

"I'm starting to wonder if you're curious about me. If you are, there are a couple of things you should know. One thing is how much I like coaching kids. I know them pretty well right now, but their lives are just getting started. I'd love to know what they'll be like in twenty or thirty years.

"Another thing is how much I love history. I spend a lot of time researching the people who used to live in the neighborhood where I live. I've learned a lot, but I finally figured out that I'll never know what any of them were really like.

"And for the last two or three months I've been going over to the Veterans Hospital in Murfreesboro. I've been interviewing men who used to be soldiers. Most of them are World War Two veterans. I'm curious about how they look at the world, but I probably haven't asked them enough personal questions."

I reached down and plugged in the tape recorder. "So I guess you and I have something in common. I research people, and it seems like you're researching me.

"I think about you a lot. I've been wondering who you are and how you feel about what you're doing with your life. And like I said, I wonder if you're curious about me. About how I see the world. If you are, I want to tell you some things you'll never find out by listening to me through headphones."

I wouldn't be down in the basement, but I could still get away. As soon as I heard them breaking through one of the doors, I'd go out through one of my windows and start running for the Belle Meade police station.

"I've been trying to write a parable. At first, I just wanted to write something for my parents. Even though they wouldn't admit it, I've been a disappointment to them for a lot of my life. But I'm starting to understand a few things. I want them to know that I might be turning out okay after all.

"And after a while, I decided that some of the kids I've coached might eventually want to know what I think. I didn't get anywhere at first, but then I had a dream and I've written down a lot of what I want to say. I'm going to read it to you, but first I want to tell you a few other things."

I sensed that they were about to come for me. They probably had Mr. Anderson. If they'd already tortured him, they knew what I'd done. They'd hear the tape and know I was home, and then they'd come for me. The tape still had to be playing when they got to my house. I thought they'd get there during the parable.

I turned on the tape recorder, and went over and sat down on my bed. I made sure they didn't hear me. There was too much light in the room. I lay back and closed my eyes. I was so tired. The voice on the tape didn't sound like my voice.

I heard myself talking about kids I'd coached and the history of the neighborhood, and what I'd learned from Palani and Ann and Edge, and then I started nodding off. I knew I was on my bed in my room, and I heard a car coming down Clearview. It seemed to take a while to go by. It wasn't long before I was floating away from the neighborhood. I could see my house and the school growing smaller and smaller as I drifted away.

I was a spirit. I could still hear my voice coming from the tape recorder, but I was in another dimension. Soon I could only see the Earth, and watching it get smaller was like watching the disappearance of a dream.

When the Earth was barely visible, I saw a light out in the cosmos. I was moving toward it, and I heard the sound of scraping metal. The light began to flicker, and when I heard the scraping again, the light disappeared and I was back in my room.

I heard splintering wood and breaking glass, and I lurched all the way awake. Then there was a crash. I thought somebody was breaking into the house. I was afraid, but when I recognized the mechanical clattering of a bulldozer, I understood.

I disguised the transition to the next tape with a few coughs. While Woodmont School was being turned into rubble less than 250 yards away, I listened to the parable. Along with my voice, I could hear the strain of the bulldozer engine and the clanking of its tracks. By the time I got to the part where the Movement was able to expand beyond Etharyos, the sounds of destruction had gotten louder.

'Within another lifetime, Etharyos had colonized the nearest habitable planet within our astral system. Other life-sustaining planets were colonized over several more generations, and only then was the next step taken. A project was launched to identify and evaluate each habitable planet within the Sphere of Exploration.

'In examining one section of the outer reaches of the Sphere, a robotic probe finally detected an Omega. The atmospheric signature of the planet you call Earth indicated that you had entered your industrial age. It was decided that Earth would be observed in advance of a possible interaction. A mission was generated, and I was selected to lead the mission.'

'Our vessel was launched and our crew had been in a state of suspension for many astral cycles when we were awakened by an emergency transmission. Radical shifts in temperature were taking place across the surface of the star of Etharyos.

'As signs of its internal instability grew more ominous, our star began sending out solar flares of a magnitude never previously observed. After two of our colonized planets were incinerated by flares, it was understood that Etharyos had a high probability of sharing a similar fate.

The agent was somewhere listening. Others would be coming. I could feel it.

'A message announcing the likely demise of Etharyos was sent to all exploratory vessels. Vessels close enough to Etharyos were commanded to return and aid in the evacuation of the planet. Our vessel was at too great a distance to render assistance. We were ordered to proceed toward Earth and await further instructions.

'There were no subsequent transmissions. It is all but certain that a flare erupted from our dying star and passed close enough to Etharyos to consume it. It was thought that Etharyos was already extinct by the time the final communication had reached us.

'We set aside our grief, and a council was conducted. We decided that as survivors of Etharyos, we had *become* Etharyos. We were within range of several uninhabited planets that have a biological signature similar to that of Etharyos. Our vessel contains what was carried on all exploratory missions – a detailed record of our history and the seeds of our planet's biological heritage. When we establish ourselves, the seeds we brought will be planted, and the luminescent forest that once grew on Etharyos will eventually grow again.

'And we have decided that because the cosmos lost Etharyos in a random cataclysm, we should attempt to restore a degree of balance. We are enhancing the opportunity for an additional planet to blossom.

'We have decided that Earth shall receive a legacy from Etharyos. Your legacy is to see your planet through the lens of an advanced perspective. I have come to you in an auxiliary vessel.

After I deliver this message, I will rejoin the others and we will travel to our new home.'

I was vaguely aware of the bulldozer, and then I heard a crash. I pulled the pillow off my head and listened for the sound of somebody breaking through one of the doors. I kept listening and then there was a second crash. I was almost sure that it came from the school. One of the walls in the lunchroom must've been pushed over.

I imagined bricks falling onto the place where lunches and school plays and Spaghetti Suppers and carnival auctions and games of bingo and PTA meetings had taken place year after year, and decade after decade.

Maybe I was trying too hard to survive. There was less to live for than there was before. Maybe it didn't matter. Maybe I should just let go.

'A great many lifetimes before its destruction, the struggles of Etharyos were the struggles with which Earth now contends. Your technology is more powerful than your wisdom. You lack the will to eliminate your most powerful weapons of war, or to restrain your environmental self-destruction. Being in your collective adolescence, you have little recognition of your possible place in the cosmos. As it once was with Etharyos, it is with you. A lack of perspective is allowing the few to jeopardize the future of a civilization.

'You are following a path that will lead to your destruction. The withering of Earth is well underway. A deepening shadow has fallen over your planet. Earth will not endure unless it moves from the shadows into the light. Humanity must become dedicated to the blossoming of its journey.

'Otherwise, Earth will merely become one more lifeless planet drifting into oblivion. Humanity is being given the opportunity to see itself within the context of the cosmos, but it must blossom of its own accord. Beyond offering this legacy, I shall remain passive. If in the end Earth allows itself to wither, then wither it will.'

I got off the bed and went over to my desk. I coughed again to cover up the sound of the tape recorder being turned off. I needed to say something else to whoever was listening. "Well I'm pretty sure you didn't get up this morning expecting to hear a parable, but at least you know how I see the world."

There was a crash when another cafeteria wall came down.

"I don't know if your equipment is picking it up, but a bulldozer is tearing down my old grammar school. If you listened to what I was saying, you understand the way I feel about its destruction.

"Woodmont School was a light on my journey. There are places like Woodmont all across the planet – places that are inspirational parts of people's lives. I believe that by lighting the way for individual journeys, the places people love help illuminate the human journey."

They hadn't come for me. Maybe I hadn't given them enough time. Maybe they still didn't know what I'd done. Or maybe they didn't have Mr. Anderson. I'd done everything I could to sound like somebody who couldn't have possibly been involved in espionage. All I could do was wait. Wait and hope that I pulled it off.

Chapter 117

I didn't drive past Woodmont when I finally left home. It would've been like seeing the mutilated corpse of somebody I loved. I thought about driving out into the country again, but it would look suspicious if I disappeared twice in three days.

I wondered if anybody was closing in on the rogue agents. If Mr. Anderson was still alive, I wondered where he was. I kept imagining him in a locked room with no windows. I needed to think about something else.

I went to the State Library to kill some time. I ended up looking through microfilm copies of the *Nashville Tennessean* from the month when I came into the world. Two of the stories seemed like they were waiting for me to find them.

One was an article from ten days before I was born. It was about the baseball field behind Woodmont School being built. A member of the Woodmont Men's Club had brought a bulldozer and leveled off the lot behind the school. There was a photograph of the man on the bulldozer, and several other men were clearing away brush.

The second story appeared five days later. It announced that the Central Intelligence Agency had gone into operation.

I didn't want to go back home. I went to a restaurant and ate dinner, and I thought about seeing a movie. *Marathon Man* was playing at Green Hills Theater. I hadn't been there since I saw *The Odessa Files.* But alarms might've gone off if I went to see a movie about a guy who was caught up in a web of espionage and double agents. A movie involving spies was probably the last thing I needed to see, but seeing somebody else suffer might've taken my mind off what I was going through.

It had been dark for a while by the time I got home. None of the threads were broken and I went inside. I wanted to say something else to whoever was listening to me. I didn't turn on the light when I went to my room. I just lay down on my bed.

I tried not to sound worried. "You know what I've been imagining? All morning I've been imagining that when I was halfway through my parable, you were so bored that you started screaming. I pictured you tearing off your headphones and running away from wherever you are. But you're probably still listening, and I might as well talk to you like you're here.

"I want to tell you a little more about the parable. Humanity really is on a journey. Ten thousand years ago we didn't even know that plants grew from seeds. A few hundred years ago we still thought that the sun and the other stars revolved around the Earth. Now people have walked on the moon and we're finally starting to understand the universe.

"Our ancient ancestors couldn't do much more than sing and beat on logs and blow into reeds. What would they have thought about Handel's Messiah? And what about medicine? In a couple of centuries, we've gone from using leeches and bleeding people, to performing heart transplants.

"Humanity has developed the same way individual humans develop. When humanity was in its infancy, we didn't know how to do very much. The only perspective he had was what was right in front of us. Now we're like a teenager – we have a lot of power, but we don't have much sense.

"Writers and poets and philosophers and historians keep trying to tell the world about the human journey, but the world doesn't listen. Maybe somebody will come along at some point and use just the right words and explain the journey in just the right way. Maybe it's like Excalibur. Maybe somebody will eventually show up and pull the sword out of the stone. However it ends up happening, the message has to get out if the world is going to save itself.

"When I was a kid I'd hear my parents fighting, and if I got scared I started praying. And one night – right here in this room – I felt fire come into my body. I still wonder if it could've been the spirit of Jesus. Ever since then, I've wanted to know the truth.

"I've noticed the way the teachings of Jesus fit in with the human journey. I'm talking about when Jesus said we should love our neighbors as ourselves and turn the other cheek and forgive each other and help the poor. And I'm talking about how Jesus wanted children to be treated.

"What I'm trying to say is that part of what Jesus taught two thousand years ago wasn't just about saving souls, it applied to saving *humanity*. Maybe that's why there were times I thought I might be feeling the spirit of Jesus when I was writing the parable.

"And I keep thinking about awareness. I wouldn't be surprised if our consciousness is part of God's consciousness. Especially when we pray. If that's the way it is, maybe God feels both our joy and our pain."

I yawned and rolled onto my side, but I made myself keep talking. I talked about my parents and wanting them to be proud of me, and how I hoped they'd live long enough to watch me get married – and maybe see a grandchild. I talked about Callie and Claire and how authentic and strong they were. And what big hearts they had, and how much I hoped that they'd both end up with guys who deserved them.

My brain was slowing down. I felt like I was pedaling a bicycle up a hill that was getting steeper. I'd been making myself sound better than I was, and I wanted to tell the truth.

"And there's this other girl. Her name is Elinor. I had a dream about her the other night. She's in high school just like Callie and Claire, so I guess I'm still crazy or perverted or whatever it is that's wrong with me.

"Sometimes I think what draws me to girls that age might be their spirit. Callie and Claire have both been through a lot, but they haven't been crushed by the world like some of the women I've known. They still have music in their voices. They haven't lost who they've always been. Girls like that, and like Elinor, are full of light.

"I'd love to run into Elinor in another eight or ten years, but she lives out of town. I don't know if I'll ever even see her again. But maybe I will, and maybe I will have grown up a little by then. Or maybe I'll eventually run into somebody who's as bright and alive as she is. Maybe I'll find somebody else with her kind of spirit."

I was conscious of how slowly I was talking. I was getting lost in the shadows of my fatigue. "I want to keep on working with kids. Maybe I'm starting to understand the way I should've been coaching all along.

"I've spent ten years trying to get my players ready to play on high school teams. I should've done a lot more for the guys who were struggling. It shouldn't have taken me so long to change. I wish there was a way to go back... be better than I... was." I was drifting away.

I didn't know how long I'd been asleep when I heard a gasp. It sounded like it came from inside my bedroom. I lay in the dark and tried to tell myself that I was dreaming. I kept listening, but the house was quiet.

The minutes drew out. The night was emptier than it was back when I lay in the dark listening to my father snoring. Deeper than when I'd listened to the barking of the dog in the distance. I was cold. I felt like I was in a crypt.

I remembered when I was little. How I thought that after I died, I'd be trapped in my coffin forever. I wanted to crawl out through the window and try to get away, but I sensed somebody waiting in the darkness. I would've gone down to the basement, but the basement seemed like death.

I kept listening, but I still didn't hear anybody else in the house. I could feel my heart beating. The fear flowed out of me like blood, and I saw myself drowning in my own tomb. I tried to slow down my breathing. I thought about talking again, but the guy who was listening would know something was wrong. He'd hear it in my voice.

A car was coming up Clearview Drive. I saw the light build up behind the blinds, and after I watched the shadows glide across the ceiling, I drifted out into the darkness. I was in our backyard, and then I was out on the playground of the country school riding the merry-go-round beneath the night sky. I could hear the breathing of unseen children straining as they pushed against the metal bars.

The merry-go-round moved faster and faster, and I tried to hold on. The front edge of the seat dug deeper and deeper into the backs of my legs, and I was spinning around and my arms were getting weaker and I could sense a presence behind me, waiting for me to let go.

When I couldn't stand the pain anymore, I swung my legs out behind me. I was hanging on and I wanted to turn loose and drift away, but I heard a gasp and I was awake again and scared again and quiet again and I listened again, but I didn't hear anything else. I was tired and tangled up in fear, and I knew it wouldn't be long before they found out who I really was. I knew that if I didn't escape then, I would never escape.

I started saying my old prayers, but then I heard myself say that I feared no evil. It was a lie, and I went back to what was true and honest, and to what was just and what was pure.

I started thinking about Mother and about my father and the hope they had for me. How much they both believed in my soul. Another car coming down Clearview. I thought about the source of the love they gave me. How the source of that love must have always existed in the cosmos. How that eternal love could be the same love that shined through Jesus and through the sacred figures of other religions. The light built up behind the blinds, and I could feel myself getting warmer as it began to glide across the ceiling.

The light was getting hot and it lifted me into the darkness, and it was around Mother and around my father. And it was around Ann as she peered at me through her glasses and painted what she saw in my eyes. The light burning inside me was around Palani as he gave me guidance in the middle of the night with the sea rolling beneath the pier. It was around Edge as he sat on a box and described the nightmare he had survived. It was around Mike Higgins as he risked his life for something larger than himself, and it was around Mr. Anderson as he worked quietly through the years using the scientific gift he was given. It was around Claire as she drew in a deep breath that echoed in the wake of her heartbreak, it was around Callie as she overcame her own heartbreak and stood by her wounded friend. It was around Elinor as her love for her father shined in her eyes, and it was around Carla as she gave me her friendship. It was around Whiting as he made himself get up off the ground again and again, and it was around David as he protected Whiting. And it was around Hill Murray as he reached out and handed me the bullet, and around so many of the other kids I coached, and the people I knew as their journeys unfolded within the larger journey of which they were all a part.

The last thing I remembered from that night was feeling like I was burning up. Soaking with sweat. Thrashing around and not being able to keep still. Not knowing whether I was asleep or awake. When I woke up the next morning, all the windows of my room were wide open.

Chapter 118

I was still afraid the next morning, but I wasn't as afraid as I'd been. And over the next few nights, what was true and honest and just and pure continued to bring light into the darkness. I kept talking to whoever was listening, but nobody came for me and my anxiety began to disappear like poison evaporating from a glass. And nobody came and nobody came and nobody came, and after a while, there was only the stain that fear left behind.

I ended up thinking that Mr. Anderson wasn't abducted. I think he slipped away from the hospital and went into hiding. If they got him, they would've broken him down and he would've told them what I did. But nobody ever came for me.

I keep wondering about the last thing Mr. Anderson said – about wanting to take me down into the cellar of the house where he grew up in Cross Keys. He kept staring into my eyes, and there was a look on his face I hadn't seen before. There must be something in the cellar he wanted me to see, but they were listening when he said it, and if they're still operating, they could be monitoring the old house.

In the end, I think they didn't come for me because after hearing the parable and everything else I said, they believed what I hoped they'd believe. I was just somebody who happened to show up to interview old soldiers.

The information from Mr. Anderson might have reached the right group inside the CIA, and the rogue agents might've been killed or hunted down. But it's possible that nothing happened to them. There are times when I imagine that they're still operating – still betraying America. Still betraying humanity. I understand that Mike could be dead, but I choose to think he's in hiding, and that he'll show up in a couple of years and tell me everything I want to know.

I'm still trying to stop thinking about it. Mike is either alive, or he isn't. I'll either hear from him again, or I won't. Mr. Anderson is either alive, or he's dead. I'll either find out what happened to him and to the cell of rogue agents, or I never will. And the technology I passed along either reached the right scientists and will be a gift to the world, or it will end up making money for some corrupt corporation. Or maybe it will just get locked away somewhere in a corporate safe.

My parents looked a lot healthier when they got back from Europe. By then I'd gotten rid of all the nails and tacks and pieces of thread, and covered up all the holes I'd drilled. And by then I'd unloaded my father's pistol and put it back in his top drawer under his socks. I didn't say anything about what happened, but I left the bug under my desk. I still look at it sometimes.

It bothers me that Ann and Palani are growing old alone. I've been thinking about how to get them together. Carla got back right after Christmas. Her latest lover is a quiet man from some little town in southern Spain. He used to be a matador. She flirts with me every time I see her. He doesn't seem to mind.

Edge finished his book and dedicated it to Addie. He told me that she cries every time she reads it. When Edge and Inez got married, I sat beside Addie at the wedding. Stan Smithson came back to Miss Young's last spring. Edge and I got to sit on our boxes and spend a few more days screening dirt. Then Stan said he had a large enough sample of animal bones.

It turned out that the slave diet at the Williams plantation was nearly identical to what Andrew Jackson's slaves and the slaves at Belle Meade had eaten. Stan said he was determined to find out why the slaves on all three places were fed the same proportions of meat.

After I went by the State Library and donated the tapes of the interviews I did in Murfreesboro, I recorded several interviews with Miss Young. Then I started interviewing some of the other longtime residents of the Woodmont neighborhood.

Basketball cranked up in early December. Whiting was the first kid at practice. He smiled the whole time he was there. He was a little taller and he'd lost some weight. Although he was still a terrible shooter, he did pretty well when we ran our press, and every now and then he got a rebound. Not to mention an occasional loose ball. David Dobbins was our best player. He was a little better than Jake Colbert had been.

A few months later, when Jones Colbert got into financial difficulty, Ellen Caswell quietly offered to pay Jake's tuition. But Carla said that after the details of their trip to see Armand Hammer *somehow* leaked out, Jones and Mary Ann didn't want to face any further shame. With so many members of the Ensworth community aware of their difficulties, they enrolled Jake and his siblings in a somewhat less prestigious private school.

I wanted to write the history of Cross Keys, but I couldn't get focused. Then I tried to get started on the history of the Woodmont neighborhood, and I didn't get very far on that either. It wasn't long before I understood there was something else I needed to write first.

I had been on a journey, and I needed to write about it. I wanted to tell the story that started when I was a teenager – and ended when I finished my mission with Mike Higgins and Mr. Anderson. And I decided that the story should include the parable.

I got out all my journals right after Christmas. I wrote through basketball and baseball seasons, and for the rest of the summer. Football will be over in another week, and I'm almost finished.

Since Mike Higgins and Bob Asberry and Mr. Anderson and the rogue agents are all part of the story, I won't be able to show it to anybody for a while. The guy who received the information on Halloween said I couldn't ever talk about it, but I'm not going to hide what happened forever.

Forty or fifty years should be long enough. Maybe at that point, I'll try to get this published. In the meantime, I'll keep it in a lockbox at the bank, and I'll leave instructions with a law firm about what to do with it if I'm not around by then.

I wonder how old I'll be if I ever read this again. By then I hope I've written a book about my neighborhood and another one about Cross Keys. And by then I hope that Elinor and Claire and Callie and Ann and Palani and Edge and Hill and Davey Austin and Inman Roberts and Whiting – and all the other people I care about – have had good lives.

By then I hope I'll know what became of Mike Higgins and Mr. Anderson and the agents, and whether what Dr. Asberry and Mr. Anderson invented made an impact on the world. And by then – if I'm still around and if I'm in my right mind – I guess I'll know what became of me.

October 26, 1977

Stopping by just after dark,
I return to the place
Where Woodmont School
Once stood.
The scars on the earth
Are covered with grass,
But my foot grazes the corner
Of a left-behind brick.
I leave it where it is.
Fifteen years ago tonight –
Half of my lifetime ago
And just above the place
Where I'm standing –
I sat in my sixth-grade classroom
When humanity stumbled
And nearly ended its journey.
I remember.
Behind me,

Beyond my house
And the old mansion
And the haunts
Of forgotten people
And the sites
Of forgotten places,
The sky darkens.
When the tip of the full moon
Appears above the eastern horizon
And begins to shine through the trees,
A dog starts barking in the distance.
Shadows form
As the moon rises
In the night sky,
Illuminating the neighborhood
And the world,
And as the moon glows
And the shadows deepen,
The stars beckon
And the dog falls silent.

www.ingramcontent.com/pod-product-compliance
Lightning Source LLC
Chambersburg PA
CBHW060540310726
48982CB00009B/1327/J

9780578434520